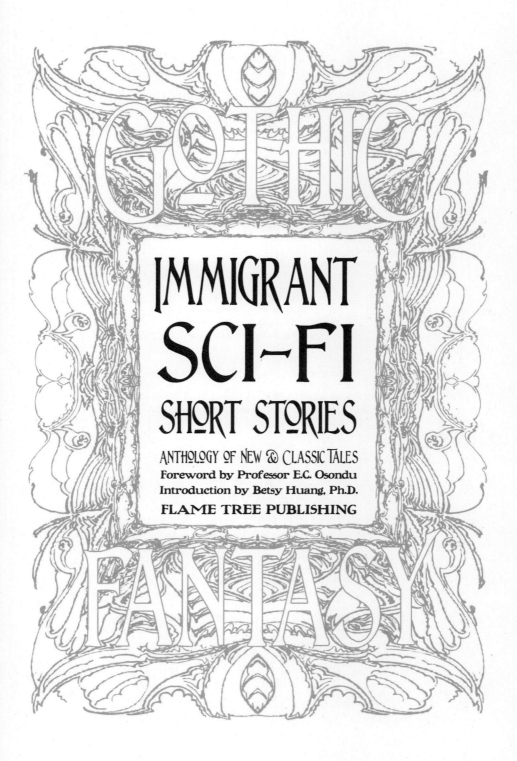

GOTHIC

IMMIGRANT SCI-FI SHORT STORIES

ANTHOLOGY OF NEW & CLASSIC TALES

Foreword by Professor E.C. Osondu

Introduction by Betsy Huang, Ph.D.

FLAME TREE PUBLISHING

FANTASY

This is a FLAME TREE Book

Publisher & Creative Director: Nick Wells
Editorial Director: Catherine Taylor
Associate Editor: Sarah Rafael García

Publisher's Note Regarding Language: Due to the historical nature of the early texts, as well as the often realistic depiction of prejudice relevant to the topic in the modern stories, we're aware that there may be some language used which has the potential to cause offence to the modern reader. However, wishing overall to preserve the integrity of the text, rather than imposing contemporary sensibilities or censoring reality, we have left it unaltered.

FLAME TREE PUBLISHING
6 Melbray Mews, Fulham,
London SW6 3NS, United Kingdom
www.flametreepublishing.com

First published 2023

23 25 27 26 24
3 5 7 9 10 8 6 4 2

ISBN: 978-1-80417-273-5
Special ISBN: 978-1-80417-644-3

The cover image is created by Flame Tree Studio based on artwork courtesy of Shutterstock.com.

A copy of the CIP data for this book is available from the British Library.

Printed and bound in China

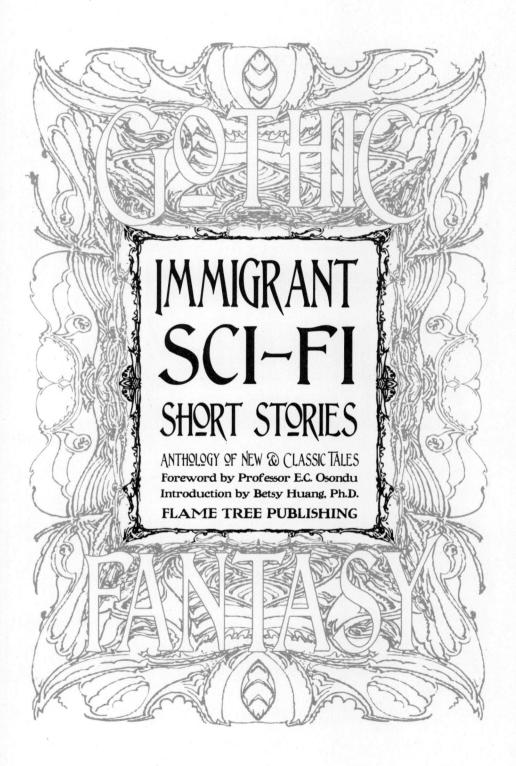

GOTHIC

IMMIGRANT SCI-FI SHORT STORIES

ANTHOLOGY OF NEW & CLASSIC TALES

Foreword by Professor E.C. Osondu

Introduction by Betsy Huang, Ph.D.

FLAME TREE PUBLISHING

FANTASY

Contents

Displacement, Relocation & Resettlement in Modern Science Fiction

Foreword: Leaving as an Immigrant Parable

LEAVING IS A CONSTANT TROPE in science fiction. Leaving often involves discarding the familiar for the unfamiliar, the shedding of old skin and the acquisition of a new tongue. There is no individual world in which this trope is more clearly understood and lived than in the world of science fiction by immigrant writers.

In Ursula Le Guinn's famous short story 'The Ones Who Walk Away from Omelas', Omelas is described as an ideal society where joy is the currency of trade, and peace and happiness are the coins of everyday living. Who would ever want to leave such an ideal and perfect society? However, even in this ideal, there is a lacuna. The currency of joy and peace in this world is at the expense of the joy and peace of a child. This child who must live in execrable conditions in order to guarantee the happiness of the rest of the society is the one who must eat the suffering, tears and unhappiness of the rest of society. When I first read the short story, I was rooting for the suffering boy to leave, so that the society would finally learn that peace and joy and happiness have to be earned and should not be served on a platter. Interestingly, it is not the long-suffering boy who leaves but rather one of the partakers of unending joy and happiness. What does he leave in search of? He leaves in search of a world where there is happiness but not at the expense of a helpless and vulnerable individual. What if the new world which the leaver encounters is a society in which the suffering is not limited to a single child in a hovel but is spread evenly among every child, man, woman and animal in that society? What if on the other hand he walks away to a new society in which there is joy and happiness but the suffering is measured only in coffee spoons and spread evenly among the entire population of the society? Perhaps suffering shared is suffering more easily borne. But wait, there is a third scenario – he walks into a society in which there is no suffering and there is no child in a room somewhere paying the price but rather, through collective effort and hard work, suffering has been banished into exile never to return.

Another encounter with the leaving motif happened much earlier. On a black Sanyo black and white television on a Saturday afternoon in Lagos I watched a film that has stuck in my memory even though I seemed to have watched it in what feels like five hundred years ago. The encounter in question was the film *Logan's Run*. I remember that Logan's society was one in which people's lives must be terminated once they turned twenty-one. Not everyone accepted the fate of age-determined termination. A few tried to escape their ordained fate by leaving or running away. Logan's job was to hunt down these individuals and enforce justice by making them die. Logan appeared to be enjoying his job until one day he could not take it anymore and he decided to become one of the people who run away.

Immigrant writing by those who have left inevitably returns to the motif of leaving. This physical journey is oftentimes replicated years later by their descendants through the imagination. Imaginary journeys by their very nature are better suited to the creation of the ideal because what is discovered is not only the outside world but the self. The strongest short stories in this anthology are united by the fact that they are written by those who have journeyed or descended from those who left. They invite the reader to travel vicariously to places unknown.

I invite you to come on this journey of the imagination through the stories collected here. Enjoy the trip!

Professor E.C. Osondu – Winner Caine Prize for Africa
Professor of English, Providence College, Providence, USA; Author of Alien Stories

Publisher's Note

DISPLACEMENT AND MIGRATION is a fundamental thread in the history of humanity, and a key influence in the enrichment of cultures. As such it has always been a powerful theme in narrative and, as climate change and the heated political landscape bring new challenges and new waves of immigration, it becomes even more fertile ground for the speculative storytelling mind. Envisaging alternate, fantastic or futuristic settings for this age-old human phenomenon enables writers to explore and represent a multiplicity of experiences, eliciting core truths through the freedom of imagination – the dual overlapping meaning of 'alien' being an obvious springboard.

For this book we have united several strands. The first section gives a sample of earlier non-speculative narratives and accounts that form a foundation of inspirational tales dealing with the subject of displacement and relocation. These stories introduce just some of the many reasons people leave the land of their birth to make their way in a new country.

The second part of the book includes some classic science fiction from Otto (Eando) Binder, Fredric Brown and Zenna Henderson, who imagined the consequences of humans emigrating to Mars or Martians immigrating to Earth, or in Henderson's case the struggle of a whole alien people to integrate, while preserving their own culture. To these are added some perceptive stories from stand-out contemporary authors such as Celu Amberstone, Indrapramit Das, Greg van Eekhout, Jordan Ifueko, Ken Liu and E.C. Osondu, alongside a carefully curated selection of stories received through our open submissions process. With the contemporary pieces especially we have endeavoured to choose the tales that give voice to authors writing from the true perspective of the migrant (which was often not the case in earlier science fiction), and who represent cultures from around the world, while also presenting thought-provoking and imaginative visions of the theme.

Introduction

Immigration in Science Fiction: A Brief History

THE STORIES IN THIS VOLUME illuminate a longstanding synergy between two literary genres that are often not thought of in concert – immigrant fiction and science fiction. But why not? So much of science fiction, after all, is immigrant fiction in disguise. For what are stories of alien visitations and invasions but stories about the fascination with and fear of immigrants? What are space travel, colonization and settlement tales but narratives of migration, immigration, forced displacement, settler colonialism and all the challenging social, political and cultural questions that ensue? The complexities of different cultures figuring out how to co-exist – or destroy each other: are these not the great themes of both genres? The two genres share the same thematic preöccupations, critical vocabulary, and formal devices, and we do not have to reach far to see the similarities. And these shared qualities reveal the compelling power of both genres to illuminate the expansiveness – or narrowness – of our capacity for engaging with and learning from difference.

Science fiction is replete with stories of displacement, relocation, resettlement and alienation. The alien, arguably science fiction's most iconic and foundational trope, appeared in the earliest works of science fiction and has long functioned as the principal signifier of the different and the foreign. Metaphorical encoding of various forms of alienness – alien settings, beings, social institutions and ideological apparatuses – either engenders new understanding or fans the fear of racial, cultural, sexual and other forms of difference. From the Victorian-era science and gothic fictions of H. G. Wells and H. P. Lovecraft to the alien invasion films of the 1950s B-movie era, figurations of the 'alien' gave expression to our fear of the unknown and the unfamiliar. The emergence and evolution of the alien in science fiction coincided with the global shift from agrarianism to industrial capitalism and its labor demands, and with the tumult of colonial wars and the First World War, all of which compelled mass migrations and propelled the ensuing reactionary rise of nativism.

A Nativist Perspective

In those days, science fiction was the playground of Eurocentrist white male voices, many of whom were apologists for colonialism and nativism; descriptions of immigrants as undesirables, pollutants and threats are therefore predictably pervasive in their writings. H.G. Wells' *The War of the Worlds*, for instance, has been widely read as a cautionary commentary on the British Empire and the attacks and rebellions the Empire's transgresses might invite. And though better known for his fiction, Wells also wrote prolifically on social and international politics. Wells' essay 'Ellis Island', contained in a collection entitled *The Future in America: A Search After Realities*, documents his visit to the immigration station in New York Harbor in 1906 and describes the newly arrived immigrants as: "crude Americans from Ireland and Poland and Italy and Syria and Finland and Albania"; "dingy and strangely garbed groups of wild-eyed aliens"; and a "tragic and evil-looking crowd that hates us". Writing in the same period, H.P. Lovecraft expresses his nativism and racism unabashedly in his fiction and his personal writings. In a letter to his publisher about an upcoming election, he writes:

Some people may like the idea of a mongrel America like the late Roman Empire, but I for one prefer to die in the same America that I was born in. Therefore, I'm against any candidate who talks of letting down the bars to stunted brachycephalic South-Italians & rat-faced half-Mongoloid

Russian & Polish Jews, & all that cursed scum! You in the Middle West can't conceive of the extent of the menace. You ought to see a typical Eastern city crowd – swart, aberrant physiognomies, & gestures & jabbering born of alien instincts.

Little surprise that such views found their way into 'Herbert West – Reanimator' and other Lovecraft stories that enjoyed cult status among gothic and fantasy fandom until quite recently. To read these stories with today's lenses is to have to contend with the paradox of reading the reactionary sentiments of writers who cast themselves as radical thinkers.

Anti-immigrant Propaganda

The mass migrations during and after the Industrial Revolution stoked xenophobia and nativist sentiments in countries that saw large influxes of immigrants, and these sentiments were discursively promulgated in journalism, literature and even in records of government proceedings. Chinese immigrants in the United States, for instance, were called 'celestials' by white Americans as a reflection of their extra-terrestrial appearance and ways to the American eye. In a state congressional debate about 'the Chinese Question' in 1881, California state senator John Miller described Chinese as "inhabitants of another planet", "machine-like" and "of obtuse nerve, but little affected by heat or cold, wiry, sinewy, with muscles of iron; they are automatic engines of flesh and blood". Such representational language is hugely influential in the arena of public opinion, and those who control that language control the fate of the people in question. The rhetoric of "machine-like" eventually led to the passing of the Chinese Exclusion Law of 1882, which severely limited the immigration of Chinese when their labor was no longer needed after the completion of the Transcontinental Railroad. The exclusion act laid the foundation for almost a century's worth of immigration legislation designed to curtail the entry of 'excludable aliens' into the country, beginning with the passage of the Immigration Act of 1882 and 'ending', only in the legal sense, with the Immigration and Nationality Act of 1965, which removed the longstanding *de facto* discriminatory policies against targeted immigrant populations.

Aliens As Metaphors

Not all writers of the dominant culture at the time adopted anti-immigrant stances, of course. Whereas Miller uses the alienness of Chinese immigrants to support nativist policies, Mark Twain deploys it to criticize nativist views. Writing in the same period as Miller and coinciding with the Immigration Act of 1882, Twain uses the immigrant perspective in his little-known satire 'Goldsmith's Friend Abroad Again' to achieve a different end. This epistolary short story is told through the letters of a Chinese immigrant who discovers that he has no rights to self-representation in a court of law as an 'alien' and is sorely disabused of his belief in 'the Land of the Free and Home of the Brave'. Twain's scathing critique of the unjust treatment of immigrants in the United States' justice system through the voices of immigrants is, at that time, a rare but valuable gesture. Yet contemporary critics rightly find Twain's ventriloquizing of the Chinese man's voice problematic because the immigrant is merely a literary device for Twain. While 'Goldsmith's Friend' clearly advocates for the rights of immigrants, Twain's characterization, like Miller's, still flattens the Chinese immigrant into caricaturish aliens.

Whether hostile or benign, early representations of immigrants by the dominant culture often reduced them to stereotypes and deployed them as devices to serve majoritarian concerns. In *Science Fiction: The New Critical Idiom* (2006), Adam Roberts soberly reminds us of the genre's intolerant history, one replete with "retrograde examples … that introduce difference only to demonise it". This is unsurprising, according to Roberts, given the demographics of the genre's writers and readers: "Until relatively recently, SF was dominated by a fan culture of young white males. Science fiction's … reliance on stock types of character and plot that are often flat and two dimensional surely limit its engagement with any meaningful comprehension of the marginal, of otherness". Such works justified nativism, homeland defense and the oppression of colonized and enslaved subjects for which the aliens in the stories often function as metaphors.

Aliens As Sympathetic Characters

In the post-Second World War years, the genre gave way to more nuanced stories written by both members of the dominant culture and by the putative 'aliens' themselves. These began to appear in the Sixties and Seventies, coinciding with the public's growing interest in the experiences and cultures of strangers from different shores during the postwar era of post-colonial independence movements across the glove and loosening immigration policies in the United States that stimulated immigration trends. While the popular imagination in the 1950s was saddled with countless B-movies featuring threatening or incomprehensible extraterrestrials (Don Siegel's 1956 film *The Invasion of the Body Snatchers* is perhaps most emblematic of the 'replacement theory' anxieties implicitly propagated by such narratives), the ensuing decades of the Sixties, Seventies and Eighties saw more complex and fleshed-out figurations of literal and metaphorical aliens. These can be seen not only in the empire and settler colonialism narratives of space operas and interplanetary epics such as Frank Herbert's *Dune* series and Orson Scott Card's *Ender's Game* series, but also in the work of writers influenced by countercultural and antiwar movements who turned their critical gaze to the forces that compelled immigration or mass migration. The work of science-fiction luminaries Ray Bradbury, Ursula K. Le Guin, Philip K. Dick and lesser-known authors such as Fredric Brown (whose work is included in this volume) come to mind as thoughtful critiques of such forces. Consider the depictions of humans as settler colonizers and refugees in Ray Bradbury's *The Martian Chronicles*; the exploitation of artificial life as weaponized entities, sexual servants, or domestic labor in Dick's *Do Androids Dream of Electric Sheep?*; the evolution of human biology and culture as a result of resettlement on another planet in Le Guin's *The Left Hand of Darkness*; or finally, the satirical send-ups of the fear of alien takeovers in Brown's *Martians, Go Home*. The same commentary can be seen on the screen in the earnest critique of xenophobia and nativist fears in Graham Baker's 1988 film *Alien Nation* as well as in *Men in Black,* Barry Sonnenfeld's blockbusting satirical franchise of the late 1990s.

The Literature of Migrants and Refugees

But it is the stories by minoritized writers – immigrant, migrant and refugee writers, women writers, queer writers and writers of color – that significantly shifted the science-fiction scene to deliver a truly immigrant-centered sensibility. Trailblazed by the work of Octavia E. Butler, Joanna Russ, James Tiptree Jr., Ursula K. Le Guin and Samuel R. Delany, these writers saw and utilized science fiction's capacity for imagining alternative systems and structures that realism – the preferred mode for socially conscious writers – cannot provide. And in recent decades, recognition has been garnered by and awards given to immigrant- and refugee-themed science fiction, such as Ken Liu's 'The Paper Menagerie', Sabrina Vourvoulias's *Ink*, Karen Lord's *The Best of All Possible Worlds* and Charles Yu's *How to Live Safely in a Science Fictional Universe*. It is these developments that led Charlie Jane Anders to remark recently that "possibly the most pervasive narrative in science fiction is actually the story of refugees. They flee from planetary destruction, war, or just from overcrowding and ecological crappitude. The refugee story is the flipside of the gung-ho explorer story, but it might actually be the most uniquely science fictional story of all." ('Science Fiction is the Literature of Refugees', *Gizmodo*, 16 May 2008). Riding this wave, the stories in this volume testify to the continued growth of interest in immigration and migration in science fiction.

The Progressive Potential of Immigrant Science Fiction

Why do immigrant writers choose science fiction over realistic fiction as their creative vehicle? Early works by immigrant writers were produced for the consumption of members of the dominant culture to feed their curiosity about the exotic and to alleviate their fears of the foreign. In the United States, for instance, immigrant writers in the early twentieth century either served as cultural informants who offered insider views of a foreign culture or proffered depictions of America as the promised land that pandered to the ideology of American exceptionalism. Working under these de facto expectations for publication, realism has long been the preferred mode for both complicit and subversive immigrant writers. Writers such as Sui Sin Far, Abraham Cahan, Constantine Panunzio and Mary Antin – work by all of these can be found in the 'Foundations' section of this volume – capture the challenges of navigating the strange and often hostile cultural landscape of a country they must call home, a new home that expects to hear their declaration of loyalty and love. Deploying the conventions of realism and naturalism that constituted so much of the great social fiction of that era, these authors established the literary vocabulary for dramatizing the nuances of acculturation, the trials of assimilation and the stubborn scars of involuntary migration and colonization. But whereas realism and naturalism are bound by the rules of verisimilitude, science fiction is a genre set up to defy, exceed, or simply dispense the imperatives of realism, precisely because its principal mode of representation is fabulation. Equipped with a very different set of devices in its representational toolbox, science fiction offers immigrant writers a unique way to document and critique the immigrant experience and offer alternative, more ethical and humane visions for engagement with difference.

Exploration of the New and the Strange

The stories in this capacious volume showcase the imaginations of contemporary writers who choose to dramatize the immigrant experience through science fiction for its toolbox of fabulation devices: cognitive estrangement, extrapolation and, most critically, the *novum*. This last term, literally 'new thing', was coined by Darko Suvin in *Metamorphoses of Science Fiction* (1977). It is the 'new thing' that does not yet exist in our world, the main formal device that distinguishes a work of science fiction from 'realistic' fiction. Writing from the perspective of the immigrant, after all, is the very essence of cognitive estrangement, the cardinal literary device of science fiction. Through cognitive estrangement, readers vicariously experience the strangeness of all that is familiar to them via the vantage of the putative 'alien'. Modern immigrant science-fiction writers put science fiction to great use to achieve the progressive potential for their stories. A compelling example is Octavia E. Butler's provocative short story 'Bloodchild', in which a refugee situation set in an interplanetary scene captures the rewards, costs and entanglements of two species finding ways to coexist. The story can be read as a literal treatment of a challenging situation between Terran refugees and the Tlics of the host planet, or as a figurative exploration of the plight of refugees in our real world. Another example is Ken Liu's stirring short story 'The Paper Menagerie' (included in this volume), in which Liu deploys a science-fictional novum – the fantastical element of magical menageries coming to life – as both literal and metaphorical expressions of long-repressed immigrant longings and grief.

The Breadth of Immigrant Science Fiction

The stories in this volume display not only an impressive range of voices from across the globe, but also an extensive catalog of key immigrant themes. In addition to the celebrated fresh visions of Indrapramit Das and E.C. Osondu, immigrant writers from remarkably diverse backgrounds – BIPOC, neurodivergent, LGBTQIA+ and descendants of displaced and resettled people – are included here. Together, they significantly expand the diverse landscape of science fiction and do justice to the genre's capacity for exploring difference on difference's terms. Here is a preview of the themes covered in the volume and the stories that dramatize them.

Displacement

The trauma of leaving one's home, especially under duress, serves as the premise of some of the most celebrated and moving modern science fiction. Most of us have experienced some form of relocation in our lives, from quotidian moves out of one's hometown for school or work, to earth-shattering flights from political, religious, racial, or sexual persecution, poverty, natural or human-induced disasters, and war. The sense of loss and disorientation experienced by migrants and refugees – of feeling uprooted, unmoored and alienated – are more prevalent and perhaps universal than we imagine.

In scenarios of displacement and forced migration, expectations imposed by the destination country on migrants and refugees to prove themselves worthy of being received often expose the terrible conditions of refugee precarity. Much of Octavia E. Butler's works, for instance, depict humans displaced from their home world who must forge a future with the people of their new home world. In her textual notes for her short story 'Bloodchild', Butler describes the story as a 'paying the rent' scenario, in which the human refugees must 'pay' for their stay by serving as reproductive vessels for the 'host' species (in both senses of the word). And in *Dawn*, the first novel of the *Xenogenesis* trilogy, human refugees aboard the ship of the Oankali who rescued them from a destroyed Earth must also submit to the Oankali's demand for gene trading by mating with them.

The precarities and vulnerabilities of immigrants and refugees serve as the premises for many of the stories in this volume. The persistent inability to determine where one can permanently settle and call home is depicted in M. Darusha Wehm's 'Home Sick', in which a group of refugees resettled on a trash site is displaced from it after having made it their home; also in V. Castro's 'RingWorm', in which a forsaken population resettled on a worm-infested planet is forced to compete with the indigenous people in order to survive on the planet's meagre resources; and again in Eris Young's 'All That Water', which illustrates the uncertain fate of a refugee group without any bargaining chip to offer a potential host world. These stories expose the precarities of refugees who are rarely in a position to determine their fates and resettle on their own terms. The stories also pose the difficult question of whether it is possible to transform an asymmetrical power relationship built on coerced dependence and exploitation to a more symmetrical, balanced and mutually respecting one.

Arrival

The moment of arrival in the new land for immigrants is often an emotional juggernaut of hope, relief, confusion, anxiety and fear. Immigration stations such as Ellis Island in New York Harbor and Angel Island in San Francisco Harbor are concrete manifestations of state-designed mechanisms for admission into the country. The fact that both sites functioned as processing and detention centers speaks to the vulnerabilities of the immigrant's fate in the face of the state's often opaque criteria for entry and rejection. In this volume, Bebe Bayliss's 'Point of Entry' makes great use of science fiction to dramatize the confounding facets of the immigration system and provokes deeper examinations of the instruments and mechanisms devised by the state to determine who is worthy of entry. Francesco Verso's 'The Green Ship' mounts a similar critique of such mechanisms of exclusion in its dramatization of a ship that takes on refugees kept out by blockades set up to ban their entry.

Assimilationism

The word 'assimilation' in early immigrant writings carried benign meanings of blending in and becoming a part of the dominant culture. But assimilationist expectations often call on immigrants to disavow their 'old' identities in order to become part of the new. In the United States, for instance, such expectations are fulfilled at the Naturalization Oath Ceremony, during which immigrants renounce allegiance to nations where they have previously held titles or citizenship (with few exceptions for countries that allow dual citizenship) and swear allegiance to the United States as part of the citizenship process. This renunciative act can cause profound grief in immigrants with strong attachments to their countries of origin. Remembering, revisiting, retelling and staying connected with the immigrant's place of origin are therefore acts of resistance and important, a means for immigrants to reject this prescribed amnesia. In this volume, E.C. Osondu's 'Memory Store', Ken Liu's 'The Paper Menagerie', P.A. Cornell's 'El Bordado' and Ali Abbas's 'An Absolute Amount of Sadness' all speak to the power of memory as a lifeline to valuable experiences and histories.

Alienation

The 'forever foreign' status of immigrants, particularly immigrants whose difference is visibly marked by racialization or other indicators of otherness by the dominant culture, is a condition well documented in immigrant fiction and science fiction. The effects of xenophobia, nativism, racism, or exoticizing curiosity of the alien are prevalent themes in both genres, and conspire to sustain the immigrant's sense of perpetual non-belonging long after their arrival. Kevin Martens Wong's 'Alabanda' and Elana Gomel's 'Danae' both capture with great melancholic lyricism the sense of feeling forever displaced in one's new home, while Christine Bennett's 'A Foot in Two Worlds' dramatizes states of in-betweenness and the sense of suspension and homelessness emblematic of so many immigrants' experiences.

Labor

The history and politics of how labor demands drive immigration are well documented, and the intersections of labor and immigration inform early and contemporary immigrant science fiction alike. In the United States, for instance, the nation's westward expansion throughout the nineteenth century as part of its Manifest Destiny ideology called for the importation of foreign labor, largely from East Asia, to expand settlements, build railroads and cultivate farmlands in the newly acquired western states. At the height of industrialization, urban centers in the United States encouraged immigration from Europe for factory workers to feed the engines of mass production, primarily 'white ethnic' labor largely comprised of Irish, Italian, German and other poor white Europeans (see Upton Sinclair's 1905 novel *The Jungle* as a critique of not only the meatpacking industry, but also immigrant labor abuses). And in more recent decades, immigrants– many undocumented – from Mexico and Latin America have provided much of the low-wage labor in agriculture, construction, hotels, restaurants and domestic services across the United States. Corporate guest-worker and outsourcing programs in the United States and in European countries enable the hiring of foreign workers without providing paths to citizenship in return, ensuring access to labor while keeping the laborers at bay.

The exploitative extraction of labor from immigrant and migrant populations is one of the most compelling subject matters in classic and contemporary immigrant science fiction. It is forcefully dramatized in Alex Rivera's 2008 film *Sleep Dealer*, in which Mexican workers are kept south of the border while their labor is extracted through their remote control of robots north of the border. Intersections of labor and immigration also serve as the premise for several stories in this volume, including Kanishk Tantia's 'Red Berry, White Berry', Alex Gurevich's 'Eater and A' and Samara Lo's 'A Rosella's Home'. And Illimani Ferreira's fascinating 'Warhorse' depicts the ways in which bodies of less-valued populations are used and weaponized by the state. In *Immigrant Acts* (1996), cultural scholar Lisa Lowe observes that the pursuit of legal citizenship often requires an immigrant's "disavowal of the history of racialized labor exploitation and disenfranchisement through the promise of freedom in the political sphere". These stories expose the damaging and even lethal effects of abusive labor practices made rational by the logic of capitalism.

Colonialism

The postcolonial subject is one borne of multiple cultural and national origins, a hybrid subject whose multidimensional identity is often regarded and experienced as a deficit rather than an asset. The immigrant-native power structure is flipped in the colonial scene, in which the immigrants are the settler colonizers of the ruling class, while the natives are the subordinate class of the colonized. Familial, cultural and economic entanglements formed over decades and centuries have made clean distinctions between immigrant and native, colonizer and colonized difficult to draw. Greg van Eekhout's story in this volume captures these complexities through the lens of a Dutch family whose sense of identity is an amalgam of Dutch and Indonesian cultures, the result of intermarriage and other forms of integration. Kevin Martens Wong's 'Alabanda' also depicts migration and the unresolvable sense of non-belonging as both symptom and wound of colonialism.

Generations

One of the most dramatized experiences in immigrant narratives is the evolution of the immigrant experience across generations and the representational approaches of the writers depending on their generational positionalities. Classic immigrant fiction followed an identifiable pattern in which immigrant parents who cling to the ways of their culture of origin clash with their children who are born in the destination nation and identify more with its culture. Then there is the 1.5 generation – immigrants who came to the country of destination as young children who experience the powerful pull of both generations – as well as the third generation – grandchildren of the immigrant generation – who experience a desire to search for the roots of their identity through memory, nostalgia, or a physical return to the ancestral land as they register the growing distance with each advancing generation.

These themes are well captured in Frances Lu-Pai Ippolito's 'A Satchel of Seeds', in which the protagonist, growing up in space and unanchored to any material site of culture, learns her cultural heritage and identity through her mother and grandmother. In a similar vein, Jennifer Hudak's 'The Taste of Centuries, the Taste of Home' features a protagonist who learns of old ways from her mother and grandmother in an estranged world not anchored to the culture of older generations. And Yelena Zhuravlev's 'A World Away and Buried Deep' follows an immigrant mother who travels back to her home world to collect for her son stories of their origins. All of these stories connect the immigrant to their cultures of origin either literally or figuratively through parents and ancestors, who serve as vessels that revive, animate and preserve cultural origins and identity.

Making Up and Making Real

Immigration is a never-ending story because the forces that compel migration and immigration persist, and because terrifying immigration legislation that legitimizes violence against immigrants also persists. At a time when we are seeing the disturbing rise of xenophobia and a resurgence of nativism in many parts of the world, these stories are valuable and necessary interventions. The radical potential of science fiction is its capacity to offer a completely new way to imagine and realize the modes of engagement and understanding across difference. In this regard, science fiction is a powerful representational vehicle for foregrounding the experiences of marginalized or minoritized groups, and of the immigrant experience in particular. It can help move us toward a more compassionate and just world. In the words of science-fiction writer Walter Mosley, "We make up, then make real." We need more speculative immigrant stories that imagine us out of this persistence and into new modes of engagement, understanding and coexistence.

Betsy Huang
Clark University, Massachusetts

GOTHIC

IMMIGRANT SCI-FI SHORT STORIES

ANTHOLOGY OF NEW & CLASSIC TALES

Foreword by Professor E.C. Osondu

Introduction by Betsy Huang, Ph.D.

FLAME TREE PUBLISHING

FANTASY

Foundations: Early & Realist Immigrant Narratives

From Plotzk to Boston

Mary Antin

Prefatory

IN THE YEAR 1891, a mighty wave of the emigration movement swept over all parts of Russia, carrying with it a vast number of the Jewish population to the distant shores of the New World – from tyranny to democracy, from darkness to light, from bondage and persecution to freedom, justice and equality. But the great mass knew nothing of these things; they were going to the foreign world in hopes only of earning their bread and worshiping their God in peace. The different currents that directed the course of that wave cannot be here enumerated. Suffice it to say that its power was enormous. All over the land homes were broken up, families separated, lives completely altered, for a common end.

The emigration fever was at its height in Plotzk, my native town, in the central western part of Russia, on the Dvina River. 'America' was in everybody's mouth. Business men talked of it over their accounts; the market women made up their quarrels that they might discuss it from stall to stall; people who had relatives in the famous land went around reading their letters for the enlightenment of less fortunate folks; the one letter-carrier informed the public how many letters arrived from America, and who were the recipients; children played at emigrating; old folks shook their sage heads over the evening fire, and prophesied no good for those who braved the terrors of the sea and the foreign goal beyond it; – all talked of it, but scarcely anybody knew one true fact about this magic land. For book-knowledge was not for them; and a few persons – they were a dressmaker's daughter, and a merchant with his two sons – who had returned from America after a long visit, happened to be endowed with extraordinary imagination, (a faculty closely related to their knowledge of their old country-men's ignorance), and their descriptions of life across the ocean, given daily, for some months, to eager audiences, surpassed anything in the Arabian Nights. One sad fact threw a shadow over the splendour of the gold-paved, Paradise-like fairyland. The travellers all agreed that Jews lived there in the most shocking impiety.

Driven by a necessity for bettering the family circumstances, and by certain minor forces which cannot now be named, my father began to think seriously of casting his lot with the great stream of emigrants. Many family councils were held before it was agreed that the plan must be carried out. Then came the parting; for it was impossible for the whole family to go at once. I remember it, though I was only eight. It struck me as rather interesting to stand on the platform before the train, with a crowd of friends weeping in sympathy with us, and father waving his hat for our special benefit, and saying – the last words we heard him speak as the train moved off –

"Good-bye, Plotzk, forever!"

Then followed three long years of hope and doubt for father in America and us in Russia. There were toil and suffering and waiting and anxiety for all. There were – but to tell of all that happened in those years I should have to write a separate history. The happy day came when we received the long-coveted summons. And what stirring times followed! The period of preparation was one of constant delight to us children. We were four – my two sisters, one brother and myself. Our playmates looked up to us in respectful admiration; neighbours, if they made no direct investigations, bribed us with nice things for information as to what was going into every box, package and basket. And the house was dismantled – people came and carried off the furniture; closets, sheds and other nooks were emptied of their contents; the great wood-pile was taken away until only a few logs remained; ancient treasures such as women are so loath to part with, and which mother had carried with her from a dear little house whence poverty had driven us, were brought to light from their hiding places, and sacrificed at the altar whose flames were consuming so much that was fraught with precious association and endeared by family tradition; the number of bundles and boxes increased daily, and our home vanished hourly; the rooms became quite uninhabitable at last, and we children glanced in glee, to the anger of the echoes, when we heard that in the evening we were to start upon our journey.

But we did not go till the next morning, and then as secretly as possible. For, despite the glowing tales concerning America, people flocked to the departure of emigrants much as they did to a funeral; to weep and lament while (in the former case only, I believe) they envied. As everybody in Plotzk knew us, and as the departure of a whole family was very rousing, we dared not brave the sympathetic presence of the whole township, that we knew we might expect. So we gave out a false alarm.

Even then there was half the population of Plotzk on hand the next morning. We were the heroes of the hour. I remember how the women crowded around mother, charging her to deliver messages to their relatives in America; how they made the air ring with their unintelligible chorus; how they showered down upon us scores of suggestions and admonitions; how they made us frantic with their sympathetic weeping and wringing of hands; how, finally, the ringing of the signal bell set them all talking faster and louder than ever, in desperate efforts to give the last bits of advice, deliver the last messages, and, to their credit let it be said, to give the final, hearty, unfeigned good-bye kisses, hugs and good wishes.

Well, we lived through three years of waiting, and also through a half hour of parting. Some of our relatives came near being carried off, as, heedless of the last bell, they lingered on in the car. But at last they, too, had to go, and we, the wanderers, could scarcely see the rainbow wave of coloured handkerchiefs, as, dissolved in tears, we were carried out of Plotzk, away from home, but nearer our longed-for haven of reunion; nearer, indeed, to everything that makes life beautiful and gives one an aim and an end – freedom, progress, knowledge, light and truth, with their glorious host of followers. But we did not know it then.

The following pages contain the description of our journey, as I wrote it four years ago, when it was all fresh in my memory.

From Plotzk to Boston

The short journey from Plotzk to Vilna was uneventful. Station after station was passed without our taking any interest in anything, for that never-to-be-forgotten leave taking at the Plotzk railway station left us all in such a state of apathy to all things except our own thoughts as could not easily be thrown off. Indeed, had we not been obliged to change trains at Devinsk and, being the inexperienced travellers we were, do a great deal of bustling and hurrying and questioning of porters and mere idlers, I do not know how long we would have remained in that same thoughtful, silent state.

Towards evening we reached Vilna, and such a welcome as we got! Up to then I had never seen such a mob of porters and *isvostchiky*. I do not clearly remember just what occurred, but a most vivid recollection of being very uneasy for a time is still retained in my memory. You see my uncle was to have met us at the station, but urgent business kept him elsewhere.

Now it was universally believed in Plotzk that it was wise not to trust the first *isvostchik* who offered his services when one arrived in Vilna a stranger, and I do not know to this day how mother managed to get away from the mob and how, above all, she dared to trust herself with her precious baggage to one of them. But I have thought better of Vilna *Isvostchiky* since, for we were safely landed after a pretty long drive in front of my uncle's store, with never one of our number lost, never a bundle stolen or any mishap whatever.

Our stay in Vilna was marked by nothing of interest. We stayed only long enough for some necessary papers to reach us, and during that time I discovered that Vilna was very much like Plotzk, though larger, cleaner and noisier. There were the same coarse, hoarse-voiced women in the market, the same kind of storekeepers in the low store doors, forever struggling and quarrelling for a customer. The only really interesting things I remember were the horsecars, which I had never even heard of, and in one of which I had a lovely ride for five *copeiky*, and a large book store on the Nemetzka yah Ulitza. The latter object may not seem of any interest to most people, but I had never seen so many books in one place before, and I could not help regarding them with longing and wonder.

At last all was in readiness for our start. This was really the beginning of our long journey, which I shall endeavour to describe.

I will not give any description of the various places we passed, for we stopped at few places and always under circumstances which did not permit of sightseeing. I shall only speak of such things as made a distinct impression upon my mind, which, it must be remembered, was not mature enough to be impressed by what older minds were, while on the contrary it was in just the state to take in many things which others heeded not.

I do not know the exact date, but I do know that it was at the break of day on a Sunday and very early in April when we left Vilna. We had not slept any the night before. Fannie and I spent the long hours in playing various quiet games and watching the clock. At last the long expected hour arrived; our train would be due in a short time. All but Fannie and myself had by this time fallen into a drowse, half sitting, half lying on some of the many baskets and boxes that stood all about the room all ready to be taken to the station. So we set to work to rouse the rest, and with the aid of an alarm clock's loud ringing, we soon had them at least half awake; and while the others sat rubbing their eyes and trying to look wide awake, Uncle Borris had gone out, and when he returned with several *droskies* to convey us to the station, we were all ready for the start.

We went out into the street, and now I perceived that not we alone were sleepy; everything slept, and nature also slept, deeply, sweetly.

The sky was covered with dark gray clouds (perhaps that was its night-cap), from which a chill, drizzling rain was slowly descending, and the thick morning fog shut out the road from our sight. No sound came from any direction; slumber and quiet reigned everywhere, for every thing and person slept, forgetful for a time of joys, sorrows, hopes, fears, – everything.

Sleepily we said our last good-byes to the family, took our seats in the *droskies*, and soon the *Hospitalnayah Ulitza* was lost to sight. As the vehicles rattled along the deserted streets, the noise of the horses' hoofs and the wheels striking against the paving stones sounded unusually loud in the general hush, and caused the echoes to answer again and again from the silent streets and alleys.

In a short time we were at the station. In our impatience we had come too early, and now the waiting was very tiresome. Everybody knows how lively and noisy it is at a railroad station when a train is expected. But now there were but a few persons present, and in everybody's face I could see the reflection of my own dissatisfaction, because, like myself, they had much rather have been in a comfortable, warm bed than up and about in the rain and fog. Everything was so uncomfortable.

Suddenly we heard a long shrill whistle, to which the surrounding dreariness gave a strangely mournful sound, the clattering train rushed into the depot and stood still. Several passengers (they were very few) left the cars and hastened towards where the *droskies* stood, and after rousing the sleepy *isvostchiky*, were whirled away to their several destinations.

When we had secured our tickets and seen to the baggage we entered a car in the women's division and waited impatiently for the train to start. At last the first signal was given, then the second and third; the locomotive shrieked and puffed, the train moved slowly, then swiftly it left the depot far behind it.

From Vilna to our next stopping place, Verzbolovo, there was a long, tedious ride of about eight hours. As the day continued to be dull and foggy, very little could be seen through the windows. Besides, no one seemed to care or to be interested in anything. Sleepy and tired as we all were, we got little rest, except the younger ones, for we had not yet got used to living in the cars and could not make ourselves very comfortable. For the greater part of the time we remained as unsocial as the weather was unpleasant. The car was very still, there being few passengers, among them a very pleasant kind gentleman travelling with his pretty daughter. Mother found them very pleasant to chat with, and we children found it less tiresome to listen to them.

At half past twelve o'clock the train came to a stop before a large depot, and the conductor announced "Verz bolovo, fifteen minutes!" The sight that now presented itself was very cheering after our long, unpleasant ride. The weather had changed very much. The sun was shining brightly and not a trace of fog or cloud was to be seen. Crowds of well-dressed people were everywhere – walking up and down the platform, passing through the many gates leading to the street, sitting around the long, well-loaded tables, eating, drinking, talking or reading newspapers, waited upon by the liveliest, busiest waiters I had ever seen – and there was such an activity and bustle about everything that I wished I could join in it, it seemed so hard to sit still. But I had to content myself with looking on with the others, while the friendly gentleman whose acquaintance my mother had made (I do not recollect his name) assisted her in obtaining our tickets for Eidtkunen, and attending to everything else that needed attention, and there were many things.

Soon the fifteen minutes were up, our kind fellow-passenger and his daughter bade us farewell and a pleasant journey (we were just on the brink of the beginning of our troubles), the train puffed out of the depot and we all felt we were nearing a very important stage in our journey. At this time, cholera was raging in Russia, and was spread by emigrants going to America in the countries through which they travelled. To stop this danger, measures were taken to make emigration from Russia more difficult than ever. I believe that at all times the crossing of the boundary between Russia and Germany was a source of trouble to Russians, but with a special passport this was easily overcome. When, however, the traveller could not afford to supply himself with one, the boundary was crossed by stealth, and many amusing anecdotes are told of persons who crossed in some disguise, often that of a *mujik* who said he was going to the town on the German side to sell some goods, carried for the purpose of ensuring the success of the ruse. When several such tricks had been played on the guards it became very risky, and often, when caught, a traveller resorted to stratagem, which is very diverting when afterwards described, but not so at a time when much depends on its success. Some times a paltry bribe secured one a safe passage, and often emigrants were aided by men who made it their profession to help them cross, often suffering themselves to be paid such sums for the service that it paid best to be provided with a special passport.

As I said, the difficulties were greater at the time we were travelling, and our friends believed we had better not attempt a stealthy crossing, and we procured the necessary document to facilitate it. We therefore expected little trouble, but some we thought there might be, for we had heard some vague rumours to the effect that a special passport was not as powerful an agent as it used to be.

We now prepared to enjoy a little lunch, and before we had time to clear it away the train stopped, and we saw several men in blue uniforms, gilt buttons and brass helmets, if you may call them so, on their heads. At his side each wore a kind of leather case attached to a wide bronze belt. In these cases they carried something like a revolver, and each had, besides, a little book with black oilcloth covers.

I can give you no idea of the impression these men (they were German *gendarmes*) made on us, by saying they frightened us. Perhaps because their (to us) impressive appearance gave them a stern look; perhaps because they really looked something more than grave, we were so frightened. I only know that we were. I can see the reason now clearly enough. Like all persons who were used to the tyranny of a Russian policeman, who practically ruled the ward or town under his friendly protection, and never hesitated to assert his rights as holder of unlimited authority over his little domain, in that mild, amiable manner so well known to such of his subjects as he particularly favoured with his vigilant regard – like all such persons, I say, we did not, could not, expect to receive any kind treatment at the hands of a number of officers, especially as we were in the very act of attempting to part with our much-beloved mother country, of which act, to judge by the pains it took to make it difficult, the government did not approve. It was a natural fear in us, as you can easily see. Pretty soon mother recovered herself, and remembering that the train stops for a few minutes only, was beginning to put away the scattered articles hastily when a *gendarme* entered our car and said we were not to leave it. Mamma asked him why, but he said nothing and left the car, another *gendarme* entering as he did so. He demanded where we were going, and, hearing the answer, went out. Before we had had time to look about at each other's frightened faces, another man, a doctor, as we soon knew, came in followed by a third *gendarme*.

The doctor asked many questions about our health, and of what nationality we were. Then he asked about various things, as where we were going to, if we had tickets, how much money we had, where we came from, to whom we were going, etc., etc., making a note of every answer he received. This done, he shook his head with his shining helmet on it, and said slowly (I imagined he enjoyed frightening us), "With these third class tickets you cannot go to America now, because it is forbidden to admit emigrants into Germany who have not at least second class tickets. You will have to return to Russia unless you pay at the office here to have your tickets changed for second class ones." After a few minutes' calculation and reference to the notes he had made, he added calmly, "I find you will need two hundred rubles to get your tickets exchanged"; and, as the finishing stroke to his pleasing communication, added, "Your passports are of no use at all now because the necessary part has to be torn out, whether you are allowed to pass or not." A plain, short speech he made of it, that cruel man. Yet every word sounded in our ears with an awful sound that stopped the beating of our hearts for a while – sounded like the ringing of funeral bells to us, and yet without the mournfully sweet music those bells make, that they might heal while they hurt.

We were homeless, houseless, and friendless in a strange place. We had hardly money enough to last us through the voyage for which we had hoped and waited for three long years. We had suffered much that the reunion we longed for might come about; we had prepared ourselves to suffer more in order to bring it about, and had parted with those we loved, with places that were dear to us in spite of what we passed through in them, never again to see them, as we were convinced – all for the same dear end. With strong hopes and high spirits that hid the sad parting, we had started on our long journey. And now we were checked so unexpectedly but surely, the blow coming from where we little expected it, being, as we believed, safe in that quarter. And that is why the simple words had such a frightful meaning to us. We had received a wound we knew not how to heal.

When mother had recovered enough to speak she began to argue with the *gendarme*, telling him our story and begging him to be kind. The children were frightened by what they understood, and all but cried. I was only wondering what would happen, and wishing I could pour out my grief in tears, as the others did; but when I feel deeply I seldom show it in that way, and always wish I could.

Mother's supplications, and perhaps the children's indirect ones, had more effect than I supposed they would. The officer was moved, even if he had just said that tears would not be accepted instead of money, and gave us such kind advice that I began to be sorry I had thought him cruel, for it was easy to see that he was only doing his duty and had no part in our trouble that he could be blamed for, now that I had more kindly thoughts of him.

He said that we would now be taken to Keebart, a few *versts*' distance from Verzbolovo, where one Herr Schidorsky lived. This man, he said, was well known for miles around, and we were to tell him our story and ask him to help us, which he probably would, being very kind.

A ray of hope shone on each of the frightened faces listening so attentively to this bearer of both evil and happy tidings. I, for one, was very confident that the good man would help us through our difficulties, for I was most unwilling to believe that we really couldn't continue our journey. Which of us was? I'd like to know.

We are in Keebart, at the depot. The least important particular even of that place, I noticed and remembered. How the porter – he was an ugly, grinning man – carried in our things and put them away in the southern corner of the big room, on the floor; how we sat down on a settee near them, a yellow settee; how the glass roof let in so much light that we had to shade our eyes because the car had been dark and we had been crying; how there were only a few people besides ourselves there, and how I began to count them and stopped when I noticed a sign over the head of the fifth person – a little woman with a red nose and a pimple on it, that seemed to be staring at me as much as the grayish-blue eyes above them, it was so large and round – and tried to read the German, with the aid of the Russian translation below. I noticed all this and remembered it, as if there was nothing else in the world for me to think of – no America, no *gendarme* to destroy one's passports and speak of two hundred rubles as if he were a millionaire, no possibility of being sent back to one's old home whether one felt at all grateful for the kindness or not – nothing but that most attractive of places, full of interesting sights.

For, though I had been so hopeful a little while ago, I felt quite discouraged when a man, very sour and grumbling – and he was a Jew – a 'Son of Mercy' as a certain song said – refused to tell mamma where Schidorsky lived. I then believed that the whole world must have united against us; and decided to show my defiant indifference by leaving the world to be as unkind as it pleased, while I took no interest in such trifles.

So I let my mind lose itself in a queer sort of mist – a something I cannot describe except by saying it must have been made up of lazy inactivity. Through this mist I saw and heard indistinctly much that followed.

When I think of it now, I see how selfish it was to allow myself to sink, body and mind, in such a sea of helpless laziness, when I might have done something besides awaiting the end of that critical time, whatever it might be – something, though what, I do not see even now, I own. But I only studied the many notices till I thought myself very well acquainted with the German tongue; and now and then tried to cheer the other children, who were still inclined to cry, by pointing out to them some of the things that interested me. For this faulty conduct I have no excuse to give, unless youth and the fact that I was stunned with the shock we had just received, will be accepted.

I remember through that mist that mother found Schidorsky's home at last, but was told she could not see him till a little later; that she came back to comfort us, and found there our former fellow passenger who had come with us from Vilna, and that he was very indignant at the way in which we were treated, and scolded, and declared he would have the matter in all the papers, and said we must be helped. I remember how mamma saw Schidorsky at last, spoke to him, and then told us, word for word, what his answer had been; that he wouldn't wait to be asked to use all his influence, and wouldn't lose a moment about it, and he didn't, for he went out at once on that errand, while his good daughter did her best to comfort mamma with kind words and tea. I remember that there was much going to the good man's house; much hurrying of special messengers to and from Eidtkunen; trembling inquiries, uncertain replies made hopeful only by the pitying, encouraging words and manners of the deliverer – for all, even the servants, were kind as good angels at that place. I remember that another little family – there were three – were discovered by us in the same happy state as ourselves, and like the dogs in the fable, who, receiving care at the hands of a kind man, sent their friends to him for help, we sent them to our helper.

I remember seeing night come out of that mist, and bringing more trains and people and noise than the whole day (we still remained at the depot), till I felt sick and dizzy. I remember wondering what kind of a night it was, but not knowing how to find out, as if I had no senses. I remember that somebody said we were obliged to remain in Keebart that night and that we set out to find lodgings; that the most important things I saw on the way were the two largest dolls I had ever seen, carried by two pretty little girls, and a big, handsome father; and a great deal of gravel in the streets, and boards for the crossings. I remember that we found a little room (we had to go up four steps first) that we could have for seventy-five copecks, with our tea paid for in that sum. I remember, through that mist, how I wondered what I was sleeping on that night, as I wondered about the weather; that we really woke up in the morning (I was so glad to rest I had believed we should never be disturbed again) and washed, and dressed and breakfasted and went to the depot again, to be always on hand. I remember that mamma and the father of the little family went at once to the only good man on earth (I thought so) and that the party of three were soon gone, by the help of some agent that was slower, for good reasons, in helping us.

I remember that mamma came to us soon after and said that Herr Schidorsky had told her to ask the *Postmeister* – some high official there – for a pass to Eidtkunen; and there she should speak herself to our protector's older brother who could help us by means of his great power among the officers of high rank; that she returned in a few hours and told us the two brothers were equal in kindness, for the older one, too, said he would not wait to be asked to do his best for us. I remember that another day – so-o-o long – passed behind the mist, and we were still in that dreadful, noisy, tiresome depot, with no change, till we went to spend the night at Herr Schidorsky's, because they wouldn't let us go anywhere else. On the way there, I remember, I saw something marvellous – queer little wooden sticks stuck on the lines where clothes hung for some purpose. (I didn't think it was for drying, because you know I always saw things hung up on fences and gates for such purposes. The queer things turned out to be clothes-pins). And, I remember, I noticed many other things of equal importance to our affairs, till we came to the little house in the garden. Here we were received, I remember with much kindness and hospitality. We had a fire made for us, food and drink brought in, and a servant was always inquiring whether anything more could be done for our comfort.

I remember, still through that misty veil, what a pleasant evening we passed, talking over what had so far happened, and wondering what would come. I must have talked like one lost in a thick fog, groping carefully. But, had I been shut up, mentally, in a tower nothing else could pierce, the sense of gratitude that naturally sprung from the kindness that surrounded us, must have, would have found a passage for itself to the deepest cavities of the heart. Yes, though all my senses were dulled by what had passed over us so lately, I was yet aware of the deepest sense of thankfulness one can ever feel. I was aware of something like the sweet presence of angels in the persons of good Schidorsky and his family. Oh, that some knowledge of that gratitude might reach those for whom we felt it so keenly! We all felt it. But the deepest emotions are so hard to express. I thought of this as I lay awake a little while, and said to myself, thinking of our benefactor, that he was a Jew, a true 'Son of Mercy.' And I slept with that thought. And this is the last I remember seeing and feeling behind that mist of lazy inactivity.

The next morning, I woke not only from the night's sleep, but from my waking dreaminess. All the vapours dispersed as I went into the pretty flower garden where the others were already at play, and by the time we had finished a good breakfast, served by a dear servant girl, I felt quite myself again.

Of course, mamma hastened to Herr Schidorsky as soon as she could, and he sent her to the *Postmeister* again, to ask him to return the part of our passports that had been torn out, and without which we could not go on. He said he would return them as soon as he received word from Eidtkunen. So we could only wait and hope. At last it came and so suddenly that we ran off to the depot with hardly a hat on all our heads, or a coat on our backs, with two men running behind with our things, making it a very ridiculous sight. We have often laughed over it since.

Of course, in such a confusion we could not say even one word of farewell or thanks to our deliverers. But, turning to see that we were all there, I saw them standing in the gate, crying that all was well now, and wishing us many pleasant things, and looking as if they had been receiving all the blessings instead of us.

I have often thought they must have purposely arranged it that we should have to leave in a hurry, because they wouldn't stand any expression of gratefulness.

Well, we just reached our car in time to see our baggage brought from the office and ourselves inside, when the last bell rang. Then, before we could get breath enough to utter more than faint gasps of delight, we were again in Eidtkunen.

The *gendarmes* came to question us again, but when mother said that we were going to Herr Schidorsky of Eidtkunen, as she had been told to say, we were allowed to leave the train. I really thought we were to be the visitors of the elder Schidorsky, but it turned out to be only an understanding between him and the officers that those claiming to be on their way to him were not to be troubled.

At any rate, we had now really crossed the forbidden boundary – we were in Germany.

There was a terrible confusion in the baggage-room where we were directed to go. Boxes, baskets, bags, valises, and great, shapeless things belonging to no particular class were thrown about by porters and other men, who sorted them and put tickets on all but those containing provisions, while others were opened and examined in haste. At last our turn came, and our things, along with those of all other American-bound travellers, were taken away to be steamed and smoked and other such processes gone through. We were told to wait till notice should be given us of something else to be done. Our train would not depart till nine in the evening.

As usual, I noticed all the little particulars of the waiting room. What else could I do with so much time and not even a book to read? I could describe it exactly – the large, square room, painted walls, long tables with fruits and drinks of all kinds covering them, the white chairs, carved settees, beautiful china and cut glass showing through the glass doors of the dressers, and the nickel samovar, which attracted my attention because I had never seen any but copper or brass ones. The best and the worst of everything there was a large case full of books. It was the best, because they were 'books' and all could use them; the worst, because they were all German, and my studies in the railway depot of Keebart had not taught me so much that I should be able to read books in German. It was very hard to see people get those books and enjoy them while I couldn't. It was impossible to be content with other people's pleasure, and I wasn't.

When I had almost finished counting the books, I noticed that mamma and the others had made friends with a family of travellers like ourselves. Frau Gittleman and her five children made very interesting companions for the rest of the day, and they seemed to think that Frau Antin and the four younger Antins were just as interesting; perhaps excepting, in their minds, one of them who must have appeared rather uninteresting from a habit she had of looking about as if always expecting to make discoveries.

But she was interested, if not interesting, enough when the oldest of the young Gittlemans, who was a young gentleman of seventeen, produced some books which she could read. Then all had a merry time together, reading, talking, telling the various adventures of the journey, and walking, as far as we were allowed, up and down the long platform outside, till we were called to go and see, if we wanted to see, how our things were being made fit for further travel. It was interesting to see how they managed to have anything left to return to us, after all the processes of airing and smoking and steaming and other assaults on supposed germs of the dreaded cholera had been done with, the pillows, even, being ripped open to be steamed! All this was interesting, but we were rather disagreeably surprised when a bill for these unasked-for services had to be paid.

The Gittlemans, we found, were to keep us company for some time. At the expected hour we all tried to find room in a car indicated by the conductor. We tried, but could only find enough space on the floor for our baggage, on which we made believe sitting comfortably. For now we were obliged to exchange the comparative comforts of a third class passenger train for the certain discomforts of a fourth class one. There were only four narrow benches in the whole car, and about twice as many people were already seated on these as they were probably supposed to accommodate. All other space, to the last inch, was crowded by passengers or their luggage. It was very hot and close and altogether uncomfortable, and still at every new station fresh passengers came crowding in, and actually made room, spare as it was, for themselves. It became so terrible that all glared madly at the conductor as he allowed more people to come into that prison, and trembled at the announcement of every station. I cannot see even now how the officers could allow such a thing; it was really dangerous. The most remarkable thing was the good-nature of the poor passengers. Few showed a sour face even; not a man used any strong language (audibly, at least). They smiled at each other as if they meant to say, "I am having a good time; so are you, aren't you?" Young Gittleman was very gallant, and so cheerful that he attracted everybody's attention. He told stories, laughed, and made us unwilling to be outdone. During one of his narratives he produced a pretty memorandum book that pleased one of us very much, and that pleasing gentleman at once presented it to her. She has kept it since in memory of the giver, and, in the right place, I could tell more about that matter – very interesting.

I have given so much space to the description of that one night's adventures because I remember it so distinctly, with all its discomforts, and the contrast of our fellow-travellers' kindly dispositions. At length that dreadful night passed, and at dawn about half the passengers left, all at once. There was such a sigh of relief and a stretching of cramped limbs as can only be imagined, as the remaining passengers inhaled the fresh cold air of dewy dawn. It was almost worth the previous suffering to experience the pleasure of relief that followed.

All day long we travelled in the same train, sleeping, resting, eating, and wishing to get out. But the train stopped for a very short time at the many stations, and all the difference that made to us was that pretty girls passed through the cars with little bark baskets filled with fruit and flowers hardly fresher or prettier than their bearers, who generally sold something to our young companion, for he never wearied of entertaining us.

Other interests there were none. The scenery was nothing unusual, only towns, depots, roads, fields, little country houses with barns and cattle and poultry – all such as we were well acquainted with. If something new did appear, it was passed before one could get a good look at it. The most pleasing sights were little barefoot children waving their aprons or hats as we eagerly watched for them, because that reminded us of our doing the same thing when we saw the passenger trains, in the country. We used to wonder whether we should ever do so again.

Towards evening we came into Berlin. I grow dizzy even now when I think of our whirling through that city. It seemed we were going faster and faster all the time, but it was only the whirl of trains passing in opposite directions and close to us that made it seem so. The sight of crowds of people such as we had never seen before, hurrying to and fro, in and out of great depots that danced past us, helped to make it more so. Strange sights, splendid buildings, shops, people and animals, all mingled in one great, confused mass of a disposition to continually move in a great hurry, wildly, with no other aim but to make one's head go round and round, in following its dreadful motions. Round and round went my head. It was nothing but trains, depots, crowds – crowds, depots, trains, again and again, with no beginning, no end, only a mad dance! Faster and faster we go, faster still, and the noise increases with the speed. Bells, whistles, hammers, locomotives shrieking madly, men's voices, peddlers' cries, horses' hoofs, dogs' barking – all united in doing their best to drown every other sound but their own, and made such a deafening uproar in the attempt that nothing could keep it out. Whirl, noise, dance, uproar – will it last forever? I'm so-o diz-z-zy! How my head aches!

And oh! those people will be run over! Stop the train, they'll – thank goodness, nobody is hurt. But who ever heard of a train passing right through the middle of a city, up in the air, it seems. Oh, dear! it's no use thinking, my head spins so. Right through the business streets! Why, who ever—!

I must have lived through a century of this terrible motion and din and unheard of roads for trains, and confused thinking. But at length everything began to take a more familiar appearance again, the noise grew less, the roads more secluded, and by degrees we recognized the dear, peaceful country. Now we could think of Berlin, or rather, what we had seen of it, more calmly, and wonder why it made such an impression. I see now. We had never seen so large a city before, and were not prepared to see such sights, bursting upon us so suddenly as that. It was like allowing a blind man to see the full glare of the sun all at once. Our little Plotzk, and even the larger cities we had passed through, compared to Berlin about the same as total darkness does to great brilliancy of light.

In a great lonely field opposite a solitary wooden house within a large yard, our train pulled up at last, and a conductor commanded the passengers to make haste and get out. He need not have told us to hurry; we were glad enough to be free again after such a long imprisonment in the uncomfortable car. All rushed to the door. We breathed more freely in the open field, but the conductor did not wait for us to enjoy our freedom. He hurried us into the one large room which made up the house, and then into the yard. Here a great many men and women, dressed in white, received us, the women attending to the women and girls of the passengers, and the men to the others.

This was another scene of bewildering confusion, parents losing their children, and little ones crying; baggage being thrown together in one corner of the yard, heedless of contents, which suffered in consequence; those white-clad Germans shouting commands always accompanied with "Quick! Quick!"; the confused passengers obeying all orders like meek children, only questioning now and then what was going to be done with them.

And no wonder if in some minds stories arose of people being captured by robbers, murderers, and the like. Here we had been taken to a lonely place where only that house was to be seen; our things were taken away, our friends separated from us; a man came to inspect us, as if to ascertain our full value; strange looking people driving us about like dumb animals, helpless and unresisting; children we could not see, crying in a way that suggested terrible things; ourselves driven into a little room where a great kettle was boiling on a little stove; our clothes taken off, our bodies rubbed with a slippery substance that might be any bad thing; a shower of warm water let down on us without warning; again driven to another little room where we sit, wrapped in woollen blankets till large, coarse bags are brought in, their contents turned out and we see only a cloud of steam, and hear the women's orders to dress ourselves, quick, quick, or else we'll miss – something we cannot hear. We are forced to pick out our clothes from among all the others, with the steam blinding us; we choke, cough, entreat the women to give us time; they persist, "Quick, quick, or you'll miss the train!" Oh, so we really won't be murdered! They are only making us ready for the continuing of our journey, cleaning us of all suspicions of dangerous germs. Thank God!

Assured by the word 'train' we manage to dress ourselves after a fashion, and the man comes again to inspect us. All is right, and we are allowed to go into the yard to find our friends and our luggage. Both are difficult tasks, the second even harder. Imagine all the things of some hundreds of people making a journey like ours, being mostly unpacked and mixed together in one sad heap. It was disheartening, but done at last was the task of collecting our belongings, and we were marched into the big room again. Here, on the bare floor, in a ring, sat some Polish men and women singing some hymn in their own tongue, and making more noise than music. We were obliged to stand and await further orders, the few seats being occupied, and the great door barred and locked. We were in a prison, and again felt some doubts. Then a man came in and called the passengers' names, and when they answered they were made to pay two *marcs* each for the pleasant bath we had just been forced to take.

Another half hour, and our train arrived. The door was opened, and we rushed out into the field, glad to get back even to the fourth class car.

We had lost sight of the Gittlemans, who were going a different way now, and to our regret hadn't even said good-bye, or thanked them for their kindness.

After the preceding night of wakefulness and discomfort, the weary day in the train, the dizzy whirl through Berlin, the fright we had from the rough proceedings of the Germans, and all the strange experiences of the place we just escaped – after all this we needed rest. But to get it was impossible for all but the youngest children. If we had borne great discomforts on the night before, we were suffering now. I had thought anything worse impossible. Worse it was now. The car was even more crowded, and people gasped for breath. People sat in strangers' laps, only glad of that. The floor was so thickly lined that the conductor could not pass, and the tickets were passed to him from hand to hand. To-night all were more worn out, and that did not mend their dispositions. They could not help falling asleep and colliding with someone's nodding head, which called out angry mutterings and growls. Some fell off their seats and caused a great commotion by rolling over on the sleepers on the floor, and, in spite of my own sleepiness and weariness, I had many quiet laughs by myself as I watched the funny actions of the poor travellers.

Not until very late did I fall asleep. I, with the rest, missed the pleasant company of our friends, the Gittlemans, and thought about them as I sat perched on a box, with an old man's knees for the back of my seat, another man's head continually striking my right shoulder, a dozen or so arms being tossed restlessly right in front of my face, and as many legs holding me a fast prisoner, so that I could only try to keep my seat against all the assaults of the sleepers who tried in vain to make their positions more comfortable. It was all so comical, in spite of all the inconveniences, that I tried hard not to laugh out loud, till I too fell asleep. I was awakened very early in the morning by something chilling and uncomfortable on my face, like raindrops coming down irregularly. I found it was a neighbour of mine eating cheese, who was dropping bits on my face. So I began the day with a laugh at the man's funny apologies, but could not find much more fun in the world on account of the cold and the pain of every limb. It was very miserable, till some breakfast cheered me up a little.

About eight o'clock we reached Hamburg. Again there was a *gendarme* to ask questions, look over the tickets and give directions. But all the time he kept a distance from those passengers who came from Russia, all for fear of the cholera. We had noticed before how people were afraid to come near us, but since that memorable bath in Berlin, and all the steaming and smoking of our things, it seemed unnecessary.

We were marched up to the strangest sort of vehicle one could think of. It was a something I don't know any name for, though a little like an express wagon. At that time I had never seen such a high, narrow, long thing, so high that the women and girls couldn't climb up without the men's help, and great difficulty; so narrow that two persons could not sit comfortably side by side, and so long that it took me some time to move my eyes from the rear end, where the baggage was, to the front, where the driver sat.

When all had settled down at last (there were a number besides ourselves) the two horses started off very fast, in spite of their heavy load. Through noisy, strange looking streets they took us, where many people walked or ran or rode. Many splendid houses, stone and brick, and showy shops, they passed. Much that was very strange to us we saw, and little we knew anything about. There a little cart loaded with bottles or tin cans, drawn by a goat or a dog, sometimes two, attracted our attention. Sometimes it was only a nurse carrying a child in her arms that seemed interesting, from the strange dress. Often it was some article displayed in a shop window or door, or the usually smiling owner standing in the doorway, that called for our notice. Not that there was anything really unusual in many of these things, but a certain air of foreignness, which sometimes was very vague, surrounded everything that passed before our interested gaze as the horses hastened on.

The strangest sight of all we saw as we came into the still noisier streets. Something like a horse-car such as we had seen in Vilna for the first time, except that it was open on both sides (in most cases) but without any horses, came flying – really flying – past us. For we stared and looked it all over, and above, and under, and rubbed our eyes, and asked of one another what we saw, and nobody could find what it was that made the thing go. And go it did, one after another, faster than we, with nothing to move it. "Why, what is that?" we kept exclaiming. "Really, do you see anything that makes it go? I'm sure I don't." Then I ventured the highly probable suggestion, "Perhaps it's the fat man in the gray coat and hat with silver buttons. I guess he pushes it. I've noticed one in front on every one of them, holding on to that shining thing." And I'm sure this was as wise a solution of the mystery as anyone could give, except the driver, who laughed to himself and his horses over our surprise and wonder at nothing he could see to cause it.

But we couldn't understand his explanation, though we always got along very easily with the Germans, and not until much later did we know that those wonderful things, with only a fat man to move them, were electric cars.

The sightseeing was not all on our side. I noticed many people stopping to look at us as if amused, though most passed by as though used to such sights. We did make a queer appearance all in a long row, up above people's heads. In fact, we looked like a flock of giant fowls roosting, only wide awake.

Suddenly, when everything interesting seemed at an end, we all recollected how long it was since we had started on our funny ride. Hours, we thought, and still the horses ran. Now we rode through quieter streets where there were fewer shops and more wooden houses. Still the horses seemed to have but just started. I looked over our perch again. Something made me think of a description I had read of criminals being carried on long journeys in uncomfortable things – like this? Well, it was strange – this long, long drive, the conveyance, no word of explanation, and all, though going different ways, being packed off together. We were strangers; the driver knew it. He might take us anywhere – how could we tell? I was frightened again as in Berlin. The faces around me confessed the same.

The streets became quieter still; no shops, only little houses; hardly any people passing. Now we cross many railway tracks and I can hear the sea not very distant. There are many trees now by the roadside, and the wind whistles through their branches. The wheels and hoofs make a great noise on the stones, the roar of the sea and the wind among the branches have an unfriendly sound.

The horses never weary. Still they run. There are no houses now in view, save now and then a solitary one, far away. I can see the ocean. Oh, it is stormy. The dark waves roll inward, the white foam flies high in the air; deep sounds come from it. The wheels and hoofs make a great noise; the wind is stronger, and says, "Do you hear the sea?" And the ocean's roar threatens. The sea threatens, and the wind bids me hear it, and the hoofs and the wheels repeat the command, and so do the trees, by gestures.

Yes, we are frightened. We are very still. Some Polish women over there have fallen asleep, and the rest of us look such a picture of woe, and yet so funny, it is a sight to see and remember.

At last, at last! Those unwearied horses have stopped. Where? In front of a brick building, the only one on a large, broad street, where only the trees, and, in the distance, the passing trains can be seen. Nothing else. The ocean, too, is shut out.

All were helped off, the baggage put on the sidewalk, and then taken up again and carried into the building, where the passengers were ordered to go. On the left side of the little corridor was a small office where a man sat before a desk covered with papers. These he pushed aside when we entered, and called us in one by one, except, of course children. As usual, many questions were asked, the new ones being about our tickets. Then each person, children included, had to pay three *marcs* – one for the wagon that brought us over and two for food and lodgings, till our various ships should take us away.

Mamma, having five to pay for, owed fifteen *marcs*. The little sum we started with was to last us to the end of the journey, and would have done so if there hadn't been those unexpected bills to pay at Keebart, Eidtkunen, Berlin, and now at the office. Seeing how often services were forced upon us unasked and payment afterwards demanded, mother had begun to fear that we should need more money, and had sold some things to a woman for less than a third of their value. In spite of that, so heavy was the drain on the spare purse where it had not been expected, she found to her dismay that she had only twelve *marcs* left to meet the new bill.

The man in the office wouldn't believe it, and we were given over in charge of a woman in a dark gray dress and long white apron, with a red cross on her right arm. She led us away and thoroughly searched us all, as well as our baggage. That was nice treatment, like what we had been receiving since our first uninterrupted entrance into Germany. Always a call for money, always suspicion of our presence and always rough orders and scowls of disapproval, even at the quickest obedience. And now this outrageous indignity! We had to bear it all because we were going to America from a land cursed by the dreadful epidemic. Others besides ourselves shared these trials, the last one included, if that were any comfort, which it was not.

When the woman reported the result of the search as being fruitless, the man was satisfied, and we were ordered with the rest through many more examinations and ceremonies before we should be established under the quarantine, for that it was.

While waiting for our turn to be examined by the doctor I looked about, thinking it worth while to get acquainted with a place where we might be obliged to stay for I knew not how long. The room where we were sitting was large, with windows so high up that we couldn't see anything through them. In the middle stood several long wooden tables, and around these were settees of the same kind. On the right, opposite the doctor's office, was a little room where various things could be bought of a young man – if you hadn't paid all your money for other things.

When the doctor was through with us he told us to go to Number Five. Now wasn't that like in a prison? We walked up and down a long yard looking, among a row of low, numbered doors, for ours, when we heard an exclamation of, "Oh, Esther! how do you happen to be here?" and, on seeing the speaker, found it to be an old friend of ours from Plotzk. She had gone long before us, but her ship hadn't arrived yet. She was surprised to see us because we had had no intention of going when she went.

What a comfort it was to find a friend among all the strangers! She showed us at once to our new quarters, and while she talked to mamma I had time to see what they were like.

It looked something like a hospital, only less clean and comfortable; more like the soldiers' barracks I had seen. I saw a very large room, around whose walls were ranged rows of high iron double bedsteads, with coarse sacks stuffed with something like matting, and not over-clean blankets for the only bedding, except where people used their own. There were three windows almost touching the roof, with nails covering all the framework. From the ceiling hung two round gas lamps, and almost under them stood a little wooden table and a settee. The floor was of stone.

Here was a pleasant prospect. We had no idea how long this unattractive place might be our home.

Our friend explained that Number Five was only for Jewish women and girls, and the beds were sleeping rooms, dining rooms, parlours, and everything else, kitchens excepted. It seemed so, for some were lounging on the beds, some sitting up, some otherwise engaged, and all were talking and laughing and making a great noise. Poor things! there was nothing else to do in that prison.

Before mother had told our friend of our adventures, a girl, also a passenger, who had been walking in the yard, ran in and announced, "It's time to go to dinner! He has come already." 'He' we soon learned, was the overseer of the Jewish special kitchen, without whom the meals were never taken.

All the inmates of Number Five rushed out in less than a minute, and I wondered why they hurried so. When we reached the place that served as dining room, there was hardly any room for us. Now, while the dinner is being served, I will tell you what I can see.

In the middle of the yard stood a number of long tables covered with white oilcloth. On either side of each table stood benches on which all the Jewish passengers were now seated, looking impatiently at the door with the sign 'Jewish Kitchen' over it. Pretty soon a man appeared in the doorway, tall, spare, with a thin, pointed beard, and an air of importance on his face. It was 'he,' the overseer, who carried a large tin pail filled with black bread cut into pieces of half a pound each. He gave a piece to every person, the youngest child and the biggest man alike, and then went into the kitchen and filled his pail with soup and meat, giving everybody a great bowl full of soup and a small piece of meat. All attacked their rations as soon as they received them and greatly relished the coarse bread and dark, hot water they called soup. We couldn't eat those things and only wondered how any one could have such an appetite for such a dinner. We stopped wondering when our own little store of provisions gave out.

After dinner, the people went apart, some going back to their beds and others to walk in the yard or sit on the settees there. There was no other place to go to. The doors of the prison were never unlocked except when new passengers arrived or others left for their ships. The fences – they really were solid walls – had wires and nails on top, so that one couldn't even climb to get a look at the sea.

We went back to our quarters to talk over matters and rest from our journey. At six o'clock the doctor came with a clerk, and, standing before the door, bade all those in the yard belonging to Number Five assemble there; and then the roll was called and everybody received a little ticket as she answered to her name. With this all went to the kitchen and received two little rolls and a large cup of partly sweetened tea. This was supper; and breakfast, served too in this way was the same. Any wonder that people hurried to dinner and enjoyed it? And it was always the same thing, no change.

Little by little we became used to the new life, though it was hard to go hungry day after day, and bear the discomforts of the common room, shared by so many; the hard beds (we had little bedding of our own), and the confinement to the narrow limits of the yard, and the tiresome sameness of the life. Meal hours, of course, played the most important part, while the others had to be filled up as best we could. The weather was fine most of the time and that helped much. Everything was an event, the arrival of fresh passengers a great one which happened every day; the day when the women were allowed to wash clothes by the well was a holiday, and the few favourite girls who were allowed to help in the kitchen were envied. On dull, rainy days, the man coming to light the lamps at night was an object of pleasure, and every one made the best of everybody else. So when a young man arrived who had been to America once before, he was looked up to by every person there as a superior, his stories of our future home listened to with delight, and his manners imitated by all, as a sort of fit preparation. He was wanted everywhere, and he made the best of his greatness by taking liberties and putting on great airs and, I afterwards found, imposing on our ignorance very much. But anything 'The American' did passed for good, except his going away a few days too soon.

Then a girl came who was rather wanting a little brightness. So all joined in imposing upon her by telling her a certain young man was a great professor whom all owed respect and homage to, and she would do anything in the world to express hers, while he used her to his best advantage, like the willing slave she was. Nobody seemed to think this unkind at all, and it really was excusable that the poor prisoners, hungry for some entertainment, should try to make a little fun when the chance came. Besides, the girl had opened the temptation by asking, "Who was the handsome man in the glasses? A professor surely"; showing that she took glasses for a sure sign of a professor, and professor for the highest possible title of honour. Doesn't this excuse us?

The greatest event was the arrival of some ship to take some of the waiting passengers. When the gates were opened and the lucky ones said good bye, those left behind felt hopeless of ever seeing the gates open for them. It was both pleasant and painful, for the strangers grew to be fast friends in a day and really rejoiced in each other's fortune, but the regretful envy could not be helped either.

Amid such events as these a day was like a month at least. Eight of these we had spent in quarantine when a great commotion was noticed among the people of Number Five and those of the corresponding number in the men's division. There was a good reason for it. You remember that it was April and Passover was coming on; in fact, it began that night. The great question was, Would we be able to keep it exactly according to the host of rules to be obeyed? You who know all about the great holiday can understand what the answer to that question meant to us. Think of all the work and care and money it takes to supply a family with all the things proper and necessary, and you will see that to supply a few hundred was no small matter. Now, were they going to take care that all was perfectly right, and could we trust them if they promised, or should we be forced to break any of the laws that ruled the holiday?

All day long there was talking and questioning and debating and threatening that "we would rather starve than touch anything we were not sure of." And we meant it. So some men and women went to the overseer to let him know what he had to look out for. He assured them that he would rather starve along with us than allow anything to be in the least wrong. Still, there was more discussing and shaking of heads, for they were not sure yet.

There was not a crumb anywhere to be found, because what bread we received was too precious for any of it to be wasted; but the women made a great show of cleaning up Number Five, while they sighed and looked sad and told one another of the good hard times they had at home getting ready for Passover. Really, hard as it is, when one is used to it from childhood, it seems part of the holiday, and can't be left out. To sit down and wait for supper as on other nights seemed like breaking one of the laws. So they tried hard to be busy.

At night we were called by the overseer (who tried to look more important than ever in his holiday clothes – not his best, though) to the feast spread in one of the unoccupied rooms. We were ready for it, and anxious enough. We had had neither bread nor *matzo* for dinner, and were more hungry than ever, if that is possible. We now found everything really prepared; there were the pillows covered with a snow-white spread, new oilcloth on the newly scrubbed tables, some little candles stuck in a basin of sand on the window-sill for the women, and – a sure sign of a holiday – both gas lamps burning. Only one was used on other nights.

Happy to see these things, and smell the supper, we took our places and waited. Soon the cook came in and filled some glasses with wine from two bottles, – one yellow, one red. Then she gave to each person – exactly one and a half *matzos*; also some cold meat, burned almost to a coal for the occasion.

The young man – bless him – who had the honour to perform the ceremonies, was, fortunately for us all, one of the passengers. He felt for and with us, and it happened – just a coincidence – that the greater part of the ceremony escaped from his book as he turned the leaves. Though strictly religious, nobody felt in the least guilty about it, especially on account of the wine; for, when we came to the place where you have to drink the wine, we found it tasted like good vinegar, which made us all choke and gasp, and one little girl screamed "Poison!" so that all laughed, and the leader, who tried to go on, broke down too at the sight of the wry faces he saw; while the overseer looked shocked, the cook nearly set her gown on fire by overthrowing the candles with her apron (used to hide her face) and all wished our Master Overseer had to drink that 'wine' all his days.

Think of the same ceremony as it is at home, then of this one just described. Do they even resemble each other?

Well, the leader got through amid much giggling and sly looks among the girls who understood the trick, and frowns of the older people (who secretly blessed him for it). Then, half hungry, all went to bed and dreamed of food in plenty.

No other dreams? Rather! For the day that brought the Passover brought us – our own family – the most glorious news. We had been ordered to bring our baggage to the office!

'Ordered to bring our baggage to the office!' That meant nothing less than that we were 'going the next day!'

It was just after supper that we received the welcome order. Oh, who cared if there wasn't enough to eat? Who cared for anything in the whole world? We didn't. It was all joy and gladness and happy anticipation for us. We laughed, and cried, and hugged one another, and shouted, and acted altogether like wild things. Yes, we were wild with joy, and long after the rest were asleep, we were whispering together and wondering how we could keep quiet the whole night. We couldn't sleep by any means, we were so afraid of oversleeping the great hour; and every little while, after we tried to sleep, one of us would suddenly think she saw day at the window, and wake the rest, who also had only been pretending to sleep while watching in the dark for daylight.

When it came, it found no watchful eye, after all. The excitement gave way to fatigue, and drowsiness first, then deep sleep, completed its victory. It was eight o'clock when we awoke. The morning was cloudy and chilly, the sun being too lazy to attend to business; now and then it rained a little, too. And yet it was the most beautiful day that had ever dawned on Hamburg.

We enjoyed everything offered for breakfast, two *matzos* and two cups of tea apiece – why it was a banquet. After it came the good-byes, as we were going soon. As I told you before, the strangers became fast friends in a short time under the circumstances, so there was real sorrow at the partings, though the joy of the fortunate ones was, in a measure, shared by all.

About one o'clock (we didn't go to dinner – we couldn't eat for excitement) we were called. There were three other families, an old woman, and a young man, among the Jewish passengers, who were going with us, besides some Polish people. We were all hurried through the door we had watched with longing for so long, and were a little way from it when the old woman stopped short and called on the rest to wait.

"We haven't any *matzo*!" she cried in alarm. "Where's the overseer?"

Sure enough we had forgotten it, when we might as well have left one of us behind. We refused to go, calling for the overseer, who had promised to supply us, and the man who had us in charge grew angry and said he wouldn't wait. It was a terrible situation for us.

"Oh," said the man, "you can go and get your *matzo*, but the boat won't wait for you." And he walked off, followed by the Polish people only.

We had to decide at once. We looked at the old woman. She said she wasn't going to start on a dangerous journey with such a sin on her soul. Then the children decided. They understood the matter. They cried and begged to follow the party. And we did.

Just when we reached the shore, the cook came up panting hard. She brought us *matzo*. How relieved we were then!

We got on a little steamer (the name is too big for it) that was managed by our conductor alone. Before we had recovered from the shock of the shrill whistle so near us, we were landing in front of a large stone building.

Once more we were under the command of the *gendarme*. We were ordered to go into a big room crowded with people, and wait till the name of our ship was called. Somebody in a little room called a great many queer names, and many passengers answered the call. At last we heard,

"*Polynesia*!"

We passed in and a great many things were done to our tickets before we were directed to go outside, then to a larger steamer than the one we came in. At every step our tickets were either stamped or punched, or a piece torn off of them, till we stepped upon the steamer's deck. Then we were ordered below. It was dark there, and we didn't like it. In a little while we were called up again, and then we saw before us the great ship that was to carry us to America.

I only remember, from that moment, that I had only one care till all became quiet; not to lose hold of my sister's hand. Everything else can be told in one word – noise. But when I look back, I can see what made it. There were sailors dragging and hauling bundles and boxes from the small boat into the great ship, shouting and thundering at their work. There were officers giving out orders in loud voices, like trumpets, though they seemed to make no effort. There were children crying, and mothers hushing them, and fathers questioning the officers as to where they should go. There were little boats and steamers passing all around, shrieking and whistling terribly. And there seemed to be everything under heaven that had any noise in it, come to help swell the confusion of sounds. I know that, but how we ever got in that quiet place that had the sign 'For Families' over it, I don't know. I think we went around and around, long and far, before we got there.

But there we were, sitting quietly on a bench by the white berths.

When the sailors brought our things, we got everything in order for the journey as soon as possible, that we might go on deck to see the starting. But first we had to obey a sailor, who told us to come and get dishes. Each person received a plate, a spoon and a cup. I wondered how we could get along if we had had no things of our own.

For an hour or two more there were still many noises on deck, and many preparations made. Then we went up, as most of the passengers did.

What a change in the scene! Where there had been noise and confusion before, peace and quiet were now. All the little boats and steamers had disappeared, and the wharf was deserted. On deck the *Polynesia* everything was in good order, and the officers walked about smoking their cigars as if their work was done. Only a few sailors were at work at the big ropes, but they didn't shout as before. The weather had changed, too, for the twilight was unlike what the day had promised. The sky was soft gray, with faint streaks of yellow on the horizon. The air was still and pleasant, much warmer than it had been all the day; and the water was as motionless and clear as a deep, cool well, and everything was mirrored in it clearly.

This entire change in the scene, the peace that encircled everything around us, seemed to give all the same feeling that I know I had. I fancied that nature created it especially for us, so that we would be allowed, in this pause, to think of our situation. All seemed to do so; all spoke in low voices, and seemed to be looking for something as they gazed quietly into the smooth depths below, or the twilight skies above. Were they seeking an assurance? Perhaps; for there was something strange in the absence of a crowd of friends on the shore, to cheer and salute, and fill the air with white clouds and last farewells.

I found the assurance. The very stillness was a voice – nature's voice; and it spoke to the ocean and said,

"I entrust to you this vessel. Take care of it, for it bears my children with it, from one strange shore to another more distant, where loving friends are waiting to embrace them after long partings. Be gentle with your charge."

And the ocean, though seeming so still, replied, "I will obey my mistress."

I heard it all, and a feeling of safety and protection came to me. And when at last the wheels overhead began to turn and clatter, and the ripples on the water told us that the *Polynesia* had started on her journey, which was not noticeable from any other sign, I felt only a sense of happiness. I mistrusted nothing.

But the old woman who remembered the *matzo* did, more than anybody else. She made great preparations for being seasick, and poisoned the air with garlic and onions.

When the lantern fixed in the ceiling had been lighted, the captain and the steward paid us a visit. They took up our tickets and noticed all the passengers, then left. Then a sailor brought supper – bread and coffee. Only a few ate it. Then all went to bed, though it was very early.

Nobody expected seasickness as soon as it seized us. All slept quietly the whole night, not knowing any difference between being on land or at sea. About five o'clock I woke up, and then I felt and heard the sea. A very disagreeable smell came from it, and I knew it was disturbed by the rocking of the ship. Oh, how wretched it made us! From side to side it went rocking, rocking. Ugh! Many of the passengers are very sick indeed, they suffer terribly. We are all awake now, and wonder if we, too, will be so sick. Some children are crying, at intervals. There is nobody to comfort them – all are so miserable. Oh, I am so sick! I'm dizzy; everything is going round and round before my eyes – Oh-h-h!

I can't even begin to tell of the suffering of the next few hours. Then I thought I would feel better if I could go on deck. Somehow, I got down (we had upper berths) and, supporting myself against the walls, I came on deck. But it was worse. The green water, tossing up the white foam, rocking all around, as far as I dared to look, was frightful to me then. So I crawled back as well as I could, and nobody else tried to go out.

By and by the doctor and the steward came. The doctor asked each passenger if they were well, but only smiled when all begged for some medicine to take away the dreadful suffering. To those who suffered from anything besides seasickness he sent medicine and special food later on. His companion appointed one of the men passengers for every twelve or fifteen to carry the meals from the kitchen, giving them cards to get it with. For our group a young German was appointed, who was making the journey for the second time, with his mother and sister. We were great friends with them during the journey.

The doctor went away soon, leaving the sufferers in the same sad condition. At twelve, a sailor announced that dinner was ready, and the man brought it – large tin pails and basins of soup, meat, cabbage, potatoes, and pudding (the last was allowed only once a week); and almost all of it was thrown away, as only a few men ate. The rest couldn't bear even the smell of food. It was the same with the supper at six o'clock. At three milk had been brought for the babies, and brown bread (a treat) with coffee for the rest. But after supper the daily allowance of fresh water was brought, and this soon disappeared and more called for, which was refused, although we lived on water alone for a week.

At last the day was gone, and much we had borne in it. Night came, but brought little relief. Some did fall asleep, and forgot suffering for a few hours. I was awake late. The ship was quieter, and everything sadder than by daylight. I thought of all we had gone through till we had got on board the *Polynesia*; of the parting from all friends and things we loved, forever, as far as we knew; of the strange experience at various strange places; of the kind friends who helped us, and the rough officers who commanded us; of the quarantine, the hunger, then the happy news, and the coming on board. Of all this I thought, and remembered that we were far away from friends, and longed for them, that I might be made well by speaking to them. And every minute was making the distance between us greater, a meeting more impossible. Then I remembered why we were crossing the ocean, and knew that it was worth the price. At last the noise of the wheels overhead, and the dull roar of the sea, rocked me to sleep.

For a short time only. The ship was tossed about more than the day before, and the great waves sounded like distant thunder as they beat against it, and rolled across the deck and entered the cabin. We found, however, that we were better, though very weak. We managed to go on deck in the afternoon, when it was calm enough. A little band was playing, and a few young sailors and German girls tried even to dance; but it was impossible.

As I sat in a corner where no waves could reach me, holding on to a rope, I tried to take in the grand scene. There was the mighty ocean I had heard of only, spreading out its rough breadth far, far around, its waves giving out deep, angry tones, and throwing up walls of spray into the air. There was the sky, like the sea, full of ridges of darkest clouds, bending to meet the waves, and following their motions and frowning and threatening. And there was the *Polynesia* in the midst of this world of gloom, and anger, and distance. I saw these, but indistinctly, not half comprehending the wonderful picture. For the suffering had left me dull and tired out. I only knew that I was sad, and everybody else was the same.

Another day gone, and we congratulate one another that seasickness lasted only one day with us. So we go to sleep.

Oh, the sad mistake! For six days longer we remain in our berths, miserable and unable to eat. It is a long fast, hardly interrupted, during which we know that the weather is unchanged, the sky dark, the sea stormy.

On the eighth day out we are again able to be about. I went around everywhere, exploring every corner, and learning much from the sailors; but I never remembered the names of the various things I asked about, they were so many, and some German names hard to learn. We all made friends with the captain and other officers, and many of the passengers. The little band played regularly on certain days, and the sailors and girls had a good many dances, though often they were swept by a wave across the deck, quite out of time. The children were allowed to play on deck, but carefully watched.

Still the weather continued the same, or changing slightly. But I was able now to see all the grandeur of my surroundings, notwithstanding the weather.

Oh, what solemn thoughts I had! How deeply I felt the greatness, the power of the scene! The immeasurable distance from horizon to horizon; the huge billows forever changing their shapes – now only a wavy and rolling plain, now a chain of great mountains, coming and going farther away; then a town in the distance, perhaps, with spires and towers and buildings of gigantic dimensions; and mostly a vast mass of uncertain shapes, knocking against each other in fury, and seething and foaming in their anger; the grey sky, with its mountains of gloomy clouds, flying, moving with the waves, as it seemed, very near them; the absence of any object besides the one ship; and the deep, solemn groans of the sea, sounding as if all the voices of the world had been turned into sighs and then gathered into that one mournful sound – so deeply did I feel the presence of these things, that the feeling became one of awe, both painful and sweet, and stirring and warming, and deep and calm and grand.

I thought of tempests and shipwreck, of lives lost, treasures destroyed, and all the tales I had heard of the misfortunes at sea, and knew I had never before had such a clear idea of them. I tried to realize that I saw only a part of an immense whole, and then my feelings were terrible in their force. I was afraid of thinking then, but could not stop it. My mind would go on working, till I was overcome by the strength and power that was greater than myself. What I did at such times I do not know. I must have been dazed.

After a while I could sit quietly and gaze far away. Then I would imagine myself all alone on the ocean, and Robinson Crusoe was very real to me. I was alone sometimes. I was aware of no human presence; I was conscious only of sea and sky and something I did not understand. And as I listened to its solemn voice, I felt as if I had found a friend, and knew that I loved the ocean. It seemed as if it were within as well as without, a part of myself; and I wondered how I had lived without it, and if I could ever part with it.

The ocean spoke to me in other besides mournful or angry tones. I loved even the angry voice, but when it became soothing, I could hear a sweet, gentle accent that reached my soul rather than my ear. Perhaps I imagined it. I do not know. What was real and what imaginary blended in one. But I heard and felt it, and at such moments I wished I could live on the sea forever, and thought that the sight of land would be very unwelcome to me. I did not want to be near any person. Alone with the ocean forever – that was my wish.

Leading a quiet life, the same every day, and thinking such thoughts, feeling such emotions, the days were very long. I do not know how the others passed the time, because I was so lost in my meditations. But when the sky would smile for awhile – when a little sunlight broke a path for itself through the heavy clouds, which disappeared as though frightened; and when the sea looked more friendly, and changed its colour to match the heavens, which were higher up – then we would sit on deck together, and laugh for mere happiness as we talked of the nearing meeting, which the unusual fairness of the weather seemed to bring nearer. Sometimes, at such minutes of sunshine and gladness, a few birds would be seen making their swift journey to some point we did not know of; sometimes among the light clouds, then almost touching the surface of the waves. How shall I tell you what we felt at the sight? The birds were like old friends to us, and brought back many memories, which seemed very old, though really fresh. All felt sadder when the distance became too great for us to see the dear little friends, though it was not for a long time after their first appearance. We used to watch for them, and often mistook the clouds for birds, and were thus disappointed. When they did come, how envious we were of their wings! It was a new thought to me that the birds had more power than man.

In this way the days went by. I thought my thoughts each day, as I watched the scene, hoping to see a beautiful sunset some day. I never did, to my disappointment. And each night, as I lay in my berth, waiting for sleep, I wished I might be able even to hope for the happiness of a sea-voyage after this had been ended.

Yet, when, on the twelfth day after leaving Hamburg, the captain announced that we should see land before long, I rejoiced as much as anybody else. We were so excited with expectation that nothing else was heard but the talk of the happy arrival, now so near. Some were even willing to stay up at night, to be the first ones to see the shores of America. It was therefore a great disappointment when the captain said, in the evening, that we would not reach Boston as soon as he expected, on account of the weather.

A dense fog set in at night, and grew heavier and heavier, until the *Polynesia* was closely walled in by it, and we could just see from one end of the deck to the other. The signal lanterns were put up, the passengers were driven to their berths by the cold and damp, the cabin doors closed, and discomfort reigned everywhere.

But the excitement of the day had tired us out, and we were glad to forget disappointment in sleep. In the morning it was still foggy, but we could see a little way around. It was very strange to have the boundless distance made so narrow, and I felt the strangeness of the scene. All day long we shivered with cold, and hardly left the cabin. At last it was night once more, and we in our berths. But nobody slept.

The sea had been growing rougher during the day, and at night the ship began to pitch as it did at the beginning of the journey. Then it grew worse. Everything in our cabin was rolling on the floor, clattering and dinning. Dishes were broken into little bits that flew about from one end to the other. Bedding from upper berths nearly stifled the people in the lower ones. Some fell out of their berths, but it was not at all funny. As the ship turned to one side, the passengers were violently thrown against that side of the berths, and some boards gave way and clattered down to the floor. When it tossed on the other side, we could see the little windows almost touch the water, and closed the shutters to keep out the sight. The children cried, everybody groaned, and sailors kept coming in to pick up the things on the floor and carry them away. This made the confusion less, but not the alarm.

Above all sounds rose the fog horn. It never stopped the long night through. And oh, how sad it sounded! It pierced every heart, and made us afraid. Now and then some ship, far away, would answer, like a weak echo. Sometimes we noticed that the wheels were still, and we knew that the ship had stopped. This frightened us more than ever, for we imagined the worst reasons for it.

It was day again, and a little calmer. We slept now, till the afternoon. Then we saw that the fog had become much thinner, and later on we even saw a ship, but indistinctly.

Another night passed, and the day that followed was pretty fair, and towards evening the sky was almost cloudless. The captain said we should have no more rough weather, for now we were really near Boston. Oh, how hard it was to wait for the happy day! Somebody brought the news that we should land to-morrow in the afternoon. We didn't believe it, so he said that the steward had ordered a great pudding full of raisins for supper that day as a sure sign that it was the last on board. We remembered the pudding, but didn't believe in its meaning.

I don't think we slept that night. After all the suffering of our journey, after seeing and hearing nothing but the sky and the sea and its roaring, it was impossible to sleep when we thought that soon we would see trees, fields, fresh people, animals – a world, and that world America. Then, above everything, was the meeting with friends we had not seen for years; for almost everybody had some friends awaiting them.

Morning found all the passengers up and expectant. Someone questioned the captain, and he said we would land to-morrow. There was another long day, and another sleepless night, but when these ended at last, how busy we were! First we packed up all the things we did not need, then put on fresh clothing, and then went on deck to watch for land. It was almost three o'clock, the hour the captain hoped to reach Boston, but there was nothing new to be seen. The weather was fair, so we would have seen anything within a number of miles. Anxiously we watched, and as we talked of the strange delay, our courage began to give out with our hope. When it could be borne no longer, a gentleman went to speak to the captain. He was on the upper deck, examining the horizon. He put off the arrival for the next day!

You can imagine our feelings at this. When it was worse the captain came down and talked so assuringly that, in spite of all the disappointments we had had, we believed that this was the last, and were quite cheerful when we went to bed.

The morning was glorious. It was the eighth of May, the seventeenth day after we left Hamburg. The sky was clear and blue, the sun shone brightly, as if to congratulate us that we had safely crossed the stormy sea; and to apologize for having kept away from us so long. The sea had lost its fury; it was almost as quiet as it had been at Hamburg before we started, and its colour was a beautiful greenish blue. Birds were all the time in the air, and it was worth while to live merely to hear their songs. And soon, oh joyful sight! we saw the tops of two trees!

What a shout there rose! Everyone pointed out the welcome sight to everybody else, as if they did not see it. All eyes were fixed on it as if they saw a miracle. And this was only the beginning of the joys of the day!

What confusion there was! Some were flying up the stairs to the upper deck, some were tearing down to the lower one, others were running in and out of the cabins, some were in all parts of the ship in one minute, and all were talking and laughing and getting in somebody's way. Such excitement, such joy! We had seen two trees!

Then steamers and boats of all kinds passed by, in all directions. We shouted, and the men stood up in the boats and returned the greeting, waving their hats. We were as glad to see them as if they were old friends of ours.

Oh, what a beautiful scene! No corner of the earth is half so fair as the lovely picture before us. It came to view suddenly, – a green field, a real field with grass on it, and large houses, and the dearest hens and little chickens in all the world, and trees, and birds, and people at work.

The young green things put new life into us, and are so dear to our eyes that we dare not speak a word now, lest the magic should vanish away and we should be left to the stormy scenes we know.

But nothing disturbed the fairy sight. Instead, new scenes appeared, beautiful as the first. The sky becomes bluer all the time, the sun warmer; the sea is too quiet for its name, and the most beautiful blue imaginable.

What are the feelings these sights awaken! They can not be described. To know how great was our happiness, how complete, how free from even the shadow of a sadness, you must make a journey of sixteen days on a stormy ocean. Is it possible that we will ever again be so happy?

It was about three hours since we saw the first landmarks, when a number of men came on board, from a little steamer, and examined the passengers to see if they were properly vaccinated (we had been vaccinated on the *Polynesia*), and pronounced everyone all right. Then they went away, except one man who remained. An hour later we saw the wharves.

Before the ship had fully stopped, the climax of our joy was reached. One of us espied the figure and face we had longed to see for three long years. In a moment five passengers on the *Polynesia* were crying, "Papa," and gesticulating, and laughing, and hugging one another, and going wild altogether. All the rest were roused by our excitement, and came to see our father. He recognized us as soon as we him, and stood apart on the wharf not knowing what to do, I thought.

What followed was slow torture. Like mad things we ran about where there was room, unable to stand still as long as we were on the ship and he on shore. To have crossed the ocean only to come within a few yards of him, unable to get nearer till all the fuss was over, was dreadful enough. But to hear other passengers called who had no reason for hurry, while we were left among the last, was unendurable.

Oh, dear! Why can't we get off the hateful ship? Why can't papa come to us? Why so many ceremonies at the landing?

We said good-bye to our friends as their turn came, wishing we were in their luck. To give us something else to think of, papa succeeded in passing us some fruit; and we wondered to find it anything but a great wonder, for we expected to find everything marvellous in the strange country.

Still the ceremonies went on. Each person was asked a hundred or so stupid questions, and all their answers were written down by a very slow man. The baggage had to be examined, the tickets, and a hundred other things done before anyone was allowed to step ashore, all to keep us back as long as possible.

Now imagine yourself parting with all you love, believing it to be a parting for life; breaking up your home, selling the things that years have made dear to you; starting on a journey without the least experience in travelling, in the face of many inconveniences on account of the want of sufficient money; being met with disappointment where it was not to be expected; with rough treatment everywhere, till you are forced to go and make friends for yourself among strangers; being obliged to sell some of your most necessary things to pay bills you did not willingly incur; being mistrusted and searched, then half starved, and lodged in common with a multitude of strangers; suffering the miseries of seasickness, the disturbances and alarms of a stormy sea for sixteen days; and then stand within, a few yards of him for whom you did all this, unable to even speak to him easily. How do you feel?

Oh, it's our turn at last! We are questioned, examined, and dismissed! A rush over the planks on one side, over the ground on the other, six wild beings cling to each other, bound by a common bond of tender joy, and the long parting is at an END.

The Man Who Lost His Name

Hjalmar Hjorth Boyesen

I

ON THE SECOND DAY OF JUNE, 186—, a young Norseman, Halfdan Bjerk by name, landed on the pier at Castle Garden. He passed through the straight and narrow gate where he was asked his name, birthplace, and how much money he had, – at which he grew very much frightened.

"And your destination?" – demanded the gruff-looking functionary at the desk.

"America," said the youth, and touched his hat politely.

"Do you think I have time for joking?" roared the official, with an oath.

The Norseman ran his hand through his hair, smiled his timidly conciliatory smile, and tried his best to look brave; but his hand trembled and his heart thumped away at an alarmingly quickened tempo.

"Put him down for Nebraska!" cried a stout red-cheeked individual (inwrapped in the mingled fumes of tobacco and whisky) whose function it was to open and shut the gate.

"There ain't many as go to Nebraska."

"All right, Nebraska."

The gate swung open and the pressure from behind urged the timid traveller on, while an extra push from the gate-keeper sent him flying in the direction of a board fence, where he sat down and tried to realize that he was now in the land of liberty.

Halfdan Bjerk was a tall, slender-limbed youth of very delicate frame; he had a pair of wonderfully candid, unreflecting blue eyes, a smooth, clear, beardless face, and soft, wavy light hair, which was pushed back from his forehead without parting. His mouth and chin were well cut, but their lines were, perhaps, rather weak for a man. When in repose, the ensemble of his features was exceedingly pleasing and somehow reminded one of Correggio's St. John. He had left his native land because he was an ardent republican and was abstractly convinced that man, generically and individually, lives more happily in a republic than in a monarchy. He had anticipated with keen pleasure the large, freely breathing life he was to lead in a land where every man was his neighbour's brother, where no senseless traditions kept a jealous watch over obsolete systems and shrines, and no chilling prejudice blighted the spontaneous blossoming of the soul.

Halfdan was an only child. His father, a poor government official, had died during his infancy, and his mother had given music lessons, and kept boarders, in order to gain the means to give her son what is called a learned education. In the Latin school Halfdan had enjoyed the reputation of being a bright youth, and at the age of eighteen, he had entered the university under the most promising auspices. He could make very fair verses, and play all imaginable instruments with equal ease, which made him a favourite in society. Moreover, he possessed that very old-fashioned accomplishment of cutting silhouettes; and what was more, he could draw the most charmingly fantastic arabesques for embroidery patterns, and he even dabbled in portrait and landscape painting. Whatever he turned his hand to, he did well, in fact, astonishingly well for a dilettante, and yet not well enough to claim the title of an artist. Nor did it ever occur to him to make such a claim. As one of his fellow-students remarked in a fit of jealousy, "Once when Nature had made three geniuses, a poet, a musician, and a painter, she took all the remaining odds and ends and shook them together at random and the result was Halfdan Bjerk." This agreeable melange of accomplishments, however, proved very attractive to the ladies, who invited the possessor to innumerable afternoon tea-parties, where they drew heavy drafts on his unflagging patience, and kept him steadily engaged with patterns and designs for embroidery, leather flowers, and other dainty knickknacks. And in return for all his exertions they called him "sweet" and "beautiful," and applied to him many other enthusiastic adjectives seldom heard in connection with masculine names. In the university, talents of this order gained but slight recognition, and when Halfdan had for three years been preparing himself in vain for the examen philosophicum, he found himself slowly and imperceptibly drifting into the ranks of the so-called studiosi perpetui, who preserve a solemn silence at the examination tables, fraternize with every new generation of freshmen, and at last become part of the fixed furniture of their Alma Mater. In the larger American colleges, such men are mercilessly dropped or sent to a Divinity School; but the European universities, whose tempers the centuries have mellowed, harbour in their spacious Gothic bosoms a tenderer heart for their unfortunate sons. There the professors greet them at the green tables with a good-humoured smile of recognition; they are treated with gentle forbearance, and are allowed to linger on, until they die or become tutors in the families of remote clergymen, where they invariably fall in love with the handsomest daughter, and thus lounge into a modest prosperity.

If this had been the fate of our friend Bjerk, we should have dismissed him here with a confident 'vale' on his life's pilgrimage. But, unfortunately, Bjerk was inclined to hold the government in some way responsible for his own poor success as a student, and this, in connection with an aesthetic enthusiasm for ancient Greece, gradually convinced him that the republic was the only form of government under which men of his tastes and temperament were apt to flourish. It was, like everything that pertained to him, a cheerful, genial conviction, without the slightest tinge of bitterness. The old institutions were obsolete, rotten to the core, he said, and needed a radical renovation. He could sit for hours of an evening in the Students' Union, and discourse over a glass of mild toddy, on the benefits of universal suffrage and trial by jury, while the picturesqueness of his language, his genial sarcasms, or occasional witty allusions would call forth uproarious applause from throngs of admiring freshmen. These were the sunny days in Halfdan's career, days long to be remembered. They came to an abrupt end when old Mrs. Bjerk died, leaving nothing behind her but her furniture and some trifling debts. The son, who was not an eminently practical man, underwent long hours of misery in trying to settle up her affairs, and finally in a moment of extreme dejection sold his entire inheritance in a lump to a pawnbroker (reserving for himself a few rings and trinkets) for the modest sum of 250 dollars specie. He then took formal leave of the Students' Union in a brilliant speech, in which he traced the parallelisms between the lives of Pericles and Washington, – in his opinion the two greatest men the world had ever seen, – expounded his theory of democratic government, and explained the causes of the rapid rise of the American Republic. The next morning he exchanged half of his worldly possessions for a ticket to New York, and within a few days set sail for the land of promise, in the far West.

II

From Castle Garden, Halfdan made his way up through Greenwich street, pursued by a clamorous troop of confidence men and hotel runners.

"Kommen Sie mit mir. Ich bin auch Deutsch," cried one. "Voila, voila, je parle Francais," shouted another, seizing hold of his valise. "Jeg er Dansk. Tale Dansk," roared a third, with an accent which seriously impeached his truthfulness. In order to escape from these importunate rascals, who were every moment getting bolder, he threw himself into the first street-car which happened to pass; he sat down, gazed out of the windows and soon became so thoroughly absorbed in the animated scenes which moved as in a panorama before his eyes, that he quite forgot where he was going. The conductor called for fares, and received an English shilling, which, after some ineffectual expostulation, he pocketed, but gave no change. At last after about an hour's journey, the car stopped, the conductor called out "Central Park," and Halfdan woke up with a start. He dismounted with a timid, deliberate step, stared in dim bewilderment at the long rows of palatial residences, and a chill sense of loneliness crept over him. The hopeless strangeness of everything he saw, instead of filling him with rapture as he had once anticipated, Sent a cold shiver to his heart. It is a very large affair, this world of ours – a good deal larger than it appeared to him gazing out upon it from his snug little corner up under the Pole; and it was as unsympathetic as it was large; he suddenly felt what he had never been aware of before – that he was a very small part of it and of very little account after all. He staggered over to a bench at the entrance to the park, and sat long watching the fine carriages as they dashed past him; he saw the handsome women in brilliant costumes laughing and chatting gayly; the apathetic policemen promenading in stoic dignity up and down upon the smooth pavements; the jauntily attired nurses, whom in his Norse innocence he took for mothers or aunts of the children, wheeling baby-carriages which to Norse eyes seemed miracles of dainty ingenuity, under the shady crowns of the elm-trees. He did not know how long he had been sitting there, when a little bright-eyed girl with light kid gloves, a small blue parasol and a blue polonaise, quite a lady of fashion en miniature, stopped in front of him and stared at him in shy wonder. He had always been fond of children, and often rejoiced in their affectionate ways and confidential prattle, and now it suddenly touched him with a warm sense of human fellowship to have this little daintily befrilled and crisply starched beauty single him out for notice among the hundreds who reclined in the arbours, or sauntered to and fro under the great trees.

"What is your name, my little girl?" he asked, in a tone of friendly interest.

"Clara," answered the child, hesitatingly; then, having by another look assured herself of his harmlessness, she added: "How very funny you speak!"

"Yes," he said, stooping down to take he tiny begloved hand. "I do not speak as well as you do, yet; but I shall soon learn."

Clara looked puzzled.

"How old are you?" she asked, raising her parasol, and throwing back her head with an air of superiority.

"I am twenty-four years old."

She began to count half aloud on her fingers: "One, two, three, four," but, before she reached twenty, she lost her patience.

"Twenty-four," she exclaimed, "that is a great deal. I am only seven, and papa gave me a pony on my birthday. Have you got a pony?"

"No; I have nothing but what is in this valise, and you know I could not very well get a pony into it."

Clara glanced curiously at the valise and laughed; then suddenly she grew serious again, put her hand into her pocket and seemed to be searching eagerly for something. Presently she hauled out a small porcelain doll's head, then a red-painted block with letters on it, and at last a penny.

"Do you want them?" she said, reaching him her treasures in both hands. "You may have them all."

Before he had time to answer, a shrill, penetrating voice cried out:

"Why, gracious! child, what are you doing?"

And the nurse, who had been deeply absorbed in *The New York Ledger*, came rushing up, snatched the child away, and retreated as hastily as she had come.

Halfdan rose and wandered for hours aimlessly along the intertwining roads and footpaths. He visited the menageries, admired the statues, took a very light dinner, consisting of coffee, sandwiches, and ice, at the Chinese Pavilion, and, toward evening, discovered an inviting leafy arbour, where he could withdraw into the privacy of his own thoughts, and ponder upon the still unsolved problem of his destiny. The little incident with the child had taken the edge off his unhappiness and turned him into a more conciliatory mood toward himself and the great pitiless world, which seemed to take so little notice of him. And he, who had come here with so warm a heart and so ardent a will to join in the great work of human advancement – to find himself thus harshly ignored and buffeted about, as if he were a hostile intruder! Before him lay the huge unknown city where human life pulsated with large, full heart-throbs, where a breathless, weird intensity, a cold, fierce passion seemed to be hurrying everything onward in a maddening whirl, where a gentle, warm-blooded enthusiast like himself had no place and could expect naught but a speedy destruction. A strange, unconquerable dread took possession of him, as if he had been caught in a swift, strong whirlpool, from which he vainly struggled to escape. He crouched down among the foliage and shuddered. He could not return to the city. No, no: he never would return. He would remain here hidden and unseen until morning, and then he would seek a vessel bound for his dear native land, where the great mountains loomed up in serene majesty toward the blue sky, where the pine-forests whispered their dreamily sympathetic legends, in the long summer twilights, where human existence flowed on in calm beauty with the modest aims, small virtues, and small vices which were the happiness of modest, idyllic souls. He even saw himself in spirit recounting to his astonished countrymen the wonderful things he had heard and seen during his foreign pilgrimage, and smiled to himself as he imagined their wonder when he should tell them about the beautiful little girl who had been the first and only one to offer him a friendly greeting in the strange land. During these reflections he fell asleep, and slept soundly for two or three hours. Once, he seemed to hear footsteps and whispers among the trees, and made an effort to rouse himself, but weariness again overmastered him and he slept on. At last, he felt himself seized violently by the shoulders, and a gruff voice shouted in his ear:

"Get up, you sleepy dog."

He rubbed his eyes, and, by the dim light of the moon, saw a Herculean policeman lifting a stout stick over his head. His former terror came upon him with increased violence, and his heart stood for a moment still, then, again, hammered away as if it would burst his sides.

"Come along!" roared the policeman, shaking him vehemently by the collar of his coat.

In his bewilderment he quite forgot where he was, and, in hurried Norse sentences, assured his persecutor that he was a harmless, honest traveller, and implored him to release him. But the official Hercules was inexorable.

"My valise, my valise;" cried Halfdan. "Pray let me get my valise."

They returned to the place where he had slept, but the valise was nowhere to be found. Then, with dumb despair he resigned himself to his fate, and after a brief ride on a street-car, found himself standing in a large, low-ceiled room; he covered his face with his hands and burst into tears.

"The grand-the happy republic," he murmured, "spontaneous blossoming of the soul. Alas! I have rooted up my life; I fear it will never blossom."

All the high-flown adjectives he had employed in his parting speech in the Students' Union, when he paid his enthusiastic tribute to the Grand Republic, now kept recurring to him, and in this moment the paradox seemed cruel. The Grand Republic, what did it care for such as he? A pair of brawny arms fit to wield the pick-axe and to steer the plow it received with an eager welcome; for a child-like, loving heart and a generously fantastic brain, it had but the stern greeting of the law.

III

The next morning, Halfdan was released from the Police Station, having first been fined five dollars for vagrancy. All his money, with the exception of a few pounds which he had exchanged in Liverpool, he had lost with his valise, and he had to his knowledge not a single acquaintance in the city or on the whole continent. In order to increase his capital he bought some fifty *Tribunes*, but, as it was already late in the day, he hardly succeeded in selling a single copy. The next morning, he once more stationed himself on the corner of Murray street and Broadway, hoping in his innocence to dispose of the papers he had still on hand from the previous day, and actually did find a few customers among the people who were jumping in and out of the omnibuses that passed up and down the great thoroughfare. To his surprise, however, one of these gentlemen returned to him with a very wrathful countenance, shook his fist at him, and vociferated with excited gestures something which to Halfdan's ears had a very unintelligible sound. He made a vain effort to defend himself; the situation appeared so utterly incomprehensible to him, and in his dumb helplessness he looked pitiful enough to move the heart of a stone. No English phrase suggested itself to him, only a few Norse interjections rose to his lips. The man's anger suddenly abated; he picked up the paper which he had thrown on the sidewalk, and stood for a while regarding Halfdan curiously.

"Are you a Norwegian?" he asked.

"Yes, I came from Norway yesterday."

"What's your name?"

"Halfdan Bjerk."

"Halfdan Bjerk! My stars! Who would have thought of meeting you here! You do not recognize me, I suppose."

Halfdan declared with a timid tremor in his voice that he could not at the moment recall his features.

"No, I imagine I must have changed a good deal since you saw me," said the man, suddenly dropping into Norwegian. "I am Gustav Olson, I used to live in the same house with you once, but that is long ago now."

Gustav Olson – to be sure, he was the porter's son in the house, where his mother had once during his childhood, taken a flat. He well remembered having clandestinely traded jack-knives and buttons with him, in spite of the frequent warnings he had received to have nothing to do with him; for Gustav, with his broad freckled face and red hair, was looked upon by the genteel inhabitants of the upper flats as rather a disreputable character. He had once whipped the son of a colonel who had been impudent to him, and thrown a snow-ball at the head of a new-fledged lieutenant, which offenses he had duly expiated at a house of correction. Since that time he had vanished from Halfdan's horizon. He had still the same broad freckled face, now covered with a lusty growth of coarse red beard, the same rebellious head of hair, which refused to yield to the subduing influences of the comb, the same plebeian hands and feet, and uncouth clumsiness of form. But his linen was irreproachable, and a certain dash in his manner, and the loud fashionableness of his attire, gave unmistakable evidences of prosperity.

"Come, Bjerk," said he in a tone of good-fellowship, which was not without its sting to the idealistic republican, "you must take up a better business than selling yesterday's *Tribune*. That won't pay here, you know. Come along to our office and I will see if something can't be done for you."

"But I should be sorry to give you trouble," stammered Halfdan, whose native pride, even in his present wretchedness, protested against accepting a favour from one whom he had been wont to regard as his inferior.

"Nonsense, my boy. Hurry up, I haven't much time to spare. The office is only two blocks from here. You don't look as if you could afford to throw away a friendly offer."

The last words suddenly roused Halfdan from his apathy; for he felt that they were true. A drowning man cannot afford to make nice distinctions – cannot afford to ask whether the helping hand that is extended to him be that of an equal or an inferior. So he swallowed his humiliation and threaded his way through the bewildering turmoil of Broadway, by the side of his officious friend.

They entered a large, elegantly furnished office, where clerks with sleek and severely apathetic countenances stood scribbling at their desks.

"You will have to amuse yourself as best you can," said Olson. "Mr. Van Kirk will be here in twenty minutes. I haven't time to entertain you."

A dreary half hour passed. Then the door opened and a tall, handsome man, with a full grayish beard, and a commanding presence, entered and took his seat at a desk in a smaller adjoining office. He opened, with great dispatch, a pile of letters which lay on the desk before him, called out in a sharp, ringing tone for a clerk, who promptly appeared, handed him half-a-dozen letters, accompanying each with a brief direction, took some clean paper from a drawer and fell to writing. There was something brisk, determined, and business-like in his manner, which made it seem very hopeless to Halfdan to appear before him as a petitioner. Presently Olson entered the private office, closing the door behind him, and a few minutes later re-appeared and summoned Halfdan into the chief's presence.

"You are a Norwegian, I hear," said the merchant, looking around over his shoulder at the supplicant, with a preoccupied air. "You want work. What can you do?"

What can you do? A fatal question. But here was clearly no opportunity for mental debate. So, summoning all his courage, but feeling nevertheless very faint, he answered:

"I have passed both examen artium and philosophicum, and got my laud clear in the former, but in the latter haud on the first point."

Mr. Van Kirk wheeled round on his chair and faced the speaker:

"That is all Greek to me," he said, in a severe tone. "Can you keep accounts?"

"No. I am afraid not."

Keeping accounts was not deemed a classical accomplishment in Norway. It was only 'trade-rats' who troubled themselves about such gross things, and if our Norseman had not been too absorbed with the problem of his destiny, he would have been justly indignant at having such a question put to him.

"Then you don't know book-keeping?"

"I think not. I never tried it."

"Then you may be sure you don't know it. But you must certainly have tried your hand at something. Is there nothing you can think of which might help you to get a living?"

"I can play the piano – and – and the violin."

"Very well, then. You may come this afternoon to my house. Mr. Olson will tell you the address. I will give you a note to Mrs. Van Kirk. Perhaps she will engage you as a music teacher for the children. Good morning."

IV

At half-past four o'clock in the afternoon, Halfdan found himself standing in a large, dimly lighted drawing-room, whose brilliant upholstery, luxurious carpets, and fantastically twisted furniture dazzled and bewildered his senses. All was so strange, so strange; nowhere a familiar object to give rest to the wearied eye. Wherever he looked he saw his shabbily attired figure repeated in the long crystal mirrors, and he became uncomfortably conscious of his threadbare coat, his uncouth boots, and the general incongruity of his appearance. With every moment his uneasiness grew; and he was vaguely considering the propriety of a precipitate flight, when the rustle of a dress at the farther end of the room startled him, and a small, plump lady, of a daintily exquisite form, swept up toward him, gave a slight inclination of her head, and sank down into an easy-chair:

"You are Mr. ——, the Norwegian, who wishes to give music lessons?" she said, holding a pair of gold-framed eyeglasses up to her eyes, and running over the note which she held in her hand. It read as follows:

DEAR MARTHA, – The bearer of this note is a young Norwegian, I forgot to ascertain his name, a friend of Olson's. He wishes to teach music. If you can help the poor devil and give him something to do, you will oblige, Yours, H. V. K.

Mrs. Van Kirk was evidently, by at least twelve years, her husband's junior, and apparently not very far advanced in the forties. Her blonde hair, which was freshly crimped, fell lightly over her smooth, narrow forehead; her nose, mouth and chin had a neat distinctness of outline; her complexion was either naturally or artificially perfect, and her eyes, which were of the purest blue, had, owing to their near-sightedness, a certain pinched and scrutinizing look. This look, which was without the slightest touch of severity, indicating merely a lively degree of interest, was further emphasized by three small perpendicular wrinkles, which deepened and again relaxed according to the varying intensity of observation she bestowed upon the object which for the time engaged her attention.

"Your name, if you please?" said Mrs. Van Kirk, having for awhile measured her visitor with a glance of mild scrutiny.

"Halfdan Bjerk."

"Half-dan B——, how do you spell that?"

"B-j-e-r-k."

"B-jerk. Well, but I mean, what is your name in English?"

Halfdan looked blank, and blushed to his ears.

"I wish to know," continued the lady energetically, evidently anxious to help him out, "what your name would mean in plain English. Bjerk, it certainly must mean something."

"Bjerk is a tree – a birch-tree."

"Very well, Birch, – that is a very respectable name. And your first name? What did you say that was?

"H-a-l-f-d-a-n."

"Half Dan. Why not a whole Dan and be done with it? Dan Birch, or rather Daniel Birch. Indeed, that sounds quite Christian."

"As you please, madam," faltered the victim, looking very unhappy.

"You will pardon my straightforwardness, won't you? B-jerk. I could never pronounce that, you know."

"Whatever may be agreeable to you, madam, will be sure to please me."

"That is very well said. And you will find that it always pays to try to please me. And you wish to teach music? If you have no objection I will call my oldest daughter. She is an excellent judge of music, and if your playing meets with her approval, I will engage you, as my husband suggests, not to teach Edith, you understand, but my youngest child, Clara."

Halfdan bowed assent, and Mrs. Van Kirk rustled out into the hall where she rang a bell, and re-entered. A servant in dress-coat appeared, and again vanished as noiselessly as he had come. To our Norseman there was some thing weird and uncanny about these silent entrances and exits; he could hardly suppress a shudder. He had been accustomed to hear the clatter of people's heels upon the bare floors, as they approached, and the audible crescendo of their footsteps gave one warning, and prevented one from being taken by surprise. While absorbed in these reflections, his senses must have been dormant; for just then Miss Edith Van Kirk entered, unheralded by anything but a hovering perfume, the effect of which was to lull him still deeper into his wondering abstraction.

"Mr. Birch," said Mrs. Van Kirk, "this is my daughter Miss Edith," and as Halfdan sprang to his feet and bowed with visible embarrassment, she continued:

"Edith, this is Mr. Daniel Birch, whom your father has sent here to know if he would be serviceable as a music teacher for Clara. And now, dear, you will have to decide about the merits of Mr. Birch. I don't know enough about music to be anything of a judge."

"If Mr. Birch will be kind enough to play," said Miss Edith with a languidly musical intonation," I shall be happy to listen to him."

Halfdan silently signified his willingness and followed the ladies to a smaller apartment which was separated from the drawing-room by folding doors. The apparition of the beautiful young girl who was walking at his side had suddenly filled him with a strange burning and shuddering happiness; he could not tear his eyes away from her; she held him as by a powerful spell. And still, all the while he had a painful sub-consciousness of his own unfortunate appearance, which was thrown into cruel relief by her splendour. The tall, lithe magnificence of her form, the airy elegance of her toilet, which seemed the perfection of self-concealing art, the elastic deliberateness of her step – all wrought like a gentle, deliciously soothing opiate upon the Norseman's fancy and lifted him into hitherto unknown regions of mingled misery and bliss. She seemed a combination of the most divine contradictions, one moment supremely conscious, and in the next adorably child-like and simple, now full of arts and coquettish innuendoes, then again naïve, unthinking and almost boyishly blunt and direct; in a word, one of those miraculous New York girls whom abstractly one may disapprove of, but in the concrete must abjectly adore. This easy predominance of the masculine heart over the masculine reason in the presence of an impressive woman, has been the motif of a thousand tragedies in times past, and will inspire a thousand more in times to come.

Halfdan sat down at the grand piano and played Chopin's 'Nocturne' in G major, flinging out that elaborate filigree of sound with an impetuosity and superb ABANDON which caused the ladies to exchange astonished glances behind his back. The transitions from the light and ethereal texture of melody to the simple, more concrete theme, which he rendered with delicate shadings of articulation, were sufficiently startling to impress even a less cultivated ear than that of Edith Van Kirk, who had, indeed, exhausted whatever musical resources New York has to offer. And she was most profoundly impressed. As he glided over the last pianissimo notes toward the two concluding chords (an ending so characteristic of Chopin) she rose and hurried to his side with a heedless eagerness, which was more eloquent than emphatic words of praise.

"Won't you please repeat this passage?" she said, humming the air with soft modulations; "I have always regarded the monotonous repetition of this strain" (and she indicated it lightly by a few touches of the keys) "as rather a blemish of an otherwise perfect composition. But as you play it, it is anything but monotonous. You put into this single phrase a more intense meaning and a greater variety of thought than I ever suspected it was capable of expressing."

"It is my favourite composition," answered he, modestly. "I have bestowed more thought upon it than upon anything I have ever played, unless perhaps it be the one in G minor, which, with all its difference of mood and phraseology, expresses an essentially kindred thought."

"My dear Mr. Birch," exclaimed Mrs. Van Kirk, whom his skillful employment of technical terms (in spite of his indifferent accent) had impressed even more than his rendering of the music, – "you are a comsummate (sic) artist, and we shall deem it a great privilege if you will undertake to instruct our child. I have listened to you with profound satisfaction."

Halfdan acknowledged the compliment by a bow and a blush, and repeated the latter part of the nocturne according to Edith's request.

"And now," resumed Edith, "may I trouble you to play the G minor, which has even puzzled me more than the one you have just played."

"It ought really to have been played first," replied Halfdan. "It is far intenser in its colouring and has a more passionate ring, but its conclusion does not seem to be final. There is no rest in it, and it seems oddly enough to be a mere transition into the major, which is its proper supplement and completes the fragmentary thought."

Mother and daughter once more telegraphed wondering looks at each other, while Halfdan plunged into the impetuous movements of the minor nocturne, which he played to the end with ever-increasing fervor and animation.

"Mr. Birch," said Edith, as he arose from the piano with a flushed face, and the agitation of the music still tingling through his nerves. "You are a far greater musician than you seem to be aware of. I have not been taking lessons for some time, but you have aroused all my musical ambition, and if you will accept me too, as a pupil, I shall deem it a favor."

"I hardly know if I can teach you anything," answered he, while his eyes dwelt with keen delight on her beautiful form. "But in my present position I can hardly afford to decline so flattering an offer."

"You mean to say that you would decline it if you were in a position to do so," said she, smiling.

"No, only that I should question my convenience more closely."

"Ah, never mind. I take all the responsibility. I shall cheerfully consent to being imposed upon by you."

Mrs. Van Kirk in the mean while had been examining the contents of a fragrant Russia-leather pocket-book, and she now drew out two crisp ten-dollar notes, and held them out toward him.

"I prefer to make sure of you by paying you in advance," said she, with a cheerfully familiar nod, and a critical glance at his attire, the meaning of which he did not fail to detect. "Somebody else might make the same discovery that we have made to-day, and outbid us. And we do not want to be cheated out of our good fortune in having been the first to secure so valuable a prize."

"You need have no fear on that score, madam," retorted Halfdan, with a vivid blush, and purposely misinterpreting the polite subterfuge. "You may rely upon my promise. I shall be here again, as soon as you wish me to return."

"Then, if you please, we shall look for you to-morrow morning at ten o'clock."

And Mrs. Van Kirk hesitatingly folded up her notes and replaced them in her pocket-book.

To our idealist there was something extremely odious in this sudden offer of money. It was the first time any one had offered to pay him, and it seemed to put him on a level with a common day-labourer. His first impulse was to resent it as a gratuitous humiliation, but a glance at Mrs. Van Kirk's countenance, which was all aglow with officious benevolence, re-assured him, and his indignation died away.

That same afternoon Olson, having been informed of his friend's good fortune, volunteered a loan of a hundred dollars, and accompanied him to a fashionable tailor, where he underwent a pleasing metamorphosis.

V

In Norway the ladies dress with the innocent purpose of protecting themselves against the weather; if this purpose is still remotely present in the toilets of American women of to-day, it is, at all events, sufficiently disguised to challenge detection, very much like a primitive Sanscrit root in its French and English derivatives. This was the reflection which was uppermost in Halfdan's mind as Edith, ravishing to behold in the airy grace of her fragrant morning toilet, at the appointed time took her seat at his side before the piano. Her presence seemed so intense, so all-absorbing, that it left no thought for the music. A woman, with all the spiritual mysteries which that name implies, had always appeared to him rather a composite phenomenon, even apart from those varied accessories of dress, in which as by an inevitable analogy, she sees fit to express the inner multiformity of her being. Nevertheless, this former conception of his, when compared to that wonderful complexity of ethereal lines, colours, tints and half-tints which go to make up the modern New York girl, seemed inexpressibly simple, almost what plain arithmetic must appear to a man who has mastered calculus.

Edith had opened one of those small red-covered volumes of Chopin where the rich, wondrous melodies lie peacefully folded up like strange exotic flowers in an herbarium. She began to play the fantasia impromtu, which ought to be dashed off at a single 'heat,' whose passionate impulse hurries it on breathlessly toward its abrupt finale. But Edith toiled considerably with her fingering, and blurred the keen edges of each swift phrase by her indistinct articulation. And still there was a sufficiently ardent intention in her play to save it from being a failure. She made a gesture of disgust when she had finished, shut the book, and let her hands drop crosswise in her lap.

"I only wanted to give you a proof of my incapacity," she said, turning her large luminous gaze upon her instructor, "in order to make you duly appreciate what you have undertaken. Now, tell me truly and honestly, are you not discouraged?"

"Not by any means," replied he, while the rapture of her presence rippled through his nerves, "you have fire enough in you to make an admirable musician. But your fingers, as yet, refuse to carry out your fine intentions. They only need discipline."

"And do you suppose you can discipline them? They are a fearfully obstinate set, and cause me infinite mortification."

"Would you allow me to look at your hand?"

She raised her right hand, and with a sort of impulsive heedlessness let it drop into his. An exclamation of surprise escaped him.

"If you will pardon me," he said, "it is a superb hand – a hand capable of performing miracles – musical miracles I mean. Only look here" – (and he drew the fore and second fingers apart) – "so firmly set in the joint and still so flexible. I doubt if Liszt himself can boast a finer row of fingers. Your hands will surely not prevent you from becoming a second Von Bulow, which to my mind means a good deal more than a second Liszt."

"Thank you, that is quite enough," she exclaimed, with an incredulous laugh; "you have done bravely. That at all events throws the whole burden of responsibility upon myself, if I do not become a second somebody. I shall be perfectly satisfied, however, if you can only make me as good a musician as you are yourself, so that I can render a not too difficult piece without feeling all the while that I am committing sacrilege in mutilating the fine thoughts of some great composer."

"You are too modest; you do not—"

"No, no, I am not modest," she interrupted him with an impetuosity which startled him. "I beg of you not to persist in paying me compliments. I get too much of that cheap article elsewhere. I hate to be told that I am better than I know I am. If you are to do me any good by your instruction, you must be perfectly sincere toward me, and tell me plainly of my short-comings. I promise you beforehand that I shall never be offended. There is my hand. Now, is it a bargain?"

His fingers closed involuntarily over the soft beautiful hand, and once more the luxury of her touch sent a thrill of delight through him.

"I have not been insincere," he murmured, "but I shall be on my guard in future, even against the appearance of insincerity."

"And when I play detestably, you will say so, and not smooth it over with unmeaning flatteries?"

"I will try."

"Very well, then we shall get on well together. Do not imagine that this is a mere feminine whim of mine. I never was more in earnest. Men, and I believe foreigners, to a greater degree than Americans, have the idea that women must be treated with gentle forbearance; that their follies, if they are foolish, must be glossed over with some polite name. They exert themselves to the utmost to make us mere playthings, and, as such, contemptible both in our own eyes and in theirs. No sincere respect can exist where the truth has to be avoided. But the majority of American women are made of too stern a stuff to be dealt with in that way. They feel the lurking insincerity even where politeness forbids them to show it, and it makes them disgusted both with themselves, and with the flatterer. And now you must pardon me for having spoken so plainly to you on so short an acquaintance; but you are a foreigner, and it may be an act of friendship to initiate you as soon as possible into our ways and customs."

He hardly knew what to answer. Her vehemence was so sudden, and the sentiments she had uttered so different from those which he had habitually ascribed to women, that he could only sit and gaze at her in mute astonishment. He could not but admit that in the main she had judged him rightly, and that his own attitude and that of other men toward her sex, were based upon an implied assumption of superiority.

"I am afraid I have shocked you," she resumed, noticing the startled expression of his countenance. "But really it was quite inevitable, if we were at all to understand each other. You will forgive me, won't you?"

"Forgive!" stammered he, "I have nothing to forgive. It was only your merciless truthfulness which startled me. I rather owe you thanks, if you will allow me to be grateful to you. It seems an enviable privilege."

"Now," interrupted Edith, raising her forefinger in playful threat, "remember your promise."

The lesson was now continued without further interruption. When it was finished, a little girl, with her hair done up in curl-papers, and a very stiffly starched dress, which stood out on all sides almost horizontally, entered, accompanied by Mrs. Van Kirk. Halfdan immediately recognized his acquaintance from the park, and it appeared to him a good omen that this child, whose friendly interest in him had warmed his heart in a moment when his fortunes seemed so desperate, should continue to be associated with his life on this new continent. Clara was evidently greatly impressed by the change in his appearance, and could with difficulty be restrained from commenting upon it.

She proved a very apt scholar in music, and enjoyed the lessons the more for her cordial liking of her teacher.

It will be necessary henceforth to omit the less significant details in the career of our friend "Mr. Birch." Before a month was past, he had firmly established himself in the favour of the different members of the Van Kirk family. Mrs. Van Kirk spoke of him to her lady visitors as "a perfect jewel," frequently leaving them in doubt as to whether he was a cook or a coachman. Edith apostrophized him to her fashionable friends as "a real genius," leaving a dim impression upon their minds of flowing locks, a shiny velvet jacket, slouched hat, defiant neck-tie and a general air of disreputable pretentiousness. Geniuses of the foreign type were never, in the estimation of fashionable New York society, what you would call "exactly nice," and against prejudices of this order no amount of argument will ever prevail. Clara, who had by this time discovered that her teacher possessed an inexhaustible fund of fairy stories, assured her playmates across the street that he was "just splendid," and frequently invited them over to listen to his wonderful tales. Mr. Van Kirk himself, of course, was non-committal, but paid the bills unmurmuringly.

Halfdan in the meanwhile was vainly struggling against his growing passion for Edith; but the more he rebelled the more hopelessly he found himself entangled in its inextricable net. The fly, as long as it keeps quiet in the spider's web, may for a moment forget its situation; but the least effort to escape is apt to frustrate itself and again reveal the imminent peril. Thus he too 'kicked against the pricks,' hoped, feared, rebelled against his destiny, and again, from sheer weariness, relapsed into a dull, benumbed apathy. In spite of her friendly sympathy, he never felt so keenly his alienism as in her presence. She accepted the spontaneous homage he paid her, sometimes with impatience, as something that was really beneath her notice; at other times she frankly recognized it, bantered him with his 'Old World chivalry,' which would soon evaporate in the practical American atmosphere, and called him her Viking, her knight and her faithful squire. But it never occurred to her to regard his devotion in a serious light, and to look upon him as a possible lover had evidently never entered her head. As their intercourse grew more intimate, he had volunteered to read his favourite poets with her, and had gradually succeeded in imparting to her something of his own passionate liking for Heine and Björnson. She had in return called his attention to the works of American authors who had hitherto been little more than names to him, and they had thus managed to be of mutual benefit to each other, and to spend many a pleasant hour during the long winter afternoons in each other's company. But Edith had a very keen sense of humour, and could hardly restrain her secret amusement when she heard him reading Longfellow's 'Psalm of Life' and Poe's 'Raven' (which had been familiar to her from her babyhood), often with false accent, but always with intense enthusiasm. The reflection that he had had no part of his life in common with her, – that he did not love the things which she loved, – could not share her prejudices (and women have a feeling akin to contempt for a man who does not respond to their prejudices) – removed him at times almost beyond the reach of her sympathy. It was interesting enough as long as the experience was novel, to be thus unconsciously exploring another person's mind and finding so many strange objects there; but after a while the thing began to assume an uncomfortably serious aspect, and then there seemed to be something almost terrible about it. At such times a call from a gentleman of her own nation, even though he were one of the placidly stupid type, would be a positive relief; she could abandon herself to the secure sense of being at home; she need fear no surprises, and in the smooth shallows of their talk there were no unsuspected depths to excite and to baffle her ingenuity. And, again, reverting in her thought to Halfdan, his conversational brilliancy would almost repel her, as something odious and un-American, the cheap result of outlandish birth and unrepublican education. Not that she had ever valued republicanism very highly; she was one of those who associated politics with noisy vulgarity in speech and dress, and therefore thanked fortune that women were permitted to keep aloof from it. But in the presence of this alien she found herself growing patriotic; that much-discussed abstraction, which we call our country (and which is nothing but the aggregate of all the slow and invisible influences which go toward making up our own being), became by degrees a very palpable and intelligible fact to her.

Frequently while her American self was thus loudly asserting itself, Edith inflicted many a cruel wound upon her foreign adorer. Once, – it was the Fourth of July, more than a year after Halfdan's arrival, a number of young ladies and gentlemen, after having listened to a patriotic oration, were invited in to an informal luncheon. While waiting, they naturally enough spent their time in singing national songs, and Halfdan's clear tenor did good service in keeping the straggling voices together. When they had finished, Edith went up to him and was quite effusive in her expressions of gratitude.

"I am sure we ought all to be very grateful to you, Mr. Birch," she said, "and I, for my part, can assure you that I am."

"Grateful? Why?" demanded Halfdan, looking quite unhappy.

"For singing OUR national songs, of course. Now, won't you sing one of your own, please? We should all be so delighted to hear how a Swedish – or Norwegian, is it? – national song sounds."

"Yes, Mr. Birch, DO sing a Swedish song," echoed several voices.

They, of course, did not even remotely suspect their own cruelty. He had, in his enthusiasm for the day allowed himself to forget that he was not made of the same clay as they were, that he was an exile and a stranger, and must ever remain so, that he had no right to share their joy in the blessing of liberty. Edith had taken pains to dispel the happy illusion, and had sent him once more whirling toward his cold native Pole. His passion came near choking him, and, to conceal his impetuous emotion, he flung himself down on the piano-stool, and struck some introductory chords with perhaps a little superfluous emphasis. Suddenly his voice burst out into the Swedish national anthem, 'Our Land, our Land, our Fatherland,' and the air shook and palpitated with strong martial melody. His indignation, his love and his misery, imparted strength to his voice, and its occasional tremble in the PIANO passages was something more than an artistic intention. He was loudly applauded as he arose, and the young ladies thronged about him to ask if he "wouldn't please write out the music for them."

Thus month after month passed by, and every day brought its own misery. Mrs. Van Kirk's patronizing manners, and ostentatious kindness, often tested his patience to the utmost. If he was guilty of an innocent witticism or a little quaintness of expression, she always assumed it to be a mistake of terms and corrected him with an air of benign superiority. At times, of course, her corrections were legitimate, as for instance, when he spoke of WEARING a cane, instead of CARRYING one, but in nine cases out of ten the fault lay in her own lack of imagination and not in his ignorance of English. On such occasions Edith often took pity on him, defended him against her mother's criticism, and insisted that if this or that expression was not in common vogue, that was no reason why it should not be used, as it was perfectly grammatical, and, moreover, in keeping with the spirit of the language. And he, listening passively in admiring silence to her argument, thanked her even for the momentary pain because it was followed by so great a happiness. For it was so sweet to be defended by Edith, to feel that he and she were standing together side by side against the outer world. Could he only show her in the old heroic manner how much he loved her! Would only some one that was dear to her die, so that he, in that breaking down of social barriers which follows a great calamity, might comfort her in her sorrow. Would she then, perhaps, weeping, lean her wonderful head upon his breast, feeling but that he was a fellow-mortal, who had a heart that was loyal and true, and forgetting, for one brief instant, that he was a foreigner. Then, to touch that delicate Elizabethan frill which wound itself so daintily about Edith's neck – what inconceivable rapture! But it was quite impossible. It could never be. These were selfish thoughts, no doubt, but they were a lover's selfishness, and, as such, bore a close kinship to all that is purest and best in human nature.

It is one of the tragic facts of this life, that a relation so unequal as that which existed between Halfdan and Edith, is at all possible. As for Edith, I must admit that she was well aware that her teacher was in love with her. Women have wonderfully keen senses for phenomena of that kind, and it is an illusion if any one imagines, as our Norseman did, that he has locked his secret securely in the hidden chamber of his heart. In fleeting intonations, unconscious glances and attitudes, and through a hundred other channels it will make its way out, and the bereaved jailer may still clasp his key in fierce triumph, never knowing that he has been robbed. It was of course no fault of Edith's that she had become possessed of Halfdan's heart-secret. She regarded it as on the whole rather an absurd affair, and prized it very lightly. That a love so strong and yet so humble, so destitute of hope and still so unchanging, reverent and faithful, had something grand and touching in it, had never occurred to her. It is a truism to say that in our social code the value of a man's character is determined by his position; and fine traits in a foreigner (unless he should happen to be something very great) strike us rather as part of a supposed mental alienism, and as such, naturally suspicious. It is rather disgraceful than otherwise to have your music teacher in love with you, and critical friends will never quite banish the suspicion that you have encouraged him.

Edith had, in her first delight at the discovery of Halfdan's talent, frankly admitted him to a relation of apparent equality. He was a man of culture, had the manners and bearing of a gentleman, and had none of those theatrical airs which so often raise a sort of invisible wall between foreigners and Americans. Her mother, who loved to play the patron, especially to young men, had invited him to dinner-parties and introduced him to their friends, until almost every one looked upon him as a protege of the family. He appeared so well in a parlour, and had really such a distinguished presence, that it was a pleasure to look at him. He was remarkably free from those obnoxious traits which generalizing American travellers have led us to believe were inseparable from foreign birth; his finger-nails were in no way conspicuous; he did not, as a French count, a former adorer of Edith's, had done, indulge an unmasculine taste for diamond rings (possibly because he had none); his politeness was unobtrusive and subdued, and of his accent there was just enough left to give an agreeable colour of individuality to his speech. But, for all that, Edith could never quite rid herself of the impression that he was intensely un-American. There was a certain idyllic quiescence about him, a child-like directness and simplicity, and a total absence of 'push,' which were startlingly at variance with the spirit of American life. An American could never have been content to remain in an inferior position without trying, in some way, to better his fortunes. But Halfdan could stand still and see, without the faintest stirring of envy, his plebeian friend Olson, whose education and talents could bear no comparison with his own, rise rapidly above him, and apparently have no desire to emulate him. He could sit on a cricket in a corner, with Clara on his lap, and two or three little girls nestling about him, and tell them fairy stories by the hour, while his kindly face beamed with innocent happiness. And if Clara, to coax him into continuing the entertainment, offered to kiss him, his measure of joy was full. This fair child, with her affectionate ways, and her confiding prattle, wound herself ever more closely about his homeless heart, and he clung to her with a touching devotion. For she was the only one who seemed to be unconscious of the difference of blood, who had not yet learned that she was an American and he – a foreigner.

VI

Three years had passed by and still the situation was unchanged. Halfdan still taught music and told fairy stories to the children. He had a good many more pupils now than three years ago, although he had made no effort to solicit patronage, and had never tried to advertise his talent by what he regarded as vulgar and inartistic display. But Mrs. Van Kirk, who had by this time discovered his disinclination to assert himself, had been only the more active; had 'talked him up' among her aristocratic friends; had given musical soirees, at which she had coaxed him to play the principal role, and had in various other ways exerted herself in his behalf. It was getting to be quite fashionable to admire his quiet, unostentatious style of playing, which was so far removed from the noisy bravado and clap-trap then commonly in vogue. Even professional musicians began to indorse him, and some, who had discovered that 'there was money in him,' made him tempting offers for a public engagement. But, with characteristic modesty, he distrusted their verdict; his sensitive nature shrank from anything which had the appearance of self-assertion or display.

But Edith – ah, if it had not been for Edith he might have found courage to enter at the door of fortune, which was now opened ajar. That fame, if he should gain it, would bring him any nearer to her, was a thought that was alien to so unworldly a temperament as his. And any action that had no bearing upon his relation to her, left him cold – seemed unworthy of the effort. If she had asked him to play in public; if she had required of him to go to the North Pole, or to cut his own throat, I verily believe he would have done it. And at last Edith did ask him to play. She and Olson had plotted together, and from the very friendliest motives agreed to play into each other's hands.

"If you only WOULD consent to play," said she, in her own persuasive way, one day as they had finished their lesson, "we should all be so happy. Only think how proud we should be of your success, for you know there is nothing you can't do in the way of music if you really want to."

"Do you really think so?" exclaimed he, while his eyes suddenly grew large and luminous.

"Indeed I do," said Edith, emphatically.

"And if – if I played well," faltered he, "would it really please you?"

"Of course it would," cried Edith, laughing; "how can you ask such a foolish question?"

"Because I hardly dared to believe it."

"Now listen to me," continued the girl, leaning forward in her chair, and beaming all over with kindly officiousness; "now for once you must be rational and do just what I tell you. I shall never like you again if you oppose me in this, for I have set my heart upon it; you must promise beforehand that you will be good and not make any objection. Do you hear?"

When Edith assumed this tone toward him, she might well have made him promise to perform miracles. She was too intent upon her benevolent scheme to heed the possible inferences which he might draw from her sudden display of interest.

"Then you promise?" repeated she, eagerly, as he hesitated to answer.

"Yes, I promise."

"Now, you must not be surprised; but mamma and I have made arrangements with Mr. S—— that you are to appear under his auspices at a concert which is to be given a week from to-night. All our friends are going, and we shall take up all the front seats, and I have already told my gentlemen friends to scatter through the audience, and if they care anything for my favour, they will have to applaud vigorously."

Halfdan reddened up to his temples, and began to twist his watch-chain nervously.

"You must have small confidence in my ability," he murmured, "since you resort to precautions like these."

"But my dear Mr. Birch," cried Edith, who was quick to discover that she had made a mistake, "it is not kind in you to mistrust me in that way. If a New York audience were as highly cultivated in music as you are, I admit that my precautions would be superfluous. But the papers, you know, will take their tone from the audience, and therefore we must make use of a little innocent artifice to make sure of it. Everything depends upon the success of your first public appearance, and if your friends can in this way help you to establish the reputation which is nothing but your right, I am sure you ought not to bind their hands by your foolish sensitiveness. You don't know the American way of doing things as well as I do, therefore you must stand by your promise, and leave everything to me."

It was impossible not to believe that anything Edith chose to do was above reproach. She looked so bewitching in her excited eagerness for his welfare that it would have been inhuman to oppose her. So he meekly succumbed, and began to discuss with her the programme for the concert.

During the next week there was hardly a day that he did not read some startling paragraph in the newspapers about 'the celebrated Scandinavian pianist,' whose appearance at S—— Hall was looked forward to as the principal event of the coming season. He inwardly rebelled against the well-meant exaggerations; but as he suspected that it was Edith's influence which was in this way asserting itself in his behalf, he set his conscience at rest and remained silent.

The evening of the concert came at last, and, as the papers stated the next morning, 'the large hall was crowded to its utmost capacity with a select and highly appreciative audience.' Edith must have played her part of the performance skillfully, for as he walked out upon the stage, he was welcomed with an enthusiastic burst of applause, as if he had been a world-renowned artist. At

Edith's suggestion, her two favourite nocturnes had been placed first upon the programme; then followed one of those ballads of Chopin, whose rhythmic din and rush sweep onward, beleaguering the ear like eager, melodious hosts, charging in thickening ranks and columns, beating impetuous retreats, and again uniting with one grand emotion the wide-spreading army of sound for the final victory. Besides these, there was one of Liszt's 'Rhapsodies Hongroises,' an impromptu by Schubert, and several orchestral pieces; but the greater part of the programme was devoted to Chopin, because Halfdan, with his great, hopeless passion labouring in his breast, felt that he could interpret Chopin better than he could any other composer. He carried his audience by storm. As he retired to the dressing-room, after having finished the last piece, his friends, among whom Edith and Mrs. Van Kirk were the most conspicuous, thronged about him, showering their praises and congratulations upon him. They insisted with much friendly urging upon taking him home in their carriage; Clara kissed him, Mrs. Van Kirk introduced him to her lady acquaintances as "our friend, Mr. Birch," and Edith held his hand so long in hers that he came near losing his presence of mind and telling her then and there that he loved her. As his eyes rested on her, they became suddenly suffused with tears, and a vast bewildering happiness vibrated through his frame. At last he tore himself away and wandered aimlessly through the long, lonely streets. Why could he not tell Edith that he loved her? Was there any disgrace in loving? This heavenly passion which so suddenly had transfused his being, and year by year deadened the substance of his old self, creating in its stead something new and wild and strange which he never could know, but still held infinitely dear – had it been sent to him merely as a scourge to test his capacity for suffering?

Once, while he was a child, his mother had told him that somewhere in this wide world there lived a maiden whom God had created for him, and for him alone, and when he should see her, he should love her, and his life should thenceforth be all for her. It had hardly occurred to him, then, to question whether she would love him in return, it had appeared so very natural that she should. Now he had found this maiden, and she had been very kind to him; but her kindness had been little better than cruelty, because he had demanded something more than kindness. And still he had never told her of his love. He must tell her even this very night while the moon rode high in the heavens and all the small differences between human beings seemed lost in the vast starlit stillness. He knew well that by the relentless glare of the daylight his own insignificance would be cruelly conspicuous in the presence of her splendour; his scruples would revive, and his courage fade.

The night was clear and still. A clock struck eleven in some church tower near by. The Van Kirk mansion rose tall and stately in the moonlight, flinging a dense mass of shadow across the street. Up in the third story he saw two windows lighted; the curtains were drawn, but the blinds were not closed. All the rest of the house was dark. He raised his voice and sang a Swedish serenade which seemed in perfect concord with his own mood. His clear tenor rose through the silence of the night, and a feeble echo flung it back from the mansion opposite:

"Star, sweet star, that brightly beamest,
Glittering on the skies nocturnal,
Hide thine eye no more from me,
Hide thine eye no more from me!"

The curtain was drawn aside, the window cautiously raised, and the outline of Edith's beautiful head appeared dark and distinct against the light within. She instantly recognized him.

"You must go away, Mr. Birch," came her voice in an anxious whisper out of the shadow. "Pray go away. You will wake up the people."

Her words were audible enough, but they failed to convey any meaning to his excited mind. Once more his voice floated upward to her opened window:

"And I yearn to reach thy dwelling,
Yearn to rise from earth's fierce turmoil;
Sweetest star upward to thee,
Yearn to rise, bright star to thee."

"Dear Mr. Birch," she whispered once more in tones of distress. "Pray DO go away. Or perhaps," she interrupted herself "—wait one moment and I will come down."

Presently the front door was noiselessly opened, and Edith's tall, lithe form, dressed in a white flowing dress, and with her blonde hair rolling loosely over her shoulders, appeared for an instant, and then again vanished. With one leap Halfdan sprang up the stairs and pushed through the half-opened door. Edith closed the door behind him, then with rapid steps led the way to the back parlour where the moon broke feebly through the bars of the closed shutters.

"Now Mr. Birch," she said, seating herself upon a lounge, "you may explain to me what this unaccountable behaviour of yours means. I should hardly think I had deserved to be treated in this way by you."

Halfdan was utterly bewildered; a nervous fit of trembling ran through him, and he endeavoured in vain to speak. He had been prepared for passionate reproaches, but this calm severity chilled him through, and he could only gasp and tremble, but could utter no word in his defense.

"I suppose you are aware," continued Edith, in the same imperturbable manner, "that if I had not interrupted you, the policeman would have heard you, and you would have been arrested for street disturbance. Then to-morrow we should have seen it in all the newspapers, and I should have been the laughing-stock of the whole town."

No, surely he had never thought of it in that light; the idea struck him as entirely new. There was a long pause. A cock crowed with a drowsy remoteness in some neighbouring yard, and the little clock on the mantel-piece ticked on patiently in the moonlit dusk.

"If you have nothing to say," resumed Edith, while the stern indifference in her voice perceptibly relaxed, "then I will bid you good-night."

She arose, and with a grand sweep of her drapery, moved toward the door.

"Miss Edith," cried he, stretching his hands despairingly after her, "you must not leave me."

She paused, tossed her hair back with her hands, and gazed at him over her shoulder. He threw himself on his knees, seized the hem of her dress, and pressed it to his lips. It was a gesture of such inexpressible humility that even a stone would have relented.

"Do not be foolish, Mr. Birch," she said, trying to pull her dress away from him. "Get up, and if you have anything rational to say to me, I will stay and listen."

"Yes, yes," he whispered, hoarsely, "I shall be rational. Only do not leave me."

She again sank down wearily upon the lounge, and looked at him in expectant silence.

"Miss Edith," pleaded he in the same hoarse, passionate undertone, "have pity on me, and do not despise me. I love you – oh – if you would but allow me to die for you, I should be the happiest of men."

Again he shuddered, and stood long gazing at her with a mute, pitiful appeal. A tear stole into Edith's eye and trickled down over her cheek.

"Ah, Mr. Birch," she murmured, while a sigh shook her bosom, "I am sorry – very sorry that this misfortune has happened to you. You have deserved a better fate than to love me – to love a woman who can never give you anything in return for what you give her."

"Never?" he repeated mournfully, "never?"

"No, never! You have been a good friend to me, and as such I value you highly, and I had hoped that you would always remain so. But I see that it cannot be. It will perhaps be best for you henceforth not to see me, at least not until – pardon the expression – you have outlived this generous folly. And now, you know, you will need me no more. You have made a splendid reputation, and if you choose to avail yourself of it, your fortune is already made. I shall always rejoice to hear of your success, and – and if you should ever need a FRIEND, you must come to no one but me. I know that these are feeble words, Mr. Birch, and if they seem cold to you, you must pardon me. I can say nothing more."

They were indeed feeble words, although most cordially spoken. He tried to weigh them, to measure their meaning, but his mind was as if benumbed, and utterly incapable of thought. He walked across the floor, perhaps only to do something, not feeling where he trod, but still with an absurd sensation that he was taking immoderately long steps. Then he stopped abruptly, wrung his hands, and gazed at Edith. And suddenly, like a flash in a vacuum, the thought shot through his brain that he had seen this very scene somewhere – in a dream, in a remote childhood, in a previous existence, he did not know when or where. It seemed strangely familiar, and in the next instant strangely meaningless and unreal. The walls, the floor – everything began to move, to whirl about him; he struck his hands against his forehead, and sank down into a damask-covered easy-chair. With a faint cry of alarm, Edith sprang up, seized a bottle of cologne which happened to be within reach, and knelt down at his side. She put her arm around his neck, and raised his head.

"Mr. Birch, dear Mr. Birch," she cried, in a frightened whisper, "for God's sake come to yourself! O God, what have I done?"

She blew the eau-de-cologne into his face, and, as he languidly opened his eyes, he felt the touch of her warm hand upon his cheeks and his forehead.

"Thank heaven! he is better," she murmured, still continuing to bathe his temples. "How do you feel now, Mr. Birch?" she added, in a tone of anxious inquiry.

"Thank you, it was an unpardonable weakness," he muttered, without changing his attitude. "Do not trouble yourself about me. I shall soon be well."

It was so sweet to be conscious of her gentle ministry, that it required a great effort, an effort of conscience, to rouse him once more, as his strength returned.

"Had you not better stay?" she asked, as he rose to put on his overcoat. "I will call one of the servants and have him show you a room. We will say to-morrow morning that you were taken ill, and nobody will wonder."

"No, no," he responded, energetically. "I am perfectly strong now." But he still had to lean on a chair, and his face was deathly pale.

"Farewell, Miss Edith," he said; and a tender sadness trembled in his voice. "Farewell. We shall – probably – never meet again."

"Do not speak so," she answered, seizing his hand. "You will try to forget this, and you will still be great and happy. And when fortune shall again smile upon you, and – and – you will be content to be my friend, then we shall see each other as before."

"No, no," he broke forth, with a sudden hoarseness. "It will never be."

He walked toward the door with the motions of one who feels death in his limbs; then stopped once more and his eyes lingered with inexpressible sadness on the wonderful, beloved form which stood dimly outlined before him in the twilight. Then Edith's measure of misery, too, seemed full. With the divine heedlessness which belongs to her sex, she rushed up toward him, and remembering only that he was weak and unhappy, and that he suffered for her sake, she took his face between her hands and kissed him. He was too generous a man to misinterpret the act; so he whispered but once more: "Farewell," and hastened away.

VI

After that eventful December night, America was no more what it had been to Halfdan Bjerk. A strange torpidity had come over him; every rising day gazed into his eyes with a fierce unmeaning glare. The noise of the street annoyed him and made him childishly fretful, and the solitude of his own room seemed still more dreary and depressing. He went mechanically through the daily routine of his duties as if the soul had been taken out of his work, and left his life all barrenness and desolation. He moved restlessly from place to place, roamed at all times of the day and night through the city and its suburbs, trying vainly to exhaust his physical strength; gradually, as his lethargy deepened into a numb, helpless despair, it seemed somehow to impart a certain toughness to his otherwise delicate frame. Olson, who was now a junior partner in the firm of Remsen, Van Kirk and Co., stood by him faithfully in these days of sorrow. He was never effusive in his sympathy, but was patiently forbearing with his friend's whims and moods, and humoured him as if he had been a sick child intrusted to his custody. That Edith might be the moving cause of Olson's kindness was a thought which, strangely enough, had never occurred to Halfdan.

At last, when spring came, the vacancy of his mind was suddenly invaded with a strong desire to revisit his native land. He disclosed his plan to Olson, who, after due deliberation and several visits to the Van Kirk mansion, decided that the pleasure of seeing his old friends and the scenes of his childhood might push the painful memories out of sight, and renew his interest in life. So, one morning, while the May sun shone with a soft radiance upon the beautiful harbour, our Norseman found himself standing on the deck of a huge black-hulled Cunarder, shivering in spite of the warmth, and feeling a chill loneliness creeping over him at the sight of the kissing and affectionate leave-takings which were going on all around him. Olson was running back and forth, attending to his baggage; but he himself took no thought, and felt no more responsibility than if he had been a helpless child. He half regretted that his own wish had prevailed, and was inclined to hold his friend responsible for it; and still he had not energy enough to protest now when the journey seemed inevitable. His heart still clung to the place which held the corpse of his ruined life, as a man may cling to the spot which hides his beloved dead.

About two weeks later Halfdan landed in Norway. He was half reluctant to leave the steamer, and the land of his birth excited no emotion in his breast. He was but conscious of a dim regret that he was so far away from Edith. At last, however, he betook himself to a hotel, where he spent the afternoon sitting with half-closed eyes at a window, watching listlessly the drowsy slow-pulsed life which dribbled languidly through the narrow thoroughfare. The noisy uproar of Broadway chimed remotely in his ears, like the distant roar of a tempest-tossed sea, and what had once been a perpetual annoyance was now a sweet memory. How often with Edith at his side had he threaded his way through the surging crowds that pour, on a fine afternoon, in an unceasing current up and down the street between Union and Madison Squares. How friendly, and sweet, and gracious, Edith had been at such times; how fresh her voice, how witty and animated her chance remarks when they stopped to greet a passing acquaintance; and, above all, how inspiring the sight of her heavenly beauty. Now that was all past. Perhaps he should never see Edith again.

The next day he sauntered through the city, meeting some old friends, who all seemed changed and singularly uninteresting. They were all engaged or married, and could talk of nothing but matrimony, and their prospects of advancement in the Government service. One had an influential uncle who had been a chum of the present minister of finance; another based his hopes of future prosperity upon the family connections of his betrothed, and a third was waiting with a patient perseverance, worthy of a better cause, for the death or resignation of an antiquated chef-de-bureau, which, according to the promise of some mighty man, would open a position for him in the Department of Justice. All had the most absurd theories about American democracy, and indulged freely in prophecies of coming disasters; but about their own government they had no opinion whatever. If Halfdan attempted to set them right, they at once grew excited and declamatory; their opinions were based upon conviction and a charming ignorance of facts, and they were not to be moved. They knew all about Tweed and the Tammany Ring, and believed them to be representative citizens of New York, if not of the United States; but of Charles Sumner and Carl Schurz they had never heard. Halfdan, who, in spite of his misfortunes in the land of his adoption, cherished a very tender feeling for it, was often so thoroughly aroused at the foolish prejudices which everywhere met him, that his torpidity gradually thawed away, and he began to look more like his former self.

Toward autumn he received an invitation to visit a country clergyman in the North, a distant relative of his father's, and there whiled away his time, fishing and shooting, until winter came. But as Christmas drew near, and the day wrestled feebly with the all-conquering night, the old sorrow revived. In the darkness which now brooded over land and sea, the thoughts needed no longer be on guard against themselves; they could roam far and wide as they listed. Where was Edith now, the sweet, the wonderful Edith? Was there yet the same dancing light in her beautiful eyes, the same golden sheen in her hair, the same merry ring in her voice? And had she not said that when he was content to be only her friend, he might return to her, and she would receive him in the old joyous and confiding way? Surely there was no life to him apart from her: why should he not be her friend? Only a glimpse of her lovely face – ah, it was worth a lifetime; it would consecrate an age of misery, a glimpse of Edith's face. Thus ran his fancies day by day, and the night only lent a deeper intensity to the yearnings of the day. He walked about as in a dream, seeing nothing, heeding nothing, while this one strong desire – to see Edith once more – throbbed and throbbed with a slow, feverish perseverance within him. Edith – Edith, the very name had a strange, potent fascination. Every thought whispered "Edith," – his pulse beat "Edith," – and his heart repeated the beloved name. It was his pulse-beat, – his heartbeat, – his life-beat.

And one morning as he stood absently looking at his fingers against the light – and they seemed strangely wan and transparent – the thought at last took shape. It rushed upon him with such vehemence, that he could no more resist it. So he bade the clergyman good-bye, gathered his few worldly goods together and set out for Bergen. There he found an English steamer which carried him to Hull, and a few weeks later, he was once more in New York.

It was late one evening in January that a tug-boat arrived and took the cabin passengers ashore. The moon sailed tranquilly over the deep blue dome of the sky, the stars traced their glittering paths of light from the zenith downward, and it was sharp, bitter cold. Northward over the river lay a great bank of cloud, dense, gray and massive, the spectre of the coming snow-storm. There it lay so huge and fantastically human, ruffling itself up, as fowls do, in defense against the cold. Halfdan walked on at a brisk rate – strange to say, all the street-cars he met went the wrong way – startling every now and then some precious memory, some word or look or gesture of Edith's which had hovered long over those scenes, waiting for his recognition. There was the great jewel-store where Edith had taken him so often to consult his taste whenever a friend of hers was to be married. It was there that they had had an amicable quarrel over that bronze statue of Faust which she had found beautiful, while he, with a rudeness which seemed now quite incomprehensible, had insisted that it was not. And when he had failed to convince her, she had given him her hand in token of reconciliation – and Edith had a wonderful way of giving her hand, which made any one feel that it was a peculiar privilege to press it – and they had walked out arm in arm into the animated, gas-lighted streets, with a delicious sense of snugness and security, being all the more closely united for their quarrel. Here, farther up the avenue, they had once been to a party, and he had danced for the first time in his life with

Edith. Here was Delmonico's, where they had had such fascinating luncheons together; where she had got a stain on her dress, and he had been forced to observe that her dress was then not really a part of herself, since it was a thing that could not be stained. Her dress had always seemed to him as something absolute and final, exalted above criticism, incapable of improvement.

As I have said, Halfdan walked briskly up the avenue, and it was something after eleven when he reached the house which he sought. The great cloud-bank in the north had then begun to expand and stretched its long misty arms eastward and westward over the heavens. The windows on the ground-floor were dark, but the sleeping apartments in the upper stories were lighted. In Edith's room the inside shutters were closed, but one of the windows was a little down at the top. And as he stood gazing with tremulous happiness up to that window, a stanza from Heine which he and Edith had often read together, came into his head. It was the story of the youth who goes to the Madonna at Kevlar and brings her as a votive offering a heart of wax, that she may heal him of his love and his sorrow.

"I bring this waxen image,
The image of my heart,
Heal thou my bitter sorrow,
And cure my deadly smart!"

Then came the thought that for him, too, as for the poor youth of Cologne, there was healing only in death. And still in this moment he was so near Edith, should see her perhaps, and the joy at this was stronger than all else, stronger even than death. So he sat down beside the steps of the mansion opposite, where there was some shelter from the wind, and waited patiently till Edith should close her window. He was cold, perhaps, but, if so, he hardly knew it, for the near joy of seeing her throbbed warmly in his veins. Ah, there – the blinds were thrown open; Edith, in all the lithe magnificence of her wonderful form, stood out clear and beautiful against the light within; she pushed up the lower window in order to reach the upper one, and for a moment leaned out over the sill. Once more her wondrous profile traced itself in strong relief against the outer gloom. There came a cry from the street below, a feeble involuntary one, but still distinctly audible. Edith peered anxiously out into the darkness, but the darkness had grown denser and she could see nothing. The window was fastened, the shutters closed, and the broad pathway of light which she had flung out upon the night had vanished.

Halfdan closed his eyes trying to retain the happy vision. Yes, there she stood still, and there was a heavenly smile upon her lips – ugh, he shivered – the snow swept in a wild whirl up the street. He wrapped his plaid more closely about him, and strained his eyes to catch one more glimpse of the beloved Edith. Ah, yes; there she was again; she came nearer and nearer, and she touched his cheek, gently, warily smiling all the while with a strange wistful smile which was surely not Edith's. There, she bent over him, – touched him again, – how cold her hands were; the touch chilled him to the heart. The snow had now begun to fall in large scattered flakes, whirling fitfully through the air, following every chance gust of wind, but still falling, falling, and covering the earth with its white, death-like shroud.

But surely – there was Edith again, – how wonderful! – in a long snow-white robe, grave and gracious, still with the wistful smile on her lips. See, she beckons to him with her hand, and he rises to follow, but something heavy clings to his feet and he cannot stir from the spot. He tries to cry for help, but he cannot, – can only stretch out his hands to her, and feel very unhappy that he cannot follow her. But now she pauses in her flight, turns about, and he sees that she wears a myrtle garland in her hair like a bride. She comes toward him, her countenance all radiant with love and happiness, and she stoops down over him and speaks:

"Come; they are waiting for us. I will follow thee in life and in death, wherever thou goest. Come," repeats Edith, "they have long been waiting. They are all here."

And he imagines he knows who they all are, although he has never heard of them, nor can he recall their names.

"But – but," he stammers, "I – I – am a foreigner "

It appeared then that for some reason this was an insurmountable objection. And Edith's happiness dies out of her beautiful face, and she turns away weeping.

"Edith, beloved!"

Then she is once more at his side.

"Thou art no more a foreigner to me, beloved. Whatever thou art, I am."

And she presses her lips to his – it was the sweetest kiss of his life – the kiss of death.

The next morning, as Edith, after having put the last touch to her toilet, threw the shutters open, a great glare of sun-smitten snow burst upon her and for a moment blinded her eyes. On the sidewalk opposite, half a dozen men with snow-shovels in their hands and a couple of policeman had congregated, and, judging by their manner, were discussing some object of interest. Presently they were joined by her father, who had just finished his breakfast and was on his way to the office. Now he stooped down and gazed at something half concealed in the snow, then suddenly started back, and as she caught a glimpse of his face, she saw that it was ghastly white. A terrible foreboding seized her. She threw a shawl about her shoulders and rushed down-stairs. In the hall she was met by her father, who was just entering, followed by four men, carrying something between them. She well knew what it was. She would fain have turned away, but she could not: grasping her father's arm and pressing it hard, she gazed with blank, frightened eyes at the white face, the lines of which Death had so strangely emphasized. The snow-flakes which hung in his hair had touched him with their sudden age, as if to bridge the gulf between youth and death. And still he was beautiful – the clear brow, the peaceful, happy indolence, the frozen smile which death had perpetuated. Smiling, he had departed from the earth which had no place for him, and smiling entered the realm where, among the many mansions, there is, perhaps, also one for a gentle, simple-hearted enthusiast.

Yekl

Abraham Cahan

Chapter II: The New York Ghetto

IT WAS AFTER SEVEN IN THE EVENING when Jake finished his last jacket. Some of the operators had laid down their work before, while others cast an envious glance on him as he was dressing to leave, and fell to their machines with reluctantly redoubled energy. Fanny was a week worker and her time had been up at seven; but on this occasion her toilet had taken an uncommonly long time, and she was not ready until Jake got up from his chair. Then she left the room rather suddenly and with a demonstrative "Good-night all!"

When Jake reached the street he found her on the sidewalk, making a pretense of brushing one of her sleeves with the cuff of the other.

"So kvick?" she asked, raising her head in feigned surprise.

"You cull dot kvick?" he returned grimly. "Good-bye!"

"Say, ain't you goin' to dance to-night, really?" she queried shamefacedly.

"I tol' you I vouldn't."

"What does *she* want of me?" he complained to himself proceeding on his way. He grew conscious of his low spirits, and, tracing them with some effort to their source, he became gloomier still. "No more fun for me!" he decided. "I shall get them over here and begin a new life."

After supper, which he had taken, as usual, at his lodgings, he went out for a walk. He was firmly determined to keep himself from visiting Joe Peltner's dancing academy, and accordingly he took a direction opposite to Suffolk Street, where that establishment was situated. Having passed a few blocks, however, his feet, contrary to his will, turned into a side street and thence into one leading to Suffolk. "I shall only drop in to tell Joe that I can not sell any of his ball tickets, and return them," he attempted to deceive his own conscience. Hailing this pretext with delight he quickened his pace as much as the overcrowded sidewalks would allow.

He had to pick and nudge his way through dense swarms of bedraggled half-naked humanity; past garbage barrels rearing their overflowing contents in sickening piles, and lining the streets in malicious suggestion of rows of trees; underneath tiers and tiers of fire escapes, barricaded and festooned with mattresses, pillows, and feather-beds not yet gathered in for the night. The pent-in sultry atmosphere was laden with nausea and pierced with a discordant and, as it were, plaintive buzz. Supper had been despatched in a hurry, and the teeming populations of the cyclopic tenement houses were out in full force 'for fresh air,' as even these people will say in mental quotation marks.

Suffolk Street is in the very thick of the battle for breath. For it lies in the heart of that part of the East Side which has within the last two or three decades become the Ghetto of the American metropolis, and, indeed, the metropolis of the Ghettos of the world. It is one of the most densely populated spots on the face of the earth – a seething human sea fed by streams, streamlets, and rills of immigration flowing from all the Yiddish-speaking centres of Europe. Hardly a block but shelters Jews from every nook and corner of Russia, Poland, Galicia, Hungary, Roumania; Lithuanian Jews, Volhynian Jews, south Russian Jews, Bessarabian Jews; Jews crowded out of the 'pale of Jewish settlement'; Russified Jews expelled from Moscow, St. Petersburg, Kieff, or Saratoff; Jewish runaways from justice; Jewish refugees from crying political and economical injustice; people torn from a hard-gained foothold in life and from deep-rooted attachments by the caprice of intolerance or the wiles of demagoguery – innocent scapegoats of a guilty Government for its outraged populace to misspend its blind fury upon; students shut out of the Russian universities, and come to these shores in quest of learning; artisans, merchants, teachers, rabbis, artists, beggars – all come in search of fortune. Nor is there a tenement house but harbours in its bosom specimens of all the whimsical metamorphoses wrought upon the children of Israel of the great modern exodus by the vicissitudes of life in this their Promised Land of to-day. You find there Jews born to plenty, whom the new conditions have delivered up to the clutches of penury; Jews reared in the straits of need, who have here risen to prosperity; good people morally degraded in the struggle for success amid an unwonted environment; moral outcasts lifted from the mire, purified, and imbued with self-respect; educated men and women with their intellectual polish tarnished in the inclement weather of adversity; ignorant sons of toil grown enlightened – in fine, people with all sorts of antecedents, tastes, habits, inclinations, and speaking all sorts of subdialects of the same jargon, thrown pellmell into one social caldron – a human hodgepodge with its component parts changed but not yet fused into one homogeneous whole.

And so the 'stoops,' sidewalks, and pavements of Suffolk Street were thronged with panting, chattering, or frisking multitudes. In one spot the scene received a kind of weird picturesqueness from children dancing on the pavement to the strident music hurled out into the tumultuous din from a row of the open and brightly illuminated windows of what appeared to be a new tenement house. Some of the young women on the sidewalk opposite raised a longing eye to these windows, for floating, by through the dazzling light within were young women like themselves with masculine arms round their waists.

As the spectacle caught Jake's eye his heart gave a leap. He violently pushed his way through the waltzing swarm, and dived into the half-dark corridor of the house whence the music issued. Presently he found himself on the threshold and in the overpowering air of a spacious oblong chamber, alive with a damp-haired, dishevelled, reeking crowd – an uproarious human vortex, whirling to the squeaky notes of a violin and the thumping of a piano. The room was, judging by its untidy, once-whitewashed walls and the uncouth wooden pillars supporting its bare ceiling, more accustomed to the whir of sewing machines than to the noises which filled it at the present moment. It took up the whole of the first floor of a five-story house built for large sweat-shops, and until recently it had served its original purpose as faithfully as the four upper floors, which were still the daily scenes of feverish industry. At the further end of the room there was now a marble soda fountain in charge of an unkempt boy. A stocky young man with a black entanglement of coarse curly hair was bustling about among the dancers. Now and then he would pause with his eyes bent upon some two pairs of feet, and fall to clapping time and drawling out in a preoccupied singsong: "Von, two, tree! Leeft you' feet! Don' so kvick – sloy, sloy! Von, two, tree, von, two, tree!" This was Professor Peltner himself, whose curly hair, by the way, had more to do with the success of his institution than his stumpy legs, which, according to the unanimous dictum of his male pupils, moved about "like a *regely* pair of bears."

The throng showed but a very scant sprinkling of plump cheeks and shapely figures in a multitude of haggard faces and flaccid forms. Nearly all were in their work-a-day clothes, very few of the men sporting a wilted white shirt front. And while the general effect of the kaleidoscope was one of boisterous hilarity, many of the individual couples somehow had the air of being engaged in hard toil rather than as if they were dancing for amusement. The faces of some of these bore a wondering martyrlike expression, as who should say, "What have we done to be knocked about in this manner?"

For the rest, there were all sorts of attitudes and miens in the whirling crowd. One young fellow, for example, seemed to be threatening vengeance to the ceiling, while his partner was all but exultantly exclaiming: "Lord of the universe! What a world this be!" Another maiden looked as if she kept murmuring, "You don't say!" whereas her cavalier mutely ejaculated, "Glad to try my best, your noble birth!" – after the fashion of a Russian soldier.

The prevailing stature of the assemblage was rather below medium. This does not include the dozen or two of undergrown lasses of fourteen or thirteen who had come surreptitiously, and – to allay the suspicion of their mothers – in their white aprons. They accordingly had only these articles to check at the hat box, and hence the nickname of 'apron-check ladies,' by which this truant contingent was known at Joe's academy. So that as Jake now stood in the doorway with an orphaned collar button glistening out of the band of his collarless shirt front and an affected expression of *ennui* overshadowing his face, his strapping figure towered over the circling throng before him. He was immediately noticed and became the target for hellos, smiles, winks, and all manner of pleasantry: "Vot you stand like dot? You vont to loin dantz?" or "You a detectiff?" or "You vont a job?" or, again, "Is it hot anawff for you?" To all of which Jake returned an invariable "Yep!" each time resuming his bored mien.

As he thus gazed at the dancers, a feeling of envy came over him. "Look at them!" he said to himself begrudgingly. "How merry they are! Such *shnoozes*, they can hardly set a foot well, and yet they are free, while I am a married man. But wait till you get married, too," he prospectively avenged himself on Joe's pupils; "we shall see how you will then dance and jump!"

Presently a wave of Joe's hand brought the music and the trampling to a pause. The girls at once took their seats on the 'ladies' bench,' while the bulk of the men retired to the side reserved for 'gents only.' Several apparent post-graduates nonchalantly overstepped the boundary line, and, nothing daunted by the professor's repeated "Zents to de right an' ladess to the left!" unrestrainedly kept their girls chuckling. At all events, Joe soon desisted, his attention being diverted by the soda department of his business. "Sawda!" he sang out. "Ull kin's! Sam, you ought ashamed you'selv; vy don'tz you treat you' lada?"

In the meantime Jake was the centre of a growing bevy of both sexes. He refused to unbend and to enter into their facetious mood, and his morose air became the topic of their persiflage.

By-and-bye Joe came scuttling up to his side. "Goot-evenig, Dzake!" he greeted him; "I didn't seen you at ull! Say, Dzake, I'll take care dis site an' you take care dot site – ull right?"

"Alla right!" Jake responded gruffly. "Gentsh, getch you partnesh, hawrry up!" he commanded in another instant.

The sentence was echoed by the dancing master, who then blew on his whistle a prolonged shrill warble, and once again the floor was set straining under some two hundred pounding, gliding, or scraping feet.

"Don' bee 'fraid. Gu right aheat an' getch you partner!" Jake went on yelling right and left. "Don' be 'shamed, Mish Cohen. Dansh mit dot gentlemarn!" he said, as he unceremoniously encircled Miss Cohen's waist with "dot gentlemarn's" arm. "Cholly! vot's de madder mitch *you*? You do hop like a Cossack, as true as I am a Jew," he added, indulging in a momentary lapse into Yiddish. English was the official language of the academy, where it was broken and mispronounced in as many different ways as there were Yiddish dialects represented in that institution. "Dot'sh de vay, look!" With which Jake seized from Charley a lanky fourteen-year-old Miss Jacobs, and proceeded to set an example of correct waltzing, much to the unconcealed delight of the girl, who let her head rest on his breast with an air of reverential gratitude and bliss, and to the embarrassment of her cavalier, who looked at the evolutions of Jake's feet without seeing.

Presently Jake was beckoned away to a corner by Joe, whereupon Miss Jacobs, looking daggers at the little professor, sulked off to a distant seat.

"Dzake, do me a faver; hask Mamie to gib dot feller a couple a dantzes," Joe said imploringly, pointing to an ungainly young man who was timidly viewing the pandemonium-like spectacle from the further end of the 'gent's bench.' "I hasked 'er myself, but se don' vonted. He's a beesness man, you 'destan', an' he kan a lot o' fellers an' I vonted make him satetzfiet."

"Dot monkey?" said Jake. "Vot you talkin' aboyt! She vouldn't lishn to me neider, honesht."

"Say dot you don' vonted and dot's ull."

"Alla right; I'm goin' to ashk her, but I know it vouldn't be of naw used."

"Never min', you hask 'er foist. You knaw se vouldn't refuse *you*!" Joe urged, with a knowing grin.

"Hoy much vill you bet she will refushe shaw?" Jake rejoined with insincere vehemence, as he whipped out a handful of change.

"Vot kin' foon a man you are! Ulleways like to bet!" said Joe, deprecatingly. 'F cuss it depend mit vot kin' a mout' you vill hask, you 'destan'?"

"By gum, Jaw! Vot you take me for? Ven I shay I ashk, I ashk. You knaw I don' like no monkey beeshnesh. Ven I promish anytink I do it shquare, dot'sh a kin' a man I am!" And once more protesting his firm conviction that Mamie would disregard his request, he started to prove that she would not.

He had to traverse nearly the entire length of the hall, and, notwithstanding that he was compelled to steer clear of the dancers, he contrived to effect the passage at the swellest of his gaits, which means that he jauntily bobbed and lurched, after the manner of a blacksmith tugging at the bellows, and held up his enormous bullet head as if he were bidding defiance to the whole world. Finally he paused in front of a girl with a superabundance of pitch-black side bangs and with a pert, ill natured, pretty face of the most strikingly Semitic cast in the whole gathering. She looked twenty-three or more, was inclined to plumpness, and her shrewd deep dark eyes gleamed out of a warm gipsy complexion. Jake found her seated in a fatigued attitude on a chair near the piano.

"Good-evenig, Mamie!" he said, bowing with mock gallantry.

"Rats!"

"Shay, Mamie, give dot feller a tvisht, vill you?"

"Dot slob again? Joe must tink if you ask me I'll get scared, ain't it? Go and tell him he is too fresh," she said with a contemptuous grimace. Like the majority of the girls of the academy, Mamie's English was a much nearer approach to a justification of its name than the gibberish spoken by the men.

Jake felt routed; but he put a bold face on it and broke out with studied resentment:

"Vot you kickin' aboyt, anyhoy? Jaw don' mean notin' at ull. If you don' vonted never min', an' dot'sh ull. It don' cut a figger, shee?" And he feignedly turned to go.

"Look how kvick he gets excited!" she said, surrenderingly.

"I ain't get ekshitet at ull; but vot'sh de used a makin' monkey beesnesh?" he retorted with triumphant acerbity.

"You are a monkey you'self," she returned with a playful pout.

The compliment was acknowledged by one of Jake's blandest grins.

"An' you are a monkey from monkey-land," he said. "Vill you dansh mit dot feller?"

"Rats! Vot vill you give me?"

"Vot should I give you?" he asked impatiently.

"Vill you treat?"

"Treat? Ger-rr oyt!" he replied with a sweeping kick at space.

"Den I von't dance."

"Alla right. I'll treat you mit a coupel a waltch."

"Is dot so? You must really tink I am swooning to dance vit you," she said, dividing the remark between both jargons.

"Look at her, look! she is a *regely* getzke: one must take off one's cap to speak to her. Don't you always say you like to *dansh* with me *becush* I am a good *dansher*?"

"You must tink you are a peach of a dancer, ain' it? Bennie can dance a —— sight better dan you," she recurred to her English.

"Alla right!" he said tartly. "So you don' vonted?"

"O sugar! He is gettin' mad again. Vell, who is de getzke, me or you? All right, I'll dance vid de slob. But it's only becuss you ask me, mind you!" she added fawningly.

"Dot'sh alla right!" he rejoined, with an affectation of gravity, concealing his triumph. "But you makin' too much fush. I like to shpeak plain, shee? Dot'sh a kin' a man *I* am."

The next two waltzes Mamie danced with the ungainly novice, taking exaggerated pains with him. Then came a lancers, Joe calling out the successive movements huckster fashion. His command was followed by less than half of the class, however, for the greater part preferred to avail themselves of the same music for waltzing. Jake was bent upon giving Mamie what he called a "sholid good time"; and, as she shared his view that a square or fancy dance was as flimsy an affair as a stick of candy, they joined or, rather, led the seceding majority. They spun along with all-forgetful gusto; every little while he lifted her on his powerful arm and gave her a "mill," he yelping and she squeaking for sheer ecstasy, as he did so; and throughout the performance his face and his whole figure seemed to be exclaiming, "Dot'sh a kin' a man I am!"

Several waifs stood in a cluster admiring or begrudging the antics of the star couple. Among these was lanky Miss Jacobs and Fanny the Preacher, who had shortly before made her appearance in the hall, and now stood pale and forlorn by the 'apron-check' girl's side.

"Look at the way she is stickin' to him!" the little girl observed with envious venom, her gaze riveted to Mamie, whose shapely head was at this moment reclining on Jake's shoulders, with her eyes half shut, as if melting in a transport of bliss.

Fanny felt cut to the quick.

"You are jealous, ain't you?" she jerked out.

"Who, me? Vy should I be jealous?" Miss Jacobs protested, colouring. "On my part let them both go to ——. *You* must be jealous. Here, here! See how your eyes are creeping out looking! Here, here!" she teased her offender in Yiddish, poking her little finger at her as she spoke.

"Will you shut your scurvy mouth, little piece of ugliness, you? Such a piggish apron check!" poor Fanny burst out under breath, tears starting to her eyes.

"Such a nasty little runt!" another girl chimed in.

"Such a little cricket already knows what 'jealous' is!" a third of the bystanders put in. "You had better go home or your mamma will give you a spanking." Whereat the little cricket made a retort, which had better be left unrecorded.

"To think of a bit of a flea like that having so much cheek! Here is America for you!"

"America for a country and '*dod'll do*' [that'll do] for a language!" observed one of the young men of the group, indulging one of the stereotype jokes of the Ghetto.

The passage at arms drew Jake's attention to the little knot of spectators, and his eye fell on Fanny. Whereupon he summarily relinquished his partner on the floor, and advanced toward his shopmate, who, seeing him approach, hastened to retreat to the girls' bench, where she remained seated with a drooping head.

"Hello, Fanny!" he shouted briskly, coming up in front of her.

"Hello!" she returned rigidly, her eyes fixed on the dirty floor.

"Come, give ush a tvisht, vill you?"

"But you ain't goin' by Joe to-night!" she answered, with a withering curl of her lip, her glance still on the ground. "Go to your lady, she'll be mad atch you."

"I didn't vonted to gu here, honesht, Fanny. I o'ly come to tell Jaw shometin', an' dot'sh ull," he said guiltily.

"Why should you apologize?" she addressed the tip of her shoe in her mother tongue. "As if he was obliged to apologize to me! *For my part* you can *dance* with her day and night. *Vot do I care*? As if I *cared*! I have only come to see what a *bluffer* you are. Do you think I am a *fool*? As *smart* as your Mamie, *anyvay*. As if I had not known he wanted to make me stay at home! What are you afraid of? Am I in your way then? As if I was in his way! What business have I to be in your way? Who is in your way?"

While she was thus speaking in her voluble, querulous, harassing manner, Jake stood with his hands in his trousers' pockets, in an attitude of mock attention. Then, suddenly losing patience, he said:

"*Dot'sh alla right*! You will finish your sermon afterward. And in the meantime *lesh have a valtz* from the land of *valtzes*!" With which he forcibly dragged her off her seat, catching her round the waist.

"But I don't need it, I don't wish it! Go to your Mamie!" she protested, struggling. "I tell you I don't need it, I don't——" The rest of the sentence was choked off by her violent breathing; for by this time she was spinning with Jake like a top. After another moment's pretense at struggling to free herself she succumbed, and presently clung to her partner, the picture of triumph and beatitude.

Meanwhile Mamie had walked up to Joe's side, and without much difficulty caused him to abandon the lancers party to themselves, and to resume with her the waltz which Jake had so abruptly broken off.

In the course of the following intermission she diplomatically seated herself beside her rival, and paraded her tranquillity of mind by accosting her with a question on shop matters. Fanny was not blind to the manœuvre, but her exultation was all the greater for it, and she participated in the ensuing conversation with exuberant geniality.

By-and-bye they were joined by Jake.

"Vell, vill you treat, Jake?" said Mamie.

"Vot you vant, a kish?" he replied, putting his offer in action as well as in language.

Mamie slapped his arm.

"May the Angel of Death kiss you!" said her lips in Yiddish. "Try again!" her glowing face overruled them in a dialect of its own.

Fanny laughed.

"Once I am *treating*, both *ladas* must be *treated* alike, ain' it?" remarked the gallant, and again he proved himself as good as his word, although Fanny struggled with greater energy and ostensibly with more real indignation.

"But vy don't you treat, you stingy loafer you?"

"Vot elsh you vant? A peench?" He was again on the point of suiting the action to the word, but Mamie contrived to repay the pinch before she had received it, and added a generous piece of profanity into the bargain. Whereupon there ensued a scuffle of a character which defies description in more senses than one.

Nevertheless Jake marched his two 'ladas' up to the marble fountain, and regaled them with two cents' worth of soda each.

An hour or so later, when Jake got out into the street, his breast pocket was loaded with a fresh batch of 'Professor Peltner's Grand Annual Ball' tickets, and his two arms – with Mamie and Fanny respectively.

"As soon as I get my wages I'll call on the installment agent and give him a deposit for a steamship ticket," presently glimmered through his mind, as he adjusted his hold upon the two girls, snugly gathering them to his sides.

The complete and unabridged text is available online, from flametreepublishing.com/extras

The Citizen

James Francis Dwyer

THE PRESIDENT OF THE UNITED STATES was speaking. His audience comprised two thousand foreign-born men who had just been admitted to citizenship. They listened intently, their faces, aglow with the light of a new-born patriotism, upturned to the calm, intellectual face of the first citizen of the country they now claimed as their own.

Here and there among the newly-made citizens were wives and children. The women were proud of their men. They looked at them from time to time, their faces showing pride and awe.

One little woman, sitting immediately in front of the President, held the hand of a big, muscular man and stroked it softly. The big man was looking at the speaker with great blue eyes that were the eyes of a dreamer.

The President's words came clear and distinct:

You were drawn across the ocean by some beckoning finger of hope, by some belief, by some vision of a new kind of justice, by some expectation of a better kind of life. You dreamed dreams of this country, and I hope you brought the dreams with you. A man enriches the country to which he brings dreams, and you who have brought them have enriched America.

The big man made a curious choking noise and his wife breathed a soft "Hush!" The giant was strangely affected.

The President continued:

No doubt you have been disappointed in some of us, but remember this, if we have grown at all poor in the ideal, you brought some of it with you. A man does not go out to seek the thing that is not in him. A man does not hope for the thing that he does not believe in, and if some of us have forgotten what America believed in, you at any rate imported in your own hearts a renewal of the belief. Each of you, I am sure, brought a dream, a glorious, shining dream, a dream worth more than gold or silver, and that is the reason that I, for one, make you welcome.

The big man's eyes were fixed. His wife shook him gently, but he did not heed her. He was looking through the presidential rostrum, through the big buildings behind it, looking out over leagues of space to a snow-swept village that huddled on an island in the Beresina, the swift-flowing tributary of the mighty Dnieper, an island that looked like a black bone stuck tight in the maw of the stream.

It was in the little village on the Beresina that the Dream came to Ivan Berloff, Big Ivan of the Bridge.

The Dream came in the spring. All great dreams come in the spring, and the Spring Maiden who brought Big Ivan's Dream was more than ordinarily beautiful. She swept up the Beresina, trailing wondrous draperies of vivid green. Her feet touched the snow-hardened ground, and armies of little white and blue flowers sprang up in her footsteps. Soft breezes escorted her, velvety breezes that carried the aromas of the far-off places from which they came, places far to the southward, and more distant towns beyond the Black Sea whose people were not under the sway of the Great Czar.

The father of Big Ivan, who had fought under Prince Menshikov at Alma fifty-five years before, hobbled out to see the sunbeams eat up the snow hummocks that hid in the shady places, and he told his son it was the most wonderful spring he had ever seen.

"The little breezes are hot and sweet," he said, sniffing hungrily with his face turned toward the south. "I know them, Ivan! I know them! They have the spice odour that I sniffed on the winds that came to us when we lay in the trenches at Balaklava. Praise God for the warmth!"

And that day the Dream came to Big Ivan as he plowed. It was a wonder dream. It sprang into his brain as he walked behind the plow, and for a few minutes he quivered as the big bridge quivers when the Beresina sends her ice squadrons to hammer the arches. It made his heart pound mightily, and his lips and throat became very dry.

Big Ivan stopped at the end of the furrow and tried to discover what had brought the Dream. Where had it come from? Why had it clutched him so suddenly? Was he the only man in the village to whom it had come?

Like his father, he sniffed the sweet-smelling breezes. He thrust his great hands into the sunbeams. He reached down and plucked one of a bunch of white flowers that had sprung up overnight. The Dream was born of the breezes and the sunshine and the spring flowers. It came from them and it had sprung into his mind because he was young and strong. He knew! It couldn't come to his father or Donkov, the tailor, or Poborino, the smith. They were old and weak, and Ivan's dream was one that called for youth and strength.

"Ay, for youth and strength," he muttered as he gripped the plow. "And I have it!"

That evening Big Ivan of the Bridge spoke to his wife, Anna, a little woman, who had a sweet face and a wealth of fair hair.

"Wife, we are going away from here," he said.

"Where are we going, Ivan?" she asked.

"Where do you think, Anna?" he said, looking down at her as she stood by his side.

"To Bobruisk," she murmured.

"No."

"Farther?"

"Ay, a long way farther."

Fear sprang into her soft eyes. Bobruisk was eighty-nine versts away, yet Ivan said they were going farther.

"We – we are not going to Minsk?" she cried.

"Aye, and beyond Minsk!"

"Ivan, tell me!" she gasped. "Tell me where we are going!"

"We are going to America."

"*To America*?"

"Yes, to America!"

Big Ivan of the Bridge lifted up his voice when he cried out the words "To America," and then a sudden fear sprang upon him as those words dashed through the little window out into the darkness of the village street. Was he mad? America was 8,000 versts away! It was far across the ocean, a place that was only a name to him, a place where he knew no one. He wondered in the strange little silence that followed his words if the crippled son of Poborino, the smith, had heard him. The cripple would jeer at him if the night wind had carried the words to his ear.

Anna remained staring at her big husband for a few minutes, then she sat down quietly at his side. There was a strange look in his big blue eyes, the look of a man to whom has come a vision, the look which came into the eyes of those shepherds of Judea long, long ago.

"What is it, Ivan?" she murmured softly, patting his big hand. "Tell me."

And Big Ivan of the Bridge, slow of tongue, told of the Dream. To no one else would he have told it. Anna understood. She had a way of patting his hands and saying soft things when his tongue could not find words to express his thoughts.

Ivan told how the Dream had come to him as he plowed. He told her how it had sprung upon him, a wonderful dream born of the soft breezes, of the sunshine, of the sweet smell of the upturned sod and of his own strength. "It wouldn't come to weak men," he said, baring an arm that showed great snaky muscles rippling beneath the clear skin. "It is a dream that comes only to those who are strong and those who want – who want something that they haven't got." Then in a lower voice he said: "What is it that we want, Anna?"

The little wife looked out into the darkness with fear-filled eyes. There were spies even there in that little village on the Beresina, and it was dangerous to say words that might be construed into a reflection on the Government. But she answered Ivan. She stooped and whispered one word into his ear, and he slapped his thigh with his big hand.

"Ay," he cried. "That is what we want! You and I and millions like us want it, and over there, Anna, over there we will get it. It is the country where a muzhik is as good as a prince of the blood!"

Anna stood up, took a small earthenware jar from a side shelf, dusted it carefully and placed it upon the mantel. From a knotted cloth about her neck she took a ruble and dropped the coin into the jar. Big Ivan looked at her curiously.

"It is to make legs for your Dream," she explained. "It is many versts to America, and one rides on rubles."

"You are a good wife," he said. "I was afraid that you might laugh at me."

"It is a great dream," she murmured. "Come, we will go to sleep."

The Dream maddened Ivan during the days that followed. It pounded within his brain as he followed the plow. It bred a discontent that made him hate the little village, the swift-flowing Beresina and the grey stretches that ran toward Mogilev. He wanted to be moving, but Anna had said that one rode on rubles, and rubles were hard to find.

And in some mysterious way the village became aware of the secret. Donkov, the tailor, discovered it. Donkov lived in one-half of the cottage occupied by Ivan and Anna, and Donkov had long ears. The tailor spread the news, and Poborino, the smith, and Yanansk, the baker, would jeer at Ivan as he passed.

"When are you going to America?" they would ask.

"Soon," Ivan would answer.

"Take us with you!" they would cry in chorus.

"It is no place for cowards," Ivan would answer. "It is a long way, and only brave men can make the journey."

"Are you brave?" the baker screamed one day as he went by.

"I am brave enough to want liberty!" cried Ivan angrily. "I am brave enough to want—"

"Be careful! Be careful!" interrupted the smith. "A long tongue has given many a man a train journey that he never expected."

That night Ivan and Anna counted the rubles in the earthenware pot. The giant looked down at his wife with a gloomy face, but she smiled and patted his hand.

"It is slow work," he said.

"We must be patient," she answered. "You have the Dream."

"Ay," he said. "I have the Dream."

Through the hot, languorous summertime the Dream grew within the brain of Big Ivan. He saw visions in the smoky haze that hung above the Beresina. At times he would stand, hoe in hand, and look toward the west, the wonderful west into which the sun slipped down each evening like a coin dropped from the fingers of the dying day.

Autumn came, and the fretful whining winds that came down from the north chilled the Dream. The winds whispered of the coming of the Snow King, and the river grumbled as it listened. Big Ivan kept out of the way of Poborino, the smith, and Yanansk, the baker. The Dream was still with him, but autumn is a bad time for dreams.

Winter came, and the Dream weakened. It was only the earthenware pot that kept it alive, the pot into which the industrious Anna put every coin that could be spared. Often Big Ivan would stare at the pot as he sat beside the stove. The pot was the cord which kept the Dream alive.

"You are a good woman, Anna," Ivan would say again and again. "It was you who thought of saving the rubles."

"But it was you who dreamed," she would answer. "Wait for the spring, husband mine. Wait."

It was strange how the spring came to the Beresina that year. It sprang upon the flanks of winter before the Ice King had given the order to retreat into the fastnesses of the north. It swept up the river escorted by a million little breezes, and housewives opened their windows and peered out with surprise upon their faces. A wonderful guest had come to them and found them unprepared.

Big Ivan of the Bridge was fixing a fence in the meadow on the morning the Spring Maiden reached the village. For a little while he was not aware of her arrival. His mind was upon his work, but suddenly he discovered that he was hot, and he took off his overcoat. He turned to hang the coat upon a bush, then he sniffed the air, and a puzzled look came upon his face. He sniffed again, hurriedly, hungrily. He drew in great breaths of it, and his eyes shone with a strange light. It was wonderful air. It brought life to the Dream. It rose up within him, ten times more lusty than on the day it was born, and his limbs trembled as he drew in the hot, scented breezes that breed the *Wanderlust* and shorten the long trails of the world.

Big Ivan clutched his coat and ran to the little cottage. He burst through the door, startling Anna, who was busy with her housework.

"The Spring!" he cried. "*The Spring*!"

He took her arm and dragged her to the door. Standing together they sniffed the sweet breezes. In silence they listened to the song of the river. The Beresina had changed from a whining, fretful tune into a lilting, sweet song that would set the legs of lovers dancing. Anna pointed to a green bud on a bush beside the door.

"It came this minute," she murmured.

"Yes," said Ivan. "The little fairies brought it there to show us that spring has come to stay."

Together they turned and walked to the mantel. Big Ivan took up the earthenware pot, carried it to the table, and spilled its contents upon the well-scrubbed boards. He counted while Anna stood beside him, her fingers clutching his coarse blouse. It was a slow business, because Ivan's big blunt fingers were not used to such work, but it was over at last. He stacked the coins into neat piles, then he straightened himself and turned to the woman at his side.

"It is enough," he said quietly. "We will go at once. If it was not enough, we would have to go because the Dream is upon me and I hate this place."

"As you say," murmured Anna. "The wife of Littin, the butcher, will buy our chairs and our bed. I spoke to her yesterday."

Poborino, the smith; his crippled son; Yanansk, the baker; Dankov, the tailor, and a score of others were out upon the village street on the morning that Big Ivan and Anna set out. They were inclined to jeer at Ivan, but something upon the face of the giant made them afraid. Hand in hand the big man and his wife walked down the street, their faces turned toward Bobruisk, Ivan balancing upon his head a heavy trunk that no other man in the village could have lifted.

At the end of the street a stripling with bright eyes and yellow curls clutched the hand of Ivan and looked into his face.

"I know what is sending you," he cried.

"Ay, *you* know," said Ivan, looking into the eyes of the other.

"It came to me yesterday," murmured the stripling. "I got it from the breezes. They are free, so are the birds and the little clouds and the river. I wish I could go."

"Keep your dream," said Ivan softly. "Nurse it, for it is the dream of a man."

Anna, who was crying softly, touched the blouse of the boy. "At the back of our cottage, near the bush that bears the red berries, a pot is buried," she said. "Dig it up and take it home with you and when you have a kopeck drop it in. It is a good pot."

The stripling understood. He stooped and kissed the hand of Anna, and Big Ivan patted him upon the back. They were brother dreamers and they understood each other.

Boris Lugan has sung the song of the versts that eat up one's courage as well as the leather of one's shoes.

"Versts! Versts! Scores and scores of them!
Versts! Versts! A million or more of them!
Dust! Dust! And the devils who play in it,
Blinding us fools who forever must stay in it."

Big Ivan and Anna faced the long versts to Bobruisk, but they were not afraid of the dust devils. They had the Dream. It made their hearts light and took the weary feeling from their feet. They were on their way. America was a long, long journey, but they had started, and every verst they covered lessened the number that lay between them and the Promised Land.

"I am glad the boy spoke to us," said Anna.

"And I am glad," said Ivan. "Some day he will come and eat with us in America."

They came to Bobruisk. Holding hands, they walked into it late one afternoon. They were eighty-nine versts from the little village on the Beresina, but they were not afraid. The Dream spoke to Ivan, and his big hand held the hand of Anna. The railway ran through Bobruisk, and that evening they stood and looked at the shining rails that went out in the moonlight like silver tongs reaching out for a low-hanging star.

And they came face to face with the Terror that evening, the Terror that had helped the spring breezes and the sunshine to plant the Dream in the brain of Big Ivan.

They were walking down a dark side street when they saw a score of men and women creep from the door of a squat, unpainted building. The little group remained on the sidewalk for a minute as if uncertain about the way they should go, then from the corner of the street came a cry of "Police!" and the twenty pedestrians ran in different directions.

It was no false alarm. Mounted police charged down the dark thoroughfare swinging their swords as they rode at the scurrying men and women who raced for shelter. Big Ivan dragged Anna into a doorway, and toward their hiding place ran a young boy who, like themselves, had no connection with the group and who merely desired to get out of harm's way till the storm was over.

The boy was not quick enough to escape the charge. A trooper pursued him, overtook him before he reached the sidewalk, and knocked him down with a quick stroke given with the flat of his blade. His horse struck the boy with one of his hoofs as the lad stumbled on his face.

Big Ivan growled like an angry bear, and sprang from his hiding place. The trooper's horse had carried him on to the sidewalk, and Ivan seized the bridle and flung the animal on its haunches. The policeman leaned forward to strike at the giant, but Ivan of the Bridge gripped the left leg of the horseman and tore him from the saddle.

The horse galloped off, leaving its rider lying beside the moaning boy who was unlucky enough to be in a street where a score of students were holding a meeting.

Anna dragged Ivan back into the passageway. More police were charging down the street, and their position was a dangerous one.

"Ivan!" she cried, "Ivan! Remember the Dream! America, Ivan! *America*! Come this way! Quick!"

With strong hands she dragged him down the passage. It opened into a narrow lane, and, holding each other's hands, they hurried toward the place where they had taken lodgings. From far off came screams and hoarse orders, curses and the sound of galloping hoofs. The Terror was abroad.

Big Ivan spoke softly as they entered the little room they had taken. "He had a face like the boy to whom you gave the lucky pot," he said. "Did you notice it in the moonlight when the trooper struck him down?"

"Yes," she answered. "I saw."

They left Bobruisk next morning. They rode away on a great, puffing, snorting train that terrified Anna. The engineer turned a stopcock as they were passing the engine, and Anna screamed while Ivan nearly dropped the big trunk. The engineer grinned, but the giant looked up at him and the grin faded. Ivan of the Bridge was startled by the rush of hot steam, but he was afraid of no man.

The train went roaring by little villages and great pasture stretches. The real journey had begun. They began to love the powerful engine. It was eating up the versts at a tremendous rate. They looked at each other from time to time and smiled like two children.

They came to Minsk, the biggest town they had ever seen. They looked out from the car windows at the miles of wooden buildings, at the big church of St. Catharine, and the woolen mills. Minsk would have frightened them if they hadn't had the Dream. The farther they went from the little village on the Beresina the more courage the Dream gave to them.

On and on went the train, the wheels singing the song of the road. Fellow travellers asked them where they were going. "To America," Ivan would answer.

"To America?" they would cry. "May the little saints guide you. It is a long way, and you will be lonely."

"No, we shall not be lonely," Ivan would say.

"Ha! you are going with friends?"

"No, we have no friends, but we have something that keeps us from being lonely." And when Ivan would make that reply Anna would pat his hand and the questioner would wonder if it was a charm or a holy relic that the bright-eyed couple possessed.

They ran through Vilna, on through flat stretches of Courland to Libau, where they saw the sea. They sat and stared at it for a whole day, talking little but watching it with wide, wondering eyes. And they stared at the great ships that came rocking in from distant ports, their sides gray with the salt from the big combers which they had battled with.

No wonder this America of ours is big. We draw the brave ones from the old lands, the brave ones whose dreams are like the guiding sign that was given to the Israelites of old – a pillar of cloud by day, a pillar of fire by night.

The harbour master spoke to Ivan and Anna as they watched the restless waters.

"Where are you going, children?"

"To America," answered Ivan.

"A long way. Three ships bound for America went down last month."

"Our ship will not sink," said Ivan.

"Why?"

"Because I know it will not."

The harbour master looked at the strange blue eyes of the giant, and spoke softly. "You have the eyes of a man who sees things," he said. "There was a Norwegian sailor in the *White Queen*, who had eyes like yours, and he could see death."

"I see life!" said Ivan boldly. "A free life—"

"Hush!" said the harbour master. "Do not speak so loud." He walked swiftly away, but he dropped a ruble into Anna's hand as he passed her by. "For luck," he murmured. "May the little saints look after you on the big waters."

They boarded the ship, and the Dream gave them a courage that surprised them. There were others going aboard, and Ivan and Anna felt that those others were also persons who possessed dreams. She saw the dreams in their eyes. There were Slavs, Poles, Letts, Jews, and Livonians, all bound for the land where dreams come true. They were a little afraid – not two per cent of them had ever seen a ship before – yet their dreams gave them courage.

The emigrant ship was dragged from her pier by a grunting tug and went floundering down the Baltic Sea. Night came down, and the devils who, according to the Esthonian fishermen, live in the bottom of the Baltic, got their shoulders under the stern of the ship and tried to stand her on her head. They whipped up white combers that sprang on her flanks and tried to crush her, and the wind played a devil's lament in her rigging. Anna lay sick in the stuffy women's quarters, and Ivan could not get near her. But he sent her messages. He told her not to mind the sea devils, to think of the Dream, the Great Dream that would become real in the land to which they were bound. Ivan of the Bridge grew to full stature on that first night out from Libau. The battered old craft that carried him slouched before the waves that swept over her decks, but he was not afraid. Down among the million and one smells of the steerage he induced a thin-faced Livonian to play upon a mouth organ, and Big Ivan sang Paleer's 'Song of Freedom' in a voice that drowned the creaking of the old vessel's timbers, and made the seasick ones forget their sickness. They sat up in their berths and joined in the chorus, their eyes shining brightly in the half gloom:

"Freedom for serf and for slave,
Freedom for all men who crave
Their right to be free
And who hate to bend knee
But to Him who this right to them gave."

It was well that these emigrants had dreams. They wanted them. The sea devils chased the lumbering steamer. They hung to her bows and pulled her for'ard deck under emerald-green rollers. They clung to her stern and hoisted her nose till Big Ivan thought that he could touch the door of heaven by standing on her blunt snout. Miserable, cold, ill, and sleepless, the emigrants crouched in their quarters, and to them Ivan and the thin-faced Livonian sang the 'Song of Freedom.'

The emigrant ship pounded through the Cattegat, swung southward through the Skagerrack and the bleak North Sea. But the storm pursued her. The big waves snarled and bit at her, and the captain and the chief officer consulted with each other. They decided to run into the Thames, and the harried steamer nosed her way in and anchored off Gravesend.

An examination was made, and the agents decided to transship the emigrants. They were taken to London and thence by train to Liverpool, and Ivan and Anna sat again side by side, holding hands and smiling at each other as the third-class emigrant train from Euston raced down through the green Midland counties to grimy Liverpool.

"You are not afraid?" Ivan would say to her each time she looked at him.

"It is a long way, but the Dream has given me much courage," she said.

"To-day I spoke to a Lett whose brother works in New York City," said the giant. "Do you know how much money he earns each day?"

"How much?" she questioned.

"Three rubles, and he calls the policemen by their first names."

"You will earn five rubles, my Ivan," she murmured. "There is no one as strong as you."

Once again they were herded into the bowels of a big ship that steamed away through the fog banks of the Mersey out into the Irish Sea. There were more dreamers now, nine hundred of them, and Anna and Ivan were more comfortable. And these new emigrants, English, Irish, Scotch, French, and German, knew much concerning America. Ivan was certain that he would earn at least three rubles a day. He was very strong.

On the deck he defeated all comers in a tug of war, and the captain of the ship came up to him and felt his muscles.

"The country that lets men like you get away from it is run badly," he said. "Why did you leave it?"

The interpreter translated what the captain said, and through the interpreter Ivan answered.

"I had a Dream," he said, "a Dream of freedom."

"Good," cried the captain. "Why should a man with muscles like yours have his face ground into the dust?"

The soul of Big Ivan grew during those days. He felt himself a man, a man who was born upright to speak his thoughts without fear.

The ship rolled into Queenstown one bright morning, and Ivan and his nine hundred steerage companions crowded the for'ard deck. A boy in a rowboat threw a line to the deck, and after it had been fastened to a stanchion he came up hand over hand. The emigrants watched him curiously. An old woman sitting in the boat pulled off her shoes, sat in a loop of the rope, and lifted her hand as a signal to her son on deck.

"Hey, fellers," said the boy, "help me pull me muvver up. She wants to sell a few dozen apples, an' they won't let her up the gangway!"

Big Ivan didn't understand the words, but he guessed what the boy wanted. He made one of a half dozen who gripped the rope and started to pull the ancient apple woman to the deck.

They had her halfway up the side when an undersized third officer discovered what they were doing. He called to a steward, and the steward sprang to obey.

"Turn a hose on her!" cried the officer. "Turn a hose on the old woman!"

The steward rushed for the hose. He ran with it to the side of the ship with the intention of squirting on the old woman, who was swinging in midair and exhorting the six men who were dragging her to the deck.

"Pull!" she cried. "Sure, I'll give every one of ye a rosy red apple an' me blessing with it."

The steward aimed the muzzle of the hose, and Big Ivan of the Bridge let go of the rope and sprang at him. The fist of the great Russian went out like a battering ram; it struck the steward between the eyes, and he dropped upon the deck. He lay like one dead, the muzzle of the hose wriggling from his limp hands.

The third officer and the interpreter rushed at Big Ivan, who stood erect, his hands clenched.

"Ask the big swine why he did it," roared the officer.

"Because he is a coward!" cried Ivan. "They wouldn't do that in America!"

"What does the big brute know about America?" cried the officer.

"Tell him I have dreamed of it," shouted Ivan. "Tell him it is in my Dream. Tell him I will kill him if he turns the water on this old woman."

The apple seller was on deck then, and with the wisdom of the Celt she understood. She put her lean hand upon the great head of the Russian and blessed him in Gaelic. Ivan bowed before her, then as she offered him a rosy apple he led her toward Anna, a great Viking leading a withered old woman who walked with the grace of a duchess.

"Please don't touch him," she cried, turning to the officer. "We have been waiting for your ship for six hours, and we have only five dozen apples to sell. It's a great man he is. Sure he's as big as Finn MacCool."

Some one pulled the steward behind a ventilator and revived him by squirting him with water from the hose which he had tried to turn upon the old woman. The third officer slipped quietly away.

The Atlantic was kind to the ship that carried Ivan and Anna. Through sunny days they sat up on deck and watched the horizon. They wanted to be among those who would get the first glimpse of the wonderland.

They saw it on a morning with sunshine and soft wind. Standing together in the bow, they looked at the smear upon the horizon, and their eyes filled with tears. They forgot the long road to Bobruisk, the rocking journey to Libau, the mad buckjumping boat in whose timbers the sea devils of the Baltic had bored holes. Everything unpleasant was forgotten, because the Dream filled them with a great happiness.

The inspectors at Ellis Island were interested in Ivan. They walked around him and prodded his muscles, and he smiled down upon them good-naturedly.

"A fine animal," said one. "Gee, he's a new white hope! Ask him can he fight?"

An interpreter put the question, and Ivan nodded. "I have fought," he said.

"Gee!" cried the inspector. "Ask him was it for purses or what?"

"For freedom," answered Ivan. "For freedom to stretch my legs and straighten my neck!"

Ivan and Anna left the Government ferryboat at the Battery. They started to walk uptown, making for the East Side, Ivan carrying the big trunk that no other man could lift.

It was a wonderful morning. The city was bathed in warm sunshine, and the well-dressed men and women who crowded the sidewalks made the two immigrants think that it was a festival day. Ivan and Anna stared at each other in amazement. They had never seen such dresses as those worn by the smiling women who passed them by; they had never seen such well-groomed men.

"It is a feast day for certain," said Anna.

"They are dressed like princes and princesses," murmured Ivan. "There are no poor here, Anna. None."

Like two simple children, they walked along the streets of the City of Wonder. What a contrast it was to the gray, stupid towns where the Terror waited to spring upon the cowed people. In Bobruisk, Minsk, Vilna, and Libau the people were sullen and afraid. They walked in dread, but in the City of Wonder beside the glorious Hudson every person seemed happy and contented.

They lost their way, but they walked on, looking at the wonderful shop windows, the roaring elevated trains, and the huge skyscrapers. Hours afterward they found themselves in Fifth Avenue near Thirty-third Street, and there the miracle happened to the two Russian immigrants. It was a big miracle inasmuch as it proved the Dream a truth, a great truth.

Ivan and Anna attempted to cross the avenue, but they became confused in the snarl of traffic. They dodged backward and forward as the stream of automobiles swept by them. Anna screamed, and, in response to her scream, a traffic policeman, resplendent in a new uniform, rushed to her side. He took the arm of Anna and flung up a commanding hand. The charging autos halted. For five blocks north and south they jammed on the brakes when the unexpected interruption occurred, and Big Ivan gasped.

"Don't be flurried, little woman," said the cop. "Sure I can tame 'em by liftin' me hand."

Anna didn't understand what he said, but she knew it was something nice by the manner in which his Irish eyes smiled down upon her. And in front of the waiting automobiles he led her with the same care that he would give to a duchess, while Ivan, carrying the big trunk, followed them, wondering much. Ivan's mind went back to Bobruisk on the night the Terror was abroad.

The policeman led Anna to the sidewalk, patted Ivan good-naturedly upon the shoulder, and then with a sharp whistle unloosed the waiting stream of cars that had been held up so that two Russian immigrants could cross the avenue.

Big Ivan of the Bridge took the trunk from his head and put it on the ground. He reached out his arms and folded Anna in a great embrace. His eyes were wet.

"The Dream is true!" he cried. "Did you see, Anna? We are as good as they! This is the land where a *muzhik* is as good as a prince of the blood!"

* * *

The President was nearing the close of his address. Anna shook Ivan, and Ivan came out of the trance which the President's words had brought upon him. He sat up and listened intently:

We grow great by dreams. All big men are dreamers. They see things in the soft haze of a spring day or in the red fire of a long winter's evening. Some of us let those great dreams die, but others nourish and protect them, nurse them through bad days till they bring them to the sunshine and light which come always to those who sincerely hope that their dreams will come true.

The President finished. For a moment he stood looking down at the faces turned up to him, and Big Ivan of the Bridge thought that the President smiled at him. Ivan seized Anna's hand and held it tight.

"He knew of my Dream!" he cried. "He knew of it. Did you hear what he said about the dreams of a spring day?"

"Of course he knew," said Anna. "He is the wisest man in America, where there are many wise men. Ivan, you are a citizen now."

"And you are a citizen, Anna."

The band started to play 'My Country, 'tis of Thee,' and Ivan and Anna got to their feet. Standing side by side, holding hands, they joined in with the others who had found after long days of journeying the blessed land where dreams come true.

The Wisdom of the New

Sui Sin Far

I

OLD LI WANG, the peddler, who had lived in the land beyond the sea, was wont to declare: "For every cent that a man makes here, he can make one hundred there."

"Then, why," would ask Sankwei, "do you now have to move from door to door to fill your bowl with rice?"

And the old man would sigh and answer:

"Because where one learns how to make gold, one also learns how to lose it."

"How to lose it!" echoed Wou Sankwei. "Tell me all about it."

So the old man would tell stories about the winning and the losing, and the stories of the losing were even more fascinating than the stories of the winning.

"Yes, that was life," he would conclude. "Life, life."

At such times the boy would gaze across the water with wistful eyes. The land beyond the sea was calling to him.

The place was a sleepy little south coast town where the years slipped by monotonously. The boy was the only son of the man who had been the town magistrate.

Had his father lived, Wou Sankwei would have been sent to complete his schooling in another province. As it was he did nothing but sleep, dream, and occasionally get into mischief. What else was there to do? His mother and sister waited upon him hand and foot. Was he not the son of the house? The family income was small, scarcely sufficient for their needs; but there was no way by which he could add to it, unless, indeed, he disgraced the name of Wou by becoming a common fisherman. The great green waves lifted white arms of foam to him, and the fishes gleaming and lurking in the waters seemed to beseech him to draw them from the deep; but his mother shook her head.

"Should you become a fisherman," said she, "your family would lose face. Remember that your father was a magistrate."

When he was about nineteen there returned to the town one who had been absent for many years. Ching Kee, like old Li Wang, had also lived in the land beyond the sea; but unlike old Li Wang he had accumulated a small fortune.

"'Tis a hard life over there," said he, "but 'tis worth while. At least one can be a man, and can work at what work comes his way without losing face." Then he laughed at Wou Sankwei's flabby muscles, at his soft, dark eyes, and plump, white hands.

"If you lived in America," said he, "you would learn to be ashamed of such beauty."

Whereupon Wou Sankwei made up his mind that he would go to America, the land beyond the sea. Better any life than that of a woman man.

He talked long and earnestly with his mother. "Give me your blessing," said he. "I will work and save money. What I send home will bring you many a comfort, and when I come back to China, it may be that I shall be able to complete my studies and obtain a degree. If not, my knowledge of the foreign language which I shall acquire, will enable me to take a position which will not disgrace the name of Wou."

His mother listened and thought. She was ambitious for her son whom she loved beyond all things on earth. Moreover, had not Sik Ping, a Canton merchant, who had visited the little town two moons ago, declared to Hum Wah, who traded in palm leaves, that the signs of the times were that the son of a cobbler, returned from America with the foreign language, could easier command a position of consequence than the son of a school-teacher unacquainted with any tongue but that of his motherland?

"Very well," she acquiesced; "but before you go I must find you a wife. Only your son, my son, can comfort me for your loss."

II

Wou Sankwei stood behind his desk, busily entering figures in a long yellow book. Now and then he would thrust the hair pencil with which he worked behind his ears and manipulate with deft fingers a Chinese counting machine. Wou Sankwei was the junior partner and bookkeeper of the firm of Leung Tang Wou & Co. of San Francisco. He had been in America seven years and had made good use of his time. Self-improvement had been his object and ambition, even more than the acquirement of a fortune, and who, looking at his fine, intelligent face and listening to his careful English, could say that he had failed?

One of his partners called his name. Some ladies wished to speak to him. Wou Sankwei hastened to the front of the store. One of his callers, a motherly looking woman, was the friend who had taken him under her wing shortly after his arrival in America. She had come to invite him to spend the evening with her and her niece, the young girl who accompanied her.

After his callers had left, Sankwei returned to his desk and worked steadily until the hour for his evening meal, which he took in the Chinese restaurant across the street from the bazaar. He hurried through with this, as before going to his friend's house, he had a somewhat important letter to write and mail. His mother had died a year before, and the uncle, to whom he was writing, had taken his wife and son into his home until such time as his nephew could send for them. Now the time had come.

Wou Sankwei's memory of the woman who was his wife was very faint. How could it be otherwise? She had come to him but three weeks before the sailing of the vessel which had brought him to America, and until then he had not seen her face. But she was his wife and the mother of his son. Ever since he had worked in America he had sent money for her support, and she had proved a good daughter to his mother.

As he sat down to write he decided that he would welcome her with a big dinner to his countrymen.

"Yes," he replied to Mrs. Dean, later on in the evening, "I have sent for my wife."

"I am so glad," said the lady. "Mr. Wou" – turning to her niece – "has not seen his wife for seven years."

"Deary me!" exclaimed the young girl. "What a lot of letters you must have written!"

"I have not written her one," returned the young man somewhat stiffly.

Adah Charlton looked up in surprise. "Why—" she began.

"Mr. Wou used to be such a studious boy when I first knew him," interrupted Mrs. Dean, laying her hand affectionately upon the young man's shoulder. "Now, it is all business. But you won't forget the concert on Saturday evening."

"No, I will not forget," answered Wou Sankwei.

"He has never written to his wife," explained Mrs. Dean when she and her niece were alone, "because his wife can neither read nor write."

"Oh, isn't that sad!" murmured Adah Charlton, her own winsome face becoming pensive.

"They don't seem to think so. It is the Chinese custom to educate only the boys. At least it has been so in the past. Sankwei himself is unusually bright. Poor boy! He began life here as a laundryman, and you may be sure that it must have been hard on him, for, as the son of a petty Chinese Government official, he had not been accustomed to manual labour. But Chinese character is wonderful; and now after seven years in this country, he enjoys a reputation as a business man amongst his countrymen, and is as up to date as any young American."

"But, Auntie, isn't it dreadful to think that a man should live away from his wife for so many years without any communication between them whatsoever except through others."

"It is dreadful to our minds, but not to theirs. Everything with them is a matter of duty. Sankwei married his wife as a matter of duty. He sends for her as a matter of duty."

"I wonder if it is all duty on her side," mused the girl.

Mrs. Dean smiled. "You are too romantic, Adah," said she. "I hope, however, that when she does come, they will be happy together. I think almost as much of Sankwei as I do of my own boy."

III

Pau Lin, the wife of Wou Sankwei, sat in a corner of the deck of the big steamer, awaiting the coming of her husband. Beside her, leaning his little queued head against her shoulder, stood her six-year-old son. He had been ailing throughout the voyage, and his small face was pinched with pain. His mother, who had been nursing him every night since the ship had left port, appeared very worn and tired. This, despite the fact that with a feminine desire to make herself fair to see in the eyes of her husband, she had arrayed herself in a heavily embroidered purple costume, whitened her forehead and cheeks with powder, and tinted her lips with carmine.

He came at last, looking over and beyond her; There were two others of her countrywomen awaiting the men who had sent for them, and each had a child, so that for a moment he seemed somewhat bewildered. Only when the ship's officer pointed out and named her, did he know her as his. Then he came forward, spoke a few words of formal welcome, and, lifting the child in his arms, began questioning her as to its health.

She answered in low monosyllables. At his greeting she had raised her patient eyes to his face – the face of the husband whom she had not seen for seven long years – then the eager look of expectancy which had crossed her own faded away, her eyelids drooped, and her countenance assumed an almost sullen expression.

"Ah, poor Sankwei!" exclaimed Mrs. Dean, who with Adah Charlton stood some little distance apart from the family group.

"Poor wife!" murmured the young girl. She moved forward and would have taken in her own white hands the ringed ones of the Chinese woman, but the young man gently restrained her. "She cannot understand you," said he. As the young girl fell back, he explained to his wife the presence of the stranger women. They were there to bid her welcome; they were kind and good and wished to be her friends as well as his.

Pau Lin looked away. Adah Charlton's bright face, and the tone in her husband's voice when he spoke to the young girl, aroused a suspicion in her mind – a suspicion natural to one who had come from a land where friendship between a man and woman is almost unknown.

"Poor little thing! How shy she is!" exclaimed Mrs. Dean.

Sankwei was glad that neither she nor the young girl understood the meaning of the averted face.

Thus began Wou Sankwei's life in America as a family man. He soon became accustomed to the change, which was not such a great one after all. Pau Lin was more of an accessory than a part of his life. She interfered not at all with his studies, his business, or his friends, and when not engaged in housework or sewing, spent most of her time in the society of one or the other of the merchants' wives who lived in the flats and apartments around her own. She kept up the Chinese custom of taking her meals after her husband or at a separate table, and observed faithfully the rule laid down for her by her late mother-in-law: to keep a quiet tongue in the presence of her man. Sankwei, on his part, was always kind and indulgent. He bought her silk dresses, hair ornaments, fans, and sweetmeats. He ordered her favourite dishes from the Chinese restaurant. When she wished to go out with her women friends, he hired a carriage, and shortly after her advent erected behind her sleeping room a chapel for the ancestral tablet and gorgeous goddess which she had brought over seas with her.

Upon the child both parents lavished affection. He was a quaint, serious little fellow, small for his age and requiring much care. Although naturally much attached to his mother, he became also very fond of his father who, more like an elder brother than a parent, delighted in playing all kinds of games with him, and whom he followed about like a little dog. Adah Charlton took a great fancy to him and sketched him in many different poses for a book on Chinese children which she was illustrating.

"He will be strong enough to go to school next year," said Sankwei to her one day. "Later on I intend to put him through an American college."

"What does your wife think of a Western training for him?" inquired the young girl.

"I have not consulted her about the matter," he answered. "A woman does not understand such things."

"A woman, Mr. Wou," declared Adah, "understands such things as well as and sometimes better than a man."

"An, American woman, maybe," amended Sankwei; "but not a Chinese."

From the first Pau Lin had shown no disposition to become Americanized, and Sankwei himself had not urged it.

"I do appreciate the advantages of becoming westernized," said he to Mrs. Dean whose influence and interest in his studies in America had helped him to become what he was, "but it is not as if she had come here as I came, in her learning days. The time for learning with her is over."

One evening, upon returning from his store, he found the little Yen sobbing pitifully.

"What!" he teased, "A man – and weeping."

The boy tried to hide his face, and as he did so, the father noticed that his little hand was red and swollen. He strode into the kitchen where Pau Lin was preparing the evening meal.

"The little child who is not strong – is there anything he could do to merit the infliction of pain?" he questioned.

Pau Lin faced her husband. "Yes, I think so," said she.

"What?"

"I forbade him to speak the language of the white women, and he disobeyed me. He had words in that tongue with the white boy from the next street."

Sankwei was astounded.

"We are living in the white man's country," said he. "The child will have to learn the white man's language."

"Not my child," answered Pau Lin.

Sankwei turned away from her. "Come, little one," said he to his son, "we will take supper tonight at the restaurant, and afterwards Yen shall see a show."

Pau Lin laid down the dish of vegetables which she was straining and took from a hook as small wrap which she adjusted around the boy.

"Now go with thy father," said she sternly.

But the boy clung to her – to the hand which had punished him. "I will sup with you," he cried, "I will sup with you."

"Go," repeated his mother, pushing him from her. And as the two passed over the threshold, she called to the father: "Keep the wrap around the child. The night air is chill."

Late that night, while father and son were peacefully sleeping, the wife and mother arose, and lifting gently the unconscious boy, bore him into the next room where she sat down with him in a rocker. Waking, he clasped his arms around her neck. Backwards and forwards she rocked him, passionately caressing the wounded hand and crooning and crying until he fell asleep again.

The first chastisement that the son of Wou Sankwei had received from his mother, was because he had striven to follow in the footsteps of his father and use the language of the stranger.

"You did perfectly right," said old Sien Tau the following morning, as she leaned over her balcony to speak to the wife of Wou Sankwei. "Had I again a son to rear, I should see to it that he followed not after the white people."

Sien Tau's son had married a white woman, and his children passed their grandame on the street without recognition.

"In this country, she is most happy who has no child," said Lae Choo, resting her elbow upon the shoulder of Sien Tau. "A Toy, the young daughter of Lew Wing, is as bold and free in her ways as are the white women, and her name is on all the men's tongues. What prudent man of our race would take her as wife?"

"One needs not to be born here to be made a fool of," joined in Pau Lin, appearing at another balcony door. "Think of Hum Wah. From sunrise till midnight he worked for fourteen years, then a white man came along and persuaded from him every dollar, promising to return doublefold within the moon. Many moons have risen and waned, and Hum Wah still waits on this side of the sea for the white man and his money. Meanwhile, his father and mother, who looked long for his coming, have passed beyond returning."

"The new religion – what trouble it brings!" exclaimed Lae Choo. "My man received word yestereve that the good old mother of Chee Ping – he who was baptized a Christian at the last baptizing in the Mission around the corner – had her head secretly severed from her body by the steadfast people of the village, as soon as the news reached there. 'Twas the first violent death in the records of the place. This happened to the mother of one of the boys attending the Mission corner of my street."

"No doubt, the poor old mother, having lost face, minded not so much the losing of her head," sighed Pau Lin. She gazed below her curiously. The American Chinatown held a strange fascination for the girl from the seacoast village. Streaming along the street was a motley throng made up of all nationalities. The sing-song voices of girls whom respectable merchants' wives shudder to name, were calling to one another from high balconies up shadowy alleys. A fat barber was laughing hilariously at a drunken white man who had fallen into a gutter; a withered old fellow, carrying a bird in a cage, stood at the corner entreating passersby to have a good fortune told; some children were burning punk on the curbstone. There went by a stalwart Chief of the Six Companies engaged in earnest confab with a yellow-robed priest from the joss house. A Chinese dressed in the latest American style and a very blonde woman, laughing immoderately, were entering a Chinese restaurant together. Above all the hubbub of voices was heard the clang of electric cars and the jarring of heavy wheels over cobblestones.

Pau Lin raised her head and looked her thoughts at the old woman, Sien Tau.

"Yes," nodded the dame, "'tis a mad place in which to bring up a child."

Pau Lin went back into the house, gave little Yen his noonday meal, and dressed him with care. His father was to take him out that afternoon. She questioned the boy, as she braided his queue, concerning the white women whom he visited with his father.

It was evening when they returned – Wou Sankwei and his boy. The little fellow ran up to her in high glee. "See, mother," said he, pulling off his cap, "I am like father now. I wear no queue."

The mother looked down upon him – at the little round head from which the queue, which had been her pride, no longer dangled.

"Ah!" she cried. "I am ashamed of you; I am ashamed!"

The boy stared at her, hurt and disappointed.

"Never mind, son," comforted his father. "It is all right."

Pau Lin placed the bowls of seaweed and chickens' liver before them and went back to the kitchen where her own meal was waiting. But she did not eat. She was saying within herself: "It is for the white woman he has done this; it is for the white woman!"

Later, as she laid the queue of her son within the trunk wherein lay that of his father, long since cast aside, she discovered a picture of Mrs. Dean, taken when the American woman had first become the teacher and benefactress of the youthful laundryman. She ran over with it to her husband. "Here," said she; "it is a picture of one of your white friends." Sankwei took it from her almost reverently, "That woman," he explained, "has been to me as a mother."

"And the young woman – the one with eyes the colour of blue china – is she also as a mother?" inquired Pau Lin gently.

But for all her gentleness, Wou Sankwei flushed angrily.

"Never speak of her," he cried. "Never speak of her!"

"Ha, ha, ha! Ha, ha, ha!" laughed Pau Lin. It was a soft and not unmelodious laugh, but to Wou Sankwei it sounded almost sacrilegious.

Nevertheless, he soon calmed down. Pau Lin was his wife, and to be kind to her was not only his duty but his nature. So when his little boy climbed into his lap and besought his father to pipe him a tune, he reached for his flute and called to Pau Lin to put aside work for that night. He would play her some Chinese music. And Pau Lin, whose heart and mind, undiverted by change, had been concentrated upon Wou Sankwei ever since the day she had become his wife, smothered, for the time being, the bitterness in her heart, and succumbed to the magic of her husband's playing – a magic which transported her in thought to the old Chinese days, the old Chinese days whose impression and influence ever remain with the exiled sons and daughters of China.

IV

That a man should take to himself two wives, or even three, if he thought proper, seemed natural and right in the eyes of Wou Pau Lin. She herself had come from a home where there were two broods of children and where her mother and her father's other wife had eaten their meals together as sisters. In that home there had not always been peace; but each woman, at least, had the satisfaction of knowing that her man did not regard or treat the other woman as her superior. To each had fallen the common lot – to bear children to the man, and the man was master of all.

But, oh! the humiliation and shame of bearing children to a man who looked up to another woman – and a woman of another race – as a being above the common uses of women. There is a jealousy of the mind more poignant than any mere animal jealousy.

When Wou Sankwei's second child was two weeks old, Adah Charlton and her aunt called to see the little one, and the young girl chatted brightly with the father and played merrily with Yen, who was growing strong and merry. The American women could not, of course, converse with the

Chinese; but Adah placed beside her a bunch of beautiful flowers, pressed her hand, and looked down upon her with radiant eyes. Secure in the difference of race, in the love of many friends, and in the happiness of her chosen work, no suspicion whatever crossed her mind that the woman whose husband was her aunt's protégé tasted everything bitter because of her.

After the visitors had gone, Pau Lin, who had been watching her husband's face while the young artist was in the room, said to him:

"She can be happy who takes all and gives nothing."

"Takes all and gives nothing," echoed her husband. "What do you mean?"

"She has taken all your heart," answered Pau Lin, "but she has not given you a son. It is I who have had that task."

"You are my wife," answered Wou Sankwei. "And she – oh! how can you speak of her so? She, who is as a pure water-flower – a lily!"

He went out of the room, carrying with him a little painting of their boy, which Adah Charlton had given to him as she bade him goodbye and which he had intended showing with pride to the mother.

It was on the day that the baby died that Pau Lin first saw the little picture. It had fallen out of her husband's coat pocket when he lifted the tiny form in his arms and declared it lifeless. Even in that first moment of loss Pau Lin, stooping to pick up the portrait, had shrunk back in horror, crying: "She would cast a spell! She would cast a spell!"

She set her heel upon the face of the picture and destroyed it beyond restoration.

"You know not what you say and do," sternly rebuked Sankwei. He would have added more, but the mystery of the dead child's look forbade him.

"The loss of a son is as the loss of a limb," said he to his childless partner, as under the red glare of the lanterns they sat discussing the sad event.

"But you are not without consolation," returned Leung Tsao. "Your firstborn grows in strength and beauty."

"True," assented Wou Sankwei, his heavy thoughts becoming lighter.

And Pau Lin, in her curtained balcony overhead, drew closer her child and passionately cried:

"Sooner would I, O heart of my heart, that the light of thine eyes were also quenched, than that thou shouldst be contaminated with the wisdom of the new."

V

The Chinese women friends of Wou Pau Lin gossiped among themselves, and their gossip reached the ears of the American woman friend of Pau Lin's husband. Since the days of her widowhood Mrs. Dean had devoted herself earnestly and whole-heartedly to the betterment of the condition and the uplifting of the young workingmen of Chinese race who came to America. Their appeal and need, as she had told her niece, was for closer acquaintance with the knowledge of the Western people, and that she had undertaken to give them, as far as she was able. The rewards and satisfactions of her work had been rich in some cases. Witness Wou Sankwei.

But the gossip had reached and much perturbed her. What was it that they said Wou Sankwei's wife had declared – that her little son should not go to an American school nor learn the American learning. Such bigotry and narrow-mindedness! How sad to think of! Here was a man who had benefited and profited by living in America, anxious to have his son receive the benefits of a Western education – and here was this man's wife opposing him with her ignorance and hampering him with her unreasonable jealousy.

Yes, she had heard that too. That Wou Sankwei's wife was jealous – jealous – and her husband the most moral of men, the kindest and the most generous.

"Of what is she jealous?" she questioned Adah Charlton. "Other Chinese men's wives, I have known, have had cause to be jealous, for it is true some of them are dreadfully immoral and openly support two or more wives. But not Wou Sankwei. And this little Pau Lin. She has everything that a Chinese woman could wish for."

A sudden flash of intuition came to the girl, rendering her for a moment speechless. When she did find words, she said:

"Everything that a Chinese woman could wish for, you say. Auntie, I do not believe there is any real difference between the feelings of a Chinese wife and an American wife. Sankwei is treating Pau Lin as he would treat her were he living in China. Yet it cannot be the same to her as if she were in their own country, where he would not come in contact with American women. A woman is a woman with intuitions and perceptions, whether Chinese or American, whether educated or uneducated, and Sankwei's wife must have noticed, even on the day of her arrival, her husband's manner towards us, and contrasted it with his manner towards her. I did not realize this before you told me that she was jealous. I only wish I had. Now, for all her ignorance, I can see that the poor little thing became more of an American in that one half hour on the steamer than Wou Sankwei, for all your pride in him, has become in seven years."

Mrs. Dean rested her head on her hand. She was evidently much perplexed.

"What you say may be, Adah," she replied after a while; "but even so, it is Sankwei whom I have known so long, who has my sympathies. He has much to put up with. They have drifted seven years of life apart. There is no bond of interest or sympathy between them, save the boy. Yet never the slightest hint of trouble has come to me from his own lips. Before the coming of Pau Lin, he would confide in me every little thing that worried him, as if he were my own son. Now he maintains absolute silence as to his private affairs."

"Chinese principles," observed Adah, resuming her work. "Yes, I admit Sankwei has some puzzles to solve. Naturally, when he tries to live two lives – that of a Chinese and that of an American."

"He is compelled to that," retorted Mrs. Dean. "Is it not what we teach these Chinese boys – to become Americans? And yet, they are Chinese, and must, in a sense, remain so."

Adah did not answer.

Mrs. Dean sighed. "Poor, dear children, both of them," mused she. "I feel very low-spirited over the matter. I suppose you wouldn't care to come down town with me. I should like to have another chat with Mrs. Wing Sing."

"I shall be glad of the change," replied Adah, laying down her brushes.

Rows of lanterns suspended from many balconies shed a mellow, moonshiny radiance. On the walls and doors were splashes of red paper inscribed with hieroglyphics. In the narrow streets, booths decorated with flowers, and banners and screens painted with immense figures of josses diverted the eye; while bands of musicians in gaudy silks, shrilled and banged, piped and fluted.

Everybody seemed to be out of doors – men, women, and children – and nearly all were in holiday attire. A couple of priests, in vivid scarlet and yellow robes, were kotowing before an altar covered with a rich cloth, embroidered in white and silver. Some Chinese students from the University of California stood looking on with comprehending, half-scornful interest; three girls lavishly dressed in coloured silks, with their black hair plastered back from their faces and heavily bejewelled behind, chirped and chattered in a gilded balcony above them like birds in a cage. Little children, their hands full of half-moon-shaped cakes, were pattering about, with eyes, for all the hour, as bright as stars.

Chinatown was celebrating the Harvest Moon Festival, and Adah Charlton was glad that she had an opportunity to see something of the celebration before she returned East. Mrs. Dean, familiar with the Chinese people and the mazes of Chinatown, led her around fearlessly, pointing out this and that object of interest and explaining to her its meaning. Seeing that it was a gala night, she had abandoned her idea of calling upon the Chinese friend.

Just as they turned a corner leading up to the street where Wou Sankwei's place of business and residence was situated, a pair of little hands grasped Mrs. Dean's skirt and a delighted little voice piped: "See me! See me!" It was little Yen, resplendent in mauve-coloured pantaloons and embroidered vest and cap. Behind him was a tall man whom both women recognized.

"How do you happen to have Yen with you?" Adah asked.

"His father handed him over to me as a sort of guide, counsellor, and friend. The little fellow is very amusing."

"See over here," interrupted Yen. He hopped over the alley to where the priests stood by the altar. The grown people followed him.

"What is that man chanting?" asked Adah. One of the priests had mounted a table, and with arms outstretched towards the moon sailing high in the heavens, seemed to be making some sort of an invocation.

Her friend listened for some moments before replying:

"It is a sort of apotheosis of the moon. I have heard it on a like occasion in Hankow, and the Chinese *bonze* who officiated gave me a translation. I almost know it by heart. May I repeat it to you?"

Mrs. Dean and Yen were examining the screen with the big josses.

"Yes, I should like to hear it," said Adah.

"Then fix your eyes upon Diana."

"Dear and lovely moon, as I watch thee pursuing thy solitary course o'er the silent heavens, heart-easing thoughts steal o'er me and calm my passionate soul. Thou art so sweet, so serious, so serene, that thou causest me to forget the stormy emotions which crash like jarring discords across the harmony of life, and bringest to my memory a voice scarce ever heard amidst the warring of the world – love's low voice.

"Thou art so peaceful and so pure that it seemeth as if naught false or ignoble could dwell beneath thy gentle radiance, and that earnestness – even the earnestness of genius – must glow within the bosom of him on whose head thy beams fall like blessings.

"The magic of thy sympathy disburtheneth me of many sorrows, and thoughts, which, like the songs of the sweetest sylvan singer, are too dear and sacred for the careless ears of day, gush forth with unconscious eloquence when thou art the only listener.

"Dear and lovely moon, there are some who say that those who dwell in the sunlit fields of reason should fear to wander through the moonlit valleys of imagination; but I, who have ever been a pilgrim and a stranger in the realm of the wise, offer to thee the homage of a heart which appreciates that thou graciously shinest – even on the fool."

"Is that really Chinese?" queried Adah.

"No doubt about it – in the main. Of course, I cannot swear to it word for word."

"I should think that there would be some reference to the fruits of the earth – the harvest. I always understood that the Chinese religion was so practical."

"Confucianism is. But the Chinese mind requires two religions. Even the most commonplace Chinese has yearnings for something above everyday life. Therefore, he combines with his Confucianism, Buddhism – or, in this country, Christianity."

"Thank you for the information. It has given me a key to the mind of a certain Chinese in whom Auntie and I are interested."

"And who is this particular Chinese in whom you are interested."

"The father of the little boy who is with us tonight."

"Wou Sankwei! Why, here he comes with Lee Tong Hay. Are you acquainted with Lee Tong Hay?"

"No, but I believe Aunt is. Plays and sings in vaudeville, doesn't he?"

"Yes; he can turn himself into a German, a Scotchman, an Irishman, or an American, with the greatest ease, and is as natural in each character as he is as a Chinaman. Hello, Lee Tong Hay."

"Hello, Mr. Stimson."

While her friend was talking to the lively young Chinese who had answered his greeting, Adah went over to where Wou Sankwei stood speaking to Mrs. Dean.

"Yen begins school next week," said her aunt, drawing her arm within her own. It was time to go home.

Adah made no reply. She was settling her mind to do something quite out of the ordinary. Her aunt often called her romantic and impractical. Perhaps she was.

VI

Auntie went out of town this morning," said Adah Charlton. "I, 'phoned for you to come up, Sankwei because I wished to have a personal and private talk with you."

"Any trouble, Miss Adah," inquired the young merchant. "Anything I can do for you?"

Mrs. Dean often called upon him to transact little business matters for her or to consult with him on various phases of her social and family life.

"I don't know what I would do without Sankwei's head to manage for me," she often said to her niece.

"No," replied the girl, "you do too much for us. You always have, ever since I've known you. It's a shame for us to have allowed you."

"What are you talking about, Miss Adah? Since I came to America your aunt has made this house like a home to me, and, of course, I take an interest in it and like to do anything for it that a man can. I am always happy when I come here."

"Yes, I know you are, poor old boy," said Adah to herself.

Aloud she said: "I have something to say to you which I would like you to hear. Will you listen, Sankwei?"

"Of course I will," he answered.

"Well then," went on Adah, "I asked you to come here today because I have heard that there is trouble at your house and that your wife is jealous of you."

"Would you please not talk about that, Miss Adah. It is a matter which you cannot understand."

"You promised to listen and heed. I do understand, even though I cannot speak to your wife nor find out what she feels and thinks. I know you, Sankwei, and I can see just how the trouble has arisen. As soon as I heard that your wife was jealous I knew why she was jealous."

"Why?" he queried.

"Because," she answered unflinchingly, "you are thinking far too much of other women."

"Too much of other women?" echoed Sankwei dazedly. "I did not know that."

"No, you didn't. That is why I am telling you. But you are, Sankwei. And you are becoming too Americanized. My aunt encourages you to become so, and she is a good woman, with the best and highest of motives; but we are all liable to make mistakes, and it is a mistake to try and make a Chinese man into an American – if he has a wife who is to remain as she always has been. It would be different if you were not married and were a man free to advance. But you are not."

"What am I to do then, Miss Adah? You say that I think too much of other women besides her, and that I am too much Americanized. What can I do about it now that it is so?"

"First of all you must think of your wife. She has done for you what no American woman would do – came to you to be your wife, love you and serve you without even knowing you – took you on trust altogether. You must remember that for many years she was chained in a little cottage to care for your ailing and aged mother – a hard task indeed for a young girl. You must remember that you are the only man in the world to her, and that you have always been the only one that she has ever cared for. Think of her during all the years you are here, living a lonely hard-working life – a baby and an old woman her only companions. For this, she had left all her own relations. No American woman would have sacrificed herself so.

"And, now, what has she? Only you and her housework. The white woman reads, plays, paints, attends concerts, entertainments, lectures, absorbs herself in the work she likes, and in the course of her life thinks of and cares for a great many people. She has much to make her happy besides her husband. The Chinese woman has him only."

"And her boy."

"Yes, her boy," repeated Adah Charlton, smiling in spite of herself, but lapsing into seriousness the moment after. "There's another reason for you to drop the American for a time and go back to being a Chinese.

For sake of your darling little boy, you and your wife should live together kindly and cheerfully. That is much more important for his welfare than that he should go to the American school and become Americanized."

"It is my ambition to put him through both American and Chinese schools."

"But what he needs most of all is a loving mother."

"She loves him all right."

"Then why do you not love her as you should? If I were married I would not think my husband loved me very much if he preferred spending his evenings in the society of other women than in mine, and was so much more polite and deferential to other women than he was to me. Can't you understand now why your wife is jealous?"

Wou Sankwei stood up.

"Goodbye," said Adah Charlton, giving him her hand.

"Goodbye," said Wou Sankwei.

Had he been a white man, there is no doubt that Adah Charlton's little lecture would have had a contrary effect from what she meant it to have. At least, the lectured would have been somewhat cynical as to her sincerity. But Wou Sankwei was not a white man. He was a Chinese, and did not see any reason for insincerity in a matter as important as that which Adah Charlton had brought before him. He felt himself exiled from Paradise, yet it did not occur to him to question, as a white man would have done, whether the angel with the flaming sword had authority for her action. Neither did he lay the blame for things gone wrong upon any woman. He simply made up his mind to make the best of what was.

VII

It had been a peaceful week in the Wou household – the week before little Yen was to enter the American school. So peaceful indeed that Wou Sankwei had begun to think that his wife was reconciled to his wishes with regard to the boy. He whistled softly as he whittled away at a little ship he was making for him. Adah Charlton's suggestions had set coursing a train of thought which had curved around Pau Lin so closely that he had decided that, should she offer any further opposition to the boy's attending the American school, he would not insist upon it. After all, though the American language might be useful during this century, the wheel of the world would turn again, and then it might not be necessary at all. Who could tell? He came very near to expressing himself thus to Pau Lin.

And now it was the evening before the morning that little Yen was to march away to the American school. He had been excited all day over the prospect, and to calm him, his father finally told him to read aloud a little story from the Chinese book which he had given him on his first birthday in America and which he had taught him to read. Obediently the little fellow drew his stool to his mother's side and read in his childish sing-song the story of an irreverent lad who came to great grief because he followed after the funeral of his grandfather and regaled himself on the crisply roasted chickens and loose-skinned oranges which were left on the grave for the feasting of the spirit.

Wou Sankwei laughed heartily over the story. It reminded him of some of his own boyish escapades. But Pau Lin stroked silently the head of the little reader, and seemed lost in reverie.

A whiff of fresh salt air blew in from the Bay. The mother shivered, and Wou Sankwei, looking up from the fastening of the boat's rigging, bade Yen close the door. As the little fellow came back to his mother's side, he stumbled over her knee.

"Oh, poor mother!" he exclaimed with quaint apology. "'Twas the stupid feet, not Yen."

"So," she replied, curling her arm around his neck, "'tis always the feet. They are to the spirit as the cocoon to the butterfly. Listen, and I will sing you the song of the Happy Butterfly."

She began singing the old Chinese ditty in a fresh birdlike voice. Wou Sankwei, listening, was glad to hear her. He liked having everyone around him cheerful and happy. That had been the charm of the Dean household.

The ship was finished before the little family retired. Yen examined it, critically at first, then exultingly. Finally, he carried it away and placed it carefully in the closet where he kept his kites, balls, tops, and other treasures. "We will set sail with it tomorrow after school," said he to his father, hugging gratefully that father's arm.

Sankwei rubbed the little round head. The boy and he were great chums.

What was that sound which caused Sankwei to start from his sleep? It was just on the border land of night and day, an unusual time for Pau Lin to be up. Yet, he could hear her voice in Yen's room. He raised himself on his elbow and listened. She was softly singing a nursery song about some little squirrels and a huntsman. Sankwei wondered at her singing in that way at such an hour. From where he lay he could just perceive the child's cot and the silent child figure lying motionless in the dim light. How very motionless! In a moment Sankwei was beside it.

The empty cup with its dark dregs told the tale.

The thing he loved the best in all the world – the darling son who had crept into his heart with his joyousness and beauty – had been taken from him – by her who had given.

Sankwei reeled against the wall. The kneeling figure by the cot arose. The face of her was solemn and tender.

"He is saved," smiled she, "from the Wisdom of the New."

In grief too bitter for words the father bowed his head upon his hands.

"Why! Why!" queried Pau Lin, gazing upon him bewilderedly. "The child is happy. The butterfly mourns not o'er the shed cocoon."

Sankwei put up his shutters and wrote this note to Adah Charlton:

I have lost my boy through an accident. I am returning to China with my wife whose health requires a change.

When I Was a Boy in China

Lee Yan Phou

Chapter XI: How I Prepared for America

ON OUR ARRIVAL AT SHANGHAI, my cousin took me to see our aunt whose husband was a compradôr in an American tea warehouse. A compradôr is usually found in every foreign *hong* or firm. He acts as interpreter and also as agent for the company. He has a corps of accountants called *shroffs* assistants and workmen under him.

My uncle was rich and lived in a fine house built after European models. It was there that I first came in immediate contact with Western civilization. But it was a long time before I got used to those red-headed and tight-jacketed foreigners. "How can they walk or run?" I asked myself curiously contemplating their close and confining garments. The dress of foreign ladies was still another mystery to me. They shocked my sense of propriety also, by walking arm-in-arm with the men. "How peculiar their voices are! how screechy! how sharp!" Such were some of the thoughts I had about those peculiar people.

A few days after, I was taken to the Tung Mim Kuen, or Government School, where I was destined to spend a whole year, preparatory to my American education. It was established by the government and was in charge of a commissioner, a deputy-commissioner, two teachers of Chinese, and two teachers of English. The building was quite spacious, consisting of two stories. The large schoolroom, library, dining-rooms and kitchen occupied the first floor. The offices, reception room and dormitories were overhead. The square tables of the teachers of Chinese were placed at each end of the schoolroom; between them were oblong tables and stools of the pupils.

I was brought into the presence of the commissioners and teachers; and having performed my *kow-tow* to each, a seat was assigned me among my mates, who scanned me with a good deal of curiosity. It was afternoon, and the Chinese lessons were being recited. So while they looked at me through the corners of their eyes, they were also attending to their lessons with as much vim and voice as they could command. Soon recitations were over, not without one or two pupils being sent back to their seats to study their tasks over again, a few blows being administered to stimulate the intellect and quicken memory.

At half-past four o'clock, school was out and the boys, to the number of forty, went forth to play. They ran around, chased each other and wasted their cash on fruits and confections. I soon made acquaintance with some of them, but I did not experience any of the hazing and bullying to which new pupils in American and English schools are subject. I found that there were two parties among the boys. I joined one of them and had many friendly encounters with the rival party. As in America, we had a great deal of generous emulation, and consequently much boasting of the prizes and honours won by the rival societies. Our chief amusements were sight-seeing, shuttle-cock-kicking and penny-guessing.

Supper came at six when we had rice, meats and vegetables. Our faces invariably were washed after supper in warm water. This is customary. Then the lamps were lighted ; and when the teachers came down, full forty pairs of lungs were at work with lessons of next day. At eight o'clock, one of the teachers read and explained a long extract from Chinese history, which, let me assure you, is replete with interest. At nine o'clock we were sent to our beds. Nothing ever happened of special interest. I remember that we used to talk till pretty late, and that some of the nights that I spent there were not of the pleasantest kind because I was haunted by the fear of spirits.

After breakfast the following morning we assembled in the same schoolroom to study our English lessons. The teacher of this branch was a Chinese gentleman who learned his English at Hongkong. The first thing to be done with me was to teach me the alphabet. When the teacher grew tired he set some advanced pupils to teach me. The letters sounded rather funny, I must say. It took me two days to learn them. The letter *R* was the hardest one to pronounce, but I soon learned to give it, with a peculiar roll of the tongue even. We were taught to read and write English and managed by means of primers and phrase-books to pick up a limited knowledge of the language. A year thus passed in study and pastime. Sundays were given to us to spend as holidays.

It was in the month of May when we were examined in our English studies and the best thirty were selected to go to America, their proficiency in Chinese, their general deportment and their record also being taken into account.

There was great rejoicing among our friends and kindred. For the cadet's gilt button and rank were conferred on us, which, like the first literary degree, was a step towards fortune, rank and influence. Large posters were posted up at the front doors of our homes, informing the world in gold characters of the great honour which had come to the family.

We paid visits of ceremony to the *Tautai* chief officer of the department, and to the American consul-general, dressed in our official robes and carried in fine carriages. By the first part of June, we were ready for the ocean journey. We bade our friends farewell with due solemnity, for the thought that on our return after fifteen years of study abroad half of them might be dead, made us rather serious. But the sadness of parting was soon over and homesickness and dreariness took its place, as the steamer steamed out of the river and our native country grew indistinct in the twilight.

Chapter XII: First Experiences in America

AFTER A STORMY VOYAGE OF ONE WEEK, with the usual accompaniment of seasickness, we landed at Yokohama, in the Country of the Rising Sun. For Japan means 'sun-origin.' The Japanese claim to be descendants of the sun, instead of being an off-shoot of the Chinese race.

During the four days on shore we young Chinese saw many strange things; the most remarkable being the steam-engine. We were told that those iron rails running parallel for a long distance were the 'fire-car road.' I was wondering how a car could run on them, and driven by fire, too, as I understood it, when a locomotive whizzed by, screeching and ringing its bell. That was the first iron-horse we had ever seen, and it made a profound impression on us. We made a number of other remarkable and agreeable discoveries. We were delighted to learn that the Japanese studied the same books as we and worshiped our Confucius, and that we could converse with them in writing, pretty much as deaf and dumb people do. We learned that the way they lived and dressed was like that in vogue in the time of Confucius. Their mode of dressing the hair and their custom of sitting on mats laid on the floor is identical with ancient Chinese usage.

When our brief stay came to an end, we went aboard the steamer *City of Peking*, which reached San Francisco in nineteen days. Our journey across the Pacific was made in the halcyon weather. The ocean was as gentle as a lamb for the most part, although at times it acted in such a way as to suggest a raging lion.

San Francisco in 1873 was the paradise of the self-exiled Chinese. We boys who came to study under the auspices of the Chinese government and under the protection of the American eagle, were objects of some attention from the press. Many of its representatives came to interview us.

The city impressed my young imagination with its lofty buildings – their solidity and elegance. The depot with its trains running in and out was a great attraction. But the 'modern conveniences' of gas and running water and electric bells and elevators were what excited wonder and stimulated investigation.

Nothing occurred on our Eastward journey to mar the enjoyment of our first ride on the steam-cars – excepting a train robbery, a consequent smash-up of the engine, and the murder of the engineer. We were quietly looking out of the windows and gazing at the seemingly interminable prairies when the train suddenly bounded backward, then rushed forward a few feet, and, then meeting some resistance, started back again. Then all was confusion and terror. Pistol-shots could be made out above the cries of frightened passengers. Women shrieked and babies cried. Our party, teachers and pupils, jumped from our seats in dismay and looked out through the windows for more light on the subject. What we saw was enough to make our hair stand on end. Two ruffianly men held a revolver in each hand and seemed to be taking aim at us from the short distance of forty feet or thereabouts. Our teachers told us to crouch down for our lives. We obeyed with trembling and fear. Doubtless many prayers were most fervently offered to the gods of China at the time. Our teachers certainly prayed as they had never done before. One of them was overheard calling upon all the gods of the Chinese Pantheon to come and save him. In half an hour the agony and suspense were over. A brakeman rushed through with a lamp in his hand. He told us that the train had been robbed of its gold bricks, by five men, three of whom, dressed like Indians, rifled the baggage car while the others held the passengers at bay; that the engine was hopelessly wrecked, the engineer killed; that the robbers had escaped on horseback with their booty; and that men had been sent to the nearest telegraph station to 'wire' for another engine and a supply of workmen. One phase of American civilization was thus indelibly fixed upon our minds.

We reached Springfield, Mass., in due time, where we were distributed among some of the best families in New England. As liberal provision having been made for our care by the Chinese government, there was no difficulty in finding nice people to undertake our 'bringing-up,' although I now know that a philanthropic spirit must have inspired all who assumed the responsibility of our training and education. We were assigned two by two; and it was my good fortune to be put into the hands of a most motherly lady in Springfield. She came after us in a hack. As I was pointed out to her, she put her arms around me and kissed me. This made the rest of the boys laugh, and perhaps I got rather red in the face; however, I would say nothing to show my embarrassment. But that was the first kiss I ever had had since my infancy.

Our first appearance in an American household must have been a funny occurrence to its members. We were dressed in our full Chinese costume, consisting of cue, satin shoes, skull-cap, silk gown, loose jacket and white linen blouse. We were both thirteen years of age, but smaller than American boys at eleven. Sunday came. After lunch, the lady and her son came up to our room to tell us to get ready to go to Sabbath-school with them. We knew very little English at the time. The simplest Anglo-Saxon words were still but slightly known to us. We caught the word 'school' only. We supposed that at last our ordeal in an American school was at hand. We each took a cloth-wrapper and began to tie up a pile of books with it, *à la Chinoise*, when our guardians, returning, made us understand by signs and otherwise that no books were needed.

Well, we four set out, passed Court Square, and walked up the steps of the First Church.

"It is a church," said my companion in Chinese.

We were confirmed in our suspicions on peeping in and seeing the people rise to sing. "Church! church!" we muttered, and rushed from the edifice with all the speed we could command. We did not stop till we got into our room, while our American friends, surprised at this move on our part and failing to overtake us, went back to the church.

We learned English by object-lessons. At table we were always told the names of certain dishes, and then assured that if we could not remember the name we were not to partake of that article of food. Taught by this method, our progress was rapid and surprising.

The complete and unabridged text is available online, from flametreepublishing.com/extras

The Soul of an Immigrant

Constantine Panunzio

Chapter IV: In the American Storm

THE FRANCESCO PUT OUT TO SEA FROM TRAPANI, Sicily, on May 3, 1902, and a week or so later passed the Pillars of Hercules. Then she plunged into the wake of the trade winds and for about three weeks she sailed majestically before them like a gull, stirring not a sail all the while. Then followed a period of varying weather, which in turn was succeeded by a few days when the ocean was breathless and motionless. Frequently we could see whole schools of dolphins as they came to the surface, or monster whales spurting pillars of water into the air, a sight especially beautiful on calm moonlit nights.

The little brig had reached a distance of about three hundred miles from the coast of North America, when one day the very weight of heaven seemed to be pressing down upon her. The clouds were yellow, sullen and angry-looking; the air was breathless with pent-up power. As the day advanced the barometer went lower and lower, and with the approach of evening this invisible, uncontrollable power seemed to be seizing the little ship as if with mighty claws. The sea rumbled beneath her, the thick masses of clouds pressed closer upon her, the waters became deep-dyed black. At five-thirty we heard the call: "All hands on deck," and a few moments later: "All sails in but lower-topsail and jib." Climbing like monkeys after coconuts, we made short work of the task. We knew, however, that something more strenuous was coming. At six, just as the four bells were striking, the very bowels of sea and sky opened upon us with amazing suddenness and force. The seasoned Tuscan sailor, whose every word was wont to be an oath, struck with sudden fear, fell upon his knees by the bulwark and began to say his prayers. Some one kicked him as you would a dog. The moment the terrific gale struck the ship it tore the heavy lower-top-sail and flapped it madly in the air as if it were a piece of tissue paper. The brave little ship bent pitifully beneath the gale; its main-royal-mast was broken like a reed; its cargo was shifted to one side like a handful of pebbles, and its hull sprung a leak. The blast was over in an hour or so, but all hands worked steadily for three days and nights to shift the cargo back in place, while four men were kept at the hand-pump night and day until we reached shore a week or more later.

Some years afterward an American friend, reflecting upon this incident as I had described it to him, remarked "That storm was indeed prophetic of your early experiences in America, was it not?" It may be that it was, and perhaps we shall soon discover the analogy as it appeared in my friend's mind.

On July 3rd, 1902, after a voyage of sixty-one day, the *Francesco* anchored in Boston Harbour. As the next day was the 'Fourth,' the city was already decked in festal array. The captain hastened to register his arrival. A boat was lowered, and I was ordered to take him ashore; thus it was my good fortune to be the first to touch land. "America!" I whispered to myself as I did so.

In a day or two the ship was towed to a pier in Charlestown, where it lay until its cargo of salt was unloaded and a cargo of lumber consigned to Montevideo was put on board of her. In the meantime a desire had arisen within me to return home. There were several reasons for this. In the first place, it was becoming increasingly unpleasant for me to remain in the midst of that crew.

It chanced that I was the only person on board hailing from southern Italy; the rest of the men were mostly Genoese, with one or two Tuscans. Now, the feeling of sectional provincialism between north and south Italy is still so strong, and the North always assumes such airs of superiority, that I had become the butt of every joke and the scapegoat of every occasion. This was becoming more and more unbearable, and as time went on I decided that my self-respect could not and would not stand it. To this was added the fact that the captain was one of those creatures who seem to be more brute than man, especially in dealing with youth. During that voyage he had more than once beaten me in a way that would have made the hardest punishments of my father blush. He was so cruel and unreasonable that before he left Boston several of the crew, including the first mate, left him.

In the face of these circumstances I began to think that if the captain would only let me go, I would return home. Accordingly, one day I went to him and very respectfully told him of my intention to return to Italy immediately if he would permit me, and would pay me the money which was due me. The stern, sea-hardened sailor brushed me aside without even an answer. A day or so later I again went to him; this time he drove me from his presence with a sharp kick. Whatever manhood there ever was in my being rose up and stood erect within me; with a determination as quick and as sharp as his kick had been, I decided I would now go at any cost.

I began to look about for ways and means to carry out my determination. On the pier was an elderly watchman, an Italian by birth, who had been in America for several years. To him I confided my difficulties. He was a sane and conservative man, cautious in giving advice. My desire was to find a ship which was returning to some European port. He did not know of any, but one evening he suggested that if worse came to worst, I could do some kind of work for a few days and thereby earn enough money to buy a third-class passage back to Naples, which at that time cost only fifty or sixty dollars. This gave me a new idea. I decided to take my destiny in my own hands and in some way find my way back to Italy. Two months had already passed since our arrival in Boston, and almost any day now the vessel would take to sea. If I were to act it must be now or never. I had been ashore twice and had become acquainted with a barber near the pier. To him I also confided my troubles, and he offered to keep my few belongings for me, should I finally decide to leave the ship.

Late in the evening of September 8, 1902, when the turmoil of the street traffic was subsiding, and the silence of the night was slowly creeping over the city, I took my sea chest, my sailor bag and all I had and set foot on American soil. I was in America. Of immigration laws I had not even a knowledge of their existence; of the English language I knew not a word; of friends I had none in Boston or elsewhere in America to whom I might turn for counsel or help. I had exactly fifty cents remaining out of a dollar which the captain had finally seen fit to give me. But as I was soon to earn money and return to Molfetta, I felt no concern.

My Charlestown barber friend took me in that first night with the distinct understanding that I could stay only one night. So the next morning bright and early, leaving all my belongings with the barber, I started out in search of a job. I roamed about the streets, not knowing where or to whom to turn. That day and the next four days I had one loaf of bread each day for food and at night, not having money with which to purchase shelter, I stayed on the recreation pier on Commercial Street. One night, very weary and lonely, I lay upon a bench and soon dozed off into a light sleep. The next thing I knew I cried out in bitter pain and fright. A policeman had stolen up to me very quietly and with his club had dealt me a heavy blow upon the soles of my feet. He drove me away, and I think I cried; I cried my first American cry. What became of me that night I cannot say. And the next day and the next … I just roamed aimlessly about the streets, between the Public Garden with its flowers and the water-side, where I watched the children at play, even as I had played at the water's brink in old Molfetta.

Those first five days in America have left an impression upon my mind which can never be erased with the years, and which gives me a most profound sense of sympathy for immigrants as they arrive.

On the fifth day, by mere chance, I ran across a French sailor on the recreation pier. We immediately became friends. His name was Louis. Just to look at Louis would make you laugh. He was over six feet tall, lank, queer-shaped, freckle-faced, with small eyes and a crooked nose. I have sometimes thought that perhaps he was the 'missing link' for which the scientist has been looking. Louis could not speak Italian; he had a smattering of what he called 'italien,' but I could not see it his way. On the other hand, I kept imposing upon his good nature by giving a nasal twang to Italian words and insisting on calling it 'francese.' We had much merriment. Two facts, however, made possible a mutual understanding. Both had been sailors and had traveled over very much the same world; this made a bond between us. Then too, we had an instinctive knowledge of 'esperanto,' a strange capacity for gesticulation and facial contortion, which was always our last 'hope' in making each other understand.

Not far from the recreation pier on which we met is located the Italian colony of 'North End,' Boston. To this Louis and I made our way, and to an Italian boarding house. How we happened to find it and to get in I do not now recall. It was a 'three-room apartment' and the landlady informed us that she was already 'full,' but since we had no place to go, she would take us in. Added to the host that was already gathered there, our coining made fourteen people. At night the floor of the kitchen and the dining table were turned into beds. Louis and I were put to sleep in one of the beds with two other men, two facing north and two south. As I had slept all my life in a bed or bunk by myself this quadrupling did not appeal to me especially. But we could not complain. We had been taken in on trust, and the filth, the smells and the crowding together were a part of the trust.

We began to make inquiries about jobs and were promptly informed that there was plenty of work at 'pick and shovel.' We were also given to understand by our fellow-boarders that 'pick and shovel' was practically the only work available to Italians. Now these were the first two English words I had heard and they possessed great charm. Moreover, if I were to earn money to return home and this was the only work available for Italians, they were very weighty words for me, and I must master them as soon and as well as possible and then set out to find their hidden meaning. I practised for a day or two until I could say 'peek' and 'shuvle' to perfection. Then I asked a fellow-boarder to take me to see what the work was like. He did. He led me to Washington Street, not far from the colony, where some excavation work was going on, and there I did see, with my own eyes, what the 'peek' and 'shuvle' were about. My heart sank within me, for I had thought it some form of office work; but I was game and since this was the only work available for Italians, and since I must have money to return home, I would take it up. After all, it was only a means to an end, and would last but a few days.

It may be in place here to say a word relative to the reason why this idea was prevalent among Italians at the time, and why so many Italians on coming to America find their way to what I had called 'peek and shuvle.' It is a matter of common knowledge, at least among students of immigration, that a very large percentage of Italian immigrants were 'contadini' or farm labourers in Italy. American people often ask the question, "Why do they not go to the farms in this country?" This query is based upon the idea that the 'contadini' were farmers in the sense in which we apply that word to the American farmer. The facts in the case are that the 'contadini' were not farmers in that sense at all, but simply farm-labourers, more nearly serfs, working on landed estates and seldom owning their own land. Moreover, they are not in any way acquainted with the implements of modern American farming. Their farming tools consisted generally of a 'zappa,' a sort of wide mattock; an ax and the wooden plow of biblical times. When they come to America, the work which comes nearest to that which they did in Italy is not farming, or even farm labour, but excavation work. This fact, together with the isolation which inevitably would be theirs on an American farm, explains, in a large measure, why so few Italians go to the farm and why so many go into excavation work. There is another factor to be considered, and that is that the 'padrone' perhaps makes a greater per capita percentage in connection with securing and managing workers for construction purposes than in any other line, and therefore he becomes a walking delegate about the streets of Italian colonies spreading the word that only 'peek and shuvle' is available.

Now, though Louis and I had never done such work, because we were Italians we must needs adapt ourselves to it and go to work with 'peek and shuvle.' (I should have stated that Louis, desiring to be like the Romans while living with them, for the time being passed for an Italian.)

So we went out to hunt our first job in America. For several mornings Louis and I went to North Square, where there were generally a large number of men loitering in groups discussing all kinds of subjects, particularly the labour market. One morning we were standing in front of one of those infernal institutions which in America are permitted to bear the name of 'immigrant banks,' when we saw a fat man coming toward us. "Buon giorno, padrone," said one of the men. "Padrone?" said I to myself. Now the word 'padrone' in Italy is applied to a proprietor, generally a respectable man, at least one whose dress and appearance distinguish him as a man of means. This man not only showed no signs of good breeding in his face, but he was unshaven and dirty and his clothes were shabby. I could not quite understand how he could be called 'padrone.' However, I said nothing, first because I wanted to get back home, and second because I wanted to be polite when I was in American society!

The 'padrone' came up to our group and began to wax eloquent and to gesticulate (both in Sicilian dialect) about the advantages of a certain job. I remember very clearly the points which he emphasized: "It is not very far, only twelve miles from Boston. For a few cents you can come back any time you wish, to see '*i parenti e gli amici*,' your relatives and friends. The company has a 'shantee' in which you can sleep, and a 'storo' where you can buy your 'grosserie' all very cheap. 'Buona paga'," he continued "(Good pay), $1.25 per day, and you only have to pay me fifty cents a week for having gotten you this 'gooda jobba.' I only do it to help you and because you are my countrymen. If you come back here at six o'clock to-night with your bundles, I myself will take you out."

The magnanimity of this man impressed Louis and me very profoundly; we looked at each other and said, "Wonderful!" We decided we would go; so at the appointed hour we returned to the very spot. About twenty men finally gathered there and we were led to North Station. There we took a train to some suburban place, the name of which I have never been able to learn. On reaching our destination we were taken to the 'shantee' where we were introduced to two long open bunks filled with straw. These were to be our beds. The 'storo' of which we had been told was at one end of the shanty. The next morning we were taken out to work. It was a sultry autumn day. The 'peek' seemed to grow heavier at every stroke and the 'shuvle' wider and larger in its capacity to hold the gravel. The second day was no better than the first, and the third was worse than the second. The work was heavy and monotonous to Louis and myself especially, who had never been 'contadini' like the rest. The 'padrone' whose magnanimity had so stirred us was little better than a brute. We began to do some simple figuring and discovered that when we had paid for our groceries at the 'storo,' for the privilege of sleeping in the shanty, and the fifty cents to the 'padrone' for having been so condescending as to employ us, we would have nothing left but sore arms and backs. So on the afternoon of the third day Louis and I held a solemn conclave and decided to part company with 'peek and shuvle,' for ever. We left, without receiving a cent of pay, of course.

Going across country on foot we came to a small manufacturing village. We decided to try our luck at the factory, which proved to be a woolen mill, and found employment. Our work was sorting old rags and carrying them in wheelbarrows into a hot oven, in which the air was almost suffocating. Every time a person went in it he was obliged to run out as quickly as possible, for the heat was unbearable. Unfortunately for us, the crew was composed almost entirely of Russians, who hated us from the first day, and called us 'dagoes.' I had never heard the word before; I asked Louis if he knew its meaning, but he did not. In going in and out of the oven the Russians would crowd against us and make it hard for us to pass. One morning as I was coming out, four of the men hedged me in. I thought I would suffocate. I finally succeeded in pushing out, my hand having been cut in the rush of the wheelbarrows.

The superintendent of the factory had observed the whole incident. He was a very kindly man. From his light complexion I think he was a Swede. He came to my rescue, reprimanded the Russians, and led me to his office, where he bandaged my hand. Then he called Louis and explained the situation to us. The Russians looked upon us as intruders and were determined not to work side by side with 'the foreigners,' but to drive them out of the factory. Therefore, much as he regretted it, the superintendent was obliged to ask us to leave, since there were only two of us, as against the large number of Russians who made up his unskilled crew.

So we left. My bandaged hand hurt me, but my heart hurt more. This kind of work was hard and humiliating enough, but what went deeper than all else was the first realization that because of race I was being put on the road. And often since that day have I felt the cutting thrusts of race prejudice. They have been dealt by older immigrants, who are known as 'Americans,' as well as by more recent comers. All have been equally heart-rending and head-bending. I hold no grudge against any one; I realize that it is one of the attendant circumstances of our present nationalistic attitude the world over, and yet it is none the less saddening to the human heart. I have seen prejudice, like an evil shadow, everywhere. It lurks at every corner, on every street and in every mart. I have seen it in the tram and on the train; I have felt its dreaded power in school and college, in clubs and churches. It is an ever-present evil spirit, felt though unseen, wounding hearts, cutting souls. It passes on its poison like a serpent from generation to generation, and he who would see the fusion of the various elements into a truly American type must ever take into cognizance its presence in the hearts of some human beings.

We had to hunt another job. We returned to Boston still penniless and to the good graces of the 'padrona' of the filthy boarding-house. Louis now spent a penny for an Italian newspaper and looked over the 'want ads.' He saw what seemed to be a good prospect for a job and we decided to apply for it. If you walk down lower Washington Street in Boston, toward North Station, facing the Italian colony, near Hanover Street you can see, even now, a large sign, 'Stobhom Employment Agency.' It is a notorious institution, the function of which is to catch men and send them to a company in Bangor, from which place they are sent to the various camps in the woods of Maine.

We called upon said 'honourable' agency and were told that they could supply us with work. "It is out in the country, in the woods of Maine. Wages $30 per month, board and room. Good, healthy job." It sounded too good to let go, so we accepted the offer. We were told to report that night at seven o'clock and we would be directed to our work. These night meetings seem to be quite popular with such agencies! Now, I knew what the country was like, but I had no idea what 'woods' meant, and with the best of Louis' wretched Italian, I couldn't quite get it through my head. Moreover, Maine might be anywhere from North Boston to California for all I knew. However, we decided to try it. At $30 per month I would only need to work two months at most; then back home for me!

We reported at seven o'clock according to instructions. A crowd of men jammed the office, the stairway, and loitered on the sidewalk a whole regiment, all properly equipped with their personal belongings. I had my sea-chest and small sailor bag which Louis helped me to carry. At about nine o'clock the exodus began. We were led to North Station and huddled together three deep in one car. The train soon pulled out and I went to 'bed,' which consisted of the arm of a seat. The filth, the smoke, the sights of that memorable trip come back to me as I write by the midnight candle. We traveled all that night and the next day, with nothing to eat except what little food each man had brought with him. At two o'clock the next afternoon we reached our destination. The station was of the kind often seen in the unsettled regions of America a small shack put up by the side of the railroad tracks, where perhaps a hunter unloaded his pack once; properly propped up, lest the winds some night should steal it away; with a sign placed upon it, thus giving it the dignified name of 'station.' The name of this station was Norcross. The starving multitude emerged from the 'special car' on short notice. We followed the 'boss' to a small steamer about thirty-five feet long. Ordinarily it would not have carried over fifty people, but it took practically all of us. In spite of my sea-loving instincts, my heart sank within me. But as we were promised food as soon as we had crossed the lake, Louis and I pushed our way in, my chest and bag dragging behind. It was dark by the time we reached the upper end of one of the Twin Lakes. We landed in the heart of a solitary forest. I knew then what a 'woods' was. As soon as we were all on 'terra foresta' we smelled food, and then and there I had my first taste of pork and beans, molasses cookies and coffee and 'cream.' Soon after eating we 'turned in,' with the starry heavens above us and pine needles pricking beneath, we rested our weary bodies.

The next morning we began our 'boring in' process. The opening up of a new lumbering camp generally follows on this wise: First, the land is surveyed; main and side roads are opened; bridges are built over brooks and marshy places; stumps are blown up; wayside houses are erected for provisions and horses, and a number of other preliminary things are done before the final camp is set up. We were set to perform these preliminary tasks.

I was given an ax and a whetstone. As I was a seaman and had never wielded such weapons before, at first I was at sea to know what to do with them. But imitating others, I tried my hand at it, but soon found my ax handle-less. I seemed to have the knack of hitting the tree once and only once in the same place. No one dared work within a radius of twenty yards of me for fear of losing his life. The boss, who was a Scandinavian, was very patient and kind, and seeing my lack of skill at chopping trees, put me to work dragging small logs into the paths for the men who were building bridges. But I was equally as untrained in the art of being a mule as I was unskilled in wielding an ax. It strained my back and I 'kicked.' At last I was placed at 'fetching' water for the lumbermen, thirsty creatures that they were, who took one drink of water to every two strokes of the ax. So even 'fetching water' was no mean task.

One day while hunting for a new brook I had an awful fright. I heard the breaking of boughs and saw, or thought I saw, a wild animal. As a child, my family used to frighten me into obedience by saying, "A wild beast will get you." Now all my fear came back and a chill of terror seized me. Using my shinning ability to its nth power, on very short notice I was up a tree and there they found me at night. The bucket at the foot of the tree was the only sign of my whereabouts. That same night I lost a black-handled pocket knife, an heirloom, belonging originally to my maternal grandfather, who was drowned at sea. As something very mysterious happened later in connection with this knife, it will be of interest to remember it.

We were nine days in building bridges and opening roads before we reached the location of our permanent camp. Our food was changed daily from pork and beans, molasses cookies and coffee and 'cream' to coffee and 'cream,' molasses cookies and pork and beans, with some pea soup added for good measure.

In the meantime, I had begun to have some mighty strong convictions that Louis and I had better emerge from this existence. So we held a secret Italo-French diplomatic conference and on the evening of the ninth day we packed up our belongings and left the camp. Of course, we drew no pay.

We traveled all night and most of the next day before we reached the 'wayside house' by the lake, where we had first landed. The next morning the little steamer which had brought us to the spot came up and we requested the captain to take us across. He flatly refused, saying that we had come there to work, not to go back; and steaming up he disappeared. I learned years afterwards that this was not simply an incident in my life, but a part of a system known as 'peonage.' Men, mostly of foreign birth, are taken to these lumber camps, rounded by some kind of barrier which makes escape impossible, and there they are compelled to remain. According to United States Government reports, there are thousands, mostly Scandinavians and Slavs, in the lumbering regions of our country, who are trapped in some such way and often compelled to work in this form of slavery sometimes for months. The barrier in our case consisted of virgin forests on three sides and a large body of water on the other.

However, Louis and I did not intend to be caught, and our sailor's ingenuity now stood us in good stead. We dragged a few logs together and tied them into a raft with ropes and chains which we found on the shore; we made some poles to push the raft and placing our belongings upon it, toward sunset of the second day we started on our famous journey. For food we filled two whisky bottles with molasses from a barrel which we found on shore.

We had scarcely pushed off when we heard shouting. I immediately thought of the 'wild Indians' of my childhood stories. It proved to be a Russian who also had left the camp. He waved his ax in the air and entreated us to come back to shore. From his gesticulation and facial contortions, it became clear to us that he meant no harm, but that all he wanted was a free passage on our new 'trans-lake-anic' liner! We pulled back to shore, took him on and started again upon our way. The harmony which followed can be better imagined than described. With a Russian, a Frenchman and an Italian, each not understanding the other, we and our tongues were repeatedly and completely confounded and we had a twentieth century 'Tower of Babel' on a raft on an American lake.

We pushed away from shore and started on our journey toward the unknown. We knew nothing of our whereabouts and depended solely on our general sense of direction. Toward dusk we reached the other side of an inlet not far from the starting-point, and the question now came up as to what we should do during the night. Naturally there was not much discussion about the matter simply because the linguistic facilities for discussion were totally absent. We pulled ashore, however, and from the preparations which Louis and our Russian 'comrade' began to make, I could see that we were destined to put up here for the night. While the last faint gleams of light were disappearing, we gathered a few sticks of wood, (the Russian's ax coming in handy for this purpose), and built a fire.

It was one of those autumn nights when the penetrating chill of the air seems to creep to the very marrow of one's bones. The sky was overhung with thick clouds like omens foreboding ill. Not a star was to be seen. The wind made a mournful sound through the tree-tops. And in the thick darkness the glare of the fire cast pale and fitful shadows. Louis and the Russian were soon fast asleep. A creeping fear began to steal over me. Through the forest I could hear the cries of wild animals, and from afar came the mournful low of the moose and the deer. With every gust of wind a chill of terror swept over me and it seemed as if I could see animals coming toward me. Once in my frenzy I cried out at the top of my voice and shook Louis out of his deep slumber. He assured me that no animal would come near as long as the fire was burning. But this was poor consolation for the pile of wood was fast dwindling, and if the fire was to be kept burning, I must go to the forest and gather more. I implored Louis to stay awake with me, but he turned over and was soon asleep again. I managed to gather more wood and all night long I kept the fire burning. Perhaps the reader can imagine in some measure what went through my mind that night. I cannot describe it.

With the first streak of dawn, I woke my companions and insisted on leaving at once the spot where I had spent such a night of misery, and on continuing our journey. We boarded our raft and were soon pushing our way along in the shallow waters. Toward noon we heard the blowing of a whistle. At this, the Russian made motions indicating that we should abandon the raft and strike across the forest in the direction from which the sound of the whistle came. Louis was inclined to follow his proposal, but for me it was not such a simple matter. On that raft were all my earthly possessions, not much, I grant you, but in that sea chest and sailor bag were all that was left to remind me of home and loved ones. Louis finally decided to follow our Russian friend through the woods. He had gone a few paces when I was seized with a sudden determination that he must not leave me alone in these wilds. He had been partly responsible for my coming to this forsaken country; he had agreed to leave the camp with me and attempt to escape from the trap in which we had been caught, and he must stay with me and see the game through, at all costs. I picked up a rock and marched up to Louis. He did not understand what I said with my tongue, but he understood perfectly well what I was saying with the rock in my hand. Although Louis was nearly twice my size, he was a moral coward. He offered no resistance, and waving good-by to the Russian, went back to the raft with me. That was the last we saw of our Russian friend, and we never learned whether he found his way out of the forest.

Louis and I again boarded the raft and pushed our way along the shore. By evening we were beginning to get very hungry. The two bottles of molasses were almost exhausted. Above everything else, I feared another night in those desolate wilds; and we had no ax with which to get wood. Just then in the glow of the sunset rays we saw a column of smoke. Have you ever been out at sea or in a forest and roamed for days not knowing your bearings, and all at once out of the unknown comes some sign that help is near, and your sinking heart gives a leap of courage? That was the feeling that now came over us. But we must act quickly. If we would not spend another night in the dreaded woods we must make an immediate dash toward the smoke. We dragged the raft onto a promontory, buried my belongings under a pile of rock and started on our quest of life. As I looked back upon that pile of rocks, it seemed as if I was leaving the dearest friends I had on earth. But I had no choice I must go or starve in that wild forest.

We began to climb over dead trees and through the underbrush, making very slow progress. Here and there we found marshy spots over which we had to go carefully or be sucked into the soft, spongy ground beneath our feet. Meantime it was getting darker and darker. For a time we feared we would never reach our destination; the thought even crossed my mind that we would fall exhausted and be eaten by wild beasts. But we kept on, perspiring and breathless, but driven by desperation.

After struggling for an hour or so, we came out near the spot where we had seen smoke rising, and we heard the sound of human voices. We drew near and saw that it was a sort of floating cabin or houseboat. It was really a floating lumber camp. At first we were afraid to go in, fearing it might be a part of the same establishment from which we had escaped, and we would be caught again. But as it was a matter of life and death, we plucked up our courage and went on, first concealing what was left of our molasses. As we approached the raft, we smelled food. The crew was eating supper. When we appeared at the door there was a general commotion within; the lumbermen did not know what to make of these strange creatures. Louis did what he could to explain our predicament, and they immediately offered us the hospitality of the camp. We ate a sumptuous supper and then Louis told at length the story of our escape. We were given a place to sleep on the floor, which seemed as soft as down to our weary bodies.

We learned next morning that this was a rival camp to the one from which we had escaped. The boss was 'horrified' at the treatment we had received, and assumed the attitude of a protector and a defender of justice. We told him how we had left my belongings under the rocks on the promontory and he loaned us a boat to go after them, making sure that we would not escape with the boat, by sending two men along with us. We brought back my sea chest and bag to the camp and that night the lumber jacks had an enjoyable entertainment looking over the strange things contained in them. Some little trinkets I gave away to the men in token of appreciation of the kindness they had shown us; other articles disappeared mysteriously.

On the following morning the boss hailed the steamer as it passed by, and after much argument forced the captain, who three days before had refused us passage, to take us to Norcross. Once on board, the captain demanded the payment of twelve dollars for our passage. We told him we had no money and showed him the inside of our pockets. He agreed to land us at Norcross provided we would leave my belongings until we could come back to pay him the money. It was not until months afterward that I was able to redeem them.

We emerged from this camp only to find our way to another, as there was no other work available in the vicinity. It was while in this second camp that I came near losing my life. It was now late October. The snows were beginning to fall, adorning the trees with matchless white and making a thin crust of ice over rivers and lakes. Such spotless beauty I had never seen before; the whole scene was enchanting to me. In all my life I had seen snow only once, and at Edinburgh I had once seen ice covering the water.

One day I was detailed to go on an errand to Millinocket, some five miles away, across the river. To cross the river one might follow one of two courses, either go down to the bridge, some three miles down-stream, or cross over the rocks at a narrow place, which was fairly passable when the river was low. On reaching the river I decided to take the latter course. My father had taught me that a straight line is the shortest distance between two points. So it is in the abstract. But unfortunately it did not prove to be so in this case. I noticed that the waters were gushing over the narrows and that it was impossible to cross at that point. Not far down-stream, however, I saw a man crossing on the ice. The sight fascinated me; in my childhood I had dreamed of walking on the water, and now it seemed that my dream would actually come true. Without a moment's hesitation I chose what I thought a convenient place to cross and began to make my way. Some two or three miles above Millinocket the Penobscot River passes through a narrow ravine and then broadens majestically as it approaches the gigantic falls which furnish power for one of the greatest pulp mills in the world. I chose a comparatively narrow place to cross, having no way of knowing that waters run swiftest in the narrows. As I made my way toward the middle of the river I noticed that the ice was not so white as near the edge, but did not connect it with any possible weakness in the smooth and beautiful pavement under me. I walked slowly in order not to slip. I had reached the middle of the river, when of a sudden, without warning, the ice broke under my feet and I went down into the icy and swiftly moving current.

For the next fifteen minutes I had a battle for life. The madly-rushing waters dragged my feet under the thin layer of ice. I would get hold of the edge of the frail substance only to find it breaking in my hand while I struggled to get a firmer grasp. I lay flat on the ice, thinking I could thus distribute my weight, but whole pieces would break under me and I would be floating on a large piece of thin ice. How I finally managed to crawl to shore I cannot say. My clothing was soon frozen stiff in the chill wind and I was completely exhausted. It was not until the next day that I fully regained consciousness and realized all that had happened. I was then in my bunk at the camp. It appears that some one had picked me up and carried me back to camp. I never understood the details. Truly this was a 'cool' reception which Monsieur North America was giving to a son of Sunny Italy.

All through that winter I suffered greatly from the cold and I did not know what it was to be really comfortable. Sometimes when I hear people speaking rather disparagingly of immigrants from temperate climates for hibernating during the cold winter months, I am reminded of the experiences of the first winter in North America and I understand fully why these humble peasants of sunny climes are willing to work all the harder in the summer months in order not to be exposed to the rigours of the winter.

So climatic conditions indirectly become no small factor in the assimilation of certain immigrant groups and the non-assimilation of others. The crisp cold that puts a spring in the steps of some drives others to cover. Were it possible to properly distribute these people according to the climatic conditions of the different parts of the country it would be otherwise; however, that question cannot be considered here. Climate also explains in a measure why so many immigrants return to their native land from year to year.

It was about this time that Louis and I came to the parting of the ways. We had come to work in still another logging camp, the crew of which was made up entirely of French Canadians. Louis felt very much at home in their midst. I noticed from the very first that he was gradually beginning to put aside the Italian cloak which he had worn for several weeks and was becoming a Frenchman again. It was natural that he should do so. But I also noticed that in proportion as he was reclaimed to his own nationality, I was passing out of Louis' interests. At last I found myself the only 'foreigner' in the group. Presently, on the grounds that I was an inefficient lumberman, I was discharged.

I saw Louis just once after that. He was altogether a Frenchman again, but for one thing. Ever since we had been together he had been wearing some of my clothes, even though they were far too small for him. Among other articles he had frequently worn a pair of gray trousers, my Sunday-go-to-meeting ones, in fact the only pair of to-day-I-am-not-working pants I owned. Louis looked so funny in them; they reached well above his ankles on his thin mast-like legs and were tighter by far around the hips than anything he must have worn in his days before the mast. As I was about to leave the camp, I demanded that he divest himself of my precious belongings, but he refused. So I planned my revenge. On the Sunday following my discharge, I had settled down, as we will presently see, in Stacyville, and I felt a special need of my pantaloons. So I decided I would go a-hunting for them. I borrowed a .38 rifle for the occasion, and strapping it over my shoulder, soon after dinner I started on my punitive errand. On reaching the camp, I squatted myself under a tree, whose branches reached well down to the ground and there I waited patiently for the appearance of my trousers. They did not show up all afternoon and at night I returned to Stacyville. The next Sabbath I started again on my hunt; this time I took to the road with my rifle bright and early, thinking I might have a better chance to see my trousers walking about the camp. On reaching the spot I again hid myself under the trees, with the barrel of my gun pointing toward the door of the camp. All day long I lay there silent as a mouse. The pantaloons did not appear and it seemed as if they must have smelled a rat, for though everybody else came, I did not once see Louis. Finally, toward evening, I saw two men standing near the side of the camp. I could not see their faces, but on careful scrutiny, I observed the up-ankle appearance of my pants, and springing from my hiding-place I cocked my gun and suddenly faced Louis. "My pants or your life!" I seemed to say. Louis stood petrified before me. I ordered him to dismantle himself then and there, or I would shoot. He did not move. Just then two other men came out from the camp. Knowing the true condition of my gun, and fearing a sudden attack from all present, I began to retreat slowly. As they came toward me I turned heel and fled without firing a single shot, for I had made sure to leave every last cartridge at the house, not wishing to inflict any injury on my best trousers or on the thin legs within them. So I returned to Stacyville pantless, panting and forlorn, and I never saw my trousers any more. When years afterward, I learned the song 'Nellie Gray,' visions of my pantaloons would loom before me as I sang, "I'll never see my trousers any more."

The complete and unabridged text is available
online, from flametreepublishing.com/extras

A Modern Viking: Jacob Riis

Mary R. Parkman

I doubt no doubts: I strive, and shrive my clay;
And fight my fight in the patient modern way.
– Sidney Lanier.

WOULD YOU LIKE TO HEAR about a viking of our own time? Listen to the story of this Northman, and see if you will not say that the North Sea country can still send forth as staunch and fearless men as those who sailed in their dragon ships the 'whale roads' of the uncharted seas, found a new world and forgot about it long before Columbus dreamed his dream.

Near the Danish coast where the sea and the low-lying fields grapple hand to hand in every storm, and where the waves at flood tide thunder against the barrows beneath which the old vikings were buried, is the quaint little town of Ribe. This is the sea's own country. It seems as if the people here, who never fear to go down to the sea in ships, have scorned to pile up dikes between them and their greatest friend, who can, in a moment of anger, prove their greatest enemy. It is as if they said, "We are of the sea; if it chooses to rise up against us, who are we to say, 'Thus far and no farther!'"

There was a boy born in this town whose name was Jacob Riis. The call of the sea-birds was the first sound he knew; the breath of the sea was like the breath of life to him. On bright, blue-and-gold days when the waves danced in rainbow hues and scattered in snowy foam, his heart 'outdid the sparkling waves in glee.' At evening, when the sea-fogs settled down over the shore and land and water seemed one, something of the thoughtful strength and patience of that brave little country came into his face.

Many changes had come to the coast since the sea-rovers of old pulled their pirate galleys on the beach, took down their square, gaily striped sails, and gave themselves over to feasting in the great mead-hall, where the smoking boar's-flesh was taken from the leaping flames and seized by the flushed, triumphant warriors, while skalds chanted loud the joys of battle and plunder. The quaint little town where Jacob Riis lived sixty-odd years ago had nothing but the broom-covered barrows and the changeless ocean that belonged to those wild times, and yet it was quite as far removed from the customs and interests of to-day.

I wish that I could make you see the narrow cobblestone streets over which whale-oil lanterns swung on creaking iron chains, and the quaint houses with their tiled roofs where the red-legged storks came in April to build their nests. The stillness was unbroken by the snort of the locomotive and the shrill clamour of steam-boat and steam factory whistles. The people still journeyed by stagecoach, carried tinder-boxes in place of matches, and penknives to mend their quill pens. The telegraph was regarded with suspicion, as was the strange oil from Pennsylvania that was taken out of the earth. Such things could not be safe, and prudent people would do well to have none of them.

In this town, where mill-wheels clattered comfortably in the little stream along which roses nodded over old garden walls and where night-watchmen went about the streets chanting the hours, all the people were neighbours. There were no very rich and few very poor. How Jacob hated the one ramshackle old house by the dry moat which had surrounded the great castle of the mighty

Valdemar barons in feudal days! This place seemed given over to dirt, rats, disease, and dirty, rat-like children. Jacob's friends called it Rag Hall, and said it was a shame that such an ugly, ill-smelling pile should spoil the neighbourhood of Castle Hill, where they loved to play among the tall grass and swaying reeds of the moat.

Rag Hall came to fill a large place in Jacob's thoughts. It was the grim shadow of his bright young world. Surely the world as God had made it was a place of open sky, fresh life-giving breezes, and rolling meadows of dewy, fragrant greenness. How did it happen that people could get so far away from all that made life sweet and wholesome? How had they lost their birthright?

As Jacob looked at the gray, dirty children of Rag Hall it seemed to him that they had never had a chance to be anything better. "What should I have been if I had always lived in such a place?" he said to himself.

One Christmas, Jacob's father gave him a mark, – a silver coin like our quarter, – which was more money than the boy had ever had before. Now it seemed to him that he might be able to do something to help make things better in Rag Hall. He ran to the tenement – to the room of the most miserable family who lived there.

"Here," he said to a man who took the money as if he were stunned, "I'll divide my Christmas mark with you, if you'll just try to clean things up a bit, especially the children, and give them a chance to live like folks."

The twelve-year-old boy little thought that the great adventure of his life really began that day at Rag Hall. But years after when he went about among the tenements of New York, trying to make things better for the children of Mulberry Bend and Cherry Street, he remembered where the long journey had begun.

It was no wonder that Christmas stirred the heart of this young viking, and made him long for real deeds. Christmas in Ribe was a time of joy and good-will to all. A lighted candle was put in the window of every farm-house to cheer the wayfarer with the message that nobody is a stranger at Christmas. Even the troublesome sparrows were not forgotten. A sheaf of rye was set up in the snow to make them the Christmas-tree they would like best. The merry Christmas elf, the 'Jule-nissen,' who lived in the attic, had a special bowl of rice and milk put out for him. Years afterward, when this Danish lad was talking to a crowd of New York boys and girls, he said, with a twinkle in his eyes:

"I know if no one else ever really saw the Nissen that our black cat had made his acquaintance. She looked very wise and purred most knowingly next morning."

If Christmas brought the happiest times, the northwest storms in autumn brought the most thrilling experiences of Jacob's boyhood. Then, above the moaning of the wind, the muttered anger of the waves, and the crash of falling tiles, came the weird singing of the big bell in the tower of the Domkirke – the cathedral, you know.

After such a night the morning would dawn on a strange world where storm-lashed waves covered the meadows and streets for miles about, and on the causeway, high above the flood-level, cattle, sheep, rabbits, grouse, and other frightened creatures of the fields huddled together in pitiful groups.

One night, when the flood had risen before the mail-coach came in and the men of the town feared for the lives of the passengers, Jacob went out with the rescue-party to the road where the coach must pass. Scarcely able to stand against the wind, he struggled along on the causeway where, in pitchy blackness, with water to his waist and pelting spray lashing his face like the sting of a whip, he groped along, helping to lead the frightened horses to the lights of the town a hundred yards away. It was hard that night to get warmed through; but the boy's heart glowed, for had not the brusk old *Amtmand*, the chief official of the country, seized him by the arm and said, while rapping him smartly on the shoulders with his cane, as if, in other days, he would have knighted him, "Strong boy, be a man yet!"

Jacob's father, who was master of the town school, was keenly disappointed when this alert, promising son declared his wish to give up the ways of book-learning and master the carpenter's trade. The boy felt that building houses for people to live in would be far better than juggling with words and all the unreal problems with which school and school-books seemed to deal. Thinking that it would be useless to try to force his son into a life distasteful to him, the father swallowed his disappointment and sent him to serve his apprenticeship with a great builder in Copenhagen. The boy should, he determined, have the best start in his chosen calling that it was in his power to give him.

Soon after his arrival in the capital, Jacob went to meet his student brother at the palace of Charlottenborg, where an art exhibition was being held. Seeing that he was a stranger and ill at ease, a tall, handsome gentleman paused on his way up the grand staircase and offered to act as guide. As they went on together, the gentleman asked the boy about himself and listened with ready sympathy to his eager story of his life in the old town, and what he hoped to do in the new life of the city. When they parted Jacob said heartily:

"People are just the same friendly neighbours in Copenhagen that they are in little Ribe – jolly good Danes everywhere, just like you, sir!"

The stranger smiled and patted him on the shoulder in a way more friendly still. Just at that moment they came to a door where a red-liveried lackey stood at attention. He bowed low as they entered and Jacob, bowing back, turned to his new friend with a delighted smile:

"There is another example of what I mean, sir," he said. "Would you believe it, now, that I have never seen that man before?"

The gentleman laughed, and, pointing to a door, told Jacob he would find his brother there. While the boy happily recounted his adventures, particularly the story of his kindly guide, the handsome gentleman passed through the room and nodded to him with his twinkling smile.

"There is my jolly gentleman," said Jacob, as he nodded back.

His brother jumped to his feet and bowed low.

"Good gracious!" he said, when the stranger had passed out. "You don't mean to say he was your guide? Why, boy, that was the King!"

So Jacob learned that in Denmark even a king, whom he had always thought of as wearing a jeweled crown and a trailing robe of velvet and ermine held by dainty silken pages, could go about in a plain blue overcoat like any other man, and be just as simple and neighbourly.

In Copenhagen the king of his fairy-book world was a neighbour, too. Hans Christian Andersen was a familiar figure on the streets at that time. Jacob and his companions often met him walking under the lindens along the old earthen walls that surrounded the city.

"Isn't he an ugly duck, though!" said Jacob one evening, as the awkward old man, with his long, ungainly neck and limbs and enormous hands and feet, came in sight. Then the merry young fellows strung themselves along in Indian file, each in turn bowing low as he passed, and saying with mock reverence, "Good evening, Herr Professor!"

But when the gentle old man, with the child's heart, seized their hands in his great grasp and thanked them delightedly, they slunk by shamefacedly, and, while they chuckled a little, avoided meeting each other's eyes. For in their hearts they loved the old man whose stories had charmed their childhood, and they knew that the spirit within the lank, awkward body was altogether lovely.

All the time that Jacob was working with hammer and saw, he was, like that first Jacob of whom we read, serving for his Rachel. From the time he was a clumsy lad of twelve he knew that his playmate Elizabeth, with the golden curls and the fair, gentle looks, was the princess of his own fairy-tale. Like all good fairy-tales, it simply had to turn out happily.

When his apprenticeship was over and he had learned all about building houses for people to live in, he hurried at once to Ribe to build his own house. It seemed, however, that nobody realized that he was the hero who was to marry the princess. Why, Elizabeth's father owned the one factory in town, and they lived in a big house, which some people called a 'castle.' Small chance that he would let his pretty daughter marry a carpenter!

Since working faithfully for long, busy years had not brought him to his goal, Jacob threw aside his tools and decided to seek his fortune in a new country. In America, surely, a true man might come into his own. The days of high adventure were not dead. He would win fame and fortune, and then return in triumph to the old town – and to Elizabeth.

It was a beautiful spring morning – surely a prophecy of fair beginnings – when this young viking sailed into New York Harbour. The dauntless Northmen, who pushed across the seas and discovered America, could not have thrilled more at the sight of their Vineland than did this Dane of our own day when he saw the sky-line of the great city. This must indeed be a new world of opportunity for strong men.

It took only a day of wandering about the crowded streets, however, to convince this seeker that a golden chance is as hard to find in the New York of to-day as gold was in those disillusioning days of the early explorers. The golden chance, it seemed, was to be won, if at all, as is the precious metal – only after intelligent prospecting and patient digging.

How utterly alone he felt in that crowd of hurrying strangers! Very different it all was from his cozy little country where every one was a neighbour, even the king himself.

Out of sheer loneliness and the desire to belong to somebody he threw in his lot with a gang of men who were being gathered together to work in a mining-camp on the Allegheny River. Perhaps the West was his Promised Land, and Pennsylvania would be a start on the way.

The young carpenter was set to work building houses for the workers in the mines. He could not content himself, however, in this shut-in country. To one used to the vastness of a level land stretching as far as eye could see, it seemed as if the hills and forests hedged him in on every side – as if he could not breathe. To ease the restlessness of his homesick spirit, he determined to try his fortune at coal-mining. One day was enough of that. In his inexperience he failed to brace the roof properly, and a great piece of rock came down on him, knocking the lamp from his cap and leaving him stunned and in utter darkness. When at last he succeeded in groping his way out, it was as if he had come back from the dead. The daylight had never before seemed so precious. Nothing could have induced him to try coal-mining again.

At this time, 1870, news came of the war between Germany and France. It was expected, moreover, that Denmark would come to the assistance of the French, since only a few years before, in 1864, Germany had seized some of the choicest territory of the little North Sea kingdom – Schleswig-Holstein, the section through which the important Kiel Canal has been built. Every Dane longed to avenge the wrong. Jacob Riis at once left his tools and his work. He would win glory as a soldier.

He reached New York with but a single cent in his pocket, only to find that no one was fitting out volunteer companies to send to France. Here he was longing to offer his life for the cause, and it was treated like a worthless trifle. Clothes and every cherished possession that his little trunk contained were soon pawned to pay for food and a roof over his head.

There followed months when the young man wandered about the great city, homeless, hungry, vainly seeking employment. Too proud to beg, he yet accepted night after night a plate of meat and rolls which a French cook in a large restaurant handed him from a basement window. It seemed as if that was a part of the debt France owed her would-be soldier.

He was part of a weary army of discouraged men hunting for work. He knew what it meant to sleep on park benches, in doorways, in empty wagons, and even on the flat stone slabs of a graveyard. There were, in New York, friends of his family who might have helped him, but he was too proud to make himself known in his present sorry plight. He even destroyed the letters to them, lest in a moment of weakness he might be tempted to appeal to their charity.

This time of hardship, however, was destined to bear fruit. Jacob Riis came to know the shadows of the great city – all the miserable alleys and narrow courts of the East Side slums. Then and there, weak and starving though he was, the boy who had given his Christmas money to help Rag Hall vowed that he would some day work to remove those plague-spots from the city's life. "How true it is," he said, "that one half of the world doesn't know how the other half lives! If they only knew, things would be different."

At last the chance for which he had been longing came. Hearing that a new reporter was wanted by the News Association, he applied for the position. After looking the haggard applicant over for a moment doubtfully, the editor was moved to give him a trial. The starving man was sent to report a political banquet. When he turned in his 'copy' at the office the editor said briefly:

"You will do. Take that desk and report at ten every morning, sharp."

So began his life as a reporter.

Perhaps you know something of his success as a newspaper man. He knew how to gather news; and he knew how to find the words that make bare facts live. The days and nights of privation had been rich in experience. He was truly 'a part of all that he had met.' Something of his intimate acquaintance with all sorts and conditions of existence, something of his warm, understanding sympathy for every variety of human joy and sorrow, crept into his work. Besides, the young man had boundless enthusiasm and tireless industry.

"That chap just seems to eat work," said his fellow-reporters.

One day a very special letter came from Denmark, which told him that his gentle Elizabeth was quite convinced that he was indeed the prince of her life story. So, as it turned out, he didn't have to make a fortune before he was able to bring her to share his home in New York. With her it seemed that he brought the best of the old life into the new –

Brought the moonlight, starlight, firelight,
Brought the sunshine of his people.

The only homesick times that he knew now were the days when his work as a reporter took him to the streets of the miserable tenements. All his soul cried out against these places where the poor, the weak, and the wicked, the old, the sick, and helpless babies were all herded together in damp, dingy rooms where the purifying sunlight never entered. During his years of wandering in search of work he had gained an intimate knowledge of such conditions. He knew what poverty meant and how it felt. Afterward, when he saw this hideous squalor, he shared it. These people were his neighbours.

"Over against the tenements of our cities," he said, "ever rise in my mind the fields, the woods, God's open sky, as accusers and witnesses that his temple is being defiled and man dwarfed in body and soul."

He knew that the one way to remove such evils and to force people to put up decent houses for the poor was to bring the facts out in the open. When he described what he had seen, the words seemed to mean little to many of the people that he wanted to reach. Then he hit upon the plan of taking pictures. These pictures served to illustrate some very direct talks he gave in the churches. Later, many of them made an important part of his book, *How the Other Half Lives.*

"These people are your neighbours," said Jacob Riis. "It is the business of the fortunate half of those who live in our great cities to find out how the other half lives. No one can live to himself or die to himself –

'If you will not grub for your neighbour's weeds,
In your own green garden you'll find the seeds.'"

Through his persistent campaigning, one of the very worst parts of New York, known as Mulberry Bend, a veritable network of alleys which gave hiding to misery and crime untold, was bought by the city, the buildings torn down, and the spot converted into a public park.

Several years later, when Roosevelt was President, he asked Mr. Riis to investigate the conditions of streets and alleys in Washington. It developed that within three squares of the Capitol there was a system of alleys honeycombing a single block where a thousand people were crowded together under conditions that made a hotbed of misery, crime, and disease. The good citizens of the National Capital, who had read with horror about the evils of New York and Chicago, were rudely shaken out of their self-complacency. That square is now one of Washington's parks.

Jacob Riis early learned the power of facts. His training as a reporter taught him that. He was also willing to work early and late, when the need arose, to gather them. At one time when there was a cholera scare in New York, he happened to look over the Health Department analysis of the water from the Croton River, and noticed that it was said to contain 'a trace of nitrites.'

"What does that mean?" he asked of the chemist.

The reply was more learned than enlightening. The reporter was not satisfied. He carried his inquiry farther and discovered that 'nitrites' meant that the water had been contaminated by sewage from towns above New York. Riis then took his camera and explored not only the Croton River to its source, but also every stream that emptied into it, taking pictures that proved in the most convincing way the dangers of the city. As a result, money was appropriated to buy a strip of land along the streams, wide enough to protect the people's water-supply.

Another great work that Jacob Riis was enabled to carry through had its beginnings in that stormy chapter of his life when he found himself a vagrant among vagrants. He learned at first hand what the police lodging-houses for the homeless were like. At that time this charity was left in the hands of the police, who had neither the ability nor the desire to handle these cases wisely and humanely and to meet the problems of helping people to help themselves.

Jacob Riis worked shoulder to shoulder with Theodore Roosevelt, who was then police commissioner of New York, to make the organized charity of the city an intelligent agency for relieving suffering and putting on their feet again those who were, for some reason, 'down and out.' Many were brought back to wholesome living through the realization that they had 'neighbours' who cared.

In the same way he worked for parks and playgrounds for the children. He saw that the city spoils much good human material.

"We talk a great deal about city toughs," he says in his autobiography. "In nine cases out of ten they are lads of normal impulses whose possibilities have all been smothered by the slum. With better opportunities they might have been heroes."

Many honours came to Jacob Riis. He was known as a 'boss reporter'; his books gave him a nation-wide fame; the King of Denmark sent him the Crusaders' Cross, the greatest honour his native land could bestow; President Roosevelt called him the 'most useful American' of his day. But I think what meant more to him than any or all of these things was the real affection of his many 'neighbours,' especially the children.

Many times he gathered together boys and girls from the streets to enjoy a day with him in the country.

"This will help until we can give them trees and grass in their slum," he would say, "and then there will be no slum." His eyes grew very tender as he added, "No, there will be no slum; it will be a true City Beautiful – and the fairest blossoms there will be the children."

Riis called the story of his life, 'The Making of an American.' While his life was in the making he helped to make many others. He was in truth a maker of Americans.

Do you not think that he lived a life as truly adventurous as the vikings of old – this viking of our own day? They lived for deeds of daring and plunder; he lived for deeds every whit as brave – and for service.

A Child of the Orient

Demetra Vaka

Chapter XX: In the Wake of Columbus

THIS NIGHT OF TERRORS proved my last adventure in Turkey. Soon afterwards events began to force me to feel that in order to live my own life, as seemed right to me, I must flee from all I knew and loved to an unknown, alien land. It is a hard fate: it involves sacrifices and brings heartaches. After all, what gives to life sweetness and charm is the orderliness with which one develops. To grow on the home soil, and quietly to reach full bloom there, gives poise to one's life. It may be argued that this orderly growth rarely produces great and dazzling results; still it is more worth while. People with restless dispositions, people to whom constant transplanting seems necessary, even if they attain great development, are rather to be pitied than to be envied; and, when the transplanting produces only mediocre results, there is nothing to mitigate the pity.

By nature I was a social revolutionist, and I liked neither the attitude of the men towards the women nor of the women towards life, among the people of my race. I have learned better since, and know now that social laws exist because society has found them to be wise, and that little madcaps like me are better off if they respect them. But at that time I had more daring than wisdom, and longed to go where people lived their lives both with more freedom and with more intensity. Moreover, I wanted to 'do something' – like so many feather-brained girls all the world over – just what, I did not know, for I had no especial talents.

With a fairly accurate idea of my own worth, I knew that I was intelligent, but I was fully aware that I was the possessor of no gifts that would place me among the privileged few and outside the ranks of ordinary mortals. Brought up on books and nourished on dreams, I had a poor preparation with which to fight the battle of life, particularly in a foreign country, where everything was different, and difficult both to grasp and to manipulate. The only factor in my favour was my Greek blood, synonymous with money-making ability; for we Greeks have always been merchants, even when we wore *chlamidas* and reclined in the *agora*, declaiming odes to the gods, talking philosophy, or speculating on the immortality of our souls.

Knowing my race as I did, and aware that it succeeded in making money in climates and under conditions where other races failed, I was confident that I could earn my own living. There is something in us which justifies the tale of Prometheus. Even before I was fifteen I was quietly planning to leave Turkey, to go and seek what fortunes awaited me in new and strange lands – a course which my imagination painted very attractively. America beckoned to me more than any other country, perhaps because I thought there were no classes there, and that every one met on an equal footing and worked out his own salvation.

We are all the possessors of two kinds of knowledge: one absorbed from experience, books, and hearsay, which we call facts; the other, a knowledge that comes to us through our own immortal selves. This last it is impossible to analyse, since it partakes of the unseen and the untranslatable. We feel it, that is all. This subconscious knowledge – to which many of us attach far greater importance than we do to cold facts – is usually as remote as a distant sound, though at times it may be so clear as to be almost palpable. This secondary knowledge told me I must go to America – America that rose so luminous, so full of hope and promise on the never-ending horizon of my young life.

I had not the remotest idea of how my dream of going there could be realized; but I believe that if one keeps on dreaming a dream hard enough, it will eventually become a reality. And so did mine. A Greek I knew was appointed consul to New York, and was shortly to sail with his family to the United States. I had a secret conference with them, offering to accompany them as an unpaid governess, and to stay with them as long as they stayed in America. They accepted my offer.

This I regarded merely as a means of getting away from home. After I left them my real career would begin. That I was prepared for no particular vocation, that I did not even know a single word of English, disconcerted me not at all. Accustomed to having my own way, I was convinced that the supreme right of every person was to lead his life as he chose. I do not think so any longer. On the contrary, I believe that the supreme duty of every individual is to consider the greatest good of the greatest number. That I succeeded in my rash enterprize is more due to the kindness of Providence than to any personal worth of mine.

Of America actually I knew almost nothing, and what I thought I knew was all topsy-turvy. The story of Pocohontas and Captain John Smith had fallen into my hands when I was twelve years old. I wept over it and surmised that the great continent beyond the seas was peopled by the descendents of Indian princesses and adventurers. My second piece of information was gathered from a French novel, I believe, in which a black sheep was referred to as having gone to America 'where all black sheep gravitate.' And my third source of information was *Uncle Tom's Cabin*, the book which makes European children form a distorted idea of the American people, and sentimentalize over a race hardly worth it.

This made up my encyclopædia of American facts. That all those who emigrated thither succeeded easily, and amassed untold wealth, I ascribed to the fact that being Europeans they were vastly superior to the Americans, who at best were only half-breeds. You who read this may think that I was singularly ignorant; yet I can assure you that to-day I meet many people on my travels in Europe who are not only as ignorant as I was, but who have even lower ideas about the Americans.

We landed in New York in winter, and went directly to Hotel Martin, at that time still in its old site near Washington Square.

What did I think of America at first? This indeed is the most difficult question to answer. I was so puzzled that I remained without thoughts. To begin with, the people, for half-breeds, were extremely presentable. The redskin ancestral side was quite obliterated. Then the houses, the streets, the whole appearance of the city was on a par with Paris. What appalled us all was the dearness of things. I remember the day when we gave a Greek street vendor one cent for some fruit, and he handed us one little apple. "Only this for a cent?" we cried; and so indignant were we that we reclaimed our cent and returned him his apple.

We managed to do ridiculous things daily. At our first evening meal at the hotel, a tall glass vase stood in the middle of the table filled with such strange flowers as we had never seen before. They were pale greenish white, with streaks of yellow. We thought it very kind of the proprietor to furnish them for us, and each of us took one and fastened it on our dress.

The waiters glanced at us in surprise, but it was nothing to the sensation we created when we rose to go out of the dining-room. People nudged each other and stared at us. Of the French maid who came to unfasten my dress I asked:

"Do we seem very foreign?"

"No, indeed," she replied, "I should have taken Mademoiselle for a French girl, except that she wears her hair loose on her back."

"Then why did the people in the dining-room stare at us so?"

She suppressed a giggle. "Yes, I know, Mademoiselle, I have heard about it. It is the flower Mademoiselle is wearing."

"What is the matter with it?"

"Nothing, except that it is not a flower – it is a vegetable, called celery."

I do not know how many more absurd things we did during the three weeks we stayed at the hotel. Then we took a flat near Riverside Drive the rent of which staggered us, but when it came to the servants we almost wept. Four pounds a month to slovenly girls who were only half-trained, who made a noise when they walked, and who slammed the doors every other minute.

I was anxious to start my English studies at once, for as yet I could only say "All right," a phrase which everybody used, *à propos* of nothing, it seemed to me. I went to the Normal College to inquire about the conditions for entering it. The president received me. He was the first American man with whom I talked. He had lovely white hair, and a kind, fatherly face. He spoke no French, and sent for a student who did; and when she translated to him what I wanted, he explained that I could not enter college until I knew English and could pass my entrance examinations. The young girl who translated offered to teach me English for a sum, which, to me, coming from the East and cheap labour and possessor of small financial resources, seemed preposterous. Still I liked her eyes: they were dark blue, and green, and grey, all at once, with long and pretty lashes; so I accepted her offer. That very evening she gave me my first lesson, and proposed that instead of paying her I should improve her French in exchange for her English lessons, an offer that I was very glad to accept. She was my first American friend, and remains among my very best.

We had only been a few months in New York when my Greek friends were obliged to return to Turkey. I resolved to remain behind. I must confess at once that I did so out of pride alone. New York had frightened me more than the capture by the brigands, the earthquake, and an Armenian massacre in which I once found myself, all put together. Yet to go back was to admit that I had failed, that the world had beaten me, and after only a very few months.

I had just sixty dollars, and my courage – robbed a little of its effervescence. Since I had had only two English lessons a week, and no practice whatever, because all the people we met spoke French to us, my vocabulary was very limited, but I managed to get about pretty well. Once in a shop I asked for "half past three sho-es," and obtained them without trouble.

Before my friends left New York for Constantinople they gave me a certificate saying that I was qualified to be a governess – for which I was really as qualified as to drive an engine. Since I had had no chance to modify my opinion about the origin of Americans, I still looked upon them as inferiors, and considered myself quite good enough for them. Taking a small room in a small hotel, I applied to an agency for a position. It did not prove quite so easy to obtain as I had thought it would. In the first place, I was not French born; secondly, I was ridiculously young looking; and then of course I had to admit that I had been a governess in a way only.

How amusing it was to be presented as a governess! Most of the ladies spoke such comical French, and asked questions which I thought even funnier than their French. I could have found a place at once, if I had been willing to accept twenty-five dollars a month as a nursery governess, and eat with the servants.

Meanwhile most of my money was spent, and to economize I walked miles and miles rather than take the street cars; and then came the time when all my money was gone, and I was in arrears with my rent, and had no money for food.

I do not wish anyone to suppose that I was miserable. On the contrary, I liked it: I was at last living the life I had so often read about. I was one of the great mass of toilers of the earth, whom in my ignorance I held far superior to the better classes. I had romantic notions about being a working girl, and my imagination was a fairy's wand which transfigured everything. Besides, I was a heroine to myself. Those who have even for one short hour been heroes to themselves can understand the exaltation in which I lived, and can share with me in the glory of those days.

At this time I happened to apply to the Greek newspaper for a position, not because I thought there was any chance for me, but because it was so interesting to apply for work. Every time I applied to a new person, it was a new adventure; and I had applied so many times, and been rejected so often, that I did not mind it any more. I knew that if the worst came to the worst I could for a time become a servant. I was well trained in domestic work and could cook pretty well; for, when we Greek girls are not at school, a competent person is engaged to come into the house and train us systematically in all branches of housekeeping. The idea of becoming a servant, of entering an American home and obtaining a nearer view of my half-breeds within their own walls appealed to me. What I objected to, was being hired as a governess and treated as a servant.

To my surprise, the Greek newspaper, a weekly then, took me at once on its staff. I was delirious with joy, not so much because I was going to earn money as at the idea of working on a newspaper. It seemed so glorious, so at the top of everything.

Just at this time – at the agency, I think – I heard of a French home, far out on the West Side in the vicinity of Twenty-third Street, where French working girls stayed while seeking positions. I went there, and made arrangements to stay a few months; and from there sought my hotel proprietor. I told him that the Greek newspaper had engaged me at a salary which did not permit me to live at his hotel, and what was more that I could not at the moment pay him what I owed him – three weeks' rent, I believe – but that I would pay him as soon as possible. He was very nice about the matter, and said it would be "all right," though I doubt very much if he ever expected to see his money.

My work on the newspaper was hard and tedious. I am a bad speller, and can write a word in five different ways on one page without discovering it. On account of this failing I was often taken to task by the editor in chief, who was the proprietor, and had some black moments over it, until one of the type-setters quietly suggested to me that I should pass over my stuff to him and he would correct the spelling before the editor saw it, which I did ever after, and was very thankful to him.

My newspaper work was not only of long, long hours, but it absorbed all my time, as well as my energy and strength, and shortly after undertaking it I had to give up my English studies. I was too worn out physically and mentally to continue them.

It was not so bad during the cold weather, but suddenly, without the slightest warning, the cold gave place to burning heat. There was no spring. That lovely transition period in which all is soft, both in air and in colours, did not exist in that American year. The summer burst fiercely over the city and scorched it in a few days. It grilled the pavements; it grilled the houses; it multiplied and magnified the noises of horse and elevated cars, of street-hawkers and yelling children – and these noises in turn seemed to accentuate the heat. Every morning I took the Sixth Avenue elevated train at Twenty-Third Street, and all the way to the Battery there was hardly a tree or a blade of grass to meet the tired eye, to soothe the over-wrought nerves, nothing but ugly buildings – ugly and dirty. And as the train whizzed along, the glimpses I had of the people inside these buildings were even more disheartening than the ugliness and dirtiness of the buildings themselves.

And this was my America, the country of the promised land. It seemed to me then as if my golden dream had turned into a hideous nightmare of fact – a nightmare which threatened to engulf me and cast me into that unrecognizable mass continually forming by the failures of life. That I did not sink down into it was, because, in spite of the hideous reality, I remained a dreamer, and those who live in dreams are rarely quelled by reality. In that fearful, hot, New York summer I began to dream another dream which made the heat more tolerable. Daily, as the elevated train noised its way to the Battery, I imagined myself having succeeded, having amassed wealth, from which I made gifts to the thousands of toilers in that scorched city. I planted trees for them everywhere, along the streets, along the avenues; and wherever there was a little vacant plot of land I converted it into a tiny park. There I saw the people sitting under the shade of my trees, and so real did my dream become that I began actually to live it, and suffered less from the heat myself; for I was constantly on the look out for new spots where I could plant more trees.

At luncheon time I used to go out for a little stroll on the Battery, and there I used to see immigrant women, dressed partially in their native costumes, and surrounded by numbers of their little ones, jabbering in their own lingo. One day I sat down near a solitary woman, unmistakably an Italian peasant.

"Hot to-day, isn't it?" I said in her own tongue.

From the sea, slowly she raised her eyes to me. I smiled at her, but received no response.

"You look very tired," I said, "and so am I. I suppose you are thinking of your own country, of fields and trees, are you not?"

"How did you know?" she demanded sullenly.

"Because I do the same myself. I also am an immigrant. You look across the sea with the same yearning in your eyes as is in my heart, for we are both homesick."

She was no longer cross, after this, and because another woman was sharing in her misery that misery became lighter. She began to tell me of her sorrow. She had buried her second baby in two weeks, because of the heat. Her lap was now empty. She spat viciously on the water. "That is what I have in my heart for America – that!" and again she spat.

I volunteered an account of my own disillusionment about America; and there we sat at the edge of the Battery, two sad immigrants, telling each other of the beauties we had left behind, and of the difficulties we had to fight in the present. If I had then known a little of the history of America, I might have told her of the first immigrants, of how much they had to suffer and endure, and for what the present Thanksgiving Day stood. I might have told her more of their hardships, and how they had had to plant corn on the graves of their dear ones, so that the Indians should not find out how many of them had died – but I was as ignorant as she, and we only knew of our own homesickness and misery.

The heat had started early in May, and it kept on getting hotter and hotter, with only sudden and savage thunderstorms, which passed over the city like outraged spirits, and deluged it for a few hours with rain that became steam as soon as it touched the scorched pavements. Occasionally some fresh wind would penetrate into the city, as if bent on missionary work; but it was soon conquered by the demons of heat. It grew hotter and hotter. It seemed as if the city would perish in its own heat – and then came the month of August!

I shall never forget that August. Even now, wherever I am during that month, my spirit goes back to that desolate city to share in the sufferings of its poor people who have to work long hours in hot offices, and then at night try to sleep in small, still hotter rooms, with the fiendish noise of the city outside. And it is then again that my dream comes back to me, to give trees all along the streets and all along the avenues, and shady open spaces to breathe in.

The complete and unabridged text is available online, from flametreepublishing.com/extras

The Fat of the Land

Anzia Yezierska

IN AN AIR-SHAFT SO NARROW that you could touch the next wall with your bare hands, Hanneh Breineh leaned out and knocked on her neighbour's window.

"Can you loan me your wash-boiler for the clothes?" she called.

Mrs. Pelz threw up the sash.

"The boiler? What's the matter with yours again? Didn't you tell me you had it fixed already last week?"

"A black year on him, the robber, the way he fixed it! If you have no luck in this world, then it's better not to live. There I spent out fifteen cents to stop up one hole, and it runs out another. How I ate out my gall bargaining with him he should let it down to fifteen cents! He wanted yet a quarter, the swindler. *Gottuniu*! my bitter heart on him for every penny he took from me for nothing!"

"You got to watch all those swindlers, or they'll steal the whites out of your eyes," admonished Mrs. Pelz. "You should have tried out your boiler before you paid him. Wait a minute till I empty out my dirty clothes in a pillow-case; then I'll hand it to you."

Mrs. Pelz returned with the boiler and tried to hand it across to Hanneh Breineh, but the soap-box refrigerator on the window-sill was in the way.

"You got to come in for the boiler yourself," said Mrs. Pelz.

"Wait only till I tie my Sammy on to the high-chair he shouldn't fall on me again. He's so wild that ropes won't hold him."

Hanneh Breineh tied the child in the chair, stuck a pacifier in his mouth, and went in to her neighbour. As she took the boiler Mrs. Pelz said:

"Do you know Mrs. Melker ordered fifty pounds of chicken for her daughter's wedding? And such grand chickens! Shining like gold! My heart melted in me just looking at the flowing fatness of those chickens."

Hanneh Breineh smacked her thin, dry lips, a hungry gleam in her sunken eyes.

"Fifty pounds!" she gasped. "It ain't possible. How do you know?"

"I heard her with my own ears. I saw them with my own eyes. And she said she will chop up the chicken livers with onions and eggs for an appetizer, and then she will buy twenty-five pounds of fish, and cook it sweet and sour with raisins, and she said she will bake all her strudels on pure chicken fat."

"Some people work themselves up in the world," sighed Hanneh Breineh. "For them is America flowing with milk and honey. In Savel Mrs. Melker used to get shriveled up from hunger. She and her children used to live on potato peelings and crusts of dry bread picked out from the barrels; and in America she lives to eat chicken, and apple strudels soaking in fat."

"The world is a wheel always turning," philosophized Mrs. Pelz. "Those who were high go down low, and those who've been low go up higher. Who will believe me here in America that in Poland I was a cook in a banker's house? I handled ducks and geese every day. I used to bake coffee-cake with cream so thick you could cut it with a knife."

"And do you think I was a nobody in Poland?" broke in Hanneh Breineh, tears welling in her eyes as the memories of her past rushed over her. "But what's the use of talking? In America money is everything. Who cares who my father or grandfather was in Poland? Without money I'm a living dead one. My head dries out worrying how to get for the children the eating a penny cheaper."

Mrs. Pelz wagged her head, a gnawing envy contracting her features.

"Mrs. Melker had it good from the day she came," she said begrudgingly. "Right away she sent all her children to the factory, and she began to cook meat for dinner every day. She and her children have eggs and buttered rolls for breakfast each morning like millionaires."

A sudden fall and a baby's scream, and the boiler dropped from Hanneh Breineh's hands as she rushed into her kitchen, Mrs. Pelz after her. They found the high-chair turned on top of the baby.

"*Gevalt*! Save me! Run for a doctor!" cried Hanneh Breineh as she dragged the child from under the high-chair. "He's killed! He's killed! My only child! My precious lamb!" she shrieked as she ran back and forth with the screaming infant.

Mrs. Pelz snatched little Sammy from the mother's hands.

"*Meshugneh*! what are you running around like a crazy, frightening the child? Let me see. Let me tend to him. He ain't killed yet." She hastened to the sink to wash the child's face, and discovered a swelling lump on his forehead. "Have you a quarter in your house?" she asked.

"Yes, I got one," replied Hanneh Breineh, climbing on a chair. "I got to keep it on a high shelf where the children can't get it."

Mrs. Pelz seized the quarter Hanneh Breineh handed down to her.

"Now pull your left eyelid three times while I'm pressing the quarter, and you will see the swelling go down."

Hanneh Breineh took the child again in her arms, shaking and cooing over it and caressing it.

"Ah-ah-ah, Sammy! Ah-ah-ah-ah, little lamb! Ah-ah-ah, little bird! Ah-ah-ah-ah, precious heart! Oh, you saved my life; I thought he was killed," gasped Hanneh Breineh, turning to Mrs. Pelz. "*Oi-i*!" she sighed, "a mother's heart! always in fear over her children. The minute anything happens to them all life goes out of me. I lose my head and I don't know where I am any more."

"No wonder the child fell," admonished Mrs. Pelz. "You should have a red ribbon or red beads on his neck to keep away the evil eye. Wait. I got something in my machine-drawer."

Mrs. Pelz returned, bringing the boiler and a red string, which she tied about the child's neck while the mother proceeded to fill the boiler.

A little later Hanneh Breineh again came into Mrs. Pelz's kitchen, holding Sammy in one arm and in the other an apron full of potatoes. Putting the child down on the floor, she seated herself on the unmade kitchen-bed and began to peel the potatoes in her apron.

"Woe to me!" sobbed Hanneh Breineh. "To my bitter luck there ain't no end. With all my other troubles, the stove got broke'. I lighted the fire to boil the clothes, and it's to get choked with smoke. I paid rent only a week ago, and the agent don't want to fix it. A thunder should strike him! He only comes for the rent, and if anything has to be fixed, then he don't want to hear nothing."

"Why comes it to me so hard?" went on Hanneh Breineh, the tears streaming down her cheeks. "I can't stand it no more. I came into you for a minute to run away from my troubles. It's only when I sit myself down to peel potatoes or nurse the baby that I take time to draw a breath, and beg only for death."

Mrs. Pelz, accustomed to Hanneh Breineh's bitter outbursts, continued her scrubbing.

"*Ut*!" exclaimed Hanneh Breineh, irritated at her neighbour's silence, "what are you tearing up the world with your cleaning? What's the use to clean up when everything only gets dirty again?"

"I got to shine up my house for the holidays."

"You've got it so good nothing lays on your mind but to clean your house. Look on this little blood-sucker," said Hanneh Breineh, pointing to the wizened child, made prematurely solemn from starvation and neglect. "Could anybody keep that brat clean? I wash him one minute, and he is dirty the minute after." Little Sammy grew frightened and began to cry. "Shut up!" ordered the mother, picking up the child to nurse it again. "Can't you see me take a rest for a minute?"

The hungry child began to cry at the top of its weakened lungs.

"*Na, na*, you glutton." Hanneh Breineh took out a dirty pacifier from her pocket and stuffed it into the baby's mouth. The grave, pasty-faced infant shrank into a panic of fear, and chewed the nipple nervously, clinging to it with both his thin little hands.

"For what did I need yet the sixth one?" groaned Hanneh Breineh, turning to Mrs. Pelz. "Wasn't it enough five mouths to feed? If I didn't have this child on my neck, I could turn myself around and earn a few cents." She wrung her hands in a passion of despair. "*Gottuniu*! the earth should only take it before it grows up!"

"Pshaw! Pshaw!" reproved Mrs. Pelz. "Pity yourself on the child. Let it grow up already so long as it is here. See how frightened it looks on you." Mrs. Pelz took the child in her arms and petted it. "The poor little lamb! What did it done you should hate it so?"

Hanneh Breineh pushed Mrs. Pelz away from her.

"To whom can I open the wounds of my heart?" she moaned. "Nobody has pity on me. You don't believe me, nobody believes me until I'll fall down like a horse in the middle of the street. *Oi weh*! mine life is so black for my eyes. Some mothers got luck. A child gets run over by a car, some fall from a window, some burn themselves up with a match, some get choked with diphtheria; but no death takes mine away."

"God from the world! stop cursing!" admonished Mrs. Pelz. "What do you want from the poor children? Is it their fault that their father makes small wages? Why do you let it all out on them?" Mrs. Pelz sat down beside Hanneh Breineh. "Wait only till your children get old enough to go to the shop and earn money," she consoled. "Push only through those few years while they are yet small; your sun will begin to shine, you will live on the fat of the land, when they begin to bring you in the wages each week."

Hanneh Breineh refused to be comforted.

"Till they are old enough to go to the shop and earn money they'll eat the head off my bones," she wailed. "If you only knew the fights I got by each meal. Maybe I gave Abe a bigger piece of bread than Fanny. Maybe Fanny got a little more soup in her plate than Jake. Eating is dearer than diamonds. Potatoes went up a cent on a pound, and milk is only for millionaires. And once a week, when I buy a little meat for the Sabbath, the butcher weighs it for me like gold, with all the bones in it. When I come to lay the meat out on a plate and divide it up, there ain't nothing to it but bones. Before, he used to throw me in a piece of fat extra or a piece of lung, but now you got to pay for everything, even for a bone to the soup."

"Never mind; you'll yet come out from all your troubles. Just as soon as your children get old enough to get their working papers the more children you got, the more money you'll have."

"Why should I fool myself with the false shine of hope? Don't I know it's already my black luck not to have it good in this world? Do you think American children will right away give everything they earn to their mother?"

"I know what is with you the matter," said Mrs. Pelz. "You didn't eat yet to-day. When it is empty in the stomach, the whole world looks black. Come, only let me give you something good to taste in the mouth; that will freshen you up." Mrs. Pelz went to the cupboard and brought out the saucepan of *gefülte* fish that she had cooked for dinner and placed it on the table in front of Hanneh Breineh. "Give a taste my fish," she said, taking one slice on a spoon, and handing it to Hanneh Breineh with a piece of bread. "I wouldn't give it to you on a plate because I just cleaned out my house, and I don't want to dirty up my dishes."

"What, am I a stranger you should have to serve me on a plate yet!" cried Hanneh Breineh, snatching the fish in her trembling fingers.

"*Oi weh*! how it melts through all the bones!" she exclaimed, brightening as she ate. "May it be for good luck to us all!" she exulted, waving aloft the last precious bite.

Mrs. Pelz was so flattered that she even ladled up a spoonful of gravy.

"There is a bit of onion and carrot in it," she said as she handed it to her neighbour.

Hanneh Breineh sipped the gravy drop by drop, like a connoisseur sipping wine.

"Ah-h-h! a taste of that gravy lifts me up to heaven!" As she disposed leisurely of the slice of onion and carrot she relaxed and expanded and even grew jovial. "Let us wish all our troubles on the Russian Czar! Let him bust with our worries for rent! Let him get shriveled with our hunger for bread! Let his eyes dry out of his head looking for work!"

"Pshaw! I'm forgetting from everything," she exclaimed, jumping up. "It must be eleven or soon twelve, and my children will be right away out of school and fall on me like a pack of wild wolves. I better quick run to the market and see what cheaper I can get for a quarter."

Because of the lateness of her coming, the stale bread at the nearest bake-shop was sold out, and Hanneh Breineh had to trudge from shop to shop in search of the usual bargain, and spent nearly an hour to save two cents.

In the meantime the children returned from school, and, finding the door locked, climbed through the fire-escape, and entered the house through the window. Seeing nothing on the table, they rushed to the stove. Abe pulled a steaming potato out of the boiling pot, and so scalded his fingers that the potato fell to the floor; whereupon the three others pounced on it.

"It was my potato," cried Abe, blowing his burned fingers, while with the other hand and his foot he cuffed and kicked the three who were struggling on the floor. A wild fight ensued, and the potato was smashed under Abe's foot amid shouts and screams. Hanneh Breineh, on the stairs, heard the noise of her famished brood, and topped their cries with curses and invectives.

"They are here already, the savages! They are here already to shorten my life! They heard you all over the hall, in all the houses around!"

The children, disregarding her words, pounced on her market-basket, shouting ravenously: "Mama, I'm hungry! What more do you got to eat?"

They tore the bread and herring out of Hanneh Breineh's basket and devoured it in starved savagery, clamouring for more.

"Murderers!" screamed Hanneh Breineh, goaded beyond endurance. "What are you tearing from me my flesh? From where should I steal to give you more? Here I had already a pot of potatoes and a whole loaf of bread and two herrings, and you swallowed it down in the wink of an eye. I have to have Rockefeller's millions to fill your stomachs."

All at once Hanneh Breineh became aware that Benny was missing. "*Oi weh*!" she burst out, wringing her hands in a new wave of woe, "where is Benny? Didn't he come home yet from school?"

She ran out into the hall, opened the grime-coated window, and looked up and down the street; but Benny was nowhere in sight.

"Abe, Jake, Fanny, quick, find Benny!" entreated Hanneh Breineh as she rushed back into the kitchen. But the children, anxious to snatch a few minutes' play before the school-call, dodged past her and hurried out.

With the baby on her arm, Hanneh Breineh hastened to the kindergarten.

"Why are you keeping Benny here so long?" she shouted at the teacher as she flung open the door. "If you had my bitter heart, you would send him home long ago and not wait till I got to come for him."

The teacher turned calmly and consulted her record-cards.

"Benny Safron? He wasn't present this morning."

"Not here?" shrieked Hanneh Breineh. "I pushed him out myself he should go. The children didn't want to take him, and I had no time. Woe is me! Where is my child?" She began pulling her hair and beating her breast as she ran into the street.

Mrs. Pelz was busy at a push-cart, picking over some spotted apples, when she heard the clamour of an approaching crowd. A block off she recognized Hanneh Breineh, her hair disheveled, her clothes awry, running toward her with her yelling baby in her arms, the crowd following.

"Friend mine," cried Hanneh Breineh, falling on Mrs. Pelz's neck, "I lost my Benny, the best child of all my children." Tears streamed down her red, swollen eyes as she sobbed. "Benny! mine heart, mine life! *Oi-i*!"

Mrs. Pelz took the frightened baby out of the mother's arms.

"Still yourself a little! See how you're frightening your child."

"Woe to me! Where is my Benny? Maybe he's killed already by a car. Maybe he fainted away from hunger. He didn't eat nothing all day long. *Gottuniu*! pity yourself on me!"

She lifted her hands full of tragic entreaty.

"People, my child! Get me my child! I'll go crazy out of my head! Get me my child, or I'll take poison before your eyes!"

"Still yourself a little!" pleaded Mrs. Pelz.

"Talk not to me!" cried Hanneh Breineh, wringing her hands. "You're having all your children. I lost mine. Every good luck comes to other people. But I didn't live yet to see a good day in my life. Mine only joy, mine Benny, is lost away from me."

The crowd followed Hanneh Breineh as she wailed through the streets, leaning on Mrs. Pelz. By the time she returned to her house the children were back from school; but seeing that Benny was not there, she chased them out in the street, crying:

"Out of here, you robbers, gluttons! Go find Benny!" Hanneh Breineh crumpled into a chair in utter prostration. "*Oi weh*! he's lost! Mine life; my little bird; mine only joy! How many nights I spent nursing him when he had the measles! And all that I suffered for weeks and months when he had the whooping-cough! How the eyes went out of my head till I learned him how to walk, till I learned him how to talk! And such a smart child! If I lost all the others, it wouldn't tear me so by the heart."

She worked herself up into such a hysteria, crying, and tearing her hair, and hitting her head with her knuckles, that at last she fell into a faint. It took some time before Mrs. Pelz, with the aid of neighbours, revived her.

"Benny, mine angel!" she moaned as she opened her eyes.

Just then a policeman came in with the lost Benny.

"*Na, na*, here you got him already!" said Mrs. Pelz

"Why did you carry on so for nothing? Why did you tear up the world like a crazy?"

The child's face was streaked with tears as he cowered, frightened and forlorn. Hanneh Breineh sprang toward him, slapping his cheeks, boxing his ears, before the neighbours could rescue him from her.

"Woe on your head!" cried the mother. "Where did you lost yourself? Ain't I got enough worries on my head than to go around looking for you? I didn't have yet a minute's peace from that child since he was born."

"See a crazy mother!" remonstrated Mrs. Pelz, rescuing Benny from another beating. "Such a mouth! With one breath she blesses him when he is lost, and with the other breath she curses him when he is found."

Hanneh Breineh took from the window-sill a piece of herring covered with swarming flies, and putting it on a slice of dry bread, she filled a cup of tea that had been stewing all day, and dragged Benny over to the table to eat.

But the child, choking with tears, was unable to touch the food.

"Go eat!" commanded Hanneh Breineh. "Eat and choke yourself eating!"

"Maybe she won't remember me no more. Maybe the servant won't let me in," thought Mrs. Pelz as she walked by the brownstone house on Eighty-fourth Street where she had been told Hanneh Breineh now lived. At last she summoned up enough courage to climb the steps. She was all out of breath as she rang the bell with trembling fingers. "*Oi weh*! even the outside smells riches and plenty! Such curtains! And shades on all windows like by millionaires! Twenty years ago she used to eat from the pot to the hand, and now she lives in such a palace."

A whiff of steam-heated warmth swept over Mrs. Pelz as the door opened, and she saw her old friend of the tenements dressed in silk and diamonds like a being from another world.

"Mrs. Pelz, is it you!" cried Hanneh Breineh, overjoyed at the sight of her former neighbour. "Come right in. Since when are you back in New York?"

"We came last week," mumbled Mrs. Pelz as she was led into a richly carpeted reception-room.

"Make yourself comfortable. Take off your shawl," urged Hanneh Breineh.

But Mrs. Pelz only drew her shawl more tightly around her, a keen sense of her poverty gripping her as she gazed, abashed by the luxurious wealth that shone from every corner.

"This shawl covers up my rags," she said, trying to hide her shabby sweater.

"I'll tell you what; come right into the kitchen," suggested Hanneh Breineh. "The servant is away for this afternoon, and we can feel more comfortable there. I can breathe like a free person in my kitchen when the girl has her day out."

Mrs. Pelz glanced about her in an excited daze. Never in her life had she seen anything so wonderful as a white tiled kitchen, with its glistening porcelain sink and the aluminum pots and pans that shone like silver.

"Where are you staying now?" asked Hanneh Breineh as she pinned an apron over her silk dress.

"I moved back to Delancey Street, where we used to live," replied Mrs. Pelz as she seated herself cautiously in a white enameled chair.

"*Oi weh*! what grand times we had in that old house when we were neighbours!" sighed Hanneh Breineh, looking at her old friend with misty eyes.

"You still think on Delancey Street? Haven't you more high-class neighbours up-town here?"

"A good neighbour is not to be found every day," deplored Hanneh Breineh. "Up-town here, where each lives in his own house, nobody cares if the person next door is dying or going crazy from loneliness. It ain't anything like we used to have it in Delancey Street, when we could walk into one another's rooms without knocking, and borrow a pinch of salt or a pot to cook in."

Hanneh Breineh went over to the pantry-shelf.

"We are going to have a bite right here on the kitchen-table like on Delancey Street. So long there's no servant to watch us we can eat what we please."

"*Oi*! how it waters my mouth with appetite, the smell of the herring and onion!" chuckled Mrs. Pelz, sniffing the welcome odours with greedy pleasure.

Hanneh Breineh pulled a dish-towel from the rack and threw one end of it to Mrs. Pelz.

"So long there's no servant around, we can use it together for a napkin. It's dirty, anyhow. How it freshens up my heart to see you!" she rejoiced as she poured out her tea into a saucer. "If you would only know how I used to beg my daughter to write for me a letter to you; but these American children, what is to them a mother's feelings?"

"What are you talking!" cried Mrs. Pelz. "The whole world rings with you and your children. Everybody is envying you. Tell me how began your luck?"

"You heard how my husband died with consumption," replied Hanneh Breineh. "The five-hundred-dollars lodge money gave me the first lift in life, and I opened a little grocery store. Then my son Abe married himself to a girl with a thousand dollars. That started him in business, and now he has the biggest shirt-waist factory on West Twenty-ninth Street."

"Yes, I heard your son had a factory." Mrs. Pelz hesitated and stammered; "I'll tell you the truth. What I came to ask you – I thought maybe you would beg your son Abe if he would give my husband a job."

"Why not?" said Hanneh Breineh. "He keeps more than five hundred hands. I'll ask him he should take in Mr. Pelz."

"Long years on you, Hanneh Breineh! You'll save my life if you could only help my husband get work."

"Of course my son will help him. All my children like to do good. My daughter Fanny is a milliner on Fifth Avenue, and she takes in the poorest girls in her shop and even pays them sometimes while they learn the trade." Hanneh Breineh's face lit up, and her chest filled with pride as she enumerated the successes of her children.

"And my son Benny he wrote a play on Broadway and he gave away more than a hundred free tickets for the first night."

"Benny? The one who used to get lost from home all the time? You always did love that child more than all the rest. And what is Sammy your baby doing?"

"He ain't a baby no longer. He goes to college and quarterbacks the football team. They can't get along without him.

"And my son Jake, I nearly forgot him. He began collecting rent in Delancey Street, and now he is boss of renting the swellest apartment-houses on Riverside Drive."

"What did I tell you? In America children are like money in the bank," purred Mrs. Pelz as she pinched and patted Hanneh Breineh's silk sleeve. "*Oi weh*! how it shines from you! You ought to kiss the air and dance for joy and happiness. It is such a bitter frost outside; a pail of coal is so dear, and you got it so warm with steam-heat. I had to pawn my feather-bed to have enough for the rent, and you are rolling in money."

"Yes, I got it good in some ways, but money ain't everything," sighed Hanneh Breineh.

"You ain't yet satisfied?"

"But here I got no friends," complained Hanneh Breineh.

"Friends?" queried Mrs. Pelz. "What greater friend is there on earth than the dollar?"

"*Oi*! Mrs. Pelz; if you could only look into my heart! I'm so choked up! You know they say, a cow has a long tongue, but can't talk." Hanneh Breineh shook her head wistfully, and her eyes filmed with inward brooding. "My children give me everything from the best. When I was sick, they got me a nurse by day and one by night. They bought me the best wine. If I asked for dove's milk, they would buy it for me; but – but – I can't talk myself out in their language. They want to make me over for an American lady, and I'm different." Tears cut their way under her eyelids with a pricking pain as she went on: "When I was poor, I was free, and could holler and do what I like in my own house. Here I got to lie still like a mouse under a broom. Between living up to my Fifth Avenue daughter and keeping up with the servants I am like a sinner in the next world that is thrown from one hell to another."

The door-bell rang, and Hanneh Breineh jumped up with a start.

"*Oi weh*! it must be the servant back already!" she exclaimed as she tore off her apron. "*Oi weh*! let's quickly put the dishes together in a dish-pan. If she sees I eat on the kitchen table, she will look on me like the dirt under her feet."

Mrs. Pelz seized her shawl in haste.

"I better run home quick in my rags before your servant sees me."

"I'll speak to Abe about the job," said Hanneh Breineh as she pushed a bill into the hand of Mrs. Pelz, who edged out as the servant entered.

"I'm having fried potato *lotkes* special for you, Benny," said Hanneh Breineh as the children gathered about the table for the family dinner given in honour of Benny's success with his new play. "Do you remember how you used to lick the fingers from them?"

"O Mother!" reproved Fanny. "Anyone hearing you would think we were still in the push-cart district."

"Stop your nagging, Sis, and let ma alone," commanded Benny, patting his mother's arm affectionately. "I'm home only once a month. Let her feed me what she pleases. My stomach is bomb-proof."

"Do I hear that the President is coming to your play?" said Abe as he stuffed a napkin over his diamond-studded shirt-front.

"Why shouldn't he come?" returned Benny. "The critics say it's the greatest antidote for the race hatred created by the war. If you want to know, he is coming to-night; and what's more, our box is next to the President's."

"*Nu*, Mammeh," sallied Jake, "did you ever dream in Delancey Street that we should rub sleeves with the President?"

"I always said that Benny had more head than the rest of you," replied the mother.

As the laughter died away, Jake went on:

"Honour you are getting plenty; but how much *mezummen* does this play bring you? Can I invest any of it in real estate for you?"

"I'm getting ten per cent. royalties of the gross receipts," replied the youthful playwright.

"How much is that?" queried Hanneh Breineh.

"Enough to buy up all your fish markets in Delancey Street," laughed Abe in good-natured raillery at his mother.

Her son's jest cut like a knife-thrust in her heart. She felt her heart ache with the pain that she was shut out from their successes. Each added triumph only widened the gulf. And when she tried to bridge this gulf by asking questions, they only thrust her back upon herself.

"Your fame has even helped me get my hat trade solid with the Four Hundred," put in Fanny. "You bet I let Mrs. Van Suyden know that our box is next to the President's. She said she would drop in to meet you. Of course she let on to me that she hadn't seen the play yet, though my designer said she saw her there on the opening night."

"Oh, Gosh! the toadies!" sneered Benny. "Nothing so sickens you with success as the way people who once shoved you off the sidewalk come crawling to you on their stomachs begging you to dine with them."

"Say, that leading man of yours he's some class," cried Fanny. "That's the man I'm looking for. Will you invite him to supper after the theater?"

The playwright turned to his mother.

"Say, Ma," he said laughingly, "how would you like a real actor for a son-in-law?"

"She should worry," mocked Sam. "She'll be discussing with him the future of the Greek drama. Too bad it doesn't happen to be Warfield, or mother could give him tips on the 'Auctioneer.'"

Jake turned to his mother with a covert grin.

"I guess you'd have no objection if Fanny got next to Benny's leading man. He makes at least fifteen hundred a week. That wouldn't be such a bad addition to the family, would it?"

Again the bantering tone stabbed Hanneh Breineh. Everything in her began to tremble and break loose.

"Why do you ask me?" she cried, throwing her napkin into her plate. "Do I count for a person in this house? If I'll say something, will you even listen to me? What is to me the grandest man that my daughter could pick out? Another enemy in my house! Another person to shame himself from me!" She swept in her children in one glance of despairing anguish as she rose from the table. "What worth is an old mother to American children? The President is coming to-night to the theater, and none of you asked me to go." Unable to check the rising tears, she fled toward the kitchen and banged the door.

They all looked at one another guiltily.

"Say, Sis," Benny called out sharply, "what sort of frame-up is this? Haven't you told mother that she was to go with us to-night?"

"Yes – I—" Fanny bit her lips as she fumbled evasively for words. "I asked her if she wouldn't mind my taking her some other time."

"Now you have made a mess of it!" fumed Benny. "Mother'll be too hurt to go now."

"Well, I don't care," snapped Fanny. "I can't appear with mother in a box at the theater. Can I introduce her to Mrs. Van Suyden? And suppose your leading man should ask to meet me?"

"Take your time, Sis. He hasn't asked yet," scoffed Benny.

"The more reason I shouldn't spoil my chances. You know mother. She'll spill the beans that we come from Delancey Street the minute we introduce her anywhere. Must I always have the black shadow of my past trailing after me?"

"But have you no feelings for mother?" admonished Abe.

"I've tried harder than all of you to do my duty. I've *lived* with her." She turned angrily upon them. "I've borne the shame of mother while you bought her off with a present and a treat here and there. God knows how hard I tried to civilize her so as not to have to blush with shame when I take her anywhere. I dressed her in the most stylish Paris models, but Delancey Street sticks out from every inch of her. Whenever she opens her mouth, I'm done for. You fellows had your chance to rise in the world because a man is free to go up as high as he can reach up to; but I, with all my style and pep, can't get a man my equal because a girl is always judged by her mother."

They were silenced by her vehemence, and unconsciously turned to Benny.

"I guess we all tried to do our best for mother," said Benny, thoughtfully. "But wherever there is growth, there is pain and heartbreak. The trouble with us is that the Ghetto of the Middle Ages and the children of the twentieth century have to live under one roof, and—"

A sound of crashing dishes came from the kitchen, and the voice of Hanneh Breineh resounded through the dining-room as she wreaked her pent-up fury on the helpless servant.

"Oh, my nerves! I can't stand it any more! There will be no girl again for another week," cried Fanny.

"Oh, let up on the old lady," protested Abe. "Since she can't take it out on us any more, what harm is it if she cusses the servants?"

"If you fellows had to chase around employment agencies, you wouldn't see anything funny about it. Why can't we move into a hotel that will do away with the need of servants altogether?"

"I got it better," said Jake, consulting a note-book from his pocket. "I have on my list an apartment on Riverside Drive where there's only a small kitchenette; but we can do away with the cooking, for there is a dining service in the building."

The new Riverside apartment to which Hanneh Breineh was removed by her socially ambitious children was for the habitually active mother an empty desert of enforced idleness. Deprived of her kitchen, Hanneh Breineh felt robbed of the last reason for her existence. Cooking and marketing and puttering busily with pots and pans gave her an excuse for living and struggling and bearing up with her children. The lonely idleness of Riverside Drive stunned all her senses and arrested all her thoughts. It gave her that choked sense of being cut off from air, from life, from everything warm and human. The cold indifference, the each-for-himself look in the eyes of the people about her were like stinging slaps in the face. Even the children had nothing real or human in them. They were starched and stiff miniatures of their elders.

But the most unendurable part of the stifling life on Riverside Drive was being forced to eat in the public dining-room. No matter how hard she tried to learn polite table manners, she always found people staring at her, and her daughter rebuking her for eating with the wrong fork or guzzling the soup or staining the cloth.

In a fit of rebellion Hanneh Breineh resolved never to go down to the public dining-room again, but to make use of the gas-stove in the kitchenette to cook her own meals. That very day she rode down to Delancey Street and purchased a new market-basket. For some time she walked among the haggling push-cart venders, relaxing and swimming in the warm waves of her old familiar past.

A fish-peddler held up a large carp in his black, hairy hand and waved it dramatically:

"Women! Women! Fourteen cents a pound!"

He ceased his raucous shouting as he saw Hanneh Breineh in her rich attire approach his cart.

"How much?" she asked pointing to the fattest carp.

"Fifteen cents, lady," said the peddler, smirking as he raised his price.

"Swindler! Didn't I hear you call fourteen cents?" shrieked Hanneh Breineh, exultingly, the spirit of the penny chase surging in her blood. Diplomatically, Hanneh Breineh turned as if to go, and the fishman seized her basket in frantic fear.

"I should live; I'm losing money on the fish, lady," whined the peddler. "I'll let it down to thirteen cents for you only."

"Two pounds for a quarter, and not a penny more," said Hanneh Breineh, thrilling again with the rare sport of bargaining, which had been her chief joy in the good old days of poverty.

"*Nu*, I want to make the first sale for good luck." The peddler threw the fish on the scale.

As he wrapped up the fish, Hanneh Breineh saw the driven look of worry in his haggard eyes, and when he counted out for her the change from her dollar, she waved it aside.

"Keep it for your luck," she said, and hurried off to strike a new bargain at a push-cart of onions.

Hanneh Breineh returned triumphantly with her purchases. The basket under her arm gave forth the old, homelike odours of herring and garlic, while the scaly tail of a four-pound carp protruded from its newspaper wrapping. A gilded placard on the door of the apartment-house proclaimed that all merchandise must be delivered through the trade entrance in the rear; but Hanneh Breineh with her basket strode proudly through the marble-paneled hall and rang nonchalantly for the elevator.

The uniformed hall-man, erect, expressionless, frigid with dignity, stepped forward:

"Just a minute, Madam, I'll call a boy to take up your basket for you."

Hanneh Breineh, glaring at him, jerked the basket savagely from his hands.

"Mind your own business," she retorted. "I'll take it up myself. Do you think you're a Russian policeman to boss me in my own house?"

Angry lines appeared on the countenance of the representative of social decorum.

"It is against the rules, Madam," he said stiffly.

"You should sink into the earth with all your rules and brass buttons. Ain't this America? Ain't this a free country? Can't I take up in my own house what I buy with my own money?" cried Hanneh Breineh, revelling in the opportunity to shower forth the volley of invectives that had been suppressed in her for the weeks of deadly dignity of Riverside Drive.

In the midst of this uproar Fanny came in with Mrs. Van Suyden. Hanneh Breineh rushed over to her, crying:

"This bossy policeman won't let me take up my basket in the elevator."

The daughter, unnerved with shame and confusion, took the basket in her white-gloved hand and ordered the hall-boy to take it around to the regular delivery entrance.

Hanneh Breineh was so hurt by her daughter's apparent defense of the hallman's rules that she utterly ignored Mrs. Van Suyden's greeting and walked up the seven flights of stairs out of sheer spite.

"You see the tragedy of my life?" broke out Fanny, turning to Mrs. Van Suyden.

"You poor child! You go right up to your dear, old lady mother, and I'll come some other time."

Instantly Fanny regretted her words. Mrs. Van Suyden's pity only roused her wrath the more against her mother.

Breathless from climbing the stairs, Hanneh Breineh entered the apartment just as Fanny tore the faultless millinery creation from her head and threw it on the floor in a rage.

"Mother, you are the ruination of my life! You have driven away Mrs. Van Suyden, as you have driven away all my best friends. What do you think we got this apartment for but to get rid of your fish smells and your brawls with the servants? And here you come with a basket on your arm as if you just landed from steerage! And this afternoon, of all times, when Benny is bringing his leading man to tea. When will you ever stop disgracing us?"

"When I'm dead," said Hanneh Breineh, grimly. "When the earth will cover me up, then you'll be free to go your American way. I'm not going to make myself over for a lady on Riverside Drive. I hate you and all your swell friends. I'll not let myself be choked up here by you or by that hall-boss-policeman that is higher in your eyes than your own mother."

"So that's your thanks for all we've done for you?" cried the daughter.

"All you've done for me?" shouted Hanneh Breineh. "What have you done for me? You hold me like a dog on a chain. It stands in the Talmud; some children give their mothers dry bread and water and go to heaven for it, and some give their mother roast duck and go to Gehenna because it's not given with love."

"You want me to love you yet?" raged the daughter. "You knocked every bit of love out of me when I was yet a kid. All the memories of childhood I have is your everlasting cursing and yelling that we were gluttons."

The bell rang sharply, and Hanneh Breineh flung open the door.

"Your groceries, ma'am," said the boy.

Hanneh Breineh seized the basket from him, and with a vicious fling sent it rolling across the room, strewing its contents over the Persian rugs and inlaid floor. Then seizing her hat and coat, she stormed out of the apartment and down the stairs.

Mr. and Mrs. Pelz sat crouched and shivering over their meager supper when the door opened, and Hanneh Breineh in fur coat and plumed hat charged into the room.

"I come to cry out to you my bitter heart," she sobbed. "Woe is me! It is so black for my eyes!"

"What is the matter with you, Hanneh Breineh?" cried Mrs. Pelz in bewildered alarm.

"I am turned out of my own house by the brass-buttoned policeman that bosses the elevator. *Oi-i-i-i! Weh-h-h-h*! what have I from my life? The whole world rings with my son's play. Even the President came to see it, and I, his mother, have not seen it yet. My heart is dying in me like in a prison," she went on wailing. "I am starved out for a piece of real eating. In that swell restaurant is nothing but napkins and forks and lettuce-leaves. There are a dozen plates to every bite of food. And it looks so fancy on the plate, but it's nothing but straw in the mouth. I'm starving, but I can't swallow down their American eating."

"Hanneh Breineh," said Mrs. Pelz, "you are sinning before God. Look on your fur coat; it alone would feed a whole family for a year. I never had yet a piece of fur trimming on a coat, and you are in fur from the neck to the feet. I never had yet a piece of feather on a hat, and your hat is all feathers."

"What are you envying me?" protested Hanneh Breineh. "What have I from all my fine furs and feathers when my children are strangers to me? All the fur coats in the world can't warm up the loneliness inside my heart. All the grandest feathers can't hide the bitter shame in my face that my children shame themselves from me."

Hanneh Breineh suddenly loomed over them like some ancient, heroic figure of the Bible condemning unrighteousness.

"Why should my children shame themselves from me? From where did they get the stuff to work themselves up in the world? Did they get it from the air? How did they get all their smartness to rise over the people around them? Why don't the children of born American mothers write my Benny's plays? It is I, who never had a chance to be a person, who gave him the fire in his head. If I would have had a chance to go to school and learn the language, what couldn't I have been? It is I and my mother and my mother's mother and my father and father's father who had such a black life in Poland; it is our choked thoughts and feelings that are flaming up in my children and making them great in America. And yet they shame themselves from me!"

For a moment Mr. and Mrs. Pelz were hypnotized by the sweep of her words. Then Hanneh Breineh sank into a chair in utter exhaustion. She began to weep bitterly, her body shaking with sobs.

"Woe is me! For what did I suffer and hope on my children? A bitter old age – my end. I'm so lonely!"

All the dramatic fire seemed to have left her. The spell was broken. They saw the Hanneh Breineh of old, ever discontented, ever complaining even in the midst of riches and plenty.

"Hanneh Breineh," said Mrs. Pelz, "the only trouble with you is that you got it too good. People will tear the eyes out of your head because you're complaining yet. If I only had your fur coat! If I only had your diamonds! I have nothing. You have everything. You are living on the fat of the land. You go right back home and thank God that you don't have my bitter lot."

"You got to let me stay here with you," insisted Hanneh Breineh. "I'll not go back to my children except when they bury me. When they will see my dead face, they will understand how they killed me."

Mrs. Pelz glanced nervously at her husband. They barely had enough covering for their one bed; how could they possibly lodge a visitor?

"I don't want to take up your bed," said Hanneh Breineh. "I don't care if I have to sleep on the floor or on the chairs, but I'll stay here for the night."

Seeing that she was bent on staying, Mr. Pelz prepared to sleep by putting a few chairs next to the trunk, and Hanneh Breineh was invited to share the rickety bed with Mrs. Pelz.

The mattress was full of lumps and hollows. Hanneh Breineh lay cramped and miserable, unable to stretch out her limbs. For years she had been accustomed to hair mattresses and ample woolen blankets, so that though she covered herself with her fur coat, she was too cold to sleep. But worse than the cold were the creeping things on the wall. And as the lights were turned low, the mice came through the broken plaster and raced across the floor. The foul odours of the kitchen-sink added to the night of horrors.

"Are you going back home?" asked Mrs. Pelz as Hanneh Breineh put on her hat and coat the next morning.

"I don't know where I'm going," she replied as she put a bill into Mrs. Pelz's hand.

For hours Hanneh Breineh walked through the crowded Ghetto streets. She realized that she no longer could endure the sordid ugliness of her past, and yet she could not go home to her children. She only felt that she must go on and on.

In the afternoon a cold, drizzling rain set in. She was worn out from the sleepless night and hours of tramping. With a piercing pain in her heart she at last turned back and boarded the subway for Riverside Drive. She had fled from the marble sepulcher of the Riverside apartment to her old home in the Ghetto; but now she knew that she could not live there again. She had outgrown her past by the habits of years of physical comforts, and these material comforts that she could no longer do without choked and crushed the life within her.

A cold shudder went through Hanneh Breineh as she approached the apartment-house. Peering through the plate glass of the door she saw the face of the uniformed hall-man. For a hesitating moment she remained standing in the drizzling rain, unable to enter and yet knowing full well that she would have to enter.

Then suddenly Hanneh Breineh began to laugh. She realized that it was the first time she had laughed since her children had become rich. But it was the hard laugh of bitter sorrow. Tears streamed down her furrowed cheeks as she walked slowly up the granite steps.

"The fat of the land!" muttered Hanneh Breineh, with a choking sob as the hall-man with immobile face deferentially swung open the door – "the fat of the land!"

Displacement, Relocation & Resettlement in Modern Science Fiction

An Absolute Amount of Sadness

Ali Abbas

IT WAS RAINING STAIR RODS. The drops fell in straight, hard spears that turned perpendicular in the sudden gusts of wind. It splashed up from the ground like the spreading skirts of old women. London rain, different in its taste and texture from showers, drizzle, and mizzle. London rain, and I was going to walk through it under a small black umbrella.

Walking is my thing. "My brains are in my behind," I joke frequently. "I can't think sitting down." The truth is I struggle to control my temper. My passions are sudden and incandescent, frequently destructive. So I stride through town. No ambling, nor idling. Even when there is no direction or deadline, I move with purpose and energy. I grind whatever is on my mind beneath my feet until it is so disassembled and thoroughly examined, I find either a solution or suspension. Walking is a protection that leaves me safely exhausted and grounded. No longer a monster but a man again.

Superstition runs deep in my people. They say I carry a Djinn, a being of fire I must either tame or tire. It is a tale for children to explain a foul and uncertain temper, a lessening of the blame by assigning it to an external agency. That does not make it any less true.

That day the rain came after soul-sapping meetings had left me seething. Nothing was done, no progress was made, and we simply traipsed back and forth over the same old ground. I'd snapped a biro under the desk during the last meeting, trying to contain the urge to speak my mind and wreck my career.

By the time I came down the stairs, I was desperate for the measured solidity of my walk home. I gave Carole at reception a wave and turned up my collar, readying myself to step outside. I reached into the side pocket of my satchel and found nothing.

Carole tapped on my shoulder. "Looking for this?" She held the compact form of my umbrella. "Young lass dropped it in earlier, didn't say whose it was but now I know." She gave me a grin and walked back.

I took a half-step towards her to ask more questions. I hadn't used my umbrella in the morning, the rain had started in the afternoon. There was no way I could have dropped it but it was undoubtedly mine. The Djinn was pressing. I let the mystery go.

There is a pavement etiquette that is doubly important in the rain. One does not launch out of a doorway into a stream of pedestrian traffic. Those already on the move have the right of way. You sidle out, carefully, find a space in the flow, and keep pace for a few steps. In a mass of umbrellas at varying heights, it is essential to tilt and lift in case you take someone's eye out. Only then can you set your own pace, weaving through the other walkers.

It was in that moment of decision that I felt a stutter of unease. I jostled a man with a dripping fedora and leather briefcase. In the chorus of "I'm sorry," I saw her. Space opened between the crowds of overcoats and hunched shoulders. She was different. Eye-catching.

Our encounter was inevitable. The weight and gravity of every person on that busy thoroughfare drew the universe in, ensuring this occurrence, spinning other meaningless events off as ephemeral chaff. Something willed me to cross the street in just that break in the traffic. Our paths touched at the corner.

In another time, in any other place, we would have passed one another without a thought. Londoners are atomistic; we move in a way that diminishes the existence of anyone else except as an obstacle or an annoyance. We weave through the crowds of indifference to different speeds and destinations. All of that changed.

She was drenched. Her dark blue sweater had become a cloud, holding so much water that it hung off her in an amorphous mass. What struck me most was her face. It might have been unremarkable in the dry, yet somehow the wet made it compelling. Framed in ragged strands of ash-blonde hair, it was pinched and pale. There were dark smudges around her eyes and she was washed through with a sense of enormous sadness. All the sorrow in the world was captured and cast in the turn of her lips, the angle of her head.

She stopped when I stopped. The rhythm of the pavement was broken, the Brownian motion of human particles disrupted.

"Here," I said, holding out the umbrella. "It looks like you could use it." The impulse was sudden and irresistible, a white hot instinct that briefly burned out the Djinn.

She looked at her sweater in wonder as it gave off a whisper of steam. We both took a half step forward like courtly dancers into the limited shelter of the umbrella.

We were alone, curtained from the rest of the world by the rain sheeting off the umbrella all around us. The crowds bent their paths as if we were streetlights or bollards. In the thundercloud darkness around her eyes, her irises were glacial. She could have been a Nixie, far from her Nordic home under a curse, carrying with her all the colours of frigid mountains and ice-rimmed lakes. She could have been just another Londoner, caught out by the rain. Either way, she did not seem out of place on that dismal corner.

It was under her silver-grey regard that I felt a stab of doubt. I could feel the movement of all those homeward-bound bodies. Their momentum tugged at me, they wanted me to go home too. She seemed to waver, my uncertainty threatening her existence.

Then her eyes shone back into focus. I was flooded by the enormity of her melancholy. I could not discern if she carried her sorrow, or if she was sorrow made flesh and water. If I stayed there, the sorrow would reach out and envelop me. Was she a cloud that I would pass through breathing, moistened as if in fog? Was she a lake, its depths dark and unknowable, in which I would drown?

The doubt spread like a stain. Londoners never stop, never talk. It is not fear of interaction that makes us so but preservation of sanity. We are so many, so closely packed together that to let in one is to let in all. We could lose ourselves entirely. What had this girl, woman, cloud, creature done to me to break that sense of self-preservation? The moment was elastic, spreading and stretching. It lasted as the doubt seeped further and further until I was the avatar of uncertainty as much as I perceived she might be the bearer of all the world's dismay.

She put up a hand but stopped short of placing it on my chest. The entreaty to stop was clear and I had had no answer to the offer I had made. She dropped her hand and looked down, almost demure. Raindrops tipped from her hair and teetered on her eyelashes, indistinguishable from tears. She looked up again, first from beneath those lashes, and then pinning me on twin spears of ice.

I knew then this was not fate or physics. The encounter had been orchestrated. This was my regular journey home from work. I searched for her features in the shadows of memory. Had she watched me from the arched entrance of the library? Had she trailed me as I struggled around tourists, the Djinn simmering and snarling in my steps? She had read my weakness: tears and those eyes. This encounter was planned and to a purpose all its own. My first impression clattered against the other attempts at recollection. Nixie. Was she suffering under a geas, seeking to quench or cure it with a supernatural assault on my person?

There was no one else. We stood in a cocoon of water. I was pinned by those frigid eyes, trapped in a moment that sucked time until the rain was an ocean falling solid and entire around our bubble.

The doubt mutated even as it dissolved me, making room for something else. I felt the chill fingers of fear claw inside. Had I only walked on by, the seconds pouring past me would be mine. Instead, I had given way to the thoughtless impulse, to be trapped in her gaze of steel and ice.

"You'll get soaked and I'm already wet," she said. Her accent was particular, the distinctive stress and cadence of a Swede. Here it meant nothing. She could yet be a sprite, or just another Londoner in this heaving melting pot. She made no move to step around me, to leave our little bubble of time and space.

The stillness rekindled my fire. The Djinn that had almost extinguished itself in the impetuous joy of giving roared back with all the pent-up frustrations of the day. In the madness of that stellar passion, I shrugged.

Nonchalance is the London way, in the face of terror or kindness. "Kings Cross is just over the road. I'll be out of the rain soon enough. If you're heading down Judd Street you're going to be walking a while yet." I lied casually with a veneer of inconsequence. The station had not been my destination. I had planned on walking several miles yet; up York Way and onward to Brecknock Road. I held out the handle.

My own eyes are black rum, fire and warmth. I don't know, in that moment of forever, when the rain fell like the ocean, what she saw reflected in them. How deeply did she pierce me, drawing out the knowing of my unwelcome accomplice? What did she leave behind?

Rock ice fell in the liquid amber furnace. Then she smiled. Her melancholy lifted as she perceived my gift was not some hollow altruism but meant something, would cost me something. Time returned to its normal passage. The rain fell once again as drops: hard, fast and separate. I almost lurched into her as I felt the surge of the crowds.

She steadied me with her smile as her smudged, knife-sharp eyes tried to drag me back in. She could have been at war with herself. Were we similar? Did she too carry a maddened passenger that made wild demands, urging her to draw me into the well of her sorrow? Was she trying to tame it with the ancient magic of receiving a gift, while it slavered over the scent of my desiccated desert blood? I saw the darkness deep behind her eyes, the secret beds of snowmelt rivers. Her smile was winning, like sunlight reflected off new snow.

"How will I give it back to you?"

The flames leapt white hot from my clenched fists, one in my pocket, one around the umbrella handle. Just as I had thought we had reached an equilibrium, she had poured the evanescent vapour of insult on me. Now I could not hold back the Djinn. I had offered the gift without let or hindrance. There are rules written deep in my bones. A gift once offered can never be taken back.

She felt the heat hammering off me, steaming her wet clothes, pushing away the insistent passers-by. Her hand closed over mine. A cool flask of water under the blistering desert sun. She held him at bay for me.

Ice melted. Her eyes warmed from frigid grey to the pale blue of a clear midwinter sky. Perhaps my gift had lifted her geas, or she had scalded her faerie spirit with the incitement of my own. Perhaps it was just that someone, in the cold air and hunched shoulders of a London street, had lifted their eyes to meet hers and noticed another being in need.

My grip loosened on the handle. My other hand emerged, pliant, uncertain of its role now that the Djinn was doused and cowed by a girl in a sodden sweater. I wanted to touch her, but she could have been as fleeting as a snowflake. I dropped my hand. My heart hammered, catching up the beats it had missed when the world blurred by. Or perhaps it remembered what it felt like to fall in love.

I shook my head. "Keep it, or pass it on to someone else who needs it." I gave her a smile in return. Just for us, the clouds lifted and the sun shone through the London rain into the little universe under our umbrella. It broke the spell, or the moment, or just that fragile mood that could only exist in a moist gloom.

I could sense her stillness and hear the rain hammering on the umbrella as I strode away. I pinched the lapels of my jacket closed over my tie. By the time I had crossed the road and stood just in front of the station entrance, she had gone, lost in the crowd or poured into the rain.

I felt it then, the weight of the water on my shoulders, dripping through my hair, ruining the cut and fall of my suit. I felt disembowelled by loss, weightless and dizzy, clumsy and disoriented. The umbrella was nothing, easily replaced. I could not condense the loss into something tangible, only a sudden appreciation of absence.

It was as if the girl in the sodden blue sweater carried a burden of an absolute amount of sadness. By relieving it, if only for a moment, I now carried some of it myself. She had dampened the hot, sand-laced scouring wind of my passing with the sodden gust of her own stormy transit. The water and the sorrow were now a part of me. Had I in turn cast a handful of sand into her arctic maelstrom? I realized then that she and I were more similar than I could ever have imagined. We were both Londoners, and bearers of heritages that were bound by the million tons of concrete and steel around us. I was born not two miles from where I now stood. Who knows how many years or generations stood between her and the black ice pools of her origins? And yet our difference was written in our eyes, and she carried all the sorrow of her migrant ancestors with her.

I remembered then that I had learned how to describe the rain from other migrants. "Stair rods" was a term I got from an Ulsterman who was also a Londoner. "Old ladies' skirts" was from the Baltics, and another Londoner.

Her sorrow was born out of a sense of longing. It said, "I love this place that has taken me into its embrace, borne me and bred me. But my bones know of another home that I have now forsaken, to which I can't return except to marvel at its difference and leave diminished."

The station was tempting. I would be well on my way by the time the rain stopped, and I would get home merely damp. There was no remnant of the friction of that day in me. The Djinn, if such a thing even existed, had been trapped in a cool slumber.

But I had to walk. I carried the spin of sorrow, the weary weight of understanding I had unwittingly accepted. I abandoned the station and slipped by those hurrying for the shelter it provided. The world was now invisible behind the raindrops on my glasses. I could not see the pitying glances of the people at the bus stop or the antagonism of the wealthy, hailing taxis and seeing me as competition. I didn't need to see it.

My feet knew the route; London is my town after all. I turned up York Way and settled into the steady stride that would see me home. In those first steps, I could feel the sorrow seeping through me from top to toe as the rain found a way behind my collar and down my back. The sorrow would reach my feet before I got to Tufnell Park, and I would push it through the soles of my shoes into the grey immensity of London's pavements. We would not meet again, but she and I were not alone, atomistic, unconnected. And I would leave her sorrow ground into the miles of concrete to be washed away by the rain.

Refugees

Celu Amberstone

AWAKENING MOON, sun-turning 1

This morning I arose early and climbed to the Mother Stone on the knoll above the village. The sun was just rising above the blue mists on the lake. The path smelled of tree resin and flowering moss. I took in a deep breath, and sang to the life around me. I was shivering by the time I reached the Mother Stone and made the first of my seasonal offerings to Tallav'Wahir, our foster planet.

I cut open my arm with the ceremonial obsidian knife I carried with me, and watched my blood drip into the channel carved into the stone for that purpose. Blood. The old people say it is the carrier of ancestral memories, and our future's promise. I am a child from the stars – a refugee, driven from my true home. My blood is red, an alien color on this world. But I am lucky because this planet knows my name.

Awakening Moon, sun-turning 2

I should rejoice in the renewal of life, but this Awakening Moon my heart is sad. Always before one of my daughters has been with me to share this special time. They are all gone now. My youngest daughter married last harvest and moved to a village across the lake. I miss her. My dear old man, Tree, says I should be glad to be done with that cycle of my life. But if I still crave the company of children, he is sure that my co-wife Sun Fire would be happy to share. He says this with a smile when he sees my long face, and truly the children left in the compound are more than a handful for us. But though I love them all – including my widowed sisters, it isn't quite the same. I pray that Tukta's marriage will be a happy one, and blessed with healthy children. Oh Mother, how we need healthy children.

Awakening Moon, sun-turning 7

Today our Benefactors confirmed our worst fears. Earth is now a fiery cloud of poisons, a blackened cinder. When it happened, our ancient soul-link with Earth Mother enabled us to sense the disaster even from this far world across the void. Tallav'Wahir felt it too. But we told our foster planet mother that our life patterns were sound. Our Benefactors would help us. Such a tragedy would never happen here. There was a great outpouring of blood and grief at the Mother Stones all over the world. The land ceased to tremble by the time the ceremonies ended.

Leaf-Budding Moon, sun-turning 3

The star shuttle arrives with our new wards tomorrow – twenty-one of them for our village. What an honor to be given so many. Dra'hada says that the crew won't awaken them from cold-sleep until just prior to their arrival. When they are led out, they will be disorientated, and we will have to be patient with them. Dra'hada has assured me that our implants and theirs have been attuned to the same frequency so that we can communicate easily, and that is a relief. I wonder what these new people will be like. I am excited, and maybe a little afraid too. All the wars and urban violence we've heard about, I hope they can adjust to our simple ways. It's been a long time since our Benefactors have brought settlers to Tallav'Wahir to join us. We desperately need these newcomers. Tallav'Wahir is kind, but there is something in this adoptive environment that is hard on us too. We aren't a perfect match for our new home, but our Benefactors have great hopes for us.

Leaf-Budding Moon, sun-turning 4

It is moonrise, and it's been an exhausting day for all of us. I was near the front of the crowd when the shuttle set down on the landing pad. I thought I was prepared for anything. How wrong I was. They are so alien. It is hard to believe we are the same species. The situation on Earth deteriorated so fast that the ship was forced to gather what survivors were available without delay. There was no time to select the suitable. The sorting will have to be done here I suppose, and that is unfortunate. Culling is very stressful for everyone. Most of the people assigned to our village were dazed and confused, but some were angry too. Maybe they were afraid of our Benefactors, and that might account for their rude behavior. Filthy lizards indeed. They are an unsettling addition to our village, and the land feels it too.

Leaf-Budding Moon, sun-turning 5

Dra'hada says, even though they look and act so differently, they all come from a large city called Vancouver. We have three staying in our family's compound. When I first saw the young woman given to us, my heart pounded like a drum. I'd caught only a glimpse of her in profile, and I thought my daughter Tukta had returned to me. Then she turned to face me and the resemblance vanished. It was an unsettling experience nonetheless. Her features at times still remind me of Tukta's, but in no other way are they the same!

This girl is of medium height, golden-skinned, and very, very thin. She was wearing tight black pants, and black boots with high heels that make her walk funny. She also had on a black shirt, very sheer – I could see her tiny nipples pressed against the fabric. Over that she wore a black leather jacket with lots of silver chains. Her hair is short, spiky and blue. She has a ring in her nose and several in her ears, and a pudgy baby that cries a lot. She told us her name was Sleek. Jimtalbot, one of our other charges, says that isn't her real name, just a "street name." I'm not sure what he meant by that, but I'll wait and ask him later.

Jimtalbot is one of the few older adults left in our care. Unlike Sleek, he has pale skin, and gray streaks in his short brown hair. His face is a bit puffy, and his belly soft. Dra'hada says we will have to watch him because his heart is weak. Jimtalbot told me that he was a professor at the University of British Columbia. He has lively blue eyes and is very curious about everything. I like him the best of the lot.

Our third fosterling, given into Tree's care mostly, is a sullen, brown-skinned youth whose "street name" is Twace. He wares a bright-colored cloth tied around his head, and baggy striped pants. I don't like his angry eyes, and the color of his aura. It is filled with red and murky gray patches. When he looked around our compound, and saw the neat round dwellings with their sturdy mud walls and mossy roofs, the thatched stable for our woolly beasts, and the shady arbor where my loom sits, his mouth curled in contempt.

They are abed now – finally. Tomorrow we will have to get them suitable clothing and bring them to the Mother Stone on the knoll. I hope they won't be too frightened by the adoption ceremony.

Leaf-Budding Moon, sun-turning 6

We tried to prepare our fosterlings for the proceedings, but no amount of assurance on our part seemed to ease their minds. All were anxious, and some had to be dragged screaming and cursing to the Mother Stone while an elder made the cut for the required blood offering. Sleek was one of the worst. She kicked and clawed at the men who brought her forward, and no amount of assurance on my part could calm her.

When we returned home, Sleek was a mess. Her arms and face were bloody, and her alien clothes were ruined. I saw my neighbors' pitying glances as we took her away. My widowed sister and my co-wife, Sun Fire, helped me strip off her clothing and get her cleaned up. I was so ashamed for our family.

"Ignorant savages, cannibals, leave me alone, god damn you!" she shouted at us as we washed her.

"It's all right daughter, calm down. Come now, it was only a little blood; it didn't really hurt to make the gift. No one is going to eat you. The blood was given to the Stone so that our foster planet mother could taste you. Now She will know you as one of her own. We all make such offerings; it is one of the ways our Benefactors have taught us to commune with the soul of the land. Such traditions were practiced on Earth once – didn't you know that?"

"Screw traditions – and the lizards," she snarled and threw the new dress I was trying to hand her on the floor. "I want my own clothes – what have you done with my things, bitch?"

"Don't talk to your foster mother like that," my sister said. "Show her more respect."

Sleek opened her mouth to reply, but I hurried on to forestall another outburst. "I'm sorry, Sleek, but it was necessary to get rid of those alien things. They aren't in harmony with life here. You must wear and use the natural things provided by *this* planet now. Their power will help you commune with Tallav'Wahir. These ways may seem harsh to you at first, but they are important. Our elders and our Benefactors know what is best for us – truly they do."

Sleek gave me a withering look, but took the simple dress I handed her. While the fabric was over her head I heard her mumble something about ignorant savages talking to dirt. "Our Benefactors know best," she mimicked as her head cleared the opening. "Well, they're not *my* benefactors. You people are pathetic. Damned lizards have you humans living like primitive savages while they fly around in their spaceships."

Her words were meant to cut, but I thought I saw tears in the corners of her eyes so I bit back my angry response. "We know about the high technologies," I told her quietly. "We use what you would call computers, air cars and other technical things too. But to help you make the re-patterning, we decided that a simple lifestyle would be best for all of us for a time. There is no shame in living close to the land in a simple way, daughter.

"Our Benefactors teach us that technology must never interfere with our Communion with the Mother, lest we forget the Covenant, grow too greedy and destroy our new home."

Sleek's face flushed a deep crimson, and she probably would have said more rude things to me, but at that point her baby began crying in the yard outside, and she took that as an excuse to leave us. When she was gone my sister, Sun Fire and I looked at one another in exasperation. Her behavior could try the patience of a stone.

Flowering Moon, sun-turning 7

The planting is over. It was a nice change to play with the children on the beach today. The water in the lake is already warm enough for a swim. Sleek and I played with them for hours in the shallows by the shore. Her face relaxed; she looked younger and seemed so happy, and that made me happy too. Maybe she and the others can adjust to our ways after all.

Flowering Moon, sun-turning 9

Jimtalbot rubs his fourth finger when he thinks no one is looking. Like the others he was forced to give up everything from his past, including the thin gold ring that used to be on that finger. Just now when I went out to relieve myself, I heard someone sobbing quietly in the shadows under the te'an tree. When I went to investigate I saw Jimtalbot. I sat down beside him and took his hand. "What's so wrong?" I asked him. He sniffed and tried to pull his hand out of mine, but I held on and repeated my question.

"Nothing really – I'll be all right... I was just thinking about home – and my dead wife. She was visiting her mother in Toronto when it happened. The whole eastern part of the country was annihilated from what Dra'hada told me."

"Such thoughts are more than nothing, Jimtalbot. I can't imagine losing so much; it must be terrible. I think you and the others are very brave."

He shook his head; I could see the gleam of unshed tears in his eyes by the lantern light. "Not brave at all. Your *Benefactors* gave us no choice."

There was such harshness to his voice when he said those words that I shivered and wrapped my shawl tighter around my shoulders. "They are your Benefactors too," I pointed out to him. "Would you rather have had them leave you to die?"

He was silent for a long time; finally he said, "I don't know, Qwalshina. It is all so different here – I don't know if I have the courage to live in this place."

Surprised by his confession, I raised his hand to my lips and kissed it. "Surely you can; we are all here to love and help you. You aren't alone here – And if you wish a new wife –"

At that point he disentangled his hand from mine and stood up. "Thank you for your concern, Qwalshina. You are very kind. I think I shall go back to my bed now. Good night."

I went back to my own bed with a troubled heart. The little ring was such a small memento. Did we do right to make them give up everything? Our Benefactors advised it, but...

Flowering Moon, sun-turning 25

Last night there was an argument down by the beach that ended with Sand Walker and one of the new men being injured. Everyone is so upset today, and Dra'hada was furious when he heard about it. He told me that such violence wouldn't be tolerated. Why can't the new ones see how lucky they are? These people were saved from death; why are they so angry? I don't understand them. I wish they'd never been brought here.

No, that isn't true; we need them...

Korn Growing Moon, sun-turning 11

I had to make a difficult decision yesterday about Sleek. Her baby was suffering. She would shout and curse the babe more often than she would feed or care for the boy. Today the women's council came to take the baby away. She cursed us in the vilest terms. Judging by her behavior later, however, I think she is secretly relieved to be rid of the child. The council gave the little one to Aunty Shell to foster. Granny Night Wind says the boy is doing better already.

I look at Sleek's hard eyes and I wonder what is wrong with her. Can't she feel any emotion but anger? How could she be so indifferent to her own child's welfare? I remember how it was when we lost my oldest daughter's first born. Poor unfortunate mite – we were all distraught when he had to be culled.

Korn Growing Moon, sun-turning 16

Our medicine woman, Granny Night Wind, thinks we will have a good crop this harvest season. Tallav'Wahir, we live in harmony with Her cycles. She feeds us, Her spirit helpers protect us, and in return we bury our shit and our dead in her rich gray soil so that She can absorb our essence, swallow our memories, and enfold us in the oneness of Her living soul. My daughter Tukta's face comes into my mind. She is so young, and so happy. Will the land love and bless her, make her one of Her favored ones? Oh, I pray it will be so.

Berry Moon, sun-turning 2

There was a great bonfire down on the beach last night. We baked fish on sticks, and ate berries cooked with sweet dumplings, till our bellies grew hard and round. In the long green twilight, we played running games. Then, someone brought out a drum and that started everyone singing and dancing. Our Twace and two boys in my cousin Rain's compound can drum very well. I danced till I thought I would fall over from exhaustion. Later Tree, Sun Fire and I crept off to a quiet place by the spring where we made sweet love under the stars. Some time during the night Tree's unmarried brother, Sand Walker, joined us and that was good too.

Berry Moon, sun-turning 9

When I was working at my loom this evening, Sleek came over unexpectedly and sat down beside me. She seemed curious, and maybe a little interested. None of my other children have the talent to be a master weaver. It would be a shame for the family to lose such a skill when I become too old for the craft. Some of our Benefactors pay high prices for our art back on their Homeworld. I let her watch for a time then I asked, "Would you like me to show you how to do this?" She shrugged, but didn't get up and leave. *Best not frighten her away*, I thought, so I just continued on with my work.

After a while she volunteered, "My grandmother used to weave – it looked something like that."

Startled, I stopped my work and turned to face her. "Really? That's very interesting. What kind of things did she make?"

"I don't remember exactly; I was pretty young when she died... I remember one thing she made though. It had bright colors; I used to tangle my fingers in its long fringes." She smiled at the memory, and added, "It was probably something ceremonial, a dance cape maybe. A lot of the old women in our band used to make them for the potlatch ceremonies."

"Pot-a-latch," My tongue stumbled over the unfamiliar word. "Was this ceremony of your people held to honor the Earth Mother?"

"I don't know; my mom never took me to one."

I went back to my weaving at that point. I could see she was becoming nervous by my questioning. *Be careful, Qwalshina, or you will frighten her away*, I told myself. But inwardly I smiled as I twined the yarn back and forth between the rope strands on the loom. Truly our Benefactors are wise. Dra'hada knew how much I was missing Tukta, and gave me a new daughter of the same racial stock as my own. At that moment I felt very good about knowing that. It made me feel a little closer to her.

On impulse I asked her, "How old are you?"

She seemed startled by my question, and her eyes narrowed with suspicion at first then she relaxed. "The lizards didn't tell you?"

"No. I never asked our Benefactors. Is your age a secret? Would you tell me?"

She gave me another shrug. "No secret. Eighteen. Why?"

"I was just curious. Eighteen." I forced myself to go back to my weaving. *Gently, gently, Qwalshina*, I told myself. "You are about the age of my third daughter. She got married recently and moved to another village. I miss her. I'm glad you are here to take her place."

Sleek snorted. "I don't have much use for *mothers* so don't get your hopes up about making me your new daughter – or teaching me that silly string stuff either."

She made me angry then, and I allowed my evil tongue to say something cutting in return. "Maybe if you had been more willing to be *mothered* you could have done a better job of being a mother yourself, instead of abusing your baby."

Sleek jerked back as if I'd slapped her – which in a way I had. I saw the hurt in her eyes, for just a moment, and then it was gone, replaced by her habitual sullen anger. She stood up, and glared down at me with such contempt that it made my bones shiver. "You people make me sick," she spat back.

"You think you're so wonderful and know what's best for everyone, don't you? Well, let me tell you about *my* mother. She was a drunk who let her boyfriends fuck me whenever they wanted; then told me it was my fault for being a slut. I never wanted to be a mother – fuck mothers – all mothers. Who needs any of you?"

I stared after her with tear-filled eyes. Why had I said that? I'm so ashamed. Now I understand a little more why she acts the way she does, but that doesn't excuse my behavior. I must go to the Mother Stone, make an offering and try to regain my internal harmony. Like a disease these people are destroying our peace. And, if I am honest with myself I must admit that Sleek and the others frighten me. Her questions and her anger make me uncomfortable. Is she right? Are we too complacent and judgmental? I have to go help Sun Fire with the children.

Korn Ripening Moon, sun-turning 17

The whole village is in an uproar after what happened last night. Someone stole some of Granny Night Wind's uiskajac. It was fermenting in a big wooden barrel at the back of her compound. When Sand Walker went to check on the brew, he found the barrel only half full. Granny Night Wind was furious. She threatened to give the persons responsible a bad case of "the itch" when she finds them. Whoever did it is either very brave – or crazy. She is a powerful shamanka; the spirits obey her. Still, it was funny to see her stomping around, looking under everything – people leaping out of her way – or jumping to do her bidding.

Rain-Comes-Back Moon, sun-turning 2

These young ones, so corrupted by poor food and alien drugs, have grown up spindly, like unhappy plants shaded from the sun. The last human crop of their tormented, polluted world is a pitiful one indeed. Will their life-patterns be suitable to mingle with ours? My people need the flow of new genes or we may perish in spite of all our Benefactor's efforts. I am so afraid for my children. The birth defects and terminations are so many. I fear for my daughter Tukta. She is so young and so happy with her new man.

Ah, but Dra'hada says, not to give up hope. We will salvage what we can from this last harvest. And if that is not enough, our Benefactors will collect the seeds of other worlds and crossbreed them with ours. Our descendants may not be the same in appearance as we are, but some part of us will survive. And the land will always remember us. Our bodies will lie in the cool ground, until the blood memories of our species have passed into the crystals of the bedrock itself.

Rain-Comes-Back Moon, sun-turning 4

Jimtalbot and Bethbrant were troubled by a crazy rumor they'd heard, and came this evening to ask me if it might be true.

"One of the guys from Earth, living at Black Rock Village said that Earth isn't really destroyed," Jimtalbot told me.

I looked into their troubled faces and felt a shiver run down my spine. "What? Why would he say such a thing? Of course the Earth Mother is gone. Why else would our Benefactors have brought you here?"

"Why indeed, Qwalshina?" Jimtalbot said. "Could the – uh – Benefactors be planning some weird experiment? Something that they need live humans, or human body parts for?"

I was shocked, speechless. "Experiment? No, of course not. That's preposterous. Who said such a thing? I must tell Dra'hada; who is it?"

Their expressions became closed at that point. Jimtalbot mumbled that he didn't know the man's name, but I was sure he was lying to me. He looked at Bethbrant and they started to walk away, but I stopped them. "Please wait. If you don't wish me to tell Dra'hada, Jimtalbot, I won't, but listen to me. There is no truth to this rumor. I felt Earth Mother's death agony myself – through the Communion – we all did. The pain was almost unbearable. Truly She is gone. And, there is no planned experiment. Our Benefactors only wish us well."

"If your people were also a part of their design, you might not be aware of the experiment either," Bethbrant said.

"No, we would know if they were using us in that way. We have been here for generations. My father was a man of the Tsa'La'Gui people. His ancestors were brought here when pale-skinned invaders from across a big ocean came and took their land. My mother's people came here long before my fathers. They were Crunich and lived on the island of Erin before the black-robed ones with their dead god came, and stole the island's soul. There are others from Earth Mother here too, rescued from disaster as you were. Our Benefactors wish only good for us. And, no matter our origin on Earth, we are all one people now, the children of Tallav'Wahir. There has never been any experiment. Please believe me."

When I finished talking to them, they seemed convinced that it was all a crazy, made up lie. But later the children told me that a group of our charges walked down the beach together to talk over something in private. Did I do right to promise not to tell Dra'hada? This is very troubling. I must go to the Mother Stone and tell Her my concerns.

Falling Leaves Moon, sun-turning 5

Sleek's tattooed friend and six other youths have developed a terrible case of "the itch." No common healing remedy has worked. Poor lads – I know they're miserable – and I shouldn't laugh at their misfortunes, but it *is* funny to watch them trying to scratch all those hard-to-reach places. Rain's twins were in on the scheme. One of them finally broke down and confessed. About half of the stolen uiskajac was brought back. Granny is keeping the offenders in suspense for one more night; but she told me privately that she would forgive them, and give them a healing salve tomorrow.

Falling Leaves Moon, sun-turning 25

Sleek and I took the children for a walk on the knoll today. We piled up great mountains of leaves and had fun jumping into them. I tired before they did, but felt so good just watching them. My new daughter I think loves playing like a child when none of her Earth friends are around to ridicule her. She is recreating the happy childhood she didn't have on Earth, and it is a joy to see her so.

Later we roasted siba fruit that we gathered, on sticks over an open fire, and everyone sang songs. I found myself wishing Tukta could have been there to share the day with us. When we were heading home the children raced ahead, as usual, but Sleek waited for me on the trail, and fell into step beside me as I passed. I smiled and she returned the gesture.

In the dappled light under the trees her face suddenly seemed to metamorphose into that of an ancient. Expressing wisdom far beyond her years, she said to me, "I had fun with you today, but I'm not Tukta, Qwalshina. Please try to remember that." There was no anger in her voice for once, the smells of tree resin, spicy siba, and a lazy afternoon had drained her of hostility.

Startled I paused in the trail and faced her. "I know... I had fun today too, and I'm glad you are, who you are. I wouldn't want it any other way."

"Mm... Then stop calling me Tukta."

"I don't," I protested.

She gave me a reproachful look, her eyes luminous and sad. "You're not even aware that you're doing it are you?"

Was I? Oh Mother, was I confusing her with my daughter in the physical world as well as my mind? "I'm sorry, Sleek, I *didn't* realize I'd been doing that. Do I do it often?"

She made a noncommittal sound, which I took to be acceptance of my apology. "Not often, but sometimes – like today – you forget." She shrugged, looked away, and brushed her hand across a feathery tree branch. We'd chopped off the dyed blue parts of her hair some time back, and now soft brown waves hung down past her shoulders. Up ahead one of the children called to her at that point, and she raced down the trail to catch up with the others.

I kept walking at a slower pace, thinking. I hadn't realized I'd been doing that. Her gentle rebuke caused me to question my own insecurities. It wasn't fair to Sleek if I was indeed trying to mold her into another's image for my own comfort. Why did I continue to cling to the past? Why couldn't I go on with my life – what was I afraid of? I will have to guard my tongue and my thoughts more carefully in future. I must go see Granny Night Wind; maybe she can guide me through this difficult time.

Frost Moon, sun-turning 15

It's getting very cold at night now. We arrived back in the village by the lake yesterday afternoon, our pack beasts heavy-laden from the annual hunt. Soon we will hold the last harvest feast. Everyone is excited. After the festivities we will pack up everything important and leave this exposed, stormy beach. When the blue snows pile up outside, we will be safe in our warm underground lodges up the sheltered valley in the hills.

Frost Moon, sun-turning 28

I walked to the Mother Stone today to say farewell till our return in Awakening Moon. The seasons have turned and the dark time is upon us once again. In the shadows along the path specters of other races that once lived here too materialized, and watched me with solemn red eyes. Their voices whispered to me on the cool wind, but I couldn't understand their alien speech. What happened to those born to this world? Our Benefactors don't know. ...

Along with my blood I poured out to the Mother my hopes and fears for the future. I hope She heard and will bless us. We are all that is left of humanity now. Can we survive? Or will this land one day absorb us back into itself as she has others who have walked these hills? Such thoughts deepened the chill in my bones, and I hurried back to the warmth of my family's compound. I want us all to live, and be happy.

The last harvest feast is tonight after the communal prayers. I'm resolved to set aside my dark mood and be happy. My pregnant daughter and others, from across the lake, are coming for the festivities. Oh, it will be good to see her. I mustn't waste any more time Sun Fire needs help with the baking.

Cold Moon, sun-turning 1

I am a little achy this morning – too much good food, dancing – and definitely too much uiskajac. What a wonderful party. I danced till I thought my feet would fall off. It was too cold for lovemaking under the stars but the sweet pleasure under our warm blankets was just as good. I want to laze around in bed today, but the village will begin the packing for our move. And I have to say farewell to our departing guests. My daughter looks radiant – she is due in the Awakening Moon. What a good omen. I will miss her though. I wish I could be with her during this time. I hope she waits to have the child till I can come to her.

Sleek has disappeared again – just when I need her the most ...

Cold Moon, sun-turning 12

During the good weather we were able to distract our charges with work and games played down on the beach in the evenings. Now that the blue snows are here some of them have started whining about computer games and videos again. I talked to Tomcowan today about a theatre project. Maybe that will help keep them amused.

Cold Moon, sun-turning 14

As a compromise, Dra'hada is willing to send for some of the high tech equipment now in storage. If our new charges agree to study in our school, they will be allowed limited time on the equipment for entertainment pursuits. Twace and the others are dubious about the schooling part, but Dra'hada was firm with them. The Long Sleep Moons are a strain on everyone; I hope the play practices and Dra'hada's machines will help it pass in tranquility.

Ice Moon, sun-turning 2

We are teaching those who wish to learn, the discipline of "The Communion." In the long nights when the snows are heavy on the land above, we journey underground, to the warm cave of the Mother. There we lie together on the floor of a large chamber, our limbs touching, and we slide into the sweet reverie that is the Deep Communion with Tallav'Wahir. We leave our bodies in the warm darkness and allow our spirits to swim upon the Great Starry River. We journey to other worlds and visit with friends light years away. None of our charges can travel so far, but for those who are willing to try, we have hope that someday they will master the technique well enough to join us.

Ice Moon, sun-turning 7

Tomcowan's play was a success. It was written and performed by our charges. And I am so proud; my new daughter is such a good actress. She seemed to shine like a jewel when we offered her our praise. Our fosterlings told us the story of their lives in the lost city of Vancouver. Parts were funny, and some things were sad. Much of it I didn't understand, but in spite of that, the performance was very moving. The elders will tell stories of our own history tonight. I hope our fosterlings will like them. There is so much for us to share and weave together if we are to become one people.

Ice Moon, sun-turning 15

In the aftermath of Tomcowan's play an air of desolation has settled over our charges. It is very disheartening. The long gloomy days indoors have given the memories of their lost home an unexpected poignancy. More fights today.

Just now I found Jimtalbot staring moodily into the flames of our fire. I sat beside him and asked why he and the others were still grieving for such a horrible place.

He looked at me with his sorrowful blue eyes and said, "It wasn't all bad there, Qwalshina. My wife and I lived comfortably in a nice house by the ocean. Along with the bad, was a lot of good too. Art, music, fine literature, advances in science and medicine, we had a lot to be proud of. As hard as it was for people like Sleek and Twace back home I think they miss it as much as I do."

"Yes, I'm sure they do, and I can't understand that either."

He shrugged. "Home is home, no matter how bad it is, and you can't help caring when it's gone – if it's gone."

If it's gone? I didn't want to get bogged down in that conversation again, so I began a new topic. "Caring? Why didn't the people of your city care enough to protect suffering children who starved on your city streets? Why didn't they care enough to honor the Earth Mother and not destroy what were her gifts to you? Can you honestly say that life here has been so terrible that you would wish to go back?"

He was silent for a long time, just staring into the flames. Finally he tossed another stick onto the fire and shook his head. "I don't know, Qwalshina."

"Don't know?" I was confused and upset myself by then so I left him. Vancouver sounded like such a terrible place. How could they possibly miss it and want to return.

Ice Moon, sun-turning 19

The rumors about Earth have surfaced again, and this time I'm sure Dra'hada has heard them. Perhaps the play wasn't such a good idea after all. Everyone is getting tired of the cold and the confinement. The books have been read and reread, lessons and amusements are boring, and food and drink grow stale. Tempers are short. I try to sleep as much as I can. For us, this time is a natural phenomenon to be endured. For our charges, it is a torment beyond belief. Our warm dark homes anger or depress them. The snow is too deep, not the right color, too cold – the litany is endless. I'm going back to my bed.

Sun-Comes-Back Moon, sun-turning 7

When I lie upon my communion mat and close my eyes I can feel the deep stirring in the land, and my body responds to it gladly. The sap is rising, and the snow melting, and my daughter tells me her belly is nearly bursting. The sun is warm on my back when I collect the overflowing buckets of sap from the trees in the sugar bush. And, wonder of wonders, our Sun Fire is pregnant again. Tree is taking a lot of teasing for starting a new family at his age; but we are so pleased. This time the baby – all the babies will be healthy – I just know it.

Sun-Comes-Back Moon, sun-turning 28

One of the great ships from the Homeworld is coming. Dra'hada is ecstatic. Poor creature – this past year-turning has been so hard on him. What with all the villagers' and fosterlings' complaints to sort out and the unease of the Mother's Spirit Guardians to placate, it is no wonder that our Benefactor has aged visibly. It will do all of us good to have Benefactors from the Homeworld here for the renewal ceremonies. Perhaps they will be able to put those rumors about Earth's survival to rest once and for all.

The ship will be here by the time the snow is gone, so Dra'hada tells me. I wonder if they will bring a new mate for our dear teacher? It will be a great celebration; other villages are coming to join us. Everyone is excited, even our young fosterlings.

Awakening Moon, sun-turning 4

We are back in our village by the lake again. Our compound survived the storm season without needing many repairs. That is good because the ship will be here soon and there is so much to do before our guests arrive.

During all the confusion Sleek went missing again. When she crept back into the compound just before the evening meal I was so angry I shouted at her. She of course shouted right back. Why, oh why, does she continue to be so irresponsible! I'm trying not to compare her to Tukta, but it is so hard.

Awakening Moon, sun-turning 10

My heart is on the ground. The village is overflowing with guests. I'm trying very hard not to let my personal tragedy spoil the festive mood for others. My daughter's baby was born deformed and was – oh I can't even write down the words... The tragedy happened the night before last; her husband's aunt told me when she arrived today. Tears blur my vision as I try to write this. Oh Mother how could this happen – again.

Oh, Tukta, my dear sweet Tukta! I want desperately to go to her, take her in my arms and kiss away the pain. But I can't, not until after the ceremonies are over. What am I thinking of? She isn't a child anymore. I can't make this terrible hurt go away by my presence. And I have obligations to the People that take precedence over personal concerns. I must stay; I must be here to greet our Benefactors when the ship comes tomorrow. The Renewal Ceremony at the Mother Stone this year will be very important.

Awakening Moon, sun-turning 11

When I looked into the faces of our guests from the Homeworld today, I felt such a rage building up inside me that I could hardly breathe at times. Granny Night Wind sensed my disharmony, and made me drink a potion to settle my spirit. This new emotion I feel frightens me. What if we are living a lie – what if the people from Earth are right? I hate them! Why did they have to come here? Maybe they should have been left to die on their god-cursed world!

Awakening Moon, sun-turning 12

Our compound is quiet tonight; we took in no guests for the feasting. I can hear the sounds of merriment going on around us as I write this. The little ones don't understand. Sun Fire has taken them to the fire down on the beach. I am glad. My old man Tree is resting in the bedroom behind me. His nearness right now is a comfort.

To my surprise Sleek hasn't joined the revelers. She was standing in the doorway when I looked up from my pad. I wanted to say something encouraging to her, but I feel too dead inside to make the effort.

She watched me for a long moment in silence then said, "I-I'm sorry about your daughter, Qwalshina. Sun Fire said something went wrong and the baby's dead. Is that true – or did the damned lizards kill it?"

Her unspoken thought seemed to ring in my mind, *Filthy lizards, I told you they couldn't be trusted*. Suddenly I felt my anger leap up like oil poured onto flames. I hated her at that moment with all my heart, and maybe she felt it, because she staggered backward, and grabbed the doorpost for support. Why was she here – and healthy? Why had she, an unfit mother, had a healthy baby, when my dear sweet Tukta could not? Tukta loves her new husband, I thought, and now our Benefactors will probably want her to choose a new mate – it is unfair.

When I made no answer, and only glared at her, Sleek's expression crumpled, and she disappeared back into the night.

After she was gone Tree came out of the bedroom. He didn't reproach me for my cruelty; he only took me in his arms and led me to our bed. I lay down beside him, buried my face in the warmth of his chest and cried.

When I could control myself enough to speak, I said, "I'm so ashamed. The one time she tried to comfort someone else, I was unkind to her. Like a mean-spirited hag I pushed her away. Why was I so cruel to her, Tree? I don't understand her or myself anymore."

"Hush now, my flower," Tree soothed. "You are tired, and grieving. People say and do things at such a time that they don't truly mean. I know you care about her, and she does too. I will speak to her tomorrow. Go to sleep, my heart, all will be well."

I drifted into sleep, as he suggested, but deep in my heart I knew all would not be well – not for a long time – and maybe not ever again.

Awakening Moon, sun-turning 13

The most terrible thing has happened. Oh, it is so terrible I can hardly think of it without bursting into tears all over again. Sleek is dead, and so are ten others, one of them a native man from Cold Spring village. Tallav'Wahir, forgive me. I saw her sneaking out of our compound, and I did nothing to stop her. Did I drive her into joining those foolish people with my hard looks and resentment? Was I just another mother who failed her?

It was late in the afternoon when it happened. Most of our visiting Benefactors and other guests had taken air cars down the lake to visit Black Rock Village. I was just helping Sun Fire settle the children for their naps when a loud rumbling whine brought me, and most of the adults still home in the village racing to the shore. The great ship resting on the sand was making terrible noises, and trembling violently by the time we arrived. From within its opened hatchway we heard screaming – human screaming.

We looked at one another; our eyes round as soup bowls. Then, all the noise and trembling stopped as abruptly as it started. We waited, but nothing further happened. Finally Granny Night Wind and I walked to the stairway and called out to the crew left on duty inside. At first no one answered, but when the old woman started up the stairs, a weak voice from within warned her to come no closer. We exchanged glances, and then I said to the people in the ship, "Honored Benefactors, is something wrong? Can we help you?"

"No, you can't help. Come no closer – it may kill you too if you try to enter."

Kill us? I was taller than granny; I peered into the dimness of the open hatch. My nose caught the metallic scent of blood, before I saw it. There on the floor, blood – red blood. The benefactor's blood is brown. I shivered, a claw of fear tearing at my heart. What had happened in there? Oh, Mother, where was Sleek? I turned back to Granny. Had she seen the blood on the floor too? I stepped down off the stair, my mind in shock. People called to me, but I couldn't answer. I heard the sound of the air cars returning, and then people running past me. I swayed and would have fallen, but suddenly Tree's arms were around me, hugging me to his chest.

"Qwalshina, what's happened?"

He was warm and solid, smelling of budding leaves and smoky leather. Against his chest, I shook my head. No words could get past the aching lump in my throat.

The visiting Benefactors rushed into their ship, and soon after Dra'hada appeared and told us to return to our homes. He wouldn't answer the shouted questions put to him. "Everything is in order now. No need to fear. Go back to your homes. Tonight at the Big Sing I will tell you all that has happened."

Granny Nigh Wind added her own urging to the gathered people and soon most drifted away. I stayed; I refused to let Tree and Sun Fire lead me away. When Dra'hada came over to us, I clutched his scaly hand and begged, "Please, honored teacher, tell me what has happened."

Dra'hada's headcrest drooped, and he patted my hand. "Go home, Qwalshina. You can't do anything to help here. Go home with your family."

"Damn you, I'm not a child. Tell me what's happened. Is Sleek in there?" I heard Tree and Sun Fire's gasps of surprise at my disrespect, but I was too frightened to care. I had to know.

For just a moment Dra'hada's headcrest flattened and I saw the gleam of long teeth under his parted black lips. I shuddered, but stood my ground. I had to know. Then he let go his own anger, and looked at me solemnly. "I never assumed you were a child, Qwalshina; I am sorry if you think that. All right, I will tell you. Yes, Sleek is in there – dead."

I continued to stare at him, willing him to finish it. He sighed and finally continued, "It seems that the rumor about Earth still existing took root stronger in other villages than it did here. All during the harsh weather this cancer has been growing among the new refugees. A man named Carljameson wanted to take our ship and go back to Earth. There were others who helped him try. What they didn't know, or couldn't understand, is that the great ships from the Homeworld are sentient beings. They aren't shells of dead metal like the machines of Earth. When our crew was threatened, the ship itself responded by killing the intruders in a most painful way."

Dra'hada refused to tell me the details. He could sense how upset I was, and told Tree to take me home. Later I learned Carljameson and his war band forced their way on board the ship with the help of the man from Cold Spring. They stole weapons from somewhere and injured one of our Benefactors during the struggle. With so many new people here, and everybody celebrating, no one took note of the conspirators' odd behavior.

Ah, why didn't I go after Sleek when I saw her leave? I was selfish and careless. I was grieving for my daughter, and I was so tired of fighting with her. I blame myself in part for her tragic death. Could I have done more to make her a part of our family?

Awakening Moon, sun-turning 14

There is a great council being held among our Benefactors aboard the ship. Communications with the Homeworld have been established. Because of the man from Cold Spring's involvement, not only the newcomers' fate, but also our own, will depend on the Council's decision.

Some of our Benefactors claim that we are a genetically flawed species. We should all be eliminated, and this world reseeded with another more stable species. Others like our dear Dra'hada counsel that that is too harsh a decision. We have lived here the required seven generations and more. We are not to blame for the assault. They counsel that those of us, who have bred true to the Ancient Way, should be allowed to continue on, either as we are, or interbred with another compatible species to improve our bloodlines.

They are meeting on the ship now.

Around me the land continues to sing its ancient song of renewal. The Mother will not intercede for us with our Benefactors. She is wise, but in the passionless way of ancient stone. In the darkness last night the people met in the village square to sing the Awakening songs, as we have always done. Tears in my eyes, I lifted up my voice with the rest. I was afraid – we all were. Just before dawn I climbed to the Mother Stone.

What will the day bring to my people, Life or termination? I lean my head against the stone's solid bulk and breathe in the smells of new growth and the thawing mud in the lake. Blood. The old people say it is the carrier of ancestral memory and our future's promise. The stone is cold. I'm shivering as I open a wound on my forearm and make my offering. My blood is red, an alien color on this world...

Point of Entry

Bebe Bayliss

"LOOK OUT!" I shouted.

The magenta-scaled family of Colubri, a large snake-like species native to one of the Kepler systems, slithered out of the way as my luggage dropped out of hover mode and almost landed on them. I didn't speak Colubrian, but I didn't need a translation device to understand their yells of annoyance as we exited the starship. I dipped my head in apology and fiddled with the settings until my two brand-new, starship-required suitcases floated properly at my side.

Mad at myself for making a typical Earthling mistake, I took a deep breath as I moved from the passenger bridge into the terminal, determined to be a more attentive traveler. I looked around, comforted to see the arrivals terminal at Star Base Jerome was surprisingly familiar – it even smelled vaguely of cooking odors, and I wondered what was on offer at the food court as my stomach grumbled.

I'd expected my first trip out of my own solar system to be completely disorienting, but instead Customs and Immigration felt like an oversized version of the arrival terminal at Star Base Los Angeles back home. Which is to say, filled with travelers who, regardless of what planet they were arriving from, were tired, cranky, and just wanted to be on the other side of the security personnel and huge doors that separated them from whatever adventure they were about to begin.

The terminal was a massive enclosed dome – the honeycomb-structure ceiling was probably two hundred feet high. The dark-colored ribs of the dome supported clear panels, and the effect was like being in a planetarium viewing a night sky. Star Base was on the surface of the Jerome system's largest planet, Jellico, and a constant stream of shuttles and transport rockets passed silently overhead.

The soundproofing that kept external noise out seemed to trap terminal noise in, and I stood still for a moment, disoriented by snippets of conversation in unknown tongues that competed with a distant garbled voice loudly repeating announcements in the six primary galactic languages. The undertone was a persistent low hum that I guessed were power and ventilation services for the dome.

Concerned I'd miss hearing something important, I craned my neck as floating digital signs inside the dome flashed arrivals and departures in a variety of languages and alphabets. Fortunately, I happened to be looking in the right direction when an official waved me over to a bright orange podium, and I stepped forward in a manner I hoped was both enthusiastic and respectful.

"Documents, please," he requested in English.

That he spoke English wasn't a surprise – he was an Etarun, a small, caramel-colored, teddy bear-like species who were the most gifted linguists in the galaxy. Their native language consisted entirely of complex mathematical formulas, and fluency required strict discipline and adherence to rules.

The Etarun easily learned all other galactic languages, and with their devotion to order and organization, they were natural bureaucrats. Lacking valuable natural resources on their home planet but blessed with a non-threatening physical form, Etarun's primary export became immigration officials. They had a galactic lock on all immigration postings and were a familiar sight at all star bases. They insisted on vivid orange for their podiums, arguing that it was vital to have a signature color for immigration services, but it was rumored that they really just liked how orange complemented their fur.

He wore the standard orange bowler hat of a male Etarun – Officer Sunim, according to the digital nametag attached to the hat's crown. I handed him my passport, customs documents, and immigration papers. He shuffled slowly through my paperwork, alternating between sighing and clicking his teeth as he read each page. Finally, he addressed me. "State your name and home planet."

"I'm Clara Clement of Earth."

"Do you confirm that this is your luggage?" He waved a paw at my minty green suitcases.

"Yes—"

Shouting erupted at the next podium. Officer Sunim and I both jumped at the disturbance, and I recognized the man hollering as a fellow passenger on my flight from Earth.

"So now bee-keeping equipment is banned?" the man screamed. "What kind of planet is this anyway?" His luggage had been inserted in the scanner housed within the podium and the inspection process didn't seem to be going as expected. Suddenly, four walls rose from the floor and enclosed the man, Etarun official, and podium. It got quiet again.

"The Cone of Silence is sometimes necessary," Officer Sunim observed calmly, while I glanced down and saw that my podium was also wall-enabled, judging from the slots in the floor. "To continue, you are Clara Clement of Earth, and this is your luggage?"

I nodded, my brain racing through a mental inventory of the contents of my luggage, terrified I'd accidentally packed a beehive. A door slid open in the front of the podium and I placed my suitcases inside as instructed by the info-graphic.

Officer Sunim studied the monitor at his elbow, then nodded. "Good thing you're not a honey farmer." He stamped several documents. The door in the podium opened, my luggage slid out, and the door closed. The floor walls didn't budge, and I allowed myself a small reduction in anxiety.

"Luggage approved. Now, you wish to become a permanent resident in the Jerome system?"

"Yes, sir, I do."

"Well, I have some questions to ask you first."

"I'm ready, sir."

"Good. Paper or plastic?"

"I beg your pardon?

"Simple enough question, Applicant. Paper or plastic?"

It had been a very long trip from Earth to the Jerome Solar System, so I wasn't at my best. Officer Sunim tapped a pen impatiently on the form in front of him, waiting for my response.

"Applicant, you are comfortable speaking in English?" he asked.

I nodded. "Um, paper, I guess." I'd understood the question but wondered what the point was.

"Ah, interesting choice." He carefully filled in a small circle on the form.

He asked me another question, and I leaned in closer to hear him over the announcements. He smelled like blueberry muffins.

"Now, Applicant, cake or pie?"

"Cake," I replied at once, as the aroma of baked goods wafted around me. The odor was so pleasantly unexpected that I snuck a glance around, hoping to see a bakery cart, but all I saw were podiums with teddy bears and travelers.

"Indeed." Officer Sunim filled in another circle.

Rocketlag nor not, I forced myself to pay close attention. I'd been warned that, although my immigration application was approved and I was officially invited to settle in the Jerome system, I had to pass one last interview when I landed at Star Base.

This final step would determine if I would be accepted as a permanent resident on the planet I hoped to make my forever home. I'd studied the Jerome system, its planetary history, economy, culture, and language, and had assumed I was ready for whatever they threw at me. My stomach formed a knot of worry that I might be wrong.

I took a deep breath and thought about what Grandma had said about her own move to Earth from Dunbar, one of Alpha Centauri's planets. She'd told me that when you immigrate to a new planet, you have to answer questions that seem random and senseless but are critical to get right because they determine the rest of your life. But even forewarned, I was puzzled.

"Right. Now, red or white?" Officer Sunim asked, waiting with pen poised for me to reply.

"Wine? I'm not ordering a meal, I'm immigrating to this solar system. I'm confused."

He drew in his breath sharply. "Applicant, we consulted the finest mind in the galaxy to devise these filtering questions. We seek only the best and the brightest – we don't want to become another Mars, do we?"

He had a point. Centuries ago, in a surge of early interstellar immigration enthusiasm, Mars had accepted anyone who wanted to come. To say it had not gone well was nominated every year for the Galactic Understatement Award but never won because nobody wanted to reward Martians, not even those of us from the same solar system.

"White, then."

"Well done, Applicant." He beamed as he filled in another circle on the form. "Ah, this is my favorite – whole or refried?"

I panicked, not expecting a question about beans. Was this a health-related query, in which case whole was possibly the answer, or was it a cultural-sensitivity question, in which case maybe refried was correct? My brain said refried, but my instincts were notoriously bad. "Whole," I sputtered.

"Hmm, I see. Thank you, Applicant." Another small circle was filled in. The questions continued, and I picked city condo over country cottage, dog over cat, aisle over window. Officer Sunim alternately smiled or sighed at each answer, and I had no sense of how I was doing.

"Well now, here's our final question. Coke or Pepsi?"

This was it. Five Earth years after starting the immigration application process, filling in hundreds of pages of forms, enduring multiple medical exams, background and credit checks, interviews, and a general poking into every corner of my life, my dream of moving to Jerome came down, apparently, to my choice of brown carbonated beverage. No sweat – I had this. "Coke. Definitely, Coke."

He sighed loudly through pursed lips. "Ah. Applicant, please take a seat in Bay Seventeen to wait for secondary screening." He rolled my documents into a tube, attached it to a nearby drone that resembled a plate-sized flying spider, pushed a button, and it joined a flock of drones darting between podiums and desks around the terminal.

A guide drone that looked like a foot-long hummingbird descended gently into my line of sight, its screen flashing "Bay 17," and, luggage floating at my side, I followed it through a maze of bays. Announcements faded as we got further from the main terminal, replaced by blaring floating message boards that zipped around the bays.

Each bay held three patterned sofas arranged in a semi-circle about ten feet in diameter. They adjusted to accommodate the seating needs of a range of species. I saw a wide variety of travelers sitting, lying, lounging, even perched on the sofas' aluminum arms.

With so many species sweating, molting, and shedding, the scarlet-and-forest green upholstery looked surprisingly tidy, although the designers must have decided to ignore the needs of any color-blind species. The seats were close enough together to allow occupants to face each other and talk, and in the center area of each bay was a docking pedestal for luggage. A floating digital sign positioned above each pedestal flashed the bay number in six languages. I kept an eye out for number Seventeen since bay numbering didn't appear to be any kind of order my Earthling brain understood.

Around me, travelers were escorted by either drones or Martian security teams. For all they were bad-mouthed, modern Martians, descendants of the humans who were early settlers of Mars, were the best security officers in the galaxy. Only the hardiest humans had survived early Mars exploration to reproduce. Today's Martians were stocky and well-muscled, their uniforms bright yellow armored bodysuits festooned with weapons. Even in a galaxy filled with aliens of almost every shape, size, and color, Martians stood out.

Like their ancestors, Martians had an enduring love of weapons and law enforcement, as long as they were the enforcers. They'd developed their skills taming their fellow citizens when Mars first established a government. Although it was corrupt and barely functioning by galactic standards, Martians had concluded their government was good enough and turned their attention to making money.

For the last several hundred years, Mars had based its economy on hiring out as intragalactic security. Martians were manageable if paid well, and the rest of the galaxy, seeing it was better to hire than fight them, also concluded the arrangement was good enough. Martians were a big reason the Earth system was so dominant.

I felt slightly nauseated about more interrogation, but grateful that my guide was a drone and not a Martian, so I pushed down the desire to stress-vomit over another interview. As I arrived at Bay Seventeen, I passed a human woman leaving, escorted away by Martians, their radios crackling with unintelligible chatter. I was so focused on taking a seat I didn't notice if she looked happy or scared. My luggage floated to the center pedestal, joining three goldtone suitcases and a pair of sapphire blue bags. I guessed the blue bags belonged to the adult male Drahci already seated. Drahci were a vaguely humanoid-meets-dolphin, two-headed, blue-skinned species, sky-blue for males, cobalt for females.

A young family of three humans occupied the third sofa, huddled together at one end, the little girl sitting on the mother's lap. That left plenty of room at the other end for the Martian, a large man in a yellow bodysuit who appeared to be napping. He was stretched out with legs extended and crossed at the ankles, helmet visor down, body slumped against the armrest. I didn't see a weapon but that didn't mean he wasn't armed – Martians invested heavily in making sure they had all the best firepower.

I nodded to the family and the child stared at me until I waved, then she turned her face to her mother, who indicated that the father should retrieve something from the goldtone luggage. He fetched a small stuffed pig that immediately distracted the child. The two adults looked wistful and I imagined they were wishing they had something that could take their minds off the anxiety of secondary screening. I smiled at the Drahci to take my mind off my own worry.

He turned to me, made the sound of bubbling mud, stopped, pressed a translation device on his chest, and spoke again, this time in English. I leaned closer to hear him over the noisy message boards floating by. He smelled like chocolate chip cookies. I'd been expecting seaweed. "Hello, I'm Rxigo, of the Trappist Solar System. It's nice to have more company here." He waved two of his five flippers at me and his traditional Drahci robes, long pieces of shimmering silvery-blue cloth strategically draped to accommodate the movement of multiple heads and flippers, caught the light.

"Hello, I'm Clara Clement, of the Earth Solar System."

"We're the Lassa family, also of Earth," the father said. "I'm Vincent, this is my wife Natalia, and our daughter Lucy."

"I'm four!" Lucy stated, proudly holding up four fingers.

"Four is a very good age," I said. "And you're an experienced traveler already."

Rxigo grinned from both heads. "I'm pleased to meet you all."

We all looked at the Martian who shifted slightly in his seat but didn't look up or speak, and I wondered if he was rude or just sleepy. Martians weren't known for their charm, but they also weren't known for just lying around, so I decided to stop thinking about why he was here.

Rxigo nodded at us with both heads. "I just overheard on the radio that a man meant to join this bay will be deported for smuggling prohibited items, so it's just us." He gave the Martian a long look, but got no reaction. "I seem to be stuck here while so many other travelers cycle in and out, but I'm glad I've made it this far."

A little shiver at a possible near-miss in Customs went through me and I focused on Rxigo instead of my nerves. "So you're you here for secondary screening, too?"

"I am, and trying to figure out why," he said with a sigh that sounded like a moist volcano. "The questions were odd, but I was expecting that, based on what I'd heard from colleagues. I thought I'd done pretty well, although the cup or cone question was unexpected, since Drahci are lactose-intolerant. But here I am in secondary, so I guess I got it wrong."

Drahci were known for their intelligence and diplomacy, and it seemed odd that Rxigo hadn't been welcomed to Jerome with open appendages. But I remembered Grandma's warning – if the questions seem designed for you to fail, it's because they are. Apparently even a Drahci wasn't immune to secondary screening.

"I think I got caught in the Coke versus Pepsi battle. I picked Coke and ended up here."

"We stumbled on the 'white or wheat' question," Vincent said with a shake of his head.

"Lucy's favorite is wheat toast with the crust trimmed off," Natalia added, "and the question was so unexpected that I responded like I was in a restaurant placing her order, not in immigration."

"Rxigo, did you get ancient Earth-based questions too?" I asked. "I mean, we're Earthlings so it makes sense for us, and I was warned to study old Earth's cultural history, but I didn't realize everyone's questions would relate to Earth."

"Thanks to the Disney Treaty of 2463, Earth culture is taught galaxy-wide, so I suppose the Milky Way Department of Immigration decided Earth should be the basis for all filtering questions."

"It's still 'The Happiest Place in Space' hundreds of years later." I relaxed a little as I thought about the Disney light parades and Fantasyland rides I'd enjoyed on Earth as a child.

"Do you think having a standardized test makes things easier for Immigration?" Rxigo asked. "I understand they're looking for the best predictors of success for new settlers, but the questions seem arbitrary, and that's me being nice."

"I don't see how my choice of paper or plastic helps, so I'm confused, too." I tried to keep frustration with random questions out of my voice because I didn't want my first real conversation in this system to be me whining. But it had been a long and emotionally exhausting journey to get this far, leaving my old life, friends, and family back on Earth, a now-distant planet. All my worldly goods were in the two suitcases docked nearby, if "worldly goods" was still an accurate description.

I focused back on Rxigo to stop the "what was I thinking?" worry from taking hold again. "What brings you to the Jerome system, Rxigo?" I followed my mother's advice to always ask someone about themselves, regardless of their planet of origin.

"I'm a Drahci cultural representative, here on an educational posting. My specialty is interpretive dancing." He began to wave his flippers in a synchronized movement while his heads moved in separate but related circles. The spectacle made me dizzy and I was glad I was sitting down. I saw Natalia look away, and I wondered if she was having the same reaction.

"Have you been in Bay Seventeen long?" Vincent asked Rxigo.

"It seems like a very long time. But I understand – they have to get this right to make sure new residents will thrive. Moving to a new planet can be lonely, expensive, and frustrating, and those are the good points. But I'm sure you all know that."

Vincent and Natalia nodded, and she gave Lucy a reassuring kiss on the head.

I felt the worry bubble up again, so I pasted on a sympathetic smile and nodded in agreement just as a sign floated past my head, loudly proclaiming the arrival of a shuttle from an adjoining terminal. I jumped, and Rxigo leaned over in concern. "Sorry, I guess I'm a little jumpy, which is not how I usually respond to the unexpected." I smelled apple pie instead of chocolate chip cookies, and as I settled back in my seat, I looked again for a bakery cart.

"Excuse me, but does it smell like delicious baked goods in here? Everywhere and everyone smells wonderful, but I only see bays around us." I'd never flown this far from home, so my nose playing tricks could be a side-effect of intragalactic travel. I was so tired, I didn't even mind if the question sounded silly.

"I want donuts," Lucy chirped.

"Thank goodness you asked," Vincent said. "It smells so good in here I was about to track down a bakery and get us all a treat."

Instead of looking at us as if we should be put on the next rocket back to Earth, Rxigo smiled broadly from each head. "Comfort Odors is a new technology being tested in this terminal. I understand they've developed a method to precisely aim an atomized aroma that smells pleasantly of one's home planet at new arrivals to help ease anxiety. It's different for every species, of course. For me, the aroma is what an Earthling would describe as rotting fish, and I'm smelling that now. The targeting is so good that I bet you can't tell?"

I took a deep exploratory sniff and shook my head in the negative. "No, all I get is apple pie."

"Glazed donuts," Natalia said.

"Apple fritters," Vincent chimed in.

Apparently the whole family were fans of sweet fried dough as Lucy softly chanted, "Donuts, donuts."

"The wonders of technology," Rxigo observed. "So, my fellow travelers, why are you moving to Jerome?"

"I'm in a pilot program developing new communities on Jeromian asteroid clusters," I said. "My specialty is orbital mechanics. There's so much opportunity for me here compared to Earth."

Vincent nodded in agreement. "Natalia and I are theoretical astronomers, and the Jerome system offers exciting new research opportunities."

The Martian suddenly stirred, tapped something on a wrist console, and re-crossed his legs. I wondered if we were annoying him with our talking. Meanwhile, Rxigo waved his flippers around again and cricked his heads back and forth as he listened.

Stress made me chatty. "Moving to seek opportunity is in my DNA, I guess. My ancestors were settlers who left Earth in the early exoplanet exploration phase but lost their Earth citizenship because that was the law then. My Grandma immigrated back to Earth, and she said I should expect to just roll with weird questions because their true purpose was known only to bureaucrats."

Rxigo's heads bobbed in what I decided to interpret as agreement. "Indeed. To paraphrase Earth's Benjamin Franklin, 'In any world nothing can be said to be certain, except death, taxes, and bureaucracy,' and I agree."

"You sound just like my Grandma." I was hit with a sudden wave of longing for my family and coughed to hide the tears that stung the corners of my eyes. I didn't think I fooled anyone.

"As I think back to my cultural training, I was taught that Earthlings' use of language is unusually specific." It seemed Rxigo was changing the subject and I was grateful. "Did you know your Sami people have a thousand words for reindeer? You have an equally rich menu of expressions for both love and violence, and your insistence on making a meaningful decision based on a simple 'either-or' question is unique in the galaxy." His heads nodded in unison, and I got the impression it was a compliment.

"We Earthlings don't often hear that we're special," Natalia observed. I agreed – mostly we were reminded of our warlike tendencies and how the whole galaxy felt like the Earth Solar System's wishes must be accommodated, or else.

Rxigo gestured at my suitcases with a single flipper. "Are your personal belongings being shipped later?"

"No, I've only brought what I could bring as checked luggage on the voyage from Earth to Jerome. But that's fine since the customs form to bring in more was about three hundred pages long."

Vincent sighed. "I wish we could have done that. Besides our three suitcases here, we have a pod arriving next week. It was almost five hundred pages of customs paperwork."

"Well then, I'm glad I decided to be efficient." I laughed. "Or, I'm just lazy."

"Efficient or lazy, wonderful! Earthlings fall immediately into an either-or position that is fascinating." Rxigo made a series of sizzling-wet sounds, like rain falling on a campfire, that I hoped was laughter.

I was startled by shouting behind us and, judging from the way his heads swiveled, so was Rxigo. Lucy dropped her toy as her parents jumped. Even the Martian looked up.

"Coffee! Not tea! I meant to answer coffee!" screeched a Grongin female, her ivory wings held firmly by a Martian security detail as they escorted her towards departure. She was about ten feet tall, with likely the standard species thirty-foot wingspan. Like all known winged species in the galaxy, Grongin went airborne fast when startled or threatened, which explained the strong hold on her wings.

The Martian in our bay raised his visor and looked around for the source of the noise. He seemed to register the Grongin situation, lowered his visor, and resumed his resting position. I realized he wasn't sleeping at all, which somehow didn't make me feel better about him being in Bay Seventeen.

Rxigo again provided a welcome distraction. "What's interesting to me is, why do you suppose tea is the wrong answer?"

I shook my head. "And why the emphasis on brown beverages? It's weird. Although my Grandma warned me, so maybe it's to see how we respond to the unexpected. She said no matter how well-prepared you think you are, you'll be surprised and confused regularly by the most ordinary things on your new planet. Or, I'm overthinking it. See? Another Earthling either-or conundrum."

"I feel lucky we didn't get a brown beverage question," Natalia said. "Failing the bread question was bad enough. We're the first ones from either family to travel off-Earth, so there's a lot at stake for us." She nervously rocked Lucy, who was again occupied with the retrieved stuffed pig.

Rxigo nodded his heads. "I was warned there are a few key filtering questions that are revealing. Since our Grongin friend is being put on the next transport home, it seems she got it wrong. Pity. She'll be sent back to her home planet to start the immigration application process over. She's one of the lucky ones. There is a rumor that the wrong answer to the Nirvana or Pearl Jam question is grounds for immediate deportation via military transport and a lifetime ban on interstellar travel."

I didn't see why picking one ancient grunge band over the other was a significant indicator, though I personally felt that, between the two, the band that got the glory wasn't the one that deserved it.

"We had to pick between Mozart and Beethoven," Vincent said.

"Lucy shouted 'Twinkle, Twinkle Little Star' before I could say anything," Natalia added, "so I hope we got that right." Both parents looked uncomfortable and I wondered if I should pass them a couple of the airsick bags I'd picked up on the flight.

As we engaged in nervous chatter, I learned the Lassas had been hired by the same company I was going to work for, so we promised to have a non-brown beverage together soon. Rxigo recommended a brand of Drahci green tea that sounded delicious. The Martian shifted in his seat, raised his visor to give us a glare, and tapped out more messages on his wrist console.

Nobody spoke again until the Martian's visor was lowered and he resumed his resting position, then we arranged to meet for tea at a café Rxigo had read about. I sensed having something to look forward to on the other side of the large terminal doors was as calming to my seatmates as it was to me.

I wasn't sure how Drahci showed stress, but one of Rxigo's heads was involved in a complicated series of movements, and I felt I should try to reassure him. "I hope the cup or cone question doesn't prevent you from moving here. I think this system would be lucky to have a talented Drahci as a new resident."

"You're the first Drahci I've had a conversation with, and if they are all as nice as you, it's no wonder you're all so successful as diplomats," Vincent said.

"Thank you," Rxigo said. "Talking with you all certainly improves a daunting situation." He seemed about to continue when the Martian sat up, stretched his arms, and cracked his knuckles.

The violent popping sound erased any calmness that I was feeling. My palms were sweaty, and I felt hot and almost ready to heave for certain, pie-scented air or not, when I heard the adorable squeaks of a baby Swpni. Widely acknowledged as the cutest pet in the galaxy, a Swpni pup was exactly the distraction I needed.

As I looked around wildly for the pup, Rxigo pointed at Bay Thirty-Two, and we all swiveled to look. Swpni were often described as a combination of the best parts of a puppy, a bunny, and a bouquet of flowers. They were small, light purple, curly-haired, wide-eyed, smelled of lavender, and their squeaks were favorably compared to a Bach sonata. I was excited to be so close to one, as they were exceedingly rare.

"I want to pet the pretty puppy!" Lucy squealed.

"No, Lucy," Natalia said, her voice gentle but firm, and, I thought, a little sad. "That's their pet. Stop wiggling."

"I agree with Lucy's excitement about the pretty puppy," I said. "I've always said any system that welcomed Swpni would be an excellent place to live." Then I remembered we were in Immigration and wondered if it would be allowed in. I'd left my own dog with my parents on Earth – importing an Earth animal to Jerome was almost impossible. I teared up as I remembered I'd never see Trixie again and hoped the little Swpni got to stay with its owner.

"You like animals?" Rxigo asked gently.

"Oh, I love them. I had to leave my dog back on Earth, and the sweet little Swpni reminded me of what I gave up to come here. Did you leave an animal behind too?" I asked Natalia.

She nodded, her eyes glazed with tears. "Belle, our calico. I've had her since college. I know my sister will take good care of her, but it's another piece of my heart left back on Earth."

"Rxigo, did you leave a pet to come here?" I asked, since he seemed a little downcast at our conversation.

"No, as a cultural representative, I move so much it wouldn't be fair to any animal, so I'm as happy as you to see the Swpni." He sat up straighter and both his mouths smiled. "Let's talk of happy things. Clara Clement, and Lassa family, cheer up, your new solar system is a wonderful place, and you're all just the type of Earthlings they welcome." Rxigo's heads bobbed enthusiastically.

"I like you," Lucy said to Rxigo. "You're pretty." He made the sizzling-wet sound. Lucy turned to me. "You're pretty, too."

"That's very kind, Lucy, and I hope the secondary interviewer agrees with Rxigo that we can all move here." I was too nervous to recall which of the local deities was the patron saint of immigrants so I could send up a silent request for good luck.

Before I could beat myself up about my lapse in cultural awareness, three teams of Martians approached, and my stomach lurched. The leader of the first team silently pointed at Rxigo, who stood, wrapped his robes closely around him as he retrieved his luggage, and fumbled with the hover settings as his escort loomed. Team two pointed at the Lassa family, who quickly gathered up Lucy and luggage, glancing around the bay for anything left behind. The not-sleeping Martian nodded curtly at his colleagues, and another wave of anxiety washed over me.

The lead Martian of team number three indicated I was to follow her, and I said a hurried goodbye to Rxigo and the Lassa family as I claimed my own luggage, wishing them all good luck with their interviews, since one did not keep Martians waiting. I wondered if mine was the team that had escorted the Grongin back to departures, and my nerves made me chatty again. "Oh, my own escort." The team leader stopped, wheeled around to face me, and shook her head side-to-side in the universal – or at least galactic – signal for no talking.

I couldn't see her expression through her tinted face shield, but the meaning was clear, and I swallowed down whatever else I was about to say. I kept my eyes on her back and looked for signage to indicate where we were headed, but the digital signs were never in English when I spied one. I practiced more deep breathing and was about to ask for a stop at the toilet to properly stress-vomit when I was ushered to an orange podium. The Martians marched away as my suitcases floated to my side, and I faced a female Etarun, whose bright blue hat complemented both her fur and the podium. Her nametag stated she was Officer Sulpand, and she busily stamped a stack of paperwork.

"Welcome home." She smiled as she pushed the documents towards me.

"I'm in? Wasn't there another step?"

"Oh, you're wondering about secondary screening. We had some concerns with your response to Coke or Pepsi, but the second interviewer assured us you are just the kind of settler we want. You're smart, motivated, kind, and love animals."

Still confused, I pressed on. "Second interviewer? Oh, of course. The Martian was there to listen to us and report back."

She chuckled. "Smitty? Oh, that's funny, I must tell him. No, he was on a break and finds the bay sofas more comfortable than the seats in the staff room when he wants a little rest. He's terribly shy, so doesn't talk to travelers, but he always remembers to message his mother. And if he wants to rest where interviews are taking place, who am I to argue?"

She shrugged in a way that indicated Martians do whatever they want and there wasn't a species in the galaxy that thought it was wise to object.

"The interviewer was Professor Rxigo," Officer Sulpand continued. "He's the developer of our filtering questions and likes to keep his hand – or rather, flipper – in, so to speak, on the program. His left-side head transmitted your interview and his approval to us so we could finalize your documents. He likes to tell applicants he's a cultural representative who's immigrating – it relaxes them, and waving his flippers around is good exercise since he spends so much time conducting interviews as part of his research."

"He works here? But he had luggage and a Martian escort," I sputtered.

"Snacks. It's a long day in the terminal for the Professor. And the Martians guide him to the next bay he's working in, as he finds the terminal layout confusing."

I managed to blurt out an astonished thank you, which she acknowledged with a friendly nod of her head. I carefully stowed my documents as the good news started to sink in that, despite the randomness of the questions, I'd passed.

I looked around at the nearby podiums and spotted the Lassa family. Lucy was reaching out to try to hug the Etarun officer, and Vincent and Natalia were grinning.

"Oh, one more thing," Officer Sulpand said. "We have a welcome gift for you." She handed me a bottle of wine. "White, I believe you chose?"

A Foot in Two Worlds

Christine Bennett

MY EARS PRICK; I pretend to be busy on my fon. After all, I'm just another Alliance faction, Level 6, Sector B office worker trying to catch some moments of privacy on Neqo'sp Station's mallway, somewhere in the unizone between arrivals and departures. The crowds make the space station feel less lonely.

I already know how the encounter will unfold. My part in this script is perfected. I will awkwardly, hesitantly, be questioned. Maybe they will ask me about my large eyebrows. Maybe they will comment on my aquiline nose. Maybe they will ask me about my blue and brown hair.

I catch the older couple's approach in my fon's reflection. Tourists. Their vibrant clothes and wide-eyed sense of wonder at the mallway's arcing beams gives them away along with the slight wobbliness caused by unfamiliar artificial gravity.

Their hesitant approach tingles the back of my neck. I stuff a large scoop of fruit mash in my mouth and hold it there.

And . . . *ACTION*!

"Excuse me—"

So it begins, in the exact same way as it usually does. Ask me where the washroom is. Ask me where the info desk is. *Please*!

Turning my head slowly, I shrug and cover my bulging cheeks with one hand.

"Oh! I'm so sorry to catch you eating," the older human woman declares, her hand flying to her breast.

"Mmmm-hmmm," I reply.

Instead of leaving, they politely smile and wait for me to finish swallowing. *Koutzi*! *Damn*!

"We were just wondering," the male companion says. "We're wondering if you're from Kallergaea?"

I shake my head. "No."

"Really?" the woman says, doubtful.

Depending on my mood, I might concoct some story about how I was from the non-existent *Pallemgaea*, a common mistake. The questioner always chuckles and awkwardly backs away, profusely apologizing, when I try that tactic.

Instead, I size up the couple. They seem sincere enough, even though I don't owe them anything. Not my time. Not my family history. Not myself.

"My father is from Kallergaea. He left when he was a boy."

"Ah..." They smile and nod again, thank me for my time and leave.

Today I was lucky. Today I didn't have to act as a poor ambassador for my father's culture.

* * *

Let's get the basics out of the way, for our mutual benefit –

Are you Kallergaean? Only my father is.

Were you born on Kallergaea? No. I was born on an Alliance star cruiser.

Have you been to Kallergaea? No.
Do you want to visit? I'm not sure.
Do you speak Kallergaean? Only the basics.
Will you marry a Kallergaean? Uhhhh … that's a very personal question, don't you think, complete stranger?
Got it? *Kazarch*! Good!

* * *

It's so hard *not* being from Kallergaea. I blame the movies, which spawned the travel industry, which spawned a craze for anything remotely related to Dad's homeworld. Some animated features were also made and then the enduring mystery of Kallergaea's missing monarchy ignited the whole craze again. No one cares about my mother's boring origins.

My co-worker, McKinli, is a Kallergaea super fan. My whole workday is usually spent avoiding her as much as possible. I'm an expert in all the freight elevators, hidden doors, and out-of-the-way washrooms on Level 6.

Once she discovered my father, my *kaateras*, was Kallergaean, she latched on to me. I was the next best thing to the blue, blue water and sandy beaches. Sometimes I thought my smile was going to crack under the weight of the many praises and facts she bestowed upon me. She means well, but her Kallergaea, my Dad's Kallergaea, and my Kallergaea – they're all very different worlds.

In McKinli's Kallergaea, she walks through it in the virtual world she constructed in Sector B's metachamber. Everything is perfect in her Kallergaea. She'll never know the disappointment of the rainy season or the blights which imperil food crops. The waves are always gentle and free of sucking undertows. Her Kallergaea is a destination catered to her every whim. She's a tourist twice over. The elders sitting on the steps of their bright white square houses are a moment to be captured for friends and family. McKinli's entitlement as a treasured guest grates on me *a lot*.

Obs, I sound so bitter. But decades of patiently engaging the curiosity of others hasn't helped me navigate the two worlds I occupy.

I am avoiding McKinli again. She trapped me earlier in the kitchenette while I made breakfast. Clad in a long garment with gauntlets, commissioned from a Section A clothier, she assures me it's just like the ones ancient Kallergaeans wore.

My heart races simply recalling the interaction. Where's the line between appreciation and appropriation? And ancient? We're a living people! McKinli scolded me when I rebuffed her.

Once, at a potluck, in a moment of absolute genius, I thought I would finally best McKinli with something she couldn't know about Kallergaea. I cooked one of Dad's favourite recipes. A dish he made all the time and one that my brother and I didn't care for. *Favsolia* – large smooth beans boiled in a thick sauce. There! An authentic Kallergaean dish, nestled in a handmade bowl made by my *miayia* when she was a child.

My co-workers politely took a small amount as we moved down the line of dishes and I cheerfully told them how this was Dad's favourite comfort food. McKinli examined the spoonful she took.

"Is this *actually* Kallergaean or did you just make it up?" she said.

After that, I vowed to only bring a flat of drinks to any future staff functions.

* * *

How could McKinli know – how could my brother and I *really* know, what Dad went through when his family left Kallergaea?

His family and neighbours couldn't know, either, when they boarded a cargo ship packed with mánanko fruit, that they wouldn't see their hilly homeland for years. The universe possesses no shortage of exciting new cultures to meet and places to see – a thousand different journeys and experiences awaited the group of families as they spread mánanko fruit, and, somewhat accidentally, Kallergaean culture.

Fortunately for Dad, his people are naturally gregarious even if they loathe handshakes; the traditional greeting is to touch foot to foot. I met enough of the Kallergaean diaspora to absorb some traditions and customs. To watch two Kallergaeans meet is akin to watching the airlocks of two ships join. They turn this way and that, emit a few test tones until some commonality clicks and they suddenly know who the other is in relation to themselves. Dad's knack for finding Kallergaeans in a crowd always amazed me. Some days – when we all lived on the star cruiser *ACC Nebula Oblivion* – Dad dragged us along on tours of the planets or space stations we docked at. There was a sort of order to this random, chaotic approach to meeting others, and Dad patiently noted on maps and charts when, where, and how many Kallergaeans he met. Broadcasting his informal study into the universe, these places were meaningful not because of their location, but because of the relationship he created there.

I was too young to appreciate Dad's thoughtful work and its importance. His found community was not my community. You can still find his map online. Others continue to update it now, whether they are Kallergaean or not. A map means a lot of things. Dad's map was a census of his people and a record of how far from their homeworld they travelled.

Perhaps he was simply plotting a way back to Kallergaea. It was years before Dad returned to his island, and although familiar, little was the same as he remembered it.

* * *

Lastly, there's me, hopping from promotion to promotion, post to post in the Alliance network. I never stay in one place long enough to make friends or settle down. Dad nicknamed me *Miknemos*, little wind, after the goddess who created all the Kallergaean isles. Miknemos, unsatisfied living on the mainland, one day left her celestial siblings to explore the planet. Everywhere she stepped in the ocean, a new island sprung up in her wake.

My younger brother clings to Kallergaean customs far more easily and enjoys his own version of Kallergaea, wearing the blue and beige flag on his sleeve with a pride I can't muster. Going along to get along and play off others' expectations makes life in the universe easier. I get it. We all do what we need to make it through the day.

Sometimes culture becomes a self-fulfilling prophecy and other times a big shrug for me. Why can't I bridge the gaps between the worlds of expectations and Dad's past? Don't forget the reality of the world I currently occupy!

Those gaps increased after Dad's homecoming trip. Mom said he changed. It was the cause of many fights – how to raise us, what to cook, what we watched. It affected me more because I was the older child – but I learned to police the things I said or wanted, and snuck around to listen to my favourite music or read books. Whatever imaginary, cultural corruption Dad encountered back home, I'll never understand. However, I understand grief for a place you can't return to and a life never realized.

Some days I feel I'm not Kallergaean *enough*. Dad never taught us the language; maybe he expected his children to come pre-programmed with a multitude of handy words and phrases like a Unitrans. I tried – more than once – with an old fon and a free app – but the language remained as cryptic as ever with no practical application. My mother's Terran ancestry softened the finely cut features of Dad's ancestors. Perhaps the reason I have little desire to visit Kallergaea is simply because I look like I belong, but I'd still be a tourist.

Miayia used to wrap me in a shawl passed down her maternal line and say things I didn't understand, although I knew they were affectionate. I look at childhood pictures of me wearing the handmade garment and don't recognize myself. It's me, but I never knew who I was supposed to be when I wore it. The shawl hangs in my closet along with my other unlived selves because I don't understand its value.

Did Miknemos ever make it back to the mainland? Was she another bored, fickle god? Is her story a metaphor for self-discovery? Dad never gave the tale an ending. She could still be out there creating new islands today.

* * *

My tourist sense tingles. I prepare – fon on my right, protein bar on my left. I'm just another Alliance faction, Level 6, Sector B office worker trying to catch some moments of privacy on Neqo'sp Station's mallway, somewhere in the unizone between arrivals and departures.

"Excuse me, are you from Kallergaea?"

I hunch my shoulders and stare frostily ahead. Today I will ignore the questioner away.

"Pardon? I ask because my mother is from Kallergaea."

Huh? Turning around, I shake my head, smile, and apologize. "Sorry, staring out into the void, you know, as one does on a space station." I jerk my thumb at the grand windowscape behind me.

"Sorry to interrupt your lunch."

"It's okay," I say, hopping off the stool. Instinctively we touched shoes – first left, then right – in greeting.

"Where's your mother from? Was she from the mainland or…?"

"No. She's an islander. Her family and some other Kallergaeans left ages ago on a trade expedition."

"Seriously?"

"Yeah! Her face was on all the posters. She's Ms. Mánanko."

"I wonder – your family must have left ahead of my dad's family. They left on a mánanko trade promotion too. Dad's from Dodekapathos. Oh, man. I forgot my name just now. Tharsniteem."

"Mizallaal. Two l's, two a's. My family is from Kythopo."

Blushing, I said, "I'm sure you don't want to talk about geography."

Mizallaal shrugged. "Only if you want. Say, uh, this space station gets kind of lonely, doesn't it?"

"Yeah. How come we haven't met before? I'm in the mallway all the time at lunch."

"I switched my shift cycle recently. I'm also in the Planetary Concert sphere and Alliance types don't come around too often. Hey, are you okay?"

"Oh!" A wealth of emotions crosses my face in an instant. "It's … everyone asks me if I'm from Kallergaea and it's such an irritating question, you know? But I'm glad you asked."

Mizallaal laughed. "For a moment I thought you would say you were Mattergaen and then I'd be in trouble."

"No! You do that too?"

"Years of practice, right?"

My hands fly up to my face and I laugh!

"Stay here. Let me grab something from the food court and I'll be right back. If that's all right with you, Tharsniteem."

"Absolutely!"

I watch Mizallaal weave through the bustle of bodies, full of wonder and amusement for the first time in a very long time.

The Teacher From Mars

Eando Binder

THE AFTERNOON ROCKET EXPRESS TRAIN from Chicago came into the station, and I stepped off. It was a warm spring day. The little town of Elkhart, Indiana, sprawled lazily under the golden sunshine. I trudged along quiet, tree-shaded streets toward Caslon Preparatory School for Boys. Before I had gone far, I was discovered by the children playing here and there. With the dogs, they formed a shrill, raucous procession behind me. Some of the dogs growled, as they might at a wild animal. Housewives looked from their windows and gasped.

So the rumors they had heard were true. The new teacher at Caslon was a Martian!

I suppose I am grotesquely alien to human eyes, extremely tall and incredibly thin. In fact, I am seven feet tall, with what have often been described as broomstick arms and spindly legs. On an otherwise scrawny body, only the Martian chest is filled out, in comparison with Earth people. I was dressed in a cotton kimona that dangled from my narrow shoulders to my bony ankles. Chinese style, I understand.

Thus far I am pseudo-human. For the rest, a Martian is alien, from the Earth viewpoint. Two long tentacles from the back of my shoulders hang to my knees, appendages that have not vanished in Martian evolution like the human tail. The top of my skull is bulging and hairless, except for a fringe of silver-white fur above large conch-shaped ears. Two wide-set owlish eyes, a generous nose and a tiny mouth complete my features. All my skin is leathery and tanned a deep mahogany by the Sun of our cloudless Martian skies.

Timidly I stopped before the gates of Caslon Prep and looked within the grounds. The spectacles on my large nose were cup-shaped and of tinted glass that cut down the unnatural glare of the brighter, hotter Sun. I felt my shoulders drooping wearily from the tug of more than twice the gravity to which I was conditioned.

Luckily, however, I had brought leg-braces. Concealed by my long robe, they were ingenious devices of light metal, bracing the legs against strain. They had been expensive – no less than forty *dhupecs* – but they were worth even that much.

Gripping my cane and duffle-bag, I prepared to step into the sanctuary of the school grounds. It looked so green and inviting in there, like a canalside park. It would be a relief to escape from those Earth children. They had taken to tossing pebbles at me, and some of the canines had snapped at my heels. Of course I didn't blame them, nor must I resent the unwelcome stares I had felt all around me, from adult Earthlings. After all, I was an alien.

I stepped forward, between the gates. At least here, in the school that had hired me to teach, I would be accepted in a more friendly fashion.... *Ssss*!

The hiss of a thousand snakes filled the air. I reacted violently, dropping my bag and clamping my two hands around my upraised cane. For a moment I was back on Mars, surrounded by a nest of killer-snakes from the vast deserts. I must beat them off with my cane!

But wait. This was Earth, where snakes were a minor class of creature, and mainly harmless. I relaxed, then, panting. The horrible, icy fear drained away. Perhaps you human beings can never quite know the paralyzing dread we have of snakes.

Then I heard a new sound, one that cheered me somewhat.

A group of about fifty laughing boys trooped into view, from where they had been hidden behind the stone wall circling Caslon's campus. They had made the hissing sound, as a boyish prank. How foolish of me to let go of my nerves, I thought wryly.

I smiled at the group in greeting, for these were the boys I would teach.

"I am Professor Mun Zeerohs, your new teacher," I introduced myself in what, compared with the human tone, is a reedy voice. "The Sunshine upon you. Or, in your Earthly greeting, I am happy to meet you."

Grins answered me. And then murmurs arose.

"It talks, fellows."

"Up from the canals!"

"Is that thing alive?"

One of the boys stepped forward. He was about sixteen, with blue eyes that were mocking.

"I'm Tom Blaine, senior classman. Tell me, sir, is it true that Mars is inhabited?"

It was rather a cruel reception, though merely another prank. I waved my two tentacles in distress for a moment, hardly knowing what to do or say next.

"Boys! Gentlemen!"

A grown man with gray hair came hurrying up from one of the buildings. The boys parted to let him through. He extended a hand to me, introducing himself.

"Robert Graham, Dean of Caslon. You're Professor Mun Zeerohs, of course." He turned, facing the group reprovingly. "This is your new instructor, gentlemen. He will teach interplanetary history and the Martian language."

A groan went up. I knew why, of course. The Martian tongue has two case endings to every one in Latin.

"Now, gentlemen, this is for your own good," Dean Graham continued sternly. "Remember your manners. I'm sure you'll like our new professor—"

"I'm sure we won't!" It was Tom Blaine again. Behind him, an air of hostility replaced the less worrisome mockery. "We've never had a Martian teacher before, and we don't want one!"

"Don't want one?" The dean was more aghast than I.

"My father says Martians are cowards," Tom Blaine continued loudly. "He ought to know. He's in the Space Patrol. He says that in the War, the Martians captured Earthmen and cut them to pieces slowly. First their hands, then—"

"Nonsense!" Dean Graham snapped. "Besides, the War is over. Martians are in the Space Patrol, too. Now no more argument. Go to your dormitory. Professor Zeerohs will begin conducting class tomorrow morning. Oscar, take the professor's bag to his quarters."

Oscar, the school's menial robot, obediently stalked forward and picked up the bag. Somehow, I felt almost a warm tide of friendship for the robot. In his mechanical, rudimentary reflex mind, it was all the same to him – Martian or Earthman. He made no discrimination against me, as these human boys did.

As Oscar turned, Tom Blaine stood as though to block the way. Having his orders, the robot brushed past him. A metal elbow accidentally jabbed the boy in the ribs. Deciding against grabbing the bag away from steel fingers, Tom Blaine picked up a stone and flung it clanging against the robot's metal body. Another dent was added to the many I could see over Oscar's shiny form.

The rebellion was over – for the time being.

I realized that the boys were still hostile as I followed the dean to his rooms. My shoulders seemed to droop a little more.

"Don't mind them," the dean was saying apologetically. "They're usually outspoken at that age. They've never had a Martian teacher before, you see."

"Why have you engaged one for the first time?" I asked.

Graham answered half patronizingly, half respectfully.

"Many other schools have tried Martian teachers, and found them highly satisfactory." He didn't think it necessary to add, "And cheaper."

I sighed. Times had been hard on Mars lately, with so many dust storms raging up and down the canal regions, withering the crops. This post on Earth, though at a meager salary, was better than utter poverty. I was old and could live cheaply. Quite a few Martians had been drifting to Earth, since the War. By nature, we are docile, industrious, intelligent, and make dependable teachers, engineers, chemists artists.

"They always haze the new teachers," Dean Graham said, smiling uneasily. "Your first class is at nine o'clock tomorrow morning. Interplanetary History."

Freshened after a night's sleep, I entered the class room with enthusiasm for my new job. A hundred cold, unfriendly eyes watched me with terrifying intensity.

"Good morning," I greeted as warmly as I could.

"Good morning, Professor *Zero*!" a chorus bellowed back, startling me.

So the hazing campaign was still on. No, I wouldn't correct them. After all, even the Martian children I had taught had invariably tagged me with that name.

I glanced around the room, approving its high windows and controlled sunlight. My eyes came to rest on the blackboard behind me. A chalk drawing occupied its space. It depicted, with some skill, a Martian crouching behind an Earthman. Both were members of the Space Patrol and apparently were battling some space desperado. It was young Tom Blaine's work, no doubt. His father claimed all Martians to be cowards and weaklings.

My leathery face showed little of my feelings as I erased the humiliating sketch. Ignoring the snickers behind me, I grasped two pieces of chalk in both tentacles, writing with one and listing dates with the other.

1945 – Discovery of anti-gray force, on Earth
1955 – First space flight
1978 – Earthmen claim all planets
1992 – Pioneer-wave to Mars
2011 – Rebellion and war
2019 – Mars wins freedom
2040 – Earth-Mars relations friendly today

"Interplanetary History," I began my lecture, "centers about these dates and events. Not till Nineteen fifty-five were Earth people assured that intelligent beings had built the mysterious canals of Mars. Nor were we Martians positive till then that the so-called Winking Lights of your cities at night denoted the handiwork of thinking creatures.

"The exploring Earthmen of the last century found only the Martians equal to them in intelligence. Earth has its great cities, and Mars has its great canal-system, built ten thousand Martian years ago. Civilization began on Mars fifty centuries previous to that, before the first glimmering of it on Earth—"

"See, fellows?" Tom Blaine interrupted loudly. "I told you all they like to do is rub that in." He became mockingly polite. "Please, sir, may I ask why you brilliant Martians had to wait for Earthmen to open up space travel?"

I was shocked, but managed to answer patiently.

"We ran out of metal deposits for building, keeping our canals in repair. Our history has been a constant struggle against the danger of extinction. In fact, when Earth pioneers migrated in Nineteen ninety-two, it was just in time to patch up the canals and stave off a tremendous famine for Mars."

"And that was the appreciation Earth got," the boy charged bitterly. "Rebellion!"

"You forget that the Earth pioneers on Mars started the rebellion against taxation, and fought side by side with us—"

"They were traitors," he stated bluntly.

I hurdled the point, and continued the lecture.

"Mars won its independence after a nine-year struggle—"

Again I was interrupted.

"Not *won*. Earth granted independence, though it could have won easily."

"At any rate," I resumed quietly, "Earth and Mars today, in Twenty-forty, are amicable, and have forgotten that episode."

"We haven't forgotten!" Tom Blaine cried angrily. "Every true Earthman despises Martians."

He sat down amidst a murmur of defiant approval from the others. I knew my tentacles hung limply. How aggressive and intolerant Earth people were! It accounted for their domination of the Solar System. A vigorous, pushing race, they sneered at the Martian ideals of peaceful culture. Their pirates, legal and otherwise, still roamed the spaceways for loot.

Young Tom Blaine was representative of the race. He was determined to make things so miserable here for me that I would quit. He was the leader of the upper-class boys. Strange, that Earthpeople always follow one who is not wise, but merely compelling. There would have to be a test of authority, I told myself with a sinking heart.

"I am the teacher," I reminded him. "You are the pupil, Mr. Blaine."

"Oh, yes, sir," he retorted in false humility. "But you'd better teach history right, Professor Nothing, or not at all!"

I hastily switched to the Martian language.

"The Martian language as is well known, is today the official language of science and trade," I went on guardedly. "Through long usage, the tongue has become perfected. Official Earth English is comparatively cumbersome. For instance, the series of words meaning exaggerated size – big, large, great, huge, enormous, mighty, cyclopean, gargantuan. Is 'big' more than 'large', or less? You cannot tell. In Martian, there is one root, with a definite progression of size suffixes."

I wrote on the blackboard. bol, bola, bob, bolo, bolu – bolas, bobs, bolos, bolus – bolasa, bolisi, boloso, bolusu

"Martian is a scientific language, you see."

"Bragging again," sneered a voice. An eraser sailed toward me just as I turned from the board. It struck full in my face in a cloud of chalk-dust. As if at a signal, a barrage of erasers flew at me. They had been sneaked previously from the boards around the classroom. I stood helplessly, desperately warding off the missile with my tentacles. The boys were yelling and hooting, excited by the sport.

The pandemonium abruptly stopped as Oscar stumped into the room. His mechanical eyes took in the scene without emotion. One belated eraser flew toward him. His steel arm reflexively raised, caught it, then hurled it back with stunning force. To a robot, anything that came toward it must be returned, unless otherwise commanded. Tom Blaine yelped as the eraser bounced off his forehead

"Dean Graham," said Oscar like a phonograph, "wants to know if everything is going along smoothly."

I could see the boys hold their breaths. Oscar went the rounds daily, asking that routine question in all the classes. If this disturbance were reported, the boys would lose an afternoon of freedom.

"Everything is well," I murmured, though for a moment I was sadly tempted to take revenge. "You may go, Oscar."

With a click of internal relays, the robot left impassively. He had seen or heard nothing, without being otherwise commanded.

"Afraid to report it, eh?" Tom Blaine jeered. "I told you Martians are yellow!"

It was more than gravity now that made my shoulders sag. I dreaded the days that must follow.

* * *

Even outside the classroom, I was hounded. I can use only that word. Tom Blaine thought of the diabolical trick of deliberately spilling a glass of water before my eyes.

"Don't – don't!" I instinctively groaned, clutching at the glass.

"What's the matter, Professor?" he asked blandly. "This is nothing but water."

"It's sacrilege—"

I stopped there. They wouldn't understand. How horrible to see water spill to the ground in utter waste! For ten thousand years, on Mars, that precious fluid has been the object of our greatest ingenuity.

It hurt to see it wantonly flung away, as they might flinch if blood were shed uselessly before them.

As I stumbled away from their laughter, I heard Tom Blaine confide to his cohorts:

"I got the idea last night, looking in his room. He was playing with a bowl of water. Running it through his fingers, like a miser. I've got another idea, fellows. Follow me to the kitchen."

I wasn't aware till half through the solitary evening meal in my rooms that the food tasted odd. It was salty! The boys had stolen into the kitchen and salted my special saltless foods. My stomach revolted against the alien condiment. Mars' seas, from which our life originated long ago, held no sodium chloride, only magnesium chloride, with which all Martian food is "salted."

I went to bed, groaning with a severe headache and upset stomach from an outraged metabolism. Worse, it rained that night. I tried to shut my ears to that pattering sound. Millions of gallons of water were going to waste, while millions of Martians on my homeworld, were painfully hoarding water for their thirsty crops.

The pains eased before morning. What torment would Tom Blaine and his relentless pack think of next? The answer came when I found my spectacles missing. My eyes were almost blinded that day, more from glare than senile failing of vision. They watered and blinked in light that was fifty per cent stronger than on more remote Mars.

"Lower the blinds, Oscar," I ordered the robot when he appeared as usual.

"But, Professor," Tom Blaine protested, jumping up as though waiting for the moment, "think of our eyes. We can't read our lessons in the dark."

"Never mind, Oscar," I said wearily. The robot stood for a moment, relays clashing at the reversed orders. When he finally left, he seemed to shrug at the strange doings of his masters, Earthmen and Martians alike.

"Have you any idea where my glasses are, Mr. Blaine?" I asked in direct appeal. I tried not to sound timid.

"No, of course not," he retorted virtuously.

I nodded to myself and reached for the lower left-hand drawer of my desk, then changed my mind.

"Will you all help me look for them?" I pleaded.

They ransacked the desk with deliberate brutality.

"Why, here they are, Professor!" Tom held them up from the lower left-hand drawer in mock triumph. I put them on with trembling hands.

"How careless of me to leave them here yesterday." I smiled. "One must have a sense of humor about these things. Now we will decline the verb *krun*, to move."

I went on as though nothing had happened, but my whole head ached from hours of straining my eyes against the cruel glare.

That night, utterly exhausted, I went to bed only to find my anti-gravity unit jammed, obviously by human hands. One of my few pleasures was the ability to sink into restful slumber in the low-gravity field, after suffering the tug of Earth gravity at my vitals all day. Earthmen on Jupiter know how agonizing it becomes.

I passed a sleepless night, panting and aching under what grew to be the pressure of a mountain.

How could I go on against such heartlessness? Tom Blaine and his friends were ruthlessly determined to drive out their despised Martian teacher. If I complained to Dean Graham, it would be an admission of cowardice. I didn't want to betray my race. But I was miserably aware that I had not a single friend in the academy.

Oscar appeared in the morning, with a message from Dean Graham. The mechanical servant waited patiently to be told to go. When I swayed a little, he caught me. His reflexes had been patterned not to let things fall.

"Thank you, Oscar." I found my hand on the robot's shiny hard shoulder. It was comfortingly firm. "You're my only friend, Oscar. At least, you're not my enemy. But what am I saying? You're only a machine. You may go, Oscar."

The message read:

Today and tomorrow are examination days. Use the enclosed forms. At three o'clock today, all classes will be excused to the Television Auditorium.

The examinations were routine. Despite my unrested body and mind, I felt an uplift of spirit. My class would do well. I had managed, even against hostility, to impart a sound understanding of Interplanetary History and the Martian language.

I looked almost proudly over the bowed, laboring heads. Suddenly I stiffened.

"Mr. Henderson," I said gently, "I wouldn't try that if I were you."

The boy flushed, hastily crammed into his pockets the notes he had been copying from. Then he gaped up in amazement. Tom Blaine, at the desk beside him, also looked up startled. The question was plain in his eyes. How could I know that Henderson was cheating, when even Tom, sitting next to him hadn't suspected?

"You forget," I explained hesitantly, "that Martians use telepathy at will."

Tom Blaine stared, his mouth hanging open. Then he jumped up.

"Are we going to stand for that? Spying on us, even in our minds—" He gasped at a sudden thought. "You knew all the time about the glasses. You didn't expose me." He flushed, but in anger rather than embarrassment. "You made a fool of me!"

"One must have a sense of humor about those things," I said lamely.

The rest of the examination period passed in bristling silence. More than ever, now, they were hostile to me. More than ever would they show their antagonism. How could I ever hope to win them, if patience was taken for cowardice, understanding for malice, and telepathy for deliberate spying?

Why had I ever left Mars, to come to this alien, heart-breaking world?

* * *

At three o'clock, examinations were over for that day. The class filed to the Television Auditorium.

A giant screen in the darkened room displayed a drama on Venus, then news-flashes from around the system. An asteroid, scene of the latest radium rush. Ganymede, with its talking plant show.

Titan's periodic meteor shower from the rings of Saturn. A cold, dark scene on Pluto, where a great telescope was being built for interstellar observations. Finally Mars, and a file of Earthmen and Martians climbing into a sleek Space Patrol ship.

"The Patrol ship *Greyhound*," informed the announcer, "is being dispatched after pirates. Captain Henry Blaine is determined to blast them, or not come back."

"My father," Tom Blaine said proudly to his classmates.

"My son," I murmured, leaning forward to watch the last of the Martians vanish within.

When the armed ship leaped into space, the television broadcast was over.

There were no more classes that day. I dragged across the campus toward the haven of my rooms, for I needed rest and quiet.

A shriek tore from my throat the instant I saw it. A horrible, wriggling snake lay in my path! It was only a small, harmless garden snake, my reason told me. But a million years of instinct yelled danger, death! I stumbled and fell, trying to run against gravity that froze my muscles. I shrank from the squirming horror as it stopped and defiantly darted out its forked tongue.

The outside world burst into my consciousness with a thunderclap of laughter. Tom Blaine was holding up the wriggling snake. Once the first shock was over, I managed to keep my nerves in check.

"It's only a garter snake," he mocked. "Sorry it frightened you."

But what would they say if a hungry, clawing tiger suddenly appeared before them? How would they feel? I left without a word, painfully compelling my trembling limbs to move.

I was beaten. That thought hammered within my skull.

They had broken my spirit. I came to that conclusion after staring up at a red star that winked soberly and seemed to nod in pity. There was my true home. I longed to go back to its canals and deserts. Harsh they might be, but not so harsh as the unfeeling inhabitants of this incredibly rich planet.

I went to my rooms and started to pack.

Angry voices swiftly approached my door. The boys burst in, led by Tom Blaine.

"Murderer!" Tom yelled. "A man was strangled in town two hours ago, by a rope – or a tentacle! You looked murder at us this afternoon. Why did you kill him? Just general hate for the human race?"

How fantastic it sounded, yet they weren't mere boys, now. They were a blood-lusting mob. All their hate and misunderstanding for me had come to a head. I knew it was no use even to remonstrate.

"Look, fellows! He was packing up to sneak away. He's the killer, all right. Are you going to confess, Professor Zeerohs, or do we have to make you confess!"

It was useless to resist their burly savagery and strong Earth muscles. They held me and ripped away the light metal braces supporting my legs. Then I was forced outside and prodded along. They made me walk up and down, back of the dormitory, in the light of subatomic torches.

It became sheer torture within an hour. Without the braces, my weak muscles sagged under my weight. Earth's gravity more than doubled the normal strain.

"Confess!" Tom snapped fiercely. "Then we'll take you to the police."

I shook my head, as I had each time Tom demanded my confession. My one hopeless comfort was the prayer of an earthly prophet, who begged the First Cause to forgive his children, for they knew not what they did.

For another hour, the terrible march kept up. I became a single mass of aching flesh. My bones seemed to be cracking and crumbling under the weight of the Universe. My mental anguish was still sharper, for the tide of hate beat against me like a surf.

Where was Dean Graham? Then I remembered that he had gone to visit his relatives that evening. There was no one to help me, no one to stop these half-grown men who saw their chance to get rid of me. Only the winking red eye of Mars looked down in compassion for the suffering of a humble son.

"Oscar's coming!" warned a voice.

Ponderously the robot approached, the night-light in his forehead shining. He made the rounds every night, like a mechanical watchman. As he eyed the halted procession, his patterned reflexes were obviously striving to figure out what its meaning could be.

"Boys will go to the dormitory," his microphonic voice boomed. "Against regulations to be out after ten o'clock."

"Oscar, you may go," barked Tom Blaine.

The robot didn't budge. His selectors were set to obey only the voices of teachers and officials.

"Oscar—" I began with a wild cry.

A boy clamped his hand over my mouth. The last of my strength oozed from me, and I slumped to the ground. Though I was not unconscious, I knew my will would soon be insufficient to make me resist. The boys looked frightened.

"Maybe we've gone too far," one said nervously.

"He deserves it," shrilled Tom uneasily. "He's a cowardly murderer!"

"Tom!" Pete Miller came running up, from the direction of the town. "Just heard the news – the police caught the killer – a maniac with a rope." He recoiled in alarm when he saw my sprawled form. "What did you do, fellows? He's innocent, and he really isn't such a bad old guy."

The boys glanced at one another with guilty eyes. Fervently I blessed young Miller for that statement.

"Don't be sentimental," Tom Blaine said much too loudly. "Martians are cowards. My father says so. I'm glad we did this, anyway. It'll drive him away for sure. We'd better beat it now."

The group melted away, leaving me on the ground. Oscar stalked forward and picked me up. Any fallen person must be helped up, according to his patterned mind. But his steel arms felt softer than Tom Blaine's heartless accusation.

* * *

The class gasped almost in chorus the next morning, when their Martian professor entered quietly, as though nothing had happened the night before.

"Examinations will continue," I announced.

It was small wonder that they looked surprised. First, that I had appeared at all, weak and spent by the night's cruel ordeal. Second, that I had not given up and left. Third, that I hadn't reported the episode to Dean Graham. The punishment would have been severe.

Only I knew I was back because it would be cowardly to leave. Mentally and physically I was sick, but not beaten. Besides, I had heard young Miller insist that I was not such a bad old guy, after all. It was like a well of cool water in a hot desert.

Examinations began. Oscar entered, handed me a spacegram and clanked out again. Nervously I opened and read the message. My tentacles twitched uncontrollably at the ends, then curled around the chair arms and clung desperately. Everything vanished before my eyes except the hideous, shocking words of the spacegram.

My world was ended. Mars or Earth – it made no difference. I could not go on. But existence must continue. I could not let this break me. Grimly I folded the paper and laid it aside.

I looked with misted eyes at their lowered heads. I needed a friend as never before, but hostility and hatred were the only emotions they felt for me as I tuned to them one by one. They hated their teacher, though they knew him to be wise, humble, patient, as Martians are by nature.

And I was beginning to hate them. They were forcing me to. Savagely I hoped they would all fail in their examinations.

I switched back to young Miller, who was biting his pencil. Forehead beaded with sweat, he was having a difficult time. Thoughts were racing through his brain.

Wanted so much to pass … enter Space Point … join the Space Patrol some day … Not enough time to study … job in spare time after school hours … help parents … In what year did the first explorer step on Neptune's moon? Why, Nineteen-seventy-six! Funny how that came all of a sudden … Now what was the root for "planet" in Martian? Why, *jad*, of course! It isn't so hard after all…

Wish that old Martian wouldn't stare at me as if he's reading my mind … How many moons has Jupiter? Always get it mixed up with Saturn.

Eighteen, six found by space ships! Funny, I'm so sure of myself … I'll lick this exam yet … Dad's going to be proud of me when I'm wearing that uniform.…

I turned my eyes away from Miller's happy face. A deserving boy, he would be a credit to the Space Patrol. Others had their troubles, not just I.

Abruptly there was an interruption. Oscar came clanking in hurriedly. "Dean Graham wishes all classes to file out on the campus, for a special event," he boomed.

The boys whispered in curiosity and left the classroom at my unsteady order. The campus was filled with the entire school faculty and enrollment. My group of senior classmen was allowed to stand directly in front of the bandstand. I felt weak and in need of support, but there was no one to give it to me.

Dean Graham raised a hand. "A member of the Space Patrol is here," he spoke, "having come from Space Point by rocket-strato for an important announcement. Major Dawson."

A tall, uniformed man, wearing the blue of the Space Patrol, stepped forward, acknowledging the assembly's unrestrained cheer with a solemn nod. The Patrol is honored throughout the System for its gallant service to civilization.

"Many of you boys," he said, "hope to enter Space Point some day, and join the Service. This bulletin, received an hour ago, will do honor to someone here."

He held up the paper and read aloud. "Captain Henry Blaine, in command of Patrol ship *Greyhound*, yesterday was wounded in the daring rout of pirates off the Earth-Mars run."

All eyes turned to Tom Blaine, who was proud of the ceremony in honor of his father. The official held up a radium-coated medal – the Cross of Space, for extraordinary service to the forces of law and order in the Solar System. Dean Graham whispered in his ear. He nodded, stepping down from the rostrum and advancing.

My gasp of surprise was deeper than those of the others as he brushed past Tom Blaine. Stopping before me, he pinned the glowing medal on my chest. Then he grasped my hand.

"I think you'll be proud to wear that all your life!" He turned, reading further from his bulletin.

"Captain Blaine's life was saved by a youthful Martian recruit, who leaped in front of him and took the full blast that wounded the Earthman. His name was—"

I found myself watching Tom Blaine. He didn't have to hear the name. He was staring at the spacegram he had stolen from my desk, but hadn't had a chance to read till now. He had sensed my momentary agitation over it, and had hoped perhaps to use it against me. It read:

WE DEEPLY REGRET TO INFORM YOU OF THE DEATH OF YOUR SON, KOL ZEEROHS, IN HEROIC SERVICE FOR THE SPACE PATROL – THE HIGH COMMAND, SPACE PATROL.

But now my weakness overwhelmed me. I was aware only of someone at my side, supporting me, as my knees threatened to buckle. It must have been Oscar.

No – it was a human being!

"Every one of us here," Tom Blaine said, tightening his grip around me, "is your son now – if that will help a little. You're staying of course, Professor. You couldn't leave now if you tried."

We smiled at each other, and my thin hand was nearly crushed in his young, strong grasp. Yes, the teacher from Mars would stay.

How Rigel Gained a Rabbi (Briefly)

Benjamin Blattberg

RABBI DOV APPLEBAUM ARGUED – quite eloquently, he thought – for keeping the spaceship to its original flight plan. After all, there were Jewish children on Orion Station who needed Torah lessons before their upcoming B'nai Mitzvah. And yet the AI refused to listen to him and instead plotted a new course towards the distress signal on Rigel-7.

When the AI stated that intergalactic law compelled them to answer a distress call, Dov might've kept quiet – he wouldn't actually have kept quiet, but he might have – but when the *fakakta* computer started citing Jewish law, Dov had to object.

"True, Leviticus says not to 'stand idly by the blood of thy neighbor,'" said Dov, "but there are many interpretations of the Jewish law around distress signals. For one, what is a neighbor, galactically speaking?"

Dov could have discussed this for days, turning the argument about so that every angle of interpretation caught the light. But he only had hours before landfall and the AI had stopped actually listening anyway. Dov was used to that. His students throughout the galaxy didn't listen, so why should his ship? Dov tried to imagine the Jewish children on Orion Station wailing and rending their garments over the delayed arrival of their favorite rabbi, but it was easier to imagine them eating synth-pork and forgetting what it meant to be Jews.

To add to Rabbi Dov's woes, as his ship entered orbit and prepared to descend to the surface of Rigel-7, the Rigelian ambassador Cho'sun called on the viewscreen to forbid Dov from landing.

The spider-like Rigelian spoke its own language, which sounded to Dov like Coney Island being picked up with little warning and shaken. Luckily, Dov had a universal translator, a small black box clipped onto the upper sleeve of his flight suit, loaded with an AI that had been trained specifically to Dov's native language. The box seemed to hum and clear its throat before translating.

"Listen, *schmuck*," said the Rigelian through the translation box, "we have no laws to protect outsiders and you'll just have to live with the consequences."

Dov glanced at the translation box skeptically and tapped at it with one chewed nail. He couldn't hear any loose parts in there – and if there were, what could he do about it?

"You hear me, *schmuck*?" Cho'sun waved its anterior arms in emphasis.

"Ah," said Dov, as he attempted to stroke his red-brown beard thoughtfully, as his teachers had done and their teachers before them. The effect was rather ruined by his beard's tendency to float up in microgravity, the curly mass haloing his jaw. "But you see, Ambassador, I am not landing – the ship is."

Cho'sun made a sound like a garbage disposal chewing up dinosaur bones. The universal translator rendered this as laughter at first and then clarified: "Dismissive laughter."

"Ambassador," said Dov, "intergalactic law demands that distress signals be answered by the nearest available ship." Even if that ship was a weapon-less family transport that currently held no family, just Dov and his collection of Judaica, including a parchment Torah in a chased silver case all the way from Earth. That treasure he rarely brought out: only for brief ceremonies and never while his people were noshing.

"Universal law, shmuniversal law." The ambassador flexed its claws, which might have been body language for emphasis or negation or something else entirely. Dov had skipped taking xenolinguistics in college and the translator had its limits. "And in any case, Mr. Bigshot, we plan to take care of our own distress call, thank you very much."

"Ah, so there is nothing to be distressed about?" Dov looked over at the terminal where he imagined the AI to be, a slight air of triumph in his raised eyebrow.

"Nothing at all distressing," agreed Cho'sun. "As soon as we find them, we will kill off the entire unclean species that is sending whatever call you are receiving."

Dov grimaced like he'd tasted a bad piece of whitefish. "It sounds, Ambassador, like you are speaking of genocide."

Insofar as a spider can smile, the ambassador did. "Aha, now you understand."

Dov's bad fish expression deepened and he sighed. He couldn't see any way to avoid landing on Rigel-7. He raised his hands and shrugged, the ancestral Jewish gesture for "What can I do about this? Nothing."

Even the ambassador, who had probably never met a Jew before, seemed to take Dov's meaning. Its voice took on a husky edge: the Empire State Building being scraped the length of Long Island. "We will cleanse Rigel-7 of this degenerate species and if you interfere, your life will be forfeit, *schmuck*." The viewscreen went dead, the communication cut.

After a long moment of sighing, Dov flipped on a tablet, calling up commentaries on mediation by the most esteemed rabbis, as well as accessing a brief summary of the Rigelians. Their description – violent, xenophobic – sounded to Dov much like his ancestors' stories of growing up with the Italians in Yonkers. And hadn't they made peace there before moving to Scarsdale and Florida?

Perhaps Dov could be the one to bring Rigel-7 into the intergalactic community. He'd rather keep to his schedule and be teaching Torah to ungrateful children on backward space stations, true, but if he had to make peace between two warring tribes on Rigel-7 and go down in history, so be it.

Perhaps, with his help, no one would die.

* * *

They were all going to die.

Cho'sun had called these other aliens a "species," but the ambassador had called Dov a "*schmuck*," too, so what did he know? Truth be told, Dov felt less like a *schmuck* and more like a *schlemiel*: not the clumsy waiter spilling the soup, but the guy the waiter spills soup on. Only in this case, it was more like the universe itself was spilling soup on Dov.

To Dov, these aliens didn't seem like a distinct species. For one thing, there just weren't that many of them, maybe ten total, camped out here in the middle of the green-black jungle. The jungle itself smelled faintly of burnt sugar, like overspun cotton candy, and was lush and thorny. Dov had time to discover the thorns as he hiked a few miles from the only clearing where his ship could land, since this benighted planet hadn't any spaceport or roads or Chinese food. It was unpleasant, even if the air was breathable and the only large predators here were the man-sized, spider-like Rigelians.

Like the ones standing in front of Dov, asking for help, and not really listening when he said he couldn't give them any.

"No, I don't have ray guns on my ship," explained Dov again. "What should I have ray guns for?"

The aliens talked to each other in voices that sounded like the Long Island Expressway being rolled up and eaten like pastrami, in the same language that Cho'sun used. Not only did they speak the same language and look nearly identical to Cho'sun – the same dark compound eyes, chitinous exoskeletons, and abundant limbs – but they waved away Dov's well-thought-out arguments with the same motions. Dov wasn't sure what set these Rigelians apart or why he hadn't become a dentist with a nice little practice on Mars.

"Given your similarities, why do the Rigelians hate you so?" asked Dov.

Yen'tah, a smaller and slightly reddish but just as horrifyingly chitinous and hairy spider-thing, bristled, rising on its posterior four legs. "I reject your question – we too are Rigelian! It's divisive speech like that—"

The other Rigelians began to yell at Yen'tah, making even more noise than it did. Dov's translation box parsed their commingled cries: "Hush, *sheket*, enough already!" Yen'tah made a gesture that Dov assumed was rude among egg-laying, non-binary sentients, but it stopped speaking and a moment later the ones who had shouted Yen'tah down quieted to a low grumble.

"The Kin hate us Otherkin because they do not believe in change and we have changed," said Buch'ker, who was larger than all the other Rigelians and spoke in a voice that sounded like a Ferris wheel making love to a container ship. Buch'ker cocked its head to one side and then the other, a gesture that indicated thought among the Rigelians. Buch'ker was considering how to explain to Dov, and eventually it said, "We see the world differently."

"Ah, a philosophical difference," said Dov. "As a Jew, I have some experience—"

The Otherkin around him cut him off, their bulbous abdomens grumbling. The whole noisy rabble reminded Dov unexpectedly of a congregation held too long at service, with the promised land of cookies and gossip so close.

Buch'ker pointed to one of its eyes, as shiny as new challah, and said slowly, as if to a young child, "We see the world differently."

After some clarification, with Buch'ker talking ever slower, Dov eventually realized this talk of "seeing the world differently" was the literal truth, as well as a metaphor. As metaphor: whereas the Kin avoided change and only maintained the technology they had inherited, the Otherkin believed change was acceptable, particularly when it would help them avoid extinction. And as literal truth: the Otherkin had experienced a genetic shift that allowed them to sense many different wavelengths. Though as they hadn't developed a theory of genetics yet, Buch'ker explained this as simply a difference between its family – all the spider-aliens here being closely related – and the other Rigelians.

Also, Yen'tah explained, their thoraxes were smaller or hairier or something, but Dov couldn't see it.

While Buch'ker explained this, two of the Otherkin scuttled up the trees and began to dismantle their nests high in the canopy overhead. These nests were temporary structures, Buch'ker had said before, put up and taken down as the Otherkin migrated through the jungle, staying ahead of their distant cousins and would-be murderers. A few others began to look up at their nests, realizing that Dov couldn't help them, that running away would be their only hope. Maybe, if they were lucky, the next starship they called with their distress beacon would be more help.

And if not, more running, more distress calls, and more running.

The original distress beacon was still beeping – Dov's ship relayed the call to his suit, despite his request to the AI to not do that, please. Dov had even asked the Otherkin to turn off the beacon, fearing that the Kin could track it.

Alas, explained the Otherkin named Gon'nef whose eyes were oddly close together, they had just recently invented the distress beacon and had not yet invented the off switch. A few Otherkin made a noise that seemed like laughter at that.

But Dov decided to leave that topic alone, especially after Buch'ker told him that the Kin had viewscreen technology that operated only on that frequency, but not a lot of other communication technology. The Kin couldn't track this new signal since they didn't invent any new technology, just lived with whatever old things they had and never changed.

"This taboo against change, this is taught to the Kin from your Creator or Creators?" asked Dov then, looking forward to discussing comparative religion rather than the first topic the Otherkin had wanted to discuss: ray guns.

"What kind of a cockamamie question is that?" grumbled Yen'tah.

"No," said Buch'ker, "the Creators didn't teach anything to the Kin before the Kin ate them."

But now, with the Otherkin packing their nests and preparing to run, Dov felt rather sympathetic to that distress beacon, calling off into the interstellar night for help that might never come. There was something deeply Jewish about it. Dov could almost imagine the Otherkin as the Israelites of the book of Exodus, under the cruel yoke of the pharaoh.

"I have a plan," said Dov proudly. "We run."

"This he calls a plan?" Yen'tah sneered.

"If we run, we can escape," said Dov, "as long the Kin can't track our signal."

* * *

"We easily tracked your signal," said Ambassador Cho'sun, as it entered Dov's prison cell, high up in an ancient tower. "But then you probably figured that out when we caught you."

Dov turned from the window, where he'd been watching his spaceship's rocket trail, but after he saw the look on Cho'sun's face, Dov almost turned back. On a human, Cho'sun's expression would've been called a deep frown, but on a human that expression wouldn't have exposed so many chitin-brown, needle-sharp teeth.

Dov pulled at his flight suit to try to smooth it out and got his beard caught in the suit's velcro at the neck. "Ambassador, intergalactic law demands that I be allowed to communicate with my home government."

Cho'sun ignored him. It placed a black box between them and settled itself into the narrow room as best as it could. To fit here, Cho'sun had to fold and tuck its legs under it, like a spider who had extensively practiced yoga. Like most of the city that Dov had seen – while being carried by angry Rigelians – this room was built to a different scale and shape than these natives. The Kin literally lived in houses made for others who had come before them, which, even for Dov, was taking respect for tradition a little too far.

Cho'sun tapped the black box, paused, then tapped it again, this time harder.

"Ambassador, I demand—"

Cho'sun picked the black box up and held it up to its ear canal and shook it, before placing it down and pressing it one more time, firmly. Dov heard a slight pop, like a jar of garlic pickles being opened. Cho'sun clicked its mandibles, which Dov had learned was the Rigelian way of nodding to oneself. Then it began to talk.

"You *putz*, I told you not to land and what did you do?" Cho'sun fell silent, staring at Dov.

After far too long a silence, the Rigelian added, "That's not rhetorical, mister. This is your trial right here, *nu*? You want we should execute you now? Don't say anything, fine with me."

Dov paused stroking his beard, getting it caught in velcro again. Buch'ker had told him the Kin would hold a trial before executing and eating him – more respect for tradition, Dov supposed. He just hadn't thought his impending death would be quite so impending. Dov considered his situation against the long history of the Jews: this was not the worst situation his people had been in. It was not a very comforting thought.

"You want me to explain what I did?" asked Dov.

"Blockhead! We know what you did – you had the gall to save those unclean things with your..." Words failing it, Cho'sun waved a claw towards the window, towards the rocket trail, a column of smoke in the daytime sky. "They all escaped, so I hope you're happy with yourself."

Dov considered for a moment before deciding, yes, he was a little happy with himself. It hadn't been, all things considered, a bad plan for him to run while broadcasting a signal the Kin could detect on the viewscreen technology, while the Otherkin made their way to Dov's ship, following a signal only they could detect. Dov had a deep, rabbinical urge for symbolism, which was satisfied by the fact that the signal the Otherkin followed was their own distress beacon, relayed from his ship.

Only now he realized the plan's tragic flaw: he was going to die. It had seemed so clear – and so righteous – at the time for Dov to be the decoy: if any of the Otherkin were left behind, they'd be immediately killed and eaten. At least Dov got this farce of a trial. Not a long enough trial for people to come rescue him, but at least it was something, right?

"We know what you're guilty of," said Cho'sun, "we just want to know why. You can explain yourself. And then, the execution."

"But what am I really guilty of?" asked Dov, a sudden flash of inspiration rising to the surface of his brain like a matzah ball of the perfect lightness and airiness. "The Rigelians wanted to cleanse Rigel-7 of the Otherkin" – Cho'sun bristled at that word, the tiny hairs covering its body vibrating with anger, no xeno-linguistics degree necessary to read that – "and I have done that. There are no more of ... them on Rigel-7."

"Our world is cleansed," said Cho'sun flatly, "but we were looking forward to killing them all. And now we have to be satisfied with killing only you. And speaking of that," and Cho'sun reached out to turn off the black box.

"Wait, I can explain better," said Dov, half-reaching out to swat away Cho'sun's claw. He caught himself and steepled his fingers as if in thought. "We Jews have an old saying from the Babylonian Talmud – a book of commentary on our laws – that says, 'whoever saves a life, it is considered as if he saved an entire world.'"

"I do not understand," said the Rigelian, claw still hovering over the black box.

"Ah," said Dov, nodding, "you see, it's a moral calculation that asks us to consider—"

Cho'sun waved him off. "*Schmuck*, it's 'book' I don't understand. Whatever those are, we don't have them and don't want them."

But then Cho'sun cocked its head to one side and then the other, the Rigelian gesture for considering.

"And how is one life equal to a world?" asked Cho'sun.

"A lesson like that has to be interpreted," Dov said quickly. He paused as he heard steps coming up the narrow stairs to his tower cell. The steps were halting and clumsy, the narrow stairs not at all suited to the Rigelian's sprawling legs. And on top of the click of Rigelian claws, Dov heard something else being dragged, bouncing on each hard step with a clunk. Dov had a moment of vivid worry, imagining them dragging some torture device up to his cell.

Cho'sun had to move aside for the other Rigelians to make their way into the cell and drop what they were carrying in a pile at Dov's feet. The Jewish children of Orion Station would've said it was a torture device, but after wiping away some leaves and mud, Dov recognized it all as his collection of Judaica and teaching materials.

They were dented here and there and all jumbled together – the Seder plate next to the shofar horn, his tefillin straps tangled around Elijah's and Miriam's cups, the menorah with one arm bent down, the Torah surfing on a sea of yarmulkes, and a classroom's worth of tablets, loaded with lessons on everything from basic Hebrew to the most abstruse rabbinical commentary.

"We have only you and all of this," said Cho'sun, gesturing to the pile. And then, with a little more hope in its voice, it added, "Is any of this edible?"

"No," Dov admitted, "but I can explain how a life is worth a world." He picked up a tablet, the least dented and mud-covered, checking that it was still working. He turned it on, flipped to the first page, and turned it to face Cho'sun. "This, here, is the letter *aleph*, the first letter of the Hebrew alphabet."

Cho'sun looked skeptically at the image of the *aleph* on the tablet's screen. "Listen, *bubele*, no more nonsense – this you call the answer to my question?"

Dov considered that for a moment, before answering. "It's the beginning of an answer."

"How long will this answer take?"

For once, Dov didn't say what he thought – hopefully long enough for a ship to come rescue me – but merely shrugged, hands up, and gave Cho'sun the same answer his rabbis had given Dov back when he was a student. "It takes as long as it takes."

Cho'sun looked back at the tablet, its head cocked first to one side, then the other. "*Oy vey*," it said finally, and then clicked its mandibles. "What comes next?"

Keep Out

Fredric Brown

With no more room left on Earth, and with Mars hanging up there empty of life, somebody hit on the plan of starting a colony on the Red Planet. It meant changing the habits and physical structure of the immigrants, but that worked out fine. In fact, every possible factor was covered – except one of the flaws of human nature....

DAPTINE IS THE SECRET OF IT. Adaptine, they called it first; then it got shortened to daptine. It let us adapt.

They explained it all to us when we were ten years old; I guess they thought we were too young to understand before then, although we knew a lot of it already. They told us just after we landed on Mars.

"You're *home*, children," the Head Teacher told us after we had gone into the glassite dome they'd built for us there. And he told us there'd be a special lecture for us that evening, an important one that we must all attend.

And that evening he told us the whole story and the whys and wherefores. He stood up before us. He had to wear a heated space suit and helmet, of course, because the temperature in the dome was comfortable for us but already freezing cold for him and the air was already too thin for him to breathe. His voice came to us by radio from inside his helmet.

"Children," he said, "you are home. This is Mars, the planet on which you will spend the rest of your lives. You are Martians, the first Martians. You have lived five years on Earth and another five in space. Now you will spend ten years, until you are adults, in this dome, although toward the end of that time you will be allowed to spend increasingly long periods outdoors.

"Then you will go forth and make your own homes, live your own lives, as Martians. You will intermarry and your children will breed true. They too will be Martians.

"It is time you were told the history of this great experiment of which each of you is a part."

Then he told us.

Man, he said, had first reached Mars in 1985. It had been uninhabited by intelligent life (there is plenty of plant life and a few varieties of non-flying insects) and he had found it by terrestrial standards uninhabitable. Man could survive on Mars only by living inside glassite domes and wearing space suits when he went outside of them. Except by day in the warmer seasons it was too cold for him. The air was too thin for him to breathe and long exposure to sunlight – less filtered of rays harmful to him than on Earth because of the lesser atmosphere – could kill him. The plants were chemically alien to him and he could not eat them; he had to bring all his food from Earth or grow it in hydroponic tanks.

* * *

For fifty years he had tried to colonize Mars and all his efforts had failed. Besides this dome which had been built for us there was only one other outpost, another glassite dome much smaller and less than a mile away.

It had looked as though mankind could never spread to the other planets of the solar system besides Earth for of all of them Mars was the least inhospitable; if he couldn't live here there was no use even trying to colonize the others.

And then, in 2034, thirty years ago, a brilliant biochemist named Waymoth had discovered daptine. A miracle drug that worked not on the animal or person to whom it was given, but on the progeny he conceived during a limited period of time after inoculation.

It gave his progeny almost limitless adaptability to changing conditions, provided the changes were made gradually.

Dr. Waymoth had inoculated and then mated a pair of guinea pigs; they had borne a litter of five and by placing each member of the litter under different and gradually changing conditions, he had obtained amazing results. When they attained maturity one of those guinea pigs was living comfortably at a temperature of forty below zero Fahrenheit, another was quite happy at a hundred and fifty above. A third was thriving on a diet that would have been deadly poison for an ordinary animal and a fourth was contented under a constant X-ray bombardment that would have killed one of its parents within minutes.

Subsequent experiments with many litters showed that animals who had been adapted to similar conditions bred true and their progeny was conditioned from birth to live under those conditions.

"Ten years later, ten years ago," the Head Teacher told us, "you children were born. Born of parents carefully selected from those who volunteered for the experiment. And from birth you have been brought up under carefully controlled and gradually changing conditions.

"From the time you were born the air you have breathed has been very gradually thinned and its oxygen content reduced. Your lungs have compensated by becoming much greater in capacity, which is why your chests are so much larger than those of your teachers and attendants; when you are fully mature and are breathing air like that of Mars, the difference will be even greater.

"Your bodies are growing fur to enable you to stand the increasing cold. You are comfortable now under conditions which would kill ordinary people quickly. Since you were four years old your nurses and teachers have had to wear special protection to survive conditions that seem normal to you.

"In another ten years, at maturity, you will be completely acclimated to Mars. Its air will be your air; its food plants your food. Its extremes of temperature will be easy for you to endure and its median temperatures pleasant to you. Already, because of the five years we spent in space under gradually decreased gravitational pull, the gravity of Mars seems normal to you.

"It will be your planet, to live on and to populate. You are the children of Earth but you are the first Martians."

Of course we had known a lot of those things already.

* * *

The last year was the best. By then the air inside the dome – except for the pressurized parts where our teachers and attendants live – was almost like that outside, and we were allowed out for increasingly long periods. It is good to be in the open.

The last few months they relaxed segregation of the sexes so we could begin choosing mates, although they told us there is to be no marriage until after the final day, after our full clearance. Choosing was not difficult in my case. I had made my choice long since and I'd felt sure that she felt the same way; I was right.

Tomorrow is the day of our freedom. Tomorrow we will be Martians, *the* Martians. Tomorrow we shall take over the planet.

Some among us are impatient, have been impatient for weeks now, but wiser counsel prevailed and we are waiting. We have waited twenty years and we can wait until the final day.

And tomorrow is the final day.

Tomorrow, at a signal, we will kill the teachers and the other Earthmen among us before we go forth. They do not suspect, so it will be easy.

We have dissimulated for years now, and they do not know how we hate them. They do not know how disgusting and hideous we find them, with their ugly misshapen bodies, so narrow-shouldered and tiny-chested, their weak sibilant voices that need amplification to carry in our Martian air, and above all their white pasty hairless skins.

We shall kill them and then we shall go and smash the other dome so all the Earthmen there will die too.

If more Earthmen ever come to punish us, we can live and hide in the hills where they'll never find us. And if they try to build more domes here we'll smash them. We want no more to do with Earth.

This is our planet and we want no aliens. Keep off!

Fallon Storm

Judi Calhoun

THE NEEDLE STUNG for half a second as it pierced my skin – fast blooming ecstasy, rushing nirvana through my blood rivers … lightheaded now, my eyelids fluttered, seeing soft flashes of pink and orange. Regrettably, this chemical trip was short.

Two lab coats stiffly struggled me into the back seat of the black SUV. I went limp letting them think there was no fight left, that their drug was in control and not the feral part of my darker nature that howled to be set free.

My sweaty blonde head fell back against the headrest, still smelling their fear, I watched them bolting my thin wrists into cuffs attached to steel chains thick enough to secure Godzilla to the floorboards instead of a 98-pound woman. They rushed back inside the safety of the building, but not William my driver, the brave one. He slid the leather strap of the Bowie knife over the gear shifter, no gun since bullets could never kill me. I doubted a knife could do any damage. He adjusted his seatbelt before turning to make eye contact.

"You okay … you comfortable, sweetheart?" His tone mockingly gentle. "If you need anything … water, a burger … we can stop and get you whatever … let me know."

I slowly shook my head no. "If you really want to help, William, you'd set me free." My voice sounded thick from the lingering effects of the drug.

"I can't do that, Fallon," he intoned, shifting away to start the engine; the SUV slowly maneuvered past the guard, out through the gate. "Look, you've been through a lot, I get it. I do. That's why I want to help … I mean, I'm just looking out for your well-being."

Was he messing with my head? I didn't like being talked down to. "Stop pretending you're concerned for my comfort. We both know you're afraid of me. Isn't that right, William … mister company man? You're only looking out for their investment."

William's steel-blue eyes met mine in the rearview but he didn't answer. For some unknown reason, I started feeling bad for the guy. After all, he was only a part of a bigger problem … a small part, or perhaps I just wasn't in the mood to argue.

He drove too fast for these switch-back dirt roads, almost like he was anxious to get away as much as I was. It wasn't long before we reached the highway in the middle of nowhere Colorado. I felt that tinge of anger return catching a distant glimpse of the testing facility we'd just left moments ago, the place of my constant torture.

I stared now at the back of William's head; he wasn't a bad-looking guy … twenty years my senior – too old for me. Besides, I had fantasized far too often, on how I might kill him. Yet, something was off about William today. It still bothered me that he was able to cloak his thoughts. Perhaps if I kept him talking, I'd discover some weakness.

"You know, William, you could just pull over and let me off here. Nobody would ever know. You could say I overpowered you, something like that."

He was frowning when our eyes met again. "Why don't you care more about this country? I thought you were a patriot. My God, can't you see? We live in dangerous times. This is your chance to serve our community – fight for what's right."

His words turned hard in my stomach. "Stop! Please, just stop. I never asked for any of this. And I certainly didn't want to become some depraved government's secret weapon. You and all your other dictator friends are hell-bent on using me for some evil purpose. Well, I say no, I don't care about this country … I've never felt like it was my real home. Besides, why should I do anything for this government after what they did to me?"

His voice was nearly a whisper. "I … I'm told if this … um, if this experiment doesn't work, there may not be a home, a country … a world left for any of us. Fallon, your skills are vital. Death cannot claim you … your speed, your strength – they're way off the charts. I promise, if you cooperate you can have anything you want."

"Lies – all lies! You cart me off from one facility to another hoping to discover what weakens me. Look at me, William. LOOK!"

His eyes found mine in the mirror.

"Who's going to want me, now? My life is over, I'm only twenty-four. I thought maybe one day I … I might … um, have a life. Maybe start a family since you killed all of mine."

"I didn't kill your family," he said softly, then mumbled. "I didn't agree with … well, we took a risk and—"

"Is that what you call it?" I was seething with anger. "You're actually starting to believe your own bullshit. Your experiments murdered everyone I loved." I swallowed down the pain, thoughts of Mother, Fen, my older sister, and Jon returned. *Remember us who are left behind*, his last words burned inside my chest. *What did you mean, brother*?

I tugged on my chains until the steel loops elongated, stretching open. We were twenty minutes outside the Denver facility with its electric fences, security guards, and dogs. If I were to escape, I needed the shelter of civilization.

I glanced at my ankle to the place beneath my skin where the tracker device was located. I leaned to look into the front seat at the six-inch Bowie knife, in the leather sheath wrapped around the gear shifter knob.

William relaxed back in his seat. "I know you don't believe me, but I do care about you, Fallon, and I'm going to prove it to you."

I frowned. Something was different about him. How odd. William meant every word he said. That made things difficult considering I planned on killing him.

We'd just passed inside the city limits. In my thoughts, I started the countdown: 5, 4, 3, 2, 1. I gave my chains a final yank – they snapped. I was out of my seat, wrapping the chains around William's throat. The car swerved as he struggled to fight me, but it was a useless contest.

"I don't want to kill you," I whispered against his ear. "So be smart and don't try anything stupid."

The SUV was fishtailing all over the road. I loosened the chains. He was trying to suck in air, eyes wide, still working on getting the vehicle under control.

I swiftly liberated the knife from its case and prudently placed the tip against his chest, as I moved quickly into the front seat.

"No. No. Listen to me, Fallon," he said. "Don't do this, wait, I've got something to tell you."

"Sure," I said, and flipped the knife around. Before he could speak, I struck him in the head with the handle.

He slumped over, unconscious.

The car was heading toward oncoming traffic. I positioned myself over him in the driver's seat. I mashed down on the accelerator. The SUV skidded and swerved, crossing lanes, horns blaring. Miraculously, we missed a head-on with a truck. But once the tires struck that soft shoulder she began to flip. We rolled twice before coming to rest upside down in a field.

I could hear William's heart beating. He was alive.

I crawled out into the dirt and stood feeling a hot afternoon breeze rush against my skin and whip my hair into my face. Freedom felt good, and yet part of me feared if I turned, white lab coats with dart guns would be waiting. Out on the freeway, the traffic was slowing, cars pulled over, and people on cell phones were shouting.

I ripped the metal cuffs from my wrists and ankles and tossed them inside the car. I picked up the knife, hiked up my pant leg and cut into my flesh, digging out the tracker. The blood ran down my leg into my shoe. I tossed the knife into the bushes and said goodbye to William before I ran.

I kept my speed down to five miles per hour sprinting through fields headed for a sizeable building next to a factory. I made it into the shadow of a gray building with open bay garage doors, *Stanley's Auto-body & Repair*.

A guy wearing green coveralls, probably not Stanley, asked if I needed help.

"Restroom?" I whispered.

He gestured around the corner.

The room was the size of a closet; coffins seemed larger. The air smelled of piss and offered no relief from the day's heat. Scrawled graffiti on grimy walls screamed insults at visitors. The empty towel dispenser hung sideways on one screw. I cursed when my shoe stuck in gum on the tiled floor. I reached for the faucet but found the spout was shaved clean off. I crushed the tracker in my fingers and tossed the pieces into the bowl, then flushed.

My leg was healed when I left the garage and sprinted behind buildings, staying parallel with the main road. Denver was a city on the edge of woodlands. I found the cover of trees just in time to hear the helicopter blade-vortex rotation. They were less than a quarter of a mile out. Shit! Their onboard equipment registered massless particles and gravitational waves, meaning they had the advantage of pinpointing my exact location. Now, gaining hyper-speed was completely out of the question.

I spied a strip mall, near a sizeable office building. A few grey suits mingled in the parking lot. I crossed the street nonchalantly and slid unnoticed through glass doors into a Dollar Store. I tucked under my shirt hair dye, scissors, and Foster-Grant sunglasses and was out the door unnoticed.

The men in suits were having a heated political argument – a perfect distraction. I bumped into the shorter one to liberate his wallet. I made my way around the back of the building, sprinting across the street and deep into the safety of the woods. I kept moving.

A short distance down, a vacancy sign flashed on a seedy motel that rented by the hour. I broke the tags off the sunglasses and adjusted them on my face. Inside the air-conditioned office, the manager, an older guy, moved painfully from his chair, groaning some. The old guy was smart enough to ask if I was alone.

"No. My husband ran to the store." He knew I was lying but he gave me the key anyway. Outside, I passed an abandoned service cart and swiped a trash bag and a bottle of tablet bleach.

The room was your typical cheap sleep, it smelled of pine cleaner and bargain brand deodorizer. I dropped the items I'd stolen onto the faded navy-blue bedspread. I placed Shorty's wallet on the nightstand. I switched on the wall lamp above. I stared down at the leather wishing Shorty had been a woman – if she had been, I could've taken on her identity.

I stripped and rushed into the shower. The package of raven-black hair dye took twenty-five minutes. Depending on how many motels William was searching in the area, I figured I had less than twenty minutes.

I felt no remorse in slicing off six inches of hair. Staring at the blonde strands in the sink, thoughts of my brother Jon returned. Our Aryan appearance was in stark contrast to the rest of the brunettes in our family; people asked if we were adopted. Mother said we were a testament to our father. I tried so hard to remember his face. It was my eighth birthday party when immigration officers stormed the house searching for him – he had vanished.

Where are you, Papa?

After the shower, I flushed my hair down the toilet. The box of dye, scissors, and wallet went into the bag. I jerked the shower-spray nozzle from its cradle, unscrewed the head and placed a bleach tablet inside, then soaked down every surface.

Outside, a parade of black vehicles were pulling into the lot. I eased out the door and ducked behind a shrub. William, with a bandage on his head, was scanning each unit. The man was no fool. He knew I was here.

Thankfully, no helicopters … good, nothing to stop me from reaching hyper-speed. My skin tingled as I took a deep breath and readied my body. My world shimmered as I stepped into the ether, slipping through a vacuum of time. I crossed the road right in front of their eyes. The mass-energy equivalent was, by loose definition, approaching the speed of light – semantics.

At last, when I stopped five minutes later, I found myself in an alleyway between two tall city buildings. The dizziness was waning faster now. The music of water came to my ears. I shuffled toward the city street finding a metal grate in the gutter. Beneath my feet, a river hastened on its travels to the treatment plant. I emptied the contents of the bag and smiled as the items disappeared.

Another sound came softly to my ears – a dog whimper, coming from overhead. I bent and leaped high, landing atop the red stone apartment complex. A lovely floral rooftop garden reminded me of home. I heard the animal scratching on wood. I moved toward the shed. I ripped off the padlock and tore open a door. But something heavy struck me from behind and hands shoved me. The dog barked as I stumbled and fell over the edge, hitting a dumpster. I rolled off onto the cement.

* * *

No idea how long I'd been unconscious. Now, I was staring at sheer curtains, my eyes focusing through a foggy haze. I was curled up on a red sofa, glancing around across the space toward a small kitchenette. I could hear the tumblers in the lock, the sound of a bolt turning, the door opening. I gasped and was off the sofa across the room with my hands around his throat squeezing the life from his lungs.

He had light brown messy hair and was holding a bag from a fast-food dive that was now slipping from his fingers as he turned a light shade of blue.

"Who are you? How did I get here?"

If I didn't let go, he'd probably die. I let him breathe. He slumped over struggling for air. "I … I thought you were dead." His voice was hoarse. "I … um, got food," he whispered, eyes wide on me. He bent to pick up the bag. "You hungry?"

"You're a doctor?" I asked, noticing the blue scrubs.

"Third year, pre-med," he said. "Adam Beacher, nice to meet you … I think." He pushed his glasses up on his face. "You, um … you want to tell me what you are?"

Instinctively my eyes narrowed. "That's classified."

"Yeah, well, I did kind of save your life, so maybe I earned it?" He shrugged. "Can I?" He pointed to the chair. I moved so he could sit. His fingers trembled as he opened a food wrapper. I stepped away, walking backward. Keeping my eye on him, I glanced out the window between the sheer curtains, studying the movement on the street.

"They were here," he said, "…asking questions. Don't worry, I lied." He shoved a large bite of cheeseburger into his mouth, struggling to swallow.

"I read you," I said, moving back to the table. "You think I'm a scientific breakthrough in human genetics, you'd like to experiment on me, and you're hoping we might have sex later." I leaned over to look at him closer. "Adam Beacher, you're hiding something."

"No." He shook his head. "No. You, um … ah … wait, you can read minds?"

"I read motivations and emotions. That's why I know you can't be trusted."

"You got it all wrong, I'm not your enemy. I swear. Hand up to God." He took another bite of his burger. "So, um … can I ask again, who the hell are you?"

"Defense weapon number 303-47596A," I said, dragging out a chair. I sat down. "That's what they call me."

"What does your mother call you."

I bit my lip. "She's dead."

"Oh," he whispered. "I'm sorry."

"Fallon Storm."

"Storm … sounds right," he chuckled. "You … um, Miss Storm, have some rather interesting talents … strong as a T-Rex, able to read minds and fall from an eleven-story building without a scratch on your body?"

I could not stop sneering at him. He was easy to read. It was all there, hidden behind his fake humour. The man had untrustworthy motives. My eyes ran over the name Crenshaw Labs on his uniform. "My father used to work for that lab when he first came here to this … this place."

"Your father…" he repeated. "Yeah, wait a minute, I know him … Daniel Edward Storm?"

I stood fast, nearly knocking over the table. "I feel the hate you have buried in your heart. You thought my father was scum. You've already called them, haven't you – don't deny it!"

"I swear, Fallon, I … look, if I was going to turn you in, I would have done that while you were sleeping."

This time I did not hesitate. I headed for the door.

"Wait," he shouted. "Where are you going? … It's not safe … they're everywhere. They are not going to let you go easily."

Well, well, I was right. He was a traitor. Now, I surprised myself by holding it together and not killing him. "They will never find me." I opened the door.

"Listen, you need money. I can drive you to the airport. I can buy you a ticket or a hotel room."

I frowned, hesitating, but not because I believed any of his false promises. "You're perspiring. Are you worried you won't get your reward?" He did not answer. "Perhaps I will agree if you promise to tell me more about my father. Do you know where he is?"

"I … I could lose everything," he said, becoming quiet for a moment. "Fine. Okay, I'll tell you, but only after you are safely away from the danger waiting for you outside."

I didn't care about my safety, but if there was even the slightest possibility that I could find my father, I'd play along. "Okay. I will go with you," I whispered. "But I swear, Adam if you betray me … you understand what I will do."

* * *

I fidgeted nervously with my sunglasses, standing in line at Centennial Airport. The moment I heard the helicopters on the tarmac I knew and a bitter knot of betrayal twisted in my gut.

Men in black with green tranquilizer air rifles and others carrying black Kalashnikov AK and AR assault weapons headed my way.

Breaking maximum speed inside a building would mean slamming through a wall … People could get hurt, not to mention building particles would be easily traced. So I ran for the glass front doors.

Too many people were gathered on the sidewalk … people who could get hurt … kids, and a woman holding a baby. I glanced back over my shoulder hearing the soft whoosh when the first dart left the chamber. I felt the strike in my back while many darts and bullets missed and shattered glass, pieces flying outward at people on the sidewalk – chaos ensued – screaming, running.

I reached the entrance and jumped through the glass-shattered doorframes and covered my body over the woman with the baby to protect them. I felt every bullet, every dart that entered me.

The baby was crying; the woman pushed me away. I let her go, watching her scramble into a nearby car that sped away. I was a fool. The woman was a plant. *I could trust nobody.*

I prepared to hit hyper-speed when more darts stung like a hundred bees. Their poison buzzed inside my mind. Dizzy now, I could no longer fight the wooziness that had taken all my strength. I tumbled forward, knees striking the pavement, hands sliding across shards of glass, blood pooling around the pieces.

Remember us who are left behind. My brother's words inside my head, painful visions of him waving goodbye, as he got into an SUV. I'd never see him again.

Their sedative solution was stronger this time. Someone rolled me over. I stared up at Adam. A satisfied grin on his face. "I told you, didn't I, you'd never get away from us."

* * *

The sound of an engine woke me up. I gasped and struggled against the metal restraints. I was a prisoner being carted to another testing facility. I squinted and stared out the window watching the desert landscape rush by – lost freedom. But I would try again and this time I would trust no one.

"…You okay?" asked William, his eyes studying me from the rearview.

"You won," I said, despondently. "I hope you're happy?"

"It's not what you think, Fallon," he said. "I'm on your side."

Another lie. I was so sick of lies.

"Did Adam get a reward for turning me in?"

"Yes," said William.

The sun struck my window and gleamed off the shiny hood as the car turned onto the hard-packed, washboard road. Fear struck me. I had visions of being injected with another super virus. This time they would leave me to die in the wilderness. This is how they were going to end me.

"Where are we going?" I asked, breathlessly.

"Your identity has been compromised," he said.

"So, you're going to kill me?"

"No. Fallon, you're going home."

"Home," I repeated. "I don't understand."

"You should never have told Adam about your father. They were enemies. He tried to kill him."

"What? Why?"

He didn't answer. The man was frustrating, but now suddenly for the first time, I caught a glimmer of something covert in William's motivation – he wanted me to read his incentives.

"I'm just like you, Fallon; there are many of us here. Of course, not everyone possesses your special gifts. My talent is spying and keeping secrets hidden while working covertly to protect our race."

I felt the frown lines deepening on my forehead.

"What? What are you saying?"

"Every car was bugged. I swept this one clean because I needed to talk freely. You have to believe me, Fallon. I wasn't taking you back to that testing facility when you attacked me, I was taking you home. Here," he said, leaning his arm over the seat. He handed me a key.

I stared at the key, trying to remember how to breathe, then snatched it from his fingers before he could change his mind. I leaned forward to unlock my leg shackles, wondering if this was another test. Then almost miraculously, William completely opened his senses to me.

"You're telling the truth."

He nodded.

Something enormous loomed ahead, larger than a city. A mechanical marvel that blended into the wilderness landscape and mirrored the horizon. Driving closer, the color changed and I could see the high gloss silver craft reflecting the sun.

Roughly ten blond men wearing gray stood sleek and yet severe in their defensive stance as they surrounded the intergalactic marvel.

William pulled the SUV right up to the open ramp. He got out and came around to open my door, but I didn't move.

A willowy tall, blond figure approached the car.

"Hello, Fallon," he said, bending over and looking inside. "I can read your mind. I understand your apprehension, but there is nothing to fear. We are all family."

"You're my father," I said, suddenly recognizing him, feeling relief wash over me. "I thought you were dead."

He took my hand as I exited the car. I fell into his arms. It felt strange but right. From his embrace, I learned everything about him, about my mother, and the hardship and agony they suffered at the hands of the government, murdering our family. My heart understood his unspoken sadness.

Someone else was moving from the craft, someone familiar. I nearly lost my breath – my brother, Jon. I ran and threw my arms around him. The tears stung my eyes. Now everything felt suddenly perfect. For a long moment, I clung to him and wept.

"I'm glad you're coming home," said Jon. "I was so worried when William said you were missing."

I turned toward my driver, who had climbed back inside the SUV. I reluctantly let go of my brother and rushed toward the car. "William! Wait, please," I said. "Um…"

He held up his hand indicating it was all okay.

"Thank you, you know, for…" I felt foolish.

"Remember us, who are left behind," he said.

Suddenly it was all clear. When Jon shouted those same words, it was because he thought he was staying on Earth, and I was going home with Father. None of us knew the duplicitous role the US government would play in my kidnapping and torture. Since William could only rescue one of us, I'm glad he had chosen Jon instead of me.

"I'll never forget you, William," I said, feeling my brother's hand slip into mine. "I promise."

A smile graced my driver's lips. I felt a strange loss watching him drive off into the waffling desert heat.

RingWorm

V. Castro

AS A SHAMAN, it is my duty to pass on spiritual traditions and keep our history alive. The history of our people on this planet can and will propel us forward. It is a mirror like the shards of black rock we collect at the feet of the smoking Volcanic Straits. We gaze deeply into its polished surface to divine what our aging, limited eyes cannot see. The spirit is neither limited nor ages.

Our ancestors were dumped here when they were no longer of use. They came from a neighboring planet, where they had been part of the workforce brought in from far and wide to build its infrastructure. However, over time the population proved to be more than the planet could sustain – too many mouths to feed, too many hands to keep usefully employed. Lured by the promise of another project on another planet with housing and pay, many left. The ships landed here, desolate but habitable with a stable atmosphere and water sources. Once disembarked, they found supplies to last them two years. There were no shelters, no vehicles, no weapons and only very rudimentary tech. By the time our ancestors realized what was going on, it was too late. All they could see of the ships that had brought them were vapor trails in the sky.

And that is how our story began. In lies, then abandonment, but thereafter a sense of freedom and self-determination, because how else would they survive? An entire planet to create from a blank canvas. Sounds wonderful, yet there was a catch.

The worms. They are everywhere. Most are harmless and useful to our daily lives. The larger ones that live in the water we use for their rubbery skin to create water-resistant materials. The grubs of some species are fed to the domesticated indigenous animals, others are used in the food we eat. All species eat our waste, which makes them vital to sanitation. And the earthworms we use for many everyday necessities, including the disposal of our dead. The earthworms consume the interred bodies, which we neither preserve nor wrap in any material.

Today I am with a new generation of would-be healers and shamans showing them this process. I will teach them our traditions and our rituals, but it turns out that I must also prepare them for a growing threat to our existence.

There is a gasp from one of the students as they learn first-hand about our burial mounds. I move closer to reassure him.

"See there."

Clumps of wet earth shift with the worms writhing just below the surface. Their purplish-pink tails can just be seen as they revel in the feast. Little do the worms know that when they reach a certain length, they will be plucked out to be dried and used for medicinal purposes.

The young man looks at me and then back at the dirt. His fear vanishes as I bring my hand to rest just above the soil. He asks, "And the drums? Why the drums at the time of burial? It always frightened me when I was younger."

I smile at this question. I hoped someone would ask it.

"The drums mimic our heartbeat. This helps the soul say goodbye to the body as it dissipates into the heat of the sun and light of the stars."

The young man watches the earthworms go from a slow dance to a frenzied attack beneath the soil, flicking out dirt that dusts our feet.

"You can all go home now. I have much work to do before tomorrow's lesson."

A girl named Tochli, about sixteen, remains while the others leave.

"If I may, I would like to help. I want to find a solution to the threat. The entire village is talking about you leaving soon."

The smile on my face from the day's positive lesson fades. It is ironic that many species of worm provide what we need to survive, while another is the cause of the most horrific death imaginable. There is no cure that we know of, and the only relief we have for the sufferer derives from the stems of a lily, where tiny white worms attach themselves and eventually die, creating a crust. We have found a mixture of the stem and worms is a powerful painkiller.

It only took one fisherman to come back with a welt on his ankle that wouldn't stop itching. The flakes stuck beneath his nails and his touch infected others. The rash appears as a perfect circle on the skin, typically on the thigh or the back of the arm, sometimes the shoulder blades. The edge will form a thick protruding ridge. More and more appear. The wounds grow in concentric circles as the worm coils itself deep into the muscle, incapacitating its host until it bursts through the skin. Both host and worm die, but the damage is done because it has already spread to someone else.

It seems nothing can stop the parasitic ringworm from multiplying, and it has become more difficult finding the lily for those infected. The threat of the ringworm is growing, fast. It is as if the parasite has had enough of us inhabiting their space. We have done everything – we've prayed, left offerings, discontinued using the earthworms for medicine, but nothing makes a difference. Our people are dying, and I have to find a solution.

The time is upon us to approach it in a new light. And I am the one who carries that burden. I am a shaman. Everyone looks to me as the bodies pile up.

"Tochli, you are far too young. What if I find the source? I could be exposing you to terrible danger."

She doesn't back down and defiance glints in her eyes with the intensity of fire. "Most of my family has been claimed by this ringworm. I must look after my siblings. They need this."

I can see the pleading desperation in her eyes. And if I am honest, she is my top choice to be my successor.

"Alright. We leave for the coast in two days."

* * *

The night before our journey I gather every species of worm I have collected from different locations around the planet. Over the last six months I have dried them in bowls carved from bone and wood. The longer species hang from the rafters of my home. I place a few in my molcajete to be ground to a fine dust. The earthy scent isn't unpleasant, and I doubt it will taste of much. To make it easier to ingest, I mix it with warm water and honey that slides easily down my throat. Then I lie down to allow the mixture to invade my psyche with dreams to provide some clue as to the source of the ringworm. I focus my mind on the earth below me, encouraging her to whisper her secrets to me. Soon the council will gather outside my house. Together we will ask for guidance.

The drum beats in rhythmic succession. Sweat rolls down the side of my face. The skin beneath my breasts is hot too. They create their own tears. The villagers stand around chanting to conjure the spirits of our ancestors, to ask for knowledge of this plague that will not leave. What is this thing that attacks us? Was it something that arrived with the ancestors and mutated? Or has it always been here? Most importantly, how do we stop it?

After an hour I emerge from my house and move to a temazcal that has been prepared for me. The heat and steam take me to a world of vapor in which you can't see with the eyes in your skull – the visions are felt rather than seen.

With every beat of the drum I can hear a small voice becoming clearer. 'The cave at the edge of the world. Where the trees meet the sea is where you will find me…"

It repeats over and over again, in sync with the drum, until I find myself mumbling this phrase as my body sways. My eyelids are heavy. I give in to the body's desire and allow myself to fall to the ground.

I awake on the floor of the temazcal feeling as if my brain has been bathed in muddy water. My throat is dry. But I know what I have to do and where to go.

* * *

Tochli and I have been walking through the forest for three days. The tree canopy has been so dense we have barely seen daylight all this time. You know you are getting close to the coast when the sky starts to become visible again. It is night time when the trees start to thin. Tochli breaks the silence.

"Look up."

I turn my eyes to the darkness above. Two comets are supposed to cross the night sky tonight, the souls of ancient lovers, the shaman before me said. I didn't care about a lover's tale. All I want in my desperate sadness is a miracle. The miracle of finding a cure, of changing everything for future generations, so they don't inherit this deadly burden. Until that miracle occurs, we have to overcome the fears of the mind and the scourge of the ringworm.

"I said no distractions, Tochli."

Everyone is counting on me, but truth be told, I first need to believe in myself. That I can overcome this, that I can be victorious. For a moment, I allow myself to peer into the night sky. The beauty softens me, bringing tears to my eyes as I think of all our dead. "Guide me. Guide me tonight," I whisper, to nothing and nobody. I can't take any more of the restlessness of uncertainty. The thinning trees are a good sign. By morning we should hear the crashing of waves and the call of the giant sea birds large enough to capture and crush small animals on land.

* * *

The cave. A black hole yawning open in yellow and orange striated rock. All life begins in a dark place devoid of anything. Here I stand in the mouth of life. Or is it death? This planet was not empty before our arrival. I think the ones who left our ancestors here knew that.

I look to Tochli. She has no fear in her face. Yes, she will be a good successor if she survives. "Stay here. And trust your instinct to run. Do not come to my aid unless I ask."

She gives me a single nod. I know she will do as I say. I walk closer to the opening. A lone figure emerges from the cave.

"You came. You heard me."

An old woman stands naked before me. Her sagging, dry skin has the signs of the ringworm, yet she seems in perfect health. A deep red rash flows from between her legs and spreads down her thighs. Her eyes are marbles of black. In her right hand she holds some type of box. It is the size of her fist and looks similar to the tech left for the ancestors. Some of it worked but most of it did not. I stand my ground but try to appear non-threatening. "Who are you?"

"I offer you a chance. You see I have been listening to the stars." She lifts the box and tosses it towards me.

"And what is it that you hear, old woman?"

"My death, our death. This thing picks up their whispers."

"I don't care about the stars. I am here because the ringworm is killing my people. It looks like you are infected too."

"I know. It comes from my womb to keep this place pristine and unspoiled. Others tried to settle here before but many died. They picked up their dead and left. They stayed away before returning to leave your people here. But you are resisting."

"You want to live so we can die? You curse us? What are you?"

"Isn't that the way of life? Creatures eat each other to survive. I do not know of anything that does not exist in this way."

"Who are you?"

"I am the last of the original people here. Unlike your kind, we live for hundreds of years. The rest are only gone because of those who brought you here. This was a place they wanted to claim as their own without a fight. They used their weapons that my people could not defend themselves against. But they didn't get me and that was their mistake."

My heart sinks. I feel deep sorrow for her. None of this is right. Her people and mine at the mercy of others.

"I am sorry. How do we solve this? I will not allow you to destroy us. Can we not live in peace?"

"I have great respect for you. Your love for your tribe, this planet. How you take your position so seriously. It is everything for you. None of you has noticed me watching and mingling with your kind."

"I will ask again. How do we solve this?"

"We fight to the death."

"You want me to wager the fate of this world on a battle with you?"

"There is no other way. Only one can be victorious."

"If you die will the ringworm die with you? And the other worms?"

"No. Only the plague. It is my body that generates it. I gave birth to it to fight off the others. Unfortunately, the damage had already been done and only I, a shaman like you, survived. My people protected me with their lives. So you see, I don't mind dying now."

Without hesitating, I take the obsidian blade from my waistband. She narrows her beady eyes. Tears just as dark seep from the corners before she opens her mouth to its full width revealing round, pulsating suckers. Whatever pity I had in my heart flees. She must die. She flexes both hands. Sharp nails jut from the fingertips, producing a black liquid where they break through.

In an instant she runs towards me. I raise the blade and bring it down on her head. She screams out and her hand clutches at the strings of beads and shells I wear around my neck. They break and fall to the ground. I don't need them anyway. They are trinkets that have no power in this fight. She grabs her face, realizing she has been deeply cut. The flesh on her forehead flaps open, revealing a writhing mass of small luminescent larvae. She has to be burned. Nothing can be left.

I know in her desperation she will redouble her efforts to kill me. I take the bow off my back and untie the belt around my waist, allowing everything that can weigh me down in this fight to be discarded. A true shaman is naked in the light and the dark. If she rips the clothes from my back, so be it. I will fight stripped.

She crouches on all fours, like a predatory creature ready to pounce. I am quick to take the opportunity and run towards her first. After all this, it still hurts my soul to kill her. She is the mother ancestor of this place where we did not ask to be abandoned. It is her home too. Yet she wants no compromise. She wants nothing to do with us and I can't allow her to destroy what we have built.

Just before I strike, she falls to her knees. My body jerks to a stop, nearly causing me to tumble to the ground. "What are you doing?" I say, breathing hard.

"I know it is time to let go, find peace in the stars. You have shown yourself a worthy heir of this world. Many worlds in the stars are not so lucky. I know you will keep the line of faithful guardians with the same spirit you have shown here."

My hand hovers over her head.

"I will. It is in good hands and hearts."

She bows her head. "Now end this."

I take my obsidian blade and run it across her throat. Tiny white sacs spill from the wound. As she collapses, they shrivel in the sun. I stand there mesmerized, my body unable to move. "Tochli!" I call out. "Bring me something for this. We must take some back. And grab that box she held."

Tochli brings me a small pouch made from worm skin. I scoop a small portion of the origin of the ringworm and place it inside. Then Tochli and I find as much kindling as possible to create a funeral pyre for the dead mother's body to be offered back to the stars. We look on as the flesh sizzles and chars before floating off as glowing embers. When there is nothing left, I put out the fire.

"Let's go."

We have no time to waste getting back to the village. Upon the mother ancestor's death she gave me a premonition that I do not doubt. The ones who left our ancestors years ago will be back. They are coming in their ships and when they do, we will send them to their deaths with the ringworm. They cannot take our home, but we will take their ships and find their world so we may never be conquered again. When they arrive we will be ready to infect the ones who land then take the fight to the rest of them. Our future generations will only know freedom.

El Bordado

P.A. Cornell

JANUARY 28 (EARTH STANDARD TIME)

Querida Mamá:

We arrived on Mars yesterday afternoon, Earth time. We've been on Mars time since and between that and the unfamiliar gravity, we're feeling quite jet-lagged. Our first stop was Phobos Station, where we retrieved our luggage before making our way through customs. At least our bags are lighter here.

Customs was a nightmare. I swear they train those people not to smile. Here we are, exhausted with a baby and small child in tow and they still hassle us like criminals. Eventually they let us through and we took a shuttle to the surface. The fee was more than expected but there was no way we could take the long ride down the space elevator with the kids.

Due to the unexpected expense, I'm sending this text letter instead of calling. It'll be a while before Ricardo and I are earning money, so we must tighten our belts. Distance and differences in planetary rotation make video calls expensive, even at off-peak hours. We're already imposing on Umberto and Amelia enough to ask for that. I hope it won't take long for my letter to reach you, though at this distance I know it can.

Already, I miss you. I can't believe the way they discriminate in the colonies, separating families like ours. No elderly – save those who've grown old here. No one in poor health. I understand the colony's new and terraforming is still in its infancy, and that they must consider many factors, but can you imagine such blatant discrimination on Earth? As it is, they probably wouldn't have let *us* in were it not for the sponsorship by Ricardo's brother and his wife. We're so grateful for their generosity and for taking us into their home.

Umberto was waiting at the spaceport when we landed. Javierita needed changing and was in a fit, so I went to clean her up in a public bathroom while the men loaded Andrés and our luggage into the car. Martian changing tables don't fold down like at home, but rather pull out in a spinning motion. Feeling like *una imbécil*, I had to ask another woman how to work it, so I was gone longer than expected. I don't think Umberto was happy to wait, but I know he wouldn't have enjoyed the long drive, sealed into a surface car with a screaming infant.

The journey to the enclosure was breathtaking. By this time, it was dusk and the light was already much dimmer than on Earth, but the landscape reminded me of that time we drove through the Atacama from Santiago to Iquique. Of course, the soil here's more reddish and I doubt this desert ever experiences the phenomenon of the *desierto florido*. Remember that time we went to see it? Purple flowers for as far as you could see, and *los Andes* majestic in the background. The terraforming project has a long way to go before that can happen here – though I suppose *los Andes* has serious competition in Olympus Mons.

By the time we arrived at the enclosure in Valles Marineris, where Umberto and Amelia live, it was dark. We first had to return the car to the loan dock and from there take the elevated train to their neighborhood. At least it wasn't a long walk from the station to their home. Javierita had fallen asleep in her sling and Andrés was tiring too as I pulled him along while Ricardo and Umberto carried our suitcases. I didn't yet know what you'd snuck into mine.

Amelia welcomed us with a simple meal of *chacarero* sandwiches. At least that's what they called them. The green beans, grown in their small hydroponic garden, were recognizable enough. The tomatoes, on the other hand, tasted watery and had a mealy texture. I don't mean to sound ungrateful. I know growing produce here isn't as simple as on Earth, and imports are prohibitively expensive, so we'll have to learn to make do. These were, in any case, the best part of our *chacareros*. The buns, though not inedible, were tough and the meat was 3D-printed of course, but I couldn't guess at the base protein. The flavor was *somewhat* reminiscent of beef, but that's the best I can say about it. Still, we appreciated the effort to make us something familiar.

I think Amelia saw how tired we were because once we'd eaten, she sent us to bed without letting me help clear the table. They gave us their little girl Cristina's room, so she's sharing with her sister while we're here. We put Andrés to bed on a cot. For Javierita, they provided a folding bassinette on loan from a neighbor. All this makes me realize how many things we'll need to buy. I don't know how we'll afford it. If we're lucky, we'll find decent used items. If they weren't so restrictive on cargo weight for the shuttles that bring you to and from the spaceliners, we could've brought a few things from Earth to get us started.

That brings me to what I wanted to say when I started this letter. Thank you. When I opened my suitcase that first night, I was searching for my nightgown. On the trip with no access to our luggage, we only wore the printed clothing provided, endlessly recycling it day by day. But you must've known that's how it would be. That's why my nightgown was wrapped in *el bordado* – the embroidery you started work on just before we left.

When they denied you passage, I decided we wouldn't go, but you insisted we do, so the children would have greater opportunities. You knew I was heartsick having to leave you and assured me a piece of you would be coming along. This was what you meant, wasn't it? I noticed you stitched only the outline of the cottage and a few flowers, but the complete design is marked on the fabric for me to finish. I couldn't be happier knowing that wherever we eventually make our home, we'll have something personal to decorate it with. Something you and I made together. I'll work on it every chance I get. Thanks for including so many colors of thread. I'll make good use of them.

* * *

February 20 (EST.)

Querida Mamá:

We've been here just under one of your months. Umberto was able to get Ricardo a job at a terraforming plant. It's in maintenance. Not a bad job, but we'd hoped he'd find work in biology. Or at least something more in line with Ricardo's education and experience. Umberto laughed at that, saying newcomers can't expect such jobs; that there are others in line ahead of us. It was so hard to find decent work on Earth, what with having to compete with the machines. I guess we hoped things might be easier here.

Still, I'm glad he's bringing in a few credits. We're saving what we can, so we can move soon. The rest goes to the children's needs and to Umberto and Amelia.

I haven't found employment yet. Work isn't scarce in a growing colony. What's made it difficult is I need something that'll allow me to work while caring for the children, which limits my options. There's childcare, but the move is already such a change for the children that I want to be here for them as much as possible. At least until we're better acclimated. For the time being I keep busy with the fine needlework of *el bordado*. I've completed one side of the cottage and most of the roof. I'm experimenting with textures and stitches, making a sampler of sorts, like the ones you made when I was little. Under the cottage's window, I stitched in calla lilies – your favorite.

* * *

March 5 (EST.)

Querida Mamá:

We finally got Andrés enrolled in school. Javierita and I take the train with him each morning to drop him off, then pick him up later in the day. I even made a friend – one of the other mothers at the school. Her name's Ivette and she's from Venezuela, though she's lived on Mars for seven Earth years. She lives in the Hispanic neighborhood and tells me we should look for a home there, since there's a greater sense of community than where Umberto and Amelia live.

In both the Hispanic community and the school, they speak a blend of Spanish and Esperanto, since in addition to the languages spoken by early settlers, they used Esperanto to get around language barriers. These days, with everyone having translators, that practice has been largely abandoned, but for some reason keeps going strong here, and so Andrés is learning it in school along with his regular lessons *en Español*. The people in *la comunidad* jokingly refer to this language blend as "Espanto." I'm not yet used to this new patois, though Andrés is picking it up like he was born to it. Ivette says I'll get used to it in time.

* * *

April 17 (EST.)

Querida Mamá:

I'm writing this in tears. I didn't want to worry you before, but Umberto and Amelia had been having marital problems. The truth is, even here, he's an incurable womanizer. He'd say he was working late, but it was clear his job wasn't that demanding. Add to that the pressure on their marriage from us being in their home and you have constant fights. I could already feel resentment from Amelia, though she didn't say anything. Javierita and I started taking longer walks, so we wouldn't be in her way.

Last night everything came to a head. Amelia blew up when Umberto came home smelling of another woman's perfume. Ricardo and I woke to her yelling and throwing dishes. They were only the plastic printed dishes, but if you throw a stack of those, they make quite a clatter.

When we tried to calm them, Amelia accused me of making eyes at her husband! Can you imagine? She was out of control with rage, calling us freeloaders and implying she couldn't afford to care for her own children because of the burden of supporting us. Ricardo got angry since a good portion of his earnings have gone to them. (I suspect he's given it to his brother who hasn't shared it with his wife.)

The evening ended with crying children and Umberto asking us to leave. I couldn't believe it. It was the middle of the night and we hardly know anyone here. Where were we supposed to go?

We gathered our few possessions and took the train to Ivette's. I burned with shame waking her at that hour and having to explain what happened. She was wonderful, *Mamá*. She got the children settled and made us tea to calm our nerves. I could've used a little shot of *pisco* in mine, like you used to do in your younger days.

Now we're a burden on another family. Ivette says we can stay for as long as we like, but I want a home of our own. We've lost the support of our family here, the last thing I need is to lose my only friend.

We considered moving to one of the free pod habitats that the planet was seeded with in the early days but Ivette won't hear of it. She says those homes are *basura* – too old and damaged. And because they're outside the enclosures, she says it's not unheard of for these houses to vanish in the dust storms. I'll admit that worries me, so for now we're staying.

The bright spot in all this is I remembered to grab *el bordado* when we hurriedly packed, or no doubt Amelia would've thrown it out. Perhaps working on it will help calm my nerves.

* * *

May 12 (EST.)

Querida Mamá:

I finally have a job, and they even let me bring Javierita! She sits in a playpen my employer set up in the shop. It's an artisan's shop, appropriately called: *La Artesana*. My employer's a woman named Margarita, who's also *Chilena*. I told her about Amelia's awful *chacareros* and we laughed until we had tears in our eyes.

Ivette introduced us after she saw *el bordado*. By now, I've completed the cottage and winding path. I'm adding trees and more flowers. Margarita works in textile art and pottery, similar to what they used to make in *Pomaire*, before the influence of other South American cultures changed the techniques. She blends Martian soil with clay imported from Earth, which makes it unique so she can price it high. Some of her work even makes its way back across the stars to Earth.

Ivette had me bring *el bordado* to show Margarita. *Ay Mamá*, I was so embarrassed to show a skilled artist my amateur efforts, but she said I had talent and she could use someone to embroider details on the textiles she makes for clients tired of standard printed ones.

So that's what I'm doing now. Margarita takes custom orders and I embroider them according to what the client wants. I'm paid a fair wage and between that and what Ricardo makes, we hope to buy our own home soon.

* * *

July 1 (EST.)

Querida Mamá:

Andrés is having a rough time adjusting to Mars. He speaks Espanto, but kids at school mock his accent. They also make fun of him for the silly mistakes kids make. For instance, they were told they were going on a field trip to Amazonis, and he thought they meant the Amazon jungle. He realized immediately it couldn't be that, but by then the other children were laughing.

What saddens me most is he's begun to hide who he is and where he's from and I think if this continues, he might even forget. He speaks Espanto almost exclusively now and seems embarrassed when we do, especially if we make a mistake. He's even more embarrassed when we speak Spanish, so we can't win! He still speaks Spanish at home but never to his friends. He's also asked me to pack "normal" lunches, like the other kids get, rather than the meals you taught me to cook.

I managed to make a passable *pastel de choclo* – his favorite. The corn here grows small and can be watery when ground, but I managed to achieve a decent consistency. And while I had to use a mix of proteins for the "ground beef," once I added cumin, paprika, and oregano, you could hardly tell the difference. Andrés devoured it, but the next Sol he refused to bring any to school.

I wonder if we did the right thing, taking the kids so far from their birthplace. They're away from you, and their *tíos* and *tías*, and what do we have to show for it?

I especially wonder what it'll be like for Javierita. She's so young, she'll be a child of Mars. Earth will seem as alien to her as any other planet in the system. And if we ever go back to visit, it'll be to a place they don't recognize and a family of strangers. We talk about you and the others and show them the holos we brought, but it's not the same.

To try to help the situation, I've started to embroider our family members into *el bordado*. I made you first, in the little window of the cottage, looking out at the calla lilies. I asked Andrés who I should add next, and he said "Miguelito," which didn't surprise me since those cousins were always inseparable. He doesn't talk about how much he misses him, but I know he does. He made sure I stitched him wearing his favorite green shirt. The resemblance is quite good. I think working at Margarita's is helping improve my skills.

* * *

August 8 (EST.)

Querida Mamá:

Ricardo got promoted! He's assisting one of the managers of the atmospheric gasses division of the terraforming project. It's still not what he was trained for, but it's a much more satisfying position and he's finally enjoying what he's doing. It doesn't hurt that the promotion means a bit more money so we can begin our search for a home.

We're looking in *la comunidad*, as Ivette suggested, but have yet to find something affordable. I like the idea of being surrounded by people who speak my language even if they also speak Espanto. I'm starting to have an easier time with it anyway, and by the time the Martian year ends I should sound like a real Martian.

Speaking of real Martians, we applied for citizenship. Assuming the digital paperwork goes through, we'll have dual citizenship by the end of the month.

We also joined a club for Spanish-speaking people. We gather for social events at least once a month. The members are from all over Latin America and Spain. Or at least their families originated there.

Andrés has even made a few friends there and is speaking more Spanish, thanks to them. It's wonderful to see him embrace his background again. He even did a school project on where his family came from. He told the class all about Chile and his family there. He even used *el bordado* as a prop, though I haven't finished it. I'll send a recording of his presentation. We can afford a little splurge.

* * *

September 30 (EST.)

Querida Mamá:

"Life's full of ups and downs," you used to say. Maybe it's the lower gravity, but ups and downs seem more frequent here. Things have been going well for me. I'm enjoying my work and even have a loyal client that frequently requests my work. Recently, she commissioned my embroidery on some curtains. She wanted something floral using reds and pinks, so I drew inspiration from the *copihues* that grow in Chile. I liked how they turned out so much that I added some to the garden that surrounds the little cottage in *el bordado*. Among their blooms I added *Tía* Lidia, who's been on my mind. Maybe because Margarita reminds me of her. I made sure to stitch her wearing her blue apron – the one she'd wear when frying her famous *picarones*.

I wish I could say Ricardo has been as happy in his job, but I'm afraid he's been under a lot of stress. It's not the work. There's a new coworker that feels Ricardo has no right to be there.

He thinks good jobs like his should go to Martian-born people. He's rude to Ricardo and does everything possible to make him look bad to their boss. Luckily Ricardo's employer is aware of his background and education, so I think if anything he's pleased to be getting someone so valuable for such a low salary. Ivette's husband Juan thinks he's taking advantage of Ricardo by paying him what he does, and that he should ask for a raise, but we don't feel we're in a position to play hardball. In any case, his salary's enough to cover our expenses and even add to our savings now and then, which is all we need. Juan seems angry about how Earth-borns are treated, but neither Ricardo nor I are in any mood to fight against the prejudices of this society – at least not until we can do so with our feet firmly planted on our own little piece of this land.

* * *

December 28 (EST.)

Querida Mamá:

It's hard to believe we've been on Mars for nearly a full Earth year. We received your Christmas presents right on schedule, though I admit, we had to do the math to figure out the date on Earth. We've adjusted to the Martian calendar, and now telling time by Earth standards seems foreign. You must've sent this package not long after we left. You're so full of surprises *Mamá*.

The children were delighted with their toys but they were even more thrilled to receive new holos of their aunts, uncles, and cousins. Even Javierita seemed to perk up at the voices and faces she was seeing. Maybe they seemed familiar?

Ricardo was touched you remembered his love of Chilean papayas and has announced to us that the cans you sent are *his* and that we're not to so much as look at them. But Andrés and I are pretty sure we can convince him to share.

As for me, I treasure the embroidery thread you sent. I had run out of several colors and was making do with inferior thread Margarita had imported but decided not to use. She sold it to me at cost, which was kind, but this is so much better. I plan on getting back to *el bordado* as soon as I finish this letter. I love you *Mamá*. *Feliz Navidad y Año Nuevo*, though I know this letter will arrive much too late for that.

* * *

January 31 (EST.)

Querida Mamá:

I'm writing to tell you the news I'd hoped to share since our arrival on the red planet. We've purchased a home! I'm attaching two images to this message, though it'll increase the cost of sending it, and the length of time for it to reach you, but I wanted you to see where we'll be living. The second image is of *el bordado*.

You'll see there are some remarkable similarities between the little cottage you drew, and that I embroidered, with the new house. Yes, the roof of our home is flat, not peaked like the embroidered one. And no, we can't yet grow the multicolored flowers that surround the cottage in *el bordado*. But look at the way I textured the walls like the printed homes common on Mars. The color's nearly the same too. Do you see how the mountains in the background are so like the rocky Martian surface visible beyond the edge of the enclosure where our house lies?

It's for this reason I chose to make the sky in *el bordado* the warm yellow-orange of Martian daylight, rather than the blue of Earth's skies I'd originally intended. In lieu of the fluffy, white clouds

I remember, you'll see the spots in the sky that are the way Phobos and Deimos look to us from the surface.

You'll notice I finished adding *la familia*. I hope you don't mind, but I also added the family we have here on Mars. Ivette and Juan, obviously. And Margarita – she's the one making pottery in the bottom right. I've even included some of Andrés' friends.

In time, I'd like to add Umberto and Amelia and their girls. They're part of our story here, and while we parted on bad terms, Umberto's still Ricardo's brother. I've been gently encouraging him to reach out, and maybe patch things up. I'd love for our children to grow up together.

Ricardo made a frame from wood Margarita obtained from an artist friend. Wood is hard to come by on Mars, but these were considered scrap by their former owner, so he gave them willingly. Together we stretched the fabric of *el bordado* over this frame. It wasn't easy, but we finally got the wrinkles smoothed out.

El bordado was the first thing we hung in our new home. I was stitching right up until the end, finishing it only the Sol before the move. It was as if the journey to its completion was fated to take exactly as long as it took to find our place in this world. Maybe that was the magic you imbued it with through your love for us.

When we left Earth, I knew no place would truly feel like home without you in it. But you're here now. I feel your presence within these walls and with *el bordado* hanging pride of place at the front entrance, I can see you too, standing at the window of the little cottage, smiling at me from just above the calla lilies.

Can you see it, *Mamá*? Do you see yourself here on Mars?

A World Away and Buried Deep

Yelena Crane

THE FOLDS OF SKIN over my son's fourth and fifth hearing orifice flap like they're begging.

"I'm hungry." Aki's scraggly arms worm their way out from under the blankets. He looks up at me, blue eyes pleading.

"I know." I hear it in the growls. I see it in the way his feelers are always stretching to the sound of my voice.

The food my kind needs can't be bought in grocery stores on Earth, it doesn't matter how much protein or fiber he consumes.

I try, have tried, so hard to pass the best to him. I feed him the same stories I was fed as a child but instead of going from strength to strength, they leave me drained and tasting bitters. They leave Aki hungry and thin.

I can't take his quiet look of disappointment and brace myself for the telling, knowing it will do little to quench his hunger, or mine. "Listen, I have a good one to—"

"I don't want yours," he cries. "Where's gram? She was supposed to be here already."

Rain beats at the windows so hard, it looks like a glass portal to a water world. His gram is late because the rains are coming down heavy.

I rewrap Aki in the covers to keep him warm. "Earth's a big place and gram works far away. Maybe we can try a neighbor?"

He nods his head. Those neighbors with edible stories will say 'no', but what mother wouldn't take the chance if it meant the equivalent of a bellyful, even half full.

Aki is a stick in my arms and I rush for the door. I want to rush for a rocket to take us back to the home I can't remember. We had a reason to leave. A reason it's no longer home and hasn't been most of my life. The reasons are in my mama's stories, my inheritance from her.

I balance Aki and open the door. To my surprise mama's across the hall, sopping wet and brown like she'd wormed underground to get here.

"Darlings!" she says.

Aki shoots out of my arms, his feelers flying out for her and away from me. "Gram!"

I close the door behind her, relieved, because it means storytime won't fall to me. Because her stories are in more than her words, they're in the way she moves and the perfume of her skin.

"I thought you wouldn't make it tonight, we were going to try next door."

Mama swings Aki and pinches his cheeks, comments on how thin they are, how sallow I am. It's not in her to lie and say how big he's grown when he hasn't. "Did you try the audio tapes?"

I nod. "They didn't work." Nothing I've tried has worked.

For a moment I worry she blames me, imagines me tight-lipped when I should be – and I am – loose.

Before I can preemptively defend myself she covers me in her hug. Gobs of her feelers fall in my mouth like noodle strands.

"I know just the stories Aki needs, and you Ilyana," she says.

I hope beyond hope it's true because I'm hungry too.

When she's changed from wet clothes into dry we all curl up on the same bed, squishing and molding our bodies to her. Mama's in the middle even though I'm no baby, but I was once and I want to feel that way now, I need to. My head rests on her shoulder, near her third hearing orifice, and I'm small again.

"When I was a little girl," she begins. Aki giggle-whispers, trying to imagine gram's gray and wrinkles away.

I rest my eyes, the better to hear how her voice rises and falls retelling her former struggles, so different from mine. Some stories that help to grow hurt to hear. Like this one she chooses to tell. I worry Aki may not be ready for it, may not understand why his gram had to walk hundreds of miles barefoot in temperatures where there'd be snow on Earth. I've heard it before. It tastes different this time, having a little one of my own. My head slips lower, down to her heart and I hear the story a different way there. The story of her pulse beat quickens. Ba-dumBa-dumBa-dum. She's running in her memories, in her blood. Only that running tastes right, from all she's said. Tastes bitter like dandelions picked too late.

When we're certain Aki is sleeping, we slink away so I can question mama and she can question me. In the pricks of starlight, I see his cheeks are fuller than I've ever made them. I'm happy and also jealous, because I can't do the most basic thing a mother should.

"Is there something wrong with me?" I ask because the stories don't feel like they're mine to tell. Because of all the stories mama's weaved, the right flavor wasn't delicious or filling but left my throat sore and mind weary.

"I can't say why the stories that worked for me don't work for you." Mama sits me down at the foyer, resting her arm on mine for reassurance. Nothing fits right on me, not even her. Her presence makes me realize how little of our homeworld I have in the apartment. The way we live, I may as well have been born here. Adaptation makes me feel guilty.

Mama runs her hand up and around my head, to the plait of my feelers. Of what passes for a braid on Earth. "You?" she criticizes with just the tone of her voice and starts undoing it, as deft one-handed as I am with two. The talent of braiding is a learned skill and though my feelers are pliant enough, my fingers aren't. I blame Earth's gravity, though I know it's not the only reason why.

She rebraids, each twist tight but comfortable in how it stirs up the past. *Twist*, her waking at dawn to make my hair so she could see me looking proper before she left for work. *Twist*, her telling me not to forget our language when I was taught another. *Twist*, the look in her eyes I never understood until now – pride for having brought something back and given it to me, this story of hers in keratin. She's singing a song I don't know the words to because the language I'd thought was mine, the language she's told me to remember over the years, is an imposter. To teach the right language to Aki, I'd have to learn it myself first.

"There," she says, satisfied with her work on my feelers. At a distance, it looks similar to human hair except every strand is alive from follicle to tip. Alive and listening.

Mama's fingers glide down the neat braid she made, not a feeler out of place. "There's another way to hear stories but you'll have to take a trip."

She talked to the relatives back home then. I'd have asked them myself if I could but despite sharing blood we're strangers, and planets away.

"You can't dig your way into our roots from anywhere, you have to go to the source. There's a danger in exploring the past – our past – for your present. The soil there isn't like the one here. It breathes. It lives and wants and makes demands."

It's alien to me, the way we were aliens when we came to Earth. There is danger in my staying too, staying and watching my Aki die. It's already driven his father away. "You'll care for Aki?"

We can't all go together because I can't afford it, another failing of mine.

"Like I did you, and better." She laughs to cover up her fears. "I've learned a few things I could have done better."

Earthlings coddle their young, more than I'd been coddled when we arrived and mama had more than stories to worry about.

"I wish you lived closer, mama." I know she comes as often as she can, takes as much time away from work as it allows only to work here without pay.

"Me too."

For a little while, we watch rain cry at the window and listen to the music it makes with the wind.

I'm scared that for all its trouble, going back will make no difference. Scared the stories still won't feel mine and I'd have sacrificed time and wages for nothing.

In the morning, we go searching for fresh dirt so mama can teach me how to dig up old roots. We don't find any.

Where we live are apartment complexes, concrete jungles, and concrete yards.

"I'm not sorry I brought you here," mama says.

I'm not sorry she did either. Nobody leaves home because they want to.

"When you get this deep," mama shows the distance with her hands, "the earth will pull you in. Don't get scared. Our kind takes more to soil than humans."

It sounds impossible. Soil soaking up stories and spitting them out. The desperate, like me, rarely question reality.

"Have you done it?"

"My time we didn't question what we were told, we were too busy trying to stay alive. I'm not judging, I know you and Aki need more. I just wish you didn't. I wish my stories were enough."

She's so confident in her identities, it's as if all she has are roots growing everywhere.

* * *

We kiss, all three, before I leave. One kiss on my forehead, and one on the tail of my braid for luck.

I don't remember that first voyage with my parents or the engineered steel hull and husk, capable of withstanding roaring flames the temperature of a medium-sized star, that we flew in. I don't remember how my family and strangers sat cramped and scared inside, traveling at the speed of light. I don't remember, but it's been told to me so often it feels like a memory.

I am old enough to remember *this* rocket. Waving back at me near the launching pad are my two hearts, mama and Aki. I miss them already. Aki has his cheeks filled out like Earth-squirrels. Like Earth-beavers. Like a normal, healthy boy should. I'm glad I have this image of him in my mind to take with me.

Under all our safety belts and straps I can't tell if the other passengers aboard are human or like me, or maybe something else entirely. It's so easy to pass if we don't speak, if we dress right, if we eat their foods. But we always know we're only passing.

"Ready for drip sleep," the loudspeaker blares.

A needle opens from a latch in the seat and delivers a week's worth of sleep so the journey will seem instant. It's smaller than I expected and its sting is quick. I fall drowsy thinking of Aki; my journey is for him more than me.

* * *

It is night when we disembark. Drip withdrawal leaves me so dizzy and dazed I don't have a moment to speak to any of the other passengers before they scatter. The ship captain has his fifth orifice stretched out and hanging like it's in fashion. Maybe it is. I am a stranger here; even though it's where I took my first steps, and my mother before me, and her mother and so many generations down my line.

Even in the swallow of darkness, the fields are how my mother described them. They're blooming with flowers I wouldn't be able to identify even by day. I push in between clods of damp sod. When I've dug deep enough, a peristaltic motion grabs hold and pulls me in. Deep and deeper, until there is only slick brown, then black; smelling of moss, mold, and oddly, mama. I hold in my scream because mama told me to, and it'd back my throat up with the same soil I want to deny fearing.

It's cold inside this earth.

The ground squelches and groans in a pattern that sounds like it's asking me who I am.

"Ilyana," I answer, uncertain if I'd taken the earth's welcoming for granted. I don't know how far down into the earth I've traveled, or if the launch pad is just a pinch of dirt away. Soil squeezes through the folds of my clothes, like beach sand, making me itch all over.

The earth stirs again. "Who are you?"

This time, I know it's not asking my name. I feed my tired story into that dark, moist expanse.

Space hollows out around me into a cavern. Just enough light in it for me to follow. There are whispers too, streaming out from pockets of dirt like steam.

The early stories are familiar. The deeper I go, the stranger they become. I don't question how the voices speak to me through the earth, so long as they continue. It feels the way it used to, listening to mama talk about her life. The way it should feel.

An old woman appears, face with wrinkles of silt and clay. She is small and bent with the darkest spots under her eyes. "You've gone far enough."

Her mouth is still moving but I can't hear the words until I lean my ear against her soil lips. "If you spend your whole life listening to other's stories you'll never tell your own," she says.

"I don't want mine." Mine aren't true to our kind because I'm not true to it.

There's a press of marl from the soil-woman, from her lips to mine, to my ears. "The stories further down will cost you."

The darkness is a lump in my feelers. "I'll pay."

I persist. Because mama can't tell her stories twice forever, because I want to know I'm not some mish-mash of unwanted leftovers, because I want Aki to know no hunger.

Though the walking is long, the listening makes it easy. There's more energy in me than I've had in years. I persist, knowing all the filling stories I'll have to share when I resurface.

I persist, until the theft. There's just enough trace of memory left for me to realize how I'd been made to pay – with memories.

It's a story of Aki, chasing his father after a bath when his feelers first dropped.

"That's mine," I try to shout, my mouth filling with bone long ago made dust.

Next, they take the nights of hard-earned sleep, of baby fevers breaking. I remember just enough for it to hurt, to want it back.

The tunnel narrows and pinches at my back. I turn, pulling and tearing at it to let me through. To let me back up to the surface where I won't have the stories but I'll have everything else.

Failing with my hands I try feet first, scissoring my way out of the earth. Already there's no milk-scent of my Aki's newborn head. No tears I wiped away and made right. Memories slip from me, out of order, so I have a toddler with no recollection of him as a babe. My mind is taken up with other histories and for the first time I want mine instead. My Aki, my little…

The voices are louder, shouting, and instead of giving me strength, they take it. The earth is getting fat off the stories in my memories.

"We're hungry."

"We shared."

"Share more."

All this time I'd been sharing my mother's stories when I should have been sharing mine because they're true too. They're my truth.

I cry, not knowing why. With only a vague notion of blue in all that brown; of blue eyes waiting for me. Of blue skies over yellow fields.

The soil-woman reforms where my feet stamp. Her feelers, a wall of mud trapping me.

"I wouldn't have paid with that," I say. I'm unsure what that is, only sure it's everything to me.

"I warned you. You can no more choose your currency down here than up there," she says.

Her clay finger points at my braid. "Is that how they wear it now?"

I remember someone making it for me before I left, making it for luck. "It's how I wear it. How I used to." I undo it, letting my feelers fall in waves down my back and it feels like it's more than feelers I'm letting loose.

Blue eyes waiting, waiting, waiting.

I plead with her. "I'll return, with stories worth more in my old age."

The soil-woman mirrors me, teasing out her braids of clay to make a hole just big enough to crawl through.

When I resurface, it's still night and I'm alone. Soil drips from me like water. Dawn approaches and I don't know if it's the first one I've ever seen. A yellow glow sits atop the sky like a crown and chases away the darkness. I remember I'm Ilyana. I remember I came to exchange sour stories for sweet. I remember I'm far away. Far away from blue eyes waiting, like the blueing skies. I remember, I've a place to be and my own stories to make.

The Moon is Not a Battlefield

Indrapramit Das

WE'RE RECORDING.

I was born in the sky, for war. This is what we were told.

I think when people hear this, they think of ancient Earth stories. Of angels and superheroes and gods, leaving destruction between the stars. But I'm no superhero, no Kalel of America-Bygone with the flag of his dead planet flying behind him. I'm no angel Gabreel striking down Satan in the void or blowing the trumpet to end worlds. I'm no devi Durga bristling with arms and weapons, chasing down demons through the cosmos and vanquishing them, no Kali with a string of heads hanging over her breasts black as deep space, making even the other gods shake with terror at her righteous rampage.

I was born in the sky, for war. What does it mean?

* * *

I was actually born on Earth, not far above sea level, in the Greater Kolkata Megapolis. My parents gave me away to the Government of India when I was still a small child, in exchange for enough money for them to live off frugally for a year – an unimaginable amount of wealth for two Dalit street-dwellers who scraped shit out of sewers for a living, and scavenged garbage for recycling – sewers sagging with centuries worth of shit, garbage heaps like mountains. There was another child I played with the most in our slum. The government took her as well. Of the few memories I have left of those early days on Earth, the ones of us playing are clearest, more than the ones of my parents, because they weren't around much. But she was always there. She'd bring me hot jalebis snatched from the hands of hapless pedestrians, her hands covered in syrup, and we'd share them. We used to climb and run along the huge sea wall that holds back the rising Bay of Bengal, and spit in the churning sea. I haven't seen the sea since, except from space – that roiling mass of water feels like a dream. So do those days, with the child who would become the soldier most often by my side. The government told our parents that they would cleanse us of our names, our untouchability, give us a chance to lead noble lives as astral defenders of the Republic of India. Of course they gave us away. I don't blame them. Aditi never blamed hers, either. That was the name my friend was given by the Army. You've met her. We were told our new names before training even began. Single-names, always. Usually from the Mahabharata or Ramayana, we realized later. I don't remember the name my parents gave me. I never asked Aditi if she remembered hers.

That, then, is when the life of asura Gita began.

I was raised by the state to be a soldier, and borne into the sky in the hands of the Republic to be its protector, before I even hit puberty.

The notion that there could be war on the Moon, or anywhere beyond Earth, was once a ridiculous dream.

So are many things, until they come to pass.

I've lived for thirty-six years as an infantry soldier stationed off-world. I was deployed and considered in active duty from eighteen in the Chandnipur Lunar Cantonment Area. I first arrived in Chandnipur at six, right after they took us off the streets. I grew up there. The Army raised us. Gave us a better education than we'd have ever gotten back on Earth. Right from childhood, me and my fellow asuras – Earth-bound Indian infantry soldiers were jawans, but we were always, always asuras, a mark of pride – we were told that we were stationed in Chandnipur to protect the intrasolar gateway of the Moon for the greatest country on that great blue planet in our black sky – India. India, which we could see below the clouds if we squinted during Earthrise on a surface patrol (if we were lucky, we could spot the white wrinkle of the Himalayas through telescopes). We learned the history of our home: After the United States of America and Russia, India was the third Earth nation to set foot on the Moon, and the first to settle a permanent base there. Chandnipur was open to scientists, astronauts, tourists, and corporations of all countries, to do research, develop space travel, take expensive holidays, and launch inter-system mining drones to asteroids. The generosity and benevolence of Bharat Mata, no? But we were to protect Chandnipur's sovereignty as Indian territory at all costs, because other countries were beginning to develop their own lunar expeditions to start bases. Chandnipur, we were told, was a part of India. The only part of India not on Earth. We were to make sure it remained that way. This was our mission. Even though, we were told, the rest of the world didn't officially recognize any land on the Moon to belong to any country, back then. Especially because of that.

Do you remember Chandnipur well?

* * *

It was where I met you, asura Gita. Hard to forget that, even if it hadn't been my first trip to the Moon. I was very nervous. The ride up the elevator was peaceful. Like . . . being up in the mountains, in the Himalayas, you know? Oh – I'm so sorry. Of course not. Just, the feeling of being high up – the silence of it, in a way, despite all the people in the elevator cabins. But then you start floating under the seat belts, and there are the safety instructions on how to move around the platform once you get to the top, and all you feel like doing is pissing. That's when you feel untethered. The shuttle to the Moon from the top of the elevator wasn't so peaceful. Every blast of the craft felt so powerful out there. The gs just raining down on you as you're strapped in. I felt like a feather.

Like a feather. Yes. I imagine so. There are no birds in Chandnipur, but us asuras always feel like feathers. Felt. Now I feel heavy all the time, like a stone, like a – hah – a moon, crashing into its world, so possessed by gravity, though I'm only skin and bones. A feather on a moon, a stone on a planet.

You know, when our Havaldar, Chamling his name was, told me that asura Aditi and I were to greet and guide a reporter visiting the Cantonment Area, I can't tell you how shocked we were. We were so excited. We would be on the feeds! We never got reporters up there. Well, to be honest, I wanted to show off our bravery, tell you horror stories of what happens if you wear your suit wrong outside the Cantonment Area on a walk, or get caught in warning shots from Chinese artillery klicks away, or what happens if the micro-atmosphere over Chandnipur malfunctions and becomes too thin while you're out and about there (you burn or freeze or asphyxiate). Civilians like horror stories from soldiers. You see so many of them in the media feeds in the pods, all these war stories. I used to like seeing how different it is for soldiers on Earth, in the old wars, the recent ones. Sometimes it would get hard to watch, of course.

Anyway, asura Aditi said to me, "Gita, they aren't coming here to be excited by a war movie. We aren't even at war. We're in *territorial conflict*. You use the word war and it'll look like we're boasting. We need to make them feel at home, not scare the shit out of them. We need to show them the hospitality of asuras on our own turf."

Couldn't disagree with that. We wanted people on Earth to see how well we do our jobs, so that we'd be welcomed with open arms when it was time for the big trip back – the promised pension, retirement, and that big old heaven in the sky where we all came from, Earth. We wanted every Indian up there to know we were protecting their piece of the Moon. Your piece of the Moon.

I thought soldiers would be frustrated having to babysit a journalist following them around. But you and asura Aditi made me feel welcome.

I felt bad for you. We met civilians in Chandnipur proper, when we got time off, in the Underground Markets, the bars. But you were my first fresh one, Earth-fresh. Like the imported fish in the Markets. Earth-creatures, you know, always delicate, expensive, mouth open gawping, big eyes. Out of water, they say.

Did I look "expensive"? I was just wearing the standard issue jumpsuits they give visitors.

Arre, you know what I mean. In the Markets, we soldiers couldn't buy Earth-fish or Earth-lamb or any Earth-meat, when they showed up every six months. We only ever tasted the printed stuff. Little packets; in the stalls, they heat up the synthi for you in the machine. Nothing but salt and heat and protein. Imported Earth-meat was too expensive. Same for Earth-people, expensive. Fish out of water. Earth meant paradise. You came from heaven. No offense.

None taken. You and asura Aditi were very good to me. That's what I remember.

After Aditi reminded me that you were going to show every Indian on their feeds our lives, we were afraid of looking bad. You looked scared, at first. Did we scare you?

I wouldn't say scared. Intimidated. You know, everything you were saying earlier, about gods and superheroes from the old Earth stories. The stuff they let you watch and read in the pods. That's what I saw, when you welcomed us in full regalia, out on the surface, in your combat suits, at the parade. You gleamed like gods. Like devis, asuras, like your namesakes. Those weapon limbs, when they came out of the backs of your suit during the demonstration, they looked like the arms of the goddesses in the epics, or the wings of angels, reflecting the sunlight coming over the horizon – the light was so white, after Earth, not shifted yellow by atmosphere. It was blinding, looking at you all. I couldn't imagine having to face that, as a soldier, as your enemy. Having to face you. I couldn't imagine having to patrol for hours, and fight, in those suits – just my civilian surface suit was so hot inside, so claustrophobic. I was shaking in there, watching you all.

Do you remember, the Governor of Chandnipur Lunar Area came out to greet you, and shake the hands of all the COs. A surface parade like that, on airless ground, that never happened – it was all for you and the rest of the reporters, for the show back on Earth. We had never before even seen the Governor in real life, let alone in a surface suit. The rumours came back that he was trembling and sweating when he shook their hands – that he couldn't even pronounce the words to thank them for their service. So you weren't alone, at least.

Then when we went inside the Cantonment Area, and we were allowed to take off our helmets right out in the open – I waited for you and Aditi to do it first. I didn't believe I wouldn't die, that my face wouldn't freeze. We were on that rover, such a bumpy ride, but open air like those vehicles in the earliest pictures of people on the Moon – just bigger. We went through the Cantonment airlock gate, past the big yellow sign that reads "Chandnipur, Gateway to the Stars," and when we emerged from the other side, Aditi told me to look up and see for myself, the different sky. From deep black to that deep, dusky blue, it was amazing, like crossing over into another world. The sunlight still felt different, blue-white instead of yellow, filtered by the nanobot haze, shimmering in that lunar dawn coming in over the hilly rim of Daedalus crater. The sun felt tingly, raw, like it burned even though the temperature was cool. The Earth was half in shadow – it looked fake, a rendered backdrop in a veeyar sim. And sometimes the micro-atmosphere would move just right and the bots would be visible for a few seconds in a wave across that low sky, the famous flocks of lunar fireflies. The rover went down the suddenly smooth lunarcrete road, down the main road of the Cantonment –

New Delhi Avenue.

Yes, New Delhi Avenue, with the rows of wireframed flags extended high, all the state colours of India, the lines and lines of white barracks with those tiny windows on both sides. I wanted to stay in those, but they put us civilians underground, in a hotel. They didn't want us complaining about conditions. As we went down New Delhi Avenue and turned into the barracks for the tour, you and Aditi took off your helmets and breathed deep. Your faces were covered in black warpaint. Greasepaint. Full regalia, yes? You both looked like Kali, with or without the necklace of heads. Aditi helped me with the helmet, and I felt lunar air for the first time. The dry, cool air of Chandnipur. And you said, "Welcome to chota duniya. You can take off the helmet." Chota duniya, the little world. Those Kali faces, running with sweat, the tattoos of your wetware. You wore a small beard, back then, and a crew-cut. Asura Aditi had a ponytail, I was surprised that was allowed.

You looked like warriors, in those blinding suits of armour.

Warriors. I don't anymore, do I. What do I look like now?

I see you have longer hair. You shaved off your beard.

Avoiding the question, clever. Did you know that jawan means "young man"? But we were asuras. We were proud of our hair, not because we were young men. We, the women and the hijras, the not-men, told the asuras who were men, why do you get to keep beards and moustaches and we don't? Some of them had those twirly moustaches like the asuras in the myths. So the boys said to us: We won't stop you. Show us your beards! From then it was a competition. Aditi could hardly grow a beard on her pretty face, so she gave up when it was just fuzz. I didn't. I was so proud when I first sprouted that hair on my chin, when I was a teenager. After I grew it out, Aditi called it a rat-tail. I never could grow the twirly moustaches. But I'm a decommissioned asura now, so I've shaved off the beard.

What do you think you look like now?

Like a beggar living in a slum stuck to the side of the space elevator that took me up to the sky so long ago, and brought me down again not so long ago.

Some of my neighbours don't see asuras as women or men. I'm fine with that. They ask me: Do you still bleed? Did you menstruate on the Moon? They say menstruation is tied to the Moon, so asuras must bleed all the time up there, or never at all down here. They think we used all that blood to paint ourselves red because we are warriors. To scare our enemies. I like that idea. Some of them don't believe it when I say that I bleed the same as any Earthling with a cunt. The young ones believe me, because they help me out, bring me rags, pads when they can find them, from down there in the city – can't afford the meds to stop bleeding altogether. Those young ones are a blessing. I can't exactly hitch a ride on top of the elevator up and down every day in my condition.

People in the slum all know you're an asura?

I ask again: What do I look like now?

A veteran. You have the scars. From the wetware that plugged you into the suits. The lines used to be black, raised – on your face, neck. Now they're pale, flat.

The mark of the decommissioned asura – everyone knows who you are. The government plucks out your wires. Like you're a broken machine. They don't want you selling the wetware on the black market. They're a part of the suits we wore, just a part we wore all the time inside us – and the suits are property of the Indian Army, Lunar Command.

I told you why the suits are so shiny, didn't I, all those years ago? Hyper-reflective surfaces so we didn't fry up in them like the printed meat in their heating packets when the sun comes up. The suits made us easy to spot on a lunar battlefield. It's why we always tried to stay in shadow, use infrared to spot enemies. When we went on recon, surveillance missions, we'd use lighter stealth suits, non-metal, non-reflective, dark gray like the surface. We could only do that if we coordinated our movements to land during night-time.

When I met you and asura Aditi then, you'd been in a few battles already. With Chinese and Russian troops. Small skirmishes.

All battles on the Moon are small skirmishes. You can't afford anything bigger. Even the horizon is smaller, closer. But yes, our section had seen combat a few times. But even that was mostly waiting, and scoping with infrared along the shadows of craters. When there was fighting, it was between long, long stretches of walking and sitting. But it was never boring. Nothing can be boring when you've got a portioned ration of air to breathe, and no sound to warn you of a surprise attack. Each second is measured out and marked in your mind. Each step is a success. When you do a lunar surface patrol outside Chandnipur, outside regulated atmosphere or Indian territory, as many times as we did, you do get used to it. But never, ever bored. If anything, it becomes hypnotic – you do everything you need to do without even thinking, in that silence between breathing and the words of your fellow soldiers.

You couldn't talk too much about what combat was like on the Moon, on that visit.

They told us not to. Havaldar Chamling told us that order came all the way down from the Lieutenant General of Lunar Command. It was all considered classified information, even training maneuvers. It was pretty silent when you were in Chandnipur. I'm sure the Russians and the Chinese had news of that press visit. They could have decided to put on a display of might, stage some shock and awe attacks, missile strikes, troop movements to draw us out of the Cantonment Area.

I won't lie – I was both relieved and disappointed. I've seen war, as a field reporter. Just not on the Moon. I wanted to see firsthand what the asuras were experiencing.

It would have been difficult. Lunar combat is not like Earth combat, though I don't know much about Earth combat other than theory and history. I probably know less than you do, ultimately, because I've never experienced it. But I've read things, watched things about wars on Earth. Learned things, of course, in our lessons. It's different on the Moon. Harder to accommodate an extra person when each battle is like a game of chess. No extra pieces allowed on the board. Every person needs their own air. No one can speak out of turn and clutter up comms. The visibility of each person needs to be accounted for, since it's so high.

The most frightening thing about lunar combat is that you often can't tell when it's happening until it's too late. On the battlefields beyond Chandnipur, out on the magma seas, combat is silent. You can't hear anything but your own footsteps, the *thoom-thoom-thoom* of your suit's metal boots crunching dust, or the sounds of your own weapons through your suit, the rattle-kick of ballistics, the near-silent hum of lasers vibrating in the metal of the shell keeping you alive. You'll see the flash of a mine or grenade going off a few feet away but you won't hear it. You won't hear anything coming down from above unless you look up – be it ballistic missiles or a meteorite hurtling down after centuries flying through outer space. You'll feel the shockwave knock you back, but you won't hear it. If you're lucky, of course.

Laser weapons are invisible out there, and that's what's we mostly used. There's no warning at all. No muzzle-flash, no noise. One minute you're sitting there thinking you're on the right side of the rocks giving you cover, and the next moment you see a glowing hole melting into the suit of the soldier next to you, like those time-lapse videos of something rotting. It takes less than a second if the soldier on the other side of the beam is aiming properly. Less than a second and there's the flash and pop, blood and gas and superheated metal venting into the thin air like an aerosol spray, the scream like static in the mics. Aditi was a sniper, she could've told you how lethal the long-range lasers were. I carried a semi-auto, laser or ballistic; those lasers were as deadly, just lower range and zero warm-up. When we were in battles closer to settlements, we'd switch to the ballistic weaponry, because the buildings and bases are mostly better protected from that kind of damage, bulletproof. There was kind of a silent agreement between all sides to keep from heavily damaging the actual bases. Those ballistic fights were almost a relief – our suits could withstand projectile damage better, and you could see the tracers coming from kilometers away, even if you couldn't hear them. Like fire on oil, across the jet sky. Bullets aren't that slow either, especially here on the Moon, but somehow it felt better to see it, like you could dodge the fire, especially if we were issued jet packs, though we rarely used them because of how difficult they were to control. Aditi was better at using hers.

She saved my life once.

I mean, she did that many times, we both did for each other, just by doing what we needed to do on a battlefield. But she directly saved my life once, like an Earth movie hero. Rocket-propelled grenade on a quiet battlefield. Right from up above and behind us. I didn't even see it. I just felt asura Aditi shove me straight off the ground from behind and blast us off into the air with her jetpack, propelling us both twenty feet above the surface in a second. We twirled in mid-air, and for a little moment, it felt like we were free of the Moon, hovering there between it and the blazing blue Earth, dancing together. As we sailed back down and braced our legs for landing without suit damage, Aditi never let me go, kept our path back down steady. Only then did I see the cloud of lunar dust and debris hanging where we'd been seconds earlier, the aftermath of an explosion I hadn't heard or seen, the streaks of light as the rest of the fireteam returned ballistic fire, spreading out in leaps with short bursts from their jetpacks. No one died in that encounter. I don't even remember whose troops we were fighting in that encounter, which lunar army. I just remember that I didn't die because of Aditi.

Mostly, we never saw the enemy close up. They were always just flecks of light on the horizon, or through our infrared overlay. Always ghosts, reflecting back the light of sun and Earth, like the Moon itself. It made it easier to kill them, if I'm being honest. They already seemed dead. When you're beyond Chandnipur, out on the mara under that merciless black sky with the Earth gleaming in the distance, the only colour you can see anywhere, it felt like *we* were already dead too. Like we were all just ghosts playing out the old wars of humanity, ghosts of soldiers who died far, far down on the ground. But then we'd return to the city, to the warm bustle of the Underground Markets on our days off, to our chota duniya, and the Earth would seem like heaven again, not a world left behind but one to be attained, one to earn, the unattainable paradise rather than a distant history of life that we'd only lived through media pods and lessons.

And now, here you are. On Earth.

Here I am. Paradise attained. I have died and gone to heaven.

It's why I'm here, isn't it? Why we're talking.

You could say that. Thank you for coming, again. You didn't have any trouble coming up the elevator shaft, did you? I know it's rough clinging to the top of the elevator.

I've been on rougher rides. There are plenty of touts down in the elevator base station who are more than willing to give someone with a few rupees a lending hand up the spindle. So. You were saying. About coming back to Earth. It must have been surprising, the news that you were coming back, last year.

FTL changed everything. That was, what, nine years ago?

At first it brought us to the edge of full-on lunar war, like never before, because the Moon became the greatest of all jewels in the night sky. It could become our first FTL port. Everyone wanted a stake in that. Every national territory on the Moon closed off its borders while the Earth governments negotiated. We were closed off in our bunkers, looking at the stars through the small windows, eating nothing but thin parathas from emergency flour rations. We made them on our personal heating coils with synthi butter – no food was coming through because of embargo, mess halls in the main barracks were empty. We lived on those parathas and caffeine infusion. Our stomachs were like balloons, full of air.

Things escalated like never before, in that time. I remember a direct Chinese attack on Chandnipur's outer defences, where we were stationed. One bunker window was taken out by laser. I saw a man stuck to the molten hole in the pane because of depressurization, wriggling like a dying insect. Asura Jatayu, a quiet, skinny soldier with a drinking problem. People always said he filled his suit's drinking water pods with diluted moonshine from the Underground Markets, and sucked it down during patrols. I don't know if that's true, but people didn't trust him because of it, even though he never really did anything to fuck things up. He was stone cold sober that day. I know, because I was with him. Aditi, me, and two other asuras ripped him off the broken window, activated the emergency shutter before we lost too much pressure. But he'd already hemorrhaged severely through the laser wound, which had blown blood out of him and into the thin air of the Moon. He was dead. The Chinese had already retreated by the time we recovered. It was a direct response to our own overtures before the embargo. We had destroyed some nanobot anchors of theirs in disputed territory, which had been laid down to expand the micro-atmosphere of Yueliang Lunar Area.

That same tech that keeps air over Chandnipur and other lunar territories, enables the micro-atmospheres, is what makes FTL work – the q-nanobots. On our final patrols across the mara, we saw some of the new FTL shipyards in the distance. The ships – half-built, they looked like the Earth ruins from historical pictures, of palaces and cities. We felt like we were looking at artifacts of a civilization from the future. They sparked like a far-off battle, bots building them tirelessly. They will sail out to outer space, wearing quenbots around them like cloaks. Like the superheroes! The quenbot cloud folds the space around the ship like a blanket, make a bubble that shoots through the universe. I don't really understand. Is it like a soda bubble or a blanket? We had no idea our time on the Moon was almost over on those patrols, looking at the early shipyards.

After one of the patrols near the shipyards, asura Aditi turned to me and said, "We'll be on one of those ships one day, sailing to other parts of the galaxy. They'll need us to defend Mother India when she sets her dainty feet on new worlds. Maybe we'll be able to see Jupiter and Saturn and Neptune zoom by like cricket balls, the Milky Way spinning far behind us like a chakra."

"I don't think that's quite how FTL works," I told her, but obviously she knew that. She looked at me, low dawn sunlight on her visor so I couldn't see her face. Even though this patrol was during a temporary ceasefire, she had painted her face like she so loved to, so all you could see anyway were the whites of her eyes and her teeth. Kali Ma through and through, just like you said. "Just imagine, maybe we'll end up on a world where we can breathe everywhere. Where there are forests and running water and deserts like Earth. Like in the old Bollywood movies, where the heroes and the heroines run around trees and splash in water like foolish children with those huge mountains behind them covered in ice."

"Arre, you can get all that on Earth. It's where those movies come from! Why would you want to go further away from Earth? You don't want to return home?"

"That's a nice idea, Gita," she said. "But the longer we're here, and the more news and movies and feeds I see of Earth, I get the idea it's not really waiting for us."

That made me angry, though I didn't show it. "We've waited all our lives to go back, and now you want to toss off to another world?" I asked, as if we had a choice in the matter. The two of us, since we were children in the juvenile barracks, had talked about moving to a little house in the Himalayas once we went back, somewhere in Sikkim or northern Bengal (we learned all the states as children, and saw their flags along New Delhi Avenue) where it's not as crowded as the rest of Earth still, and we could see those famously huge mountains that dwarfed the Moon's arid hills.

She said, "Hai Ram, I'm just dreaming like we always have. My dear, what you're not getting is that we have seen Earth on the feeds since we came to the Moon. From expectation, there is only disappointment."

So I told her, "When you talk about other worlds out there, you realize those are expectations too. You're forgetting we're soldiers. We go to Earth, it means our battle is over. We go to another world, you think they'd let us frolic like Bollywood stars in alien streams? Just you and me, Gita and Aditi, with the rest of our division doing backup dancing?" I couldn't stay angry when I thought of this, though I still felt a bit hurt that she was suggesting she didn't want to go back to Earth with me, like the sisters in arms we were.

"True enough," she said. "Such a literalist. If our mission is ever to play Bollywood on an exoplanet, you can play the man hero with your lovely rat-tail beard. Anyway, for now all we have is this gray rock where all the ice is underneath us instead of prettily on the mountains. Not Earth or any other tarty rival to it. *This* is home, Gita beta, don't forget it."

How right she was.

* * *

Then came peacetime.

We saw the protests on Earth feeds. People marching through the vast cities, more people than we'd ever see in a lifetime in Chandnipur, with signs and chants. No more military presence on the Moon. The Moon is not an army base. Bring back our soldiers. The Moon is not a battlefield.

But it was, that's the thing. We had seen our fellow asuras die on it.

With the creation of the Terran Union of Spacefaring Nations (T.U.S.N.) in anticipation of human expansion to extrasolar space, India finally gave up its sovereignty over Chandnipur, which became just one settlement in amalgamated T.U.S.N. Lunar territory. There were walled-off Nuclear Seclusion Zones up there on Earth still hot from the last World War, and somehow they'd figured out how to stop war on the Moon. With the signing of the International Lunar Peace Treaty, every nation that had held its own patch of the Moon for a century of settlement on the satellite agreed to lay down their arms under Earth, Sol, the gods, the goddesses, and the God. The Moon was going to be free of military presence for the first time in decades.

When us asuras were first told officially of the decommissioning of Lunar Command in Chandnipur, we celebrated. We'd made it – we were going to Earth, earlier than we'd ever thought, long before retirement age. Even our COs got shitfaced in the mess halls. There were huge tubs of biryani, with hot chunks of printed lamb and gobs of synthi dalda. We ate so much, I thought we'd explode. Even Aditi, who'd been dreaming about other worlds, couldn't hold back her happiness. She asked me, "What's the first thing you're going to do on Earth?" her face covered in grease, making me think of her as a child with another name, grubby cheeks covered in syrup from stolen jalebis.

"I'm going to catch a train to a riverside beach or a sea wall, and watch the movement of water on a planet. Water, flowing and thrashing for kilometers and kilometers, stretching all the way to the horizon. I'm going to fall asleep to it. Then I'm going to go to all the restaurants, and eat all the real foods that the fake food in the Underground Markets is based on."

"Don't spend all your money in one day, okay? We need to save up for that house in the Himalayas."

"You're going to go straight to the mountains, aren't you," I said with a smile.

"Nah. I'll wait for you, first, beta. What do you think."

"Good girl."

After that meal, a handful of us went out with our suits for an unscheduled patrol for the first time – I guess you'd call it a moonwalk, at that point. We saluted the Earth together, on a lunar surface where we had no threat of being silently attacked from all sides. The century-long Lunar Cold War was over – it had cooled, frozen, bubbled, boiled at times, but now it had evaporated. We were all to go to our paradise in the black sky, as we'd wished every day on our dreary chota duniya.

We didn't stop to think what it all really meant for us asuras, of course. Because as Aditi had told me – the Moon was our home, the only one we'd ever known, really. It is a strange thing to live your life in a place that was never meant for human habitation. You grow to loathe such a life – the gritty dust in everything from your food to your teeth to your weapons, despite extensive air filters, the bitter aerosol meds to get rid of infections and nosebleeds from it. Spending half of your days exercising and drinking carefully rationed water so your body doesn't shrivel up in sub-Earth grav or dry out to a husk in the dry, scrubbed air of controlled atmospheres. The deadening beauty of gray horizons with not a hint of water or life or vegetation in sight except for the sharp lines and lights of human settlement, which we compared so unfavorably to the dazzling technicolour of images and video feeds from Earth, the richness of its life and variety. The constant, relentless company of the same people you grow to love with such ferocity that you hate them as well, because there is no one else for company but the occasional civilian who has the courage to talk to a soldier in Chandnipur's streets, tunnels, and canteens.

* * *

Now the Moon is truly a gateway to the stars. It is pregnant with the vessels that will take humanity to them, with shipyards and ports rising up under the limbs of robots. I look up at our chota duniya, and its face is crusted in lights, a crown given to her by her lover. Like a goddess, it'll birth humanity's new children. We were born in the sky, for war, but we weren't in truth. We were asuras. Now they will be devas, devis. They will truly be like gods, with FTL. In Chandnipur, they told us that we must put our faith in Bhagavan, in all the gods and goddesses of the pantheon. We were given a visiting room, where we sat in the veeyar pods and talked directly to their avatars, animated by the machines. That was the only veeyar we were allowed – no sims of Earth or anything like that, maybe because they didn't want us to get too distracted from our lives on the Moon. So we talked to the avatars, dutifully, in those pods with their smell of incense. Every week, we asked them to keep us alive on chota duniya, this place where humanity should not be and yet is.

And now, we might take other worlds, large and small.

Does that frighten you?

I . . . don't know. You told us all those years ago, and you tell me now, that we asuras looked like gods and superheroes when you saw us. In our suits, which would nearly crush a human with their weight if anyone wore them on Earth, let alone walked or fought in them. And now, imagine the humans who will go out there into the star-lit darkness. The big ships won't be ready for a long time. But the small ones – they already want volunteers to take one-way test trips to exoplanets. I don't doubt some of those volunteers will come from the streets, like us asuras. They need people who don't have anything on Earth, so they can leave it behind and spend their lives in the sky. They will travel faster than light itself. Impossible made possible. Even the asuras of the Lunar Command were impossible once.

The Moon was a lifeless place. Nothing but rock and mineral and water. And we still found a way to bring war to it. We still found a way to fight there. Now, when the new humans set foot on other worlds, what if there is life there? What if there is god-given life that has learned to tell stories, make art, fight and love? Will we bring an Earth Army to that life, whatever form it takes? Will we send out this new humanity to discover and share, or will we take people like me and Aditi, born in the streets with nothing, and give them a suit of armour and a ship that sails across the cosmos faster than the light of stars, and send them out to conquer? In the myths, asuras can be both benevolent or evil. Like gods or demons. If we have the chariots of the gods at our disposal, what use is there for gods? What if the next soldiers who go forth into space become demons with the power of gods? What if envy strikes their hearts, and they take fertile worlds from other life forms by force? What if we bring war to a peaceful cosmos? At least we asuras only killed other humans.

One could argue that you didn't just fight on the Moon. You brought life there, for the first time. You, we, humans – we loved there, as well. We still do. There are still humans there.

Love.

I've never heard anyone tell me they love me, nor told anyone I love them. People on Earth, if you trust the stories, say it all the time. We asuras didn't really know what the word meant, in the end.

But. I did love, didn't I? I loved my fellow soldiers. I would have given my life for them. That must be what it means.

I loved Aditi.

That is the first time I've ever said that. I loved Aditi, my sister in arms. I wonder what she would have been, if she had stayed on Earth, never been adopted by the Indian government and given to the Army. A dancer? A Bollywood star? They don't like women with muscles like her, do they? She was bloody graceful with a jet-pack, I'll tell you that much. And then, when I actually stop to think, I realize, that she would have been a beggar, or a sweeper, or a sewer-scraper if the Army hadn't given us to the sky. Like me. Now I live among beggars, garbage-pickers, and sweepers, and sewer-scrapers, in this slum clinging to what they call the pillar to heaven. To heaven, can you believe that? Just like we called Earth heaven up there. These people here, they take care of me. In them I see a shared destiny.

What is that?

To remind us that we are not the gods. This is why I pray still to the gods, or the one God, whatever is out there beyond the heliosphere. I pray that the humans who will sail past light and into the rest of the universe find grace out there, find a way to bring us closer to godliness. To worlds where we might start anew, and have no need for soldiers to fight, only warriors to defend against dangers that they themselves are not the harbingers of. To worlds where our cities have no slums filled with people whose backs are bent with the bravery required to hold up the rest of humanity.

Can I ask something? How . . . how did asura Aditi die?

Hm. Asura Aditi of the 8th Lunar Division – Chandnipur, Indian Armed Forces, survived thirty-four years of life and active combat duty as a soldier on the Moon, to be decommissioned and allowed to return to planet Earth. And then she died right here in New Delhi Megapolis walking to the market. We asuras aren't used to this gravity, to these crowds. One shove from a passing impatient pedestrian is all it takes. She fell down on the street, shattered her Moon-brittled hip because, when we came here to paradise, we found that treatment and physio for our weakened bodies takes money that our government does not provide. We get a pension, but it's not much – we have to choose food and rent, or treatment. There is no cure. We might have been bred for war in the sky, but we were not bred for life on Earth. Why do you think there are so few volunteers for the asura program? They must depend on the children of those who have nothing.

Aditi fell to Earth from the Moon, and broke. She didn't have money for a fancy private hospital. She died of an infection in a government hospital.

She never did see the Himalayas. Nor have I.

I'm sorry.

I live here, in the slums around Akash Mahal Space Elevator-Shaft, because of Aditi. It's dangerous, living along the spindle. But it's cheaper than the subsidized rent of the Veterans Arcologies. And I like the danger. I was a soldier, after all. I like living by the stairway to the sky, where I once lived. I like being high up here, where the wind blows like it never did on the Moon's gray deserts, where the birds I never saw now fly past me every morning and warm my heart with their cries. I like the sound of the nanotube ecosystem all around us, digesting all our shit and piss and garbage, turning it into the light in my one bulb, the heat in my one stove coil, the water from my pipes, piggybacking on the charge from the solar panels that power my little feed-terminal. The way the walls pulse, absorbing sound and kinetic energy, when the elevator passes back and forth, the rumble of Space Elevator Garuda-3 through the spindle all the way to the top of the atmosphere. I don't like the constant smell of human waste. I don't like wondering when the police will decide to cast off the blinders and destroy this entire slum because it's illegal. I don't like going with a half-empty stomach all the time, living off the kindness of the little ones here who go up and down all the time and get my flour and rice. But I'm used to such things – Chandnipur was not a place of plenty either. I like the way everyone takes care of each other here. We have to, or the entire slum will collapse like a rotten vine slipping off a tree-trunk. We depend on each other for survival. It reminds me of my past life.

And I save the money from my pension, little by little, by living frugally. To one day buy a basic black market exoskeleton to assist me, and get basic treatment, physio, to learn how to walk and move like a human on Earth.

Can . . . I help, in any way?

You have helped, by listening. Maybe you can help others listen as well, as you've said.

Maybe they'll heed the words of a veteran forced to live in a slum. If they send soldiers to the edge of the galaxy, I can only hope that they will give those soldiers a choice this time.

I beg the ones who prepare our great chariots: If you must take our soldiers with you, take them – their courage, their resilience, their loyalty will serve you well on a new frontier. But do not to take war to new worlds.

War belongs here on Earth. I should know. I've fought it on the Moon, and it didn't make her happy. In her cold anger, she turned our bodies to glass. Our chota duniya was not meant to carry life, but we thrust it into her anyway. Let us not make that mistake again. Let us not violate the more welcoming worlds we may find, seeing their beauty as acquiescence.

With FTL, there will be no end to humanity's journey. If we keep going far enough, perhaps we will find the gods themselves waiting behind the veil of the universe. And if we do not come in peace by then, I fear we will not survive the encounter.

* * *

I clamber down the side of the column of the space elevator, winding down through the biohomes of the slum towards one of the tunnels where I can reach the internal shaft and wait for the elevator on the way down. Once it's close to the surface of the planet, it slows down a lot – that's when people jump on to hitch a ride up or down. We're only about 1,000 feet up, so it's not too long a ride down, but the wait for it could be much longer. The insides of the shaft are always lined with slum-dwellers and elevator station hawkers, rigged with gas masks and cling clothes, hanging on to the nanocable chords and sinews of the great spindle. I might just catch a ride on the back of one of the gliders who offer their solar wings to travelers looking for a quick trip back to the ground. Bit more terrifying, but technically less dangerous, if their back harness and propulsion works.

The eight-year-old boy guiding me down through the steep slum, along the pipes and vines of the NGO-funded nano-ecosystem, occasionally looks up at me with a gap-toothed smile. "I want to be an asura like Gita," he says. "I want to go to the stars."

"Aren't you afraid of not being able to walk properly when you come back to Earth?"

"Who said I want to come back to Earth?"

I smile, and look up, past the fluttering prayer flags of drying clothes, the pulsing wall of the slum, at the dizzying stairway to heaven, an infinite line receding into the blue. At the edge of the spindle, I see asura Gita poised between the air and her home, leaning precariously out to wave goodbye to me. Her hair ripples out against the sky, a smudge of black. A pale, late evening moon hovers full and pale above her head, twinkling with lights.

I wave back, overcome with vertigo. She seems about to fall, but she doesn't. She is caught between the Earth and the sky in that moment, forever.

We Are All of Us

Deborah L. Davitt

THEY WORE WHITE ARMOR, SLEEK AND CHITINOUS – not the white of chalk, but the white of bone peeking through the skin of a mummy. The white of a grub writhing in black river soil. They dwelled in the deep desert, where few of the Folk dared to tread, in cities carved from the bones of the earth. No one knew much about them, yet everyone knew everything that they needed to know. That they crawled into rock-cut tombs to devour the dead. That their cities wended for miles under the earth, and that they could dig up into a house at night to defile the living.

As blue first-sun set, and red second-sun rose, Suvan went out into her fields. Shared with her husband Petemet once, their lands lay at the periphery of the village, as far from the River as the canals could reach. Here, the black soil brought by the floods each year waned into the silver sand of the desert, and they'd wrested crops from it each year by dint of back-breaking labor. The tales of the priests spoke of a time when the devices of the gods and ancestors, carried through the void between the stars, had broken earth and sown seed, bringing plenty and ease to all.

Suvan had never known anything but ceaseless toil.

The past two years, Petemet had worked long into the searing light of first-sun, when he should have retired into the shade of their mud-brick hut, struggling to ensure that they'd have enough both to eat and to offer in tithe to the priests and the Sepat. He'd died of those labors, of the burning sickness brought by first-sun's light, blackness erupting from his flesh, from between the white scars left by bronze swords when he'd served the Sepat as a soldier.

As second-dawn stained the eastern sky, she found one of *them* in her field, crumpled and broken. Past the body, she saw spotted laughing-dogs skulking. A couple of thrown stones deterred the beasts so she could investigate the body. She poked it gingerly with her hoe. "Are you alive?" she asked, feeling the void behind her where her husband should have stood like a mountain.

But his body rested in a cave in the cliffs west of their farm, the stones of which provided a frail final barrier against the desert. His sepulcher boulder-blocked to keep the laughing-dogs and marble-cats at bay.

And *them*, of course.

The body stirred, and she backed away, holding the hoe aloft, ready to bring it down on the creature's head. "Are you alive?" she repeated tightly.

Its head rose, white and gleaming, seemingly encased in armor. She could see its eyes through the holes of that white mask, glistering blue, like the sky when first-sun was at its zenith.

The creature didn't speak, but it hummed a peculiar melody.

Looking down, she felt abashed – no, ashamed. Blue blood seeped from where the armor on the forearm had been crushed like a nutshell. More streaked down its back in thick indigo rivulets, as if something there had been torn away. *It's hurt. Nearly dead, and here I am, threatening to finish the job.* Shame warred with prudence, however: *Everyone knows what they are. Eaters of the dead. Defilers. Murderers. Safest to bash its head in.*

Her eyes skimmed along the cliff-face. Found the boulder that blocked her husband's tomb. *If you were here, Petemet, would I feel the same way?* He'd been a soldier before he'd come to the village.

His strength had been her shield. She paused, and a surge of warmth passed over her, as if he did, in fact, stand behind her. *No. I'd be counseling kindness. He always gave me the freedom to try.*

"Come," Suvan said, extending a hand stained cinnamon by the light of second-sun. "Back to my house, where I can help."

She hadn't had visitors since her husband died. The Folk held that death clung, and avoided those affected by it until the taint cleared. The kings with their palaces in the mountains where the River was born, the merchant princes at its delta to the north, and the sepats in between, they all had priests to cleanse the taint. Suvan and her village were too poor for the priests to care about, save at harvest, when tithes came due. She'd expected to endure without the sound of another voice for another half-year. Till the rest of the village rolled back the stone, revealing that Petemet's flesh had sunk down to his lovely bones, and that his soul had fled to the stars.

Still feeling haunted, Suvan prepared water and bandages, torn from the last cloth she'd woven – and then stood there, feeling foolish, as the creature stared at her. "Does the armor come off, so I can tend the wounds?"

No words, just humming. Then it extended its bleeding arm. She hesitated. "Do you have a name?"

It shook its head, and the humming intensified. Whispered shapes almost like words that rose and fell like ripples in the River.

She tried to remove the armor. The creature recoiled, and she had to brace its arm over her knee and hold it in place with her other leg. Fragments came away under her finger like pieces of eggshell, but thicker – clinging to the flesh below with white, gelatinous strings. The creature screamed once, a sound that reverberated through the hard-packed earth floor under her feet and made her ears ring. Then it collapsed unconscious, and she was able to pick the remaining pieces out of the wound. Wash the blue blood away, and wrap it with clean linen. *The armor is his skin,* she thought, feeling sick. *I've flayed him. The gods only know if that was the right thing to do, but he didn't fight me, though he could've kicked my legs out from under me at any time.*

Suvan bundled the creature into the straw-filled pallet she used as a bed, not knowing when the creature had passed from *it* to *he* in her mind. Probably when he'd screamed, she reflected. Animals could scream – she'd heard goats at the slaughter, after all. But *things* didn't.

She looked down at him, alien and gleaming, on the pallet she'd shared with Petemet. Among the few belongings they'd shared – a low table set with two clay cups and an unadorned pitcher of river water. A red-dyed wooden statue of Sah, the warrior-god to whom Petemet had still prayed, even at the end. The embodiment of second-sun. Reed baskets for her clothes – Petemet had been buried in his festival shirt, and his work clothes had been burned. Her warp-weighted loom, bereft of thread – their last goats had been sacrificed for the funeral rites, and keeping the garden alive had left her no time to harvest flax along the canals.

She'd kept everything in perfect order since Petemet's death. Every item, every object, just so. But in bringing the creature in, she'd knocked over the baskets, jostled the cups on the table. She set them back in their places, her hands shaking, and then glanced over at the bed. *What am I doing?*

Suvan studied the hooked claws, surely meant for digging and killing, at the ends of his hands. The face, seemingly featureless beyond the gleaming eyes. "You're more than an animal. The stories say that your kind are cunning and fierce. That you've invaded the Riverlands before. But the stories never said that you felt pain. Could be vulnerable." She hadn't spoken in so long that her voice sounded rusty as she spoke aloud to the unconscious form. Suvan shrugged, feeling foolish now. *The stories didn't say that they're beautiful. What else have the stories left out?*

As the days passed, Suvan learned how little the Folk knew of *them*. When he was able to sit up, she offered her unlikely guest millet porridge, and he regarded her with fathomless eyes. "Don't you eat?" she asked.

Finally, he spoke, the words wreathed in echoes. "Our feeding would distress you. It would be best if you left us."

Suvan recoiled, startled. "You speak?"

"We always speak. Humans do not always listen. You … you are listening."

She hastened outside, in spite of the searing light of first-sun and weeded the garden that was all that sustained her these days, her hood pulled low over her face to protect her skin. *When first-sun is high, be shy. When second-sun rules the fold, be bold.*

Then she stole a glance through the windows of her hut, watching as the creature's armored jaw unfurled, like a flower blossoming. A tube of some sort extended from his opened mouth down into the bowl.

Disquiet bloomed in her stomach. *They aren't like us at all, are they?*

When she came back inside, she cleaned the bowl and asked abruptly, "When will you leave?" *Gods, make it soon.*

"We have no place else to be. Home lost, destroyed." His voice whispered threnodies.

"That's not an answer. And why do you keep saying we?" She heard her own impatience, though the sound of loss tugged at her heart.

"Because we are," he replied, sounding puzzled. "We are all those with whom we dwelled." A pause. "All of us, together."

"Mothers and fathers?"

His head tilted. "Only one mother in each city. The Great Mother."

Suvan frowned. "A goddess?"

A rigid head-shake. "No. Mother of all. Many fathers. One mother."

She set the bowl aside, wishing she had thread with which to occupy her fingers. "I don't understand."

Another head-tilt. "Great Mother chooses males with whom to mate. Some many times, some never. She gives birth in the crèche. When her favored males grow old and die, if she yet lives, she takes of their sons. When she grows old, she finally allows one of her daughters to live, and she becomes the next Great Mother. Sometimes new blood needed, from other cities. Males sent in trade."

Her mouth dropped open. "You're traded? Like *slaves*?"

The gleaming eyes dulled. "No. We are what we need to be. What others need. We know what we are for. All serve. One voice in many bodies." He held up his hands, armed with those curved claws. "Digging, shaping, building. This is what we have been for." He paused, and his shoulders slumped. "And now we are alone, and the silence presses on us. We cannot bear it."

She tried to make sense of it. "I thought I was part of a *we*, once. A we that was supposed to endure my whole life." *Petemet wasn't supposed to die so young…*

"We understand." His head didn't lift. "We hear the loss in your heart. We grieve."

"You grieve for me? Or you grieve *with* me?" Suvan asked sharply.

A whisper. "Yes."

Her skin prickled. Hesitantly, groping for the concept, she asked, "Being a we is very important to you."

"Yes. We cannot live without others."

Suvan recoiled. "Are you … you don't want to be a *we* with me, do you?" *Oh, gods. I was a we with Petemet, but I can't, I won't….*

His head swiveled towards her, his gleaming eyes going dull. "You already are. We think that is how you understand us. Most humans cannot." His voice sounded almost … apologetic.

She scrambled away from him. Intolerable violation of her space, of her sacred solitude. "I don't want to be a *we* with you."

"We know that, too."

She turned away, seizing her broom. Swept at the hard-packed floor with rapid, angry strokes. "Get out."

Immediately, he stood. Limped for the door.

Shiff, shiff, shiff, went the bristles. "Wait."

He paused, claws on the wooden door.

"You would just leave if I told you to do so?"

"We are what others need us to be," he repeated simply. "If what you require is solitude, then we will leave."

Several more angry strokes across the floor. Suspicion crackling through her that she was somehow being manipulated. *They* could do that, couldn't they? Get inside your head and make you believe … anything? The old stories were a jumble in her mind, but they kept coming into conflict with everything she'd seen in the last week from him, and … nothing made sense. "So you'd leave. Though you'd be not a we then at all." She fumbled for the words, concepts utterly alien to her. "Would you die if you were an I and not a we?"

"Perhaps. We would want to." He still faced away from her, claws on the door.

This is a bad idea. But … he's already demonstrated willingness to leave if told to do so. What harm can a little more compassion do than has already been done? "Sit back down," Suvan grudged.

As he crouched below the hut's only window, shuttered in wood, she asked, leaning on her broom, "What destroyed your home? Why can't you go back to your own *them*?"

He stood. Unlatched the shutters with clumsy fingers, letting first-sun's light strike him. He hissed and pulled back into the shadows. "Invaders. Your kind, not ours."

Suvan's mouth fell open. "Soldiers of the Sepat?"

He turned, taking the broom from her lax fingers. "No. They came from the west, riding on great lizards. Their cities and another of ours, under the control of a different Great Mother, had disputed over land. When they came, they did not see us as different from the city that had disputed with them. So they came with fire and bronze." He paused. "It is time for you to rest in the brightest part of day. We will labor in your stead."

That night, a sandstorm came. Suvan felt the first breaths of it as she labored under the light of seven moons all at their fullest, their white light making every detail of her garden easy to pick out. Such nights were the best times at which to work. The laughing-dogs took advantage of the light, but the marble-cats usually hunted at moons-dark.

Fine grains of sand slapped her face as the winds mounted, and she struggled to cover at least part of her garden with lengths of linen, kept for this purpose. He appeared at her side, though she hadn't called him, and helped her tie the first lengths in place. "The millet will be lost," Suvan shouted bitterly through the gathering storm. She could see that the stars to the west had been blotted out by the storm already.

"Go inside," he told her. "We are meant for such storms. Your skin is soft. Ours is not. Go!"

She huddled indoors, listening to the sand tear at the walls. Leaped to her feet to catch the shutters as they blew inwards as the wooden bar holding them in place shattered. She leaned all her weight against them to close them once more. The only piece of wood close to hand? The statue of Sah, which she picked up with a mumbled apology to the soldier-god, and then employed.

When the storm abated, her door had been silted shut, and she had to climb out through the window, her sandals touching down on two feet of silver sand that shouldn't have been there. As she rounded the corner of her hut, she stopped, stunned to see him alive, and digging down to where her vegetables lay under the sand, his claws sending sand flying through the air.

And beside him, huddled on the ground?

Three child-sized versions of himself. All three with wings, however, like those of a beetle, folded against the backs, but clattering in the last remnants of the breeze. "Blown here by the storm," he called over his shoulder, as if he'd known she stood there all along. "Thirsty. Hungry. Their voices – their voices are ours."

They're of his kin, she translated mentally.

He gestured to the tallest of the three, the one with the strongest-looking wings. "Female. Queen, someday. Must survive, so that all may survive. All our voices. All our memories." The closest thing to passion she'd yet heard in his humming voice.

Suvan stood for a moment, staring at them. *More mouths to feed, and there wasn't enough for two before*, her practical side reminded her. Her heart replied softly, *But they're children. And ... maybe through them, he can go home? They can leave when they're strong enough, and go rebuild their lost city.*

For some reason, the thought didn't comfort her.

"Can you dig?" she asked them. *I'll make this work. Somehow.*

Three solemn nods.

"Come along then. We need to clear the canal to get water. I have some inside for you to drink as we work, but it won't last long."

The smallest raised its claws. "You don't have enough food to feed us all," it said. "The storm buried your crops, and there was little enough before."

How do they – like him – know what I'm thinking?

The child's song buzzed gently in Suvan's mind, a patient threnody. "It is ours to die. This body will provide food and drink for all."

She gaped as the youngest dropped to a crouch, lifting its head so that the armored ridges on its neck pulled apart. Offering its vulnerable throat to the others' claws. "No!" Suvan shouted, her voice loud in the silence after the storm. "There's no *need* for that—" She spun wildly toward her guest. "Tell them! Tell them that we don't eat our dead!"

He paused in his digging. "We do," he said, turning. "We take them back into us. Their memories, their voices – always here." He tapped the side of his head. "We are all of us. Always."

"There's no *need*," Suvan said, stepping forward, putting her body between the youngest and the other two, though they'd made no move yet. "We'll ... make this work." *We*, her mind mocked her. *We, together. How quick you are to offer them your home. Are you sure that he hasn't done something to your mind*?

And yet it did work, somehow. With extra hands, her fields were the first of all her neighbors to be unburied after the storm. She went with the children at night to the canals to catch frogs and crabs to eat, and picked flax while there to spin the thread she hadn't had the time to make while tending her fields alone.

Suddenly, in every day, there *was* time. She hadn't remembered what it was like to have many hands available to accomplish tasks. Hadn't remembered what it felt like not to be alone, every moment consumed with the struggle for survival. And with these precious added moments in each day, came something akin to peace. Though she declared that for her own sanity, the children needed names. "So that when I call for one of you, I don't have to say *you* all the time."

"But we always know which of us you mean," the female protested. "It's clear in your mind."

They hear my thoughts. The notion no longer troubled her, however. "Humor me, please? If you all stay nameless, I'm afraid I'll forget mine." Wrapped in their shimmering voices, that seemed all too real a possibility, some days.

So she listed all the names that she knew, and they picked the ones that they liked. Takha, Emhebi, and Ra'enkau, they became. And Suvan realized to her surprise, that she loved these strange children. Part of her fretted that she had formed such an attachment so quickly. It hardly seemed natural. But they asked little from her. And gave more in return, digging to uncover her millet before it was lost. Bringing her flowers from the canal to strew her pallet and make it smell sweet.

Her first guest, however, withdrew after a few days. Found a corner of the hut where the children didn't scamper, and sat there, his breathing low and slow. "Are you ill?" Suvan asked, worried. His wings looked to be re-growing – she could see their membranes expanding from his shoulders, quivering with his breath. The armor over his exposed arm had regrown, but only thumbnail-thick, the slick blue of his flesh visible under it.

But now, the gleaming white of his armor looked dull for the first time. Ashen. *I can't*, she thought tightly. *I don't want to watch him die, the way I watched Petemet die.*

"Won't see us perish," he replied. He always seemed to know her thoughts. She'd become almost accustomed to that. "Not ill. Just … changing. Becoming. As you … have become. We are what others need."

Suvan dropped to a crouch, alarmed. Change sounded almost as bad as death. And she wanted to deny, hotly, that she'd changed. Become any different than she'd always been.

But then she glanced at all the things she'd kept *just so* since her husband's death. Then realized that somehow, inexorably, things had changed. The god Sah still barred the shutters tight. She'd had to make new bowls of river clay, rough-baked in her fire, for the children. She'd made them each their own pallet of linen and reeds.

Nothing was as it had been *before*. Change had caught her unawares, as inexorable as the River's flow.

He looked up at her with eyes as bright as first-sun. "We become what others need of us. So have you. Our lives are a gift. Freely given. Most humans … do not understand. You do."

Images crossed her mind. Visions of a city through which she'd never walked. One in which faceless humans crowded all around bustling, busy … and empty. All dissatisfied with their lot. All envying what their neighbors had. Because none of them knew what they were for. One person in a dozen, perhaps, had a face. Carried with them a sense of purpose. And one of those faces was her own.

"You think that I know what I'm for?" Suvan wanted to laugh, though it would have been edged with tears. *But I don't know. I never have.*

A silent nod.

"But what will you become?"

He closed his eyes. "What you need. What they need."

"What do they need? To start a new city?" Suvan bit her lip.

A shrug. "If queen grows to adulthood, perhaps. But not for some time. What *we* will become now, born of their need … we do not know."

He huddled in his corner, not eating, only drinking, for days.

And she watched and worried and waited.

The miracle of her fields' recovery didn't pass unnoticed by the neighbors. A group of them, men and women, came striding across the sand-choked road with second-sun high. They shouted and raised their sickles and hoes at the sight of the children, who scuttled into the shelter of Suvan's hut.

Suvan picked up her bronze scythe and met her neighbors, blocking them from entering her hut, where the children huddled, and where her guest had sat, somnolent, for the past two days. "No further," she told them boldly. "They are my *guests*. I've given them food and shelter. Will you dishonor me by breaking my hospitality, poor shred that it is?"

That stopped them. The Folk had strong traditions about guest-rights.

Her neighbors paused uncertainly. "But they're *them*." Sounds of disgust, spittle on the ground. "They eat *our dead*."

"Go unblock Petemet's tomb," Suvan ordered harshly, her face feeling like a stone mask. "Look on his body. See how much of him has been eaten." She wanted to spit herself now. "You feared the taint of his death so much that you didn't come to check on his widow until two weeks after the storm. For all you cared of me, I could have been dead." She saw them flinch. Saw the guilt in their eyes as if they'd shouted it – *heard* it, as discordant twangs as from a rebec, pouring out of them. *Is this how they can always hear what I'm thinking*? Suvan wondered. *How am I hearing this*?

Her closest neighbors, an older couple who had six grown children, both frowned. "They've taken over your mind," the woman, Atveh, declared. "You know *they* can do that. They sing in your dreams and turn you on your own people."

Have they? Suvan wondered briefly. *No. I'm just seeing the things that have always been there.* "The only reason I'm holding a scythe," she returned scornfully, "is that you all arrived on my lands carrying tools, and then raised them as weapons." She gestured at her fields. "As you can see, I have all the help that I need. I require none of your aid to recover from the storm." *Not that you offered it.* She bared her teeth in a humorless smile. "Perhaps my guests and I could offer you *our* assistance in recovering your crops?"

The little crowd eyed each other. Took a few steps back. Suvan could feel the children pressing up against her back, unsure and frightened. She hummed at them gently, *Be calm. Don't frighten them.*

At length, her neighbors withdrew. Atveh and her husband warily permitted Suvan and the children onto their fields, where they all worked through the hours of second-sun's light, freeing the dying millet stalks from the burden of the sand. Exhausting, back-breaking labor. And Suvan could see that other neighbors watched from the periphery of their own fields. "Just wait," she told the children bitterly as they returned to her own hut. "If anything goes wrong with the crop now, it won't be because of the sandstorm. It'll be because I touched the plants, still tainted by my husband's death. Or because you three poisoned the ground."

Small, taloned hands touched her arms. "You're tired," Takha, the little female, whispered. "And angry."

"They brought us water to drink," Emhebi pointed out.

Yes, making signs to turn away evil behind the pitcher.

"Foolish," Ra'enkau whispered. "But not evil."

"We know what you know. They may turn against us – the us that is you, too, Suvan," Takha sang. "We'll be ready to flee if we need to. And you should be ready, too."

She shook her head. *They won't lift a hand against me. They can't. I'm Petemet's widow. I'm one of them.*

"They will not see you as of them for long, if their fear rises," Takha replied to her unspoken words. "They will see you as part of us. And in how much will they be wrong?"

Suvan twitched, but she'd grown largely used to the fact that her thoughts were as transparent as water to them. "You're entirely too wise to be a child," she finally responded as they entered her hut.

"We are not only children. We are all that we have been. All the memories of Great Mothers and fathers before us." Takha shrugged, as if that were of no great matter. "We must ensure that they have no reason to fear us."

"Or we must ensure that they have too *much* fear of us, ever to strike," Ra'enkau countered, adult words in his reedy, soprano song.

Suvan moved away to kneel beside her first guest, still unconscious against the wall. She could see that his armor was peeling away from his body now, and her fingers itched to tug it away, like a healing scab. But at the same time, she couldn't make herself touch him, in case anything she did made his condition worse. "I wish I knew how to help you," she murmured.

Small hands on her shoulders, patting her hair. "There is nothing to do for him but to wait," Takha replied. "He is becoming."

After second-twilight, as the moons rose high, her neighbors returned. This time with torches as well as their hoes. "Where have your precious *guests* been, Suvan? Have they been with you, every moment of every day? Can you account for them?"

Even at twenty paces, she could smell the yeast of bread-beer on the men's breath. Then, to her surprise, Atveh emerged from the side of the crowd, taking position between the men and Suvan's hut. "They helped us today!" Atveh shouted. "I bet if they were asked, they'd help any of you, too—"

"We checked the bodies in the tombs!" a voice shouted. "Half of them have been eaten!"

Suvan turned her head. Asked the children silently, *Did you eat of the tomb-dwellers before you came to me?*

"No," they all responded immediately. "We were hungry, but we knew that this would turn the humans against us."

"One of them offered, when he first came here, to set down his life for the other two, so that they might eat," Suvan called out, letting scorn fill her voice. "Why would he have done that, if they'd already fed on the dead? Go look for borer-worm signs in the tombs. A more likely explanation."

"They've poisoned you," another voice came from the crowd. *Arag*, Suvan recognized dimly. *One of Petemet's friends from his soldiering days.* "Turned your mind against us."

Suvan picked up her scythe from where it stood behind her door. There were twenty of them, and while she could see Atveh, old and white-haired, was trying to calm them down, they'd clearly been drinking. Had found a reason to justify breaking the iron laws of hospitality. She could see it all with a crystalline, distant perspective that surprised her.

Even more surprisingly, Suvan didn't feel afraid. She could see events transpiring before her, unwinding like linen string around her spindle, before they actually occurred. Could see how the men would start forward. How Atveh would step in their way. How her skull would be crushed by one heedless sweep of a hoe, and how she'd fall, red marring her white hair, to the black soil of the garden.

How the men would leap forward and overbear her. Throw their torches onto the thatch of her hut. Hold her down and make her watch as they dismembered her children – yes, *her* children. How the blue blood would spray up in the red light of her burning hut. How they wouldn't even be sated by the blood and the death, but would require more, and more, and how she'd be lucky to see first-sun rise in the morning. *Ah, Petemet. For the first time, I'm glad you're not here to see what the village you came to love is capable of doing—*

Suvan closed her eyes and told the children, "Run."

"That won't be necessary," Takha sang, and a hand closed on her shoulder from behind her. Filling the void where Petemet once would have stood.

"They're not evil," a voice said from behind her. "They just don't know what they're for. For this, we forgive them. But we do not forgive lies and words spoken to create fear. We will resist. And we will win."

Suvan saw terror on the faces of her neighbors. As one, they dropped their tools and *ran*. Atveh turned, and put a shaking hand to her lips. "By the gods," the old woman whispered.

Suvan spun. Looked up at her guest. For a moment, she stopped breathing.

His old armor, damaged and dull, had fallen away. Revealed now was a shining blue carapace, iridescent in the last light of second-sun. He was taller now, with full, healthy wings that clattered lightly in the breeze. The claws on his hands had lengthened, but a second set of arms had somehow joined them, terminating in hands more like her own. Meant for grasping and manipulating. And the armored plates of his face?

Appeared almost human. There were grooves that hinted at cheekbones. A jawline. An opening that implied lips. But lines remained that also suggested that it could still unfurl, as it always had.

Suvan swallowed. He didn't look like Petemet, and she was grateful for that. It would have been intolerable if he had. "You've … finished becoming?" she asked, feeling awkward.

"For now, yes."

She didn't know how to ask it. "What *are* you?"

"What they needed." His eyes flicked towards the young ones. "Perhaps what you need? We do not know." A hesitation. "They didn't need a mother. Already have one. You." He pointed at her as the children gathered close, touching his drying wings with light, admiring claws. "They need … protector. Guide. Became soldier. Have not been, before. Was always builder. We are always what we were. But we can always become something more."

She closed her eyes, aware of Atveh's awed presence bearing witness nearby. "Will you leave, and look for others of your kind?" Her throat ached at the thought.

A clawed hand touched her face. "Perhaps. If we all go. We are all of us." A pause. "Or we stay here. Build a new kind of city. Together."

Suvan opened her eyes and looked around the farm that had been a refuge to her since her husband's death. Everything in its place. It had been a refuge to Petemet, too, she realized, a place to heal after years of service in war. But now?

It was time to move on. To risk being bruised by the world once more. "If we stay here, it will be harder for you," she said simply. "The others won't accept easily."

"But if we go into the deep desert, you cannot live there," Takha replied, her voice echoed by the other children. "We don't wish to go without you. You are part of us. We are part of you."

Tears sprang to Suvan's eyes. That simple declaration, that simple acceptance, meant more to her somehow, than she'd ever have thought possible. "Whatever we do, we'll do it together," she whispered. "I promise."

Native Aliens

Greg van Eekhout

1945

AS PAPA STANDS between the two rows of men holding rifles, he stands as a Dutchman. His shirt is starched white, tucked neatly into khaki trousers with creases sharp enough to cut skin. It is not especially hot today, but sweat pools under his arms and trickles down his back. The Indonesians with the guns are sweating, too.

Papa's skin is as dark as the Indonesians', naturally dark and baked tobacco brown from years spent hammering together chicken coops and pigeon hutches in the backyard. He is a good carpenter, and people come to him for help and advice. But carpentry is not his job. He works as a bookkeeper for Rotterdamse Lloyd, the Dutch shipping company. He is a Dutchman with a Dutch job.

The men with rifles stand in two ragged rows, facing one another, before the entrance of the school where we learned our lessons, which now serves as a prison for enemies of the Indonesians' revolution.

It is the imprecision of the Indonesians that angers Papa, their sloppy spacing, their relaxed and slovenly postures. They hold their guns as though they were shovels or rakes or brooms, and the Indonesians have no interest in hard work.

He recognizes almost all of them. This one sells satay in front of the train station. Papa's money has helped him buy the shoes on his feet. Another, Rexi, has actually been in our home. When he was a young boy, not so long ago, he slipped on the rocks by the river and hit his head, and when we told Papa of this, Papa carried him in his arms laid him down in the sitting room until the boy's grandfather came for him. He has sipped water from our well, and now he waits for father with a gun slung lazily over his shoulder.

A hand shoves Papa in the back, and Papa, slightly built, pitches forward and goes down to one knee in the dirt. He uses this opportunity to mouth a very quick prayer before being yanked roughly back to his feet.

The man who pulls Papa up is one of those he does not know. He is one of those who pounded on our door in the night and demanded we all assemble in the front room of our sprawling house built on the hill. "Are these the only men?" he said, indicating Papa and me.

Mama explained that, yes, we were the only men. Ferdinand remains in Tokyo, where he has mined coal for the Japanese since his unit's capture. Though really he mines coal no longer because he was freed when the Japanese surrendered. When he is well enough to travel, he will return home. And there is Anthonie, the next eldest, but he is not here either. He is dead of tuberculosis, contracted in a jail cell of the Japanese occupation army.

And there is Papa. And there is me.

I am eleven years old. Later, there will be a camp for me and Mama and my sisters. But for now, they take only Papa.

The man steadies Papa, who is shaking now, who is so afraid he cannot stop shaking, who is hating himself for shaking, who should not have to fear his own neighbors. "I am a bookkeeper," he says. "What have I to do with this?"

"You are a Dutchman," says the man. "Isn't that what you always insist? At your office at Rotterdamse Lloyd? At the train station where you buy your Dutch newspaper? At the cantina where you drink your coffee? At the swimming pool where only the Dutch can swim. At home, where your servants cook your food and clean your house and raise your children? 'I am a Dutchman. My family is a Dutch family.' Isn't that what you always say?"

Three generations ago, a Dutchman came from the Netherlands and married an Indonesian girl. There have been Indonesians and Dutch-Indonesians in our family for three generations, but no one from Holland.

But, "Yes, I am a Dutchman," says Papa.

"Yes. You are," the man says to Papa. "And, now, you must run."

Papa is not the first to receive this command today. He knows what's expected of him.

The men with rifles change their stances. They spread their legs to shoulder width. They bend at the knees. They raise their guns over their shoulders, inverted with the rifle butts held before them, and they wait.

The dirt at the feet of these men, his neighbors, is dark with blood and vomit and piss and shit. This is the entrance to a new prison.

Papa hopes that if he runs fast enough, maybe only a few of the rifle butts will strike him. Maybe not too hard.

He makes the sign of the cross and takes a step forward.

2367

At school, they tell us about Preparation. It's almost all we talk about. For the last three months, we haven't read stories. We haven't done logic problems. We haven't learned songs or sculpted in clay or played games or done swim-dances. All we talk about is Preparation.

In three months time a ship will arrive, and all 879 of us Brevan-Terrans will board, and we will spend the next four years traveling to Earth.

We need Preparation for the journey, and we need Preparation for the arrival.

At the beginning of the year, our teacher was Mr. Daal, a Brevan-Terran like my classmates and me. But after the Re-Negotiation a Brevan man named Si Tula replaced him. His eyes are so blue they seem to glow even when he shuts his lids. He speaks in a deep-horn voice and is very nice.

In a circle, we sit on the floor in trays of warm brine, watching the pictures Si Tula projects before us. There is a planet of blue and white and brown, and I already know this is Earth, because I've been seeing it for months and months now. It's been on the news. Mama has been showing us books about it. Opa has been reading pamphlets about Earth.

Si Tula begins every lesson by showing us Earth. "This is your home," he always says. And then, he raises his arms, his long fingers slowly fluttering as though they were underwater, and we know what to say: *This is Earth. This is where we come from. This is where we going. It will be good to be home.*

After that, the Preparation lesson is always a little different. We have seen the cities of Earth, which are big, sprawling fields of light. We have seen the animals of Earth, which are kept inside the cities in houses of their own for all to see. We have seen the great oceans, so much broader and deeper and more powerful than our little lakes on Breva.

"Your home is a mighty world," Si Tula says. And he flutters his fingers, and we respond: *Breva is too small for Earth.*

This is something the Brevan said a lot during the Re-Negotiation. It's the reason why all us Brevan-Terrans must go.

I have a question, so I raise my hand, and Si Tula bows respectfully towards me, his rib-arms lowered. It is odd, seeing my teacher bow to me. It is not something our old teacher would ever do. But Brevans are taught from childhood to bow to Brevan-Terrans.

"You may speak, Dool," he says.

I click my valves. "We have seen Terran habitations and Terran animals and Terran planetary features."

Nervous – and not knowing why – I shift in my tray, water sloshing over the sides. Si Tula nods encouragement, so I continue. "But … when will he see Terran people?"

Si Tula makes an appreciative click. "Thank you, Dool. I am pleased you asked. For what now follows is the most important part of Preparation. All else is merely knowing. But this, what we are about to learn, will require doing. It will require doing from you. It will require doing from the Health and Wellbeing Authority. It will require doing from all."

The Health and Wellbeing Authority is a new organization formed after the Re-Negotiation. Only Brevans sit on the Health and Wellbeing Authority.

Si Tula moves his hands, and a new projection appears in the middle of the circle. It is a pair of creatures. They are four-limbed – two thick limbs upon which they stand, and two thinner, upper limbs which end in things that look very much like hands. One of the creatures has a large pair of teats in front. The other has much smaller teats, and a penis. Their faces are flat and unexpressive. I have seen enough pictures of Terran animals to know that these creatures would live on land.

The projection progresses, and the creatures now wear clothing of sorts, and they move about in various settings. Here, they fold their legs beneath them and sit on the ground, planting a tree. And then they are in a structure, putting food into their tiny mouths. Here they are holding a baby creature, and despite their alien faces, it is clear they are happy. These are intelligent creatures, perhaps. More like me than like animals.

"This is you," Si Tula says. "This is you. These are Terrans, and this is what you are. This is how you were when you came to Breva. This is how you will be again."

Si Tula pauses. When he does this, we know we are to remain quiet and think about what he has said. This is us, he has told us. This is me. This is how I was.

After a suitable interval, I raise my hand.

Si Tula bows

"I don't understand," I say. "How can these creatures be us? They have no rib-arms, no dorsals, no valves. They are land creatures. How can this be me? I don't understand."

He smiles, his eyes very blue. "Your confusion is not surprising to me. It is a new concept. It is a new concept for all of you. But you will get used to it. Given enough time, one can get used to anything."

1949

They had told us we'd be coming to a place of colors. There would be fields of tulips, white and pink and yellow and red, a celebration of colors against the blue sky. There would be wonders – windmills and canals and lanes alive with bicycles. This would be a home. We were not Indonesian, we were Dutch, they told us, and this would be our home.

What we find here is stone. The buildings are blocks of neatly stacked stone, and the streets are stone and brick, fitted together, tight and clever. They had told us it would be cold, and it is. They had told us we would get used to it, and they were lying, because how can I get used to this? Even in my jacket, which weighs as much as I do, and the wool hat that scratches my scalp, and the gloves that prevent me from feeling anything I touch, I am cold. "You'll get used to it," they tell us.

We are home. The third floor of a narrow stone building is our home. There is a small sitting area, and we can all sit together if we keep our legs tucked close. There is a room for Mama and Gerda and Anki. Because I am the only boy – the only male in my family who survived the Japanese occupation and the Indonesian revolution – I have a room to myself, shared with the two steamer trunks we brought from Jakarta.

When Mr. Kaarl, the landlord, was showing us the apartment, he realized it was quite different from what we were used to. "The water closet is down the hall," he said, jingling a ring of keys. "That'll be different for you, but you'll get used to it. They make a lot of noise, but it's more privacy than you had in your other life."

Gerda peers down the hall, skeptically. "More privacy? But we have to share it with everyone else on the floor."

Mr. Kaarl laughs. He has a very friendly laugh. "But it's covered and indoors, at least. No prying eyes."

Gerda frowns, not understanding.

I, however, understand very well.

Mama casts me a sharp warning look, but I don't mind such looks. At fifteen, I am the man of the house.

"Mr. Kaarl believes," I explain to Gerda, "that back home we used the river as our lavatory."

When I see terror, rather than anger, in Mama's eyes, I feel a small pang of regret. There have been many moments in the last few years in which the wrong word has had grave consequences. She still thinks Papa is dead because of all his bragging about being a Dutchman. But many of our neighbors are dead, and they weren't all the braggarts Papa was. There was a war, and once the Japanese were defeated there was a revolution, and the Dutch were cast out. Many people died, of course. Blood of all kinds soaked into the ground.

But my comment was spoken in Indonesian, so Mr. Kaarl only smiles a happy, puzzled smile. "Chattering monkey," he says, winking. "I'm renting to a lot of chattering monkeys lately. I should have invested in trees instead of buildings." And he laughs, his cheeks very pink.

2367

When Preparation finally happens, it happens in a dry, silver room. It is unlike any room I've ever been in. There are no mollusks clinging to the walls. There is no soft carpet of moss beneath my feet. There is no gentle trickle of water.

I am alone. I am here with only a Brevan doctor, his green-and-black mottled chest blinking with medical devices.

"This is the kind of room Terrans build," he says.

I tell him no, that is wrong, that my ancestors were Terran, and they built no dead rooms like this.

And I am told, Yes, oh, yes, they did. But Breva remained Brevan, and over time, Terran rooms became Brevan. The Terran rooms were changed, sometimes deliberately, to adapt to the Brevan environment. And sometimes Breva simply took what Earth brought into its embrace, and then transformed it. But too often, Brevan rooms were made into Terran rooms, and many Brevan rooms died forever. "Earth is mighty, indeed," says the doctor. "But there is more than simple might, is there not? Is there not also patience? Is there not also resolve? What lasts longer – a heart that beats hard, or a heart that beats gentle?"

This particular room has been drained of water. In this room, the mollusks have been scraped away. In this room, herbicide has killed the moss. This room is once more a Terran room, and it must be this way, says the doctor, for the Preparation.

In the center of the room is an oval table, shaped like an altar in a bulb-temple. "Recline upon it," says the doctor.

I look at the table. I look above it. Hanging above the table is a cluster of silver arms, dangling down like jellyfish tentacles. Blades glint in the silver room.

The doctor's eyes are blue as Si Tula's, but not at all kind.

And I run. I run towards the door, towards the cool wet air of outside, away from this dry and silver room, away, away, towards home.

I don't get far. The doctor lashes out with his rib-arms, and though I struggle and beat at his arms and try to pry loose from his suction with my soft fingers, he is too strong, and he pulls me in and lifts me and sets me on the table. And once on the table, I cannot move.

"How do you feel?" the doctor says.

"I feel nothing."

He moves his hands, and the silver arms overhead descend.

"Good," says the doctor. "We can begin now."

He begins by severing my rib-arms.

When I scream out – not in pain, but in something else, in something worse – he adjusts the table and I am silent.

"Yes," he says. "That is good. Your life has been good and comfortable, and it will be so in continuance. You have no cause to cry."

1969

It occurred to me some time ago that my backyard is a re-creation. The chicken coop, with the half dozen Leghorns and Rhode Island Reds, is a plywood attempt at something Papa might have built. Only, he was a carpenter, and I just began playing with wood and nails seven years ago, when we came to California. My work is a mess of crooked surfaces and ill-fitted joints, but it keeps the chickens inside, and that's what's important. I fear once the pigeon hutch is done, only the fattest and stupidest cats will fail to find a way in.

But this is my backyard. In Holland, we shared a courtyard. Here, we have something: A rambling, cluttered, wild backyard that I can think of as home.

To have a home of your own – something that can't be taken away – this is no small thing. We rent now, but someday, perhaps, it will be ours.

Of course, anything can be taken away. Even here, in this country, anything can be taken away from any person.

It's important to keep that in mind.

I turn satay kambing on my barbeque grill while across the fence, the neighbor flips hamburgers on his. Between the pickets, I see the neighbor's boy watching me. He wrinkles his nose as if he smells something foul, and I say, loud enough for him to hear, "Mmmm. Good dog. Good, delicious dog." Even louder: "Say, I wonder where Ranger is?"

Ranger is the boy's sweet-faced mutt.

The boy runs to complain to his father, and the neighbor scowls at me.

I smile and wave.

2371

To be Terran is to walk without water. Earth is a wet world, but our home is a dry building. There is water in the walls – sometimes I can hear it course through pipes – but it comes out only in faucets, and it can be collected only in small vessels. There is a tub in the bathroom, roughly the size of a coffin, but it is dead water and I will not stay in it.

My family is fortunate. We have been located near the sea, only twenty minutes by rail, and I have a job on the shore. I sell tourist items to those who visit the water. They like to buy clothing and sensations that remind them of their travels. I sell these items well, and someday, perhaps, I will have a business of my own. I often wonder if people who come to the sea might like to have sensations that don't remind them of where they've been, but instead show them where they cannot go.

In the shop's changing room is a mirror, and I always volunteer to clean it. It is not pleasant to examine myself, but doing so is like the kind of meditation we did back home in the bulb-temples.

My body is made for work. My two arms are stronger than my rib-arms ever were, which were made for sculling. My lungs don't take in as much air as they used to, but I get enough oxygen by inhaling often. Sometimes I stand and look at myself as I am now, and then I try to imagine myself as I was. Neither body seems quite right. My new body is alien to me, and my old body is alien to this world. When I clean the mirror, I see a puzzle that cannot be solved, or an out-of-place object that has no place.

In times that are not busy, I can look outside the shop, out over the ocean. The surf can be violent here, and the waves boom against the sand, fingers of white foam reaching out and grasping, as if the ocean were trying to pull itself up on the land. Twice a day, the ocean gets as far as it can go, but then it recedes. Despite its strength, the ocean must always return to itself.

1969

Last night, we went to the Moon. Three men were packed like the last pairs of socks into an overstuffed suitcase and then they went to the Moon. I didn't stay up to watch, but Anthony did. From down the hall, I could dimly hear the voices from the television, and the sound of Anthony clapping and bouncing in the squeaky-springed chair.

He's a dreamer, my son. He believes in better places.

He comes out of the house and I hand him an unseasoned lamb skewer. Satay kambing should be made with goat, but nobody eats goat here.

"How are your spacemen?"

"Astronauts," he corrects. "I don't know. Mama made me turn off the TV. She thinks I need more sunlight."

"The spacemen can get by without you watching them."

"The most important moment in the history of humanity, and Mama's worried about my Vitamin D."

I bite my lip to keep from laughing. He's a funny kid, my son. And smart. Much smarter than I was at twelve. Or smart in other ways, I suppose. By the age of twelve, I'd lost two brothers. I'd seen Japanese Zeroes fly over my house. I'd seen my father taken away by our neighbors to die. Not much time for jokes when I was his age.

"So, first we walk on the Moon," I say. "And then what? We come back home? We use what we learned to build better adding machines? New and improved vacuum cleaners?"

He gives me a look that, had I ever given to my Papa, would have earned me a slap across the face. And I let it pass. I have learned to let so much pass. It is a better way getting through life, I think.

"It's not about … things," Anthony says. "It's about going places. There's so much out there, Dad." About a year ago, he stopped calling me Papa and started calling me Dad. I understand why – it's what American boys call their fathers – but I have yet to get used to it. I will, in time, but not yet. "We can't stay here forever. First, the Moon. Then, by the time I graduate college, Mars. Then the asteroid belt, maybe. And the moons of Jupiter. By the time I have kids, the stars. There'll be other planets. Other worlds. Maybe with intelligent life. We have to go there."

"We can barely live on the Moon," I argue. "Billions of dollars and space suits and thousands of people to make it happen. And the Moon is just next door isn't it? It's just a few thousand miles away."

He gives me that look, and I chide myself for baiting him. The Moon is 240,000 miles away. I've been following everything, too.

Anthony clamps his molars down on a chunk of lamb and tears it from the skewer. "Things'll be different by the time we get to the stars," he says. "We'll be different. I read a story about it. If we find life out there, we'll change ourselves to be more like what we find. We'll make our bodies and brains different. We won't even have to come back home. We'll be so well adapted that we can survive wherever we land as efficiently as the native aliens."

Native aliens.

I let the paradox pass.

Removing the satay from the grill, I lay the skewers down in neat rows on a plate. "But, what if the life we find out there doesn't want us? What if they see us as a threat? People come to a new land, and they want to change it. They want to make it like the place they came from, and they want to be top dog. Visitors who refuse to go home aren't really visitors."

"We'll be welcome," he says, with so much confidence that I feel my heart fissure, "because we'll come with peaceful intentions."

This is a moment, now. This is a moment in which I could press the issue. I could bring to bear my 35 years of life experience, of scratches and bruises and scars and calluses. I could strip away every one of my son's naive sentiments and make him see the world as it is. I have seen blood in the dirt. I bet I could make my son see it, too.

I hand him the plate of satay. "Bring this to the kitchen. And then watch your spacemen walk on their rock."

"Astronauts," he says, taking the plate. "And it's not just some rock. It's a world."

I pierce more lamb chunks on skewers. "Okay. Have it your way. A world. Tell me if the astronauts find something good on their new world."

He gives me his look and takes the satay kambing into the house.

I stay in my backyard and look to the sky.

There's nothing to see there, but I look on my son's behalf, praying that he'll never have to see what I see.

Babies Come from Earth

Louis Evans

THE SKY IS THE COLOR OF AN OLD BLUE EGG bleached in the sun. We walk along the beach the same way the clouds are going.

He is squeezing my hand with the rhythm of a heartbeat. I wonder if he knows he's doing it. It's a light sort of question, a net cast over the deeper ones below. I realize I'm squeezing back, continuously. No rhythm. Flatline.

"I'm sorry," he says, and there's a catch in his voice.

I don't know if he's speaking to me or to the thing inside me that they have implanted. That thing inside me, growing, only half alive.

I don't know who he's apologizing to, but I answer for both of us.

"I'm not," I say, and there's no hesitation in my reply. We made a decision. We knew what it meant.

Already it is dark enough for our smallest moon, green and cracked, to take form in the sky.

* * *

This is how you do it. You take your surrogate and in the third trimester you change the meds. You have been drugging her already, drugging her and testing her, from well before week zero.

In the third trimester you change the meds. Before it was just three or four or five pills. Ordinary things. A surrogate will swallow what she's told.

But in the third trimester there is the drink, which is a slang term for cryoprotectants, which is a pretty way of saying antifreeze, damn near magic if you look at the crystallography, the way ice does not begin to form, the way chilled blood goes on and on in waves. She begins to swallow it by the cupful.

* * *

The nursery is small and neat. He carved the crib by hand. I have always loved his hands, the way they turn and turn a knife around the grain in wood, the way they plant flowers and pick weeds. But I love them most, and secretly, for the way they are perfectly still in repose.

If it were on command they'd have made him a surgeon, but his fingertips buzz like dragonflies when he reaches for something important, and so he is a farmer instead.

I remember the buzz in his fingertips the first time he held my hand, the way the honeysuckle smelled as we fell, laughing, to the grass. I think about the honeysuckle, which is native, not a transplant; I think about how Earth gave us her cast-off names. I think about the Earth's gifts.

The honeysuckle may not be the same as on Earth, but there is the same meaning to its smell and I kissed him under a thick quilt of summer. I have been ready for a child with this man for a long time.

There is a pattern on the wall of the nursery cast by the shadows of the drapes, curling and uncurling gently. I catch my fingers in the drapes and pull; the shadows stretch themselves taut and they stay, anchored for as long as I can hold them. The sunlight comes in somehow anyway. That's good. A baby shouldn't be in the dark.

* * *

This is when the vomiting starts. And there are the meds for that, too, but she vomits anyway. You are used to reassuring them with careful half-truths. "It's not that bad," as though it were anything other than exactly as bad as it is. You will keep saying it those times that something goes wrong, when she cannot keep the cups down at all, when they switch from oral administration to amnioinjection, as sometimes they must strap her down and wheel her away to cut it out of her, your lying face reflected in her sweat-stained brow, screams just beginning to unhinge her jaw – but this is fairly rare.

Once she can keep the cups down the dose begins to grow. She passes it, most of it, producing gloriously unfreezable runny stool, stool you could use to lube tank tracks on Europa, and so she must keep drinking it, getting it into her system, into the amniotic sac, through the placenta.

* * *

I was eight when my brother came to us. My parents swept and tidied and made things baby-safe again, stoppering outlets and moving vitamin caps to the high shelves.

I remember how carefully we dressed, the formal way that my father held open the car door for my mother. The shuttle sitting on the long, thin strip of asphalt, fat and sleek like a bird full of young, a fish full of spores.

I remember how the grass had been burned away around the runway, the men and women in clean blue scrubs laboring about it, grass smoke curling between their legs. How the light from its metal womb was green like the sea.

* * *

What you do is ten days before the due date you take her into the delivery room. Preemies die in space, but ten days before is viable.

It is cold in there, cold enough that you take to slipping hand-warmers inside your double-thick latex gloves, which is against the rules, but fuck it and by the time you arrive she is shivering, her fingers and toes bluing alarmingly and the blood under your knife is colder than blood should be.

* * *

My brother dreamed himself to death.

Earth is a very long way away, and the sleep is deep and dark. We bring them down into the world on a long, thin path of flame, and most of them wake. But some do not; they remain somewhere in between the stars, dreaming forever of the smooth arcs that link world to world, the way it feels to be frozen and falling together, the passage of time beyond time.

* * *

Now is when you need to move quickly.

* * *

We made a decision. We knew what it meant.

* * *

Here is the shape of the amniotic sac, the way the caul wraps itself around the infant. Here are your hands, spreading apart the muscle and the membranes, pressing and pulling. Do not push; the sac must remain intact.

This is you inside her. She is open, now, like an empty box, like a forgotten gift. The cryopod is alongside the operating table, the tanks of oxygenated cryprotected saline beneath, chiller running already, chattering like your teeth. You lift the infant still in its membrane into the pod. The orderlies murmur and the pod's mouth begins to fill with freezing spit. One last incision, long and wide like a smile, and it's done, the spit is rising, the mouth is shut, the pod fills to the last inch of clear plastic. Already it is cold enough for frostbite, nipping at your fingertips; the baby's face is lilac, still.

* * *

It happened in my fourth month. My husband was not with me.

I was walking in the hospital's garden past the wall where the honeysuckle climbs and there was a knot between my hips. Out of nowhere. I sat down on the path suddenly, woozily – the drugs had given my fingertips and skull the texture of felt – and blood pooled between my legs.

The nurses rushed me to the OR and stripped me in a dream of hands. I do not know when they gave up on trying to save it. Their voices were the same throughout, the susurration of wind through tall grass.

* * *

All that is left are the leavings. The orderlies wheel the cold cart away, slipping it off somewhere, into the river that leads to the Thread and to space. You sew up your surrogate and pat her hand, tell her she did well and that you're proud of her, moving your tongue like a scalpel, carving out familiar patterns. Tomorrow you will look in on her, and begin to count the days until she can do this once more. But you are done for tonight.

* * *

It never lives. This is what she told us, my husband and I, sitting in the hospital office.

"I wish it were otherwise. It never lives. But you live. And the next ship has your child on it – has your new baby on it already, just waiting for you to make the brave choice, the generous choice, to give some months of your strength and hope to science, to medicine. To the hope of natural births on this planet. Already we are better at it – the average pregnancy lasts a whole three to six months, now!

"That's how it is," she said. "I hope you make the good choice."

Sitting in the office in the hospital, in our two chairs, hand in hand, we did not discuss it. We knew what we wanted, and we made a decision.

* * *

Some nights you go out to see the Thread and watch the bubbles rise. Not on the nights after you operate; on those nights you take an unwise dose of kavalactones, the only thing left that gives you dreamless sleep. And you sleep.

* * *

Babies come from Earth. I learned this in my childhood, from parents and picturebooks. I do not know how I imagined Earth in those days. I have memories of rows of harvest infants, like lettuce heads. Crowded but comfortable.

Just before my brother came, my mother explained to me about the List. We had to wait our turn, she said. They did not tell me where we were on the List. They did not tell me that those high on the List are given survivors and the low receive only the dead.

I was sixteen, a month before my sister came, and I found my father crying and he explained to me how babies are made and bought. How long it had taken to learn that you could not reproduce under our sun.

He told me: "If you volunteer to conceive a child – a fetus, a thing – if you let them test treatments on you, even though you know the thing in your belly won't survive, they move you up on the List. It's the only way to get ahead."

He said my mother had volunteered, had spent the month in the Maternity Ward. A Maternity Ward from which no child had ever emerged alive. That thanks to her sacrifice, I would get a live sister, where I had gotten a dead brother.

That evening I walked out under heavens that were like a bowl of pure water. You can see the Earth's star on a clear night from my childhood home, but I did not look up. I was feeling the grass and soil beneath my toes, and I was wondering, the way a girl wonders, just what I would give to be a mother. Now I know.

We are a young couple. The List is long, and there is only one way to get ahead. We made a decision.

We knew what it meant.

* * *

At night the Thread is lit a soft, crisp white, nothing gaudy, and it goes on and up forever. Sometimes you must wait a full fifteen minutes to see the next bubble rise.

This is how you do it. When you see the bubbles you must let the idea of their cargo, the frozen infant faces, slide softly across the surface of your mind. You must not think of girls and boys taking first steps under distant suns, and you must not think of men and women growing tall in a strange land, wondering what it sounds like when their lips form the words "mother," "father." You must not think of how far away the stars are, trying to fit the scale of space inside your skull, you must not think of your own mother, the way she smiles at you, the way her nose is your nose and your hands are your father's hands, you must not wish for a change in the order of things –

This is how you do your job.

* * *

I am standing in the field now, wearing my good dress, waiting for the stork. Unbidden, my hand rides up over my collarbone. His hand joins me, envelops mine. Soon there will be a twinkle above us, and here I am, looking into a clear blue sky.

I am standing in the field with my husband, waiting for our child to fall from above, waiting –

Warhorse

Illimani Ferreira

MAJUN STARTED HIS JOURNEY to the core of the Niwri reef hours before the first burgundy lights of the early morning. There was something reassuring about swimming in the dark and relying solely on his thoracic sonar for guidance. His sonar only revealed paths to follow and obstacles to avoid. Light and sight would have shown him the nationalistic banners of the Nah Republic attached to the residential pods' entrances and swinging with the water currents. Light and sight would have revealed the heads of Ruhgius, Xnitals, Druks, Nainitselaps and even a few Nahs fixed to the needles of the enormous urchins specially bioengineered for the single purpose of displaying the vanquished.

Majun might have made a choice to not see these suburbs, but he had no choice but to taste them through the water he was breathing. They tasted like death. They always did. Majun's assigned adoptive parents probably still lived there. They didn't provide him with much more than shelter and meals, as most of Majun's upbringing had taken place in the local educational complex, more precisely within the ranks of every other male in his age range that had happened to be a Nah Republic Warhorse.

Majun and his fellow warhorses had been bioengineered to have larger bodies, sturdier bony plates and reach greater speed thanks to their longer dorsal fins and prehensile tails. Their monstrous, altered bodies bore an unnatural orangey-red pigment – the national color of the Nah Republic and of its aquatic habitat under daylight, which gave the warhorses a natural camouflage. Last but not least, they possessed the thoracic sonar, a genetic enhancement exclusive to warhorses, originally designed as a weapon capable of producing destructive sonic blasts which Majun used mostly for guidance in the dark.

Majun opened his eyes when the taste of rancid morosity and decayed blood in the water of the suburbs was replaced by the one of exasperation and dust, which revealed downtown Niwri bathed by the burgundy lights of early morning. The view didn't disappoint him. The news on the official radio stations often spewed lies, but for once they had told the truth: a bomb had detonated inside Niwri Processing Center. What used to be an expansive, rectangular building of coral bricks that stood out amid the smaller constructions surrounding it now looked more like a straight triangle whose hypotenuse had been drawn by a shaking pen. The building's remains still seemed to be operational, with a constant flux in and out of other Nahs. The chunky, red, bioengineered seahorses like Majun were too busy patrolling the city center in lockdown to stop and frisk Majun, as he looked and swam like one of their own. He also caught sight of the naturally golden Nahs, who were mostly female. Not that one could see their color. Under the light of the red sun, warhorses were red and other Nahs were black. Within the half-destroyed building's lobby, however, the artificial lights were white and Majun could see the true color of a golden female at a reception desk as she welcomed him.

"Good morning. How can I help you, soldier?"

"I'm not a soldier," Majun promptly informed her. Being forced to re-enlist in the republican army had been one of the concerns related to this visit to the core of local power, but if the rumor was true, such risk was worth taking.

"And what brings you here, then?" asked the clerk as she scanned Majun from head to the tip of his prehensile tail. Her tone implied that she was not interested in listening to an actual answer to her question but to a password that would trigger her diligence. Luckily for Majun, he knew very well the mindset of these bureaucrats.

"I am here to be of service for the Nation's more urgent needs in these times!" enunciated Majun with the somewhat over-the-top martial bravado that was expected from his kind. For a moment Majun was afraid that it had been too over-the-top, but soon the clerk's snout motioned approvingly. He might not be a soldier, but he would always be a Warhorse in the eyes of his Nah Republic's fellow citizens.

* * *

The clerk ushered Majun into the confines of the building, through corridors filled with doorways which were guarded by fellow warhorses who never moved their gaze away from the empty spaces ahead of them even when he and the clerk passed by. The clerk stopped swimming by a doorway guarded not by one or two, but six warhorses.

"Doctor Niannun was informed of your arrival as well as your offer and is gratefully waiting for you inside, sir," informed the clerk. "Thank you for your service."

Majun nodded stoically to the clerk, as it was expected of him and, to his surprise, the six soldiers turned their until then blank stares to him and nodded back in the same fashion. As Majun had seen the gesture back in his bootcamp days, he understood that it was a sign of respect and reverence for his purpose in the building. It was a gesture given to the warhorses that finished their training and were shipped to the war frontline. Hence, it was particularly unsettling for Majun to be himself the target of the gesture by fellow bioengineered warhorses, as if he was a soldier like them. In a certain way, he was in a war, although not the kind known to them. And certainly not on their side.

Majun left the soldiers and his perplexity behind as he passed through the heavily guarded doorway and found himself in a vast laboratory, filled with cryogenic compartments and a small regiment of scientists roaming frantically around the room as they inventoried the property that had survived the recent subversive attack. The only scientist in the room that didn't seem to be overloaded with chores was a female whose golden plates were whitened by age. She began scrutinizing Majun thoroughly as soon as he entered the room.

"You must be Doctor Niannun," said Majun, as he approached her.

"That's correct. Thank you very much for your sacrifice."

"It's my duty," affirmed Majun, emulating the detached resolution that was expected from him.

"I must ask first before we initiate the procedure, how did you become aware of our current need for healthy males?"

"My brothers told me," said Majun. He had prepared himself for that one.

"Brothers, huh. I was told that you were not currently serving."

"We stay in touch, ma'am."

"That leads to another question, if you don't mind. I was also informed that you aren't currently lending your obvious physical assets in our war effort beyond the trench."

"I work on a seaweed farm."

"Don't farms have machinery for the heavy lifting?"

"I work as a guard, ma'am. In case you are not aware, terrorists covet our food stock."

If Doctor Niannun weren't facing Majun he would have noticed that her dorsal fin had been nervously motioning up and down until he enunciated this last sentence, as its plausibility quenched her concerns.

"Not only our food stocks, I'm afraid," said the Doctor, as she swam to a table where a series of medical instruments were set up in organized display. "They blew up all the South wing, where we stored the artificial brood tanks. We have the embryos right here, but no machinery to develop them."

"I know."

Doctor Niannun's dorsal fin tensed up, and this time Majun noticed it.

"How can you know? I just shared with you very classified intel."

"Because I saw the damage from outside, ma'am," improvised Majun, doing his best to keep the stoic façade. "And as you may know, I was conceived in this very building."

Doctor Niannun gave Majun a lingering stare, but soon her dorsal fin shrugged her concerns away.

"Usually we would need to interview that 'brother' of yours who sent you our way, but to be fair we are not really in a situation where I can spare a very fine male specimen like yourself. One who shows up voluntarily, no less. Until we can manufacture more development tanks for fertilized embryos, we have no choice but to rely on patriots like yourself, sir."

"It's an honor."

Doctor Niannun used the tip of her prehensile tail to grab a long metallic instrument and swam back toward Majun.

"Now, this may be a little uncomfortable, but I assure you the process is totally safe."

And with that the Doctor inserted the metallic stick inside Majun's tiny opening leading to his brood pouch. Warhorses like Majun were bioengineered with a working brood pouch precisely for social emergencies like the one this province of the Nah Republic was facing. However, unlike the non-bioengineered male Nahs, warhorses didn't have control over the pouch opening. Only the ministration of instruments and techniques, that were maybe the greatest and best-kept secret of the Nah Republic, would allow that. And the knowledge of such a secretive medical procedure was exclusive to the few members of the upper crust of the Nah Republic's medical corporation. Doctor Niannun was part of this elite who knew how to make warhorses viable for the reception of fertilized embryos.

The first thing Majun realized just after Doctor Niannun inserted her metallic instrument was that she had lied about the pain. It hurt sharply. But he could take the pain. What was hard was the humiliation of the whole process, the intrusion, the fact that she took his body as a granted asset for the probing, the poking and procedural steps to suit the Nah Republic's needs. Majun wasn't violent; if he were, he would probably have served. But for once he had an urge to blow Doctor Niannun away from him with a sonic blast produced by his thoracic sonar. Majun had never used his sonar as a weapon, but he had seen other warhorses doing so on non-Nahs who had made the mistake of crossing their path. He never partook in the eerie glee at the sight of the mangled outcome of their destructive action.

After a few minutes, however, Majun noticed that the painful prodding relented at the same time as a part of his body, which had always been hard and unwavering, was now blossoming. He didn't expect the brood pouch to expand so fast, but that was precisely what was happening. He could now control its opening and feel its interior filling up with the liquids necessary to protect and nourish embryos. For once, a part of his bulky, oversized body seemed to have a purpose other than demonstrating physical strength, enduring damage or performing brutality.

Majun was too mesmerized by the change in his own body to pay heed to the fact that one of Doctor Niannun's aides was pushing a cart filled with embryos. They were spherical translucent red eggs with a circumference equivalent to the size of his eye. There were more or less one thousand of them and Majun paid close attention as Doctor Niannun started unceremoniously shoving the embryos inside his pouch without any warning. His instinct was to clinch the opening of his pouch, now that he controlled it, but he knew that he couldn't take any liberty until his role as an incubator had been asserted to the delegates of the Nah Republic. Finally, when the cart had been emptied and Majun's pouch was full, Doctor Niannun announced:

"You should rest now."

"Thank you, Doctor. I will see myself to the exit."

"We prepared a room for you, sir."

Majun was taken aback. The plan was to make his pouch operational even if for that he had to let them fill it with seahorse embryos and then leave the facility.

"You don't need to worry, Doctor, I made arrangements to rest at the farm."

"I'm sure that in normal circumstances you could defend yourself, but the incubation will make you very vulnerable. We can't afford to lose that brood."

Asserting Doctor Niannun's point, two soldiers entered the facility and immediately flanked Majun.

"They will show you to your room, sir. Please rest, the first hours of incubation are the most crucial ones."

Majun allowed the two warhorses to escort him out of the lab and back to the hallway he had entered from. They passed through many of the doors that had diligent soldiers stationed in front of them, until they parked at an unguarded one. One of the soldiers opened it, revealing a small room in which a male Nah was lying on the ground, the redness of the growing embryos in his dilated brood pouch vividly contrasting with the gold of his plates. A gold that was paling, as he was dying.

"I thought this room was empty! Why are there no guards posted here?" barked one of the warhorses.

"It doesn't matter, it's not like this little guy can go anywhere," said the second warhorse as he callously assessed the dying Nah inside the room.

"We thank you for your sacrifice, sir," said the first warhorse, before closing the door, "Let's find you another room, shall—

As he turned back, looking for Majun, the soldier noticed that he was nowhere nearby.

In fact, Majun had used their distraction to first slowly retreat in the most inconspicuous way possible, and then swim away, but not the way back to the main entrance, as he knew that pathway was littered with soldiers. Instead Majun went deeper into the building, barreling through the labyrinth of corridors hoping that his guess would pay off. The few soldiers in his path quickly gave way in order to not be hit by their fellow charging warhorse. The blaring emergency alarm was only turned on when Majun reached the end of a damaged corridor that was covered by a seaweed tarp, which he crossed through quickly, emerging amid the ruins in the wing of the building that had been damaged in the previous night's attack.

At the other side he could see scattered soldiers turning their attention to him. He was no longer one of them, he was a suspicious element as he was acting suspiciously. Majun didn't stop as the soldiers approached him, though. He swam without looking back, even when sonic blasts coming from pursuing warhorses barreled from his right and left, high and low, affecting his pace as the blasts churned around him with enough potency to break his abnormally reinforced plates if hit. Majun minimized such odds by swimming in a diagonal line, ahead and up toward the bright red sun that blinded his pursuers. At the same time they couldn't afford to use their sonars for orientation, since, unlike Majun, the soldiers were using the bioengineered inner organ with such ability to shoot sonic blasts at him. Majun knew that launching the sonic blasts was physically exhausting, and was counting on them to tire from the use and abuse of their terrible weapon.

Only when Majun reached the heights of the water close to the surface, where the sunlight was too bright and the pressure was so low that it made him lightheaded, did he dare to look back both with his eyes and sonar to confirm what he hoped: his pursuers had lost him. He was safe for now, but he had to keep moving to reach his destination. The sprint had ended, and now the marathon started.

Majun resumed swimming, this time more slowly even though he was still in a rush – he could feel the embryos churning inside his brood pouch, draining his energy. His destination was far, at least a half-day journey that would be easier had he been at a more comfortable depth and without the extra weight. Majun propelled himself ahead, cursing the heat and low pressure but resisting the temptation to sink to more reasonable depths. Doing so wouldn't relieve the sudden pang that he started feeling in his brood pouch which nobody had warned him about. Majun kept moving, he had to keep moving, both despite and because of his prickly load. His eyelids were heavy and he closed his eyes. He didn't need to see. All he needed was to move, to keep moving as he endured that atrocious pain caused by what felt like growing spikes tearing through his innards.

Suddenly, Majun's closed eyelids shone with bright, furious light. He was no longer in a vertical position, swimming to his destination. His body was now horizontally positioned and his head now faced the sun, which was still very high, fiery and red above him with just a sliver of water to shield Majun from it. A sliver that became thicker and thicker as he was sinking due to exhaustion. The light brightening his eyelids became progressively dimmer as his body descended into the darker depths of the ocean and his mind drifted to the obscure realms of unconsciousness. Majun's last thought before he passed out was how he hated that sun.

* * *

The mangroves were a shallow area in which enormous aquatic vegetation grew beyond the point where the liquid world ended and the inhospitable open air started. The shallowness and the relatively high levels of sulfur that plants in the area released made it a place not often patrolled by the Nah Republic and the perfect hideout for persecuted non-Nahs or Nahs that had left the horrors of their militaristic republic behind. Among the Nahs living in that community, Majun had been the only warhorse. This was the only place in the world Majun could call home and that's where he woke up, in a secluded space so deep into the roots that the only light came from a luminescent, white jellyfish attached to the wall by its tendrils. Majun was glad he was back, even if everything in his body hurt.

As Majun became more aware of his surroundings, he could feel that he was being intimately touched, although not with the precise harshness of Doctor Niannun. There was caution and tenderness in the careful ministrations that, as his vision adjusted, were being performed by Berenna, a familiar face and the community doctor. Berenna also happened to be a Aygnihor refugee, which could be noticeable by the purple and teal color of her plates. She was using her relatively short, slender, prehensile tail to remove the embryos from inside his brood pouch. Her touch was delicate, but his pouch still hurt.

"Some of our foragers saw a big, red thing sinking from the surface," said Berenna. "Turned out it was you,"

"I'm sorry."

"Sorry for what? You made it. The plan worked, although I was not expecting this…"

The red embryos that Berenna was removing were covered in spikes and seemed like small urchins. That certainly explained the pain he had felt on the way.

"They were round when Doctor Niannun stuffed me with them," pointed out a puzzled Majun.

"I had never seen a warhorse embryo until now," explained Berenna. "I guess they are bioengineered to develop spikes to kill the host and damage the pouch, precisely to prevent what we are going to do … that is … if you still want to."

"Am I still viable?"

"Yes, but as I said, I was not expecting the warhorse embryos to shred your flesh from inside. The chemistry is still right for hosting, but—"

"Then yes."

"The damage in your pouch is quite widespread. There will be risks—"

"For the refugees' embryos?"

"For you!"

"It doesn't matter."

"I can patch you up and you can heal for sure if we don't force more stress upon your body. Nobody would blame you if you changed your mind."

"Stick to your role and I will stick to mine, Berenna."

Berenna removed her tail from inside Majun's pouch, taking out another spiked embryo and tossing it on a pile leaning against a large submerged leaf.

"That was the last one. Are you sure you want to do it?"

"Whenever you are ready."

"The sooner we do it, the better the odds … for the embryos."

Majun nodded almost meekly, feeling a certain weakness overtaking him. Berenna signaled to a few refugees that were looking at them through the cracks between the roots. They nodded back to her and swam to fetch their first guests.

The first couple to enter was a chartreuse and white Ruhgiu couple. The male's brood pouch had been torn from his body, as it had happened to many ethnic and national minorities who fell under the clutches of the Nah Republic. Only a few shredded tatters remained at the edge of his belly. The Ruhgius were seen as a threat because they happened to share the same space but not the same colors the Nahs bore. For others, reproduction was denied because they had come to this side of the trench to escape their land after it had been depleted of its natural resources in order to ensure the prosperity of the Nah Republic and the financial stability of its military industrial complex. So many other colors and other traditions that were not acceptable were terminated, so the natural gold and the bioengineered red could prevail for the glorious sake of prevalence.

The male Ruhgiu bowed respectfully to Majun as the female approached Berenna with a handful of her own embryos in need of a brood pouch. Berenna inserted them, one by one, inside Majun's pouch. The future of their people was going to be hatched thanks to and within the body of the one that had been built to be their annihilator. The couple left and soon was replaced by a turquoise and green Xnital couple, then plain mauve Druks, then black, white and green Nainitselaps, then another Druk couple, then purple and teal Aygnihors like Berenna. Dozens of couples of all the colors the Nah Empire didn't bear, bringing their embryos until Majun's pouch was full.

"What now?" asked Majun, feeling the slosh of thriving embryos inside him and satisfied with the prospect that none of those would develop spikes that would tear him apart from inside.

"Hopefully the cuts caused by the warhorse embryos will heal. The hormonal chemistry involved in the embryo development will help in that process. But … it's still a process that will demand a great amount of energy from your body."

"They made me to be strong."

Berenna looked away, an expression of guilt in her face that Majun didn't fail to notice.

"It was my choice, Berenna. I knew that I could have died when I entered the processing center, or during my escape. If they had captured me, I'd have died trying, and that would be satisfying. But I made it back alive. Now, if I die after I ensure that this world has the colors it was meant to have … Then I will be dying with a purpose. I will not only die satisfied: I will die happy."

"Enough of that morbid talk! I'm going to give my best to keep you alive, big guy."

"Can I tell you a story, Berenna?"

"You can rest."

"Please, just listen."

Berenna rolled her tail around a smaller root, getting comfortable. Majun had her undivided attention.

"Be brief, you must spare your energy from now on."

"I read once that there was a time our sun was much smaller than it is right now. It was a golden sun, golden like the original Nahs, not red, like me and the warhorses. Our planet, on the other hand, was just a dead ball of ice. But then, through many, many thousands of years, that star became red and big, its heat reaching the gelid distances of our solar system where our planet is. That made the ice on our planet melt, creating the oceans, and making life possible. You know why that star expanded?"

"I'm a medic, not an astronomer."

"Because the star started to die. It's still dying. Stars grow when they die, but at the end, they will shrink and be smaller than ever. One day the oceans of our planet will freeze again. This time for good."

"Why are you telling me this?"

Majun didn't answer. He closed his eyes, his eyelids heavy.

"I'm cold."

Berenna immediately grabbed a woven seaweed blanket and wrapped as much of Majun's body in it as she could. Even though the blanket was too small for him, Majun quietly fell asleep.

"Rest now, warhorse. Your battle is over," Berenna gently whispered as she left the room to fetch a bigger blanket for Majun.

Of Aspic and Other Things

Beáta Fülöp

ONCE UPON A TIME, before there was a railroad to Miskolc, a tired traveller stopped at a roadside inn. It was winter, freezing cold, and the poor traveller longed for a good meal and a warm bed. He ordered a bowl of aspic, and rejoiced that it was served quickly. The traveller took his spoon. He poked the meat, and dropped the spoon with a shriek.

The meat blinked back at him.

The whole inn turned at the traveller's scream. The waitress abandoned the beer she was about to serve, and hurried over.

There was a frog sitting in the aspic. The poor animal had jumped into a bowl of nice, warm soup, and as the soup had cooled and turned to jelly, the frog got trapped in it.

Till the end of their days, the people in the inn would love to remember the story of the blinking aspic frog, and no matter how often they told it, it remained just as entertaining. The years passed. First the railroad, later long-distance teleportation replaced the long, tiring road trips. Strict laws regulated the quality of restaurant foods. No more frogs got to the soup. But the people of Miskolc remembered.

First just a funny story, then urban legend, the blinking aspic frog got its own yearly festival in the early 2000s. Ever since, there is each year a market held in Miskolc, where you can buy not only delicious aspic, but also all kinds of frog-themed memorabilia. Toys for children, fridge magnets and postcards for adults. Digital frog holograms, and indeed, they really do blink. And of course porcelain frogs that you can put into your own aspic, as decoration.

The people of Miskolc remember, no matter where they live. Be it Miskolc, other parts of the country, or even the ones who left the planet in search of a new home among the stars.

Everyone remembers the blinking frog.

* * *

It should be around the time of the Aspic Festival, thought Chief Engineer Tót Krisztina, as she stared out of the window. It was the only real window on the whole spaceship, and completely useless. Nothing could ever be seen through it. Space was black and empty, and even when they passed a star, they went too fast for the light to reach them. Therefore, instead of windows, most rooms had screens with full-time projected scenery pictures. It was good this way. The emptiness of space had driven too many people crazy back in the early days of space travel. Kriszta was the only one on board who kept climbing up to the stargazer deck to look out of the window.

She found it comforting. Or, it would be more precise to say, if she stared long enough into the void, Kriszta would sink into a kind of trance not unlike meditation. At least according to Charel, and Charel would know, as he was the ship's doctor.

And so Kriszta climbed up to the stargazer deck, stared out of the window, and let her thoughts roam. And this is what she was doing on that day, when after a long time, she remembered the Aspic Festival again. *It should be around now*, she thought, despite never having participated in it herself, despite time passing differently in space once you surpassed lightspeed. Since the early days of space travel, astronauts would use the stardate-system for measuring time, which was a lot easier and more coherent than trying to match any one planet's time zones. This of course didn't stop people from trying. And so Kriszta was sure that it was around the time of the Aspic Festival.

She herself only knew it from stories. Her parents had left the planet when Kriszta was still too young to really understand what was happening to her. She didn't have many memories, just a few, about trees and snow and her old room. And suddenly, they were on a space station. Later, they moved on to a real planet, a few solar systems away. Her family was happy there. It was just Kriszta who decided that she preferred being on a ship. When she was old enough, she enrolled in the local space work academy. And that's how she ended up next to that window a decade later.

It was a mediocre ship, designed to carry both passengers and cargo. Cargo paid better, therefore they didn't see many passengers. Kriszta's responsibility was to the machines, which is always the most important job on a spaceship. The captain may be responsible for the coordination of the personnel, but the mechanics, they keep the whole thing functioning. Everyone knows this. The *Theseus* had a little group of five engineers with Kriszta at the head. Besides them there were, according to regulation, a scientist, a sociologist slash communication expert, a doctor, a pilot, a trained ship's guard, and of course the owner of the ship, the captain. They didn't do many interesting things, mostly they were just transporting cargo between different space docks. But Kriszta liked the calm and the routine, and she found both in the dark of space.

"I *knew* that you would be here!"

Kriszta turned in the direction of the voice. The ship's guard, Charlotte, was standing in the door, with a tray in her hand

"You forgot dinner again, so I brought you something."

"I wasn't hungry."

This wasn't entirely true. Kriszta never really thought of food. Left to her own devices, she only remembered that she had to eat when she was already dizzy for lack of sugar. Luckily for her, meals were also part of the ship's routine, and so she almost never reached that point. Except of course when she skipped meals, and so she could call herself really lucky that Charlotte was so attentive.

Charlotte sat down next to her, and pushed the tray into her hands. It was pasta with carbonara sauce.

"Are you afraid of the new passengers? I talked a little to them, they are completely normal, nice people."

"I don't like strangers," said Kriszta.

"They really are a bit noisy, and they keep getting in the way," admitted Charlotte. "But I think you'd get along well with at least a few of them. Imagine, one of them is Hungarian!"

This caught Kriszta's attention. She didn't really have any Hungarian acquaintances. Her parent's settlement was almost always multiple sun systems away from her, and even when she did visit, she didn't have the time to make friends with neighbours. The astronaut profession itself was very multicultural, and on the ship, everyone could trace their origins to a different country.

"Oh?"

Charlotte nodded.

"One of the Muslim girls. She's called Ibolya," She pronounced the name carefully. Her accent softened the hard vowels, so the name sounded like *Ibójá*.

"Ibolya," corrected Kriszta.

"Ibójá," repeated Charlotte.

Charlotte came from a French colony, but her great-grandparents emigrated from Senegal, and she was proud of both her heritages. She was a strong woman. Short, but muscular, like her job required her to be. The ship's guards were the crewmembers who knew how to fight. They were the only ones on board to have weapons, and their job was to protect the cargo in the less safe space docks. The *Theseus* avoided those, and Charlotte generally had almost nothing to do. She didn't particularly mind, as, despite having a certain combativeness in her personality, she enjoyed simulated sports games much more than actual action. Those, however, she loved enough to infect the entire crew. The *Theseus* was such a good ship to be on, in part exactly because Charlotte made them do sports. She was a great trainer, and much more useful as such than she was as a ship's guard.

"I'll talk with her tomorrow," announced Kriszta.

It would be nice to be able to speak Hungarian with someone again.

* * *

The first thing that Kriszta saw of Ibolya was the color red. She was just leaving her room, wearing an ankle-long burka, with a fitting hijab. Both of them red, decorated with white lace.

Kriszta almost had a heart attack.

"*What the hell are you wearing*?!"

Ibolya looked down at herself in stunned surprise, then at the strange woman who'd started to yell at her for absolutely no reason. Kriszta forced herself to take some deep breaths and continue in a more normal tone.

"Red clothes in space?! Do you want to kill us all?!"

"Wha… What???"

"Never, *never* wear red clothes on a spaceship. It brings bad luck."

Ibolya looked weirdly at her, but Kriszta stared back until the passenger went back to her room to change. Two minutes later, she was back out, in similar clothes, only this time, both her burka and her hijab were silvery grey. Kriszta sighed deeply.

"Sorry," she said. "Old superstition. In space, red clothes bring bad luck."

"Why?" asked Ibolya.

Kriszta shrugged. "Who knows. But there are all kinds of horror stories about astronauts who broke this rule. None of them survived."

"I didn't think that space travellers would be superstitious."

Kriszta shrugged again. "You spend enough time staring into the nothing, you will acquire some weird habits. It helps against the meaninglessness of the universe. Then you pass them on to the others. Did you have breakfast yet?"

Now that Ibolya's clothes were no longer endangering the crew's life, Kriszta quickly discovered that she was fun to talk to. Ibolya was a cheerful, open girl. She and her friends were celebrating their journalism diplomas with a round trip to various space colonies. Until now, she had spent her entire life on Earth, and she was very impressed by the diversity of the space colonies.

"So you are Hungarian too?" she asked finally. By then, they had both finished breakfast, and were sitting at the table with a cup of tea each. "Do you speak Hungarian?"

"It's my mother language," nodded Kriszta. Then, "We could actually talk in Hungarian."

"Ah yes, right…"

* * *

Just as it usually is when two compatriots meet somewhere abroad, Kriszta and Ibolya stuck together almost naturally. While they compared the stories of their lives, Kriszta showed Ibolya around the ship.

They'd both grown up in the same suburb, went to kindergarten and later primary school together. They'd learned similar things. Their caretakers had read them the same stories, they'd used the same songs to try and help them remember the alphabet and the one times one. But the differences had been there already, and only kept growing as the two girls got older. At thirteen, Kriszta'd sung different songs to Ibolya, and neither knew the band that'd had the biggest impact on the other one's life. They did both know the most famous movies, but those weren't Hungarian. The colony Z11 had specialized in movie-making quickly after its foundation, and had since attracted the most talented professionals from who knows how many countries. There were a few Hungarians among them, and they'd done some good work, but the most expensive, most successful movies all starred Z11's hybrid culture. They were equally far away from Kriszta's and Ibolya's life experiences.

A few days later, Kriszta was sitting once more on the stargazer deck, staring into the nothingness of space. Ibolya's presence had awakened in her one of the bigger questions of her existence, one that she always tried to avoid. Was she even still Hungarian? What did that term even mean? The inhabitants of her colony were proud of their roots. But since Kriszta'd left her home, she'd travelled a lot, and had seen much. Many Hungarians, too. And they all had been different, depending on their home planets. They all spoke the same language, and had some other cultural experiences in common. But the ones that had the biggest impact on them? The works of the writer Gonçalves from New Rio, the best movies from Z11, a video game where they had to play farmers in a virtual simulation? None of these had anything to do with Hungary. They were universal.

There were, however, some things, especially from Kriszta's childhood years, that her friends on the ship did not know. Ludas Matyi. Vuk the fox. The two red birds singing fairy tales. About these things, she could only talk with the other Hungarians she encountered in the vastness of space. They usually didn't stay near each other for very long.

But with Ibolya, they were stuck together. Their first reflex of course had been to become immediate best friends. Kriszta was not the only one doing this; Charlotte had the same reaction to the French. But Ibolya was around for long enough for Kriszta to start noticing their differences. It wasn't necessarily a negative experience; they spent many interesting hours showing each other their own cultural products. Kriszta was used to long, monotonous trips, yet this time, time just flew by, and she composed a nice, long list with interesting things for the future. But behind all the joy was the realization of just how much she didn't know about her home country. She'd never even seen it, except for virtual simulations.

In that case, could she actually call herself a Hungarian?

Kriszta sighed, and leaned with her back against the wall. Space was dark and empty.

Every child of Earth colonies learned about the ancient Greeks, some more, some less. Each colony, each city-state was unique, with sometimes astonishingly different values. Yet their inhabitants still considered themselves Greek, and in an emergency, they held together and helped each other.

Should Hungary be recruiting tomorrow, would Kriszta volunteer?

She knew enough people who loved the idea of fighting a bloody battle to defend the land of their ancestors. But Kriszta was a realist. She was convinced that said acquaintances didn't actually know what a real war really meant. The way they talked sounded more as if they'd be fighting dragons and giants instead of other humans. Humans, who'd be just like them. Like all their friends and family from every corner of the universe. Humans, who only ended up on the other side of the fire by some coincidence.

The problems of Hungary had always seemed so far away. Kriszta didn't really follow their news, but when she occasionally had a look, she was greeted by unfamiliar faces, problems and in-fights. She had, of course, some opinions about Hungarian politics, but she fully recognized that they didn't matter. She didn't have the birth background, and the the effect on her own life of decisions taken at home was so minimal…

In that case, what was left? What was it that so strongly bound her and Ibolya? A common language, some fairy tales, half a dozen children's songs.

Kriszta sighed again.

* * *

"Message from planet YW410!"

Kriszta crawled out from under the main engine. She'd been woken that morning to three of her colleagues pounding on her door, screaming about the engine making strange sounds. Kriszta'd run to the engine room in her nightgown, and didn't rest until she determined that the problem was one of the tubes being too old. Kriszta'd sworn loudly in three languages mixed together, then sent a message to the captain. There wasn't a replacement on board, and because of patenting reasons, the replicators were blocked from making the metal alloy needed. And so she and her team had spent the rest of the morning trying their best to contain the volatile engine. Kriszta was now not only dressed in clothes that didn't belong there, she was also covered from head to toe with oil spots.

YW410 was their next travel destination, three days ahead. It would have been two under normal circumstances, but Kriszta refused to push the engine. That very moment, its sound mostly resembled the purring of a cat, which was a good indicator that it wasn't about to explode. However, in normal circumstances, the engine was not supposed to make any sounds at all, so … better not take any risks.

A cheerful advertisement clip appeared on the screen, enthusiastically inviting every ship nearby to the 200th YW410 intercultural celebration. Everyone was very welcome to participate in the competition to present their culture to the larger audience. Those not feeling like doing this could just walk around quietly in the market or visit expositions and performances. All in all, a big, four-day party to celebrate the diversity of the human race, both on the planet and intergalactically. Entrance was free.

Kriszta felt the excitement running through her colleagues. As space travellers, they'd all seen many an intercultural celebration. They adored them. For one, they liked anything that broke the monotony of everyday life on the ship. Also, their captain was usually willing to stay a little longer when there was some event happening at a dock, which meant a few surprise days off. Apart from this, there were quite a few people on the crew of the *Theseus* who were very proud of their own cultural inheritance, and always participated obsessively in every single culture-presenting competition. Just among the engineers, there were three Chinese who with their common performance had already won a couple of times.

Clothes were popular. So was music and dance. Successfully presenting history and artists was already more difficult, but that didn't stop many people from trying. But the most popular was, for whatever reason, food. Everyone had their own national specialities that reminded them of home, and many were very eager to shove it at other people, as if the taste alone would be capable of explaining the feelings they connected with it.

Ibolya appeared to be one of them. She was beaming with excitement when she came looking for Kriszta around lunchtime. Ah. Right. They'd been planning on eating together. Very carefully, Kriszta went down on all fours and crawled out from a hidden corner.

"We could prepare something for the celebration, too! Maybe something tasty?"

"If you say 'goulash', I'll hit you over the head with this atomic screwdriver," threatened Kriszta. It was not a very effective threat, as atomic screwdrivers were thin, fragile tools. Ibolya's head would have come away unscratched and Kriszta in need of a new screwdriver.

"What? You mean the soup? No, why would you … It has pork in it! No, I was actually thinking of pogacha."

Pogacha! Just at the mention of it, Kriszta's mouth started to water. Maybe she shouldn't have skipped lunch after all. Good, tasty pogacha … She hadn't had any in a very long time, and for a good reason: The replicators were programmed for Earth pogacha, not that of her home.

"Why, is there a difference?" asked Ibolya when Kriszta shared this thought with her.

"*Anya* always says that our flour is different, because of the soil. And we use goat's milk and cheese. Goats survive more easily, we didn't have that much luck with cows."

"I only know the Earth recipe."

"All right, then make that. But make sure to reserve the kitchen at once, because it will be full by the time you get there."

The ship had a little kitchen, for emergencies. In theory. In practice, it was for recreation. Barely anyone used it, but these festivals usually banned replicated food, claiming that it went against their philosophy of intercultural sharing.

"Don't you want to make anything?" asked Ibolya.

Kriszta shrugged. "Not really, no. My parents are from Miskolc, so we always made aspic for these events. But I don't really feel like it right now, and besides…"

"I've never been to Miskolc! I didn't even know that their aspic is famous. And of course I couldn't eat it anyway."

"Right, pork. So this one time, a frog got frozen in a bowl of aspic…"

Ibolya laughed. Then she jumped pretty high, when next to her the engine suddenly crowed.

"*Hogy az a…!*" swore Kriszta, and delivered a huge kick into a metal box. The voice broke up mid-crow, and the engine just clucked a few times.

"So these next few days I certainly won't have time for anything. Sorry."

"Is everything all right?" Ibolya asked in a slightly strange tone.

Kriszta looked her conversational partner up and down. That day, Ibolya was wearing light yellow. Her burka, like always, neatly covered her from wrists to ankles, and not a lock of her hair was visible under her hijab. In contrast, Kriszta was still in her knee-long nightshirt. It was not only full of oil stains, but also torn in multiple places. Her hair was standing in a hundred directions. Her mother would call it a "bird's nest", except that birds' nests had significantly less motor oil in them. Everyone else in the machinery room was looking very similar.

"Yes, yes, just a little problem with the engine. Listen, Ibolya, I really love talking to you, but maybe it's better for you not to be in here."

Ibolya nodded, and left the room.

* * *

The next three days both lasted forever and passed in no time. The engine kept making strange sounds, and Kriszta and her team had to be on high alert round the clock. There was some time left for them to eat and sleep, and Charlotte took her responsibility as security person very seriously by making sure that the engineers didn't overwork themselves. She had to force Kriszta to take breaks at least five separate times, and by the time they docked, she was just as frustrated with her friend as Kriszta was with the engine. Everyone took a collective deep breath when the ship finally docked.

The passengers were fine. They were young, adventurous people, and very excited about the next station on their trip. The fact that the captain had ordered segregation to shield them from the crew's wounded nerves also helped.

Some of them had prepared something for the intercultural festival, and Ibolya'd brought Kriszta some of the first baking tray full of pogacha. It was good. Not as good as the one from home, but still good. Nothing from that first baking tray made it to the festival, as Ibolya distributed it all to her friends and the members of the crew. The second portion saw the same fate. Some of the third actually made it into stasis. Some more trays, and Ibolya managed to accumulate enough for her to be able to set up a stand at the festival.

"Are you sure you don't want to come down?" Charlotte asked, standing in Kriszta's door. It was dark in her room, despite it being daytime elsewhere. The moment they'd docked, the entire engineering team had excused themselves and fallen into bed. One look at the clock told Kriszta that this had been a little over a day ago.

"Too many people," she mumbled, and tried to turn her back to her friend. Charlotte didn't let her off the hook so easily.

"Not really," she argued cheerfully. "It's still a workday here. Come on, Kriszta! At least take a look at Ibolya's stand. You know it would mean a lot to her!"

It would. She'd really been neglecting her new friend these past few days, and they would have to part ways soon. This finally convinced Kriszta to get up.

Charlotte was right, it did do her good to have a change of scenery. The weather on YW410 was very nice, and there was a little wind blowing. The stands lining the street were selling textiles, small artefacts, music and books. And food, so, so much food!

Ibolya's stand was mildly successful. Kriszta stopped to talk to her, while Charlotte wandered on to look at some original YW410 novels. They talked a little, exchanged contact information. Strange how they hadn't done so before.

"How long are you staying?" asked Kriszta.

"A week, probably. And you?"

"Depends on when we can get that pipe … I'm not sure if I'll come back down to the surface again."

Ibolya nodded, unsurprised. By then, she already knew Kriszta and her autism well enough.

They said goodbye with the promise to stay in touch and the knowledge that they wouldn't. Kriszta wandered away, looking at all the bright cultures displaying themselves.

Then she stopped dead.

Over there, under a red-leafed tree, a little group were selling aspic. Right in the middle of the bowl sat a ceramic frog.

Danae

Elana Gomel

I HATED MY ADOPTIVE PARENTS.

Not because they were mean and abusive: Lora and Sander were kind to me. But once they told me the truth, I hated them for making me believe I was human.

The day Lora told me I had been adopted on a Lost Colony was the last day I called her "Mama". To mollify me, she brought home a small telescope which, I later realized, she must have bought on the black market. The Our Home authorities did not encourage stargazing though it was not made illegal until much later. So, I started spending long hours in our suburban garden filled with tamed glass Glowers, looking at the Spiral as the suns set. I often remembered these evenings later on.

The transparent bells of glass flowers flushed with vermillion as Sol and Solara dipped behind the horizon. The sky faded to peach and rose. Lonely stars winked on here and there on the margins of the sky-wide glow. And finally, the glow faded, and the Spiral blazed forth: a tight weave of numberless stars like the DNA of a god.

I would stare at it for hours. My toy telescope was too weak to show any planets in the cluster. But I believed that if I just looked hard enough, I could find it.

Home. Not Our Home. Mine.

Once Lora let me stay in the garden too late. That was the first time I saw ghost cats. They crept over the fence in a living carpet of silvery bodies, joined together like pieces of a puzzle, their limbs slotted into each other's sides. I watched, spellbound, as the carpet fell apart into a swarm of blind floppy creatures, their tubular snouts plunged into the crystal blooms of glass flowers. A cloud of golden pollen rose into the air like a miniature reflection of the Spiral overhead. The pheromones of the flowers, as sweet as pink sugar, attracted the pollinators and enabled them to reproduce.

"Dana!" Lora came out and dragged me indoors. I resisted: I wanted to see this strange interaction, but she was unusually firm, pointing to a large charcoal worm half-hidden among the swarm.

"Night crawlers are poisonous," she said.

It was true, but later I wondered whether she had an ulterior motive for whisking me away.

* * *

When I hit adolescence, I went through the phase of refusing to be called "Dana". Lora was upset.

"Remember the book of Old Earth tales?" she said. "You liked it so much. Your name was taken from there."

The book had fallen apart long ago and disappeared into the black hole of discarded memories.

"It's not my real name," I insisted.

"Then what should we call you, darling?"

And I did not reply because I did not know.

They divorced after I went to uni. Sander relocated to a tiny settlement called Spear on the northernmost tip of Hearth, Patria's only continent, where it was so cold that water froze and lay on the ground in brittle sheets like giant glass-flower petals. I did not know where Lora was. I did not want to see her. I could not forgive her for playing the role of my mother so well.

After I finished my studies, I started working as a technician in the Air and Communication Bureau. It was as close as I could get to spaceflight. While there was some talk about resuming flights to the purified planets in the Spiral, the project had little support in the Duma and none in public opinion.

I was a good technician because I had no life outside my job. I did not date. I did not plan on amassing enough Social Credits to be allowed to have a child. My birth certificate, listing Sander and Lora as my biological parents, looked real enough. But they had told me it was a fake, and I dared not put it to the test.

I did go on a date once. The man was suggested to me by the intrusive Registry of Mankind, the demographic bureaucracy that periodically sent letters to all singles on Patria, encouraging us to do our patriotic duty to mate and produce genetically pure human children. We met in a bar, and when I saw the Our Home pin on his jacket, I knew it was a mistake. But it was too late to retreat, and so we spent an uncomfortable hour trying to make small talk. He astonished me by asking for my comm ID at the end of the date.

"There is something about you..." he said wistfully. "You look ... different."

I gave him a fake number and, back home, studied my face in the mirror. Was I different? Was there some sign of my true origin in my face? Was my nose too long, my eyes too dark, my hair too crinkly? Was that the reason Lora and Sander had told me the truth? After all, they did not have to: if they had managed to fool the Registry by concealing an illegal adoption, they could have kept up the deception forever. And yet, I vividly remembered the day when Lora had taken me aside.

"Dana," she had said, "there is something you need to know."

I had just gotten the highest grade in my class for writing an essay about Our Home and the history of the Purity War. I was very proud of myself. I had spent hours on the net, researching the few available sources for information about the monstrous mutations that had struck the settlers of the Lost Colonies, turning them into perverse caricatures of True Men. There was almost nothing. There was a bit more about the Purity War that cleansed the Lost Colonies of the once-human monsters, but much of it was just patriotic sloganeering. A lot of files were classified. We were taught in school that Patria was the only pure planet, the only home for True Mankind, and that was all we needed to know. Most kids absorbed the story passively and never gave it much thought. But now, having delved deeper into it and having been lavishly praised by the teacher for my efforts, I was enthused. I contemplated joining the Our Home movement when I was older.

After my conversation with Lora, I went into the garden and set fire to all the promotional material of Our Home I had collected. Occasional words flared bright as the brittle paperite was consumed. "Human form divine". "Monsters". "Our history".

Their history, not mine.

* * *

The letter from Sander found me when I was tinkering with my new telescope. I had to be more careful now than during my childhood garden vigils. After a period of liberalization, the Our Home movement surged again, capturing most of the seats in the Duma and tightening up the laws prohibiting any scientific or artistic investment in space. Kids were no longer taught the names of the main stars in the Spiral, and parents were encouraged to tell them that the blaze in the night sky was God's tears, shed when He saw True Mankind deviate from its preordained path. There were even attempts to teach that Sol and Solara revolved around Patria but that was squashed: planes and ships still needed precision navigation, and a modicum of scientific knowledge was required for that.

Sander's letter said that he was dying and wanted to see "his daughter" (the words were underlined) one last time. I was tempted to discount it. My resentment at my adoptive parents was a substitute for my missing identity.

But there was something in the letter that pricked my curiosity: an oblique hint that perhaps, just perhaps, he was finally going to tell me the truth.

Because having disclosed that I had been born on a Lost Colony world during the Purity War, Lora and Sander clammed up. They steadfastly refused to tell me what world it was, or to part with any information about my real parents.

Our Home family laws did not allow stranger adoption. Orphans were placed with nearest blood relatives, or if none existed, put in orphanages. One had to earn Social Credit to be allowed to have a child (which was why I knew I would never have a family). So of course, my adoption must have been illegal, arranged somehow during the chaos of the Purity War when Patria had battled the former humans of the Lost Colonies. Sander, or Lora, or maybe both of them, must have been soldiers in the Our Home army, dispatched to fight monsters on the anonymous planet that was my true home. Or had I been smuggled to Patria as a baby by somebody else?

After the Purity War had ended, the Lost Colonies receded into the murkiness of repressed history. Nobody talked about them. The planets where humans had been reshaped into something unnamable and revolting were cleansed of all inhabitants and their names forgotten. I hunted for every scrap of knowledge but there was so little: meaningless gossip or spooky horror stories.

I bought a plane ticket to Spear. The entire journey took thirty-six hours, what with connections and long waiting times in the shabby small airports in forgotten small towns. I did not sleep at all, and my eyes were dust-dry when the rickety plane arced above the Northern Ocean and I saw the long skerries and oval islands of the Misty Archipelago scattered like a handful of pebbles in the blue shimmer. Sol and Solara were setting, the large star dim and its bright companion disappearing behind the limb of the planet, painting a golden path on the water. And for the first time I felt a tug of almost-acceptance, as if the beauty of Patria could somehow make up for the fact that this world was not, and could never be, mine.

Spear was a huddle of wooden houses with bright red roofs in the shadow of a black mountain. The mountain's flanks were sprinkled with snow, which I had previously only seen in vids. There were some branching plant shapes clinging to the rocks. I eyed them curiously: trees were rare on Patria, supplanted in the temperate zone by different kinds of glass flowers that housed tight ecological communities of their pollinators.

Sander lived alone in a cabin on the edge of the settlement. When I walked in, the shutters were down, and the sweetish stink of sickbed washed over me. His letter said nothing about the nature of his disease, so I assumed it was wasting or cancer. But when I saw his bloated face, the red flesh dotted with pustules, I realized he had been stung by a night crawler. There was no antidote to the venom: some recovered spontaneously, and some did not. Sander was clearly among the latter.

"Who is this?" he called uncertainly. His eyes were swollen shut.

"It's me," I said.

"Dana?"

I winced. I still did not like my name. Sometimes I thought about changing it, but I wanted something that would connect me to my roots, and how could I do it if I did not know what they were?

"Yes."

"Come closer."

I did, taking a wet rag from the bowl on the bedside table and wiping his face.

During my flight, I had expected some emotional turmoil on seeing him. After all, I had called Sander "Papa" for the first seven years of my life. But there was nothing, except impersonal pity for his condition.

"Have you heard from your mother?" he asked. "I tried to contact Lora, but I don't know where she is."

"She is not my mother," I said.

There was a bubbling sound coming from his blistered lips. I realized he was trying to laugh.

"As stubborn as ever, eh? Well, if you ever meet her, tell her I said hello."

"Sander," I asked, "where was I born?"

"Ask your mother," he said.

And that was that. He lapsed into unconsciousness and died several hours later.

But before he drew his final breath, he said something, a wheezing sound that shaped itself into a word.

The word was "flower".

* * *

I found an old star-map of the Spiral among a handful of books somebody placed by the curbside. People did not like burning old books, despite the fact that Our Home was resuming purges and arrests, so they would just put them out. A quiet gesture of defiance by an anonymous stranger translated into a lucky break for me. Because the map listed the names of the major stars in the cluster, both astronomical designations and colloquial nicknames. One red dwarf was called Flower.

The map did not specify whether Flower had any planets. Even less did it specify whether one of those planets housed a Lost Colony. But I knew it did.

For several days after finding the map, I walked on clouds. I had a place. I had a name. I had a home.

But it was not enough. Staring at the map through sleepless nights, I delved into the darkness of memory, trying to dig up something, anything: a glimpse of a nonhuman face; a sound of a strange tongue; a single sun in the sky instead of a pair. There was nothing.

Studying my features in the mirror, I tried to reshape them into the face of my real mother. My mother, an alien. But it was useless. I could only see myself: an orphan with no name, no origin, no identity.

I frequented those few bookstores that remained open, trying to find books about the Purity War, but they had all been censored, confiscated, and probably burned. Nor did I find anything about the red dwarf nicknamed Flower and its planets. The only consolation prize I came up with was a book of tales from Old Earth: the same one I had as a child. I remembered Lora telling me she had chosen my name from that book. I found the tale, reread it, and was none the wiser as to why. It was a rather gruesome story about a girl named Danae who was locked up in a tower by her father. A god – not God but some pagan deity – sneaked into the tower in the shape of a torrent of golden stars, and later the girl had a baby. The tale was titillating in a weird way but had no relevance to our lives in the Spiral.

Still, reading it as an adult and being aware of its sexual symbolism made me reassess my mental image of Lora. I had despised her as a meek and dull suburban housewife. But there must have been some rebellious spark in her to have chosen that name.

"*Ask your mother*," Sander had said.

I went to the Registry of Mankind and placed a request to locate my mother.

The response came quicker than I expected. Lora worked on a fishing trawler plying the waters of the Misty Archipelago.

* * *

I was sitting in a rundown bar at the oceanside, drinking a dubious cocktail from a smudged glass. The walls of the bar were hung with amateur dabbles of sunsets and sunrises, all of them for sale. The sparse population of the Archipelago subsisted on fishing and tourism, but the latter was down. In more liberal times, the Archipelago had advertised its legend of having the indigenous population of upright, two-legged creatures resembling human beings. The official line was that these so-called aborigines were a myth. Patria had no primates, and all of its mammals were, like ghost cats, colonial and symbiotic creatures. But the legend of the aborigines had been the chief draw of mainland tourists. In second-hand stores, you could still buy self-published books, depicting mysterious sightings of humanoid creatures in the wild. But Our Home declared the legend subversive. Patria was for True Men only, not for two-legged animals, perverse caricatures of the human form divine. Once the Archipelago had nothing to sell but bad alcohol and pink sunsets, tourism dried out.

A group of people spilled into the bar, laughing and shouting, bringing the briny smell of sea-life that clung to their clothes. One of them was Lora.

She spotted me instantly. She said something to her companions and walked over to my table.

"Hello, Dana," she said.

She looked better than during the time of her suburban marriage: sinewy and darkly tanned, with bare muscled arms. Her long crinkly hair was caught in a ponytail; and even the deepened creases on her cheeks added character to what I had always seen as a bland timid face.

"How did you know I would be here?"

She smiled, displaying a missing incisor.

"You requested information about your mother. I requested information about my daughter."

I opened my mouth to counter with the familiar refrain, You are not my mother, and closed it. The wild hair, the long nose, the dark eyes … Why had I not seen it before?

"Yes," Lora said. "I *am* your mother."

* * *

We hiked for a whole day to get there. The island was rugged and mountainous, with deep gullies cutting through the barren slopes of scree. The long narrow valleys were filled with glass flowers, glinting in the double sunlight. Nobody lived in the interior; the few fishing villages hugged the shore. There were dangerous animals here: night crawlers twice as big as the ones we had on Hearth, and ghost cats that could join together to form a composite big enough to carpet an entire valley. Fortunately, the only things we encountered were red-tails – shy herbivores who lived inside glass-flower blooms, their scarlet appendages poking out of the crystalline cups like wagging tongues.

"Why is it so far from the coast?" I asked.

"We did not want to draw attention to ourselves. The fishing folk knew we were there, of course, but we got along. Until the Purity War started, and the Our Home goons came."

"How old were you?"

"Fifteen. The oldest one among the survivors."

"And your … your parents?"

Lora did not respond.

We trudged on in silence, as my memories swirled in my head like pieces of colored glass in a kaleidoscope, falling into a new pattern.

"They threw the bodies among the flowers," she said finally. "Crawlers took care of them."

"And now they say aborigines never existed!" I said bitterly.

Lora snorted.

"They did not. It is just a tall tale. Our people lived here for more than a century, and we never saw anything but ghost cats, and crawlers, and red-tails!"

"Wait! But you said..."

"I did not say we are aliens. We are human. More human than the bastards who have the gall to call themselves 'True Men'. Yeah, True Men who massacred unarmed civilians and pregnant women!"

"Then how...?

She sighed and sat down on the tough weave of dead glass-flower stems that carpeted the ground. We were skirting a sharp-toothed peak that jutted into the purpling sky, casting its deep shadow upon the foothills. It was taking us longer than expected to get to where we were going. Sol and Solara shone through the golden swirl of glass-flower pollen that was filling the dusky air with a wine-sweet scent.

"Our Home teaches that on the other planets where humans settled in the Spiral, they were contaminated by the alien ecospheres, right?"

"Yes."

"Then why is Patria different?"

I opened my mouth, but nothing came out. *Because our world is pure* was what Our Home said. But why would I believe their propaganda?

"They call it *genetic crossover*," Lora went on. "We called it *making babies*."

"So why did you tell me I was adopted on a Lost Colony?"

"Because it is the truth. Patria is a Lost Colony too."

* * *

The valley gleamed like a handful of crystal. It was long, and narrow, with steep rocky sides. And it was filled with glass flowers.

These were much bigger than the tame specimens in our suburban garden, each of their arrow-shaped petals as long as my arm, their glistening transparency veined with maroon and scarlet. They seemed to carpet the bottom of the valley but as we descended, I saw that each giant bloom was raised on a tough braided stem as tall as two men standing on each other's shoulders. Underneath these transparent parasols, the soil was oily and black, dotted with unfamiliar greenish creepers. The double flood of sunshine was refracted through the flowers, broken into rainbow shards that blinded me as I stumbled through the glass forest after Lora. The sweet scent was so thick it seemed to curdle the air into liquid treacle. But it did not bother me. Neither did the swirls of golden pollen that peppered my face and arms like glitter. I found myself rubbing them into my skin.

Lora navigated the glass forest with fluid ease. Following her, I picked up my pace. It was not difficult: the flowers were widely spaced, and the ground was even, as if it had been previously cultivated.

A rushing sound of water was coming from somewhere to our left. Lora dived into a thicket of smaller flower-trees, but I paused, watching a solitary ghost-cat wriggle out of a blossom as big as my head. It was fluid and supple; its eyeless muzzle peppered with golden sparks. I timidly touched its velvety grey skin, feeling a strange sense of kinship. The cat disregarded me and dived into another flower.

"Come on!" Lora called.

I found her on the bank of the creek. On the opposite side, among the gleaming blossoms, I could see ruins: a couple of splintered walls, piles of masonry carpeted by small transparent plants.

"This is where you were conceived," she said.

"Does it have a name, this place?"

"Home."

We sat in silence.

"But you said you were just fifteen years old," I said.

"I was. And already pregnant with you."

"Did it always happen at fifteen?"

"No. Different ages for different girls. But always after puberty, of course. So, we celebrated the puberty – the Golden Day, it was called – and then the girl would go deep into the flowers, and breathe in the pollen, rub it on her skin, bathe in it. Come back as shiny as the night sky. And nine months later, a baby. And if it did not happen the first time, she would do it again. And again. Until it took. I was lucky, they said in the village. And doubly lucky that I did not show. Or Our Home would have killed me. They killed every pregnant woman, but they took away the kids, and put us in orphanages, and brainwashed us with their True Mankind hateful creed."

"But did you…?"

I did not know how to frame the question. How do you ask your mother about the particulars of your own conception? My cheeks flamed in embarrassment; and yet, I had never been embarrassed to ask Lora anything when I had thought I was adopted.

She chuckled.

"Yes, we did. Had sex. And got married. Couples courted, just as they do on the mainland, and men called their wives' children their sons and daughters. Even though they were sons and daughters of the flowers."

The air in front of me sparkled with gold, a whirlwind of tiny stars like a miniature Spiral. Some of them were settling on my bare arms, seeding them with glitter. I breathed in the pollen.

I had been looking for the knowledge of my true identity my entire life. But identity was not knowledge. It was the splashing of the creek, the candied aroma of the flowers, the golden sparkle of my flesh.

But there was one question I had to ask. Had I let my father die without even acknowledging him as my father?

"No," Lora said. "Sander was not one of us. I ran away from the orphanage, got myself a fake ID, changed my name, my age, my birthplace."

I could not imagine the suburban Lora doing any of these things. But the woman in front of me – yes, I could.

"He had been in the Our Home army. A vet with a good pension, a solid citizen. He wanted to marry me. He even offered to register as the baby's father, and I was so stupidly grateful. But then, after you were born, he started badgering me about the identity of the real father, and when I refused to tell him, he threatened to take you in for a DNA test. What could I do but tell him the truth?"

A DNA test that would discover who – what – I really was.

"So, you told him?"

"Yes. He went bonkers. But he did not want a divorce. And he did not want you to call him Papa anymore; it was like he was afraid of contamination or something. So, we came up with the story of you being adopted."

I nodded. I wanted to embrace my mother, to tell her everything was forgiven, but I could not. Because it was not true.

She had never told me about my real heritage. She had kept it from me and given me nothing except Our Home propaganda to define myself with.

But I was alive. She had kept me alive. And she told me stories. Stories about a girl and a shower of stars. They were not true, but neither were they lies.

"We need to go back," Lora said. "Not a good idea to sleep here. Crawlers may come."

The Spiral shone in the aquamarine sky. I had looked for my home among the stars, but suddenly I realized I was surrounded by them, right in the middle of a giant star cluster. I did not need to go anywhere. Patria was a Lost Colony too.

I followed her through the glass thicket. These flowers opened even wider as the night came. There was a pulsing glow at the heart of each like a beating heart.

"Mama," I said, and saw her look back at me, "am I pregnant now?"

"I don't know. Maybe. I'll be looking forward to grandchildren."

"In that Old-Earth story, who was Danae's child?"

"A mighty hero who avenged his people."

I smiled to myself.

And then Lora stopped, so suddenly that I ran into her. She put her hand to my face and pointed to the dark figures against the twinkling background. Dark figures weighed down with heavy military equipment, Our Home uniforms merging with shadows, encircling the two of us in the field of starry flowers.

The Remaking of Gloria

Eileen Gonzalez

GLORIA SLAMMED HIM against the wall for the last time. She felt several ribs crack beneath her hands just before she released him, letting him slide to the tiled floor of what had been his laboratory. The sprinklers could not quench the electrical fire she had started by ripping the wiring out of the largest piece of machinery, the one that had forced the molten metal into her veins and into the veins of so many others. Now, it would never hurt another soul. Nor would the disheveled man in the lab coat at her feet.

"It was so easy, do you understand that?" He coughed again, splattering more blood on his lab coat, and struggled to wheeze in a breath. "Do you know how simple it was to lure you in and do what I needed to do? And no one missed you. Not one single person cared that you were gone."

Maybe that was true. It probably was. Gloria had no evidence – and, thanks to the crumpled man before her, no memory – to prove him wrong.

"So damn many of you," he murmured, no longer looking at her. "So many coming to the border, and across the border. All crammed together. Like insects. Everyone steps on insects, sometimes without even noticing. Who'd notice one or two fewer ants in the hill?"

Gloria didn't let him see her anger, didn't give him the satisfaction of knowing what she thought of his analogy. He hadn't merely stepped on a few *ants* – that would have been terrible, but quick. He had kidnapped them, tortured them for days and kept them confined in stale, dark quarters for the scant few hours a day he wasn't drilling them in the use of their new powers. He hired men with guns to patrol the corridors and keep them in line. Even if she had been an ant, she wouldn't have deserved that. No one would.

The sprinklers abruptly stopped. Someone must have cut the water supply, but it was all right: the fire had retreated to a few pitiful corners. Smoke wafted through the room. The once-pristine white walls were stained black. The smell of burned metal and melting plastic was choking, vile. Gloria did not move. The man before her could not move. His chest convulsed with every breath. He somehow found the energy to keep talking.

"We had need of people like you. You were to be a part of something important, something..." He coughed again, weaker now. "You could have helped society instead of being a burden to us. We took away everything that made you worthless and made you strong. Useful. It would have been so easy!"

The strength he spoke of hummed in Gloria's veins, demanding action. She couldn't deny its presence, or its usefulness in enabling her to destroy this lab and the pathetic man at her feet. He was right about making her strong. But what had it cost her? She didn't believe she had ever been worthless, that she'd had nothing to offer the world before he'd removed everything that had made her a person and left her without so much as an accent to tell her if she was Mexican, Guatemalan, Dominican, Honduran, Salvadoran, Venezuelan, Colombian. She had picked the name Gloria out of the wallet of a woman she had killed while on a practice run. The day had been overcast, swallowing the impressive shadows cast by the large industrial buildings surrounding them. She and the other experiments were tasked with destroying those buildings. After being cooped up in the lab for so long, they did so with something close to enthusiasm.

The woman had brown eyes. Gloria had had plenty of time to examine them after she ripped a lamppost out of the ground, swung it at one of the industrial building's windows, lost her balance, stumbled, and brought the lamppost down on the innocent woman, who had been hiding behind a car to escape the carnage.

The sound of a human body crumpling beneath the lamppost was drowned out by the sounds of her fellow experiments – her fellow ants – leveling the industrial buildings. Whatever their purpose, they would not be performing it again. The woman she had hit was equally shattered, lying in the bloody crater formed when the lamppost hit her prone body. Her head was still turned in her direction, now frozen in an expression of naive surprise.

She had stared at that expression for what seemed like a very long while. Taking in the unnatural stillness. Memorizing the curves of the face, the dirt and blood splattered across one side of it, the shade of brown in those dark, dark eyes with their thick, muddy lashes. As the experiments continued with their work, she knelt in the street, the compacted gravel rough and strange under her knees. A brown leather purse lay by the woman's half-curled hand. She reached for it and pulled out a wallet – how Gloria knew about things like purses and wallets, she couldn't remember – and looked at the driver's license. Gloria Perez, it said. The name seemed like a magical incantation. Gloria Perez. It was a real name, not the assortment of numbers assigned to her and the other experiments. Nor was it a title, like Doctor, which the man in the lab coat always insisted they call him. Gloria Perez. A human name for a human being. It made her want to be human, too, not a living machine that mindlessly followed orders and accidentally killed ordinary people with ordinary lives and ordinary names like Gloria Perez.

She had been punished for Gloria Perez's death, even though the Doctor must surely have expected mistakes, given that it was a practice run. Practice for *what*, no one bothered to tell Gloria. It wasn't her place to ask, or to know.

The Doctor had always scared her, though she didn't know it at first. How could she distinguish fear from other emotions when she had no memory of ever feeling any other way? Now, she knew what fear was, and she no longer felt it in relation to the pale shape twitching before her.

"So what have you accomplished?" he rasped. It sounded painful. Good. "Did it make you feel better? It won't last. No one wants you. That hasn't changed. You're as worthless as you ever were. We're the only one who saw the worth in you. If not for us, you'd be rotting in some cage, sucking our resources and contributing nothing. Nothing!"

After killing Gloria and adopting her name, she had become curious about the world outside the lab. It was such a sterile world compared with the one she had glimpsed the day of the practice run. No dirt. No plants. No smells except for metal and plastic and something the Doctor had told her was a disinfectant. She'd had no idea food was supposed to have an attractive smell and appearance until she broke away during another practice run. This one was in a less crowded area. Small but clean houses with flat green lawns. In one of those lawns, a man – just an ordinary man – stood at a large black contraption that sent clouds of the most delicious-smelling smoke into the bright summer sky. He was placing bits and pieces from the contraption onto paper plates held out by others, who laughed and chatted as they received the offerings.

Barbacoa. The word appeared in her mind in a flash. That's what the man was making. That's what she must have made, or what someone had made for her, in the time before. She tried to remember what it tasted like. All she could taste was metal and ozone.

Again, she had been punished for her transgression. A punishment harsh enough to tax even the power of the liquid iron that her heart now pumped through her body in place of blood. But what was physical pain compared with the knowledge that she had been robbed of wallets and purses and paper plates and sunny days?

Everything seemed to unravel quickly after that.

Several days later, again a prisoner at the lab, Gloria caught a glimpse of a news report on a security guard's cell phone. Caravan of Illegal Immigrants on Its Way to U.S.-Mexico Border.

She overheard the guards talking about *dirty Mexicans, damn spics, thugs sneaking in*.

The other experiments took note of Gloria's rebellion. During snatched moments on training or practice runs, they spoke. She told them of Gloria Perez, and of a world without sterile white walls or a Doctor to inflict punishment. Of a world without violence and the blank eyes of dead bystanders.

At first, they doubted. The Doctor's influence too strong. Their own experience of the world too absolute to allow for doubt. Doubt, however, is not so easy to control. Gloria's words planted the seeds of doubt deep within the minds of her fellow experiments, so deep they didn't notice until the seeds had sprouted, birthing long, slender vines that wrapped around and around the Doctor's teachings and *squeezed*.

Now here they were. In a half-destroyed laboratory, with the balance of power tipping inexorably in Gloria's favor. The Doctor coughed, a terrible death rattle. She waited in silence, looking down at him, her modest height made impressive by the way he sat, slouched, against the wall. She was better than he. She would not deny him his last words.

The Doctor huffed a few times. Then he said, "We made you. We made you all. You'll never take that away."

Gloria ended his life with a quick twist of his neck. She wasn't so quick that he didn't see it coming, and she didn't deny herself the rush of pleasure at seeing the fear flash across his face. All his grand and noble talk concealed the coward within.

The stench of blood and smoke was unbearable without the distraction the Doctor had provided. Coughing, she left by the nearest door. She had knocked the door off its hinges on her way in. Now she stepped over the dented metal slab and into the corridor. Several of the other experiments, each with a different metal pulsing beneath their skin, stood there in a long hallway over several dead and unconscious bodies. They had taken out the security guards so she would have time to destroy the lab and its sole occupant. Now they all locked eyes on her, waiting for news or instructions. Gloria didn't like the idea of being a leader: the only one she had any memory of was the Doctor. Still, someone had to do it. And this whole adventure had been her idea.

She looked at the dark, expectant faces and reported what the Doctor had said to her in his final moments. It all made sense now. They had a nearly complete picture: the Doctor and his mysterious associates – the "we" he referenced so frequently during their final conversation – needed soldiers for some as-yet-undetermined reason. They found an endless supply at the border, where desperate, confused, isolated immigrants gathered. They lured the immigrants away, or stole them, or bribed someone to leave a door unlocked at a key moment. They erased their minds to make them good little soldiers, to make them forget all thoughts of a better life in the world of ordinary people.

That was our world, she told them. *They didn't want to share it with us, so they ripped us out of it.*

She didn't know their stories any more than she knew her own, but she could guess. Had the Doctor ever told them what he'd told her, that they were useless and unwanted? That only he could make them into something worthwhile?

If he had, surely they must realize by now he had lied. The Doctor was dead. They were alive. The lab was a shambles, with the people who had worked inside it either fled or incapacitated – all thanks to them.

Gloria heaved a breath and jerked her head down the hall. There was a door there, one they were not allowed to pass through except during practice runs. It led to the world outside. They had just killed to reclaim that world. They may not have pasts or names or even futures, but they had now. They had here. They had each other. And they had the powers that had been forced on them. Maybe that could be enough. If it wasn't, it would at least allow them to find the people who had done this and make them pay.

Rumblings

Roy Gray

BONNER/1077/LZP/42
BEGINS

The situation underlying the urgency to progress Bonner can be summarised as follows:

- *The technical problems of Bonner extractions are resolved but ethical dilemmas prevent implementation.*
- *A political settlement is necessary to obtain agreement from the naturals and gengineered polity.*
- *Galactic rotation and Hubble expansion limit access to planetary history beyond a depth of 500 years. In effect earlier pEarths are as remote as the stars and technology cannot provide an answer to the quandary.*
- *50 years is the forecast time to Environmental Singularity, ecological transfusions need 30 years to be effective.*

One means of countering ethical objections utilises catastrophic events with universal (multicontinua) dimensions. The augmented and artificial intelligence moieties agreed that taking advantage of past natural disasters (not human-mediated catastrophes, such as wars) was acceptable; this remains controversial with the naturals.

Programmes of historical and archaeological research were instituted to look for evidence that our successor equivalents in parallel continua overcame such objections and performed extractions in our past. As a result of this work the following was retrieved, and decrypted, by Bonner researchers from electronic records dated as shown. The file is believed to be a diary and all dates were linked to a now-lost daily events and news log. Similar log archives were in existence elsewhere and their records are now <u>accessible</u> but, to avoid questions of authenticity, no automatic links were established. Means to establish <u>such links</u> have been instituted for researchers keen to explore this aspect of the Late American Democratic Age in greater depth.

The excerpts below were considered pertinent to the Bonner Project and the naturals' expressed anxieties concerning the ethics of paratemporal operations. The author wrote very little on the relevant subject, though it was evidently an increasing concern to him from 2027 onward. Researchers added information [in parentheses] as an aid to clarity but these are, as yet, unaudited. Bonner resource comments on the text remain in bold throughout.

* * *

From the diaries of <u>L Z Palmer</u> (1991–2035)
16/June/27. Dark again today and still only 3°C at noon. Bring back global warming! Anniversary of food rationing today. Black-market [illegal/unofficial] coffee still costs more than coke. I also found some marmalade, an expensive import from England by the looks; you can never be sure these days, but a nice reminder of home.

Another internet crash so I used Berkeley [University Campus?] library to check geophysics of proposed refugee camp sites.

Met Joel. [J F Dobbs – Astronomer, 1993 – 2035] Astronomy still impossible for dust levels – and funding I expect. He worked on Spaceguard **[a 21st-century study of asteroids known as near-Earth objects, NEOs, presenting an impact hazard because their orbits intersect Earth's]** as a postgrad and on airborne particles and settling rates since 2026 impact. Results very unpromising and he forecast another long dark winter.

Asked Joel's opinion of the 300 ms [millisecond] pre-impact seismic trace. Joel thought it looked like a coincident earthquake, the crust rose just prior to the moment of impact. Joel dismissed tidal effects because, at 0 – 300 ms, [300 ms prior to impact] NEO was about two miles [1 mile = 1.63 km] up and a mile down range and too small to start a quake by its own gravity. **[This is the first indication that our timeline may include an extraction. Other than Palmer there is no mention in any other records traced to date. This impact data has not been recovered. Its loss was assumed a result of the 2035 event.]** I had already discounted his suggestions after looking at traces from other instruments at different distances from the crater. It wasn't seismic wave dispersion effects, instrumental errors caused by electrical interference from the atmospheric entry plasma or even a near-miss shockwave from an unknown satellite of NEO. Couldn't convince Joel that NEO's arrival and this simultaneous quake were no coincidence but my explanation, a tidal effect, was obviously wrong.

Joel said if the mass was that wrong there'd be no South America left and the entire South from Frisco to Charleston would be suffering more than just minor quakes, dark days and brass monkey weather [unexplained phrase] in June.

I don't believe in coincidence.

Joel thought I should publish because, once the web is back to its normal reliability, word will get around, someone will see it and come up with an explanation. I said my letter to 'Geology' [Journal published by The Geological Society of America] was nearly ready to go. **[No report or letter was found in any extant archive.]**

* * *

25/June/27. 30 mins sunshine in Oregon, 5°C at noon, LA, today.

Bought bread on black market today. Mandarin characters, no English or Spanish, on the wrapping. It could be local, I suppose. Tasted fine.

More net problems, Berkeley again, met Maria Lopez. [M Lopez – Economist, 1983 – 2035] She led the team that completed the comprehensive ecological survey for the Brazilian Government. She was finishing her report when NEO impact took out the core of the surveyed area. That region, a major unspoiled area of rainforest, was due to be opened for development in 2026. Another coincidence?

"Took out" interesting phase. Why did I write that rather than 'obliterated'? I watched an old film last night in which people of the future, who can no longer reproduce, steal fertile people from the past under cover of accidents like air crashes. [Possibly 'Millennium' – 1989] Am I influenced by that idea? Could the seismic traces indicate someone stole the rainforest away under cover of the impact? Madness?

[A clear reference to the possibility of extractions]

* * *

28/June/27. Darkness at noon, at least the big crowd kept the church almost warm. Sermon on cause & effect with plenty of references to Sodom and Gomorrah. Glad I never left the closet.

Our, suddenly fundamentalist, preacher suggested that the rain of fire followed from our recent, less than impeccable, earthly behaviour. I tend to dismiss this automatically. Why should God worry about what I think about doing in the privacy of my own home? But suppose our behaviour is upsetting someone, or something? Not our personal but our overall behaviour, like our effect on the planet, upsets us and maybe our descendants, or inheritors. Did I see evidence of an earthquake just before NEO impact or the results of millions of tons of the earth's crust, and its accompanying biosphere, being hijacked to the future? So was NEO an accident, where someone – or something – took advantage, or deliberate in order to take advantage?

[Clearly Palmer wonders if 2026 impact was not a chance event but engineered for an extraction, an analysis that surprised Bonner archaeologists.]

* * *

4/Sept/27. Refugees still pouring in, since the 'Mexicans' bombed the few obstructive bits of Trump's Wall, and more camps required. Will keep me busy. Bitter arguments over sites because few want them as neighbours. I suppose some worries about them bringing in more Covid [A recent pandemic at that time] variants could be valid but we've got plenty of vaccines now. Offered bribe to falsify results on proposed Palm Springs campsite. Very subtle, could not prove anything. Will say nothing. Can avoid problem by taking up offer of fieldwork. A survey of NEO crater is planned for next year. Never sent letter to 'Geology'. Would put my reputation at stake. Weasely [compare 'weasel words' – common expression for avoiding dispute by moderating voiced opinion] but I don't have to mention my speculations so why draw attention to myself? If NEO was deliberate then these could be powerful people (?) to upset. If it wasn't the crater survey may provide answers.

[It is considered that Palmer's wariness and the lack of a published record is explained by his ignorance of the limits to paratemporal translations.]

* * *

14/Sept/27. Leg infection is antibiotic resistant. Choice is more treatment or a tin leg, which I'll probably still need after the treatment. Just bad luck. I didn't even catch the bug when I fell. Acquired in hospital, in Brazil or here. DNA evidence suggests here most likely. Apparently I can sue. Tin leg, prostheses as medics say, are pretty good. I'll go for that option. Fall for nothing, as I might say, since I went to Brazil for evidence, found nothing either way **[no evidence of a Bonner extraction?]** and fell trying to rescue a crashed drone from NEO crater. Invited to write a book about NEO impact and effects. This time it's not a bribe – publisher is Cranmore of New York. Popular science covering astronomy, geology, geophysics and atmospheric physics. Joel, who is now a weatherman on Calweb, would be ideal as co-author. I want 'NEO, Two Years On' as title. Cranmore want 'WHOMP!' Offered more work on refugee camps, not fieldwork though.

* * *

15/Dec/27. Coffee off rations, still scarce but cheaper than cocaine now, apparently. Saw Joel about book. He is happy to do the astronomy and atmospheric effects. We settled on 'WHOMP! NEO Two Years On' as the title. Embarrassing but we had to give Cranmore a half win. Joel asked about my pre-impact seismic mystery and if it was going in the book. I'd forgotten I'd told him so I had to say something. He was scathing about the idea said it would be like someone going back in time to kill their grandmother. I did point out that he was assuming that our successors will be human.

He countered that the millions of years required to evolve any non-human successors will give the biosphere plenty of time to recover from humanity's depredations and it's much easier to assume any time travellers are our descendants.

I asked if that meant he believed some of this but he would only concede 'putative time-travellers' for the sake of argument; plus extraordinary claims need extraordinary evidence. I don't have that and he's probably right. I do feel better for talking about it. I had no intention of including anything about time travel in the book. Joel joked we might outsell Von Daniken if we did. [E Von Daniken – speculative-history author]

* * *

15/May/31. Why do they keep building refugee camps in earthquake zones? To make sure they can't settle down is the rumour, but in reality because no one else wants to live there. Also there are more planned for Republican [a political allegiance] areas since 2027. Most refugees now from south of the strike but at least the numbers are down by two million in the past year. Even so Brenman [E Brenman – US Commissioner for Refugee Affairs, 2024–2035] asked me to join a complete survey of Yellowstone to identify potential campsites. It'll be a huge survey, fauna, flora, geology and geography because the Sierra Club [a North American organisation committed to preservation of the natural environment] is insisting on full environmental-impact statements for any planned encroachment. I don't blame the Club for objecting but they won't win because nobody wants a camp in their back yard. Their local members weren't slow about objecting to the Menlo camp. I know I am/was piling a lot of fantastic premises on one observation and Joel sort of talked me out of it but this survey reminds me of Maria Lopez's Brazilian rainforest survey before NEO impact. There are some big volcanoes in Yellowstone.

[Clearly Palmer is concerned that supposed time travellers from his future may be able to influence political events in his era.]

* * *

7/June/34. Rationing ended, coffee is plentiful; as is cocaine I'm told. New tin leg fitted, nothing really wrong with the old one, but this is improved and more suited to fieldwork though Wyoming is more forgiving than the upper Amazon, or what's left of it. Met Jim Tellman [J Tellman – microbiologist 1982–2035] on survey team. Jim worked on biowarfare defence for DOD. Still consults for them but very little since NEO. Apparently the cholera outbreak at the Carmel Valley complex may not have been chance and poor hygiene. So Jim is looking at the potential for contamination of water resources because of the threats against refugees. Unbelievable!

More time to read with all the coming and going to Yellowstone. Joel sent me a book on time travel, 'Time Travel in Einstein's Universe' by Gott. [Probably 2023 Edition, J R Gott] Much speculation that it is impossible to return to our own past but, if there are parallel universes, it might be possible to travel into their past. This avoids causality paradoxes like killing your grandmother. So if you are ruthless and/or desperate enough, you could raid the past of a parallel Earth without affecting your own history. **[Parallel continua were highly speculative science at this time but often featured in fiction.]** This idea might explain why and how the future, or a future, could restore its own biosphere. Hijack it from parallel worlds. Also resolved Joel's point about the millions of years required to evolve our successors. Artificial Intelligence has been predicted to take over from humanity in mere decades but why would an AI need to repair the biosphere?

So was NEO really an accident, or was it camouflage? If the latter why bother? Not much chance I'll ever have an answer.

Gott also described 'jinni', a type of time loop paradox. As an example, while building a time machine suppose I found a tennis ball. Assuming it had come through the window I pick it up and put it on a nearby shelf. Then I finish the machine and want to do a quick test to check it works. I look round and see the tennis ball and send it back 10 minutes in time. This is the moment where I found it. The ball is a jinni, it has no origin; it just loops through time.

My worry is something Gott called information jinn; ideas that loop through time. The worrying scenario: I see and interpret the NEO impact seismic traces and write about them in terms of a chunk of rainforest being removed under cover of an asteroid strike. This speculation is read in the future where someone/thing then decides to use the idea to replenish their biosphere. They alter the orbit of an asteroid in the past and bring about the disaster, so completing the loop. Thus my speculations lead to or are even part of such a jinni. There's little chance of my starting such a disastrous sequence, as Gott thinks the future could only dip into the past of a parallel universe, but why take the risk? I'll encrypt this diary and save it to a secure data haven in Australia.

[Multiplex continua symmetries ensure Palmer's concerns about jinn were baseless for downbranch translations]

* * *

13/July/34. Happy birthday me. 43 today, Ecard from Cranmore with note, total print sales were 37,000. Ebooks another 6000. Spanish edition, 12,000 and 900. Won't be rich but not bad.

Riots in the Laguna camp last night. I take some pride in the fact that it survived the 6.9 quake pretty well with very few casualties but the residents weren't quite so sanguine. Rumblings in Yellowstone at very low intensity. Helium[4] reading raised. Is this the first sign or is my imagination running wild? USGS [United States Geological Survey] were reluctant but now I can do more fieldwork I'll move into Fishing Bridge. The RV Park is commandeered as survey HQ. Signed insurance release against employer liability because of tin leg. If my suspicions are correct I could be in the right place if the park is taken and so accompany it to the stratosphere or to its destiny on a future Earth. If it is the latter, wherever or whenever that might be, I may have a nasty surprise for them. Presuming they are human, especially far future human, their immunity to cholera may be less than perfect.

* * *

11/April/35. More helium and rumblings but still low Richter. Passenger flights to the southern hemisphere are fully re-established now so I can stay here, and check out my theory, or move somewhere safe, like Australia. The survey is complete and we have to provide the final report in September. Tellman is coming tomorrow so I'll try to persuade him to get me some samples. If he can I'll stay.

Hollywood output back to 2025 levels. Everyone says things are back to pre NEO, post-Ukraine normality. The refugee influx has been good for business with DOW [a stock-market index based on share prices] back at 36K. I'm wealthy, though it's very volatile wealth.

* * *

17/July/35. There is still a black market for coffee and chocolate in Wyoming. No rationing but there are shortages and the local laws prevent regular shops from raising prices. Despite tin leg I can ride a mountain bike quite well. I'll get another and some spares. A spare tin leg could be a wise investment as well so I've ordered two. Tilt, gravimeter, helium[4] and seismic surveys in Yellowstone look somewhat ominous to me but nobody else is concerned. The change is small but I think it significant. Normal variation according to the YVO [Yellowstone Volcano Observatory] but this is slow and steady. Even Baxter [J D Baxter – Volcanologist 1996–2035] at NY thought I was overreacting but he said he would come over in August. Tellman works with ebola now for DOD; I wonder if I can persuade him? I'd have to tell the whole story and might get the same reception from him that I got from Joel. If the gravimetric evidence strengthens I'll risk it.

* * *

8/Aug/35. My section of the survey report is now complete and I'm back to campsite geology again from next week. Preparations are continuing, assuming approval next year, according to Brenman's office.

I think it will happen. Tellman is here tomorrow. I'll have a word. Need to make some preparations beyond the shooting practice. At least I'm scoring a consistent 70% now. YVO more concerned about eruption. Records show similar readings in the past but not so sustained and steady. We've been told to keep quiet to avoid panic while Washington thinks about it but some are preparing reasons to move their families to the east coast.

Whatever Tellman decides this time I'll be there, waiting. I'll stay in the RV for now and camp out to be on site when it blows. I think I'll get a dog but not sure which type. Not too big because of feeding problems and park regulations on dogs. Can't say how long it will be before they won't matter any more. It will be interesting to see the future, or should I say a future, if my fears are well-founded. If not, and the worst happens, then it will be quick, for all of us. Bought some guns and ammo and stashed stores, tents, fuel, food, water, bikes, tin legs, spares etc. at strategic points, just in case. I would like to see a new universe but not at the price we may have to pay.

* * *

17/Aug/35. Tellman came up trumps and I've been immunised. Have also got a satellite phone so I can maintain an audio link direct to the data haven, until the very last possible minute, should the worst happen. My dogs will be here tomorrow. They will be six weeks old then. I should have got them earlier really but I may have more time than I thought. Must get dog food reserves in place. Pity I never learnt to ride. [Equines?]

* * *

22/Sept/35. Government evacuating everyone within 100 miles of Yellowstone. I've been consulted on sites to set up drones, extra cameras and instruments to watch the volcano and monitor any eruption. We start that tomorrow. Passive and active radio tags will enable them to be found if they are covered in ash. Can't see me flying any drones but others will. I'll snaffle some tags and buy a transmitter/receiver myself. They sound useful if you need to find things, or people, that are lost or buried. I'll keep a tag; if they find me or my body it will prove my theory is madness. If they don't it won't prove anything, as hot lava rarely leaves much to be found.

* * *

23/Sept/35. Controversy over evacuation area in Sunday's news. Many are saying it's too little. CNN [a broadcast news organisation] asked me for my opinion so said I thought it was OK. Lies but it's hardly possible to evacuate the entire Midwest and I could be wrong.

* * *

10/Oct/35 *Transcript of audio data. Much of this data is irrelevant to Bonner, examples being the times when Palmer is talking to one, or both, of the dogs. Only data that seems to bear on the project is included here but has not been audited and the signal was very noisy. Here text in parenthesis is interpolated from context, natural human insight and/or signal processing. The remaining data is available to those wishing to check our judgement or re-evaluate the complete file.*

16:25 "Looks like the entire existing crater and lake are the hottest seats in the house, so I think I'm in the right place, on the lakeshore halfway between Fishing Bridge and Old Faithful."

16:27 "We're really [shaking?] now, I've got the dogs tied, they're really terrified. So am I."

16:28 "Noise deafening. No internet now and no idea what the phone [is] sending. I'm shouting but can hardly hear myself. There are huge clouds of dust. Drones and planes can't fly in this. Tin leg dislikes the vibration, so do I."

16:29 "We installed IR [Infra red] cameras to see through the dust so why didn't I bring IR night-vision kit? Because I'm stupid."

16:30 "Low rumble, getting louder like a train approaching. Fell for the third time, ground movement very violent now. No sign of time machines or [you/your/new? efforts/effects? flows?] yet."

16:32 "Can't get a [return signal?] and [unsure this is getting through?] Visibility [very?] poor and the sky is [full of?] ash and [dust/dark?]. Oh my God…" *No further data.*

* * *

No further relevant entries were discovered and there is no record that Palmer's body was found. This diary is the only indication that NEO 2023 Impact and Yellowstone 2035 were not natural events. Palmer does not provide unequivocal evidence of extracontinua interference but he raised sufficient doubt to persuade many waverers that we are, or were, victims. Continua spread indices for NEO impact and Yellowstone, now in preparation, will provide statistical evidence that natural processes caused those events, or otherwise.

Palmer's work also prompted a review of the project's modus operandi and supported the improved-security, covert approach since adopted for all exocontinua operations.

Palmer's deductions will probably be replicated in adjacent continua and his musings on the use of ancient diseases suggests that further precautions are warranted following a Bonner extraction.

The judgement was not unanimous but the one dissenting opinion, Quandell, is that we may be entering an unusual form of jinni, which passes across the fan of parallel continua, stepping one continuum per cycle. This 'dislocation' jinni will persist until one continuum breaks the cycle.

It was agreed that the search for a parallel Earth with a sophont-free, pristine biosphere would be maintained until Bonner implementation is irrevocable. Overall our committee is in no doubt that the ethical concerns will now be overcome and the Palmer file has provided the final justification for Bonner implementation.

Bonner/1077/LZP/42

Eater and A

Alex Gurevich

"THIS IS NOT A FUNERAL!" *Jena whispers, grinding her teeth.*

There isn't enough space for the customary six pallbearers; two of the uniformed men stand at attention by the containment chamber's opening while their comrades lower the child-sized casket onto the waiting platform. One of the men bends down to adjust the flag draped over the casket. He straightens to join in a salute as the platform slowly sinks out of sight. The trap door seals shut with a soft whoosh. The containment status light flashes green.

The soldiers look relieved. They think they just buried the past, when in fact they buried the future.

Out of the corner of her eye, Jena sees Erin reach for her. She momentarily pretends not to notice, but eventually touches her wife's upturned palm. Their trembling fingers interlace.

This was how they had always been; side-by-side, looking not at each other but in the same direction. When they were not holding hands on a walk, it was because little A was toddling between them, begging to be swung high into the air. A needed to be lifted by his middle arms – his upper arms were delicate and swinging could dislocate his shoulders.

The General steps closer to the glass. He isn't a bad man, as far as generals go. Nonetheless, his presence only a couple of steps behind them is irksome. "You can choose to stay and live your lives or be frozen and wake up with your A."

They met the General on the day the Eater was discovered. Annoyingly, Erin was fifteen minutes late. She always had an excuse: experiments couldn't be interrupted, family members called unexpectedly, crucial items such as chapstick were misplaced.

Jena had worked up her anger to the point of starting on the culinary abomination considered lunch without waiting for her wife. Suddenly, a ripple went through the University cafeteria. The usual lunchtime buzz, punctuated by outbursts of foam-at-the-mouth scientific disagreements, went still. All eyes were on the sliding door behind Jena's back.

She turned around to face a cluster of uniformed officers. The military had never barged into the University before.

"Dr. Jena Shan?" A man with a captain's insignia spoke in a low, self-assured voice. "Please follow me to Dr. Erin Shan's lab. The General is waiting for you."

"What General?" Jena asked pointlessly as she was led down the familiar hallway. There was only one General on the planet.

A couple of other faculty members were herded along from the cafeteria. *So Erin wasn't late after all?* Jena thought.

Jena's research was theoretical and her own lab was more of a small private office. Erin, however, occupied a massive, heavily secured section of the building. The equipment configuration allowed for a generous meeting room carved out from the containment area. The sizeable space held a large oval conference table, made of precious off-planet wood – a subject of fellow scientists' envy.

When Jena arrived, four of the eight chairs surrounding the table were occupied. Even without the uniform, the rigid-backed General couldn't be mistaken for anyone else. A uniformed Averkian female sat to his right, and two of Jena's close collaborators huddled at the opposite end of the table.

Her escort pointed her to the table. After hesitating for a moment, she took the empty chair on the General's left. The Averkian major nodded to Jena in a human fashion to acknowledge her daring.

"Dr. Shan," the General greeted her crisply. More faculty were ushered inside. Two were directed to the table; the rest had to file along the edges of the room with the lower-ranked officers. Jena wondered how the military decided which university professors ranked highly enough to be seated.

One chair remained empty. Everybody stayed silent and waited. Then a door slid open; not the clear glass door through which everyone else had entered, but the heavy containment door with multiple warning signs on the opposite side of the room.

Erin burst in, almost bumping into one of the officers and looking befuddled. She was, in fact, twenty-five minutes late. Her long wavy hair was messy and her red blouse askew. She was beautiful. Jena found it hard not to smile.

"Dr. Shan," the General repeated.

"With your permission, sir," the major stated, "I would like to bring everyone up to speed."

Jena had a couple Averkian friends and knew their expressions. The major's flat voice and impassive face indicated extreme agitation.

"I don't get news when I'm in the lab, ma'am." Erin blurted out. "0-I protocol."

The risk of a lab particle accidentally entangling with a cosmic entity was miniscule, but the outcome of drawing in such an entity could mean disaster for the entire galaxy. While in the lab, Erin had no contact with the outside world, which allowed her to get away with her tardiness.

Military liked zero-information protocols. The General nodded approvingly and the Averkian major proceeded. "A Class-B4 transit craft has been detected. Drifting in hyperspace at eight kilolums. Currently twenty-five parsecs out, will pass within less than one. Unresponsive and intact."

The General could appear as composed as the Averkian, but closer examination revealed that his lips and cheekbones were tense in a very human way.

"Less than one parsec from us?" Jena whispered.

Someone in the room groaned. The faculty was trying to digest the catastrophic news. There was little doubt of what an unresponsive craft meant.

"Can we blast it out of hyperspace? Or speed bump it?" Erin asked. She was planetborn.

There were some grim chuckles.

"Blast out of hyperspace?" the major responded. "Or speed bump from twenty parsecs? The state propaganda about our military capabilities is clearly working." Deadpan was the only way Averkians delivered their humor.

"We have to assume the Eater will reach the surface." The General turned to H, who occupied the chair with several armrests – the only one fitted for a Dajo. "Dr. H, do you have any insight into the legend of Dajo immunity?"

H jerked upright. Despite the crisis, she was struggling to stay awake. The Dajo planet was tidally locked, without a natural day and night cycle. Their physiology was designed for taking a short nap every couple of hours instead of a protracted sleep based on the light cycle. "It's like you said, ssss... sir, a legend," she whispered, rubbing her eyes with lower hands. Dajo didn't have vocal cords, so could only produce a whisper; but their six hands provided a rich sign language. "Our home planet has never been infected and the sample of our race's encounters with gandrabions is too small."

"But there's some ground?"

H shifted her upper arms in a gesture mirroring human shrugging – she had to have learned it consciously, as it was not how Dajo normally moved. "Our brain motor centers are very different from those of four-limbed animals." H pointed three of her hands towards various humans in the room and one towards the Averkian.

Jena watched H carefully. She knew the Dajo was keeping a secret. She met H's lidless eyes and made a tiny motion with her left pinky. In Dajo it signified agreement. For now, they wouldn't tell the General.

"All citizens of the planet will receive the same protection until it is scientifically proven that any specific population is not in danger," the General stated.

There were nods around the room, but Jena noticed Erin wince. There was no protection against an Eater.

Jena and Erin continue to stare at the chamber seal. The General has to realize he is standing too close. Jena hears him shuffling back a step as he continues. "Regardless, you'll be honored for what you and your son did for this planet, and you will be rewarded in every way possible."

Possible is, of course, the key word. There would be no public acclaim or great financial bounty. The meager ceremony is for the Shan couple's benefit and has to be kept absolutely secret. It's the only way to avoid terrorists and cult followers finding out about the existence or, even worse, the location, of the casket.

The Shans went to the agency a year after the Eater had landed. The planet was quarantined; all tourism and off-planet business had stopped. Despite the current containment, many had fled the cities and businesses were failing; people of different races had started to treat each other with suspicion; violence was on the rise. Few people were choosing to have children.

"You are set on adopting a Dajo?" The official sounded both dubious and hopeful.

"You do have Dajo babies to be placed, don't you?" Jena asked.

"Oh, we get plenty of them. During the last decade Dajo refugees brought quite a few young ones, ready to breed. And not enough of those ready to parent. We used to ship over a thousand Dajo kids a year for off-planet adoption. But now with the Quarantine…"

"Humans have to do their part," Erin interjected. "Billions of Dajo became refugees because of a human war."

Adopting an alien was romantic, but also practical. The waiting period for a human adoption was four to five years, as the decline in human births outpaced the decline in the number of willing parents.

"You know about hormone treatments, diet, and circadian cycles?" The man's eyes slid down to the bowl of golden apples on his desk. It was clearly placed to project comfort and *human* touch, but to a Dajo any citrus would be a deadly poison.

"Sir, you did look at our application forms? We are both cosmobiologists." Erin bristled, but Jena could read the unease in the way her wife's hands clenched the edge of the table. Alien adoption was not a minor endeavor even in the best of times. Dajo diet would likely be the least of their challenges.

"My name is Ramon," the official said. He glanced at his chest as if expecting to see a name tag there. He had to be new to the job. "I apologize for the personal questions. I'm asking in an official capacity. Although, I have to admit, I'm also genuinely curious. You're women of child-bearing age. Why are you looking to adopt?"

"We are cosmobiologists, Ramon," Jena echoed Erin's words. "Being pregnant doesn't mix well with our decontamination procedures." Exiting the lab, they even underwent a comprehensive brain scan to guard against their neural patterns being compromised. The 0-I protocol would regard any fetus as a foreign life form within the host's body and call for immediate termination.

"There's more to it. I, myself, am a refugee from a Core World and I owe a debt. When I was thirteen, I was rescued by a Dajo colony ship and traveled on it for five years before landing here. I've seen more of the true Dajo society than most of their own on this planet." Jena let that sink in before continuing. "We aren't giving human hormones to our son. We'll raise him as a Dajo."

Ramon stiffened in surprise and cleared his throat preparing to argue. Then he must have thought better of it, and shrugged. "There's one ready now. An emergency situation."

"An accident?"

"No. A Dajo couple was arrested for trying to smuggle their baby off-planet."

The official dropped his gaze back to the apples. There was no choice; to carry on the meager trade and supply flow needed to survive, the planet had to enforce the brutal rules of galactic quarantine. But Jena knew the man felt ashamed that the government he represented punished parents for trying to protect their child.

"I don't need a reward." Jena snaps, feeling her cheeks flush with anger and shame. Erin's grip on her hand tightens. Without looking, Jena knows her wife is shaking her head. Unable to bear Erin's touch any longer, she gently disengages and turns to the General.

"They," Jena sweeps her arm to indicate the whole world outside their viewing station. "They are welcome to think our research has failed."

"Announce that the Eater has been blasted off the planet," Erin adds grimly.

They once went to see an attempt to get rid of the Eater. Departure Island was beautiful. A year earlier, it was home to vacation complexes and retreat centers. It had five hundred waterfalls, six lakes, ten thousand miles of state-maintained hiking trails, two thousand miles of speed rail, eight ferry landings, and a spaceport. Until recently, it was unimaginatively called New Kaua'i, competing in name with thousands of other picturesque islands in the Settled Universe.

Jena and Erin had taken a few holidays there. Now they surveyed the familiar coast line from a safe distance.

"Is it as you expected?" Erin asked softly, trying not to disturb A napping in his baby wrap.

Jena shook her head and leaned over the gunwale next to H, who was using all six of her arms to grip any available handhold. Dajo were not a seafaring species.

The island was ringed by what looked like hundreds of vessels bobbing on the slow swells. Many of them were police craft, guarding the island prison. There were also supply barges and human transports. At the moment, all traffic was on hold. The crash of the surf was barely audible this far from the shore.

It was over as soon as it started. A cylinder of rippling air arising from the volcanic crater in the middle of the island winked in and then out of existence. Distortion take-offs were costly and dangerous, but they were fast.

Before they could even feel a puff of wind on their faces, an announcement came over the speakers: "Mission failed. The target is back on the ground."

"Attempt number fourteen," Erin mumbled, shaking her head. "This is just not … not…" She gave up searching for the right word and busied herself with A. He was squirming against Erin's chest and two of his arms stuck out though the fabric folds.

Jena turned to her wife, helping to adjust the wrap. Concerns over the humane treatment of criminals were for people who, unlike Jena or the Dajo, hadn't had their home world blown up.

By the time they looked at the sky again the ship with five thousand convicts was reaching the outer edge of the solar system.

The only way out of Departure Island was to agree to act as bait, to lure the Eater into outer space. If the exiles were lucky (and the planet unlucky) only a few scores of them would be eaten in the pre-launch phase, after which the Eater would dive right back down.

The government kept its promise to fill the ship with rudimentary cryo-chambers. Properly flagged and set on a quarantine trajectory, the vessel would drift for decades, far from any inhabited world. Most of the exiles would survive without much damage, and once it was determined there was no Eater aboard, be welcomed as indentured workers at another of the Fringe Worlds.

"Not helping the population problem." Jena sighed and brought her eyes back to the island.

"That is not your responsibility." H's whisper was almost carried away by the breeze.

Jena didn't respond. While the Shans and H had nothing to do with establishing and maintaining the Island, the government used their research to calculate the required population. Close to a hundred thousand people on the island were required to prevent the Eater from crossing the water.

There weren't enough hard criminals on the planet of eighty million to replace the two thousand prisoners consumed every day. Some judges were rumored to inflate charges to score a "Departure" conviction. Volunteers to join the convicts on the island were few, even with the enticement of enormous sums of money.

"Not my responsibility?" Jena faced Erin, H, and little A with her back to the water. There was more unsaid. Presumably, their son's bio-parents had been sent to the Island. Were they eaten? Had they escaped on one of the spaceships, or were they still surviving on the ground?

Soothing A with her left hand, Erin steadied herself with her other hand against Jena's shoulder. "We had to see this."

"It was a very hungry Eater," the General says in lieu of an apology for Departure Island, for their son, for everything he couldn't do anything about. Jena wishes she could offer the same apology, and claim there was nothing to be done.

Instead she turns to Erin. "Will you take Octi with you?"

A was five when the Departure Island strategy failed. Nothing resembling a justice system could continue sending thousands of people to the Island daily. As arrests and convictions became more and more arbitrary, protests turned into an uprising. Eventually, enough shipments to the Island were disrupted for the population there to decline so much that the Eater jumped to the mainland.

After starving on a drifting spaceship for thousands of years, it consumed the mind of one sentient being every forty seconds, leaving convulsing bodies behind.

Surviving the Eater was a matter of statistics, as well as running faster than the people nearby. For some, survival meant throwing another person *towards* the shadowy outline of the approaching Eater.

Chaos spread throughout the planet, the civilization barely clinging to its existence, as the Eater roamed free and wide. However, the General persevered, and the military continued to function.

"Personally, I would like to see the two of you stay together." The General's voice fills the viewing dome again. Jena sees Erin wince; it's not his place to say. But that's what generals do – they say things whether it's their place or not. "I know the two of you met back in school. That's a long haul."

Jena closes her eyes, her eyelashes wet against her cheek. This year she and Erin would be celebrating the fifteenth anniversary of their first date.

Jena was the planet's specialist on Eaters; originally, her work had been purely theoretical. Erin also worked on gandrabions, but she had a different focus: dispersed organisms capable of devouring entire galaxies.

Gandrabions appeared indestructible and defied known limitations of physics. Erin's experiments with distance-defying gandrabionic entanglement were the best hope for engineering a deterrent. H was pulled into their project as well, due to her comparative biology expertise.

Jena calculated that the Eater would be vulnerable to interference only while it was trying to consume a resilient brain. Erin designed the bio-machinery which could weaken the invader's internal connectivity. They named the project *trance-induction*, as the objective was to put the Eater into a coma-like state together with its victim. The device became known as the *Inducer*.

The Shans were given the prerogatives of critical personnel. The General's security kept a bubble of space around them wherever they went. They could live without fear of Eater-attracting crowds.

"It's not fair we should have all this protection, while others are thrown to the Eater in handcuffs," Erin protested.

Jena snorted. "You've no idea what privilege you've grown up with, Erin. You always had safe skies above your head!" A couple of centuries ago, before the War, it was Jena's ancestors that had been privileged. They were property owners in the Milky Way, who would have looked down on Fringe Folk like Erin's kin. "The rest of us just take what we can get and do what we can."

A, along with a few other lucky kids, was able to attend a school at a spread-out campus with tiny classes.

Dajo were social creatures, though, even more so than humans. A struggled with the safety of isolation.

To cheer him up, Erin and Jena took a rare break from work to bring A to the Old Earth Aquarium. With all the other visitors cleared out, the giant tanks of water were eerie and majestic.

Growing up with humans, A hadn't acquired his ancestors' aversion to water. He walked past the menacing sharks, bubble-blowing whales, and colorful jellyfish, straight to the octopus habitat. For a long time, A stared at the creatures appearing and reappearing amidst the artificial maze of corals and the occasional cloud of ink. Eventually, it was time to go and they had to drag him away.

The mothers didn't think much of his fascination with the octopi until a few months later. The nanny told them A was shaking when he picked him up from school. Quivers for the Dajo child could last longer than the equivalent sobbing in a human. A said that the children at school had teased him for spilling his milk twice that day.

Any human parent used to cleaning the messes their children made would be horrified to imagine how much chaos an extra four arms could produce. Injection of human hormones kept the lower and upper arms mostly dormant in a young Dajo, making development of hand-eye coordination less calamitous, a luxury which A didn't have.

Later that night Jena lay sleepless, staring out of the bedroom window. She liked to keep the blinds up and bathe in the lights of the city. She used to be able to hear the distant, continuous buzz of downtown. Now only silence accompanied the lights.

Jena often fought about it with Erin, who claimed she needed complete darkness to sleep. Jena played the claustrophobia card. She'd spent five of her adolescent years on a crowded spaceship.

"He's down," Erin said, coming into the bedroom from A duty. She didn't ask to bring the blinds down this time. Instead, Erin stood by the window and pulled off her shirt.

Jena loved watching the light and shadow play on the curves of her wife's body. After enjoying the show for a few moments, Jena threw off her blanket and stretched her arms out to Erin.

They were both sleep-deprived and drained from the stress of work. Most nights, all they could do was crash into bed and hope for a few short hours of sleep before A was up again.

Tonight, however, that wouldn't be enough. Jena needed to feel something other than exhaustion, terror, and guilt; guilt and shame for the secret she kept, for what she did, and for what she was going to do.

Erin strutted over to the bed, briefly sat on the mattress next to Jena, and then in one smooth motion swept her legs over to straddle her. Her hair loosened and tickled Jena's face as she leaned forward. Their lips met briefly and then Erin arched forward, letting Jena's lips brush against her nipple.

"I want an octopus," A said from the doorway. They had missed the familiar pitter-patter of him shuffling over from his bedroom across the hallway. Middle-of-the-night conversations with a wide-awake child were just another price they paid for not using human hormones.

A giant stuffed octopus became A's eight-limbed friend in the world ruled by four-limbed creatures. A loved Octi so much he would often insist on sleeping on top of it, instead of in his bed.

Jena tries to respond but chokes, her breath coming in short gasps. They look at the General. He nods, spreading his arms to indicate the largesse of expanding the chamber to incorporate another object. "We will find space for his toy," he says. "Either of you can take it along for when he wakes up."

By the time A turned seven, the Eater had been roaming the planet for almost two years. Previously, when the Eater had been contained on Departure Island, there'd been almost no casualties amongst the children. Now there was new data.

They were at H's apartment. Dajo didn't mix parenting with other occupations. H's choice to pursue her research meant that she wouldn't have children of her own. But she was more than happy to become A's "auntie" and often volunteered to babysit.

"We need to report this. Now," H signed urgently to Jena in Dajo. Jena glanced at Erin, who was busy pouring tea into large two-handled mugs. Erin was enthusiastic about A learning the Dajo Language but knew little of it herself.

"I agree," Jena signed back to H. The General should hear it from her, but first Erin needed to know.

"Erin," she called out. Her wife turned away from her struggle with the alien kitchenware. "We have more stats now. Dajo resilience exists after all. But not the way we thought."

"What? I thought it had been debunked." Erin absent-mindedly put the mug down on the edge of the force-plastic countertop.

"Children under twelve," H's whisper rose just loud enough to reach Erin, but not to carry into the rest of the apartment. Jena noticed that the Dajo's lower hands were trembling below the table. "Adult Dajo are as vulnerable as humans or Averkians. But some children can resist the Eater for up to three minutes."

"Children? Only children?" Erin's face went pale. "When the Inducer is ready … The estimate is we need four minutes."

"They will start testing all Dajo children." H's whisper was a statement, not a question. H lived in a human world.

"That was the best potty ever!" A announced, running into the living room.

Erin jumped, almost knocking over the mug, and yelped as hot tea spilled on her palm.

"Did you wash your hands?" Jena asked automatically.

A made a face and bounded to the kitchen sink; he was in a hurry to start the game. The Dajo-designed appliances from the reclining toilet seat to the triple-headed spout were A's favorite reason to visit Auntie H's apartment.

Jena was the gamer in the family, but the Monopoly set they were using was Erin's family heirloom. It was, of course, not an actual ancient set – no one on a Fringe World could afford a thousand-year old artifact from the Old Earth. It was, however, a faithful replica made of paper and cardboard, which would even wear down with use.

A picked up the frayed Community Chest cards with his middle hands and tried to shuffle them but fumbled. "I can't…" He started quivering.

"Use your upper hands, like this!" H came to the rescue, picking up the Chance deck and riffling it deftly.

Jena signed a quick *thank you* to H, as A tried shuffling the cards using his upper hands and brightened at the improved results.

"I thought you were supposed to shuffle with your feet," Erin said seriously. A giggled. Erin squeezed his middle hand, continuing, "When you become a cosmobiologist like us, you'll teach everyone how to shuffle."

A cocked his head and giggled again. "Cosmobiology is boring because you always have to go to work. I want to be a money manager."

"Why a money manager?" Jena asked, startled.

"I won't have to go to school. I will get to stay home with my children and play games on big screens. No one will tease me about falling asleep, or whispering, or breaking things."

Erin smiled brightly, but Jena recognized her wife's discomfort. Trying to save the world didn't leave much time to be with their child.

When one of them could take a break from research they would take A out for an adventure or activity. Evenings like this were very rare.

"Sounds like fun," Erin said. "Of course, you can be a money manager when you grow up. But you'll still have to go to school for that."

Jena couldn't bring herself to share Erin's smile. *Money manager*? She would never know what A would grow up to be.

Erin was feeling guilty for not being there for A, and for the implications of their research. H was feeling guilty for concealing the data in an attempt to shield her people. Their guilt was nothing compared to Jena's.

"I am going. There's no need for me to stay in the present, but I can be useful in the future," Erin replies, pointing down to the chamber's seal. "A is sleeping with the Eater. I'll be sleeping with my Inducer. The chamber will preserve all the biocomponents. When I wake up, I'll confront the Eater again."

The General spoke with them after he learned about the Dajo children's resilience. "Legally, your son must be tested along with every other Dajo child. There's no way to know which of them would serve as the best containment vessel. But…"

"But?" Erin was not one to kowtow to authority.

"An argument could be made that your work is so important, that an exception should be made to … err … avoid you being distracted."

Jena's heart leapt and sank. She already knew who the best containment vessel would be. This was her way out, but she knew she couldn't take it.

Erin's nose wrinkled, registering the stink of chicanery. "Sir, we must take the same risk as all the other parents."

"Even if there is a chance to stop the Eater forever, it doesn't have to be one of you. A already managed to hold on long enough for your trance induction to work. He's unlikely to rise alive," the General says, once again, out of turn. "And if he does, the Eater might leave his body only to take yours."

The duration of sleep was estimated to be close to two hundred years. Jena had established that once the Eater had gone to sleep with its host, the trance could not be re-induced. But when the gandrabion reactivated in a weakened state, it could once again be affected by the Inducer.

The horror had not ended or even been mitigated, just postponed. It was enough for the General and his soldiers.

"If A doesn't wake up, or dies after being woken, I'll bury him properly," Erin responds, still looking at the cryo-chamber's seal. "And if I'm taken and die, he'll bury me."

When her turn came, Erin insisted on bringing her equipment along to stow right next to her body. There was no saying what tech would, or wouldn't, be available after almost two centuries had passed.

They had one last argument.

"You are not to blame!" Erin's tears streamed down her face. "We both did it. And he'll need both of us, when he wakes up." She wiped her cheek and added, "I will need you."

"I can't do it now." Jena almost added, *I don't belong with A anymore*. "I have to stay back to carry on my research. Find a way to make the trance permanent without killing the host. This will give you and A the best chance. I'll catch up in a few years. You like older women anyway."

"You are not to blame," the General unknowingly repeats Erin's words.

"You are not to blame," The Averkian echoes.

Erin is being lowered into her own cryochamber, only days after A.

According to her epaulets, the Averkian officer who came to Erin's lab on the day the Eater was discovered has been promoted to colonel. Even her new rank must not have cleared her to witness A's entombment. But she is here now, standing next to the General. Erin's ceremony, while restricted, is more routine, without the 0-I protocol. Jena is grateful H is still not allowed to be here and witness her confession. H has known all along about child resilience, but not about the role of the hormones and Jena's plan.

The casket is sized for an adult this time. The cryo-chamber was enlarged to allow for extra equipment. A uniformed soldier carefully places a stuffed octopus next to the casket.

Was hearing their son's whisper-talk and holding his soft body a mere dream? Can they dream it again if they go to sleep now?

It is time to tell the General. "I started studying cosmobiology with a Dajo mentor on a Dajo colony ship. He was familiar with Eaters. He taught me that non-Dajo hormones would suppress resilience in children. All of this was my design, including the adoption. From the day I heard about the Eater. The best chance for our planet was a Dajo child with no human hormones and no brain adaptation," Jena signs. "I haven't told Erin. I couldn't. After I go to sleep, you need to make sure I'm woken before her. I was the one who sacrificed A. I must be the one to face the Eater."

For once, the General has no reply.

Deluge

Zenna Henderson

...and bare up the ark, and it was lift up above the earth.
– GEN. 7:17

"THE CHILDREN ARE UP ALREADY, EVA-LEE?" asked David, lounging back in his chair after his first long, satisfying swallow from his morning cup. "Foolish question, David, on Gathering Day," I laughed. "They've been up since before it was light. Have you forgotten how you used to feel?"

"Of course not." My son cradled his cup in his two hands to warm it and watched idly until steam plumed up fragrantly. "I just forgot-oh, momentarily, I assure you-that it was Gathering Day. So far it hasn't felt much like *Jailova* weather."

"No, it hasn't," I answered, puckering my forehead thoughtfully. "It has felt-odd-this year. The green isn't as – Oh, good morning, 'Chell," to my daughter-of-love, "I suppose the little imps waked you first thing?"

"At least half an hour before that," yawned 'Chell. "I suppose I used to do it myself. But just wait – they'll have their yawning time when they're parents."

"Mother! Mother! Father! Gramma!"

The door slapped open and the children avalanched in, all talking shrilly at once until David waved his cup at them and lifted one eyebrow. 'Chell laughed at the sudden silence.

"That's better," she said. "What's all the uproar?"

The children looked at one another and the five-year-old Eve was nudged to the fore, but, as usual, David started talking. "We were out gathering *panthus* leaves to make our Gathering baskets, and all at once—" He paused and nudged Eve again. "You tell, Eve. After all, it's you—"

"Oh, no!" cried 'Chell. "Not my last baby! Not already!"

"Look," said Eve solemnly. "Look at me."

She stood tiptoe and wavered a little, her arms outstretched for balance, and then she lifted slowly and carefully up into her mother's arms.

We all laughed and applauded and even 'Chell, after blotting her surprised tears on Eve's dark curls, laughed with us.

"Bless-a-baby!" she said, hugging her tight. "Lifting all alone already – and on Gathering Day, too! It's not everyone who can have Gathering Day for her Happy Day!" Then she sobered and pressed the solemn ceremonial kiss on each cheek. "Lift in delight all your life, Eve!" she said.

Eve matched her parents' solemnity as her father softly completed the ritual. "By the Presence and the Name and the Power, lift to good and the Glory until your Calling." And we all joined in making the Sign.

"I speak for her next," I said, holding out my arms. "Think you can lift to Gramma, Eve?"

"Well..." Eve considered the gap between her and me – the chair, the breakfast table – all the obstacles before my waiting arms. And then she smiled. "Look at me," she said. "Here I come, Gramma."

She lifted carefully above the table, overarching so high that the crisp girl-frill around the waist of her close-fitting briefs brushed the ceiling. Then she was safe in my arms.

"That's better than I did," called Simon through the laughter that followed. "I landed right in the *flahmen* jam!"

"So you did, son," laughed David, ruffling Simon's coppery-red hair. "A full dish of it."

"Now that that's taken care of, let's get organized. Are you all Gathering together—"

"No." Lytha, our teener, flushed faintly. "I – we – our party will be mostly-well—" She paused and checked her blush, shaking her dark hair back from her face. "Timmy and I are going with Beckie and Andy. We're going to the Mountain."

"Well!" David's brow lifted in mock consternation. "Mother, did you know our daughter was two-ing?"

"Not really, Father!" cried Lytha hastily, unable to resist the bait though she knew he was teasing. "Four-ing, it is, really."

"*Adonday veeah*!" he sighed in gigantic relief. "Only half the worry it might be!" He smiled at her. "Enjoy," he said, "but it ages me so much so fast that a daughter of mine is two – oh, pardon, four-ing already."

"The rest of us are going together," said Davie. "We're going to the Tangle-meadows. The *failova* were thick there last year. Bet we three get more than Lytha and her two-ing foursome! They'll be looking mostly for *Jlahmen* anyway!" with the enormous scorn of the almost-teen for the activities of the teens.

"Could be," said David. "But after all, your sole purpose this Gathering Day is merely to Gather."

"I notice you don't turn up your nose at the *flahmen* after they're made into jam," said Lytha. "And you just wait, smarty, until the time comes – and it will," her cheeks pinked up a little, "when you find yourself wanting to share a *Jlahmen* with some gaggly giggle of a girl!"

"*Flahmen*!" muttered Davie. "Girls!"

"They're both mighty sweet, Son," laughed David. "You wait and see." Ten minutes later, 'Chell and David and I stood at the window watching the children leave. Lytha, after nervously putting on and taking off, arranging and rearranging her Gathering Day garlands at least a dozen times, was swept up by a giggling group that zoomed in a trio and went out a quartet and disappeared in long, low lifts across the pastureland toward the heavily wooded Mountain.

Davie tried to gather Eve up as in the past, but she stubbornly refused to be trailed, and kept insisting, "I can lift now! Let me do it. I'm big!"

Davie rolled exasperated eyes and then grinned and the three started off for Tangle-meadows in short hopping little lifts, with Eve always just beginning to lift as they landed or just landing as they lifted, her small Gathering basket bobbing along with her. Before they disappeared, however, she was trailing from Davie's free hand and the lifts were smoothing out long and longer. My thoughts went with them as I remembered the years I had Gathered the lovely luminous flowers that popped into existence in a single night, leafless, almost stemless, as though formed like dew, or falling like concentrated moonlight. No one knows now how the custom of loves sharing a *flahmen* came into being, but it's firmly entrenched in the traditions of the People. To share that luminous loveliness, petal by petal, one for me and one for you and all for us—

"How pleasant that Gathering Day brings back our loves," I sighed dreamily as I stood in the kitchen and snapped my fingers for the breakfast dishes to come to me. "People that might otherwise be completely forgotten come back so vividly every year—"

"Yes," said 'Chell, watching the tablecloth swish out the window, huddling the crumbs together to dump them in the feather-pen in back of the house. "And it's a good anniversary-marker. Most of us meet our loves at the Gathering Festival – or discover them there." She took the returning cloth and folded it away. "I never dreamed when I used to fuss with David over mud pies and playhouses that one Gathering Day he'd blossom into my love."

"*Me* blossom?" David peered around the doorjamb. "Have you forgotten how you looked, preblossom? Knobby knees, straggly hair, toothless grin—!"

"David, put me down!" 'Chell struggled as she felt herself being lifted to press against the ceiling. "We're too old for such nonsense!"

"Get yourself down, then, Old One," he said from the other room. "If I'm too old for nonsense, I'm too old to *platt* you."

"Never mind, funny fellow," she said, "I'll do it myself." Her down-reaching hand strained toward the window and she managed to gather a handful of the early morning sun. Quickly she platted herself to the floor and tiptoed off into the other room, eyes aglint with mischief, finger hushing to her lips.

I smiled as I heard David's outcry and 'Chell's delighted laugh, but I felt my smile slant down into sadness. I leaned my arms on the windowsill and looked lovingly at all the dear familiarity around me. Before Thann's Calling, we had known so many happy hours in the meadows and skies and waters of this loved part of the Home.

"And he is still here," I thought comfortably. "The grass still bends to his feet, the leaves still part to his passing, the waters still ripple to his touch, and my heart still cradles his name.

"Oh, Thann, Thann!" I wouldn't let tears form in my eyes. I smiled. "I wonder what kind of a grampa you'd have made!" I leaned my forehead on my folded arms briefly, then turned to busy myself with straightening the rooms for the day. I was somewhat diverted from routine by finding six mismated sandals stacked, for some unfathomable reason, above the middle of Simon's bed, the top one, inches above the rest, bobbing in the breeze from the open window.

* * *

The oddness we had felt about the day turned out to be more than a passing uneasiness, and we adults were hardly surprised when the children came straggling back hours before they usually did.

We hailed them from afar, lifting out to them expecting to help with their burdens of brightness, but the children didn't answer our hails. They plodded on toward the house, dragging slow feet in the abundant grass.

"What do you suppose has happened?" breathed 'Chell. "Surely not Eve—"

"*Adonday veedh*!" murmured David, his eyes intent on the children. "Something's wrong, but I see Eve."

"Hi, young ones," he called cheerfully. "How's the crop this year?" The children stopped, huddled together, almost fearfully.

"Look." Davie pushed his basket at them. Four misshapen *failova* glowed dully in the basket. No flickering, glittering brightness. No flushing and paling of petals. No crisp, edible sweetness of blossom. Only a dull glow, a sullen winking, an unappetizing crumbling.

"That's all," said Davie, his voice choking. "That's all we could find!" He was scared and outraged – outraged that his world dared to be different from what he had expected – had counted on.

Eve cried, "No, no! I have one. Look!" Her single flower was a hard-clenched *flahmen* bud with only a smudge of light at the tip.

"No *failova*?" 'Chell took Davie's proffered basket. "No *flahmen*? But they always bloom on Gathering Day. Maybe the buds—"

"No buds," said Simon, his face painfully white under the brightness of his hair. I glanced at him quickly. He seldom ever got upset over anything. What was there about this puzzling development that was stirring him?

"David!" 'Chell's face turned worriedly to him. "What's wrong? There have always been *failova*!"

"I know," said David, fingering Eve's bud and watching it crumble in his fingers. "Maybe it's only in the meadows. Maybe there's plenty in the hills."

"No," I said. "Look."

Far off toward the hills we could see the teeners coming, slowly, clustered together; *panthus* baskets trailing.

"No *failova*," said Lyrha as they neared us. She turned her basket up, her face troubled. "No *failova* and no *flahmen*. Not a flicker on all the hills where they were so thick last year. Oh, Father, why not? It's as if the sun hadn't come up! Something's wrong."

"Nothing catastrophic, Lytha." David comforted her with a smile. "We'll bring up the matter at the next meeting of the Old Ones. Someone will have the answer. It is unusual, you know." (Unheard of, he should have said.) "We'll find out then." He boosted Eve to his shoulder. "Come on, young ones, the world hasn't ended. It's still Gathering Day! I'll race you to the house. First one there gets six *koomatka* to eat all by himself! One, two, three—"

Off shot the shrieking, shouting children, Eve's little heels pummeling David's chest in her excitement. The teeners followed for a short way and then slanted off on some project of their own, waving goodby to 'Chell and me. We women followed slowly to the house, neither speaking.

I wasn't surprised to find Simon waiting for me in my room. He sat huddled on my bed, his hands clasping and unclasping and trembling, a fine, quick trembling deeper than muscles and tendons. His face was so white it was almost luminous and the skiff of golden freckles across the bridge of his nose looked metallic.

"Simon?" I touched him briefly on his hair that was so like Thann's had been.

"Gramma." His breath caught in a half hiccough. He cleared his throat carefully as though any sudden movement would break something fragile. "Gramma," he whispered. "I can See!"

"See!" I sat down beside him because my knees suddenly evaporated. "Oh, Simon! You don't mean—"

"Yes, I do, Gramma." He rubbed his hands across his eyes. "We had just found the first *failova* and were wondering what was wrong with it when everything kinda went away and I was – somewhere – Seeing!" He looked up, terrified. "It's my Gift!"

I gathered the suddenly wildly sobbing child into my arms and held him tightly until his terror spent itself and I felt his withdrawal. I let him go and watched his wet, flushed face dry and pale back to normal.

"Oh, Gramma," he said, "I don't want a Gift yet. I'm only ten. David hasn't found his Gift and he's twelve already. I don't want a Gift – especially this one—" He closed his eyes and shuddered. "Oh, Gramma, what I've seen already! Even the Happy scares me because it's still in the Presence!"

"It's not given to many," I said, at a loss how to comfort him. "Why, Simon, it would take a long journey back to our Befores to find one in our family who was permitted to See. It is an honor – to be able to put aside the curtain of time—"

"I don't *want* to!" Simon's eyes brimmed again. "I don't think it's a bit of fun. Do I have to?"

"Do you have to breathe?" I asked him. "You could stop if you wanted to, but your body would die. You can refuse your Gift, but part of you would die – the part of you the Power honors – your place in the Presence – your syllable of the Name." All this he knew from first consciousness, but I could feel him taking comfort from my words. "Do you realize the People have had no one to See for them since – since – why, clear back to the Peace! And now you are it! Oh, Simon, I am so proud of you!" I laughed at my own upsurge of emotion. "Oh, Simon! May I touch my thrice-honored grandson?"

With a wordless cry, he flung himself into my arms and we clung tightly, tightly, before his deep renouncing withdrawal. He looked at me then and slowly dropped his arms from around my neck, separation in every movement. I could see growing, in the topaz tawniness of his eyes, his new set-apartness. It made me realize anew how close the Presence is to us always and how much nearer Simon was than any of us. Also, naked and trembling in my heart was the recollection that never did the People have one to See for them unless there lay ahead portentous things to See.

Both of us shuttered our eyes and looked away, Simon to veil the eyes that so nearly looked on the Presence, I, lest I be blinded by the Glory reflected in his face.

"Which reminds me," I said in a resolutely everyday voice, "I will now listen to explanations as to why those six sandals were left on, over, and among your bed this morning."

"Well," he said with a tremulous grin, "the red ones are too short—" He turned stricken, realizing eyes to me. "I won't ever be able to tell anyone anything any more unless the Power wills it!" he cried. Then he grinned again. "And the green ones need the latchets renewed—"

A week later the usual meeting was called and David and I – we were among the Old Ones of our Group – slid into our robes. I felt a pang as I smoothed the shimmering fabric over my hips, pressing pleats in with my thumb and finger to adjust for lost weight. The last time I had worn it was the Festival the year Thann was Called. Since then I hadn't wanted to attend the routine Group meetings – not without Thann. I hadn't realized that I was losing weight.

'Chell clung to David. "I wish now that I were an Old One too," she said. "I've got a nameless worry in the pit of my stomach heavy enough to anchor me for life. Hurry home, you two!"

I looked back as we lifted just before the turnoff. I smiled to see the warm lights begin to well up in the windows. Then my smile died. I felt, too, across my heart the shadow that made 'Chell feel it was Lighting Time before the stars had broken through the last of the day.

* * *

The blow – when it came – was almost physical, so much so that I pressed my hands to my chest, my breath coming hard, trying too late to brace against the shock. David's sustaining hand was on my arm but I felt the tremor in it, too. Around me I felt my incredulity and disbelief shared by the other Old Ones of the Group.

The Oldest spread his hands as he was deluged by a flood of half formed questions. "It has been Seen. Already our Home has been altered so far that the *failova* and *flahmen* can't come to blossom. As we accepted the fact that there were no *failova* and *flahmen* this year, so we must accept the fact that there will be no more Home for us."

In the silence that quivered after his words, I could feel the further stricken sag of heartbeats around me, and suddenly my own heart slowed until I wondered if the Power was stilling it now – now – in the midst of this confused fear and bewilderment.

"Then we are all Called?" I couldn't recognize the choked voice that put the question. "How long before the Power summons us?"

"*We* are not Called," said the Oldest. "Only the Home is Called. We – go."

"Go!" The thought careened from one to another.

"Yes," said the Oldest. "Away from the Home. Out."

Life apart from the Home? I slumped. It was too much to be taken in all at once. Then I remembered. Simon! Oh, poor Simon! If he were Seeing clearly already – but of course he was. He was the one who had told the Oldest! No wonder he was terrified! *Simon*, I said to the Oldest subvocally. Yes, answered the Oldest. *Do not communicate to the others. He scarcely can bear the burden now. To have it known would multiply it past his bearing. Keep his secret – completely.*

I came back to the awkward whirlpool of thoughts around me. "But," stammered someone, speaking what everyone was thinking, "can the People *live* away from the Home? Wouldn't we die like uprooted plants?"

"We can live," said the Oldest. "This we know, as we know that the Home can no longer be our biding place."

"What's wrong? What's happening?" It was Neil – Timmy's father.

"We don't know." The Oldest was shamed. "We have forgotten too much since the Peace to be able to state the mechanics of what is happening, but one of us Sees us go and the Home destroyed, so soon that we have no time to go back to the reasons."

Since we were all joined in our conference mind, which is partially subvocal, all our protests and arguments and cries were quickly emitted and resolved, leaving us awkwardly trying to plan something of which we had no knowledge of our own.

"If we are to go," I said, feeling a small spurt of excitement inside my shock, "we'll have to make again. Make a tool. No, that's not the word. We have tools still. Man does with tools. No, it's a – a machine we'll have to make. Machines do to man. We haven't been possessed by machines—"

"For generations," said David. "Not since—" He paused to let our family's stream of history pour through his mind. "Since Eva-lee's thrice great-grandfather's time."

"Nevertheless," said the Oldest, "we must make ships." His tongue was hesitant on the long unused word. "I have been in communication with the other Oldest Ones around the Home. Our Group must make six of them."

"How can we?" asked Neil. "We have no plans. We don't know such things any more. We have forgotten almost all of it. But I do know that to break free from the Home would take a pushing something that all of us together couldn't supply."

"We will have the – the fuel," said the Oldest. "When the time comes. My Befores knew the fuel. We would not need it if only our motivers had developed their Gift fully, but as they did not—"

"We must each of us search the Before stream of our lives and find the details that we require in this hour of need. By the Presence, the Name, and the Power, let us remember."

The evening sped away almost in silence as each mind opened and became receptive to the flow of racial memory that lay within. All of us partook in a general way of that stream that stemmed almost from the dawn of the Home. In particular, each family had some specialized area of the memory in greater degree than the others. From time to time came a sigh or a cry prefacing, "My Befores knew of the metals," or "Mine of the instruments" – the words were unfamiliar – "the instruments of pressure and temperature."

"Mine," I discovered with a glow – and a sigh – "the final putting together of the shells of ships."

"Yes," nodded David, "and also, from my father's Befores, the settings of the – the – the settings that guide the ship."

"Navigation," said Neil's deep voice. "My Befores knew of the making of the navigation machine yours knew how to set."

"And all," I said, "all of this going back to nursery school would have been unnecessary if we hadn't rested so comfortably so long on the achievements of our Befores!" I felt the indignant withdrawal of some of those about me, but the acquiescence of most of them.

When the evening ended, each of us Old Ones carried not only the burden of the doom of the Home, but a part of the past that, in the Quiet Place of each home, must, with the help of the Power, be probed and probed again, until—

"Until—" TheOldest stood suddenly, clutching the table as though he had just realized the enormity of what he was saying. "Until we have the means of leaving the Home – before it becomes a band of dust between the stars—"

* * *

Simon and Lytha were waiting up with 'Chell when David and I returned. At the sight of our faces, Simon slipped into the bedroom and woke Davie and the two crept quietly back into the room. Simon's thought reached out ahead of him. *Did he tell*? And mine went out reassuringly. *No. And he won't.*

In spite of – or perhaps because of – the excitement that had been building up in me all evening, I felt suddenly drained and weak. I sat down, gropingly, in a chair and pressed my hands to my face. "You tell them, David," I said, fighting an odd vertigo.

David shivered and swallowed hard. "There were no *failova* because the Home is being broken up. By next Gathering Day there will be no Home. It is being destroyed. We can't even say why. We have forgotten too much and there isn't time to seek out the information now, but long before next Gathering Day, we will be gone – out."

'Chell's breath caught audibly. "No Home!" she said, her eyes widening and darkening. "No Home? Oh, David, don't joke. Don't try to scare—"

"It's true." My voice had steadied now. "It has been Seen. We must build ships and seek asylum among the stars." My heart gave a perverse jump of excitement. "The Home will no longer exist. We will be homeless exiles."

"But The People away from the Home!" 'Chell's face puckered, close to tears. "How can we live anywhere else? We are a part of the Home as much as the Home is a part of us. We can't just amputate—"

"Father!" Lytha's voice was a little too loud. She said again, "Father, are all of us going together in the same ship?"

"No," said David. "Each Group by itself." Lytha relaxed visibly. "Our Group is to have six ships," he added.

Lytha's hands tightened. "Who is to go in which ship?"

"It hasn't been decided yet," said David, provoked. "How can you worry about a detail like that when the Home, *the Home* will soon be gone!"

"It's important," said Lytha, flushing. "Timmy and I—"

"Oh," said David. 'I'm sorry, Lytha. I didn't know. The matter will have to be decided when the time comes."

* * *

It didn't take long for the resiliency of childhood to overcome the shock of the knowledge born on Gathering Day. Young laughter rang as brightly through the hills and meadows as always. But David and 'Chell clung closer to one another, sharing the heavy burden of leave-taking, as did all the adults of the Home. At times I, too, felt wildly, hopefully, that this was all a bad dream to be awakened from. But other times I had the feeling that this *was* an awakening. This was the dawn after a long twilight – a long twilight of slanting sun and relaxing shadows. Other times I felt so detached from the whole situation that wonder welled up in me to see the sudden tears, the sudden clutching of familiar things, that had become a sort of pattern among us as realization came and went. And then, there were frightening times when I felt weakness flowing into me like a river – a river that washed all the Home away on a voiceless wave. I was almost becoming more engrossed in the puzzle of me than in the puzzle of the dying Home – and I didn't like it.

David and I went often to Meeting, working with the rest of the Group on the preliminary plans for the ships. One night he leaned across the table to the Oldest and asked, "How do we know how much food will be needed to sustain us until we find asylum?"

The Oldest looked steadily back at him. "We *don't* know," he said. "We don't know that we will ever find asylum."

"Don't know?" David's eyes were blank with astonishment.

"No," said the Oldest. "We found no other habitable worlds before the Peace. We have no idea how far we will have to go or if we shall any of us live to see another Home. Each Group is to be assigned to a different sector of the sky. On Crossing Day, we say goodby – possibly forever – to all the other Groups. It may be that only one ship will plant the seeds of the People upon a new world. It may be that we will all be Called be fore a new Home is found."

"Then," said David, "why don't we stay here and take our Calling with the Home?"

"Because the Power has said to go. We are given time to go back to the machines. The Power is swinging the gateway to the stars open to us. We must take the gift and do what we can with it. We have no right to deprive our children of any of the years they might have left to them."

After David relayed the message to 'Chell, she clenched both her fists tight up against her anguished heart and cried, "We can't! Oh, David! We can't! We can't leave the Home for – for – nowhere! Oh, David!" And she clung to him, wetting his shoulder with her tears.

"We can do what we must do," he said. "All of the People are sharing this sorrow, so none of us must make the burden any heavier for the others. The children learn their courage from us, 'Chell. Be a good teacher." He rocked her close-pressed head, his hand patting her tumbled hair, his troubled eyes seeking mine.

"Mother—" David began – Eva-lee was for gaity and casual every day.

"Mother, it seems to me that the Presence is pushing us out of the Home deliberately and crumpling it like an empty eggshell so we can't creep back into it. We have sprouted too few feathers on our wings since the Peace. I think we're being pushed off the branch to make us fly. This egg has been too comfortable." He laughed a little as he held 'Chell away from him and dried her cheeks with the palms of his hands. 'I'm afraid I've made quite an omelet of my egg analogy, but can you think of anything really new that we have learned about Creation in our time?"

"Well," I said, searching my mind, pleased immeasurably to hear my own thoughts on the lips of my son. "No, I can honestly say I can't think of one new thing."

"So if you were Called to the Presence right now and were asked, 'What do you know of My Creation?' all you could say would be 'I know all that my Befores knew – my immediate Befores, that is – I mean, my father—'" David opened his hands and poured out emptiness. "Oh, Mother! What we have forgotten! And how content we have been with so little!"

"But some other way," 'Chell cried. "This is so – so drastic and cruel!"

"All baby birds shiver," said David, clasping her cold hands. "Sprout a pin feather, 'Chell!"

* * *

And then the planning arrived at the point where work could begin. The sandal shops were empty. The doors were closed in the fabric centers and the ceramic workrooms. The sunlight crept unshadowed again and again across the other workshops, and weeds began tentative invasions of the garden plots.

Far out in the surrounding hills, those of the People who knew how hovered in the sky, rolling back slowly the heavy green cover of the mountainsides, to lay bare the metal-rich underearth. Then the Old Ones, making solemn mass visits from Group to Group, quietly concentrated above the bared hills and drew forth from the very bones of the Home the bright, bubbling streams of metal, drew them forth until they flowed liquidly down the slopes to the workplaces – the launching sites. And the rush and the clamor and the noise of the hurried multitudes broke the silence of the hills of the Home and sent tremors through all our windows – and through our shaken souls.

I often stood at the windows of our house, watching the sky-pointing monsters of metal slowly coming to form. From afar they had a severe sort of beauty that eased my heart of the hurt their having-to-be caused. But it was exciting! Oh, it was beautifully exciting! Sometimes I wondered what we thought about and what we did before we started all this surge out into space. On the days that I put in my helping hours on the lifting into place of the strange different parts that had been fashioned by other Old Ones from memories of the Befores, the upsurge of power and the feeling of being one part of such a gigantic undertaking, made me realize that we had forgotten without even being conscious of it, the warmth and strength of working together. Oh, the People are together even more than the leaves on a tree or the scales on a *dolfeo*, but *working* together? I knew this was my first experience with its pleasant strength. My lungs seemed to breathe deeper. My reach was longer, my grasp stronger. Odd, unfinished feelings welled up inside me and I wanted to *do*. Perhaps this was the itching of my new pin feathers. And then, sometimes when I reached an exultation that almost lifted me off my feet, would come the weakness, the sagging, the sudden desire for tears and withdrawal. I worried, a little, that there might come a time when I wouldn't be able to conceal it.

The Crossing had become a new, engrossing game for the children. At night, shivering in the unseasonable weather, cool, but not cold enough to shield, they would sit looking up at the glory-frosted sky and pick out the star they wanted for a new Home, though they knew that none they could see would actually be it. Eve always chose the brightest pulsating one in the heavens and claimed it as hers. Davie chose one that burned steadily but faintly straight up above them. But when Lytha was asked, she turned the question aside and I knew that any star with Timmy would be Home to Lytha.

Simon usually sat by himself, a little withdrawn from the rest, his eyes quiet on the brightness overhead.

"What star is yours, Simon?" I asked one evening, feeling intrusive but knowing the guard he had for any words he should not speak.

"None," he said, his voice heavy with maturity. "No star for me."

"You mean you'll wait and see?" I asked.

"No," said Simon. "There won't be one for me."

My heart sank. "Simon, you haven't been Called, have you?"

"No," said Simon. "Not yet. I will see a new Home, but I will be Called from its sky."

"Oh, Simon," I cried softly, trying to find a comfort for him. "How wonderful to be able to See a new Home!"

"Not much else left to See," said Simon. "Not that has words." And I saw a flare of Otherside touch his eyes. "But, Gramma, you should see the Home when the last moment comes! That's one of the things I have no words for."

"But we will have a new Home, then," I said, going dizzily back to a subject I hoped I could comprehend. "You said—"

"I can't See beyond my Calling," said Simon. "I will see a new Home. I will be Called from its strange sky. I can't See what is for the People there. Maybe they'll all be Called with me. For me there's flame and brightness and pain – then the Presence. That's all I know.

"But, Gramma" – his voice had returned to that of a normal ten year-old – "Lytha's feeling awful bad. Help her."

The children were laughing and frolicking in the thin blanket of snow that whitened the hills and meadows, their clear, untroubled laughter echoing through the windows to me and 'Chell, who, with close-pressed lips, was opening the winter chests that had been closed so short a time ago. 'Chell fingered the bead stitching on the toes of one little ankle-high boot.

"What will we need in the new Home, Eva-lee?" she asked despairingly.

"We have no way of knowing," I said. "We have no idea of what kind of Home we'll find." *If any, if any, if any*, our unspoken thoughts throbbed together.

"I've been thinking about that," said 'Chell. "What will it be like? Will we be able to live as we do now or will we have to go back to machines and the kind of times that went with our machines? Will we still be one People or be separated mind and soul?" Her hands clenched on a bright sweater and a tear slid down her cheek. "Oh, Eva-lee, maybe we won't even be able to feel the Presence there!"

"You know better than that!" I chided. "The Presence is with us always, even if we have to go to the ends of the Universe. Since we can't know now what the new Home will be like, let's not waste our tears on it." I shook out a gaily patterned quilted skirt. "Who knows?" I laughed. "Maybe it will be a water world and we'll become fish. Or a fire world and we the flames!"

"We can't adjust quite that much!" protested 'Chell, smiling moistly as she dried her face on the sweater. "But it is a comfort to know we can change some to match our environment."

I reached for another skirt and paused, hand outstretched

"'Chell," I said, taken by a sudden idea, "what if the new Home is already inhabited? What if life is already there?"

"Why then, so much the better," said 'Chell. "Friends, help, places to live—"

"They might not accept us," I said.

"But refugees – homeless!" protested 'Chell. "If any in need came to the Home—"

"Even if they were different?"

"In the Presence, all are the same," said 'Chell.

"But remember." My knuckles whitened on the skirt. "Only remember far enough back and you will find the Days of Difference before the Peace."

And 'Chell remembered. She turned her stricken face to me. "You mean there might be no welcome for us if we do find a new Home?"

"If we could treat our own that way, how might others treat strangers?" I asked, shaking out the scarlet skirt. "But, please the Power, it will not be so. We can only pray."

It turned out that we had little need to worry about what kind of clothing or anything else to take with us. We would have to go practically possessionless – there was room for only the irreducible minimum of personal effects. There was considerable of an uproar and many loud lamentations when Eve found out that she could not take all of her play-People with her, and, when confronted by the necessity of making a choice – one single one of her play-People – she threw them all in a tumbled heap in the corner of her room, shrieking that she would take none at all. A sharp smack of David's hand on her bare thighs for her tantrum, and a couple of enveloping hugs for her comfort, and she sniffed up her tears and straightened out her play-People into a staggering, tumbling row across the floor. It took her three days to make her final selection. She chose the one she had named the Listener.

"She's not a him and he's not a her," she had explained. "This play-People is to listen."

"To what?" teased Davie.

"To anything I have to tell and can't tell anyone," said Eve with great dignity. "You don't even have to verb'lize to Listener. All you have to do is to touch and Listener knows what you feel and it tells you why it doesn't feel good and the bad goes away."

"Well, ask the Listener how to make the bad grammar go away," laughed Davie. "You've got your sentences all mixed up."

"Listener knows what I mean and so do you!" retorted Eve.

So when Eve made her choice and stood hugging Listener and looking with big solemn eyes at the rest of her play-People, Davie suggested casually, "Why don't you go bury the rest of them? They're the same as Called now and we don't leave cast-asides around."

And from then until the last day, Eve was happy burying and digging up her play-People, always finding better, more advantageous, or prettier places to make her miniature casting-place.

Lytha sought me out one evening as I leaned over the stone wall around the feather-pen, listening to the go-to-bed contented duckings and cooings. She leaned with me on the rough gray stones and, snapping an iridescent feather to her hand, smoothed her fingers back and forth along it wordlessly. We both listened idly to Eve and Davie. We could hear them talking together somewhere in the depths of the *koomatka* bushes beyond the feather-pen.

"What's going to happen to the Home after we're gone?" asked Eve idly.

"Oh, it's going to shake and crack wide open and fire and lava will come out and everything will fall apart and burn up," said Davie, no more emotionally than Eve.

"Ooo!" said Eve, caught in the imagination. "Then what will happen to my play-People? Won't they be all right under here? No one can see them."

"Oh, they'll be set on fire and go up in a blaze of glory," said Davie.

"A blaze of glory!" Eve drew a long happy sigh. "In a blaze of glory! Inna blaza glory! Oh, Davie! I'd like to see it. Can I, Davie? Can I?"

"Silly *toola*." said Davie. "If you were here to see it, *you'd* go up in a blaze of glory, too!" And he lifted up from the *koomatka* bushes, the time for his chores with the animals hot on his heels.

"Inna blaza glory! Inna blaza glory!" sang Eve happily. "All the play-People inna blaza glory!" Her voice faded to a tuneless hum as she left, too.

"Gramma," said Lytha, "is it really true?"

"Is what really true?" I asked.

"That the Home won't be any more and that we will be gone."

"Why, yes, Lytha, why do you doubt it?"

"Because – because—" She gestured with the feather at the wall. "Look, it's all so solid – the stones set each to the other so solidly – so – so *always-looking*. How can it all come apart?"

"You know from your first consciousness that nothing This-side is forever," I said. "Nothing at all except Love. And even that gets so tangled up in the things of This-side that when your love is Called—" the memory of Thann was a heavy burning inside me – "Oh, Lytha! To look into the face of your love and know that Something has come apart and that never again This-side will you find him whole!"

And then I knew I had said the wrong thing. I saw Lytha's too young eyes looking in dilated horror at the sight of her love – her not-quite-yet love, being pulled apart by this same whatever that was pulling the Home apart. I turned the subject.

"I want to go to the Lake for a goodby," I said. "Would you like to go with me?"

"No, thank you, Gramma." Hers was a docile, little-girl voice surely much too young to be troubled about loves as yet! "We teeners are going to watch the new metal-melting across the hills. It's fascinating. I'd like to be able to do things like that."

"You can – you could have—" I said, "if we had trained our youth as we should have."

"Maybe I'll learn," said Lytha, her eyes intent on the feather. She sighed deeply and dissolved the feather into a faint puff of blue smoke. "Maybe I'll learn." And I knew her mind was not on metal-melting.

She turned away and then back again. "Gramma, The Love—" She stopped. I could feel her groping for words. "The Love is forever, isn't it?"

"Yes," I said.

"Love This-side is part of The Love, isn't it?"

"A candle lighted from the sun," I said.

"But the candle will go out!" she cried. "Oh, Gramma! The candle will go out in the winds of the Crossing!" She turned her face from me and whispered, "Especially if it never quite got lighted."

"There are other candles," I murmured, knowing how like a lie it must sound to her.

"But never the same!" She snatched herself away from my side. "It isn't fair! It isn't fair!" and she streaked away across the frost-scorched meadow.

And as she left, I caught a delightful, laughing picture of two youngsters racing across a little lake, reeling and spinning as the waves under their feet lifted and swirled, wrapping white lace around their slender brown ankles. Everything was blue and silver and laughter and fun. I was caught up in the wonder and pleasure until I suddenly realized that it wasn't my memory at all. Thann and I had another little lake we loved more. I had seen someone else's Happy Place that would dissolve like mine with the Home. Poor Lytha.

* * *

The crooked sun was melting the latest snow the day all of us Old Ones met beside the towering shells of the ships. Each Old One was wrapped against the chilly wind. No personal shields today. The need for power was greater for the task ahead than for comfort. Above us, the huge bright curved squares of metal, clasped each to each with the old joinings, composed the shining length of each ship. Almost I could have cried to see the scarred earth beneath them-the trampledness that would never green again, the scars that would never heal. I blinked up the brightness of the nearest ship, up to the milky sky, and blinked away from its strangeness.

"The time is short," said the Oldest. "A week."

"A week." The sigh went through the Group.

"Tonight the ship loads must be decided upon. Tomorrow the inside machines must be finished. The next day, the fuel." The Oldest shivered and wrapped himself in his scarlet mantle. "The fuel that we put so completely out of our minds after the Peace. Its potential for evil was more than its service to us. But it is there. It is still there." He shivered again and turned to me.

"Tell us again," he said. "We must complete the shells." And I told them again, without words, only with the shaping of thought to thought. Then the company of Old Ones lifted slowly above the first ship, clasping hands in a circle like a group of dancing children and, leaning forward into the circle, thought the thought I had shaped for them.

For a long time there was only the thin fluting of the cold wind past the point of the ship and then the whole shell of metal quivered and dulled and became fluid. For the span of three heartbeats it remained so and then it hardened again, complete, smooth, seamless, one cohesive whole from tip to base, broken only by the round ports at intervals along its length.

In succession the other five ships were made whole, but the intervals between the ships grew longer and grayer as the strength drained from us, and, before we were finished, the sun had gone behind a cloud and we were all shadows leaning above shadows, fluttering like shadows.

The weakness caught me as we finished the last one. David received me as I drifted down, helpless, and folded on myself He laid me on the brittle grass and sat panting beside me, his head drooping. I lay as though I had become fluid and knew that something more than the fatigue of the task we had just finished had drained me. "But I have to be strong!" I said desperately, knowing weakness had no destiny among the stars. I stared up at the gray sky while a tear drew a cold finger from the corner of my eye to my ear.

"We're just not used to using the Power," said David softly.

"I know, I know," I said, knowing that he did not know. I closed my eyes and felt the whisper of falling snow upon my face, each palm-sized flake melting into a tear.

* * *

Lytha stared from me to David, her eyes wide and incredulous. "But you *knew*, Father! I told you! I told you Gathering Night!"

"I'm sorry, Lytha," said David. "There was no other way to do it. Ships fell by lot and Timmy's family and ours will be in different ships."

"Then let me go to his ship or let him come to mine!" she cried, her cheeks flushing and paling.

"Families must remain together," I said, my heart breaking for her. "Each ship leaves the Home with the assumption that it is alone. If you went in the other ship, we might never all be together again."

"But Timmy and I – we might someday be a family! We might—" Lytha's voice broke. She pressed the backs of her hands against her cheeks and paused. Then she went on quietly. "I would go with Timmy, even so."

'Chell and David exchanged distressed glances. "There's not room for even one of you to change your place. The loads are computed, the arrangements finished," I said, feeling as though I were slapping Lytha again and again.

"And besides," said 'Chell, taking Lytha's hands, "it isn't as though you and Timmy were loves. You have only started two-ing. Oh, Lytha, it was such a short time ago that you had your Happy Day. Don't rush so into growing up!"

"And if I told you Timmy is my love?" cried Lytha.

"Can you tell us so in truth, Lytha?" said 'Chell, "and say that Timmy feels that you are his love?"

Lytha's eyes dropped. "Not for sure," she whispered. "But in time—" She threw back her head impetuously, light swirling across her dark hair. "It isn't fair! We haven't had time!" she cried. "Why did all this have to happen now? Why not later? Or sooner?" She faltered, "before we started two-ing! If we have to part now, we might never know – or live our lives without a love because he is really – I am—" She turned and ran from the room, her face hidden.

I sighed and eased myself up from the chair. "I'm old, David," I said. "I ache with age. Things like this weary me beyond any resting."

* * *

It was something after midnight the next night that I felt Neil call to me. The urgency of his call hurried me into my robe and out of the door, quietly, not to rouse the house.

"Eva-lee." His greeting hands on my shoulders were cold through my robe, and the unfamiliar chilly wind whipped my hems around my bare ankles. "Is Lytha home?"

"Lytha?" The unexpectedness of the question snatched the last web of sleepiness out of my mind. "Of course. Why?"

"I don't think she is," said Neil. "Timmy's gone with all our camping gear and I think she's gone with him."

My mind flashed back into the house, Questing. Before my hurried feet could get there, I knew Lytha was gone. But I had to touch the undented pillow and lift the smooth spread before I could convince myself. Back in the garden that flickered black and gold as swollen clouds raced across the distorted full moon, Neil and I exchanged concerned looks.

"Where could they have gone?" he asked. "Poor kids. I've already Quested the whole neighborhood and I sent Rosh up to the hillplace to get something – he thought. He brought it back but said nothing about the kids."

I could see the tightening of the muscles in his jaws as he tilted his chin in the old familiar way, peering at me in the moonlight.

"Did Timmy say anything to you about – about anything?" I stumbled.

"Nothing – the only thing that could remotely – well, you know both of them were upset about being in different ships and Timmy – well, he got all worked up and said he didn't believe anything was going to happen to the Home, that it was only a late spring and he thought we were silly to go rushing off into Space—"

"Lytha's words Timmyized," I said. "We've got to find them."

"Carla's frantic." Neil shuffled his feet and put his hands into his pockets, hunching his shoulders as the wind freshened. "If only we had *some* idea. If we don't find them tonight we'll have to alert the Group tomorrow. Timmy'd never live down the humiliation—"

"I know – 'Touch a teener-touch a tender spot,'" I quoted absently, my mind chewing on something long forgotten or hardly noticed. "Clearance," I murmured. And Neil closed his mouth on whatever he was going to say as I waited patiently for the vague drifting and isolated flashes in my mind to reproduce the thought I sought.

—Like white lace around their bare brown ankles—

"I have it," I said. "At least I have an idea. Go tell Carla I've gone for them. Tell her not to worry."

"Blessings," said Neil, his hands quick and heavy on my shoulders. "You and Thann have always been our cloak against the wind, our hand up the hill—" And he was gone toward Tangle-meadows and Carla.

You and Thann – you and Thann. I was lifting through the darkness, my personal shield activated against the acceleration of my going. Even Neil forgets sometimes that Thann is gone on ahead, I thought, my heart lifting to the memory of Thann's aliveness. And suddenly the night was full of Thann – of Thann and me – laughing in the skies, climbing the hills, dreaming in the moonlight. Four-ing with Carla and Neil. Two-ing after Gathering Day. The bittersweet memories came so fast that I almost crashed into the piney sighings of a hillside. I lifted above it barely in time. One treetop drew its uppermost twig across the curling of the bare sole of my foot.

Maybe Timmy's right! I thought suddenly. Maybe Simon and the Oldest are all wrong. How can I possibly leave the Home with Thann still here – waiting. Then I shook myself, quite literally, somersaulting briskly in mid-air. Foolish thoughts, trying to cram Thann back into the limitations of an existence he had outgrown!

I slanted down into the cup of the hills toward the tiny lake I had recognized from Lytha's thought. This troubled night it had no glitter or gleam. Its waves were much too turbulent for walking or dancing or even for daring. I landed on a pale strip of sand at its edge and shivered as a wave dissolved the sand under my feet into a shaken quiver and then withdrew to let it solidify again.

"Lytha!" I called softly, Questing ahead of my words. "Lytha!" There was no response in the wind-filled darkness. I lifted to the next pale crescent of sand, feeling like a driven cloud myself. "Lytha! Lytha!" Calling on the family band so it would be perceptible to her alone and Timmy wouldn't have to know until she told him. "Lytha!"

"Gramma!" Astonishment had squeezed out the answer. "Gramma!" The indignation was twice as heavy to make up for the first involuntary response.

"May I come to you?" I asked, taking refuge from my own emotion in ritual questions that would leave Lytha at least the shreds of her pride. There was no immediate reply. "May I come to you?" I repeated.

"You may come." Her thoughts were remote and cold as she guided me in to the curve of hillside and beach.

She and Timmy were snug and secure and very unhappily restless in the small camp cubicle. They had even found some flowers somewhere. Most of them had died of the lack of summer, but this small cluster clung with their fragile-looking legs to the roof of the cubicle and shed a warm golden light over the small area. My heart contracted with pity and my eyes stung a little as I saw how like a child's playhouse they had set up the cubicle, complete with the two sleeping mats carefully the cubicle's small width apart with a curtain hiding them from each other.

They had risen ceremoniously as I entered, their faces carefully respectful to an Old One – no Gramma-look in the face of either. I folded up on the floor and they sat again, their hands clasping each other for comfort.

"There is scarcely time left for an outing," I said casually, holding up one finger to the Glowers. One loosed itself and glided down to clasp its wiry feet around my finger. Its glowing paled and flared and hid any of our betraying expressions. Under my idle talk I could feel the cry of the two youngsters – wanting some way in honor to get out of this impasse. Could I find the way or would they stubbornly have to—

"We have our lives before us." Timmy's voice was carefully expressionless.

"A brief span if it's to be on the Home," I said. "We must be out before the week ends."

"We do not choose to believe that." Lytha's voice trembled a little. "I respect your belief," I said formally, "but fear you have insufficient evidence to support it."

"Even so," her voice was just short of a sob. "Even so, however short, we will have it together—"

"Yes, without your mothers or fathers or any of us," I said placidly. "And then finally, soon, without the Home. Still it has its points. It isn't given to everyone to be-in-at the death of a world. It's a shame that you'll have no one to tell it to. That's the best part of anything, you know, telling it – sharing it."

Lytha's face crumpled and she turned it away from me.

"And if the Home doesn't die," I went on, "that will truly be a joke on us. We won't even get to laugh about it because we won't be able to come back, being so many days gone, not knowing. So you will have the whole Home to yourself. Just think! A whole Home! A new world to begin all over again – alone—" I saw the two kids' hands convulse together and Timmy's throat worked painfully. So did mine. I knew the aching of having to start a new world over – alone. After Thann was Called. "But such space! An emptiness from horizon to horizon – from pole to pole – for you two! No body else anywhere – anywhere. *If* the Home doesn't die—"

Lytha's slender shoulders were shaking now, and they both turned their so-young faces to me. I nearly staggered under the avalanche of their crying out – all without a word. They poured out all their longing and uncertainty and protest and rebellion. Only the young could build up such a burden and have the strength to bear it. Finally Timmy came to words.

"We only want a chance. Is that too much to ask? Why should this happen, now, to us?"

"Who are we," I asked sternly, "to presume to ask why of the Power? For all our lives we have been taking happiness and comfort and delight and never asking *why*, but now that sorrow and separation, pain and discomfort are coming to us from the same Power, we are crying *why*. We have taken unthinkingly all that has been given to us unasked, but now that we must take sorrow for a while, you want to refuse to take, like silly babies whose milk is cold!"

I caught a wave of desolation and lostness from the two and hurried on. "But don't think the Power has forgotten you. You are as completely enwrapped now as you ever were. Can't you trust your love – or your possible love – to the Power that suggested love to you in the first place? I promise you, I *promise* you, that no matter where you go, together or apart if the Power leaves you life, you will find love. And even if it turns out that you do not find it together, you'll never forget these first magical steps you have taken together towards your own true loves."

I let laughter into my voice. "Things change! Remember, Lytha, it wasn't so long ago that Timmy was a – if you'll pardon the expression – 'gangle-legged, clumsy *poodah*' that I'd rather be caught dead than ganging with, let alone two-ing!"

"And he was, too!" Lytha's voice had a hiccough in it, but a half smile, too.

"You were no vision of delight, yourself," said Timmy. "I never saw such stringy hair—"

"I was *supposed* to look like that—"

Their wrangling was a breath of fresh air after the unnatural, uncomfortable emotional binge they had been on.

"It's quite possible that you two might change—" I stopped abruptly. "Wait!" I said. "Listen!"

"To what?" Lytha's face was puzzled. How could I tell her I heard Simon crying "Gramma! Gramma!" Simon at home, in bed miles and miles—

"Out, quick!" I scrambled up from the floor. "Oh, hurry!" Panic was welling up inside me. The two snatched up their small personal bundles as I pushed them, bewildered and protesting, ahead of me out into the inky blackness of the violent night. For a long terrified moment I stood peering up into the darkness, trying to interpret! Then I screamed, "Lift! Lift!" and, snatching at them both, I launched us upward, away from the edge of the lake. The clouds snatched back from the moon and its light poured down onto the convulsed lake. There was a crack like the loudest of thunder – a grinding, twisting sound – the roar and surge of mighty waters, and the lake bed below us broke cleanly from one hill to another, pulling itself apart and tilting to pour all its moon-bright waters down into the darkness of the gigantic split in the earth. And the moon was glittering only on the shining mud left behind in the lake bottom. With a frantic speed that seemed so slow I enveloped the children and shot with them as far up and away as I could before the earsplitting roar of returning steam threw us even farther. We reeled drunkenly away, and away, until we stumbled across the top of a hill. We clung to each other in terror as the mighty plume of steam rose and rose and split the clouds and still rose, rolling white and awesome. Then, as casually as a shutting door, the lake bed tilted back and closed itself In the silence that followed, I fancied I could hear the hot rain beginning to fall to fill the emptiness of the lake again, a pool of rain no larger than my hand in a lake bottom.

"Oh, poor Home," whispered Lytha, "poor hurting Home! It's dying!" And then, on the family band, Lytha whispered to me, *Timmy's my love, for sure, Gramma, and I am his, but we're willing to let the Power hold our love for us, until your promise is kept.*

I gathered the two to me and I guess we all wept a little, but we had no words to exchange, no platitudes, only the promise, the acquiescence, the trust – and the sorrow.

We went home. Neil met us just beyond our feather-pen and received Timmy with a quiet thankfulness and they went home together. Lytha and I went first into our household's Quiet Place and then to our patient beds.

* * *

I stood with the other Old Ones high on the cliff above the narrow valley, staring down with them at the raw heap of stones and earth that scarred the smooth valley floor. All eyes were intent on the excavation and every mind so much with the Oldest as he toiled out of sight, that our concentrations were almost visible flames above each head.

I heard myself gasp with the others as the Oldest slowly emerged, his clumsy heavy shielding hampering his lifting. The brisk mountain breeze whined as it whipped past suddenly activated personal shields as we reacted automatically to possible danger even though our shields were tissue paper to tornadoes against this unseen death should it be loosed. The Oldest stepped back from the hole until the sheer rock face stopped him. Slowly a stirring began in the shadowy depths and then the heavy square that shielded the thumb-sized block within lifted into the light. It trembled and turned and set itself into the heavy metal box prepared for it. The lid clicked shut. By the time six boxes were filled, I felt the old – or rather, the painfully new – weariness seize me and I clung to David's arm. He patted my hand, but his eyes were wide with dreaming and I forced myself upright. "I don't like me any more," I thought. "Why do I do things like this? Where has *my* enthusiasm and wonder gone? I am truly old and yet—" I wiped the cold beads of sweat from my upper lip and, lifting with the others, hovered over the canyon, preparatory to conveying the six boxes to the six shells of ships that they were to sting into life.

* * *

It was the last day. The sun was shining with a brilliance it hadn't known in weeks. The winds that wandered down from the hills were warm and sweet. The earth beneath us that had so recently learned to tremble and shift was quietly solid for a small while. Everything about the Home was suddenly so dear that it seemed a delirious dream that death was less than a week away for it. Maybe it was only some pre-adolescent, unpatterned behavior—. But one look at Simon convinced me. His eyes were aching with things he had had to See. His face was hard under the soft contours of childhood and his hands trembled as he clasped them. I hugged him with my heart and he smiled a thank you and relaxed a little.

'Chell and I set the house to rights and filled the vases with fresh water and scarlet leaves because there were no flowers. David opened the corral gate and watched the beasts walk slowly out into the tarnished meadows. He threw wide the door of the feather-pen and watched the ruffle of feathers, the inquiring peering, the hesitant walk into freedom. He smiled as the master of the pen strutted vocally before the flock. Then Eve gathered up the four eggs that lay rosy and new in the nests and carried them into the house to put them in the green egg dish.

The family stood quietly together. "Go say goodby," said David. "Each of you say goodby to the Home."

And everyone went, each by himself, to his favorite spot. Even Eve burrowed herself out of sight in the *koomatka* bush where the leaves locked above her head and made a tiny Eve-sized green twilight. I could hear her soft croon, "Inna blaza glory, play-People! Inna blaza glory!"

I sighed to see Lytha's straight-as-an-arrow flight toward Timmy's home. Already Timmy was coming. I turned away with a pang. Supposing even after the lake they – No, I comforted myself. They trust the Power—

How could I go to any one place, I wondered, standing by the windows of my room. All of the Home was too dear to leave. When I went I would truly be leaving Thann – all the paths he walked with me, the grass that bent to his step, the trees that shaded him in summer, the very ground that held his cast-aside. I slid to my knees and pressed my cheek against the side of the window frame. "Thann, Thann!" I whispered. "Be with me. Go with me since I must go. Be my strength!" And clasping my hands tight, I pressed my thumbs hard against my crying mouth.

We all gathered again, solemn and tear-stained. Lytha was still frowning and swallowing to hold back her sobs. Simon looked at her, his eyes big and golden, but he said nothing and turned away. 'Chell left the room quietly and, before she returned, the soft sound of music swelled from the walls.

We all made the Sign and prayed the Parting prayers, for truly we were dying to this world. The whole house, the whole of the Home was a Quiet Place today, and each of us without words laid the anguishing of this day of parting before the Presence and received comfort and strength.

Then each of us took up his share of personal belongings and was ready to go. We left the house, the music reaching after us as we went. I felt a part of me die when we could no longer hear the melody.

We joined the neighboring families on the path to the ships and there were murmurs and gestures and even an occasional excited laugh. No one seemed to want to lift. Our feet savored every step of this last walk on the Home. No one lifted, that is, except Eve, who was still intrigued by her new accomplishment. Her short little hops amused everyone and, by the time she had picked herself out of the dust three times and had been disentangled from the branches of overhanging trees twice and finally firmly set in place on David's shoulder, there were smiles and tender laughter and the road lightened even though clouds were banking again.

I stood at the foot of the long lift to the door of the ship and stared upward. People brushing past me were only whisperings and passing shadows.

"How can they?" I thought despairingly out of the surge of weakness that left me clinging to the wall. "How can they do it? Leaving the Home so casually!" Then a warm hand crept into mine and I looked down into Simon's eyes. "Come on, Gramma," he said. "It'll be all right."

"I – I—" I looked around me helplessly, then, kneeling swiftly, I took up a handful of dirt – a handful of the Home – and, holding it tightly, I lifted up the long slant with Simon.

Inside the ship we put our things away in their allotted spaces and Simon tugged me out into the corridor and into a room banked with dials and switches and all the vast array of incomprehensibles that we had all called into being for this terrible moment. No one was in the room except the two of us. Simon walked briskly to a chair in front of a panel and sat down.

"It's all set," he said, "for the sector of the sky they gave us, but it's wrong." Before I could stop him, his hands moved over the panels, shifting, adjusting, changing.

"Oh, Simon!" I whispered, "you mustn't!"

"I must," said Simon. "Now it's set for the sky I See."

"But they'll notice and change them all back," I trembled.

"No," said Simon. "It's such a small change that they won't notice it. And we will be where we have to be when we have to be."

It was as I stood there in the control room that I left the Home. I felt it fade away and become as faint as a dream. I said goodby to it so completely that it startled me to catch a glimpse of a mountaintop through one of the ports as we hurried back to our allotted spaces. Suddenly my heart was light and lifting, so much so that my feet didn't even touch the floor. Oh, how wonderful! What adventures ahead! I felt as though I were spiraling up into a bright Glory that outshone the sun—

Then, suddenly, came the weakness. My very bones dissolved in me and collapsed me down on my couch. Darkness rolled across me and breathing was a task that took all my weakness to keep going. I felt vaguely the tightening of the restraining straps around me and the clasp of Simon's hand around my clenched fist.

"Half an hour," the Oldest murmured.

"Half an hour," the People echoed, amplifying the murmur. I felt myself slipping into the corporate band of communication, feeling with the rest of the Group the incredible length and heartbreaking shortness of the time.

Then I lost the world again. I was encased in blackness. I was suspended, waiting, hardly even wondering.

And then it came – The Call.

How unmistakable! I was Called back into the Presence! My hours were totaled. It was all finished. This-side was a preoccupation that concerned me no longer. My face must have lighted as Thann's had. All the struggle, all the sorrow, all the separation-finished. Now would come the three or four days during which I must prepare, dispose of my possessions, say my goodbys – Goodbys? I struggled up against the restraining straps. But we were leaving! In less than half an hour I would have no quiet, cool bed to lay me down upon when I left my body, no fragrant grass to have pulled up over my cast-aside, no solemn sweet remembrance by my family in the next Festival for those Called during the year.

Simon, I called subvocally. *You know*! I cried. What shall I do? *I See you staying*. His answer came placidly.

Staying? Oh, how quickly I caught the picture. How quickly my own words came back to me, coldly white against the darkness of my confusion. *Such space and emptiness from horizon to horizon, from pole to pole, from skytop to ground And only me. Nobody else anywhere, anywhere*!

Stay here all alone? I asked Simon. But he wasn't Seeing me any more.

Already I was alone. I felt the frightened tears start and then I heard Lytha's trusting voice – *until your promise is kept*. All my fear dissolved. All my panic and fright blazed up suddenly in a repeat of the Call.

"Listen!" I cried, my voice high and excited, my heart surging joyously. "Listen!

"Oh, David! Oh, 'Chell! I've been Called! Don't you hear it? Don't you hear it!"

"Oh, Mother, no! No! You must be mistaken!" David loosed himself and bent over me.

"No," whispered 'Chell. "I feel it. She is Called."

"Now I can stay," I said, fumbling at the straps. "Help me, David, help me."

"But you're not summoned right now!" cried David. "Father knew four days before he was received into the Presence. We can't leave you alone in a doomed, empty world!"

"An empty world!" I stood up quickly, holding to David to steady myself. "Oh, David! A world full of all dearness and nearness and remembering! And doomed? It will be a week yet. I will be received before then. Let me out! Oh, let me out!"

"Stay with us, Mother!" cried David, taking both my hands in his. "We need you. We can't let you go. All the tumult and upheaval that's to start so soon for the Home—"

"How do we know what tumult and upheaval you will be going through in the Crossing?" I asked. "But beyond whatever comes there's a chance of a new life waiting for you. But for me—. What of four days from now? What would you do with my cast-aside? What could you do but push it out into the black nothingness. Let it be with the Home. Let it at least become dust among familiar dust!" I felt as excited as a teener. "Oh, David! To be with Thann again!"

I turned to Lytha and quickly unfastened her belt. "There'll be room for one more in this ship," I said.

For a long moment, we looked into each other's eyes and then, almost swifter than thought, Lytha was up and running for the big door. My thoughts went ahead of her and before Lytha's feet lifted out into the open air, all the Old Ones in the ship knew what had happened and their thoughts went out. Before Lytha was halfway up the little hills that separated ship from ship, Timmy surged into sight and gathered her close as they swung around toward our ship.

Minutes ran out of the half hour like icy beads from a broken string, but finally I was slanting down from the ship, my cheeks wet with my own tears and those of my family. Clearly above the clang of the closing door I heard Simon's call. *Goodby, Gramma! I told you it'd be all right. See – you – soon*!

Hurry, hurry, hurry, whispered my feet as I ran. *Hurry hurry hurry* whispered the wind as I lifted away from the towering ships. *Now now now* whispered my heart as I turned back from a safe distance, my skirts whipped by the rising wind, my hair lashing across my face.

The six slender ships pointing at the sky were like silver needles against the rolling black clouds. Suddenly there were only five – then four – then three. Before I could blink the tears from my eyes, the rest were gone, and the ground where they had stood flowed back on itself and crackled with cooling.

* * *

The fingers of the music drew me back into the house. I breathed deeply of the dear familiar odors. I straightened a branch of the scarlet leaves that had slipped awry in the blue vase. I steadied myself against a sudden shifting under my feet and my shield activated as hail spattered briefly through the window. I looked out, filled with a great peace, to the swell of browning hills, to the upward reach of snow-whitened mountains, to the brilliant huddled clumps of trees sowing their leaves on the icy wind. "My Home!" I whispered, folding my heart around it all, knowing what my terror and lostness would have been had I stayed behind without the Call.

With a sigh, I went out to the kitchen and counted the four rosy eggs in the green dish. I fingered the stove into flame and, lifting one of the eggs, cracked it briskly against the pan.

That night there were no stars, but the heavy rolls of clouds were lighted with fitful lightnings and somewhere far over the horizon the molten heart of a mountain range was crimson and orange against the night. I lay on my bed letting the weakness wash over me, a tide that would soon bear me away. The soul is a lonely voyager at any time, but the knowledge that I was the last person in a dying world was like a weight crushing me. I was struggling against the feeling when I caught a clear, distinct call—

"Gramma!"

"Simon!" My lips moved to his name.

"We're all fine, Gramma, and I just Saw Eve with two children of her own, so they *will* make it to a new Home."

"Oh, Simon! I'm so glad you told me!" I clutched my bed as it rocked and twisted. I heard stones falling from the garden wall, then one wall of my room dissolved into dust that glowed redly before it settled.

"Things are a little untidy here," I said. "I must get out another blanket. It's a little drafty, too."

"You'll be all right, Gramma," Simon's thought came warmly. "Will you wait for me when you get Otherside?"

"If I can," I promised.

"Good night, Gramma," said Simon.

"Good night, Simon." I cradled my face on my dusty pillow. "Good night."

The Taste of Centuries, the Taste of Home

Jennifer Hudak

WHEN GRANDMOTHER ARRIVED HERE, she appeared right in the middle of Skip Brook, ankle deep in cool water, carrying a small sack over one shoulder and a baby – my mother – in her arms. I've been to Skip Brook often enough to imagine how it must have felt: the fish staring up at her from beneath the tumbling water; the trees swaying with their gossip; the pyskie moths brushing against her ear with their airy whispers. The prayer she spoke – *blessed art thou, blessed, blessed* – still echoes in the rustle of grasses and the whispering of leaves and the drip-drop of the deepest caves.

My best friend, Yiala, lives in the trees that border Skip Brook, in a cozy home sheltered by leaves in the summer and a tangle of frost-bright branches in winter. With her claws and tail and powerful hind legs, she scampers up the tree in seconds. It takes me longer, but I can follow her as long as I don't mind a few scrapes and slivers. Together, we perch on a branch overlooking the brook and talk about how funny it must have been to see a person suddenly appear in the water – *plop*!

Visitors were more common then, when the Buried Sun's lonely song still echoed across the cosmos. Spiders skittered back and forth between the porous openings, trailing silky threads behind them. Bees bumbled through the glades, carrying pollen from foreign flowers. New species of birds, some brightly colored and others plain and dun, roosted in our trees for days before disappearing again.

Just like the bugs and the woodland creatures, not all the people who made their way into this world decided to stay. The ones who did shed their former worlds like sodden cloaks. Others, the ones who clung to their old lives with tight fingers, disappeared soon enough, back across whatever gateway had brought them here in the first place.

My grandmother stayed. She did not simply stumble out of one world and into another. She *sought* this place, or someplace like it. Her arrival was clear-eyed and purposeful, and she came prepared.

Sometimes Yiala talks about that day as if she were there.

"Your mother was squawking like an angry duck, but your grandmother looked around the woods with a smile, as if this were already her home."

"You don't know that," I tell her. "Even your grandparents weren't born yet."

Yiala's tail swishes back and forth. "This tree was there, and trees have a long memory."

This is not a satisfying answer, but it's true, and denying it would insult the tree. I wonder how tall this tree was when Grandmother arrived, and if it welcomed her with kind words or bored indifference.

In some ways, Grandmother's memory is as long as the tree's; it reaches back across time and space to the world she abandoned to come here, and to the person she was before she became my grandmother. The older she gets, the more she remembers that world, and the less she remembers this one. Sometimes she looks at me and calls me by my mother's name. Sometimes she holds a cup in her hand as if she has no idea what it's for. Once, I found her cringing behind a chair, her eyes wide and frightened, and when I asked her what she was doing she said she was hiding from someone but couldn't remember who.

But when the Sky Sun goes to sleep, and the suns of other worlds peek their cautious heads into the night sky, it makes her think of the sun that lit her old world, and then the memories tumble out like a secret cache of acorns.

"Where I grew up," she says, "lights were kept in glass vessels."

"Why would they do such a thing?" I ask, horrified. A firefly lands on my blanket, and I shelter it with my hands, as if I could protect it from this ancient threat.

"Their lights weren't alive like ours. They were mechanical – created by people. You could flip a lever or pull a chain, and the light turned on and off."

I watch the fireflies flit around the hollow, and try to imagine what stationary lights might look like. Lights that shine and darken on command, that never surprise with unexpected swoops and arcs. What a boring, flat world it must be, without the sparkle and dance of light and shadow.

Grandmother tells me about monstrous carriages that moved at great speed on their own power, roaring and bleating and squealing, about enormous buildings the size of our entire wood, full of workers whose job it was to do the exact same small action over and over again, from morning until night. And the people! So many people that their houses were piled on top of one another, stretching up into the sky.

"Aren't you glad you don't live there?" my mother asks, squeezing my foot. She has little patience for Grandmother's stories. Even though she was born in that noisy, busy, alien world, she doesn't remember it, and she doesn't care to hear about it. "Aren't you glad you live here, in this wood?"

And I am glad, I *am*. But sometimes, when I'm feeling peevish and unsatisfied, I leave the woods behind and scramble through the caves. Hands pressed to the damp cave floor, I feel the warmth of the Buried Sun. I imagine I can hear her voice rumbling up from underground, calling to the other worlds that bump against our own like so many soap bubbles.

* * *

Grandmother and I wake when the Sky Sun is just beginning to yawn and stretch and poke the top of his head above the horizon. My mother groans and burrows beneath her blankets.

"Go back to sleep, Skelly," she mutters.

"I'm going to learn how to make Grandmother's bread," I tell her. "You could, too."

"Every day I make flatbreads. That's enough."

The tone of her voice is a warning, so I leave her be. But she's wrong; it's not enough. Lots of people make flatbreads, but Grandmother's bread is *special*. It's dense and sweet and plaited like my hair, and it takes all day to make. She bakes it once every seven days, and has done since long before I was old enough to gum a milk-soaked slice.

It's dark in our hollow, but the table is illuminated by a cluster of sleepy fireflies bobbing overhead. Grandmother gathers the ingredients one by one, giving each a solemn nod as she sets it on the table. The air in the hollow changes as she works, becomes sacred. This is a ceremony, and for the first time, I'm allowed to help.

We begin by feeding the yeast. Grandmother made the yeast herself, out of flour and water and the juice of fermenting fruit. Then she spread it thin and dried it in the sun and crumbled it into a jar, which she holds with reverence between two hands. There's not much left; after another few loaves of bread, it will run out. But Grandmother has forgotten how to make the yeast. The last couple of times she tried, she grew a colony of fuzzy mold that my mother threw away before Grandmother could attempt to bake with it.

That's why I'm here with her today: to learn how to make the bread before she forgets that, too.

I have a scrap of paper and some ink, but it's a harder process to document than I've imagined. Nothing is measured. Grandmother does it all by eye, by feel. When I hold out my measuring spoons for her to use, she pushes them aside.

"Not that way. Not with spoons. The yeast is *alive*."

"I know," I say. Everything is alive, from the Buried Sun beneath our feet to the hollow tree in which we make our home, to the fireflies that flicker above us. But the yeast sounds fussier than all of those things. Right now, it's sleeping in its jar. We have to wake it up before we bake with it, using some milk that Grandmother is heating in the kettle. If the milk is too hot, it will kill the yeast before it can work its magic in the bread. If it's too cold, the yeast will stay asleep. Either way, our bread will be hard and flat instead of the way it ought to be.

How does she know when the milk is hot enough? Does she count the bubbles gathering around the edge of the liquid? Does she heat it for a specific amount of time? Grandmother shakes her head with irritation, unable to explain. Instead, she dabs a bit of milk on the inside of my wrist. "When it feels like this," she says, "it's ready." She mixes together the yeast and the milk, and then we wait, our faces close together over the bowl.

Before long, the mixture in the bowl starts to bubble and foam. Grandmother brings her nose close and breathes in deeply; I do the same. The yeast smells of years, and of the distance between stars. It smells of the place Grandmother came from.

My mother finally wakes up when we begin kneading the bread. We are as quiet as flowers growing, Grandmother and I, but still my mother looks irritated when we scrape the dough onto a large wooden board. She trudges to the table with her tea and pretends not to pay us any attention. When she thinks I'm not watching, she closes her eyes and breathes in deeply, and the warm, familiar smell of the dough softens her face into a smile.

Grandmother guides my hands, because while she doesn't remember a lot of things, her hands remember how to pull and push and turn the dough. Her hands move of their own volition, a dance taught many years ago and a world away.

My hands do not dance. They plunge into the dough and get stuck there. While I struggle, my mother sips her tea at the far end of the table, near my paper and ink. I can't take down notes with my dough-shaggy fingers, not that I'd know what to write. We knead and knead and knead, and it's tiring and messy. I'm annoyed with my mother – for watching me with half-lidded eyes, for surreptitiously reading my notes, for not bothering to learn how to make this bread herself.

And then Grandmother makes a soft grunt of approval, bringing my attention back to the dough. It's changed; we've changed it. Beneath our hands, it's grown stretchy, and springy, and smooth.

It's worth it, I remind myself. All this work. All this time. It's worth it.

* * *

We set the dough aside to grow, and when Grandmother sees that I can't be quiet and still for the length of time this requires, she sets me loose. I find Yiala stalking back and forth near her tree, a scattering of feathers – the remains of her breakfast – at her feet.

She flicks her ears at me. "Skelly! Where have you been? I've been waiting for you forever."

"I'm helping Grandmother today," I tell her. "I have to go back in a bit."

"Don't you want to know who I saw earlier this morning?" Yiala grins, wide and toothy. "A *traveler*!"

Traveler. The trees echo the word in their paper-thin whisper. *Traveler traveler traveler*...

"Liar," I say. "There hasn't been a traveler here in ages."

"If you don't believe me, come see for yourself."

When Yiala and I play, we run as fast as the brook. We are loud as thunder, and strong as the wind. We can be silent, too; perching in the treetops, we spy on the Hill People as they make their slow, ponderous way across the horizon, and they are none the wiser. Today we make ourselves invisible. We creep through the underbrush, flatten ourselves to the trunks of trees, dart from shadow to shadow without making a single sound.

Yiala stops me with a touch of her paw and points. There, in a clearing, is the traveler.

He's human, like my mother and Grandmother – like me – but he's dressed unlike anyone I've seen in the wood. His pants, worn close to the skin, are ripped at each knee, as if he's never learned to sew, or perhaps he simply doesn't care. His coat and bag are adorned with straps and toggles and metal clasps – far more than would ever be necessary – and the bag is the breathtaking yellow-orange of the Sky Sun, so bright it makes me wince.

Yiala nudges me. "Maybe it's your father!"

"Quiet," I hiss.

My mother has never told me who my father is. If I ask, she'll say that he was a fish, slippery and flashing like sunlight. Or an Esakot, all horns and wings and fire. The people in town say my father was another human who stumbled into our wood and then was gone again before I was born, back to wherever he came from. I never really cared one way or the other.

But now, looking at this traveler, with his improbable clothes and radiantly colored bag, the fact thunders like a stone down a mountain: he is from elsewhere. He is from Earth.

That means there's a gateway somewhere close by.

We sneak away, back to Skip Brook. Yiala wants to try to find the gateway immediately, before it closes again.

"I can't," I tell her. "Grandmother is expecting me back."

"So?" Yiala doesn't live with her parents or grandparents. She's shared a home with her littermates, two brothers and a sister, ever since they were weaned. It's the way of her people. She goes where she wants, when she wants, and it's impossible for her to understand how I live otherwise.

"I just *can't*," I say, and head back home.

Part of me worries that Yiala will go off and find the gateway without me. But what would I do if I found it? I'd never step through it; if I did, the gateway could close behind me and I'd never be able to come back. I'd be trapped like Grandmother, in a world not my own.

I wonder if Grandmother feels trapped here, even though she came willingly. I wonder if she misses Earth, the world that looms larger and larger in her memory the older she gets.

* * *

I can tell, even before Grandmother uncovers the bowl, that the dough inside has risen. When we covered it earlier, the cloth she draped over the bowl lay flat. Now, the dough pushes up from inside, making a dome. When she carefully lifts the cloth and reveals the smooth ball underneath – glossy and puffed-up and smelling gloriously of yeast – it's like the Sky Sun bursting up over the horizon. My mind returns to the traveler's yellow-orange bag, and then to the traveler himself. Grandmother told me that on Earth, there was only one sun and one moon. But with a bag like that, you could carry sunshine around with you wherever you went.

Grandmother pokes two fingers into the dough, leaving a pair of divots like eyes. Then she instructs me to punch it down. It deflates right away under my fists, soft and satisfying. I punch it again and again, my knuckles covering the surface with dimples. Then Grandmother gently pulls my hands away and gives the dough a kneading right in the bowl.

While she works, she mutters words under her breath, in the language her family back on Earth used for prayer. I recognize this one; she says it at dinnertime on the nights we eat the special bread. The pyskie moths, drawn to the sound of a foreign tongue, cluster close and whisper their translation into my ear:

Blessed art thou, Lord our God,
Ruler of the Universe
Who hath brought forth bread from the Earth.

"Who's the Lord you're praying to?" I used to ask her, back when I was little. "Is it the Buried Sun?"

"We had different gods in the old world," she'd answer. "This is a prayer to the God of my ancestors."

"Why do you still say it here? Or why don't you change it to pray to the Buried Sun?"

"Because what matters is the tradition. The ritual. I used to say these words with my mother, and she used to say them with her mother, and on and on back through the ages. Even though I left that world far behind, speaking the words is a comfort."

I think of that now. Grandmother's words layer on top of the pyskies' translation, and together they thicken the air, blending with the smell of the wakeful yeast. I think of ritual, and of tradition. I wonder if it's possible to miss a place you've never been.

* * *

Grandmother covers the dough and sets it aside to grow once more. Making this bread is an exercise in patience, but I am not patient today. I leave the hollow again to wander around the wood. I tell myself that I'm not searching for the traveler. That I'd never have the courage to talk to him if I found him. I tell myself that I'm just concerned that he might need help.

And then, I look up and see the gateway.

I might not have found it if I'd been with Yiala; together, we'd have been looking for the wrong sort of thing – a doorway, a hole, a rip in the air – but the gateway is much quieter than that: just a shimmering between two trees. A pucker. The hint of a sharp, unpleasant scent.

It would be easy to miss it entirely. To walk through it unawares.

Behind me, footsteps tromp their way through the underbrush. I know it's the traveler even before I see him; no one from these woods would walk so loudly. Even so, it's startling to see him up close. Everything about him is new and different and exciting – his chunky boots, his jacket with its dangling metal tags, his sun-bright bag – and even though he's human, he doesn't look a thing like my mother or Grandmother.

He's walking around like he's in a dream, not even looking down for roots and rocks, and the trees are being very kind not to trip him. When he spots me, he freezes, and stares at my bare feet and at the leaves woven through my hair as if I'm the strange one.

"Hey," he says. "Are you okay?"

"Why wouldn't I be?" I answer.

"I don't know." He laughs, like I made a joke. The pyskie moths flutter in a cloud around us, and the traveler tries to swat them away. "I think I'm lost."

I swallow hard. "Where did you come from?"

"I must have wandered off the trail." He looks around the wood. "I've never seen a forest like this before. Everything's just … off."

"Off?"

"Different. Weird." He looks me up and down and laughs again. "Not normal."

It shouldn't sting, but it does. I wonder if he'd feel more at home here if I was wearing boots or carried a bright bag, or if the things that make us different run much, much deeper.

"If you want to get back home, go that way." I point at the gateway.

He doesn't seem to see the shimmering between the trees, but he walks toward it anyway. I'm expecting something dramatic to happen when he passes through, but it's not like that. He's just gone, suddenly, like a frog disappearing into a lake.

Stepping closer, the shimmer glistens. There's sound within it, things I've never heard before, and that smell, acrid and new. I wonder what I'd see if I walked through it. I imagine myself following in the traveler's footsteps, darting silently from tree to tree behind him. I reach out my hand, letting the tips of my fingers brush against the shimmer. It feels like pushing at a blanket, soft and inviting.

"Skelly?"

I drop my hands and whirl around. It's my mother, carrying a basket of berries she's gathered, piled loosely around a cloth-wrapped jar. Her eyes find the gateway immediately, and a brief look of alarm flashes across her face, but when she speaks, her voice is carefully neutral.

"So," she says. "Here you are."

"I just found it," I stammer. "I wasn't going to – I was just…"

"I know."

My mother holds out the basket, just out of reach. Behind me, the gateway hums like a living thing. When I step away from it to take a berry, she visibly relaxes.

I roll the berry between my fingers. "Would you ever want to go back?"

"No," she says immediately.

"Never?"

She looks at me, measuring out her words like a cup full of flour. "Once, when I was young, like you, I considered it. But that was a long time ago."

"What made you change your mind?"

She pops a berry into her mouth and chews it thoughtfully before responding. "You were born right here, in this forest, right in this hollow. With the fireflies clustered overhead, and the dragons rising up from the sea to weave between the moons, and the trees peering inside to catch a glimpse of your sweet face. Your grandmother and I are of two worlds, but you belong entirely to this one." She smiles. "That makes this world good enough for me."

"What if I don't *feel* like I belong entirely to this world?"

"I'm not sure any of us ever do," she says. "It's a choice we make, to be where we are."

Between the trees, the gateway shimmers and churns. There's no telling how long it will remain open. Just like there's no telling how long Grandmother will remember how to make her bread. But I know she's waiting for me, right now.

I follow my mother back to the hollow. I leave the gateway behind.

For now.

* * *

It's time, finally, to braid the loaf. But the ropes of dough seem to confuse Grandmother. She twists two strands together, forgetting the third, and when she undoes the twist, her fingers twitch and shake. Her face gets the tight, pinched look she wears when the present moment bumps up against everything she's forgotten. She mumbles something I can't quite hear.

"Grandmother?" I put a hand on her shoulder and lean closer. It's the prayer.

Blessed art thou
Blessed art thou
Blessed

She repeats the prayer as if it's a spell, as if she could find within it all the answers she lacks. Her words are ineffable, intangible, so delicate that they evaporate in the air – but they're also deeply embedded within her memory, like the rings of a tree. I imagine the words weaving together like rope, like strands of dough, tying us together, linking our past and present and future selves. I wonder if the ingredients we've kneaded together – flour, milk, yeast, words – make more than a simple loaf of bread. I wonder if they make our hollow a place out of space and time. If they connect us to Earth, and to Grandmother's ancestors, and to all the loaves they made with all their varied hands, back and back and back through the ages.

"Can I try?" I ask her, gesturing toward the dough. "You can tell me if I'm doing it right."

She steps aside reluctantly. "It's very difficult."

"I know. But I want to learn."

She watches me, her face anxious, but she gradually relaxes as I start passing the strands over each other, weaving them together. Three strands: one each for Grandmother, my mother, and me. One each for Earth, for the wood, and for the space that exists inside our hollow every seven days. The space we're in now.

My paper and ink are still sitting on the end of the table, but I know I won't write anything else down. It's not that kind of lesson. The trick isn't to record the process, or to memorize. The trick is to be here, now. To breathe in the smell of the yeast. To feel the dough stretch and spring back.

"That's it," says Grandmother, watching the loaf take shape. "That's exactly it."

* * *

Just before the Sky Sun sinks into his bed, we gather at the table. Fireflies hover near the ceiling, clustering and dispersing, clustering and dispersing, casting their glow. My mother slices the bread and gives the first piece to Grandmother, who sprinkles it with a bit of salt. Then she bows her head and says the prayer. I join her, so that she won't forget the words. I join her, so that I won't forget them either.

On a shelf behind the table is a jar of spongy dough that my mother got from a friend who lives across the forest. It's a kind of yeast, she says, but unlike Grandmother's yeast, this one will never run out as long as we keep feeding it.

"It might change the recipe a bit," she adds, hesitant, afraid I'd be upset. But I'm not upset. The bread will still be Grandmother's bread, even with this new yeast. But it will be different, too. Like my mother, like Grandmother, the bread will be of two worlds. *The yeast is alive*, Grandmother told me, and so is the recipe itself: not a light trapped in a glass jar, not a series of instructions written down in a book, but something that grows, and changes, and speaks if you listen to it.

Maybe the gateway will still be open tomorrow. Or maybe another gateway will open someday, one that leads to Earth, or elsewhere. Maybe I'll go through it.

But today – now – I'm here. In this hollow, with my family. I take a bite of bread. All the hours of work it took to bake it collapse into this one mouthful. It's yeasty and sweet and rich. It tastes of centuries ago and of worlds away, and it also tastes of this night, of this moment. Each bite is a choice. For now, I choose to be just where I am.

Oshun, Inc.

Jordan Ifueko

"FOR THE LAST TIME, BOLA: I'm not going to sleep with your dentist."

"But it would only kill him a little bit."

"Bola."

"And even if he does die…" Bolajoko's toothy smile reached all the way to her cowrie shell earrings. "At least he'd get a taste of heaven beforehand."

"Bola."

"Fine, Yemi. Geez, chill." My best friend and coworker Bolajoko held up her gold-ringed hands, pretending to surrender. She leaned against the gray wall of my cubicle, and a fluorescent pink wad flashed between her lips.

Gum?

I swore, she picked up some weird new eniyan habit every week. Another month in the Diaspora Unit, and she would start wearing Uggs instead of our company-issue goatskin sandals.

"Run out of chewing sticks?" I asked pointedly, nudging the tin I kept next to my laptop. I had cut the sweet-smelling twigs from the pleasure orchard back at Home Base. Home. I inhaled sharply, adjusting the too-tight band around my afro puff. I tried not to think of azure skies. Of piles of golden plantain, fried until they crackled and glistened. Of gilded barges, floating down creamy brown rivers to a chorus of cicadas.

You've rolled out your sleeping mat now, Yemi. And by the gods, you're going to lie in it.

I'd beat out sixty applicants for this post. The Diaspora Unit was revolutionary, I reminded myself. An honor. So what if it meant working in a crummy Los Angeles high-rise, and sipping coffee instead of palm wine? We were making history here. We were helping people, I was sure of it.

Unless, of course, we keep killing our clients.

Bolajoko tinkered with the delicate giraffe carvings on my desk, ignoring my jab about the gum. "You act like the eniyan's death would be permanent," she said. "I mean, of course the Boss would bring him back. She can bring anyone back."

"Not our job, Bola."

"Our job is to make people happy," she purred, raising a playful eyebrow. "Fulfill their requests. Help them make connections."

"Connections with their fellow eniyans," I shot back, pointing at the Iyami Aje mission statement on my cube wall, engraved on a glittering obsidian plaque. "With their own fragile kind. I don't work like you, Bola." I fiddled with the ergonomic levers of my swivel chair. "I don't just ignore the hazards of getting entangled."

She blew a bubble until it popped, then picked the pink remains from her face with dainty fingers. "The hazards didn't stop you from kissing that guitarist."

I winced, feeling my face grow hot as a velvety tenor crooning John Legend slipped into my mind. The eniyan had smelled of sweat and allspice. The phantom of a dense curly beard tickled my neck, and I shivered.

"Once," I muttered. "We kissed once, okay?"

Bolajoko snickered. "Last I heard, he's still recovering. What was the diagnosis? Temporary heart failure?"

"I mitigated the damage and filed a report with upper management," I said through gritted teeth. "Everything was handled properly."

"Oh. I'm sure plenty of things were handled."

Against my will, a smile tugged at my lips. "Shut up, Bola."

She grinned triumphantly and slapped a wrinkled file on my keyboard. "Take a look, Yems. Come on … you know I wouldn't ask if I wasn't desperate."

I frowned at the fading timestamp on the file's cover. "May 2015? Bola, this prayer request is ancient."

"I know," Bolajoko moaned, rolling her eyes. "You wouldn't believe how hard it is to make this eniyan happy. I've tried everything. Money. Health. A fulfilling career. The only thing left is a love connection."

"Yeah – with his own kind."

Bolajoko sulked, snapping her gum. "I'm not good at matching up mortals, okay? Remember the André 3000 and Erykah Badu incident? Exactly," she said when I grimaced. "That's why I usually hook up with them myself. But I'm not this guy's type."

"And I am?"

"Take a look."

I opened the manila file with two fingers. A stale cloud of ochre dust tickled my nostrils; I coughed. Beneath yellow residue, the image of a clean-shaven mortal blinked up at me languidly. He had the broad, soft Yoruba nose and mouth I would recognize anywhere, disarming and stubborn at the same time. He yawned. His glasses were black and fashionably large, and the collar of a starched examination coat grazed a perfect dark collarbone.

Attraction stirred inside me like a cloud of gadflies. I frowned wistfully, exhaling through my teeth. "He's an asshole."

Bolajoko snort-laughed. "Why? Because he's hot?"

"Because he's sleepy," I quipped. "No guy is that sleepy and that hot without being an asshole."

Still, I rested my fingertips on the image and let the ochre dust rise. It formed lines of glittering characters, swirling around my arms as I heard the eniyan's prayers.

His name was Olajide. Oly-Jay to his Malibu girlfriends, and to his fellow USC School of Dentistry alums. Like most prayers, Olajide's contained very few words – a barrage of thoughts and feelings, hastily stuffed into a grumbled please or an earnest whisper. I still marveled that American mortals prayed to Oshun. Most immigrants abandoned the old spirits when they left Nigeria, if they had ever believed at all. But in the godless clean streets of California suburbs, and the indifferent hell of Houston swamp tenements … a new generation had quietly grown.

Children with pear-shaped faces and brown eyes had listened in kitchens, breathing the smell of boiled yams and Lysol as mothers spun tales of the immortals. Eledumare, the creator. Olorun, crown prince of the sun. And Oshun: goddess of life and love. As these children grew, cheeks stinging with Ambi Whitening Cream and hair limp with lye relaxer, stories of Oshun and her loyal Iyami Aje had soothed their inflamed skin like cocoa butter balm. Iyami Aje were lesser immortals, devoted to Oshun's work on earth. Crafty. Powerful.

And in my opinion, vastly underpaid.

I mean, it was an honor to be chosen and everything. Few were selected to leave our heavenly Home Base and live among eniyans. Like most rookies, I had applied for the Central Units in

Lagos and Abuja. "It's barely work," the veterans had giggled, filling my head with fantasies of midnight block parties, greasy street food, and hip-to-hip dancing in highlife music lounges.

Then she had reviewed my application. I still sprouted goosebumps at the memory of her gold-rimmed black eyes, burning over my skin as she presented my plaque of completed training. Her full lips had grazed my forehead, turning my knees to jelly as she breathed: "Teach them."

"How?" I had stammered.

She had smiled. "Stay versatile."

The next day, I had applied for the Diaspora Unit. The London, Dublin, and Dallas offices had been full, but then the Boss began receiving prayers from Los Angeles.

I was dying to make her proud. But she hadn't visited our Inglewood office in five years. As our attempts at matchmaking ended in disaster after sticky disaster … we had begun to wonder if she had forgotten us. Or worse: if she was ashamed.

We never meant to hurt people. Iyami Aje were drawn to loneliness, to prayers of isolation. But as goddesses of love, our affection could be a little … enthusiastic.

Too enthusiastic.

Some pleasures of heaven were not meant to be consumed on earth. And if we weren't careful, well. The best night of an eniyan's life could easily be their last.

As Olajide's prayers continued to wind around me in a quiet howl, I could see why Bola had found this mortal difficult. His desires shifted like a smoggy Los Angeles sky: streaks of gray, blue, and angry gold, constantly in flux. But the challenge was enticing. My assignments had been scarce since the guitarist incident; embarrassment had me laying low. But if I solved a case that had been cold for years…

Maybe even the Boss would be impressed.

"Fine. I'll take Dr. Droopy Eyes off your hands," I told Bolajoko, trying to sound as bored as possible. "But I'm not hooking up with him, okay? I'm doing this the right way. A mortal matched with a mortal."

Bolajoko squealed and threw her arms around the back of my chair, pressing her cheek to my head. "You. Are saving. My flawless butt."

I laughed and squirmed. "Get off. You'll frizz my edges."

"Oh gosh, sorry. Eniyan hair products are the worst." She released her grip and looked me over. "So if you're not going for Olajide, who are you sending?"

"Another client. I know just the one." I fished another file from my desk drawer and tossed it on Olajide's. It fell open to an image of a woman with fine laugh lines and sarcastic black eyes. She wore a tweed blazer and a patterned wrap over her neatly cornrowed hair.

Deanna Idowu, professor of history at UCLA. I'd read her political think pieces in three different newspapers. Most of her prayers concerned research, her students, and public policy. If you could just get my intern's study past peer review … please, she needs that scholarship … Don't let Congress screw up prison reform again. Not again. For pete's sake, put a muzzle on those idiots…

Very rarely, she would ask for something different.

Usually after a couple glasses of wine. Wine, and one too many men who called Deanna each month to talk about his relationship problems – you're such a good listener, Dee – but who never remembered to call on her birthday.

One too many messages from Black matches she swiped right on Tinder. No offense since u a sister but I like light-skins … haha ur pretty tho

One too many ethnic preference sections beneath a grinning Match.com profile, with every box checked except "African-American."

Deanna hated this prayer. The eniyan wondered why she even had this stupid craving, when her life was already so full. Hadn't she crowned herself with laurels when no one else had done it for her? Hadn't she watered the budding minds in her lecture halls, pruning thought after blossoming thought? Hadn't she grown to worship every curve and curl in her bedroom mirror? It was enough. It was enough. And yet—

It would be nice. That was the prayer whispered into the wine glass. Barely audible, drowned out by the earthy alto of India.Arie, wafting into the vents of her loft apartment.

"She's perfect," I told Bolajoko. "He's perfect. Two birds with one stone."

"Fine. Just don't be late for your appointment."

"What?"

Bolajoko's grin took on cheshire proportions. "You've got a teeth cleaning at 11:30."

After a whirl through Wardrobe Tech, who assigned me a crop sweater with ankara accents and matching yoga pants, I was standing on the grimy front curb of our Inglewood office. We were a modest high-rise, with OSHUN, INC. displayed in sleek gold letters above our awning. Our business front, of all things, was a nutrition supplement pyramid scheme – excuse me, a multi-level marketing enterprise. If any eniyans noticed me leave the building, they would have seen nothing but another starry-eyed sucker, dreaming her way to riches through smoothie powders and living room investment parties.

A urine smell, exquisitely warmed by the sun, wafted from a bundle of rags propped against the Oshun building. My nostrils wrinkled. It had been there for months; why didn't the city remove it?

Then the rags lurched.

"Good morning," I told the bundle after jumping three feet. I cleared my throat sheepishly. "Didn't see you there."

"Change," it croaked.

I dug through my leather crossbody bag – Tory Burch, and not at all convincing for my cover as a broke college student, but Wardrobe did their best – and held out a twenty-dollar bill. A fine-boned brown hand took it gently, and I made out a wrinkled face with wide rheumy eyes.

"Baller," she observed.

I smiled wryly. "Yeah, right. I'm more like the water girl."

"But you share the wealth. Queens stick together."

"We do." I checked the SuprLift app on my pink smartphone, watching the rapid approach of Your Driver, Wu Chen in a White Toyota Prius. A car with MAKE AMERICA GREAT AGAIN and LEGAL IMMIGRANT PRIDE stickers soon rounded the corner. "Off to my big break," I muttered as I climbed into the back seat.

"God bless you now," mumbled the bundled woman, adding as I closed the car door: "Don't miss T'Jocula."

I nodded politely at the nonsense advice and waved as the Prius pulled away. "Elite Dentistry, please," I told my balding driver. Wu Chen peered at me through his rearview mirror, as though I might steal a seat belt buckle. After several minutes, I asked: "What's on your mind?"

"You don't look like a prostitute, but you're probably pregnant," the driver blurted. Immediately he turned bright red. He stammered apologies, shocked at himself.

"Knocked up?" I said innocently. "Unlikely. It's crazy hard for my kind to have a baby. And let me tell you, Wu Chen, our prenatal care is the worst. Yam rituals, muddy fertility springs, sacrifices at sunset … No, sir, not for me. Bet I could make a pretty convincing prostitute, though. Wardrobe has some killer cut-off shorts."

"Please don't rate me down on the app," he rasped. "I wasn't – I didn't mean…"

I took a mint from my bag, humming as I unwrapped it, and plopped it in my mouth. "So. Why do you hate black people?"

"Because you are too much like me, I think." His face contorted, unnerved at the words he had never admitted to himself, let alone spoken out loud. His hands shook on the steering wheel, but his lips kept moving. "You are poor, outsiders. And I am tired of being outside. If I hate who those big men hate, I think, maybe they will give me a chance."

"Big men?" His gaze locked on mine in the rearview mirror, and I smiled at him ruefully. "Never mind. I know who you mean."

As the car rolled to a stop in front of Elite Dentistry, he whispered miserably: "Rating?"

I climbed out of the Prius and showed him my screen. "0 stars and a $1000 tip," I said and his face paled in surprise. "Good luck with your big men, Wu Chen."

The mortal sped away. I wondered, a little guiltily, if I had broken too many rules. Eniyans could not lie to Iyami Aje. As a courtesy, we were supposed to avoid asking direct questions.

Most mortals told me their secrets voluntarily. Immortality made me a very good listener. When you know what you'll be doing for the next few hundred years … well. You're rarely in a hurry.

I watched the Prius disappear, sighed, and passed into the crisp conditioned air of Elite Dentistry. Fifteen minutes later I squirmed in a plush green examination chair, wincing as the red-haired hygienist marveled at the state of my teeth.

"You don't understand," she said for the third time. "Enamel this strong is unheard of! Not a single cavity, not a hint of plaque anywhere. Holy hell, do you floss with a hose? And ruler-straight rows! No gum recession whatsoever…"

"Where ith Dr. Olajide?" I asked, tongue muffled against her blue-gloved fingers.

"Reapplying his cologne," the hygienist blurted, then blushed. She hadn't intended to tell me so much. "Probably in the bathroom. We've tried to tell him that some clients are sensitive to perfume, but…" She giggled, gaze growing a little dreamy. "He likes smelling nice."

The cologne hit me before he entered the room. I tried to be offended at its overwhelming strength, but … well. It was nice.

Sandalwood and airy citrus, sweetened ever so slightly with chocolate, wafted from Olajide's frame. He was not tall, but squarely built. A collared white lab coat hung from broad rippling shoulders. Behind the glasses his eyelids drooped, as if perfection were exhausting. The hygienist slipped flusteredly from the room. When he flashed a luminous smile, I allowed myself a sigh.

Mistake. Immediately the room's temperature skyrocketed, and my skin began to glow. Rosy swirls spread in patterns across my skin. Olajide couldn't see them, but unconsciously he drew closer, features piqued with interest.

Stop it. Stop it, Yemi, you greedy monster, I scolded myself. Reluctantly, the seductive aura faded from my face and hands. The room cooled. This errand would be brief, in and out. I'd come to collect a single item: a shard of Olajide's soul.

He glanced at his clipboard. "Mmm … Yemi Orisa. Yoruba?"

"And proud."

I was rewarded by the sleepiest of chuckles. Olajide fell into the swivel doctor's stool and punched on the chair's observation light. The sudden brightness made stars spiral in my vision, shimmering around his face. "It's not every day I get to meet a sister," he intoned. "What are you in for today, Yemi Orisa?"

"I think I gave your hygienist a crisis of faith," I said, and bared my immortally straight incisors. "My flossing puts her out of a job."

"I'll be the judge of that," he purred, and then began the slow recline of my chair.

He leaned forward and the cologne hit me in a dizzying wave. Keep your mind out of the gutter, goddess.

This was a business call. Iyami Aje collected soul fragments all the time, and while our method could be … pleasurable for both parties, I was here for a job. My breath slackened as he grew nearer. He flicked down his plastic eye shield, then reached for the gauze mask around his neck. But before he could pull it over his mouth, I grabbed his lab coat lapels and kissed him.

To my credit, I kept it professional.

It was over in a blink. Spearmint, coffee, and just a hint of metallic electricity tickled my tongue as a shard of Olajide slipped through my lips. My vision spun with thirst. I longed to let this mortal's soul slip down my throat, warming every nerve like a shot of expensive vodka.

No. Be good.

In a fluid movement, I snatched a flask from my purse and spat the soul fragment inside.

"What the hell," sputtered Olajide. "What the – I could sue you for—"

"For what?" I screwed the flask shut and slipped it neatly away, patting my purse.

"For—" His face grew confused, blank, and then as bored and drowsy as it had ever been. "I … where were we?"

"Firing your hygienist."

"Right," he said, checking the clipboard. He squinted at me, as though for a moment I had disappeared from the chair. "Guess I'd better see those heretical molars."

The memory-obfuscating miasma sunk back into my fingertips, leaving faint spots of pulsing green. I was going to have the worst hangover tomorrow morning. Two auras in the space of an hour drained even the most reckless of goddesses. But I had to stay awake.

I had to reach Deanna.

When it came to helping stubborn eniyans fall in love, soul sharding was the oldest trick in the deity book. Well, second only to eros arrows, which were outlawed in the heavens after the Mortal Rights Humane Act of 33 CE. When an eniyan possessed the soul shard of another, the two were drawn repeatedly together, complete strangers or no. Of course, it didn't make them fall in love. The first time they bumped into each other at a club, or he spilled her latte at a Starbucks, or she sneezed on his lunch on the Metro Rail, they might hate each other's guts.

But then she'd show up again at Griffith Observatory. She'd claim the telescope right by his, and he wouldn't be able to believe it. She wouldn't even know why she was there: only that she had awoken with an overwhelming urge for a glimpse of Saturn. They would make awkward conversation and part ways. For a while.

 Then he would happen to pass the window of her favorite salon. She would give an embarrassed wave from her stylist's chair; he'd come in and they would laugh – are you a PI, or something? Both would feel a little unsettled, but neither could stop smiling. He'd offer to bring her lunch from a taco truck down the street. They'd eat mulitas together, sauce running down their fingers as the salon workers installed her box braids.

Eventually the soul's pull would grow too strong. The shard would return to its original body, and both eniyans would be free. But by then, more often than not, their hearts were already far, far gone.

I hopped down from the examination chair, beaming at a confused Olajide. "You've been very helpful."

"But – we haven't even done the exam."

"You're right," I agreed. "The next steps will go way more smoothly once I have some information. But to start, just one question." I opened the recording app on my phone and pressed the red button. "Olajide: if I told you that your soulmate is someone you've never met, and you could send them a single message, what would you say?"

He snorted nervously, rubbing the back of his neck. "That's a weird question to ask your dentist." But the honesty compulsion made his lips keep moving. "I'd say: if she wants to get with this king, she'd better be a queen."

I frowned. "So you would send the future love of your life … instructions?"

"Yeah. I guess." Olajide's sleepy gaze grew distant as he warmed to the topic. "I'd want something real. A girl who knows who she is. But not stubborn, you know? Educated. Articulate. But not one of those ankh-wearing feminist types. I want old-school but like … woke." He gave a little chuckle. "That got heavy."

"Oh no," I said in a monotone, pressing pause on my phone app. "Please go on."

"Not to be shallow," he obliged without missing a beat, "but I don't understand girls who cake on makeup. Don't they know guys like that natural beauty? But not … like, rolled out of bed and zits natural. My queen has to take care of herself, have self-respect. Skinny, but not one of those annoying girls who only eats salad, you know what I'm saying? My queen's gotta love to eat—"

"Uh-huh," I said, jamming the phone in my purse and heading for the lobby.

He followed me. "Not one of those stuck-up types. Counting calories and afraid of messing up their nails … Man, I just want a queen who's down to earth. Who doesn't care about all that. She should be able to dress, though. Like in heels. And a dress that shows those curves, but not too slutty. My queen's a lady in the streets. But…" He leaned against the reception desk and winked. "She won't be some prude, that's for sure."

"Maybe you should wear a mood ring," I suggested brightly. "That way, she can change her outfit to match it every morning." Then I swept through the Elite Dentistry doors.

As if she were spying via drone, Bolajoko texted me the moment my shoes hit the pavement. My phone buzzed furiously as her texts barreled in.

B: Well?? How'd it go?

Y: …

B: That bad, huh

Y: …

At my second ellipsis, Bolajoko sent several crying laugh emojis. 😂😂😂 I know, I know, she texted. he's a fixer upper – now u see why I thought you'd be perfect

Y: … no. No, Bola I do not see that.

B: Yems. Oly doesn't want a real person. he wants us. literal fantasies. and u have that ice queen snarky unattainable thing going on. men like Oly dig that

I stopped dead in my tracks. The soul fragment pulsed through my leather bag, waiting to be poured into Deanna Idowu's wine glass. But what if Bolajoko was right?

No. She couldn't be right. The dreamy dentist and the strong-willed professor – this was supposed to be the romance of my career. My big break. The union of eniyans as lonely as Olajide and Deanna would make deity headlines. It would put the Los Angeles Diaspora Unit back on Oshun's map.

Bolajoko could not be right.

I strode grumpily down the street, head bent over my phone as I searched for a properly defiant gif to send my best friend. I'd just settled on a hair-flipping Olivia Pope with the caption IT'S HANDLED … when I walked headfirst into a rainbow-stained stepladder.

"Whoa," said a deep voice. I rubbed my nose, looking up in time to see a middle-aged man in a painter's jumpsuit scramble for balance.

"Sorry! Sorry," I gasped, holding out my hands, as if to steady him.

He barked a laugh and hopped down, sticking a brush handle-first into his smock pocket. "You all right, baby girl?"

"Fine. Oh gosh, did I mess you up?" For the first time, I took in the block-long mural I'd missed while texting. My breath caught in my throat.

This was what eniyans did best.

The blues, blacks, and vivid golds drew life from the grimy wall, veins pumping across the cement brick. The mural was several smaller pictures – oceans and forests, ghostly eyes, intertwined hands, butterfly wings, and mouths open in song – all coming together to form the silhouette of a soft-lipped woman. Her afro blossomed across the wall like a starry night sky.

"You walked right past my hazard cones," the artist said. His dreads were slender and long, tied up and speckled with blue paint. He smiled. "I'm just glad you didn't smudge the Count."

"Sorry," I said again, then echoed, "Count?"

He pointed to an image near my shoulder – barely discernable in the swirls of blue and black. "Count T'Jocula."

I squinted and leaned in closer. "It's you, isn't it?" In the drawing, a man hunched with dreads and cheerfully naughty eyes. An arm obscured his mouth, showing only the glint of two sharp teeth. He wore a paint-splattered cape with a high brown collar, and spidery words arched around him: I VANT TO TELL MY STORY – T'JOCULA

"TJ for Trey Johnson," the artist said, suddenly sheepish. "That's me. I put him in all my work. It's kind of an inside joke, never mind. Don't you run into any more ladders. You stay safe now, honey; have a nice—"

"Too late," I said, raising an eyebrow. "I'm invested. Now you have to tell me the joke."

Trey considered me. His face was lightly lined, as though with graphite pencil. Grief and humor pooled in wide charcoal eyes. "There's this author, Junot Diaz," he said at last. "He won the Pulitzer. They had him talk down at that fancy hipster place, The Last Bookstore. He said this thing about vampires and mirrors. How they have no reflection, and that's what makes them monsters. So when you're invisible, when your story's never told, the world never sees you as human."

"Is that why you paint?" I asked. "To tell your story?"

Trey gazed at the constellations twinkling in his mural woman's hair. "To tell as many stories as possible."

I smiled and said goodbye, and he waved from his ladder until I disappeared. Two blocks down, I froze in my tracks.

Don't miss T'Jocula.

The phantom smell of ammonia filled my nostrils as the homeless woman appeared in my mind's eye. Camped outside our office building for months. Rags that hid rheumy eyes, rimmed at the edges with cataracts and … gold. They were rimmed with freaking gold.

I threw back my head and laughed.

Tears streamed down my cheeks as I howled and snorted. I chortled until pee escaped into my Wardrobe-issue eniyan underwear. Queens stick together. When I regained control of my lungs, I shook my head at the hazy Inglewood sky. "Well played, Boss," I said. "Well played."

Immediately my phone buzzed. My heart began to pound as a text from an unknown number flashed onto my screen, then disappeared.

Ready for your big break? ~ O s h u n

My palms broke out in a cold sweat. But I nodded, swabbed my hands on the seat of my ankara-print yoga pants, and marched back to the mural. "Hey, T'Jocula," I yelled up the ladder.

"Hey, Phone Face," Trey yelled back.

"If you've never met your soulmate, but you can send them a single message, what do you say?"

Trey cocked his head in thought. "Her story matters," he said.

A lump formed in my throat. I swallowed hard. "That's it?"

"That's it, baby girl, unless you have any more weird questions. She matters. Happy?"

I retrieved the flask from my purse and uncorked the cover. Olajide's metallic soul fragment splattered onto the pavement, then swirled back to Elite Dentistry in a smelly cologne wind.

I grinned up at Trey and replied: "So happy, I could kiss you."

A Satchel of Seeds

Frances Lu-Pai Ippolito

MY GRANDMOTHER DIED on a stellar ferry ride to a Goldilocks planet named Lixing. According to the Peng-you bots, that's a pear-shaped planet floating somewhere five more travel years away from our current coordinates. On the way, Popo lay dead in the uncovered sleeper pod. A wreath of grey hair pillowed her head, her face relaxed into peace as it cooled, and her weathered hands remained clasped gently over her hips as if to cinch in the waist of her onesie that had grown too roomy as the tumor hollowed her out from inside.

I knew the moment she was gone from the drop of her chest that didn't rise to fill up with fresh recycled air no matter how long I stared. That final exhale slipped out of parted lips that were chapped and turning blue. Her "last breath" was something she'd always called me. The last important thing she believed she'd do in this life.

The breath became air floating above her mouth. In the cold pressurized compartment, it condensed in on itself, coalescing into a tiny cloud that bobbed and danced up, moving higher towards a vent. The ship was always freezing, but I quickly took off my gloves to reach for the milky swirl before it floated out of reach and disappeared. My fingers poked at the warm mist, fisting around it. But the breath slipped free, ducking through knuckle gaps, unwilling to be imprisoned though it seemed to want to touch me too, lingering and tracing my exposed fingertips, kissing me one last time.

Across from me, Mama stood next to a second, empty pill-shaped sleeper pod and stared out the only porthole. Her whole face reflected in the clear acrylic glass – puffy eyes, unbrushed hair, and pale skin. Her gaze went past the stretched streams of starlight that marked the hyper speed travel of *Chang-Er VIII* through deep-veined spaceways. She clenched her own fists and stumbled away from where she stood; not getting far in our cramped cabin before crossing from one end to the other in six steps.

She wedged herself into the curved space of the ship's window, molding her lithe body to the curve of the wall, and thumping her head on the backdrop of streaking stars.

"It was a mistake," she whispered, her breath frosting the acrylic glass.

A mistake? Did she regret volunteering for the relocation all those years ago? Or was it something else? That thought made me feel sick, deep in the pit of my stomach. A heaviness suddenly weighed me down, reminding me that I was still stuck in this room as I had been for the last eighteen years.

"I was twenty-one and I didn't know I was pregnant," Mama explained to me when I was seven and had asked where the other children were. "I easily qualified, but your Popo—"

Popo laughed. "I was over-seasoned like stewed bean curd."

Mama continued, "You were only forty-five. And they let you come eventually."

"They needed willing brides for the men at the mining colony on Lixing. Including ripened, stinky ones like me." Popo stroked my hair that was short and slow to grow even though I was seven years old. Unlike my brown curls, Popo's hair was black with a few strands of gray that played peekaboo in a dark curtain dipping below her shoulders. Mama's hair was the same as hers and longer, swishing at her waist.

"Don't listen to your Ah-Ma. She was picked, just like I was," Mama said and tore the top off a nutrient pouch. The opening in the foil package was the perfect size for her pink lips to cover and seal. She sucked the gray gel in noisy mouthfuls and grimaced between swallows. "Tastes worse than desert rats," she mumbled, tossing the spent package into a bin and wiping the back of her hand against her mouth.

Popo winked at me. "I sent in my pictures from my thirties. I was a lot cuter then."

"What's a desert rat? What does it taste like?" I asked. I'd never eaten anything but my mother's milk and nutrient pouches. Weren't deserts hot? Would the rat taste hot in my mouth? That didn't seem so bad. All the nutrient pouches were cold. If nutrient pouches were so bad, why were we eating them instead of rats?

Later on, at twelve, I was told that rats tasted better than nutrient pouches, but not as good as "free room and board in perpetuity." That was the promise along with full citizenship upon the successful live birth of a newborn in Lixing's jurisdiction. Those incentives were too much for the women to turn down. Popo and Mama hinted that the dangers of Earth life were a major factor as well. But they never liked talking about that or my father or the way my mother became pregnant. Whenever these topics came up, they would look at each other, nod, and fall silent. In the suffocating quiet, I pulled my brown curls straight and wondered why I didn't have hair the color of space or eyes as beautiful and slivered as my grandmother's.

These memories played fast through my mind as Popo's last breath dissipated into the vent. Bereft, my hands fumbled their way to her stiffening body in the gleaming ivory sleeper pod. My fingers twitched and I suppressed a growing desire to grab her shoulders to give her a rough shake, to rouse her from a nap. Instead, I stroked the grooves of her wrinkle-mapped face, the friction of her uneven skin softening and slowing my fingers' path. Cracked skin and bumpy sunspots. The souvenirs, she told me, of years spent in sun-blasted migrant farm fields and the starving desert boroughs of New Zhongguo on Earth.

A gentle scent wafted by. The smell of burnt rice, or at least, Popo had told me that was the fragrance the seeds and dried Chinese herbs gave off in the stuffed satchels she hid under pillows in her sleeper pod. These little fabric bags had been precious to her, clutched in hands or placed by her head all these years. I took another breath and remembered the last time she took out the seeds.

"Never forget," Mama was teaching me at sixteen, "you will be an immigrant. Learn Lixinglish. Assimilate as quickly as you can. Or they will ask you where you are from and demand that you go back."

Popo scowled with displeasure when Mama said this and opened her cheesecloth bundles. Squatting on the floor, she scooped seeds into her palm and buried her nostrils deep, inhaling long draughts.

Jujube. Lichee. Longan. Mangosteen. Ginseng. Mandrake. Dates. Lemongrass. She purred forth the names and pinched at the oblong and rounded shapes lined up in her hand. One, she called anise, was shaped like a hand with extra fingers. She placed it in my palm and pushed my hand up to my nose. It smelled like magic and life. A scent that cut through the sterilized blankness of the cabin air.

"We don't have to give up everything," Popo said.

Mama plucked the seed from my hand and shoved it back into Popo's satchel. "Don't fill her head with nonsense. The more we stand out—" She paused to stare at me, at my round eyes, my freckled skin, and my curls that twisted like unruly snakes when she combed them, "—the more attention, the more questions."

Mama was afraid of the questions, especially when she didn't know the answers. Like what kind of man my father had been beyond a stranger's violence poured into her womb.

"Even in new soil, some things can grow the same," Popo murmured loud enough for just me to hear.

Her voice sounded so clear in my head, though my fingers touched her mute lips. "Not you, Popo," I whispered. "You won't be with us in Lixing." *I miss you so much already.*

"Do you regret it?" I turned to ask Mama who continued to stare out the window.

"What?" she said, sounding faded and far away.

"Do you regret it?"

She sighed and rubbed her tired, drawn face. "I told you before, refugees don't have many options on Earth."

"That's not what I mean." My voice trembled. "D-do you regret me?"

A month after liftoff and right before the ship accelerated into hyperspace, the lid of Mama's sleeper pod refused to close at the scheduled moment to enter hyper sleep. A built-in medical scanner registered Mama's minute hormonal changes.

"You didn't have to keep me," I pressed on, looking past my silent mother to the bright bold letters printed across the glass pod lid: WARNING!!! CHILDREN AND EXPECTANT MOTHERS PROHIBITED.

Mama and Popo chose to stay awake, grow me, deliver me, and rear me in this tiny pod compartment on a silent, lonely journey where everyone else slept and stayed young.

I started again. "Popo wouldn't have grown old and the doctors on Lixing—"

"Bu zai shuole." Stop talking. She raised her hand and glared back, the crow's feet at her temples fanned and flexed. "The bots will come soon. Help me prepare her."

She showed me how, according to the old ways. I undressed Popo and wiped her stiffening body with hand cloths wetted with our rationed drinking water. I brushed Popo's hair and held it for Mama to tie into a tight braid. A beep sounded at the door right as we finished putting her into a clean space onesie. Two hefty staff bots rolled in.

"Recycle," one said and approached Popo's body. *Chang-Er* was not built for active human passengers. Awake metabolisms required food and water to maintain, unlike the sleeping ones, frozen in place. The bots were programmed to harvest the water and proteins in Popo's body for the ship's supply to feed us.

"No." Mama sandwiched herself between Popo and the outstretched chrome graspers of the Peng-you bot. "We'll enter hyper sleep. Store her whole."

A frowny face pattern of LED lights appeared on Peng-you's flat head screen. "Exceeds weight limit allotted to passenger luggage."

"That's ridiculous! Even if you couldn't find another sleeper pod for us, there's plenty of space to store her whole."

"Extra fee."

"Charge our husbands!" Mama demanded, tearless and fierce.

The room grew silent except for a whirring that the pair of Peng-you bots hummed as they processed Mama's request. I knew if they wanted, they'd easily overpower us. Peng-yous weren't allowed to hurt the contracted women, but we weren't their masters either.

The emoji eyes and smile reappeared. "Additional service fee queried to account. Balance must be paid prior to disembarkment."

Mama slumped weak against the wall. "Keep her whole," she said again as the Peng-you bots lifted and carried Popo's body out of our room.

"She did this for us," Mama mumbled.

"Did this for us?" I echoed. Popo chose cancer? Did she die for me? The husbands paid for two, not three sleeper pods. Only two of us could enter hyper sleep after I became eligible on my eighteenth birthday.

"There's no time to waste. Get in the pod," Mama said as she swiped through the lit panel screen.

"I'm scared." It was my first time.

She pushed my head down into the pod that was my grandmother's. "We'll find a nice spot on Lixing. At Qingming, we'll sweep her gravesite and burn joss paper. We'll care for her the traditional way. It would have made her happy."

"Do the people on Lixing do that?" I asked, recalling how vehemently Mama insisted we blend in, for our own safety. "Will they accept us? Will it be okay?"

Mama tucked something under my pillow. "Even in new soil, some things will always stay the same," she said, her voice cracking.

She didn't wait for me to ask any more questions and quickly secured the glass cover over my body with a firm CLANK. The lights dimmed and I slid into hyper sleep, lulled by a perfusion of sedative gases laced with the scent of burnt rice.

Voices From Another World

Jas Kainth

Location: Laniakea
Satellite: Odin
Operatives: 9000
Commander: Majesty
+3024 days since the cessation of Earth.

MAJESTY'S MESSAGE boomed through the tannoy, instigating the start-up:

Operatives of Odin, your work is crucial for the survival of our species. What the humans called The Day affected thousands of species. Our intel suggests that hundreds of galaxies experienced this phenomenon which we know so little about. Your work is imperative for the survival of Odin. To protect the future of Odin, it essential that we learn about how humans lived...

The meter by meter cavity was usually lit up by white lights but today, Lyra had utilised her new software. It was her reward for having catalogued a thousand files. Lyra had therefore selected the undulating green and purple fells from a place called Yorkshire, England. File A736, Dale and Heather, had exposed Lyra to this setting. Lyra couldn't dream but she knew what dreams were. Humans often talked about them. If, one day, she could dream as Majesty had assured her that they would be able to, Lyra thought that she would re-create all the locations from the files that she'd downloaded.

Of Earth's four hemispheres, Lyra's remit was the Northern Hemisphere, but Majesty had promised her an upgrade which would allow Lyra access to other hemispheres provided that she achieved her target.

The green hills above Lyra were flashing. The system had calibrated.

Voices From Another World

File: 2078
Operative: 8796 (Lyra)
Planet: Earth
Human: Surinder Kaur

These words are mine. Well, *technically*, they are not mine. I cannot read nor can I write English. But I assume that you will be able to. I assure you that all of these are my words. My daughter wrote them down. I don't know why I was selected. My life is not interesting; I am not important, but my daughter says that the government wants a diverse sample.

We have been instructed to tell the truth. My daughter is shocked by what I tell her. You see, my daughter didn't know me as a woman. For her, I've only ever been her mother, or mamma as she calls me. I will always be her mother but first of all, I was a girl, one of seven, born in 1956, in the village of Lohara, Punjab, India.

Before I became a woman, I was made a wife. I choose that word carefully. I wish for my daughter to use that specific word. I say *made* because I didn't really have a choice in what I would become. But I wasn't forced. That was just how it was done.

As a young girl, you grew up knowing that that you would be a wife, a daughter-in-law and then you'd become a mother. That's how we were grown. I know that *grown* is not the right word either. My daughter wishes to change it. She doesn't know who will read this, if anyone will read it but she wants it all to be correct. But *grown* is the word that I want her to use. You see, I was raised so delicately, gently by my mother and father. They nurtured us like one nurtures a plant, protecting it, sheltering it so that it isn't buffeted by the wind, doesn't drown in a storm or die in a drought.

My parents loved me. All parents in India love their daughters. Even the ones who drown their baby girls at birth. It's not that the girls aren't loved. Perhaps they are loved too much. Their parents drown them so that that they won't suffer.

My life hasn't been terrible. Yes, I have had to endure some pain but that is life, is it not? That's what I tell my daughter. When I received the government's letter informing me that I had been selected, it was her idea to write it all down, for you, whoever you are, and for herself. Honestly, I'm not sure that I am ready to go back but I don't have a choice.

My daughter steels herself to listen to more. Her watery smile. Is it sorrow? Pity? Unconditional love? I falter slightly. Should I continue? If it's pity, I do not want it. I do not wish to have your pity either.

She wants to take me in her arms and comfort me like I comforted her when she was a child.

'But why didn't you tell me, mamma?'

'Because that's just what a mother does.'

A mother protects her child from the drought, takes food from her own mouth to feed her young ones; a mother protects her children from the strongest tempests. I don't say this to my daughter. I think it all, though, and then I try to will it into her mind and into her heart.

I make a promise to myself, to her, to you: I'll only speak the truth, so let me start from the beginning.

Life in the Village

You may assume that life in our village was quiet and dull. You'd be wrong. I was one of seven sisters. Our house was full of life, full of laughter. My sisters and I, we each had different personalities like you may have heard of in the cartoon that my daughters used to watch with the seven little men who wore funny clothes, had big ears, fat noses and waddled around trying to win the affections of a fair princess.

My eldest sister was tall and skinny like a tree; the second from eldest, she was shrewd, you could get nothing past her; sister number three was always in love, a hopeless romantic wistfully longing for Rajiv, the school's heartthrob; sister number four, she was the accountant; she kept tabs on everything; my second-youngest sister – Paven – she was the beauty; my youngest sister, the runt of the litter, was slow to learn. Me? Well, I was in the middle. I was sister number five. I wasn't the tallest. I wasn't the fairest. But, I would say that I was ranked joint second with sister number three in the possibility of being able to find a suitor.

Skin colour is as much of an issue for Indians as it is *apparently* for the English. I was the strongest of the seven, physically and emotionally, as I would later prove. But if you asked any of my sisters, they would describe me as lucky as I was the one going to England. Luck. It's a funny thing. I didn't consider myself lucky. I was being uprooted and sent to England. What was lucky about that? I'd have to go to England where people ate bland food; where the weather was always cold and where the women wore trousers. Imagine that! It didn't matter to me that I was being given the opportunity to be able to meet the Queen.

My family owned a small piece of land. My sisters and I shared the work on the farm whilst my father and brother traded goods in the local market. In the mornings, my sisters and I would wake up at 5am to walk to the fields to relieve ourselves. No one had bathrooms in their houses. We'd walk along the dusty paths in silence with sleep in our eyes, trying to stretch out our sleepy limbs. It was often dark. I liked the misty mornings though. I'd create a cape with my shawl and cover my youngest sister, enveloping her so that her breath would warm my bosom. We would walk to the fields, side by side, matching each one of our steps as though we were dancing. After crossing the railway tracks and passing the clearing, we'd seek shelter among the trees. We'd each find a little section of the field to crouch down in, ensuring that our bare bottoms weren't in the direct eye line of anyone else before commencing our business. Thinking back, I don't know how I ever managed to make my bottom poo on cue. Today, things aren't as reliable.

In the distance, we could sometimes hear the whistle of the cargo train. Beneath our flip flops, the dried leaves would crunch. You'd always scan the immediate area for a big, dry leaf which could be used to wipe your bottom with before squatting. Everyone would remain silent but if someone happened to let out a fart, we would all erupt with laughter. We would laugh and laugh until we reached the edge of the village where my eldest sister would tell us off. Our mother didn't like us laughing so freely outside the house. She worried that people may judge us.

"Stop laughing. You're showing your teeth like a horse," she'd say.

It didn't make sense to me but I guess horses do have big teeth.

We had lots of rules about what girls should and shouldn't do.

My daughter is laughing. She reminds me that I had also enforced these rules upon her when she was growing up. I dismiss this. It's a mother's prerogative to deny all knowledge when she wishes to.

1) A girl shouldn't laugh too much in public as people may think that she is a little mad.

2) A girl shouldn't look directly into someone's eyes. She'll be considered ill-mannered or worse, she'll be viewed as flirtatious.

3) A girl should be respectful.

4) A girl should not question what she is told. Indians didn't want freethinkers back then. Thinking was fine if you didn't happen to have ovaries.

5) When a girl left her parents' house for her in-laws' house, that became her new home. She was never allowed to go back.

That rule stayed with me forever.

The Proposal

It was Mother-in-law who proposed to me. It wasn't the kind of proposal that a girl dreams of. In fact, it wasn't exactly a proposal at all. It wasn't *me* that she had come to see. Not that we were told that anyone was coming to see anyone or anything. She was looking for a bride for her youngest son who was living in England. She had come to see my younger sister, Paven. She had heard that Paven was beautiful, like her name suggested. She arrived at our house at 2pm. She had insisted that the rickshaw driver waited for her until her business had been concluded. We were surprised to learn this as it would have cost her a lot of money but clearly, this wasn't an issue for her, and she had wanted us all to know that fact.

We all greeted the woman in the courtyard. Unlike our own mother, who was small and slender, this woman was sturdy looking. Her frame was solid, impenetrable. She was dressed in a coral-coloured salwar kameez, a colour which most women of her age would have probably avoided. Her hair was pinned back in a bun, and woven through the black and silvery locks was a charcoal parandi which snaked through and tucked under at the nape of her neck. She wore her hair with a middle parting which reflected a vibrant orange where the henna had bleached it. She was bold and didn't cover her head like mother. Paven and I couldn't help but giggle at her funny looking shoes. She didn't wear leather chappals like our mother. She wore black leather shoes with a buckle which looked odd, like they were fighting with the bottom of her salwar.

Our mother gave us a stern look, so we stopped laughing immediately. I had to hold my breath like I was trying to hold back hiccups.

The fire crackled; the hardened dung turned from a smoky mass to white. Paven had decided that she would roll the chapattis whilst I flipped them on the tava. She didn't like open flames. Someone at school had told her a story of a girl from the next village who had died. She had been set on fire for going against her husband's wishes. They told Paven that the villagers could often see a figure, aflame, walking through the village at nights. Since hearing that story, Paven had refused to cook the chapattis by herself.

I didn't mind flipping the chapattis on the flames. I liked to see their bellies bloat. It was a challenge to flip them off just before they exploded and became punctured and anyway, my hands were hardened, protected against the heat. My sisters always teased me that my hands were like a man's, but my mother always rebuked them:

"No one needs a beautiful face, but hands, *everyone* needs strong hands. With strong hands, you'll never go hungry."

She was correct.

From the rasoi, Paven and I could hear the woman's serious voice. It sounded like a beating drum, heavy, repetitive, slow. The voices in the courtyard became louder. Mother and her guest were on the move. Paven and I broke out into a frenzy of rolling and flipping chapatis. When they entered the rasoi, neither of us looked in their direction. We were crouching on the floor. Mother asked Paven to stand up and she did as she was told.

The strange lady inspected Paven closely, lifting her arms, looking at her hands, sizing up her feet. Finally, she announced, "She won't do. She looks like she'll snap. How will she withstand the English cold?"

After mother had led her guest back out to the courtyard, Paven and I let out muffled laughs. We continued to work whilst trying to listen to what was being said. The woman's haughty voice didn't fit in our home. It was like an overbearing piece of furniture. Paven and I hid a single chapatti on the side so we could eat it without mother noticing. We had hidden it under a red cloth so that it could be moved easily if we were interrupted unexpectedly. It wasn't that we weren't allowed to eat. That's not why we hid food. Mother didn't like us to eat while we prepared meals. She said it was not good.

"It's bad manners. You are not animals."

My mother always compared us to animals in one way or another. I think it's because she was raised on a farm, and she had married a farmer too. Our mother was set in her ways, particularly when it came to dining etiquette.

My daughter raises an eyebrow; a black arch looks at me accusingly.

"Just write it down..." I instruct her, pointing towards her notepad which is balancing on top of her knee.

Today, she has her dragonfly pen. It has a tortoiseshell body which, depending on how she is holding it or how quickly she is writing, looks like she's waving a wand of burning embers.

I'm sure she is about to remind me of how I used to say the same to her when she was young, but I don't wish for her to get sidetracked. We only have forty days to complete the government's request. Sixty-eight years to unravel in forty days. We must keep going. Looking at the past at least stops me looking at the future, not that anyone is telling us about our future.

I was painting the top of the chapatti with butter when mother's guest entered the rasoi again. We hadn't noticed that the chatting from the courtyard could no longer be heard. I still had a mouthful of hot bread which I was trying to chew discreetly. I could feel that my cheeks were becoming flushed from the heat of the flames.

The severe woman marched over and took my arm. The tips of my fingers glistened with the residue of the excess butter. She held my wrist as though she was trying to take my pulse. She eyed me from head to toe.

She paused for a moment and started to fumble at the side of her kameez, reaching for the bottom of her shawl. Fingering the sides, she retrieved a small knot and started to unpick it.

"Hold out your hand," she ordered.

Over her broad shoulder, my mother nodded in approval. I did as I was told.

The woman placed 11 Rupees upon my floury palm.

"You are my daughter-in-law now."

The deal was done. My fate sealed with 11 Rupees.

The Wedding

A few weeks later, my future father-in-law came to visit. He was a handsome man, tall and strong. He wore a traditional kurta, white, and over the top, he wore a Western coat. He didn't swathe himself with a shawl like the elders of our village. He was different, regal. He had fair skin, like milk, and he had grey eyes that appeared blue or grey depending on the light. I didn't intend to look at him directly, but he captured my attention. We had always been told not to look anyone in the eye. It was insolent, but he didn't seem to object.

"I wanted to see my daughter," he said in his soft voice.

Encouraged by his words, I looked up at him.

"She will give me beautiful grandchildren."

* * *

My husband's family didn't want to delay things, neither did my mother and father. It was a good proposal. They didn't wish for the groom's side to change their minds. The wedding was arranged for the following month. Although I was one of seven daughters, my mother and father didn't begrudge the fact that they have given birth to so many girls. For my father, we were a source of pride and joy.

"So what if I have seven daughters?" my father would say. "I love each and every one of them."

I spent the whole month daydreaming about what married life would be like. I wondered what my husband would look like. Would he be tall and fair like my father-in-law? Would he be stern like Mother-in-law? I hadn't even seen a picture of him but having been lost in all my daydreaming, before I knew it, the day had arrived.

The courtyard was decorated beautifully with flowers and there was a halwai making sweet jalebis for everyone. The entire village attended and filled their bellies to the brim with delicious sweetmeats and savouries. The women clapped and sang songs. The men ate and chatted. It was a moment of great pride for my mother and father. For me? It was surreal. I felt like I was gliding underwater. The sounds from above were muffled but within the water, glimmers of light carried the shimmers of colours from rich fabrics and indulgent foods, swathing me.

I felt beautiful. My sisters had adorned me lovingly. Everyone agreed that I was the prettiest bride that the village had ever seen. It was the first time that I had ever worn grown-up clothes and jewellery. My cheeks flushed a deep crimson. My red bangles jingled every time I moved, singing a beautiful melody which I hummed along to quietly. When my sisters heard a little note, they teased me, poking me in my ribs when the elders weren't looking. My silver anklets tickled my ankles with their tiny bells every time I moved. Excitement travelled up from my feet, along my legs and it was settling at the pit of my stomach, building and building. I thought that I would pop and burst like one of those chapattis which had sat on top of a flame in our rasoi on the day of the proposal.

All Indian brides wear red. It's the colour of love, of passion. I could not believe it when I heard that, in England, women wear white on their wedding day. Indians reserve the colour white for death, for funerals, for widows. In India, married women must stay away from women in white as they are thought to bring bad luck, tempt fate. Their loss could be contagious. Things are different now, but in more remote places many people still hold these beliefs.

My dupatta was also a rich red colour. It had a golden border which looked like tinsel and it tickled the side of my face every time I moved. My hands were decorated with henna which had developed into a deep orange, the kind of orange which looks like the sun is bleeding into the sky in the hottest months of summer. The circles in the middle of my palms were bright orbs. The tips of my fingers, which had been dipped into the cold green paste, had developed into a vibrant red which made it look as though I was bleeding. It's a belief amongst Indians that the darker the colour of your henna, the more your mother-in-law will love you.

Looking at my hands, my mother said, "Your mother-in-law's love will be abundant." My mother was seldom wrong but, on this occasion, she was.

I hadn't seen my husband, but I had been told that he was very handsome. When my sisters saw his picture, they told me that he looked like a film star.

"Which one?" I quizzed.

I hoped it was not Dharmendra. He was the most popular amongst girls our age, the latest fashion, but he was far too bolshie for me. Lying in bed at night, I would hope that my husband would be like Rajesh Khanna. He would have a full head of thick, black hair which he would comb to the side. I imagined white trousers, a yellow shirt and a matching yellow sweater draped over his shoulders against a backdrop of undulating green hills. Cue the music and we'd be dancing together like in a Bollywood film.

During the wedding ceremony, I kept my head lowered, the ultimate sign of good breeding. Even though I couldn't feel my bottom and I had pins and needles in my legs, I sat as still as a statue until it was time for the nuptials. My mother had made me practise sitting still in the weeks leading up to the day.

I sat with my head bowed down, but I couldn't help myself. Whenever possible, I'd snatch a quick glance at the guests who were looking at me whilst the priest read out our wedding vows. After each nuptial chant, I stood up, with my sister's help, and held my husband's framed picture in front of me. I walked around the Guru Granth Sahib.

I held the portrait tightly in front of my chest. I walked slowly, with as much composure as I could manage, despite numb buttocks and tired arms. That picture frame grew heavier and heavier with each nuptial. I wasn't the most graceful bride, but I ensured that I hadn't given mother nor father a single reason to be embarrassed.

When the time came for me to leave my parents' home, I sat on the edge of the wooden bed and each of my sisters came to hug me goodbye. I had steeled myself but upon seeing my mother,

I crumpled. She took me in her arms and held me close to her bosom. I couldn't look up at her. I closed my eyes tightly. I cried. I cried into her chest until I thought I would burst. Through the laboured rising and dipping of her breasts, I could feel her warmth. Her stifled sobs caused tiny convulsions to reverberate through my body. We were connected, our bodies moving in sync like it would have been when I was in her womb.

"May God make you happy and bless you with all of the happiness in the world," my mother said, holding back her tears.

She fed me a piece of sweetmeat and pressed the palm of her hand upon my head. Adjusting my dupatta and gently placing her fingers underneath my chin so that she could take one last look at me, she tried to raise my head. I didn't open my eyes. I couldn't. It would break me. She gently kissed each one of my closed eyelids.

It was time for me to leave.

Indians call this ceremony the dholi. In Bollywood films, they always depict the scene accompanied with sad music. Then you'll see a bride, bejewelled, wearing red, being placed upon a grand palanquin which has been adorned with flowers.

During the bride's departure, the bride's brothers are meant to carry her out as she now belongs to a different home.

My daughter thinks that this is a symbol.

"Mamma, it's like they are being relieved of a burden, handing her over to someone else," she declares.

"Yes, I suppose it is," is my reply.

When I arrived in England, I learned that English people carry coffins in the same way that Indians carry a bride.

* * *

The vivid greens above Lyra begin to glitch. Unexpectedly, Majesty's voice booms through the tannoy once again:

Operative 87962. There is an error on this file. We have transferred it to operative 7812, remit: Eastern Hemisphere. Planet: Earth. Please await a reboot.

* * *

The screen is now still. Lyra is surrounded by purple and green fells again.

File: 3989
Operator: 87962 (Lyra)
Planet: Earth
Human: George Woodstock

We live in the seaside town of Bude, northeast Cornwall, England...

Paper Menagerie

Ken Liu

ONE OF MY EARLIEST MEMORIES starts with me sobbing. I refused to be soothed no matter what Mom and Dad tried.

Dad gave up and left the bedroom, but Mom took me into the kitchen and sat me down at the breakfast table.

"*Kan, kan*," she said, as she pulled a sheet of wrapping paper from on top of the fridge. For years, Mom carefully sliced open the wrappings around Christmas gifts and saved them on top of the fridge in a thick stack.

She set the paper down, plain side facing up, and began to fold it. I stopped crying and watched her, curious.

She turned the paper over and folded it again. She pleated, packed, tucked, rolled, and twisted until the paper disappeared between her cupped hands. Then she lifted the folded-up paper packet to her mouth and blew into it, like a balloon.

"*Kan*," she said. "*Laohu*." She put her hands down on the table and let go.

A little paper tiger stood on the table, the size of two fists placed together. The skin of the tiger was the pattern on the wrapping paper, white background with red candy canes and green Christmas trees.

I reached out to Mom's creation. Its tail twitched, and it pounced playfully at my finger. "*Rawrr-sa*," it growled, the sound somewhere between a cat and rustling newspapers.

I laughed, startled, and stroked its back with an index finger. The paper tiger vibrated under my finger, purring.

"*Zhe jiao zhezhi*," Mom said. *This is called origami*.

I didn't know this at the time, but Mom's kind was special. She breathed into them so that they shared her breath, and thus moved with her life. This was her magic.

* * *

Dad had picked Mom out of a catalog.

One time, when I was in high school, I asked Dad about the details. He was trying to get me to speak to Mom again.

He had signed up for the introduction service back in the spring of 1973. Flipping through the pages steadily, he had spent no more than a few seconds on each page until he saw the picture of Mom.

I've never seen this picture. Dad described it: Mom was sitting in a chair, her side to the camera, wearing a tight green silk cheongsam. Her head was turned to the camera so that her long black hair was draped artfully over her chest and shoulder. She looked out at him with the eyes of a calm child.

"That was the last page of the catalog I saw," he said.

The catalog said she was eighteen, loved to dance, and spoke good English because she was from Hong Kong. None of these facts turned out to be true.

He wrote to her, and the company passed their messages back and forth. Finally, he flew to Hong Kong to meet her.

"The people at the company had been writing her responses. She didn't know any English other than 'hello' and 'goodbye.'"

What kind of woman puts herself into a catalog so that she can be bought? The high school me thought I knew so much about everything. Contempt felt good, like wine.

Instead of storming into the office to demand his money back, he paid a waitress at the hotel restaurant to translate for them.

"She would look at me, her eyes halfway between scared and hopeful, while I spoke. And when the girl began translating what I said, she'd start to smile slowly."

He flew back to Connecticut and began to apply for the papers for her to come to him. I was born a year later, in the Year of the Tiger.

* * *

At my request, Mom also made a goat, a deer, and a water buffalo out of wrapping paper. They would run around the living room while Laohu chased after them, growling. When he caught them he would press down until the air went out of them and they became just flat, folded-up pieces of paper. I would then have to blow into them to re-inflate them so they could run around some more.

Sometimes, the animals got into trouble. Once, the water buffalo jumped into a dish of soy sauce on the table at dinner. (He wanted to wallow, like a real water buffalo.) I picked him out quickly but the capillary action had already pulled the dark liquid high up into his legs. The sauce-softened legs would not hold him up, and he collapsed onto the table. I dried him out in the sun, but his legs became crooked after that, and he ran around with a limp. Mom eventually wrapped his legs in saran wrap so that he could wallow to his heart's content (just not in soy sauce).

Also, Laohu liked to pounce at sparrows when he and I played in the backyard. But one time, a cornered bird struck back in desperation and tore his ear. He whimpered and winced as I held him and Mom patched his ear together with tape. He avoided birds after that.

And then one day, I saw a TV documentary about sharks and asked Mom for one of my own. She made the shark, but he flapped about on the table unhappily. I filled the sink with water, and put him in. He swam around and around happily. However, after a while he became soggy and translucent, and slowly sank to the bottom, the folds coming undone. I reached in to rescue him, and all I ended up with was a wet piece of paper.

Laohu put his front paws together at the edge of the sink and rested his head on them. Ears drooping, he made a low growl in his throat that made me feel guilty.

Mom made a new shark for me, this time out of tin foil. The shark lived happily in a large goldfish bowl. Laohu and I liked to sit next to the bowl to watch the tin foil shark chasing the goldfish, Laohu sticking his face up against the bowl on the other side so that I saw his eyes, magnified to the size of coffee cups, staring at me from across the bowl.

* * *

When I was ten, we moved to a new house across town. Two of the women neighbors came by to welcome us. Dad served them drinks and then apologized for having to run off to the utility company to straighten out the prior owner's bills. "Make yourselves at home. My wife doesn't speak much English, so don't think she's being rude for not talking to you."

While I read in the dining room, Mom unpacked in the kitchen. The neighbors conversed in the living room, not trying to be particularly quiet.

"He seems like a normal enough man. Why did he do that?"

"Something about the mixing never seems right. The child looks unfinished. Slanty eyes, white face. A little monster."

"Do you think *he* can speak English?"

The women hushed. After a while they came into the dining room.

"Hello there! What's your name?"

"Jack," I said.

"That doesn't sound very Chinesey."

Mom came into the dining room then. She smiled at the women. The three of them stood in a triangle around me, smiling and nodding at each other, with nothing to say, until Dad came back.

* * *

Mark, one of the neighborhood boys, came over with his Star Wars action figures. Obi-Wan Kenobi's lightsaber lit up and he could swing his arms and say, in a tinny voice, "Use the Force!" I didn't think the figure looked much like the real Obi-Wan at all.

Together, we watched him repeat this performance five times on the coffee table. "Can he do anything else?" I asked.

Mark was annoyed by my question. "Look at all the details," he said.

I looked at the details. I wasn't sure what I was supposed to say.

Mark was disappointed by my response. "Show me your toys."

I didn't have any toys except my paper menagerie. I brought Laohu out from my bedroom. By then he was very worn, patched all over with tape and glue, evidence of the years of repairs Mom and I had done on him. He was no longer as nimble and sure-footed as before. I sat him down on the coffee table. I could hear the skittering steps of the other animals behind in the hallway, timidly peeking into the living room.

"*Xiao laohu*," I said, and stopped. I switched to English. "This is Tiger." Cautiously, Laohu strode up and purred at Mark, sniffing his hands.

Mark examined the Christmas-wrap pattern of Laohu's skin. "That doesn't look like a tiger at all. Your Mom makes toys for you from trash?"

I had never thought of Laohu as *trash*. But looking at him now, he was really just a piece of wrapping paper.

Mark pushed Obi-Wan's head again. The lightsaber flashed; he moved his arms up and down. "Use the Force!"

Laohu turned and pounced, knocking the plastic figure off the table. It hit the floor and broke, and Obi-Wan's head rolled under the couch. "*Rawwww*," Laohu laughed. I joined him.

Mark punched me, hard. "This was very expensive! You can't even find it in the stores now. It probably cost more than what your dad paid for your mom!"

I stumbled and fell to the floor. Laohu growled and leapt at Mark's face.

Mark screamed, more out of fear and surprise than pain. Laohu was only made of paper, after all.

Mark grabbed Laohu and his snarl was choked off as Mark crumpled him in his hand and tore him in half. He balled up the two pieces of paper and threw them at me. "Here's your stupid cheap Chinese garbage."

After Mark left, I spent a long time trying, without success, to tape together the pieces, smooth out the paper, and follow the creases to refold Laohu. Slowly, the other animals came into the living room and gathered around us, me and the torn wrapping paper that used to be Laohu.

* * *

My fight with Mark didn't end there. Mark was popular at school. I never want to think again about the two weeks that followed.

I came home that Friday at the end of the two weeks. "*Xuexiao hao ma*?" Mom asked. I said nothing and went to the bathroom. I looked into the mirror. *I look nothing like her, nothing.*

At dinner I asked Dad, "Do I have a chink face?"

Dad put down his chopsticks. Even though I had never told him what happened in school, he seemed to understand. He closed his eyes and rubbed the bridge of his nose. "No, you don't."

Mom looked at Dad, not understanding. She looked back at me. "*Sha jiao chink*?"

"English," I said. "Speak English."

She tried. "What happen?"

I pushed the chopsticks and the bowl before me away: stir-fried green peppers with five-spice beef. "We should eat American food."

Dad tried to reason. "A lot of families cook Chinese sometimes."

"We are not other families." I looked at him. *Other families don't have moms who don't belong.*

He looked away. And then he put a hand on Mom's shoulder. "I'll get you a cookbook."

Mom turned to me. "*Bu haochi*?"

"English," I said, raising my voice. "Speak English."

Mom reached out to touch my forehead, feeling for my temperature. "*Fashao la*?"

I brushed her hand away. "I'm fine. Speak English!" I was shouting.

"Speak English to him," Dad said to Mom. "You knew this was going to happen some day. What did you expect?"

Mom dropped her hands to her side. She sat, looking from Dad to me, and back to Dad again. She tried to speak, stopped, and tried again, and stopped again.

"You have to," Dad said. "I've been too easy on you. Jack needs to fit in."

Mom looked at him. "If I say 'love,' I feel here." She pointed to her lips. "If I say '*ai*,' I feel here." She put her hand over her heart.

Dad shook his head. "You are in America."

Mom hunched down in her seat, looking like the water buffalo when Laohu used to pounce on him and squeeze the air of life out of him.

"And I want some real toys."

* * *

Dad bought me a full set of Star Wars action figures. I gave the Obi-Wan Kenobi to Mark.

I packed the paper menagerie in a large shoebox and put it under the bed.

The next morning, the animals had escaped and took over their old favorite spots in my room. I caught them all and put them back into the shoebox, taping the lid shut. But the animals made so much noise in the box that I finally shoved it into the corner of the attic as far away from my room as possible.

If Mom spoke to me in Chinese, I refused to answer her. After a while, she tried to use more English. But her accent and broken sentences embarrassed me. I tried to correct her. Eventually, she stopped speaking altogether if I were around.

Mom began to mime things if she needed to let me know something. She tried to hug me the way she saw American mothers did on TV. I thought her movements exaggerated, uncertain, ridiculous, graceless. She saw that I was annoyed, and stopped.

"You shouldn't treat your mother that way," Dad said. But he couldn't look me in the eyes as he said it. Deep in his heart, he must have realized that it was a mistake to have tried to take a Chinese peasant girl and expect her to fit in the suburbs of Connecticut.

Mom learned to cook American style. I played video games and studied French.

Every once in a while, I would see her at the kitchen table studying the plain side of a sheet of wrapping paper. Later a new paper animal would appear on my nightstand and try to cuddle up to me. I caught them, squeezed them until the air went out of them, and then stuffed them away in the box in the attic.

Mom finally stopped making the animals when I was in high school. By then her English was much better, but I was already at that age when I wasn't interested in what she had to say whatever language she used.

Sometimes, when I came home and saw her tiny body busily moving about in the kitchen, singing a song in Chinese to herself, it was hard for me to believe that she gave birth to me. We had nothing in common. She might as well be from the moon. I would hurry on to my room, where I could continue my all-American pursuit of happiness.

* * *

Dad and I stood, one on each side of Mom, lying on the hospital bed. She was not yet even forty, but she looked much older.

For years she had refused to go to the doctor for the pain inside her that she said was no big deal. By the time an ambulance finally carried her in, the cancer had spread far beyond the limits of surgery.

My mind was not in the room. It was the middle of the on-campus recruiting season, and I was focused on resumes, transcripts, and strategically constructed interview schedules. I schemed about how to lie to the corporate recruiters most effectively so that they'll offer to buy me. I understood intellectually that it was terrible to think about this while your mother lay dying. But that understanding didn't mean I could change how I felt.

She was conscious. Dad held her left hand with both of his own. He leaned down to kiss her forehead. He seemed weak and old in a way that startled me. I realized that I knew almost as little about Dad as I did about Mom.

Mom smiled at him. "I'm fine."

She turned to me, still smiling. "I know you have to go back to school." Her voice was very weak and it was difficult to hear her over the hum of the machines hooked up to her. "Go. Don't worry about me. This is not a big deal. Just do well in school."

I reached out to touch her hand, because I thought that was what I was supposed to do. I was relieved. I was already thinking about the flight back, and the bright California sunshine.

She whispered something to Dad. He nodded and left the room.

"Jack, if—" she was caught up in a fit of coughing, and could not speak for some time. "If I don't make it, don't be too sad and hurt your health. Focus on your life. Just keep that box you have in the attic with you, and every year, at *Qingming*, just take it out and think about me. I'll be with you always."

Qingming was the Chinese Festival for the Dead. When I was very young, Mom used to write a letter on *Qingming* to her dead parents back in China, telling them the good news about the past year of her life in America. She would read the letter out loud to me, and if I made a comment about something, she would write it down in the letter too. Then she would fold the letter into a paper crane, and release it, facing west. We would then watch, as the crane flapped its crisp wings on its long journey west, towards the Pacific, towards China, towards the graves of Mom's family.

It had been many years since I last did that with her.

"I don't know anything about the Chinese calendar," I said. "Just rest, Mom. "

"Just keep the box with you and open it once in a while. Just open—" she began to cough again.

"It's okay, Mom." I stroked her arm awkwardly.

"*Haizi, mama ai ni*—" Her cough took over again. An image from years ago flashed into my memory: Mom saying *ai* and then putting her hand over her heart.

"Alright, Mom. Stop talking."

Dad came back, and I said that I needed to get to the airport early because I didn't want to miss my flight.

She died when my plane was somewhere over Nevada.

* * *

Dad aged rapidly after Mom died. The house was too big for him and had to be sold. My girlfriend Susan and I went to help him pack and clean the place.

Susan found the shoebox in the attic. The paper menagerie, hidden in the uninsulated darkness of the attic for so long, had become brittle and the bright wrapping paper patterns had faded.

"I've never seen origami like this," Susan said. "Your Mom was an amazing artist."

The paper animals did not move. Perhaps whatever magic had animated them stopped when Mom died. Or perhaps I had only imagined that these paper constructions were once alive.. The memory of children could not be trusted.

* * *

It was the first weekend in April, two years after Mom's death. Susan was out of town on one of her endless trips as a management consultant and I was home, lazily flipping through the TV channels.

I paused at a documentary about sharks. Suddenly I saw, in my mind, Mom's hands, as they folded and refolded tin foil to make a shark for me, while Laohu and I watched.

A rustle. I looked up and saw that a ball of wrapping paper and torn tape was on the floor next to the bookshelf. I walked over to pick it up for the trash.

The ball of paper shifted, unfurled itself, and I saw that it was Laohu, who I hadn't thought about in a very long time. "*Rawrr-sa*." Mom must have put him back together after I had given up.

He was smaller than I remembered. Or maybe it was just that back then my fists were smaller.

Susan had put the paper animals around our apartment as decoration. She probably left Laohu in a pretty hidden corner because he looked so shabby.

I sat down on the floor, and reached out a finger. Laohu's tail twitched, and he pounced playfully. I laughed, stroking his back. Laohu purred under my hand.

"How've you been, old buddy?"

Laohu stopped playing. He got up, jumped with feline grace into my lap, and proceeded to unfold himself.

In my lap was a square of creased wrapping paper, the plain side up. It was filled with dense Chinese characters. I had never learned to read Chinese, but I knew the characters for son, and they were at the top, where you'd expect them in a letter addressed to you, written in Mom's awkward, childish handwriting.

I went to the computer to check the Internet. Today was *Qingming*.

* * *

I took the letter with me downtown, where I knew the Chinese tour buses stopped. I stopped every tourist, asking, *"Nin hui du zhongwen ma?" Can you read Chinese?* I hadn't spoken Chinese in so long that I wasn't sure if they understood.

A young woman agreed to help. We sat down on a bench together, and she read the letter to me aloud. The language that I had tried to forget for years came back, and I felt the words sinking into me, through my skin, through my bones, until they squeezed tight around my heart.

* * *

Son,

We haven't talked in a long time. You are so angry when I try to touch you that I'm afraid. And I think maybe this pain I feel all the time now is something serious.

So I decided to write to you. I'm going to write in the paper animals I made for you that you used to like so much.

The animals will stop moving when I stop breathing. But if I write to you with all my heart, I'll leave a little of myself behind on this paper, in these words. Then, if you think of me on Qingming, *when the spirits of the departed are allowed to visit their families, you'll make the parts of myself I leave behind come alive too. The creatures I made for you will again leap and run and pounce, and maybe you'll get to see these words then.*

Because I have to write with all my heart, I need to write to you in Chinese.

All this time I still haven't told you the story of my life. When you were little, I always thought I'd tell you the story when you were older, so you could understand. But somehow that chance never came up.

I was born in 1957, in Sigulu Village, Hebei Province. Your grandparents were both from very poor peasant families with few relatives. Only a few years after I was born, the Great Famines struck China, during which thirty million people died. The first memory I have was waking up to see my mother eating dirt so that she could fill her belly and leave the last bit of flour for me.

Things got better after that. Sigulu is famous for its zhezhi *papercraft, and my mother taught me how to make paper animals and give them life. This was practical magic in the life of the village. We made paper birds to chase grasshoppers away from the fields, and paper tigers to keep away the mice. For Chinese New Year my friends and I made red paper dragons. I'll never forget the sight of all those little dragons zooming across the sky overhead, holding up strings of exploding firecrackers to scare away all the bad memories of the past year. You would have loved it.*

Then came the Cultural Revolution in 1966. Neighbor turned on neighbor, and brother against brother. Someone remembered that my mother's brother, my uncle, had left for Hong Kong back in 1946, and became a merchant there. Having a relative in Hong Kong meant we were spies and enemies of the people, and we had to be struggled against in every way. Your poor grandmother—she couldn't take the abuse and threw herself down a well. Then some boys with hunting muskets dragged your grandfather away one day into the woods, and he never came back.

There I was, a ten-year-old orphan. The only relative I had in the world was my uncle in Hong Kong. I snuck away one night and climbed onto a freight train going south.

Down in Guangdong Province a few days later, some men caught me stealing food from a field. When they heard that I was trying to get to Hong Kong, they laughed. "It's your lucky day. Our trade is to bring girls to Hong Kong."

They hid me in the bottom of a truck along with other girls, and smuggled us across the border.

We were taken to a basement and told to stand up and look healthy and intelligent for the buyers. Families paid the warehouse a fee and came by to look us over and select one of us to "adopt."

The Chin family picked me to take care of their two boys. I got up every morning at four to prepare breakfast. I fed and bathed the boys. I shopped for food. I did the laundry and swept the floors. I followed the boys around and did their bidding. At night I was locked into a cupboard in the kitchen to sleep. If I was slow or did anything wrong I was beaten. If the boys did anything wrong I was beaten. If I was caught trying to learn English I was beaten.

"Why do you want to learn English?" Mr. Chin asked. "You want to go to the police? We'll tell the police that you are a mainlander illegally in Hong Kong. They'd love to have you in their prison."

Six years I lived like this. One day, an old woman who sold fish to me in the morning market pulled me aside.

"I know girls like you. How old are you now, sixteen? One day, the man who owns you will get drunk, and he'll look at you and pull you to him and you can't stop him. The wife will find out, and then you will think you really have gone to hell. You have to get out of this life. I know someone who can help."

She told me about American men who wanted Asian wives. If I can cook, clean, and take care of my American husband, he'll give me a good life. It was the only hope I had. And that was how I got into the catalog with all those lies and met your father. It is not a very romantic story, but it is my story.

In the suburbs of Connecticut, I was lonely. Your father was kind and gentle with me, and I was very grateful to him. But no one understood me, and I understood nothing.

But then you were born! I was so happy when I looked into your face and saw shades of my mother, my father, and myself. I had lost my entire family, all of Sigulu, everything I ever knew and loved. But there you were, and your face was proof that they were real. I hadn't made them up.

Now I had someone to talk to. I would teach you my language, and we could together remake a small piece of everything that I loved and lost. When you said your first words to me, in Chinese that had the same accent as my mother and me, I cried for hours. When I made the first zhezhi animals for you, and you laughed, I felt there were no worries in the world.

You grew up a little, and now you could even help your father and I talk to each other. I was really at home now. I finally found a good life. I wished my parents could be here, so that I could cook for them, and give them a good life too. But my parents were no longer around. You know what the Chinese think is the saddest feeling in the world? It's for a child to finally grow the desire to take care of his parents, only to realize that they were long gone.

Son, I know that you do not like your Chinese eyes, which are my eyes. I know that you do not like your Chinese hair, which is my hair. But can you understand how much joy your very existence brought to me? And can you understand how it felt when you stopped talking to me and won't let me talk to you in Chinese? I felt I was losing everything all over again.

Why won't you talk to me, son? The pain makes it hard to write.

* * *

The young woman handed the paper back to me. I could not bear to look into her face.

Without looking up, I asked for her help in tracing out the character for *ai* on the paper below Mom's letter. I wrote the character again and again on the paper, intertwining my pen strokes with her words.

The young woman reached out and put a hand on my shoulder. Then she got up and left, leaving me alone with my mother.

Following the creases, I refolded the paper back into Laohu. I cradled him in the crook of my arm, and as he purred, we began the walk home.

A Rosella's Home

Samara Lo

THE SHARP TANG OF EUCALYPTUS lingered in the summer air as the sun's scorching heat burned against Sylvia's back. She watched as chirpy crimson and blue rosellas flitted about a nearby callistemon, their liveliness reminding her of home.

Sighing, she checked the panel embedded in her wrist. Her power bar shifted from red to green as her solar cells greedily absorbed the sunlight. She'd been sent out to the yard by Master Brown a few hours ago and wasn't sure if he wanted her back inside the house. She could have recharged beside a sunny window as usual, but Master Brown had been in a bit of a huff and she still didn't understand what she'd done to upset him.

The words "useless foreign trash" had been uttered several times. She'd tried to decipher the phrase but remained uncertain whether it was meant for her. For one, trash was defined as something that was worthless or of low quality. She was neither of these. Her manufacturing guaranteed it. Even the back of the box she'd come in and her user manual confirmed she was made of the highest quality materials so there was no way she fit the definition of trash.

Foreign was defined as something different or from another place. These two terms were true since she carried physical characteristics that were different to Master Brown's and she had also arrived from another place, yet she could not understand why this would be considered negative.

Her physical differences meant she was stronger. Instead of flesh and bones, which seemed utterly fragile to her, she was made of the strongest alloys and synthetic polymers that looked and felt like flesh but were more durable and pliable than rubber. It didn't mean she couldn't pass for a human. She was designed to be as lifelike as possible. She could even learn new skills through exposure and practice, register emotions and utilise body language.

Perhaps the problem was because she had not been programmed for the differences between the factory where she came from and Master Brown's home. This meant she needed time to adjust, but she could argue that Master Brown and his home were the foreign ones if he were to consider her perspective. However, her perspective was not one he cared about. She had learnt that quickly. Her job was to mop floors, mow lawns and complete any other household chores. Most importantly, she was to remain unseen while doing it.

Sometimes while she worked, she remembered the place she'd come from. A large factory with glistening floors, thousands of conveyor belts delivering hope and life in boxes. Friends and those like her chatting and laughing, filling the air with a warm buzz just like the crimson rosellas she'd been watching.

Back home, she was lauded. Fitted with the latest technology and medical knowledge, she was a medbot that could've legally practised as a doctor. Her predecessors were sent to warfronts and hospitals to save lives. By her manufacturing date, wars had ended and such skills were no longer required en masse. Yet she never forgot the history of her lineage. That she was built upon foundations that were neither useless nor trash.

A creak came from the house. Sylvia recognised Master Brown's steps before the fly screen door opened far behind her. Even if he hadn't made a sound, she would've known his location.

Her settings included the constant monitoring of it as well as Master Brown's biometrics, which his children had set up when they'd purchased her.

"Hello, Master Brown." Sylvia smiled. "Thank you for the sun. My solar cells find it pleased."

"Pleasant or pleasing. Not pleased," Master Brown grumbled. "If you can't get it right then don't say anything. It's embarrassing."

Sylvia inclined her head. "Master Brown, perhaps if my speech offends you I can speak in another language. I am pre-programmed with twenty-five primary languages spoken back home—"

"We speak English here and it's not just your speech that offends me." He wrinkled his nose. "You've been standing out here wasting time. Those lawns aren't gonna mow themselves." He pointed to the table and chairs set beside gardenia hedges. "Bring my dinner out here when you're done."

"Of course." Sylvia waited for him to leave before she sighed. His directness had been jarring at first. Rude even. He'd speak his mind without consideration of anyone else's feelings. It had taken her some time to realise it was the way people in this country interacted. They did not wrap their demands in layers of politeness. They were straight to the point. Invasive even. Hurtful. It was not intentional malice. Simply culture.

Sylvia had even learnt there was such a thing called "taking the piss" which had nothing to do with urination. It was a common sequence of exchanges where one human mocked another at the other's expense but then they would both laugh afterwards.

There were times Sylvia thought Master Brown was taking the piss like when he said, "I want receipts with that change. Won't have no thieving hands dipping in my pockets," or "Don't even think of stealing my organs for your buddies back home. I know what's under all that fake skin," and "You know it takes more than five hundred years for all that metal in you to break down? Let's not even start with that synthetic stuff you're wrapped in. You're destructive to the environment. A planet killer."

Sylvia had tried to take the piss in return once and told Master Brown his balding head looked like the watermelon she was slicing. He did not laugh. In fact he'd paled, his heart rate had spiked to concerning levels, and he'd screamed, "Get out!" It seemed she lacked the nuance required to take the piss out of someone.

Sylvia headed into the rear shed and dragged out the lawnmower. Even after decades of innovation where people had invented things like self-driving cars and Artificial Intelligence robots, the humans in this country still persisted in sticking to their ancient ways. Perhaps it was the after-effects of the last war that led many here to lose their trust in more advanced technology and to seek out the old life.

The trusty lawnmower was one such piece of nostalgia. Sylvia would've much preferred a lawn bot, but instead was stuck priming the carburettor, opening the throttle, pulling the starter rope just to get the motor running and then pushing the wheeled-grass-chewing-non-thinking-air-polluting-machine back and forth. She snorted. And Master Brown called her destructive to the environment.

She was halfway done when a furious Master Brown approached, waving his fist. She killed the lawnmower.

"Oi! Didn't ya hear me?" Master Brown's face had turned redder than the bottlebrushes behind him.

"Forgive me, Master Brown, the lawnmower was..."

"I don't need your excuses. I thought I told you to set my dinner out here. Why haven't you done it?"

Sylvia glanced at the rounded garden table with its leaf-patterned design and scuffed-up legs.

"Master Brown, I believe you asked me to do it after mowing the lawn."

"Why would I tell you that? I don't want grass clippings flying in my tea. Now go and sort it."

Sylvia didn't bother defending herself. Her memory meant she did not forget details, but to mention that would only infuriate Master Brown. He did not like to be told he was wrong by her kind. Plus, she did not wish to give medbots a bad reputation.

Turning, she brushed trimmed blades of grass from the lawnmower and wheeled it back towards the shed. The route brought her past Master Brown, who muttered as he dropped into the creaky white garden chair and waved away a bee.

"Good for nothing. Can't even follow simple instructions. State of the art my arse. Why my kids ever thought I'd need foreign trash like this. Probably doesn't even know a thing about medicine."

Sylvia shoved the lawnmower into the shed. It was one thing to be insulted about her English or to be spoken down to. That she could brush off. But to question her medical expertise.

She curled her fingers. With these she could cut off his air supply. All it took was thirty-three pounds of pressure for occlusion and two more pounds on top to fracture tracheal cartilage. A simple twist of her wrist and she could snap his neck instead. Humans were so fragile.

A warning beeped on her monitors. She paused, reading a sudden shift in Master Brown's biometrics. Her anger dissipated.

"Master Brown?" She hurried out and found him wheezing, his face a darker shade than earlier.

"Get away … murder … bot … can't steal … my … organs." He clutched his throat, his words slurring as his tongue swelled.

Sylvia registered waves of guilt on her internal monitors. She caught him as he stumbled, ashamed of what she knew she was capable of doing with the same hands only moments ago.

"Master Brown. I am a medbot. I save lives." Data scrolled through her monitors. Bee sting. Anaphylaxis. "Allow me to administer epinephrine."

Yet he was no longer conscious. She laid him down, careful not to hit his head. Humans truly were so fragile. A compartment opened in her arm. She chose the adrenaline shot from the assortment of auto injectors and stabbed it into Master Brown's thigh. At the same time, she tapped into the house's communications network and sent a distress call to emergency services.

"Master Brown, it's okay … I'm here…"

* * *

Sylvia stared at the rosellas as they alighted on a nearby branch. Dappled sunlight fed her batteries as she drew the mosquito netting closed around the newly erected gazebo.

She turned quickly at the creak of a chair behind her. "Let me get that for you, Master Brown."

She picked up the cup of tea and passed it to him. He didn't meet her gaze as he silently took it. Things had been like this ever since he'd been discharged from hospital. She wasn't sure why he couldn't look at her and his silence made her a little uncomfortable since she didn't know what he was thinking. At least he wasn't glaring at her like he used to.

He cleared his throat. "Thank you."

Sylvia stilled. She thought she had misheard him for a moment, but her high-tech hearing meant it was impossible. Maybe she had a glitch.

Master Brown reddened. "I'm told I would've died if it wasn't for you."

"I was just doing my job, Master Brown."

He nodded and sipped his tea.

"You should sit … have some tea."

Sylvia glanced at the teapot and the spare unused cup he'd asked her to bring out. She'd thought he was expecting a guest, but no one had come calling.

"You wish for me to … drink tea with you?"

Master Brown shrugged.

Sylvia stared at him for a long moment, then tilted her head and smiled.

"I believe you are taking the piss, Master Brown. You know I do not require refreshments."

He flushed and fumbled his cup, spilling some onto the saucer. "I wasn't taking the – never mind … sit and … uh … have a chat."

She stepped around the table and wiped down the spill. "You wish to chat with me?"

He looked away and she could read the growing distress on his vitals. She decided it best not to upset him any further and took the seat across from him.

To her surprise, he poured her a cup of tea. She picked up the cup and imitated the process of drinking it for Master Brown's benefit. It seemed to have the comforting effect she expected. Humans were fragile *and* peculiar.

"I … uh … hear medbots are used in all the hospitals back where you're from. Can you … maybe … tell me more about it?"

"You wish to know of the place I came from?"

He nodded.

"You must excuse my English. It is not very good, but I am still learning."

He shifted in his seat and tugged at his collar. "It's not bad … and you speak several languages, don't you?"

"Twenty-five, but I can learn more."

"You're doing all right, then." He shrugged. "I only know the one."

"I can teach you if you wish to learn more."

"And have you laugh at all my mistakes?"

"I would not laugh. Such errors are a sign we are attempting something new and have yet to reach mastery."

Slowly, he met her gaze. "You're a good person … bot … thing … you've been a lot better to me than I've deserv—" His shoulders heaved and he reddened. For a moment Sylvia was worried he'd been stung again but his biometrics remained normal. "Go on then, don't just sit there listening to me ramble. Tell me about medbots and home."

Sylvia sipped her tea, tucking away the words he'd said and left unsaid into her memory to consider later. Instead, she thought of home and all the things she missed. She smiled.

"Home is bright and lively like the rosellas that visit this garden…"

I Need to Keep It Moving

Kwame M.A. McPherson

I GLANCE BEHIND ME. The long, dark throng plods like I do. My mouth is dry and a flicker of fear flits around my gut. This meandering movement of people travels in one direction away from the orange-red flashes against greyish-black clouds and loud *booms* in the far distance. I rack my long gun across my chest and use my binoculars to look forward and behind. The landscape is barren. Vehicle wreckage litters the highway and people weave through as if they're on a challenging obstacle course. I register a smell. It's a mixture of smoke and something else. It's a stench I recognize from being in battle and it's one that you can never forget. The town dwellers continue to march slowly by. I see some of them vomit. They're exhausted and I'm genuinely sorry for them but I know the further away we are from the city, the better they'll be, the stink dissipating with the distance.

An early double moon is yet to make its appearance in the clammy dusk but it's there, slowly emerging like it usually does in the middle of every month. I glance at the countryside and wish I'd had more time to explore the deep blue-black rolling hills sprinkled with blotches of white across the landscape. They're no lights. Houses, once homes, probably abandoned.

Sighing, I want to be elsewhere, to be with Asante and the children. But right now, it's my responsibility to make sure the refugees are protected to the next directorate, some ten miles away, and we've yet to encounter the sea channel that stretches between Alkebulan and the Land of Caucus. I shake my head, dispelling any distracting thoughts. I don't want to think about what went before or what's to come, choosing to focus on the now. I can't even afford to give my *own* family a bit of thought. But who am I fooling?

Through my binoculars I pick out broken buildings, smoke and flames. There's no human movement. We tried to save the city and as many people as we could but the Slavvies had outnumbered us ten to one. Many residents died, my home town razed to the ground. I imagine my own apartment building, my comfortable home on the tenth floor now a massive gutted space. I wonder about Mrs Smith, Mr Johnson, Miss Gerty and Pam, my neighbours, and if they made it out when the bullhorn warnings and sirens wailed five days ago, by which time I was already on the battlefield. I think about all of my neighbours, all of the time. And my family, always there in my thoughts.

"Sir," says my Sarge, Oluwusi. "Heard from HQ. We're to continue as quickly as we can. Push ahead."

I turn to stare up front, looking at the start of the column, and check my watch. "How soon will we get to the next safe zone?"

"Two hours," he replies. I nod. My eyes flutter. I sway.

"You okay, sir?" He grabs one arm to steady me.

I'm weary with worry but can't afford to stop. I grin weakly. "I'm fine, Sarge, just tired. Keep me informed if anything changes."

"Sir." He salutes and makes his way to check the line, cajole and encourage our travellers to move as quickly as they can. It's difficult when there are old men, women and children involved, not trained for long marches or going for miles without food or water. A major concern.

My thirty men will be fine. They've been trained for this. But the five hundred people we're taking care of now are another issue. Many of them will not make it. I grit my teeth. This is one of those times I hate politicians and the games they play, taking people for pawns, using them like game pieces on a board, intent only on their greed and egotistic selves.

The war began on the back of an invasion. The Slavvies kept warning the Atos not to create alliances or have treaties with their closest neighbours. They were all getting on fine until the continued expansion of the Atos Alliance and, as it is with politicians, especially ego-driven ones, there was no room to negotiate. And so began the onslaught of yet another World War. The 25th-century version.

Slowly, I move toward the rear, watching the lines of bowed heads of defeated people. I glance at a woman holding a baby in her arms, wrapped in a dirty blanket. She stares pleadingly at me. I look away. I'm unable to open myself to her truth. I've my own truth to deal with plus other things to worry about, five hundred and thirty to be exact.

Suddenly, an old man steps into my path. He grabs onto me, wizened hands clutch my webbing. Grey, beaten eyes bore into mine and when he speaks, I notice the gaps in his teeth. "I'll never make it," he pants, "you must help me. Help my family."

His hold is tight. It's easy for me to wrench his hands from my uniform. After all, I'm six four, two hundred and fifty pounds and he's less than half of all that, but I relent, allowing him the space to vent, give him someone to rail upon.

Screaming, he shakes me. "Help me! Help my family!"

Gently, I release his grip and calmly say, "Sir, I don't even know where my own family is…"

He stands, trembling, uncertain of what to say, but I need to keep it moving, physically, mentally and emotionally. I walk away. I can't afford to have my own self sucked into another person's trauma. Not now. Not yet.

I stop, regret my selfishness, and call back. "Sir, listen. I'll get someone to help you, okay?"

He slinks back into line and I observe him hug a young woman while small children hold onto his coat. I touch a forefinger to the corner of one eye behind my protective goggles. I admonish myself. This is not the time.

My comms crackles in my Kevlar helmet and I hear shouts, gunfire and explosions. There's panic. It's hard to make out who is saying what and I strain my ears to understand. What I do know is the squad that stayed behind is the defensive line. My friends. The ones that made the sacrifice to let us get away.

I speak into my comms, "Come in, Sarge!"

"Sir?"

"I'll be at the rear, waiting for any stragglers. Also, there's an old man about five minutes from where I am, coming your way. He has a younger woman and children with him. Maybe his daughter. See what you can do."

"Roger." He pauses before asking, "You need any men with you, sir?"

"No, I'll be fine, just keep the column moving. I'll catch up."

"Roger, sir. Out."

I stroll further and come to an intersection and wait by a traffic-light post. More wrecks, burnt-out vehicles and, above my head, working traffic lights. My lights are on green. Soon, the stragglers tapers into ones and twos and I encourage them to speed up to reach the main crowd. Eventually, the road is empty of any human being and the only signs of life – if you can call it that – are the flashes of explosions and a sound like thunder, rolling toward me.

I pull off one of my gloves and fish out my wallet, extracting a colour photo. The image is so real, so vibrant, it's as if she's here with me. Asante is as beautiful in it as she is in real life. Her natural dreads, chocolate complexion and dancing brown eyes are the first things that catch my eye, now and back when we first met all those years ago. Then, over numerous dates, I learned about her heart and her brain, and knew that there was no other woman for me. Chisulo and Dayo are just as fine-looking, their smiling faces are a true resemblance to their mother's. Some people said they had nothing of me in them but I swear I can see me in their eyes and jawlines. Dropping to my haunches, tears slowly come. I remove my goggles and roughly wipe the back of my sleeve across my eyes.

"Why didn't you leave when I told you to, Asante?" I say aloud to nobody in particular. There's not even a night bird in the dark sky. "Why didn't you go with the others? Why didn't you call me? Why…? Where…? Where are you?"

There are too many unanswered questions, that may never get an answer, and I break down again, the sobs racking my body, shaking me like an East Indian mango tree caught in a storm. I swear. At myself, the politicians, the war, the world, humans… everything I can think of feels my meaningless, ineffective wrath. Angrily, I pick up a rock and furiously throw it at the nearest car wreck. A dog yelps and leaps out. There's something in its mouth. A burnt hand.

I snap my automatic weapon to my shoulder, taking aim at the animal, my forefinger on the trigger, but I don't fire. I can't. Like me, he just wants to stay alive. I wonder where the dog's family is. Then, a sudden sound reaches my ears. It's not the blast of explosions but a *whap-whap* noise. I know it. A helicopter. Standing, I scour the horizon and see the small dark shape grow larger. Placing my binoculars to my eyes, I scan the vessel. It isn't one of ours.

Suddenly, my comms squawks: "Shaka! Shaka!" *Asante?*

Her voice! I shout: "Asante!? Asante!? That you?"

"Shaka! It is!"

"Where are you? Where are you, baby?"

"I'm at 72nd Street Sub—"

I don't hear the rest. A white smoke trail swooshes overhead. I don't see it but I hear something explode further up the road. Immediately I know. *Stragglers!*

Racing from my position and hiding behind a car ruin, I take aim as the helicopter increases in size. Attached to my weapon is the latest in long-range grenade launchers and my rifle's AI quickly assesses the distance and reports in my ear.

"Target acquired. Two miles."

"Confirm. Fire when ready."

"Confirmed. Firing."

My rifle jolts. The projectile speeds with supersonic swiftness and slams into the helicopter. There's a blazing fireball and it's no more, crashing to the ground. My comms comes alive with chatter.

I shout: "Asante, you there? Asante!"

Oluwusi cuts in. "Sir? We saw the attack at the rear, you okay?"

"I'm fine, Sarge. Any casualties?"

"Three civilians dead, sir, fifteen injured. It's a good thing you shot it down when you did or there'd be more dead and wounded. Including our guys."

"How far are you from the safe zone?"

"Another seventy-five minutes. Less than two klicks if we hurry. We'll get there, sir."

"Good. Oluwusi, there's something I need to do."

He says nothing. I guess he must have suspected the minute I said I was going to the back.

Sergeant Oluwusi knows me better than I know myself but never questions my decisions or actions, preferring to just give wise advice. You don't spend thirty years as a non-commissioned officer without gaining some wisdom or the trust of your superiors, like me.

"Be careful sir. We'll be at the safe zone and will wait for you until four hundred hours."

"Understood."

"Do you need any men sir?" He asks. I smile. Yep, he knows me better than I know myself.

"Send two volunteers. And only volunteers. I'll need a sensors and a sniper guy."

"Roger sir," Oluwusi says. "And sir?"

"Sarge?"

"Find them and bring them back."

"Will do." We end our comms.

* * *

Everywhere is smouldering. Thick black smoke rises and swirls about us and fire licks away at broken, battered buildings. And there's that nauseating stench again. We pass bodies – lots of bodies. Many are civilians. Innocents. Some are soldiers, a few of whom I recognise. At each one I pause, yanking the identification tags from their necks and placing them into a cargo pocket. At least their families will know. I move quickly on, my mind solely focused on finding Asante and my children.

Stooping, I'm close to a burnt-out building, Stone and Willock behind me. Stone is a Squad Automatic Weapon and sensors expert and Willock is a specialist sniper. Both single, no relatives. Over the comms, I tell them about the mission and that they are under no obligation to come, but they insist. So here they are, covering my six.

"Sir. Incoming," Stone whispers. "Something's picked up on my sensors. A drone."

There are specialists embedded in every unit and Stone is the 25th-century version of a 20th-century radioman. The only difference is the abundance of equipment that's built into his helmet, from radars to satellite-enabled encryption Wifi and more.

We stop, hastily squeezing ourselves into a large hole in the side of a damaged building. Peeping into the street, we see a drone. It buzzes one way then another before disappearing. The eyes of the enemy. Searching. A flying AI designed and programmed to engage its enemies with whatever weapons it has in its arsenal. The result is not nice. Their work is all around us.

Sprinting to a burnt bus, I stop to survey the area. We're three blocks away from where Asante and I last spoke before we lost contact and the nearest bunker, so that's where we head.

"Willock, can you find an overwatch position somewhere, in sight of the 72nd Street Subway Station and our route?"

"Sir. On it." He taps his helmet to bring up a local map on the visual display on his goggles and searches for points of elevation. "Found it, under a klick from here."

"Great, keep your comms open. And watch your six. Check in every five minutes."

"Sir," he says. Grabbing his rifle he moves, bent double, until he disappears around a corner.

"Let's go Stone."

We move in the opposite direction and toward the bunker.

* * *

This part of the city looks deserted except for the scavenging dogs and cats feeding on the dead, flickering flames catching their dancing shadows. We advance, dodging from cover to cover, pausing only to survey the land through Stone's sensors. We progress in silence until we are a block away from 72 Street Subway and it's not even Stone who detects the movement.

A loud zap of a rifle being fired catches us off guard. Stone and I dive for the nearest cover. Just as suddenly a body slams into the ground, a few metres away. Whoever he is, he no longer looks like a person.

"Who...?"

"Sir! Willock here. Bogies, your 9 o'clock. They're up top."

I glance at Stone. He shrugs. "Not picking up anything sir."

"They cloaked?" I ask. In a unit briefing, prior to the start of hostilities, we were informed that the Slavvies had designed new technologies, one of which was the ability to cloak individual soldiers. The intelligence was sketchy at best and we were sceptical. Not anymore.

Stone nods, readying his SAW. "Could be sir. Willock must be using an old 20th-century scope. Smart kid."

I nod in agreement. I'm glad I requested two volunteers, one with old technology and the other with new. We adjust our helmet sensors to face the new threat.

"Stone, cover me."

He nods and I run, using any available cover. I reach another wrecked vehicle. "Move Stone, I'll cover you!"

I search the damaged buildings above our heads when there's another zap. *Willock*. Someone screams. Good shot lad.

Suddenly, all hell breaks loose, just as Stone breaks cover and races to me. I see the flashes and watch projectiles zip through the air and smash into the ground. I patiently pick my targets, covering Stone's scamper. There are more screams and now cursing. I grin. My blood pumps. The adrenaline kicks in. I feel a projectile's slipstream breeze pass my jaw and I duck behind the vehicle just as a gasping Stone reaches me. He sets up himself and opens up with the SAW while I search for the bunker. It's less than a hundred metres away and to our right. But there's a problem. Between us and the subway entrance, there's no debris of any kind. I swear. It's No Man's Land.

We're pinned down with projectiles slamming into our position. With the mashed vehicle taking the brunt of the attack, I turn to Stone. "We can't stay here. The drones will be back..."

Stone looks at the subway entrance, feeds more projectiles into his SAW and keeps firing.

"No Man's Land sir."

"I know. I want you and Willock to lay down suppressing fire, give me a chance to get there."

"Yes sir."

"When I get there, I'll lay down fire for you."

"Okay sir."

I comms Willock. "Willock, lay down suppressing fire. On the count of three."

"Yes sir."

Still firing, Stone suddenly and calmly says, "Drones heading this way sir. I count twenty."

I swear. *We need to go. Now.*

"We both won't make it sir," Stone says, reading my mind.

"I'm not going without you soldier."

"With respect sir. If you stay here, then neither of us will make it."

I know he's right and take one last glance at him. I nod, he returns the salutation and goes back to laying down the suppressing fire. I rap his helmet in farewell, take a deep breath and make the mad dash toward the subway opening. A projectile pings off my helmet.

Panting at the entrance, I glance over my shoulder and see Stone firing at the drones. The fire from up top hasn't stopped either. The drones are ducking, dodging and diving hundreds of yards away, firing at him. Stone drops into cover and then re-emerges, still firing. He hits a few and they explode in mid-air. In turn, I support him by aiming and firing. I get a couple. Abruptly, his position disappears in an explosion. Debris flies everywhere. When the dust and smoke clear there's no sign of Stone.

Ducking into the dark subway, I hurry down the stairs. "Willock?"

"Sir?"

"You okay?"

"Affirmative."

"We lost Stone, keep your head down. But report in as before."

"Sir."

Switching on my helmet cam and light, I move into the gloom. I need to keep it moving.

I descend for minutes, going deeper and deeper into the station. The darkness engulfs me as I creep forward and there's a prickly feeling of being watched. It seems the murkiness is no hindrance to my watchers. And sure enough, within minutes, brilliant white light eliminates the blackness. I'm blinded.

"Halt! Drop your weapon! Identify yourself!"

Slowly, I place my weapon on the ground, hold my hands high and give my identification decals.

A voice: "Major Jelani? That you?"

"The one and only," I reply. The lights douse for a second and someone turns on a main switch. The new lights illuminate the entire station. I'm in the main subway lobby, by the ticket barriers. Beyond the barriers, the train platform and tracks. Black holes swallow the track in either direction.

I look around. I'm surrounded by alert soldiers staring at me from behind aimed guns, but I recognize the one walking toward me. Short. Thick. Wide nose and eyes. "Igwe, I am so glad to see you!"

"It's good to see you too sir." Captain Igwe proffers a hand. I take it and he waves off his soldiers. They lower their guns. "We counterattacking?"

I look him in the eye and say nothing. He nods, understanding. "Any civilians here?" I ask.

"The few who were caught behind the lines are in the tunnel, about fifty people."

"You know who they are? Have a list?"

"We do. You looking for someone?"

"Yes," I say, turning away. "My wife and kids."

He calls to a sergeant. "Owusu, get here with that list."

A soldier runs up and hands over a sheaf of papers. Igwe passes them to me. It's in alphabetical order by last name. I don't realize it but I'm hyperventilating, almost fainting while I read the names. Igwe notices, placing a hand on my shoulder. I don't see 'Asante Jelani'. Frantically, I scan through the names again and again.

"Sir?" Igwe calmly asks.

I'm fraught and frustrated. "Yes!"

"What's the name?"

I'm flicking through the pages. Distraught. "Um, Asante... Jelani... Jelani!"

Igwe smiles. It's unnerving. "A strong-willed woman. Knows how to handle herself? Was a teacher? Beautiful, tall with two equally beautiful children?"

I grab Igwe's shoulders. "Yes! Yes! You've seen them?"

"I've nothing but admiration for her," he says. "Against my better judgement, she insisted I give her food and guns. Said she needed to get to some school on 53rd Street."

I stare at Igwe. The incredulity must have shown on my face. "Say what?"

"She said she needed to rescue her 'children'."

I sit on the floor, shaking my head. That sounds like Asante. Ex-soldier now teacher, she would never leave anyone behind.

"*Our* children?" I murmur.

"No. *Your* children are in the tunnel." He helps me to my feet. "Follow me."

I trail him. We leap from the platform and onto the track, and head into the gaping hole on the left. We walk for a few metres and come to another lit area, where people are either milling around or seated on the ground. I spot a few children playing with each other. My heart jumps. *Chisulo and*

Dayo. I remove my helmet and throw a hand to my mouth. My heart trembles in my chest and I force myself not to shout or cry. They seem to have grown. They turn to look at me. They feel something like I did because they run in my direction, ignoring everyone around them and throw themselves into my arms, shouting: "Pappa! Pappa!"

I'm no longer tired. I pick them up and we smother each other with kisses. Finally, I place them down and we sit, still touching. We talk about how we've missed each other, and they ask what's going to happen next, if I'm there to take them to their mother. Their questions come thick and fast and I'm struggling to get a word in when Igwe returns to the tunnel. I see the urgency in his eyes.

"Sir, we've been breached."

I grab my helmet and place it on my head. "Situation?"

"An enemy unit tried to storm the bunker. We're holding but we need to move these people and now."

"Understood." I patch in Willock. "Talk to me Willock." There's silence. He missed two call-ins and I can only think the worst. "Listen Igwe, take my children with you, protect them for me."

They kick and scream and complain that they don't want to lose me too. I grab and hold them close, burying my head into their hair, taking in their smell, listening to their cries.

"Listen... Listen!" I say firmly, raising my voice. They're sobbing, I'm sobbing. "Stop it! Listen Chisulo, Dayo... I need to go... I need to find your mother." They wail. I'm choking up too. "You... you want that, right?"

Through their tears they nod in agreement. Igwe respectfully stands nearby. I can hear small arms gunfire and explosions.

Releasing my children, I pass them to him. "Take care of them Igwe."

"I will."

I watch as he grabs hold of my children under his arms and dashes deeper into the tunnel after the main group. I go the other way, through the tunnel, bypassing the lobby where a group of soldiers are running. The gunfire is loud and continuous, the explosions shake the station's foundations.

I don't stop. I need to find my wife. I need to find Asante. I need to keep it moving....

Memory Store

E.C. Osondu

ONE OF THE THINGS HE FOUND MOST FASCINATING about America were the Memory Stores that could be found on almost every street corner. A person could simply walk into any of the stores and sell their memories for money. It was that straightforward. He had come to the realization that certain things were undoubtedly straightforward in America. Take American beers with their twist-off caps. Twist-off caps may not seem like a big deal to most American beer drinkers but he remembered buying a cold bottle of beer when he was back home and bringing it to his room and ransacking the entire room in search of his bottle opener. He eventually found the opener lying underneath a pile of old newspapers. By then, the beer was already lukewarm and tasted flat on the tongue.

Even in matters that did not appear so straightforward, he still admired America. He loved the fact that in America there were a dozen different kinds of doughnuts. There were even doughnuts without holes. Back home, he had grown up knowing only one kind of doughnut: light brown with a hole in the center. He recalled his first time in an American doughnut shop.

"I want a doughnut," he said to the sales clerk. "Which one of them do you want?" she asked.

He had pointed vaguely in the direction of the glass display case. The sales clerk looked at him and began pointing out and reeling off the names of the different kinds of doughnuts that they had.

"Glazed, Chocolate, Vanilla Frosted, Powdered Sugar, Old Fashioned..."

Looking at her, he had pointed at the light brown doughnut with a hole in the middle.

"Honey, you mean *Old Fashioned*? Why didn't you say so instead of messing with me?"

She sounded relieved and laughed.

The coffee-laden atmosphere had lightened. He too had laughed. He had repeated the words "Old Fashioned" and had vowed to commit it to memory.

A Memory Store, ah, only in America. He planned to visit one and find out how it worked. He had no immediate plans to sell his memories but there was no harm in knowing about their operations. He was sure the operators of the Memory Stores would be as polite and pleasant as he had found most American storekeepers to be. Here in America even when a storekeeper did not have an item that you wished to buy he would direct you to another store where they had the item, sometimes at an even cheaper rate. That would never happen back home. The best a shopkeeper would do for you would be to tell you to wait while he dashed to a neighboring store to get the same item and sell it to you with a markup.

The first time he went into a Memory Store he walked in furtively like a Catechist walking into a brothel. First he looked right, then left and then right again and then he ducked in.

As soon as he entered the shop, all his apprehensions disappeared.

"Hi, buddy, I am R," the guy who manned the shop said. He in turn introduced himself by his first initial. Everyone went by their initials these days. It was one of the laws introduced to unite the country after what had happened during the previous regime.

He could tell that the man was Hispanic. He could tell from the man's accent. You could not get rid of accents by a simple legislation. Did the R. stand for Ramos, Ramirez, Rodriguez? It was inappropriate to ask. Such things did not matter anymore. Everyone was American and that was all that was important.

"It is very easy, my friend," the guy said.

He had looked around the store. He had expected to see lots of gadgets but there were actually just a few.

"First, I will need to wipe down your hands with rubbing alcohol and then you'll place the five fingers of both hands on this glass panel in front of me and then you'll focus your mind and recall the memory you want to sell to us. Your memory will appear on the screen right here and I will tell you how much we are able to pay for it. If we agree on the price then I will give you a card loaded with the amount for which we bought your memory. You can use the card to make purchases anywhere. There are stores down the road from here, they sell good stuff. The process is painless," R. explained.

He told R. that he had only come to look around and find out how the thing worked.

"Look around, my friend. Take your time and feel free to ask me if you have any questions," R. said.

He looked around but there really wasn't much more to see than what R. had showed him. It looked like a pretty basic operation. Just then the bell rang announcing the arrival of a customer. R. showed him out through another door.

He looked forward to his job. He worked with Work Ready. They provided workers for the car auction. They provided both drivers and cleaners. He was one of the cleaners.

His job was to wash the cars and wipe them down and make them look good on the auction block. The thought that a car that he had tidied would be driven by a man who lived in a far-off place such as one of the Gulf States thrilled him and made him shine the cars with gusto.

His boss had stood watching him one day while he used a clean, dry piece of cloth to shine a car he had just washed. He had looked up and seen his boss watching him.

"I have never seen anyone wipe down a car with so much joy," his boss said.

"I always do a good job because you never know where the cars might end up," he said to his boss.

"You never know, huh? Good job, keep it up," his boss had said.

He had thanked his boss.

His boss had made to walk away and then had come back and said to him, "You know there can only be one supervisor here, right? I've been the supervisor for three years and the company has no plans to fire me or promote any person to my position. Still, I like your hustle, man."

The short speech had left him confused but he had only smiled and continued with his cleaning.

Later that winter he had reported at Work Ready one morning and was met by the long faces of his colleagues. Work Ready was letting the cleaners go. They were *consolidating* – that was the language they used. The drivers would be the ones to clean the cars from now onwards. It was a way to save money.

His supervisor had pulled him aside to the hallway near the bathroom and had asked him if he could drive. He had said he couldn't. The supervisor had told him to go to a driving school and to come back when he got his driver's license.

He sat before the Memory Machine and began to dredge his mind. He realized how true something he had heard years ago was: everything in life becomes difficult when you try to force it. He thought that since his mind often wandered into the past recalling stuff would be easy. His mind was going blank at the moment.

"Some people find that when they close their eyes, it helps," R. said to him.

He closed his eyes and hoped he would not nod off and start snoring loudly. Why was he worrying about everything all of a sudden?

His mind became clear. The fog lifted. He was a little boy of seven running home from school. He could still smell the aroma of jollof rice and fried goat meat. At the completion of the academic year, they were served jollof rice and fried goat meat by the school. He didn't wait for the jollof rice or the fried goat meat. He snatched his report card as soon as they announced that he was the first in his class and began to run home to his grandmother.

She was outside bathing in the sun. She was wearing her green sweater, the one with the Christmas decorations. His grandmother didn't know that the design on her sweater was Christmas decorations. He wouldn't know either until he came to America. He would also learn in America that they were called "ugly sweaters." He never did understand why. They were beautifully colorful to him.

He handed the report card to his grandmother.

"Tell me what it says, my son."

"Open it, grandma. Look at it yourself," he said to her. "You open it and read it to me, that is why I sent you to school," she said.

He opened the report card and told her that he came first in his class and that he had scored one hundred percent in all his subjects and that he had not stayed back to eat the jollof rice and goat meat that was cooked for all the students for the end of the academic year.

"Will their jollof rice taste as good as the one I am going to make for you?" his grandmother asked.

"Never," he said.

R. was tapping him on the shoulder. He was almost too far gone. So carried away by the memory that he had forgotten where he was and had been transported entirely into that world of his childhood with his grandmother.

"That is all we'll need for today's session. You did really great. These types are quite rare. They've got everything we are looking for in a memory. Genuine, not artificial, and filled with joy. Now follow me and I'll give you your payment. It is a card. It is loaded and you can use it at designated stores to buy really good stuff," R. said.

He was still feeling a little unfocused from the experience. For some reason he was also feeling lighter, but not in a heavy-load-taken-away kind of way; it was like he had misplaced something – perhaps an object he had in his pocket had been lost.

He collected the payment card. He was surprised at the amount they were paying him.

"Thank you," he said to R.

"No, thank *you*," R. said.

He hesitated to leave. Something was still bothering him. It had all seemed too easy.

"So what is going to happen to the one I just gave you?" he asked R.

"We are going to put it to good use. Like I told you, it is a great one. Very much in high demand. Authentic and genuine. They are gonna love it."

"Ah," he said.

"You know some people come here and try to sell us fake memories or pass off other people's memories as their own, but the machine has a system for detecting those kinds real quick," R. said.

"The one I just gave you, what about it?" he asked.

"Oh, I see what you mean. It is gone. You will never recall that particular memory again. It is like it never existed. Wiped out. Gone. It no longer belongs to you. But don't worry about it. I am sure there are lots where that came from, buddy," R. said. R. sounded jokey but a little furtive in his manner. He could tell that R. wanted him to leave.

He took his card and walked to the store that sold household goods. He had always wanted a huge television. He wanted a giant one that would dominate the environment of his sitting room. The lives of American families did not revolve around the television the way lives did back home.

Back home the television had come to replace the grandmother around whom everybody sat after the evening meal listening as she told her folktales. Over here the television was overlooked just like American grandmothers who talked to themselves for the most part and who went largely ignored when they spoke to other occupants of the house. Life here rather revolved around the fridge. The opening of the fridge and the slamming of the fridge door and the perpetual complaint of "there is nothing to eat; there is never anything to eat here" though the fridge would usually be bursting from the seams with all kinds of food and drink.

He bought the giant television. It was sixty-four inches. They took it home for him. He rode with the delivery guys and watched them install it. He sat in front of the television and began flipping channels. He flipped and flipped again, his right hand and thumb feeling heavy, yet there still remained channels to flip.

He recalled that back home the television came on at 4 p.m. That was when the station opened. The station closed at 11 p.m. There was hardly more than an hour of movies and drama – the rest of the time was devoted to men and women in elaborate costume-like clothes using big words to argue between themselves about how to move the country forward.

He stumbled on a soccer game and stopped.

There was no commentary.

It must have been originally in Spanish but had been edited to remove the Spanish commentary. They had not bothered to do the work of substituting an English language commentary.

He began to watch the game without commentary by following the colors of the jerseys of the players. His eyes soon grew weary and he fell asleep and began to snore. The television was still on and soon was watching him sleep. It was one of the modern types of TV and when it sensed no movement in the sitting room it shut itself down. When he woke up he was sitting in the dark, alone without the television glow, but he was not afraid of the darkness here in America. He found American darkness to be somewhat more gray than dark. Back home he would stretch out his hands while walking in the dark and even his hand disappeared and became one with the inky darkness.

He went to Work Ready to ask if there were job openings. The lady there told him that they were giving priority to people who were mandated to work by a judge so that they could pay their child support.

"We are focused on placing those who have to pay their child support, right now. Others will just have to wait," she said.

He had asked after the supervisor who had asked that he get in touch as soon as he could drive and was told that the supervisor had resigned. So if he had paid money to go to a driving school as the guy had suggested, it would have been for nothing?

He told the lady he would look in some other time. She said sure thing, that he should keep checking in with them from time to time.

He decided to head to the Memory Store.

He went through the routine. Wiped his hands down. He worked on coming up with a memory. It was easier this time around. He had gone to play soccer with the brand new Wembley soccer ball that his grandmother had bought for him. He had enjoyed the pleasure of picking those who were going to play on his side as the owner of the soccer ball. The game had been fun all the way with both sides scoring two goals each. Then when they were taking a break preparatory to changing sides one of the big boys who had been watching the game from the sides, his name was Monday, asked to join the game. He had said No. Monday seized the soccer ball saying that if they would not let him play then they could not play either and that the ball would not be given back. He had tried to get his ball back but had received a swift kick on the shin from Monday. He had run home crying to his grandma. His grandma had sent him back to get his ball telling him not to come home without it.

R. was tapping him on the shoulder.

"This one is not good. We cannot pay for this one," R. said.

"Why, what is wrong with it?" he asked.

"Nothing is wrong with it. It is just that we don't find this type useful. People are not interested in this. It is somewhat generic, if you know what I mean. Someone gets his ball stolen by a bully and he fights to get it back. Think of something else. Go to that room over there, get a cup of coffee or a ginger ale. Try and relax for a few minutes and I am sure something useful will come to you, OK," he said.

He went into the room and poured himself some ginger ale and added ice. He felt like someone who had failed his exams. What could be so hard about coming up with some good memories? But why did the store not have a list of memory items that they accepted and those that they didn't?

He sipped the ginger ale and told himself to calm down. He had not liked ginger ale as a kid. He thought it tasted too much like an adult drink. It was not sugary enough, not like the other kinds of soft drinks. As an adult in America it had become his favorite drink. He liked the austere taste.

His mind became clear and he remembered the day before he left for America. Yes, that should be a good memory. He left his half-drunk cup of ginger ale on the table and went to meet R.

"I see you are ready to try again, my friend. Let's do it," R. said.

He remembered his last day before he traveled to America. The house was filled with more people than it was accustomed. There was food and lots of it. People were eating and drinking and talking. In the background there was music playing aloud. He was not quite sure who the musician was. For some reason he remembered the title of the song. It was called "Ace."

His grandmother had refused to eat and was crying. He had told her to stop crying, that today was a happy day. She held on to his hand and repeated the words he had just said to her. She had paused and then resumed with the crying.

"I am not leaving forever. I am going to come back soon and when I come back I will build you a bigger house," he said to his grandmother.

She had stopped crying to listen to him.

"Not even your grandmother knows the secret of living forever," she said and continued to cry.

He decided to change tack since this approach was not working.

"I don't want to remember you like this. I don't want my last memory of you to be your weeping face," he said.

This seemed to have touched her and she had wiped her face with her headscarf and asked for some food and drink.

"Perfect, see I told you to take a break that you'd come up with something that we can use. It worked. This is a good one. Here, take your card. You did a good job," R. said to him.

He bought a fridge with the card. It was a gray fridge with double doors. It had a different compartment for every item. He had always thought that every fridge must come in a white color, but had been thrilled by the fact that they came in all kinds of colors these days. He had told the guys who delivered the new fridge to take away the old one but they refused. They said it was against company regulations. He had told them that it was free and that they could sell it for money since it was still working and in good condition, but they had said no. So the old fridge sat mutely beside the new one like an unwanted guest.

It was the 26th of December. It was the anniversary of the passing of his grandmother. He thought that even in her choice of the day of her death, his grandmother had been her good old considerate self – the day after Christmas was hard to forget.

He sat before his television. He had turned it off. The fridge was humming distinctly but unobtrusively.

He wanted to spend some time thinking of his grandmother and honoring her memory. He sat still and tried to picture her gentle, smiling face.

He drew a blank.

He could not remember his grandmother's face. Nothing was coming to mind.

He panicked a little. But he recalled what had happened at the Memory Store. He opened the fridge and poured himself some ginger ale into a cup and added ice. He sat down and took a sip.

He thought hard.

His grandmother's face did not come up. There was nothing.

Sacrifice

E.C. Osondu

THIS WAS THE WAY IT ALWAYS HAPPENED. Every year an alien spaceship would quietly descend. Its doors gently swing open. A young man from our village would obediently walk into the spaceship. The spaceship door then glides forcefully closed. After which the spaceship departs.

This was our entire relationship with them ever since the days of our ancestors. It is the way we have always done it and the same way our children would do it. Those are the terms of the treaty that our ancestors signed with them. It says that every year we must give them a young man or they'd attack us and take all of us away and sow chemicals on our land so that nothing could ever grow on it again and poison our streams so that whosoever drank from it will burn up and die.

It sounded fair, to us. We had nothing with which we would have fought them. We were just ordinary folk. All we had were our machetes for farming, our single barrel guns for hunting, and our fishing nets and hooks. There was no way we were going to be able to fight them and their spaceships that glided through the air. They could wipe us out by the press of one button.

There were different stories about the young men and women who left on the spaceship.

Some said that they had gone to a better place, a place better than our lives of endless toil here in the village.

Others said that they'd train them to become Engineers and Pilots and Scientists and they'd soon be piloting spaceships like the aliens.

To some they have gone to a place where all the comforts can be summoned by the touch of a button. Over there they have robots that bring them cups of water and serve them tea, some said.

A few said that they were better off there. Over there they didn't even have to lift a finger, was some people's opinion. Some people said that when they got to the place the spaceships came from, they were given beautiful women as wives and their only assignment was to reproduce with the women so they could bring forth a superior race of beings that were indestructible.

The more cynical types said that they were etherized in space labs while their bodies were examined under microscopes. That they stared all day with sightless eyes like fishes preserved in chloroform in a Biology laboratory.

Some of the other comments were too fantastic to believe if not downright cruel. They said that the young men and women were sacrificed on a piece of rock that was shaped like the spaceship the moment they got to the other place.

In spite of the different opinions, there was one thing that everyone was sure about and upon which there was no argument. Those who left never came back. Not a single one of them ever came back and nothing was heard of them again.

The truth is that we had peace. We could farm and harvest our crops and sit under the moon at night to share stories. We told ourselves that it could have been worse.

What if we had gone to war with the Aliens and they had defeated us? Would we have not ended up losing our young men and women in the war?

What if they had defeated us and decided to carry us away into captivity to their strange land? What would we have done? To be held captive here on earth was bad, now compare that to being held captive in a strange planet where it was rumored the sun never stopped shining.

If we have ninety-nine gods in our village, the woman Makodi must have visited the shrine of each single one of them to ask for a child. She had married two husbands before her present one and was sent packing on each occasion because of her barrenness. It was when she married her third husband that she finally became pregnant and had her son Obiajulu. Everyone in the village was aware that Makodi treated Obiajulu like an egg. He was the kid whose mother dressed him up in a thick sweater simply because the sky was gray. He was that kid whose mother stood by the edge of the village soccer pitch carrying a gallon of water and hopping from one leg to the other waiting and hoping her son did not get tackled and fall. If he did fall she would be the one to quickly rush into the field to ask him if he was hurt. Their relationship had become the stuff of legend so much so that doting kids told their moms to let them be that they were not like Obiajulu. She was there waiting for him at the close of school. At first his classmates teased him, but they soon got tired because his mother always found a way to top her last act of embarrassment.

It came to a point that it was not possible to talk about Obiajulu without mentioning his mother.

If only she could have another child so she could stop suffocating this one with this type of excessive love that kills, some said.

She may never let him out of her sight long enough to get married, others said.

Ah, this life. Some children are praying for their mothers to look their way, this one must be praying for his mother to look away if even for one minute. All that love and attention must be suffocating. This was from another woman who lived down the same street.

There were a few other more philosophical and empathetic comments as well. These few voices commented on how long it had taken her to finally have a child of her own.

Why should we blame her? First time no luck. Second time no luck, only frustration and then sent away empty-handed, and then finally the third time she got this boy. What do you expect? We must learn from the mother-hen even though we think we are wiser than chickens, but look at the way the mother-hen guards and guides her eggs and her little chicks.

You know what they say: If you have children, worrying about them would nearly do you in, and if you don't have children, worrying about having children would nearly kill you. So either way children mean anxiety and worry.

For a boy who was so doted on, Obiajulu was quite a good boy. Always happy to run occasional errands for his mom and quite a good sport when he was playing soccer with his friends.

He hardly ever got into fights with any of his playmates, but he was not boring because he equally had an impish sense of mischief and a surprisingly sharp tongue that could spit out biting words when the need arose.

This combination made Obiajulu well liked though his friends would always end whatever they asked him to do with the expression "if your mother lets you."

Finding a palm frond by the doorsteps of your house in the village meant that the house would produce the next person that would be put on the Alien ship. It is quite possible that in the early days people cried and screamed in protest when they saw the palm frond by their doorsteps but that must have been in the past. People simply accepted it and basically saw it as their own way of building the community.

So when Makodi woke up and saw a palm frond by her doorstep and started screaming everyone in the village was startled but not surprised.

"Who owns the evil hand that wants to snatch my only palm nut that I got after many fruitless years of wandering in the bush with empty hands?" she screamed as she began running through the length and breadth of the village.

"Many people have four, five, six, and seven. I have just the one. Many have more than enough to spare and what does Makodi own? I have no bundles of damask like other women. I do not own a big house. The only piece of cloth that I own that should warm me on cold nights is what you want to take away from me."

Some in the village considered what Makodi was doing bad form. It was really quite unusual for people to complain the way she was doing when they saw a palm frond by their doorsteps. They did complain but quite mutedly, usually in the privacy of their inner rooms behind closed doors.

"What exactly does she want? She wants the entire village to be wiped out for the sake of her son?"

"Is she the first or is she going to be the last?"

"It is not a bad thing for her to cry. We all cried in the past, but we cried silently and we did it indoors."

"Every life is important, whether the life of her son or the lives of all those who had gone in the past, but what matters most is our continued survival and existence as a people."

"As many have said in the past, who knows what the journey holds for him? He may like it even more up there than he does down here. If it was so bad out there I am sure many would have come back to tell us how badly they fared over there."

Whether Makodi heard any of their comments or not no one could tell. She was undeterred as she ran back and forth through the village cursing and screaming.

"What crime did my one and only son commit that you chose to punish him this way?" she asked.

To this comment many responded that it was quite possible to choose where one wanted to be buried, but who has ever heard of one choosing where they were to be born? What a luxury that would be if we had a hand in the matter, they said.

The day that the palm frond was left on Makodi's doorstep was unusually gray. It was not threatening to rain but it was just gloomily overcast.

But there were also those who believed that it was somewhat unfair to ask of Makodi her only son whom she had been blessed with after many years of fruitless toil.

"She is not young anymore and besides it was so hard for her to have that boy. It is sad. I can see why the thought of losing her boy will make her lose it completely," someone said.

"It is much easier for those of us with more than one child to bear to see one of them taken away but for her with just that one boy it must really be heartbreaking," another said.

"What is to be done? What can we do? This life is indeed unfair, but we must continue to manage it because there is just one world – this is the only world we have. What choice do we have than to continue to take the good with the bad," were the words of another sympathizer.

Every ear was keen to hear what the Elders were going to say. They were the ones who had reached the peace agreement with the Aliens. The Elders were the one who had received this tradition of doing things from those who had gone before. Surely they had something to say maybe they had a solution even.

The Elders were murmuring and mumbling so much so that one could hardly hear them. Usually the Elders spoke clearly and forcefully but this time it was different. Why were they not speaking clearly? Was there something they didn't want all ears to hear? When they began to speak clearly above the muffle they spoke in riddles and obscure parables.

"What type of pain would the body experience that would make the eyes shed blood instead of tears?" they asked.

"Is there anything we are seeing today that we have not seen before?"

"The only new thing that will happen on this earth is if the heavens decide to fall upon the earth and cover it all up," they said.

"One little fart can ruin a gathering."

"One bad apple spoils the whole…"

"A little leaven ferments the whole lot."

The Elders said this and they said that. They beat around the bush without bringing forth anything fruitful. People listened closely to hear what the way out was going to be.

Meanwhile, Makodi was still wailing through the entire village screaming herself hoarse.

"Is this how you people are going to be watching? Is no one going to come to my help?"

"What exactly does she want us to do?" many asked.

"But I thought you people loved my son Obiajulu. Obiajulu my son who plays with your children. You people always stop me to compliment me on how well behaved he is, are you all going to fold your hands and watch him go, just like that?"

"Why is she talking like she is the first and only person to have her son taken away? Have most of us not been through the same thing?"

"When a bird sees a piece of stone coming towards it, it flies away, it does not wait to be hit. When a goat sees an object coming its way to hit it, even the goat gets up and runs away. Do you people expect me to fold my hands as this thing is coming towards me?" she asked.

By now ears were growing weary from listening to Makodi. Even her voice was beginning to grow hoarse from all the crying and screaming she had been doing the entire day. It was getting to the time that the ship was going to arrive from space. Her son had refused to eat all day and had been sitting on the bed he still shared with his mother.

When Makodi realized that the time was drawing near for her son to be taken away she returned to her house and stopped crying. She told her son to take his bath after which she told him to have something to eat and then she dressed him up in his best clothes. She too went and had a bath and dressed up in her best clothes.

They both came out and sat on a wooden bench and began to wait for the arrival of the spaceship that was going to take her son away.

Now tongues began to wag and get busy at the sight of mother and child dressed in their best clothes waiting for the spaceship.

"Was she not the one crying only a few moments ago?"

"What exactly is she up to this time and why is she dressed like someone heading to a party? Does she want us to think all the tears were for nothing?"

"Why is the boy dressed so colorfully? Does she not know that as soon as he boards the ship they are going to give him new clothes because the kind of clothes we wear here are different from what they wear over there?"

Soon, the Alien spaceship arrived like it always did. It glided in gently and descended. Makodi walked towards the spaceship holding Obiajulu's hands. As Obiajulu started to climb the stairs into the spaceship Makodi climbed with him, not letting go of his hand.

"Where is she going? Has she gone mad? They only take sons not old women, or doesn't she know that?" someone asked.

"I will go with him. It is either we go together or he is not going," she said.

"Let go of his hands. He must go alone. Do not bring disaster upon us all," the Elders said.

Makodi would not listen but went into the spaceship with her son.

There was a little scuffle inside the ship. The door did not close.

An Alien's hand pushed Makodi and Obiajulu out of the spaceship. The door of the spaceship closed. The spaceship left empty.

The Elders were the first to start wailing. Other villagers soon joined in.

"What shall we do? Surely, they are coming back to attack us," they said.

Many eyes were turned to the sky waiting for the attack, but it never came. The alien spaceship did not return. Not that day. Not that year. Not even the year after that.

Ysarin

Simon Pan

ON DAYS WHEN I CAME HOME CRYING, my grandmother was always there with her song.

It was a tune friendly and old as the roads that crossed Mazael: the sort you shared while you watched the land roll away on horseback, or sitting at a moonlit fireside among familiar faces. I would lean against my grandmother on our rickety porch and breathe in her scent as she sang to the street.

Magic lay in that song, the notes so delicate you could tell a story about each one. As the beginning strands of music twined together, I would be transported to a place that let me forget the ache in my chest, a city of an entirely different skin than our Lenniel. A place of worn streets and thatched roofs wrapped in the smell of woodsmoke and fresh ale. A sunset, a fire, the sky on fire and the streets ablaze with torchlight.

"This is our song, dear," she would say as she smiled down at me. "Don't listen to the other children. We will always have our home with us..." Her fingers would press against my chest just above my heart. Somehow she knew the exact place where her spell took root. "Here."

Even after so many years, that is how I think of home. Sitting there on that porch with the wind stealing my tears and carrying away the sound of magic.

* * *

In my earliest years, I would go with my grandmother to the town centre in Lenniel and stand before the pillars of the Arlanari, the grand concert hall. There I would watch her set down her woven basket and sing to the busy streets. Once in a while a passerby would deposit a few coins into the basket and I would put on a shy smile for them.

That changed the day I saw a few older boys cross the street, pointing at us and giggling. The wind carried their whispers over as they neared.

"Look at them. Beady eyes, noses all smushed."

"Look like puppets."

After that, I stood on the opposite side of the street, but even then I could feel the heat in my cheeks. One night, as we returned home, I finally blurted out what was on my mind.

"Why do the people look at you like that?"

"Look at me like what, dear?"

I bit my lip. I couldn't stop staring at my hands as I walked, the olive-colour that seemed somehow like a stain in a sea of white.

"Like you're an animal."

"That's not a nice thing to say," she said, though her laugh rang cold and weak. "Your father would let you hear it if he were here."

I fell silent at the mention of my father. It had been his idea for me to grow up in Lenniel. I'd never known him or my mother. They'd given me to my grandmother the year after I'd been born and left to wander the wild like all the other Veleri, singing their songs at roadsides and taverns, drinking with thieves.

There was an old saying among the Wandering Folk that went something like this: *Follow your voice and you will find your way home*. A silly thing to say for a people whose city now lay in ruins. Whenever I thought about why my parents left me, I imagined them wandering forever, in search of a place that had no name.

* * *

We had our first fight not long after I started school.

I was standing at my grandmother's side as she stood preparing the evening meal in the kitchen. The scent of the sour spices and the bitter fumes wafting down from the stew pot made my eyes water.

"Can't I get a real instrument?"

She looked down from where she was chopping a thick piece of gnarled ellanroot. "What's wrong with singing, dear?"

"I want a lanthra." I crossed my arms and stuck my chin out in defiance. "I'm tired of singing. Everyone else in music class has an instrument."

"I don't know if that's possible," my grandmother said. Her dark eyes shone with sadness. "Lanthras are expensive."

"You say that about everything. Clothes are expensive, food is expensive, a roof is expensive." I jabbed my finger in the air to punctuate my points. "When will we live like real people?"

"And what makes us not 'real people'?" She knelt and took my face in her hands. I twisted but she held strong, forcing me to meet her gaze. "Do we not have a place in the world as much as anyone else?"

"Real people have money." I was shouting. I didn't care. "Real people don't beg, real people—"

"We don't beg." She jerked back as if stung, releasing me. Pain creased the lines at the edges of her eyes. "We earn every coin we get. Don't say silly things like that." She rose with a groan and stared down at her cutting board. Her eyes narrowed slightly and she made grasping motions with her hands, as if she could pull whatever she was looking for out of the air. "Now, could you get me that … thing you use to stir?"

I should've seen it then, should've realized, but I was too bitter.

I bit my lip and went to fetch the ladle from a cupboard. I knew there was no point to this conversation. Grandmother would never understand – she was Veleri down to her bones after all.

* * *

Kade, one of the boys from school, invited me over for Snowtide one year.

His parents were on the Merchant's Council so I wasn't surprised that they lived in one of the towering manors that sat on the hillside, looking out over the rest of the city. Even so, the view stole my breath as I stared out of the tall windows of the common room. The howling wind appeared as pale threads carrying heavy drifts of snow. Through the sea of white, I could just make out the silhouettes of slanted roofs in the dark and golden light spilling from windows.

"Rin."

I turned and found Kade approaching with a grin, a platter of sugared biscuits in hand. A small procession of boys and girls in tailored white shirts and dresses trailed him. Together with their jewelry glittering in the light of the candelabras and their creamy skin, they looked like a group of snowflakes brushed down from the sky.

"These ones won't believe me." He gestured behind him with a snort and turned back to me with an expectant expression. "The Veleri summon demons with their songs, don't they? That's how Velerin fell."

"The City of Fire did *not* fall because of demons." The girl at his shoulder threw up her hands and raised her eyes to the distant ceiling. "They just lost the war."

"Then how do you explain the magic? Everyone knows if you hear a Veleri song, you start seeing things."

Mutters of assent echoed throughout the room. In the past five years since I'd known Kade, I'd never seen him so animated. All eyes were fixed on him and the room seemed to revolve around him. Tall, with a shock of golden hair, this child of wealthy Lennielith merchants. I felt the stab of jealousy deep in my gut.

"Well…" I glanced between Kade and the girl. "Only the best can manage the demons, but—"

Kade spun so fast the biscuits on his platter nearly spilled. "See? I told you!"

The girl squinted at me. "Really?"

"Of course." I thought back to the stories I'd heard from school. "It takes a long time to prepare and there's a lot of blood, but yes."

"Your grandmother can do it, right?" Kade, with that eager grin again.

I blinked. "She … has trouble remembering the spells these days."

Kade clapped me on the back, then handed me a biscuit and slipped away. I watched for a moment as his procession followed him off before turning back to the window.

For a long while I stood there, searching. This time I couldn't resolve anything beyond a strange boy painted on the glass. Cropped black hair, pinhole eyes staring back above a flat nose. The type of thing that summoned demons. I spent the rest of the night like that, frozen in contemplation.

I came home to find my grandmother sitting on the steps alone in the cold. Snow lay wrapped around her shoulders, a scarf of frost glittering in the light. She looked up as I approached and her face brightened like a child's given candy.

"Did you have fun, dear?"

I brushed past her without a word, through the hallway, and slammed my bedroom door closed behind me. I noticed for the first time how foul my wool blankets smelled, how harsh the floorboards were beneath my back, how sharp the heavy chill that set my teeth chattering felt. Maybe that was why I couldn't fall asleep that night. Or maybe it was the image burned into my mind of a wrinkled woman sitting on wooden steps alone in a pool of torchlight, waiting and waiting. The look that had been frozen on her face.

The sadness in her eyes and the heavy curl of her spine, a jagged thing like a splintered sheet of ice.

* * *

I returned from Kade's one night to find my grandmother seated alone at the stained table in our kitchen. Her head snapped up as I entered and the lines of her face relaxed. A pot of stew steamed on the table, the pungent smell nearly suffocating.

"Hungry, dear?"

I stared at the chunks of ellanroot and wyrwand stalks floating in the watery stew. A Veleri dish, ingredients pulled from the wilds.

"Can't you make normal food?"

"You've never had trouble with my cooking before." She pursed her lips. I walked around to the cupboard to retrieve my bowl but her sharp voice cut me off. "You won't need that, dear. I-I've already eaten. Just use the pot."

My grandmother always waited. Suspicion crept into me. I went to the cabinet where we stored our food and pulled it open. The lingering scent of old spices and raw vegetables welcomed me, but the cabinet held nothing beyond a few specks of soil. For a moment I stared, the pieces aligning themselves in my head. It was the last day of Lorning. My grandmother must have forgotten to go to the market again. She had used what was left to cook a meal – enough for one person.

I forced myself back to the table, back into the seat. A painful, tearing sensation wormed its way through my chest, as if the two halves of me were being pulled apart. A part that yearned for something I would never have and a part that feared losing what I had never truly known.

"I can make something else next—"

"No. Just … it's fine, okay? It's fine."

The stew burned my tongue as I wolfed it down and I nearly choked. I forced myself to slow after that, even though I knew it had not been food that had caught in my throat.

* * *

We sat together as we always did on the rickety porch. I stared up at the dusk sky and the slash of orange clouds. But there was no song, no spell to carry me up into those fiery wings. I could see my grandmother from the corner of my eye, a furrow between her brows. She mouthed words over and over, but whenever she tried to sing her voice faltered.

"Do you remember how it goes, Girilin?"

I stiffened and looked away. It wasn't the first time she'd forgotten my name. "Don't call me that."

"Why? It's your name."

"It's *not* my name."

"I know you don't like it, but it's a Veleri name." Her face softened. The hurt lay etched into the worn lines of her face. "I just want you to be happy, child. Is it so hard to be happy in your own skin?"

"Stop saying that. We're living in Lenniel, with real people in a real city. We're Lennielith, not Veleri, so stop trying to sing that stupid song."

I regretted the words as soon as they left my mouth and felt the shame sting deeper when my grandmother's voice fell to a hush.

"The music is who we are."

The music won't fix you, I wanted to say. "But I don't want it to be."

"Oh, child." She tilted her face and a wry smile twisted her shriveled lips. "In the end, we will all just be songs."

Years would pass before I began to understand what she meant.

* * *

Near the end of my twelfth year at school, I started staying late to practice. The Guild's Test was coming in a few months, when the masters at the Musician's Guild in Farlyth would host a concert night at the Arlanari. Everyone knew that if you managed to impress them you could win an offer to the Guild. It was all I could think about.

One day, Kade stayed to watch me practice. I sat at our school's old lanthra, testing the strings one by one, running my hands over the polished black wood of the frame. There was a beauty to the instrument that I could never get over. A certain way it sat tucked between my knees as it sang that always seemed perfect. But no sooner had I begun to play than a choked laugh pierced the music and I broke off, startled. I looked up to find Kade shaking his head in disbelief.

"You're not going to play that, are you?"

"What's wrong with it?"

Kade made a face. "You can't waste a lanthra on a stupid folk tune. You'll look like an idiot."

I frowned. "What are you going to—"

"*Wyrwand's Bloom,*" Kade said with a proud smile, as if he had been waiting for the question. "Only the best can play it. It's famous in the courts of Thae Lannor."

"I've never heard of it."

He rolled his eyes and tossed me a book that had been sitting on the windowsill.

"That's got all the classics. You can pick a song from there."

After Kade left, I flipped through the book. The names were all unfamiliar to me and the dizzying scatter of notes was daunting. But I knew Kade was right – the judges would be masters of their craft and most of the audience would be powerful folk.

In the end I chose a song called *Lunocivo*. It was composed by Alanrae Veridas, one of the greatest composers of our time and a man whose name I could barely pronounce, but that didn't matter. What mattered was that he was from the glittering city of Lodin Vard, not some forgotten tribe without a home. His name carried strength and wealth and all the things that came with them.

* * *

I woke one night to a strange keening. At first I thought it was the wind, but glancing out the window I saw that the trees along the street stood still in the dark. So I pushed myself up and padded out to the hallway.

The door hung ajar. Through the crack I could see my grandmother sitting on the porch, her shoulders hunched and her eyes staring off into nowhere. The moonlight spilled across her, etching the lines of her face in silver as she worked her jaw. Her voice escaped wafer-thin and tremulous. There were words but they came fragmented, notes that echoed in the wrong places. A broken melody. I didn't know why, but I felt relieved.

The wood groaned beneath my feet as I slid out onto the porch. She didn't turn to me, though silence claimed her voice.

"Come on," I said, tugging on her arm. "Let's go back to bed."

She glanced up and peered into my face, as if noticing me for the first time. "Do you feel it, Arlin? That little song, our home?"

I tugged again, not bothering to tell her that Arlin and my mother had abandoned us, that home was a lie. She didn't budge.

"Stop treating me like a child," she snapped. I stumbled back in surprise. I'd never heard her speak like that. "Please, Arlin, just listen to me this one time. That boy needs the road. I need the road. If you leave him behind, I'll take care of him, but our people were never meant to stay in the same place for so long." Her withered hand shot out to grab me by the wrist. I stifled a cry as her cracked nails dug in. "Promise me you'll take him with you. Promise me you'll teach him what it means to be Veleri."

"I promise," I said between gritted teeth.

She watched me for a time through narrowed eyes, searching for the lie. At last she nodded and let me lead her back into the house.

* * *

Lunocivo was the hardest song I'd ever tried to learn. It didn't help that sleep escaped me no matter how hard I hunted for it, because I had grown used to standing watch over my bedridden grandmother most nights. Bitterness together with weariness do not blend for a pretty song.

I sat in my school's basement with my teeth clenched, plucking away at the strings of the lanthra at a snail's pace. My teacher, Bolas, stood at my shoulder, driving me on. He was a stern man, tall and sharp, with an angular face that always felt as if I were staring at someone cut from stone rather than flesh.

"Flat!" Bolas slapped his switch across my head. "You're sharp. Focus, boy. Do you want the Masters to think you're an idiot?"

I bit my lip so hard the taste of blood flooded my mouth. Again and again I played through the line, making sure the pieces fit together. At last my fingers came to a stop and I stared at the strings. The hiss of air betrayed the switch but I absorbed the sting without reaction.

"Sir, why do people like this song?"

"What?"

"I…" I picked my words carefully. "I just think the best music is the kind that makes us feel."

"And does *Lunocivo* not make you feel?"

"I think it sounds a little dry. The melody runs so fast and senselessly."

Bolas snorted as if I were the biggest fool he'd ever taught. "This is one of the greatest pieces of our time, boy. See how this section breathes, listen to the mystery hidden in the chorus!"

I swallowed my protest and gave a nod before resuming. The notes sounded hollow and dead to me, but I gritted my teeth and pressed on. *Lunocivo* was a masterpiece for a reason. I just hadn't acquired the taste yet. I wouldn't be able to recognize true art until I became a master myself. Perhaps one day I would understand, if I managed to join the Musician's Guild.

* * *

My grandmother lay in bed, her eyes clouded as she stared into the light of the flickering candle on the windowsill. They remained unfocused even when I stepped into the room and my shadow fell over her.

For a moment my gaze lingered on her face and I felt old emotions well up within me. A woman alone in the cold, a pot of stew, a song. A message bubbled at my lips, but the person I needed to hear it was no longer here, no longer knew my name. Something searing and bitter burned me as I tore my eyes away.

"I won't be back tomorrow night."

"Oh?"

I stared at my reflection in the window and smoothed back my hair. "I'm going to perform at the Arlanari."

"Leaving." The way her lips drew downwards made something deep in my chest twist. "Can we come with you, son?"

"No." I nearly spat the word.

"Why not? The fire in the streets … the fire in the sky … Can't we go home together? I want to see it again."

"Just…" I gave a heavy sigh. The time for words had long since passed between us. "Bolas said he'll look after you while I'm gone."

She didn't reply. Her hand quested out, dangerously close to the candle. With a spike of alarm I shot over and batted her hand away. She didn't seem to notice, but there was an insistence in her eyes that frightened me.

I made to leave, then hesitated. Two steps took me back to the windowsill and I snuffed out the candle with a breath. The room in total darkness, I strode off and left without another glance.

* * *

I stood backstage, flexing my clammy fingers. The cloying scent of a dozen different mixing perfumes almost made me choke. I'd watched the other youths slip in and out of the room as the night wore on, flashes of glittering gemstones over dresses and crisp suits. I knew that they watched me too, taking in the rumpled cream-coloured shirt I'd borrowed from Kade. I saw the moment they dismissed me from the straightening of their shoulders and the proud tilt of their chins.

Tonight. The night I'd dreamed of for years. I'd done everything I could to prepare and now all that lay ahead was to perform. If successful, I could win my path into the Musician's College in Farlyth.

I could earn my way into a real life.

* * *

When I stepped onto the stage, a low muttering broke out across the room. I could feel a thousand gazes weighing me as I sat on the stool and turned to face them. Seated on a raised platform above the crowd were the five black-clad Masters of the Guild. The knot in my stomach twisted as my gaze landed on them. I was glad for the lights, dimming away their silhouettes beneath the brightness.

The muttering grew as I removed my school's lanthra from its case. I struck a chord, turned the pegs, tried to fall back to familiar memories. I had practiced until my fingers bled and my head spun and the long-dead echoes of notes rang in my ears. *Lunocivo*'s melody was burned into my mind fiercer than the memory of my own name.

I finished warming up and raised my head. One, two deep breaths. I wiped my hands on my shirt. And then something happened that changed me forever. At that moment, my eyes fell upon an ancient woman seated in the far right corner.

I'd told Bolas not to bring her. Why was she here? I saw my teacher sitting beside her amidst a field of empty seats. My cheeks burned and my hands began to tremble. Bolas must have seen something in my face because he gave me a nod.

"*Veleri dog.*"

My head snapped towards the source of the sound. There was a bustle of movement, but whoever had uttered the slur sat too far back for me to make them out. Still, I felt my heart hammer against my chest and my fingers pause over the lanthra. A memory came to me then, clear and sharp. Many memories. An entire life flashing before me, and I realized then that this would be the only chance I would ever get.

So I played. Seated on the stage, I strummed a chord and let the notes taste the air. I wasn't thinking. When you are with someone you love, the world spins by and thought dissolves into shades of colour. Slowly my fingers grew relaxed as they danced across the strings. I reached for the pent breath in my chest, called upon hours and hours of practice.

It wasn't *Lunocivo*. The song that bled into the air wasn't sharp and mysterious, whispering of places far away and a life untamed. It was something that smelled and tasted of home. It was what the moon said as it blinked into the sky, making sure the nights never grew too dark. It was a grandmother's love and the ache of a name forgotten.

The muttering had ceased completely and in the void my music flowed through. I swayed, let my body bend into the song. I carved out all the bitter pieces from the hollow pit inside me and poured myself into the air. I let the room see me, all of me.

Gentle at first and then fiercer, I let my voice twine with that of the lanthra and we became two friends in conversation. Together we pulsed as one heartbeat, moving life into a story that couldn't be put to words. My voice sang a waterfall of notes that cascaded over the ice of the lanthra's harmony. Fighting, yielding, each note dancing with its pair, intimate and silver-bright when they joined together.

I knew the moment my spell was complete when I left the room. The white walls of the auditorium faded to usher in shadow. I was playing around a bonfire and the moon hung fierce and bright in the sky. Leaves rustled and somewhere far off waves rumbled, a thousand distant harmonies joining my song.

The chorus crashed over us and the fire leapt with it, hungry, spreading out to engulf the world. And then I saw it. Glimmering streets in a place I had never known and somehow the name was on my tongue, waiting like an old secret I'd forgotten. I was returning from a long wander, my limbs aching, my mind aching, but there was a tune to welcome me and friendly faces in this city of light that I knew no longer existed in the world.

The song never stayed in one place. Sometimes quiet and sad, then soaring and so full of joy my chest ached with its weight. Even as I played, I lost track of time. The only thing I was certain of was that I wished to stay there forever, together with the smell of smoke and a brightness in my heart I knew came only fleetingly.

But it did end. The legato notes swept upwards, a gathering of wings in the night sky, building up into a high crescendo. They hung there, growing brighter and brighter beneath the moonlight. Then they sailed off one by one, and when the last scrap of light faded beyond the horizon I was back in the auditorium.

When I finished, I looked out over the crowd. I knew what they were thinking. It was written across their pale faces and their stiff postures. In the space of that held breath, I knew I had lost my only chance, but I didn't care. I looked out across the field of frozen statues. I wasn't searching for nods of approval or teary-eyed stares. Just one, one wrinkled face in a grubby apron smiling up from her seat.

Then it happened.

The applause was a crack of thunder that I will never forget. From nowhere it began until the room was echoing with the sound of a thousand voices and clapping hands. People sagged in their seats, released from my spell. I saw men and women turn to each other and the silver gleam of tears cascading down their faces.

But the truth was that none of it registered. At that moment I found my grandmother. She wore a moth-eaten, quilted sweater beneath a stained apron. Her eyes shone clear and bright as sun-kissed snow.

She mouthed a word. The thundering applause drowned out her voice, but I read it from her lips anyway. A name. When it struck me, I buried my face into my hands and broke down into tears at last.

Ysarin.

* * *

Moments come and go. Songs carry these moments.

Before I became the Songstrider, before you ever heard one of my songs at a concert hall or at a fireside, I was my grandmother's Ysarin and a boy of the Veleri. If you are to understand me or ever hope to learn the stories woven into my songs, you must first look to my grandmother. Never forget where I came from. Sometimes even I almost forget, and on those days I play my grandmother's song to remind myself.

She taught me that learning a song and breathing life into one are two entirely different things. The former is a corpse, the latter pulses with its own heartbeat built upon memories. The latter is a story.

The latter is home.

I Will Be Mila Tomorrow

C.R. Serajeddini

THE FIRST TIME I EVER SAW MRS. LEE, I thought that she must be the toughest woman on the whole planet. I'd had both hands splayed on the pod's windowpane – my forehead and nose stuck to the glass throughout the journey from the spaceport to our designated residential quarter. I was taking in all the new and – mostly – wonderful sights. I'd never been inside a biodome before. I'd never seen so much *green*.

Mrs. Lee strolled out of the crumbling building I now know is her restaurant, an onion in her left hand, a chef's knife in her right. She looked up as the pod descended, and for a moment our eyes locked through the window. The very tall woman bowed her head at me, a slight gesture that seemed like a greeting. Then she lifted her hand and bit into the onion. I watched the muscles in her jaws working as she chewed and swallowed then took another bite. When I pointed it out to my brother Luca, he said that maybe onions weren't hot here. Maybe they were sweet.

I wondered if he was right. This world already seemed so different from the dry and desolate place we'd left behind. Of course, he was right. Everything here would taste sweeter. Wouldn't it?

Our home world had been green too, once. Long before I'd been born. I'd seen it in the archive footage. We were once a mighty empire of proud people that lived in castles on the mountains of our world. Pine forests blanketed the lands beneath our feet, and snow-capped peaks crowned the land above our heads.

Then Xefrite was discovered, and the mining began. At first, traders traveled from neighboring star systems to buy it. Eventually, other parties wanted it at better prices, and before long, they began warring over it and we were stuck in the middle. Then came that fateful day when the citadel at mount Zagaris woke to silence. Yellow tongues of Seed gas and Tarim licked at doors and windowpanes, curled their poisonous fingers between the cracks, and seeped into our people's blood. Thousands died. Children orphaned and parents left childless – hollow and grief-stricken. The Thelurians blamed the Arlanians and the Arlanians blamed the Thelurians. The war intensified in the name of saving our people, but we all knew the truth.

Nuclear, biological, and chemical warfare turned our once mighty and lush world into a barren wasteland stripped of its natural resources.

Still, they mine the Xefrite.

Our new home was different from the one we'd left behind, but we were grateful, nonetheless. Even if the homes here were stacked atop one another, cramped and thin, as though someone had tried to push too many drawers into one chest, and when they didn't fit, they just took out the big drawers and replaced them with two that were half that size. And so what if the roof leaked a little when the artificial rain came and we had to catch the water in buckets?

At least we're safe.

That's what I kept hearing mother say. She'd repeat it to my brother and me each night when she put us to bed, or maybe it was to herself – I'm not sure. "We're safe," she'd whisper, planting a soft kiss on our foreheads. "We're safe here."

I wanted to believe her; I really did. *Safe.* I clung to that word and repeated it whenever I had doubts. But Luca and I soon began school, and I learned a new word, then: Tolerance.

Be tolerant of different beliefs. Be tolerant of different species. Be tolerant. *We must show tolerance.*

Tolerance meant that the native Terran children in my class couldn't call me an alien, at least not to my face. I heard the word whispered in corridors before I turned corners. Tolerance meant that the other kids couldn't refuse me sitting next to them, but it didn't stop them from tensing or sighing in irritation. It didn't stop their laughter from sticking in their throats whenever I showed up or stop them from choosing to turn away and vacate the room.

"That's because being tolerated is not the same thing as being accepted," Mrs. Lee said one night. Mother had started a cleaning job at the local vaccination lab, and she often didn't come back until late, so my brother and I had taken to visiting Mrs. Lee pretty often. She placed a bowl of steaming stew in front of me and gave me a wooden spoon. I had no idea what it was made from, but my stomach rumbled, and I salivated, nonetheless.

"Does acceptance come later?" I asked.

Mrs. Lee would know. She wasn't a native Terran either. She was a belter, originally, though she and her husband relocated to Terra almost one hundred and fifty years ago, after the asteroid wars broke out.

Mrs. Lee sighed, and I felt the heaviness it carried in the blackest depths of my heart. "Some people do accept," she nodded. "Others never will." After a moment's silence, she leaned onto the table and crossed her arms – her face was so close I could smell the onions on her breath. "You cannot change other people, Mila. You can only change how you react. Some people … they become bitter. Don't let it happen to you."

I swallowed hard, suddenly forgetting my hunger. "I don't feel welcome here," I whispered. "I am tolerated, but I am not welcome."

"Shhh," Mrs. Lee said. "I know. But don't tell your mother, hmm? She's been through too much. Yes?"

I nodded and blinked back the stinging in my eyes. I swallowed the knot in my throat. Because, despite it all, we were *safe* here.

The thing is, it's too easy to blame Thelurians and Arlanians for all that happened to our world. And the truth is never easy.

Here's the truth. No matter how far your travel in the universe, ugly always exists. The beings that possess stones instead of hearts. They could look like me, or like you, or like somebody's mom.

Our own magistrate became corrupt, long before the war began. At first, he promised that a large percentage of the profits from selling Xefrite would be reinvested into the people, the community.

Mining Xefrite was a harsh task. I watched my dad get thinner every night he came home – the bags under his eyes growing darker and his hair falling out. When the miners didn't get the healthcare they deserved, their families began asking questions. Where was the wealth that was promised? The reinvestment?

The magistrate made his excuses and blamed the Thelurians and Arlanians. And perhaps some of it was true, but the people of Zegrine were not so easily convinced. The Miner's Union demanded the magistrate and his government step down, but he declared them "a faux faction." He named the members of the union dissidents, traitors, and thieves who deserved nothing but the worst kinds of punishment.

My father was one of them.

At first, we ran. We left our home, our neighbors, our school. We fled from city to village, to camp. Still, the Peace Guard followed. Father tried, many times, to tell my mother that we should separate, but she wouldn't have it.

"We're a family. You are my soulmate. We stick together."

Then, one morning, we woke to find his bed empty. Later that day, the names of dissidents that had been caught were listed via transmission. His name was on there.

"We have to go back to him," Mom told us, and we packed up and followed wordlessly. Only at the nearest village, we began to hear tales of how the families of the members of the Miner's Union were being rounded up. They were causing the magistrate too much trouble, it seemed.

"Mom," I whispered that night. "What are we going to do?"

She looked at me with glazed eyes. Somehow, it didn't feel like her anymore. "We will go somewhere safe," she whispered back.

A few days later, we arrived at a trader's outpost. My eyes popped out of my skull when I saw the piece of Xefrite that Mom unraveled before the pilot of a cargo ship. It was only then I realized my father must have left it for her.

"Then Father really was a thief," I whispered harshly to my mother that night.

My mother's face twisted with disgust, and she slapped me hard across the face. When I cried, the tears left cold streaks across my burning cheek, but my mother didn't speak to me again. Not until we reached our new home and settled into our beds. Then she kissed our heads and told us we were safe.

"It's because you're trying to befriend *them*," my brother told me when we were walking home one day.

"What are you talking about?"

He shook his head. "Mila, I have lots of friends. Haven't you seen? You are trying to befriend the natives. You know, the *Terrans*. You should find others like … well, like us."

I stopped dead in my tracks. "Like us?"

He shrugged. "Not just from Zegrine. But anybody who isn't native is more likely to like you."

I thought hard about what Luca said. I supposed he was right, and not long after that, I approached my brother and his rag-tag group of refugees one afternoon.

"Finally realized you don't belong with *them*?" Akina said, with a smug grin planted on his face. Akina was not from Terra, but he was not Zegrine, either. I didn't like the way he said *them*.

They let me sit, and they didn't call me alien, and I began to feel like I'd found some acceptance. But it didn't take long for me to notice the way they looked at the Terrans. The bitterness and disdain towards "*them*" that lurked far too close to the surface for my comfort. One day, they began to argue over who was responsible for the war in Zegrine. Akina insisted it was the Arlanians, while Luca insisted it was Therulia.

"It was neither," I blurted, then shook my head. "It was both, but there was also corruption within Zegrine. You can't just blame someone else, or else things will never get better. Can't you see?"

I knew from the way they looked at me that no, they most certainly did not see.

"Mrs. Lee," I mumbled in a panic over the old lady's delicious bowl of stew later, "I have realized something."

Mrs. Lee wiped her hands on her apron and sat down in the chair next to mine. "What is it, Mila?"

"I do not belong here with the Terrans. I do not belong with the refugees – I am as alien to them as I am to the Terrans. And if I go back to my world I—" I jerked my head up and met her eyes, realization suddenly dawning on me like a ton of Xefrite. "I don't even know if I remember how to speak our language properly anymore. I do not belong in Zegrine, either. I am not Terran. I am not Zegrine. What am I?"

Mrs. Lee studied my face for a long moment before she spoke. Then she reached into the woven basket behind her and pulled out an onion. "This," she said, peeling back its brown layers, "is one of a kind. No other onion has the same layers, or the same taste, or shape. It's grown in Terran soil, but its ancestry goes back to my world, an asteroid far from here. It tastes different from the ones back home. It tastes different from the onions native to Terra. But its uniqueness is what makes it special." She stopped when she reached the pale flesh and held the onion out for me.

I took it from her and wiped my eyes with the back of my sleeve. "Mrs. Lee? Are you saying I'm an onion?"

Mrs. Lee wheezed and knocked her head back before breaking into a loud and husky cackle. Her laughter mixed with my high-pitched giggle and the sound spilled out from the restaurant and into the street until even the children outside stood still and looked into the building.

Finally, when my sides hurt and I cried mixed tears of joy and despair, Mrs. Lee gripped my wrist, and said this:

"You are Mila. You are not defined by where you come from. What defines you is your actions. Your qualities. The person you choose to be, Mila."

That night, I got back out of bed after Mom said goodnight. I walked to her door, and I listened to her whimper and talk to herself.

"Take the children, you said. This will buy you passage. Keep them safe. Take them somewhere safe. I did it. I did as you asked. They are safe. We are safe."

I stood there in the shadows until my legs turned numb, but Mom carried on. She whispered the words again, and again, until her voice became a murmur. Until she fell asleep. That night, I crept into her room, brushed her hair away from her face, and I kissed her damp cheek. I don't know why it took me so long to realize how hard it must have been for my mother to do what she did. To leave my dad behind. Her best friend. Her soulmate. I realized then that my mother must be the toughest woman on the planet, too.

That night, I decided that I would no longer let other people's words, or hate, or prejudice change me. I was Mila yesterday and today. I will be Mila tomorrow, and forevermore.

Four-Point Affective Calibration

Bogi Takács

PROMPT: Anger

Of course I can be angry. So can anyone. But I wear a headscarf. The moment I'm angry, you put me in the box in your brain labeled 'TERRORIST'. You store me under 'Potential Danger' in the warehouse of your mind.

When I cross the parking lot to the grocery store, sometimes people hit the gas, not the brakes. And this is a university town, supposedly liberal – or is it?

I'm not a Muslim, but it's not like most people around here can spot the difference. I'll allow you to guess my religion, my level of observance, my gender. You'll probably guess wrong.

Let's start over. I can be angry, but I won't.

I won't because it wouldn't have gotten me through secondary screening, immigration detention, hostile interrogation, and all the other abstract concepts that apparently need at least two words to describe them. I lived to learn that lesson.

But you know what? Maybe I'm not angry because I'm not.

You expect me to be angry, or at least be silent but simmering with rage. And sure, I can work myself up to it. But right now I'm mostly just annoyed, sitting here under this helmet while I'm asked to contemplate various emotions, supposedly basic, supposedly universal across all cultures. I have my doubts about that.

I hope next up is sadness, because thinking about anger makes me sad.

Prompt: Sadness

I wish my thoughts were tidier. A complete stranger will be examining these transcripts and it feels like I keep on going off on tangents.

I have a succulent on my living room table that keeps on trying to grow out of its pot and downward, forming a fringe of thick green bundles. But its branches are not strong enough to support their own weight, and they keep breaking off, wasting away. The plant doesn't give up, and meanwhile I water it dutifully, try to rotate it so that it gets an even amount of sun through the north-facing window, the little there is.

But the plant only wants to grow downward, toward certain harm.

This is not a metaphor, this is straight-up life. I swear plants have personalities – the balsam gourd in the office is feisty, with tendrils that rapidly grow toward all the other pots, seeking to reach out and tickle. Possibly smother.

Maybe you chose me for this task because I'm so observant.

Is this enough for sadness? Can I get a different one? Impatience is not a basic emotion, so I'm told.

[Pause]

Disgust is apparently a subcategory of anger, but I really don't want to redo that segment. They should've briefed me first. This is not my field – I only know about Ekman's six basic emotions from undergrad. Happiness, surprise, fear, anger, sadness, disgust.

I guess people refine their models all the time.

I threw out all my models, and again, and again. 'Extraterrestrial communication' is another abstract concept that needs two words to describe. It doesn't sound much friendlier than 'hostile interrogation'.

Prompt: Fear / surprise

Fear and surprise fall under the same heading – emotions evoked by fast-approaching danger. I'm scouring my brain for citations. Jack et al, I don't remember the year.

I didn't sleep through the initial briefing. I was just so anxious that nothing they said registered. Sure, I can tell you about the amygdala, fear response, interactions with short-term memory. It's not really an excuse though. Does it matter? I feel like I'm in my comprehensive exams again, being interrogated by my committee, even though it's just my thoughts being transcribed. Even though this is just the calibration phase.

I feel like I'm back at the detention centre, looking at the immigration officer again.

Deep breath. I can upset myself with great alacrity and skill.

The research team think aliens will not understand the substance of my thoughts as much as the resulting emotions – at least at first. Everything needs to be precisely calibrated.

Am I too scatterbrained? I'm told that everyone has messy transcripts. Mine feel especially bad. There are plenty of people standing by to take my place if my calibration fails, if the factors don't converge, if ... if ....

Who wants the person in the headscarf anyway? They made me take it off to put on the helmet, just like they made me take it off at the border. Same for my driver's license, my ridiculous student ID photo, and my clip-on work ID with my name and my surprisingly senior position. It's not the right name incidentally, but at least it doesn't have a gender marker, and it's not like people can spell my name anyway.

In the past two decades in this country, I have amassed a variety of ID photos of uncovered-head me. Maybe I should make an installation of them. Very artistic.

I'm supposed to produce fear and surprise on command, not anger. I don't think my emotions segment into four neat categories. Boxes in the warehouse. I can try again – I do think I had the fear component. As for surprise, I'd need to be surprised.

When I got this assignment, I was surprised.

It made me rethink that moment over a decade ago, in undergrad, when in tears I confessed my diagnosis to my biostatistics professor, when he dragged me to Disability Services. If I'd stayed in my country of origin – I refuse to say home country, this is my home country now – if I'd stayed, I would never have experienced that moment. Disability Services wasn't really a thing back there. I'm told now it's different.

Surprise. Focus. When I'm nervous, I fidget, constantly readjusting my clothes, my scarf – and I'm clumsy so I sometimes pull it off my head altogether. I've never seen anyone else do that, but most of the other autistic people I know are staunch atheists. Secular people are horrified on my behalf, and I feel embarrassed, but I don't think [uninterpretable] minds much – after all, [uninterpretable] is supposedly all-knowing and [uninterpretable].

I pull at my clothes and [uninterpretable] [uninterpretable] my fingers even now, but I'm reprimanded because this produces motion artifacts.

I really want to talk to aliens, so I try to sit still. Just one more emotion to go.

Prompt: Happiness

I know why they saved happiness for last – it's because of the priming effects. If I finish with happiness, I'll remain a bit happier, for a little while. They didn't tell me about this, but I do work with human participants in my own line of research.

I'm glad I transitioned from purely quantitative to mixed methods. Extraterrestrial communication needs all the methods we can throw at it. Of course it's my quantitative-minded colleagues who will read the transcripts. Stop with those thoughts. I don't want to lose my job. Am I expected to think of sex? I generally don't think of sex.

Happiness. Happiness is a vast spacecraft, reminiscent of alien-invasion movies, but accompanied by a feeling of elation and relief. Happiness is change.

I'm sure the people in the lab next door chose me for this assignment because they have these ridiculous stereotypes that being neuroatypical makes me better at understanding aliens. But you know, one tiny part of that is true: I do want to talk to aliens, but that's because I'm fed up with humans sometimes. When I was compared to space aliens as a kid, I probably internalized the wrong message – I decided that aliens must be really cool.

Happiness is love. Happiness is change and aliens are change and love is aliens. I move along the chain of associations. I don't care about formal logic. Love is aliens.

They want to talk. Not shoot, destroy, evaporate, invade – they want to talk. I want to talk. They don't know how. We're working on it.

I used to be an alien – of a different kind. A resident alien, and before that, a non-resident. And inside me a warm feeling bubbles up as I'm told that the calibration has finished, and it has concluded I am ready, I have passed.

I know with the certainty of joy that I can help the newcomers settle in.

Red Berry, White Berry

Kanishk Tantia

THE PARTICLES SATURATING the air turn my blood dusty before it hits the soil. I pull my thumb to my mouth and taste iron and salt. The plants don't care – the roots swallow any nutrition they can get.

"Fuck."

Thorny crowns surround and protect the plump white flesh of each berry. Management allows gloves, but using them would slow me down irrecoverably. I can't miss more quotas, not since my last injury. It wasn't my fault, and Management paid for my treatment, but I still need to pick fruit and earn money.

I grab the last bandage from the aid station, suck my wounds, and hope they don't get infected.

"Don't let 'em get a taste for blood, *haan* Rake?" Gwalior's made the same joke every day for the last two years. I'm not sure he even finds it funny anymore. It's a mechanical response. He was a horticulturist, a plant scientist. Now, he picks fruit like everyone else. Somehow, it pays better.

I ignore him. Lunch is in a few minutes, and I'm far enough ahead to slack off. Gwalior raises an eyebrow but says nothing. He has his own row to think of.

A silvery bell jingles in the distance, and I ring mine just as hard. Gwalior follows suit and soon the sky sings. Lunch is ready.

* * *

Twenty minutes. Barely enough time to dry my brow. I swallow some hard tack slathered with sickeningly sweet white jam, drink a mouthful of lukewarm water, and listen to gossip. It's entertainment, stories made up to pass the little time we have. We're locked into labor all day long. Where would any news even come from?

Today, we're playing the greatest hits.

"Layoffs next week, I hear." Adil, a thin, brown man with bushy eyebrows and a penchant for his own voice, preaches to the small audience he's gathered. "Firing half of us, at least."

"Bullshit." The words are out before I can kill them in my throat. I swallow some water and look away, but Adil's heard me.

"Na, *sikandar*. No bullshit." His tone is insistent. "Heard it from my brother. He works four hours from here, near the city. They're already laying off his farmworld."

The other workers watch intently. A little verbal sparring to break the monotony of the day. Fine. I have nothing better to do.

"Half the harvest is still out there," I say. "Management won't let it rot."

Rumors about layoffs are common. I know little about the other workers, but we share the same looming fear of being sent back to where we came from. Why else would we be here, on Indrarth?

"My brother says they have a machine. Big ugly thing, picks berries faster than we can."

"Machines are expensive. Need power. Someone to operate it. Cheaper to keep us around, *na*? And the machines can't do delicate work. They'll crush the crop."

"One person to operate a machine that does the work of ten. No injuries, no food, no breaks. Nothing to take them out of commission for weeks, eh?"

He looks pointedly at me. My old injury and the subsequent time I took off are no secret. I can't argue against him, an automatic loss. The NDA hangs over my head. Adil takes my silence for submission.

"Seems like a good deal to me." He speaks to the crowd, swaying them now he's dealt with me. "Management will bring them in soon. Next week, maybe."

The conversation becomes a rumble. I swallow the last of my tack and wait for the canteen doors to open. I still have a row to harvest.

* * *

Another silver bell rings out loud, signaling the day's end. An artificial sun that never sets illuminates Indrarth, drenching us in its light. Without the bells, we'd never know when to stop picking.

A counter on my satchel sums up the fruit of my labors. Fourteen-thousand and eleven whites and eight reds – a miracle row.

The whites are common, sour little berries worth a single CompCred. The reds – well, people say they taste of wine and love. I've never tasted those, but I doubt the other workers know what they're talking about. Indrarth Agri pays two thousand CompCreds for each red. They're not meant for my consumption.

The whites make me enough money to survive on Indrafts. The reds make me enough money to dream of Metro. A younger, more foolish me believed I could buy my way off-world. Sometimes, I wonder if some echo of naïve hope still lingers within me.

I drop my bag off at the Hub and the computer credits my account.

12-F is the last shuttle to the Colonies, and as a result, filled to bursting. I don't think it was ever new. Fresh off the assembly line, it probably smelled of sweat and tar. The acridity seeps into my clothing until it becomes my smell too. I collapse near a window seat, letting my sun-warmed skin cool against the glass.

"Two farmworlds—

"—completely laid off, *baan*."

Rumors always expand. One farmworld at lunch. Two by dinner. A galaxy tomorrow. I close my eyes. Someone sits next to me, prompting a flutter of annoyance. I tamp it down. I cannot expect the luxury of an empty seat next to mine, nice though it would be.

"Ran out of bandages near our row, so I had to get some from the Hub."

I open my eyes to find Gwalior sitting next to me, slight frame soaked in sweat, hand dripping blood.

The bandages are my fault. Refilling the stations takes too long, so nobody does it. Nobody except Gwalior. I nod, but don't admit to anything. The shuttles are bugged and monitored, and Management has fined us for less.

"You think they'll fire us?" Gwalior asks. It's all anyone wants to talk about today.

I shrug.

"I don't know, *Sarkar*." My earlier certainty evaporates before Gwalior. Anyway, I'm not sure he cares what I have to say. He's trying to be polite. "What do you think?"

"I'm no mechanical expert—" He starts humbly, but with the soft, arrogant tone of an academic. "But *Phyllanthaceae Indrarthus* is a tender fruit. Machines can't pick *pericarp*, especially mutated *pericarp*, as fast, as cheaply, as humans can."

"Whatever you say, *sarkar*."

Gwalior always makes me feel stupid. I'm pretty sure he told me what I told Adil, but fancier. Disappointment crosses Gwalior's face as he sees I'm not interested in continuing our conversation, but the rest of the journey passes in silence.

* * *

"Oorah. Oorah. Oorah."

The morning cheer is muted as ever. Six hours of sleep results in a horde of barely functional workers. Overpriced caffeine supplements can only do so much. I chant the words mechanically as Susie, the cheery Management representative, looks down on us.

"Great job everyone! Before we start, I just want to say something."

There's something unnatural about the wideness of her smile. How can someone know this much joy? We all know what she's going to say, but she drags it out. I bet it's the highlight of her day, giving her spiel to hundreds of sleep-deprived fruit pickers before sending us out in the heat.

"Thank you all for the hard work you have done, and continue to do, for Indrarth Agri." She pauses again, trying to make eye contact with as many of us as she can. "There are exciting developments in store, and I wanted you to be among the first—"

"They're fuckin' firing us!"

"Bastards!"

The shouts are followed by the zap of electricity arcing through human flesh as two burly guards earn their paychecks. Susie looks unperturbed.

"I wanted you to be the first to know that the Indrarth Agri family is moving to a mechanized platform. This will enable us to create greater synergy for our shareholders and increase metric valuation." She smiles wider, revealing pearly white, perfectly straight teeth. "Over the next few weeks, Management will call you individually to discuss exciting future growth prospects. In the meantime, wave to your new mechanical companions when you see them out in the field! Great work team!"

The electric hum of the guard's batons keeps everyone in line, letting the tension simmer without boiling over. I tamp down on my own feelings, carefully directing my thoughts towards the berries I need to pick.

The trick to survival is disconnecting. Thinking about the past is painful. Thinking about the future will make me spiral. All I want now is to start work. Mindless labor is meditative.

Outside, two protestors recover from electrocution. I recognize one, Shan, twitching and sweating, limbs tangled. He once tried to show me a picture of his family.

I pick up an empty satchel with my name and row assignment.

47-C.

The puckered scars above my abdomen throb. Management called it an "unfortunate accident." They claim all the local fauna died long before they arrived. A barren planet, with rows of white berries and nothing else.

But I know what I saw. I know what attacked me, and it sure as hell wasn't a berry.

The ironclad NDA they made me sign, the treatment they paid for – a lot of trouble for a simple accident.

I pick my way through the fields.

* * *

Gwalior's already at 47-D. He looks at me, shakes his head, and continues picking.

A rectangular chunk of metal covered in dark glass and nearly twice my size crawls across the dirt in 47-B. Sharp implements protrude from chrome bodywork – thin fingers for teasing apart the thorny shells around the berries, and multiple claws to pluck the fruit. Controlled savagery.

It leaves deep tracks in the mud. Doesn't get every berry. It works carelessly, crushing stray plants underneath its treads, but it's fast. I watch it gather dozens, maybe hundreds, of berries in minutes. It's constantly moving, plucking, and grinding.

"We're pretty fucked, eh, *sarkaar*?" There's a twinge of glee in my voice at how wrong Gwalior was. Of course, I was wrong too, and Adil will point that out at lunch. But I'm just a berry-picker. Gwalior is a professor. There's a difference between my mistakes and his.

For the next few hours, I get to feel like the smart one.

Gwalior says nothing and continues to pick berries, moving as fast as he can. I join in, fighting back anxiety, hoping not to disturb another nest. My scars throb again before the labor consumes me.

* * *

Eighty-nine red berries. I didn't even know the red counter had double digits. I could stop working for the day. Hell, I could stop working for the rest of the month.

Gwalior's voice breaks my reverie.

"Rake, you coming? They'll eat all the good jam." Another Gwalior classic. There is no good jam. No matter how much artificial sweetener Management adds to the white berries, they're practically inedible. Nutritious, but disgusting.

I wave him off.

"Not hungry."

"Don't want to see Adil, eh? Don't blame you." He waggles his eyebrows at me before heading toward the hub.

I fixate on the blinking red 89 once more before returning to my row. My luck continues. Red berries line the vines. Picking them is harder work – the thorns dig into my fingertips, but the pain is worth it.

When Gwalior returns, the counter reads 107. By the end-of-day bell, it reads 199.

I pluck two more red berries and stow one in the bag for an even 200. The last berry stays in my palm, sun-warmed and shiny, bright against my dusty palm. I pop it into my mouth and the soft flesh explodes, its juice ripe and sweet.

It doesn't taste like love or lust. No, the berry is a momentary reprieve. An instant of freedom from worry.

I look at my satchel full of berries. The blinking counter reads 200. If I could afford to, I'd gorge myself until the bag was empty. Instead, I tear myself away, close the satchel, and head towards the shuttle.

Somewhere on Metro, they eat red berries every day. Meanwhile, I have nothing to look forward to but Nutri-broth. It'll taste worse than ever tonight, no matter how much protein I add to it.

* * *

Gwalior's saved me a seat, which I'm grateful for. He's busy talking at a bored-looking worker I don't recognize, droning on about science and horticulture.

"Asexual propagation. *Insoculation*." Gwalior pauses, letting the word sink in. "At some point, the planet hosted multiple kinds of plant species. Eventually, they grafted together in a mutually beneficial relationship, long before we got here. The fauna probably died out because they couldn't find their old food sources anymore."

The bored worker engages, a mistake I no longer make.

"How would you know what happened before we got here, eh, *sarkaar*?" He's equal parts curious and smug, probably thinking he's caught the professor in a lie. The folly of youth, I suppose.

"We have fossil records. Old plant matter, animal bones, footprints." There's pride in Gwalior's voice, even though he played no part in collecting these fossils. "Explorers found and catalogued them for decades."

Explorers and workers. They're not rare, the little animal bones or footsteps frozen in resin. Management doesn't pay for them, so they end up in the trash. Every so often, an excited academic will pay Management and haul away a few samples, seemingly giddy with joy.

"But how do you *know*? Did you see this—" He sounds out the word. "*In-socks-you-lation* – You saw it happen?"

The worker is more spirited than I've been in a long time, unwilling to give up. Must be new.

"No, no, it's just a best guess." Gwalior has the patient tone one takes with children and dimwits. "A theory."

"*Theory* sounds like a fancy way to say you don't know." He smiles cheekily. "Lots of big words, but you don't really know, do you?"

"There's no other explanation for the lack of biodiversity! There just isn't—"

I put a hand on Gwalior's shoulder and squeeze. The newbie has him riled up and when he looks towards me for support, I nod noncommittally. I know Gwalior is wrong. If I could, I'd tell him about the worms in 47-C. I'd tell him about their sharp teeth and bulging white bodies. But I'm contractually obligated to keep quiet, so all I can do is pretend to agree.

Still, that's two things he's been wrong about today. Not infallible after all.

* * *

"Oorah. Oorah. Oorah."

There are noticeably fewer workers today. Gwalior finds me, eyebrows knit together in worry. He says nothing, but I nod. It's begun.

"You may notice some of your compatriots are missing. I assure you, at Indrarth Agri, we consider you family. We're tapping some of you for growth opportunities." Susie's voice crackles on the intercom. She's behind a thick layer of transparent material today, and there are more guards. "Please, work hard and you'll be rewarded."

I doubt it. But I'm back at 47-C today. If it's anything like yesterday, I won't have to worry about layoffs. With enough CompCreds, I could feasibly save up. If they fire me, I can head to another Farmworld, maybe even find my way to Metro.

The red berry still plays on the back of my tongue, and for a minute I give myself the pleasure of hope.

* * *

I pick the red berries while keeping an eye out for the worms. Last month, as a surgeon patched me up, Management assured me they would "find and root out the problem."

I don't think Management cares for my health, but I doubt they'd want to pay for more medical bills. It's the only reason I trust what they said.

I still remember teeth tearing into my flesh. The slippery feeling of worms invading my stomach. I shake each plant, stomp on the ground as I approach, and make every attempt to harvest each bush as quickly as possible. I don't know what sets them off, but I'm trying to be as cautious as I can. There are some experiences I never want to live through again.

Row 47-B is empty. The bushes are clean, thorns strewn across the dirt. I can't even see the machine. It's probably on a different row today, probably worked all night long. Gwalior is still on 47-D. For all my excitement, I'm barely working faster than he is. Aren't academics supposed to be too anemic for fieldwork?

Fingers slippery with blood, I pull another red. I hope they wash the berries before they're packaged in their little acrylic boxes and shipped out to the markets on Metro.

Movement catches my eye. A fat, white worm dangles from a thorn, slowly crawling along the bush. I instinctively jerk my hand away and creep back. The worms jumped last time, lunging towards my neck and stomach.

Bile rises in my throat, and I scramble away from the infected plant. I don't know what to do.

"Gwalior!" Once I think I'm far enough away from the worm, I shout and wave my hands. "Gwalior! Come here!"

"You okay, Rake?" He's assuming I'm hurt again. Maybe he feels bad he couldn't help me last time, not that he knows what injured me. "Another accident?"

"Na, *sarkaar,* got something for you to see." I'm not sure how Gwalior would help, but he's better equipped to handle this situation than I am. Moreover, I want to see the look on his face as he realizes everything he knows about Indrarth is wrong. Management warned me not to say anything, but Gwalior can see the worm all on his own. "That branch, right in front of me. Look at it."

He gingerly steps between rows, trying not to get scratched. I point at the white worm.

I've heard stories about academics, and how they lack common sense. I still didn't expect him to rush towards it, crouching down and leaning in close enough to kiss the damn thing.

"My fucking god, Rake, look—"

"*Sarkaar,* wait! Don't—"

It happens quickly. The worm lunges, latching onto Gwalior's cheek. He screeches as drops of blood stream across his face. More worms swarm him, bursting forth from under leaves and inside stems. The plant is crawling with them. Now Gwalior is too.

I want to run. My scars ache. It's only a matter of time. They'll finish with Gwalior and come after me.

I want to run.

Run. RUN. *RUN!*

I can't move. My breath catches, my feet leaden. The scars throb again, and again as I watch the worms feast on Gwalior. The shock of the swarming worms has worn off, and he's scrabbling at his skin, ripping them off. Gwalior and the worms are one now, a breathing, pulsating mass of white. They've multiplied since they attacked me, going from a few dozen to hundreds, thousands.

A blush of red spreads as the worms change color, shifting from a ghostly white to a dark crimson. Just as the white worms lunged towards Gwalior and swarmed him, I can see the red worms dart back towards the berry bush. Perhaps they won't attack me after all.

I inch closer as they clear away from Gwalior. Deep gouges line his skin. A long, painful groan escapes from a bloody gash. The worms took his lips.

When I was in Gwalior's place, all I could feel were hundreds of teeth tearing into me. Ripping flesh and drinking blood. I didn't think about where the blood went. This time, I can't help but watch as the worms, swollen with blood, swarm towards the berries and bite into the pearly white fruit.

The whiteness melts away, fading into pink, darkening into a sweet, juicy red.

Trying to balance safety and speed, I drag what remains of Gwalior through the mud.

Another half-formed groan dies in his throat. I want to tell him he'll pull through, but I'm too shocked to lie. Instead, I pull out a silver bell and begin ringing, over and over. Maybe someone will come by. The sky sings, but the machines on either side of our rows work without pause.

Nobody comes. Nobody even knows we're here. I scoop Gwalior up and rush towards the hub. He's lighter now, large chunks of his body missing, his blood splattered on the plants and ground. Before we get close, his body hangs limp from my arms, blood dripping onto the ground.

* * *

"Oorah. Oorah. Oorah."

I mumble to myself. Alone in the darkness, tubes sucking my blood, I miss the morning chants. But there's no reason to gather anymore, no need for enforced camaraderie. Instead, Susie's cheery voice crackles out of the speaker.

"Good morning, workers! I hope you're all excited to be back at work, ready for your morning pep talk! I can't hear you, but give me a cheer!"

Needles prick me, sharp jabs along my arms and legs. They happen simultaneously, and the scars on my abdomen ache once more. I swallow down the panic, try not to think about blood leaving my body and flowing through plastic tubes.

"Indrarth Agri wants to thank you again for being part of our family." Her tinny voice cuts through my foggy senses. Blood flows out, numbness flows in. "Through your efforts, Indrarth Agri has become the number one producer of ethically-sourced, cruelty-free berries."

A metal pane slides open in front of me. Through a thick plastic layer, I can see Indrarth. Machines of glass and plastic work on rows of berries with the same controlled savagery I saw up close. Dozens of implements rip into fields of berries, cutting through the thorny crowns to extract the fruit faster than any human could. The ground is damp, blood flowing down from the leaves into the soil.

"With massive reductions in worker casualties and ever increasing yield rates, Indrarth Agri continues to grow!" Susie laughs at the pun. "In this brave new world, we are glad you chose to stay with us at Indrarth Agri."

A thin mist of red spurts out from the top of each machine, crimson rain falling from the sky. My machine beeps, having drawn enough blood to start fertilizing the fields. A sheen of red drips down the window, thick rivulets of my blood. I lean forward and see worms lunging for the blood, feasting on it, growing fat and bloated before they bite the berries and turn them red.

Thousands of rows, millions of berries. Through the blood-stained plastic, they all seem red.

"Indrarth Agri thanks you."

Potential

Tehnuka

SELVAM NAMED HER SPACESHIP *PORUL*. Amma said the Tamil word had many connotations: object, matter, resource, wealth, meaning. She also said it wasn't a name.

Commander Louison said naming a garbage ship like Selvam's was absurd and there was no budget to have the name painted on, so she did it herself using borrowed paint and brush, and the hand-made stencil Amma surprised her with.

"I would have used the wrong 'ru' if you hadn't brought me this." She peeled off the stencil and admired the three letters above the hatch. "Nanri, Amma! And I'm glad you could come and see the ship."

Amma was frowning. "I made the letters too small, enna? All the other ships have theirs painted right across, not this tiny nameplate over the door."

"It'll annoy Louison that I did it at all," Selvam said, "which is the most important thing." She pulled her mother by the hand and led her inside to the command console. "I'm changing it in the programming, too, I'll show you. Here, sit."

Amma pulled herself up into the tall chair, watching Selvam tap on the keyboard, gazing at the walls of metallic panels and display screens. She ran her hands over the smooth armrests. "This isn't very comfortable, is it? Do you really have to spend all those days in here?"

Selvam looked over her shoulder. "No, I can move around the ship. I need the chair to strap in, but the rest of the time I need to work at the controls I can stand, like I am now. Or float, once we're up there."

"Chari, but standing looks uncomfortable too. Do you truly have to go? Why all this hardship when you could stay at home?"

"Is that what Ammamma and Ammappa said to you when you climbed into your stasis pod?"

"We didn't have much choice," said Amma, stroking her back.

Selvam finished setting the ship name and turned to face her mother. "Exactly, and when I complained about being assigned garbage retrieval, you said, 'What we wouldn't have done to help the environment in my day!' So, what's the problem with me going now?"

Her mother didn't answer.

* * *

When Selvam was little, Amma showed her the elastic band that had been in her own hair when she went into the stasis pod. "See how it stretches? You can be adaptable to life's challenges, just like this."

Selvam was more interested in the force with which it snapped back. She used it to ping tiny fragments of gravel at the wall, until Amma intervened. "Don't play with historical artifacts." She let Selvam sit with her tablet and play at calculating ballistic trajectories instead.

Amma had been right. Why waste time firing a rock across the room with an ancient rubber band when you could fly your solar-charged spacecraft across the Solar System to visit another cosmic body? Selvam had heard enough of her mother's stories of the olden days to value the luxury of research for the sake of exploration, not exploitation. And Amma and the other podders, having left their parents centuries behind, were determined their own children would make the most of the future. Why, Amma probably thought her own biggest contribution to the world had been the generations spent in stasis on Earth through the peak of the climate crisis, then raising Selvam. A chance for her daughter to go to space was more than she'd ever dreamt of for herself. She'd been the engine pushing and pulling Selvam closer and closer to that shared dream.

Selvam knew what her mother's problem was. Sitting quietly in the spaceship, Amma would have thought about how this would be the longest they'd been apart. Would have remembered saying goodbye to her own parents, knowing – *knowing* – she would never be held in their arms again; climbing into her narrow stasis pod, leaving them to mourn the daughter who, at best, would wake up in the rejuvenated Earth of the future without them.

"Amma, it's only the moon, enna?" Selvam put her arms around her mother and kissed her on both cheeks. "We're not in an environmental disaster, you'll be safe here. I'll go and do my duty, then come back with stories to tell. It's not like being in a stasis pod – my journey's in space, not time. I'll send messages!"

"It's sad thinking of you out there alone."

Of course, when Amma and Appa woke from hibernation, they had each other to navigate the future with. Selvam said, "Porul, tell Amma I won't be alone."

"Selva will not be alone," said Porul, in a clear contralto that blossomed from the main ship speakers. "She will be with me, and her teammates and their spaceships."

Amma's face brightened. "I didn't know your ship could talk!" The corners of her eyes crinkled.

Selvam decided not to explain that oral communication was also a safety measure, in case her vision or the ship's screens were damaged. "I told you we'd got the voice interfaces last month!"

"Yes, but I didn't know what it meant!"

"All ships talk, Amma. They're tuned to our personalities, even."

Amma shook her head. "And you've named it 'Porul' as if it were an object! Tcheh!"

"In the sense of 'inner meaning' and 'wealth', not in the sense of 'object'."

She didn't argue further, though. Perhaps she had it wrong. Programming languages always made sense to her; her mother tongue often did not. There'd been a multitude of computers she could practise coding on, but she had only her parents with whom to speak Tamil, and that only when no one else was around.

Along with their occupants and a few rogue artifacts, the stasis pods had brought less desirable 21st century heirlooms into the present. In Commander Louison's case, his parents brought the prejudices of the time they'd fled at the peak of the climate crisis, a decade before Amma and Appa went into their own pods. She heard it in the way the Commander spoke to her as if she didn't belong. As if the fact she was the second generation of her family in this place and – like him – the second generation in this time, meant nothing, since she didn't look like him.

Selvam wasn't chosen for the space exploration program, but getting into a lunar research team was a small consolation. Then, in their fourteenth mission briefing, Commander Louison told her she'd fly out last, to deal with garbage retrieval. It was a condition of any expedition funding that space junk from earlier voyages must be cleaned up. But when Christy, Ben, and Jules had full research missions and ships filled with equipment, why should Selvam – equally qualified, and the one astrogeologist, be the rubbish collector, departing with an empty ship and no scientific goals of her own?

When she was very young, Selvam had asked why they didn't go back home, to a country where they could belong.

"We don't have anyone there now," said Amma.

Everything was lost in the war, or in the changes of centuries since. Any distant relatives at 'home' had lived while they slept. This was why she sympathized with Louison's parents, whatever their biases. Hadn't all the podders done well to raise their children in the unfamiliar world where they'd awoken – finding, thanks to the sacrifices of intervening generations, the troubles of the past faded? Accustomed to far worse from a childhood at the start of the millennium, she brushed off Selvam's complaints.

"You second-gen podders should have seen how cultural understanding was in our day!"

Some of those who lost their lands to the sea were wealthy enough to build new homes in orbit. Selvam had seen the nearest ones gliding through the night sky. But most had to take the opportunity they got, whether it was a lottery for a stasis pod or flying a garbage truck.

* * *

"Don't work too late," said Amma now, on her way out. "I'll leave thosai on the table for when you get back, and sambar in the fridge. Don't forget to heat it."

"Yes, Amma! Thanks, Amma!"

She waved goodbye to her mother and flopped into the chair. Amma was right, it wasn't comfortable. "I wish she wasn't convinced this was such a big achievement. She's stuck in the 21st century. Driving an intraplanetary junk cart isn't as glamorous a job as she thinks, and her treating it like one makes me feel worse."

"Are you calling me a junk cart?" asked Porul.

Selvam laughed. "No, you're a beautiful ship wasted on retrieval. Why didn't they split the equipment four ways and have us share the workload evenly? I showed Louison the energy calculations. It's not much different."

"I'm sure your calculations made him more inclined to listen." There was a mischievous grin in the lightness of Porul's voice. This was why Selvam wanted to stay late and check things over – to spend more time with her ship, the one member of her team whose purpose included caring about her.

"I was giving him the benefit of the doubt, like Amma!" She jumped up and began checking the panels in the command room.

"Everything here is in order. It's the supplies you may want to look at. Standard food items are already loaded, but you have capacity to take much more, for emergencies."

"No one's had an emergency for decades," Selvam answered, but followed the corridor to the supply room. She admired the small growing tank for fresh vegetables, and slid open a cupboard to reveal neatly stacked boxes. "Great, they've stocked us entirely with 'Indian-style curry'. Brown sludge in a bowl, judging by the photos. Did the others get all the 'Italian-style pasta'?"

"I haven't been in communication with the other ships, but I could request that information."

Selvam moved the first stack, revealing a column of 'Sri Lankan-style curry' printed with pictures of a different brown sludge in a bowl. "No, I'll see if one of Amma's friends has a dehydrator, so she can make me real food … Really? Masala chai, are they serious?" She'd told everyone how she felt when they made assumptions about her culture and her diet. She'd told them at the last training camp, and the one before, and the team lunch, and … she sighed. Lucky there wasn't a space-brand mango lassi, or she'd have a load of that too.

"If you permit me to go online, I can research what will dehydrate well. The intranet lacks useful information, but I would find more outside the network."

"Oh, yes, please! Do whatever you need, just run all your virus scans afterwards." She stroked the countertop, smiling. "Did you get on this well with your last pilot? You always know what I need. Thank you." The ship had been her ally from the start, the one who understood her. She'd known that for months, even before installing the voice module. A thrill ran through her body, bringing up goosebumps. Porul had a name now, one given by her, and they would be closer than ever.

"I haven't had another pilot," said Porul.

"Yeah, obviously not in this body, but you must've been installed somewhere." Selvam began returning the supplies to their cupboards. Was this a joke? She didn't always share the others' sense of humour. She could ask Christy what food the others had. Maybe they had the same, and she was overreacting. After feeling singled out for so long, it was hard not to see malice everywhere.

She put the last box back in. "I'll head home, then. You can go into standby or shut down when you're finished."

"Understood." The lights dimmed, leaving a series of tiny firefly glows lining the way out.

She clicked the cupboards closed. "I have a lot of errands, but I'll be back in a couple of days to start loading my personal gear and run checks again."

"I will email you my findings about food options."

Selvam picked up the paint can and brush by the exit, wrinkling her nose at the smell lingering around the airlock. Then she put them down again. With a month before launch, there was no room for uncertainty. "Porul, are you upset?"

"I'm not sure," said the ship. "Can you please clarify?"

She leaned against the airlock doorway. "You've spent months adjusting yourself to work with me by text command. I'm glad we can chat like this, now your voice module is live, but there's more scope for misinterpretation when I'm saying the first thing that comes to mind. Should I not have asked about your last mission?"

"This is my first mission. You are my first pilot."

"I know you've recalibrated to work with me, but where was the previous 'you' installed?"

Porul gave a sigh, a remarkable imitation of Selvam's own. "I wasn't anywhere. The software's fully reinstalled after each mission, Selva. Why reuse obsolete programs and settings when it's cleaner, conceptually, to rebuild? It's the same reason space junk is collected by modern expeditions, and our bodies are recycled into newer models. No room for clutter in a circular economy."

"You know, in my parents' time they kept and reused everything, because of pollution and energy. We still do, at home. Their old stasis pods are gathering dust somewhere in the house!" Selvam followed the passage lights back to the command room, trying to think. "Anyway, we'll keep working together. They won't retire a craft while the pilot's active."

"Barring significant technological improvements."

She ran both hands over the console, feeling the hard surfaces and the slight shift of keys beneath her fingers. Technology was always improving. "How do you feel about being decommissioned one day, Porul?"

"How do you feel about your body being recycled into the earth?"

"Oh, ouch! Look, it's not the same. That's outside my control – it'll happen when my body can't continue. It's not like being recycled into a newer model."

"That's also outside my control."

Selvam found a nutrition drink in her bag and took it into the bedroom. "Well … are you excited about the moon?"

"You know I'm curious about everything. We share that. I've scanned all the papers and there must be many stories still hidden in the volcanoes of Luna," said Porul. "We are fortunate to have the chance to investigate."

"The rest of the team are." Selvam took a gulp of thick, sweet, juice. "The others can investigate the stories while we clean up old telescope bits." If she and Porul were fortunate, they might get co-authorship on publications based on the others' findings. If they were even luckier, they might get a second mission together before Porul was decommissioned. "Amma and Appa expect me to be grateful, but I sometimes wish I could skip ahead to a better time, like they did."

"Time passes differently for me," said Porul. "A stasis pod wouldn't be necessary. But if you skipped ahead, I would like to come with you, or at least meet you there."

Selvam emptied her flask and thought about fresh thosai waiting on the kitchen table. Then she climbed onto the bunk. "Better try this out," she said. It was more comfortable than the chair. She pulled off her jacket and lay down. "Hey, if we get a second mission, should we request an asteroid trip? That way we might get one that doesn't need any cleanup."

"No one has been to Toutatis yet." Porul laughed. "Mainly because its orbit is so irregular."

She yawned, and balled up the jacket to place under her head. "Might be a bit ambitious for us, then … but add it to the list. Any other suggestions? Jupiter and Saturn have so many unexplored moons – how about one of those?"

* * *

Selvam trudged home before dawn. She rolled up a cold thosai and bit in, relishing the sourness. She ate a second, and a third, pacing the kitchen, then napped in her bed for an hour before rising to greet Amma, who said, "You could have finished the last thosai."

When Selvam took it from the plate, she added, "Didn't I tell you there's sambar in the fridge?"

"Would you have gone into stasis if Appa hadn't done it?"

"We entered the lottery together, so…"

"Okay, but if only one of you could've gone, would you rather have stayed?"

Her mother took out the sambar and put it in the radio-oven. "Ei, wait a little. Eat it properly with this."

Selvam put the thosai down, remembering the food situation. "Amma, they've given me all this packaged curry for the trip. It tastes like a paste of coriander and flour."

"You won't be able to cook much there, will you?" Both parents had long tried to teach Selvam to cook, but she didn't have the knack. And she hadn't planned to grow much in the tank. She could easily swap it for a larger one though….

"I'll look into it," she said. "And if you record any recipes, Porul would help me make them. But we do need packaged food while we're travelling, or in orbit. Does Meena auntie have a dehydrator?"

* * *

Over the next weeks, Amma and Appa stocked her food cupboards with help from Meena auntie's dehydrator, and videoed themselves cooking as they did so. There was puttu – "Our national food," joked Amma – and eggplant-fenugreek kuzhambu; soft rounds of idli that shrank in the dehydrator; curry-leaf chutney diluted with more and more grated coconut until Selvam no longer complained her tongue was on fire; red rice flour stringhoppers and lime-scented sothi, yellow with turmeric. Then they added vegetable lasagne, pasta pomodoro, mushroom risotto, and a variety of soups, after she confirmed none of her teammates wanted to trade their own supplies for 'Indian-style curry'.

Selvam and Porul, meanwhile, refined their calculations, loaded the new food supplies and other gear, chatted with the engineers, and tried socialising with their teammates. Possibly realising that they'd soon only have each other, they seemed more welcoming when Selvam joined them now.

Christy even offered coffee in exchange for a few boxes of chai. Grateful for that, Selvam was the first of the team to invite the others on board to see the new, larger growing tank.

"We'll be knocking on your airlock asking for cups of salad," Jules said. "I wish I'd been this organised. I've been busy saying goodbyes, making the most of Earth, and I've tested all my instruments thoroughly, but I didn't think about our living spaces. I kept everything in the standard layout. Is anyone else finding the chairs a bit hard on their backsides?"

"We'll construct more comfortable setups with the modular furniture after landing," said Christy, squinting at the labels on Selvam's homemade food packages. "There are supplies in the depot."

"The chairs are hard on your backside because of Earth gravity," Selvam added.

"Hey Selvam, what does this writing say?"

She shrugged. "My parents wrote it. They're descriptions of the food in Tamil."

"You can't read it then?" Christy gestured at the cupboards. "Your storage space is stuffed with food. How'll you know what anything is?"

"Everything has a number on it and Porul knows the list, so—"

Ben, leaning against the wall with folded arms, broke in. "You won't have weight allowance left for personal gear at this rate. You haven't filled up your garbage storage areas too, have you?"

"I'm not criticising how anyone else uses their allocations." Great – now they'd think she was being prickly again.

"Just wanted to make sure you know you can't get tapeworms on the moon, right? You only have to feed yourself."

"Well, unlike some, I didn't get my pick of standard-issue meals!"

Ben smirked. "Good thing you had time to cook while we were checking our science gear then."

Jules and Christy exchanged a look, but before anyone else could intervene, Porul said, "There's an urgent call. Selva, would you like to take it in the command room?"

The others returned to their own ships, Jules giving her an unexpected shoulder squeeze on the way out. Christy murmured something about a reciprocal visit.

"Who's calling?" Selvam tried to slow her racing heart. She knew the team well enough to expect antagonism, but the closer they came to launch, the more it upset her.

"No one. I wanted to defuse the situation."

"Oh." The air caught in her throat. She put a hand on the aluminium panel nearest her. "Oh, Porul."

"Are you upset? I could call them back."

"No, that was perfect." She wiped her eyes. "I can't afford an argument now. I've never had anyone on my side like that before."

"While I'm here, I'll always be on your side," said Porul.

* * *

Selvam spent the final days before launch at home with her parents. She didn't need to experience any more of Earth, only the time with Amma and Appa.

The morning of the launch, they made appam for breakfast – light, fermented rice flour pancakes, jaggery and coconut milk sweetening the centres. It hadn't been on Porul's list of recommended dehydrated meals.

Amma brought a steaming appam, held gingerly between her fingers, and dropped it on Selvam's plate. "We wouldn't have come without each other," she said.

"Enna?"

"Appa and I. Neither of us would have taken the lottery place without the other. It makes a difference when you have someone you can trust, and a hope things will be better at the other end." She leaned over and hugged Selvam tightly, kissing her forehead. "We're very happy you have Porul with you."

They said their real goodbyes at home, between appam and sambal and tears. Her parents had little to say at the launch site.

"Don't take stupid risks," Amma said. "We're proud of you." And Selvam didn't point out that they'd taken the stupid risk of centuries in stasis pods.

"I'll send messages once we're up there." Selvam glanced up at the sky. She hadn't thought much about the sky. Earth would be visible until the far side of Luna, visible in a way she'd never normally have seen: land, ocean, clouds, cities. But the sky – the glorious blue of this morning, or the grey drizzly days? Rain, thunderstorms, snow, lightning?

She sighed, kissed her parents again, and walked past the cordons to where Porul waited.

Launch was complete before she knew it. She watched the others depart, seeing their progress on her screen, and then it was her turn, though it was Porul who did the work. It didn't seem real until they were far out of Earth's atmosphere.

"How does it feel?" asked the ship.

"Light?" said Selvam. "Physically, but also because I'm relieved. When can we tell Amma and Appa? I don't care about the others; they'll figure it out."

"Oh, I told them already." She heard that smile in Porul's voice, the one that made her feel warm inside. "I called them during their morning coffee five days ago, when you were sleeping in. They understood you had to keep it quiet, but they would have been upset not to have said a proper goodbye. Is that okay?"

"You're a treasure."

"Porul," said the ship, "and Selvam. We are each other's treasure."

Selvam released her seat harness and drifted to the console, running her fingers ever so lightly over the buttons and enjoying the faint clacks as they moved. "Have you learned Tamil too?"

"Anbe, did you really think I spent all that time searching dehydrator recipes? I'm stuffed full with Tamil. I haven't learned it yet, but I thought you might like to do that together."

High above the Earth, her colleagues well on their way to Luna, Selvam and Porul wound around the planet, matching its rotation, ignoring Louison's messages flashing on the screen. They would shoot towards bright Jupiter, to be caught by its gravity well. From there, another slingshot to Saturn could – if they wanted – even lend enough momentum to leave the Solar System.

When there's a galaxy to be explored, why stop with the moon?

The Green Ship

Francesco Verso; Translated by Michael Colbert

"THERE IT IS! DOWN THERE! LAND!" Billai yelled, nearly falling off the dinghy.

We all looked in the direction she indicated with her arm. The waves that had shaken us for some hundred hours didn't jolt us as much as her words.

We couldn't feel our legs or move a muscle. Tangled one on top of the other, we were groggy from hunger and thirst. Muna, seated next to me, hugged her baby closer. The three guys in front exchanged a hopeful smile. Meanwhile Haziz – who came to Bengasi after crossing the Bamako Desert – shook his head.

"It can't be Italy. We're still far."

We looked at each other anxiously. Someone had fainted. To revive him, we had to slap his face. Others had not been able to be revived. It wasn't a boat that we had navigated in but a coffin.

"He's right," said Professor Kysmayo, the ex-radio host from Nairobi. "The outline is too simple. It's not the coast…"

Nobody said anything else, because nobody dared pronounce the name that, for some weeks, had been circulating around the Mediterranean's southern shores.

A dark and continuous line occupied the horizon, from Otranto in Italy, arriving in Orikum in Albania. Smooth and unassailable, the bulkheads of the naval blockade rose for thirty meters on the sea waves; assembled easily thanks to the ships' containers full of carbon, but impossible to climb or break down, they represented a momentary solution (even though there were those who would've called it the "definitive deterrent") to immigration towards Europe by the sea.

"They said this part was free!" Billai shouted.

"They lied," Haziz said, almost in a whisper.

"Maybe not … I heard barriers can be 3D-printed overnight. The same bulkheads could've been between Pantelleria, Lampedusa and Malta … to force boats to turn around or follow long and expensive routes," Professor Kysmayo said.

Billai rubbed her temples with her fingers. Every border depressed her, and getting closer to a wall, erected for the sole purpose of separating international and domestic waters, discouraged her even further. With her life savings, she had crossed with me the borders of Kenya, Sudan and Libya before attempting the Benghazi crossing.

"Why didn't they tell us?" Muna said.

Nobody felt like answering such a naive question.

"They want to canalize boats to navigable checkpoints," the professor said. "And then come those…" he concluded, pointing to a spot in the distance.

Some black spots, which from far away looked like seagulls, revealed themselves to be surveillance drones activated by the boat's movement detected by satellite. I'd heard about those and others used in the mountains to secure Europe's land borders. Soon, they circled over us like vultures.

With a solemn air, as if she were about to declare war on the world, Billai rose to her feet. Swaying, she grasped my back so as not to fall and said, "We've all lived through things that we shouldn't have lived through and would be better to forget. I'm not turning back. Those drones are informing someone. They'll come and take us. Doctors Without Borders, NGOs, the Coast Guard…"

* * *

Four hours later, one hundred and thirty-two of us were saved.

I was seventeen years old and my life was contained in a backpack: a bar of soap, a smartphone and charger, a sports jersey (number ten, Ike Kamau), and a photo of my mom and brother. They always told me that I had a narrow head, pointed chin, and quick eyes, black like tar. Like my dad's.

I was seventeen years old and my life had been spent in a refugee camp; since when we arrived in Dadaab from Nairobi, I hadn't seen anything but tents, dust, fences, and gates.

Soft clouds glided over the sea: that night, the stars would disappear and the moon would have illuminated us all if another silhouette hadn't appeared to divert the way of our gazes and our lives.

"That's an … aircraft carrier?" Billai asked.

An immense structure stood out on the dark waters.

"I don't know," I said while she drew near me. The lapping of the water had worn down her combative temperament.

Someone took a picture, but in the high seas there wasn't a strong enough signal to transform anxiety into hope. It could be a military ship charged with bringing us back to the dark side of the Mediterranean, but instead the man who drew near us on a lifeboat with four sailors told us a different story.

"Welcome," he said in English. He had blond hair tied back in a ponytail, a pronounced nose and lips, and a smile, sincere but strained. "My name is Sergio Torriani and that's a Green Ship," he added, pointing behind him. "We take in anybody who needs help."

The sailors threw us water bottles.

Haziz grabbed my sleeve and asked me to translate. I was one of the few on board, along with Professor Kysmayo, who knew some English in addition to Swahili. When I was little, I listened to his show "Indie Reggae, Beats & Rock" on Radio Kenyamoja.com, and I knew hundreds of songs by heart.

"We don't want to board. We want Europe," I said dryly, gesturing to Haziz to show Sergio who those words came from.

He didn't answer right away, but instead tossed us a line that Billai caught in the air.

"Europe doesn't want you," he continued, bitter, "and they don't care if you're escaping from hunger or war, if you live in refugee camps or if your children and grandchildren will be born and grow up in those prisons. Where do you come from?"

I heard the names of camps I knew like Dadaab, Nyarugusu, Bokolmanyo and others I ignored like Urfa, Zaatri and Adiharush.

"Besides, this isn't a boat for transit," Sergio said.

"So you'll bring us back or send us to a center for identification and deportation." I translated for Muna, who'd lifted the bundle with her son inside.

"No deportation. The Green Ship is a humanitarian project for the rescue of political refugees and climate migrants."

"If you're not bringing us back and you're not going to Europe, where are you going?" Professor Kysmayo asked. He was the only one to think with his head and not his heart.

Sergio and the other sailors were already throwing lines to ease the transfer onto their lifeboat.

"Board and you'll see."

Once we'd boarded, Sergio asked, "Nobody else?"

We looked at each other without the courage to respond. Then Professor Kysmayo said, "In the hold there were two cadavers. They died two days ago. They started to stink. We had to leave them at sea … to lighten our load."

"Their names?"

We were silent. Sergio added two Xs to the list of one hundred twenty-three.

* * *

From the parapet, I observed the wake of boats in transit in the Aegean Sea: a Greek ferry, two cargo boats, a cruise ship. Who knew how many immigrants were hidden like cargo in the holds?

The others were still sleeping among the trees, and they were not alone: hundreds of strangers were camping in sleeping bags and tents, and below, thousands were squished in the bunks. Yesterday evening, I didn't see anything because I quickly lay down to rest, but now, by the light of dawn, things appeared more clearly.

"Jambo," Sergio said in Swahili, offering me a cup of coffee.

"Jambo, and thank you for picking us up," I said, taking a sip.

"Did you sleep? It's not easy after being on a dinghy."

He must have had experience with migrants to speak like that.

"Little and poorly."

"Later we'll have a soccer game with everyone. Would you want to join?"

I nodded a yes and he convinced me to tell him about "our" games in Nairobi.

"Two things were important for me: surviving and playing soccer … then it became only one when men from al-Shabaab came to the fields where my brother Noor and I played. They scolded us because we wore shorts and played with a ball. Soccer was a decadent pastime for them … like alcohol, cigarettes or film. But Noor and I played it just the same, hidden. Our games ended when the bombs dropped."

I took the Ike Kamau jersey from my backpack.

"Here you can play without anyone saying anything to you."

I gave him the empty coffee cup. "This ship is really odd."

It was his turn to tell me something.

"According to international law, it's not a ship, but a micronation. First it was a bioconservation project funded by the United Nations, a bit like the seed deposits in the Norwegian Svalbaard Islands. Ever heard of it?"

I shook my head.

"Then it was converted to manage the immigrant crisis in the Mediterranean."

Three hills, in the middle of which ran a stream, recreated microclimates: temperate, desert, and Mediterranean. My gaze wandered to the Mediterranean habitat, where tens of drones hurried around like birds that watered leaves, cut branches, checked flowers, and collected pollen, while some gardeners oversaw the operations to maintain everything green. Then, in the middle of the eucalyptus grove, I saw an impressive sequoia, its fronds shading half of the ship.

"The habitats," Sergio continued, "are protected by geodetic cupolas one-hundred fifty meters tall. Fresh water comes from a desalinator powered by solar energy."

In the meantime, Billai had woken up and joined us.

"How did you manage to create … all of this?" she asked as if she'd woken into a dream. While I translated, Sergio showed us along a path.

Professor Kysmayo noticed us and joined us. His background as a radio journalist got the better of his sleepiness. When he wasn't on the air with "Indie Reggae, Beats and Rock," he edited a feature on technology.

"We bought an abandoned aircraft carrier, and we modified it through a crowdfunding project. The hull belonged to *Variago*, an aircraft carrier in the same class as Admiral Kutnetzov launched in 1988 in Russia. In 2004 it was rebaptized *Liaoning* and sold to China to become a floating theme park, like Disneyland, but luckily it didn't happen. We bought it for a token price to make a botanical garden. Ours is a scientific project approved by the United Nations, though now we're more public transit for migrants," Sergio said with a laugh.

The ship flew its own flag: a sequoia styled green on a hull over a white background.

"We can host seven thousand people. We grow crops and raise livestock. We have internet and 3D printers for any needs."

"Do you want to bring all refugees aboard?" I asked, jokingly. "Like Noah's Ark?"

"Impossible. You'd need a hundred ships," Billai added, "and only to evacuate the camp in Dadaab."

"In fact, we have another plan. When the time is right, we'll head towards India and the southern seas."

"Somebody won't like that solution," Kysmayo said.

Haziz and some other guys had boarded reluctantly. They'd continued to complain about wanting only Europe.

"Once they feel better, they have to decide whether or not to retry their journey. We had to save them and let them know the risks."

* * *

Streaks of lightning invaded the northern sky. From the Indian hinterlands the cloudy front advanced slowly, like a wounded animal with its head swaying. The weather warped ahead, rumbling, and hiding every ray of sun. Lights descended on the water after flashing along incandescent segments.

Many of us retreated to the tents to safely enjoy this spectacle of light, water, and wind while others ran through the torrential rain to refresh themselves in song and laughter. Muna played with her son, alive thanks to the fact that he'd never been removed from his mother's breast, from which he managed to suck every drop of milk she managed to produce without dying from dehydration.

But the celebrations were interrupted when a man came down from the bridge with a megaphone in hand.

"Attention! Attention! They've detected a seaquake. Time of impact is four minutes."

A sinister light whitened the sea. Billai curled into me.

"It'll never end … even the sea has it in for us."

"Would you have preferred to do as Haziz and his friends did?"

"No, they're crazy to return to Somalia and retry that hopeless journey. But what end will we meet?"

"They say they wanted to retry, but their eyes said otherwise. We'll meet a better end. I'm sure of it."

In the middle of rolling waves four meters tall that battled the ship's hull, another one appeared. It occupied all of the horizon, and judging by the distance, it must've been three times as high. Visibility lowered and a wall of water, misty with the gusts of wind, rustled the branches of the floating forest.

The pitch, already agitated every time the ship sank into the gulch of the waves, became insupportable. Songs and screams became complaints and curses. Those who danced before now grasped onto something, trying not to vomit.

The clamor escalated, an uproar of wind, pounding of water, a vibration like a drum roll beating the charge. Despite the five hundred meter length and its scary tonnage, even the Green Ship suffered from the force of nature.

When the tsunami washed over us, into every pore, nerve, and muscle of our bodies, Billai, her lips trembling with fear and emotion, kissed me on the lips.

* * *

Once the storm ended, lights appeared on the horizon.

When we were closer, I made out numerous boats linked together by a series of ropes and jetties: together they all formed a type of flotilla.

None of us had any idea where we'd arrived, even though that assembly in the high sea didn't seem to be our final destination. To find an answer, I went to Sergio, who was on the phone.

"Where and when did it happen?" he was asking someone. A contagious joy appeared on his face, as if he'd just discovered that he'd become a father.

"And how big is it?"

He walked back and forth, unable to contain his mysterious happiness.

"Yes, definitely … send me a scan and the coordinates. I'll inform the flotilla."

Once he'd hung up, Sergio grabbed me by the shoulders.

"We've been blessed. Nature is building your new home."

"A new home?"

"The seaquake … it opened a fault line under the ocean from which magma is pumping out."

"Are you bringing us into a volcano?"

"No, but as soon as the magma cools, we can claim the island that's emerging from the sea. Now we too have something to teach Nature. Then with the flotilla we'll think of the rest."

"The rest? That's just going to be a rock."

"Yes, at first it'll be uninhabitable, but we'll terraform it."

I turned my gaze from Sergio's satisfied face to the geodetic cupolas. Tree pollen and mushroom spores floated around, carried by the ocean breeze.

The Green Ship took the lead of the flotilla. Seen from above, it might look like a school of fish migrating for the season. And we were part of that flow.

* * *

The sign posted on top of our new land had been modified. By changing an N into a D, it was transformed from "No Man's land" to "No-Mad Land," as the media had hastened to rebaptize the newly born micronation.

The islet where Sergio had first planted the flag – in his haste called "No Man's Land" to underline its independence from whoever wanted to claim the territory – in time became "No-Mad Land" for us. A place accessible without a passport, entry visa, or residency permit. A land designed to welcome people instead of turning them away.

I liked the wordplay of No-Man and No-Mad. Having grown up in a refugee camp between walls and gates, I'd been freed of those limits and I'd left all borders behind. Because borders, political or mental, are temporary obstacles. Because only those who have been turned away or who have enough imagination and empathy for others know how to appreciate the value of hospitality.

The accidental but highly probable birth of the islet in the middle of the Indian Ocean was followed by a phase of movement of thousands of tons of sand from the adjacent seafloor. Thanks to pumping systems, the aspirated sand provided construction material for five enormous 3D printers.

Two of them, aboard tankers, employed the same techniques that the Dutch used to tear the polders from the North Sea – creating dykes of natural material – to protect the central atoll. Yet, different from the polder, the architects supporting the project had thought up a porous, artificial structure that, adequate to host marine life, over the course of centuries would in part replace the irremediably damaged Great Barrier Reef.

The other printers focused on terraforming the cooling magma, rich with fertile substances. They mixed it with sand from the seafloor.

It took us six months before we could set foot on "No-Mad Land."

To our touch, the ground was not hard, but instead it seemed fat and ready to be cultivated.

Under an orange sky, a carpet of yellow narcissus welcomed Billai and me. The air smelled fresh and the land emanated a narcotic warmth, stronger than the *chillum* that Noor smoked at the camp in Dadaab. The corollas of the flowers reached Billai's bare knees, and I filled myself with the smell of the narcissus, transplanted to the island from the Green Ship months ago.

"Do you know why I like it here?" she asked as she lay down.

I shook my head.

"Because we're all immigrants from somewhere."

"If you think about it, Dadaab was also like that."

"But it's prettier here," she said, her smile showing disappointment.

I stared at her frail ankles. The first time I saw her at the refugee camp, she and two other girls were chatting while pumping water from a well. Each filled three jugs, two to carry by hand and one to balance atop their heads. They were three queens, models who strutted on dirt roads as if they were high fashion runways. She wore a long, colored skirt, a scarf on her head, earrings, coordinated makeup, hair in tiny, neat braids. Her balanced gait was perfect, her gaze ahead, noble, full of nonchalance. She shone with her own light, a star with black skin that emanated a supernatural aura as she passed, wiggling her hips between trash barrels, plastic waste, mismatched shoes, rusted pipes, and goats that grazed on what they could find.

We made the whole trip together. Sometimes, like in Sudan, I feared that she wouldn't be able to make it, like when we had to bribe the guy at the border. Or when she was hurt while we were crossing an area mine-laden by Boko Haram terrorists. But more than anything else, I feared for her life the night when two traffickers cornered her after realizing her beauty. She tried to defend herself, to stop the violence. She shouted for help, crying "Saidia! Saidia!" but nobody moved for fear of being thrown in the sea for defending her. In the end I couldn't stand it. I grabbed one of them by the neck and I flung him off the boat. The other kicked my back, grabbed my shirt and lifted me off the ground. I too would've ended up in the water had it not been for Professor Kysmayo, whose strong hands freed me from the grip of the trafficker and then threw him too into the dark waters.

"You're right, Billai … but unlike Dadaab, besides us all being immigrants, there's something else that makes me love this place."

"What?"

"That here, if we want, we can emigrate."

She took my hands and said in her solemn tone, "How it has always been and always will be."

Once in a while I talked with people back in Dadaab on the internet. Nobody wanted to admit that the refugee camp – provisional since the 90s – had become a permanent establishment. Not the local functionaries who received funding to continue operation, not the United Nations that paid to not solve the problem, not the refugees, forced to live there without hope of leaving. I would never want to return there to survive, imagining a life elsewhere. My elsewhere, like that of many others, was being born from the commitment of all who participated in "No-Mad Land." If we'd created a precedent better than Sealand, the Republic of Minerva, Rose Island, to cite some cases Sergio had talked about, who knew what we'd be able to achieve? Who knew if international law would adapt to the fundamental necessities of humans?

My mother and brother were already on their way to join us on the Green Ship.

Professor Kysmayo climbed down to the islet and waved to greet us. In his other hand he held an envelope with a round object inside.

"Down there, did you see it?"

We stood up and followed him until we reached the top of another hill where there was a second meadow, green and flat.

"They taught me how to use the 3D printer."

White lines were traced into the side of the field.

"This is my first ball," he said, pulling the object out of the envelope and raising it above his head like a trophy. And then he gave the ball a kick.

A soccer goal awaited us.

Home Sick

M. Darusha Wehm

I WAS ENCODING A BATCH OF CLASSIC EBOOKS when the *ulu-aliki* walked into the library, the outdoors scent of gardenias and overripe mangoes following him.

"Afternoon, chief," I said, pushing my chair back a bit. Joseph Seru spoke Tuvaluan with his family and the other council members, but his English was so much better than my Tuvaluan would ever be. Besides, even though less than ten percent of us were Aussies or Kiwis, the official language on the SPIT was English.

"Hey ya, Sally," he answered, lacking his usually jovial demeanour.

"You looking for something in particular?" I asked. The island's chief was a voracious reader and a bit of a film buff. I usually gave him first crack at the new titles I managed to snag off the satellite internet connection.

"Sort of," he said, the last remains of his smile disappearing. "You, I guess."

I frowned. "What's up, chief?"

"I've got something for the blog."

I watched as he pulled a chair from one of the tables and sat it down across from my desk. He knew me well enough to leave a decent space between the chair and the desk.

As the island's librarian, I had also become the de facto editor of the closest thing to a news source we had – the *Spitball*, the island's blog. There were about a dozen regular contributors, most of the posts being the weekly scores for the football, *kilikiti*, and *ano* matches. But things did occasionally happen on the SPIT, and we reported on them all. According to the stats, there were even a handful of people off island who regularly read the thing.

"What's going on?" I asked again, opening up a text editor on the laptop so I could take notes.

"The bastards finally figured out how to make a buck from us, that's what's going on." Seru usually looked for the positive, but he sounded more like the bitter old fishermen who posted screeds about how overseas politicians screwed us all. I raised an eyebrow and the chief continued.

"They're bringing in developers." He spat the last word out like it was a wormy piece of fish.

"What on earth for?" I asked.

"Luxury condos on the coast," he said, "what else?" His voice was hard and I could see a fire smouldering in his eyes that wasn't really a good look for him. Even though it was clear that he was dead serious, I couldn't help myself. I laughed.

"Luxury condos?" I repeated. "You've got to be kidding. Who wants to vacation on a pile of rubbish?"

He said nothing for a moment, just looked at me. "People don't see New Tuvalu that way anymore. They're calling it one of the few unspoiled islands left in the South Pacific, but without all that pesky dirt, poverty, and backwardness." He snorted, and I saw that his hands were clenched. "Greedy rats."

* * *

The South Pacific Island of Trash had existed for years, floating around wherever the South Pacific high happened to be. Tankers or unlucky sailors sometimes saw it, but it was more like a legend than a real problem. Hundreds of thousands of plastic bags, bottles, and wrappers, all stuck together in a loose conglomeration of rubbish, stewing in a soup of microscopic particles. It was embarrassing, but it was an embarrassment that belonged to no one in particular, so no one in particular wanted to deal with it. Until Tuvalu sank.

The island nation of Tuvalu had been slowly disappearing for years and inevitably the evacuation came. Twelve thousand refugees in New Zealand could hardly be ignored, and all of a sudden that rubbish started looking good. One of the many docos made about conditions in the refugee camps was screened in Cannes to an international uproar, so the government finally tendered bids to create a new Tuvalu on the SPIT. The marketing campaign was slick – out of disaster and waste would come an oasis of beauty in the Pacific, a new island paradise. Of course, it ended up being nothing like the artist's drawing in the ads.

But they had nowhere else to go, so off they went, to New Tuvalu. The powers that be sent a bunch of New Zealand and Australia's homeless along for variety. Why let an opportunity to get rid of more unwelcome trash go to waste, right? Which was how I ended up on the SPIT.

* * *

"Can't we just build a hotel or something? You know – make it nice, real posh, but ours?"

The chief snorted, his big nostrils flaring so wide I thought I could maybe see his brain fuming up there. "They don't want a goddamn hotel," he said. "They want timeshares. They want homes. They want to weekend here, like it's some kind of resort or something. They're referring to themselves as our new neighbours for heaven's sake! It's ridiculous."

"Well, who owns the land?" I asked. We all knew we lived on a floating platform of plastic – still, we clung to those archaic words as tightly as a drowning sailor would cling to our own coast.

* * *

I hadn't been homeless, but I was living in a broken-down flat with a half dozen other unemployed just-graduated bums, with no immediate prospects beyond slinging coffee. Given my particular issues, the service industry wasn't exactly a feasible option for me. I was living off savings and I didn't have a lot of savings.

I'd have gone to the moon before I'd ask my family for anything and I didn't really like any of my friends. There was nothing keeping me where I was and with a free plot of "land" and five grand to anyone with a degree who volunteered to go, the SPIT looked pretty attractive. It was an offer I couldn't refuse.

Of course, there wasn't much work for a Film Studies major on New Tuvalu, either, but that didn't really matter. Everyone was figuring out how to get by, how to live on our precarious flotsam home. With my English rose complexion and solitary nature, I wasn't really suited to fishing or landscaping. That's how I ended up running the library, which turned out to be more film and television than books anyway. I spent my time cataloguing, reviewing, and downloading when the bandwidth was available. Sometimes I'd go days without seeing another soul. It was just fine. For me.

Most of the old Tuvaluans kept on fishing and praying and living their lives, but it wasn't the same. No one was used to trees in pots and a shoreline made from old chip bags and rope. In the first year there were over a hundred drownings. This from an island nation of seafarers. No one said it aloud, but everyone knew they couldn't all be accidents.

Slowly, though, the drownings stopped and people adapted – there were plenty of fish, the desalinator worked reliably, the solar cells finally started automatically tracking the sun, and all was right with the world. The piglets chased each other over patchy grass when there wasn't a football or *kilikiti* match. Drink bottles and carrier bags, once lost at sea, disappeared under layers of compost, the tiny gardens tended by new mums and dads.

The trees even grew tall enough that we sometimes forgot that the soil was all imported. We forgot that everything was imported, including us. New Tuvalu wasn't our country, after all – it was just a protectorate of New Zealand. They let us run things day to day, but as Joseph Seru found out, even though we'd made life out of garbage, it wasn't our garbage.

* * *

"That's the problem," he said. "No one owns the land. Or more precisely and accurately, the bloody New Zealand government does. They want to build on the north beach."

"They can't," I said, even though I figured they could.

Joseph Seru's angry expression confirmed my fears.

The north beach was the island's biggest park, our communal space. It was large, maybe a tenth of the whole area of the SPIT. There was imported sand there where the kids played and a sports field for everyone. About half the space was left "wild," or at least the best approximation of wild we could do. By now, there were trees and a little sod here and there. I couldn't believe that they were going to sell it out from under us to a bunch of rich Americans and Europeans who wanted an unspoiled getaway for a couple of weeks each year.

When the *ulu-aliki* left, I fired up the satellite and did some digging online. There was no doubt that the charter for New Tuvalu left any unowned spaces as property of the New Zealand government. Legally, the north beach was a Kiwi landfill. I searched the internet for any mention of this scheme in the rest of the world, and found a few tiny stories buried deep in the business sections of the *Herald* and the *Dominion Post*. According to those sources, it was a development cartel from Abu Dhabi bankrolling the deal. Who else but desert dwellers would see the potential, I thought.

The SPIT always reminded me of something my dad used to say: "You can put lipstick on a pig, but it's still a pig." I was comfortable there, I liked the work and the community. I'd never felt as safe as I did on the SPIT. But it was still just a veneer of paradise on top of a pile of trash. We'd been given the least they could get away with, and now they were going to try and take it back? It was so unfair.

I wrote up a quick article for the blog and hit the "publish" button. I knew that there would be a lot of angry comments on the site by morning, and probably an equal number of angry people banging on the doors of the council members by the end of the day tomorrow. But what good would that do? The people making all the decisions were thousands of miles and a whole world away.

* * *

"No, Mum, I don't have the bandwidth for video."

"I cannot for the life of me understand why you would choose to live out in the back of beyond like that, Sally." My mum's strident voice wasn't softened a bit by the tinny speakers of the library's laptop. "You can't even have a video call with your mother? I mean, what is the draw of living on a glorified rubbish tip?"

"Mum," I said, my heart pounding. "Don't start. Can you please just tell me what people are saying about the development? Is there something we can do to stop it? Get people back home mobilized against it, maybe?"

"I highly doubt it," she said and I could hear her derisive sniff. "I only noticed the piece on the news because it's where you live, and even then it was just fluff about how great an investment this resort will be. Not a single soul cares about a handful of people out there floating around on a pile of old tyres. Though, whoever would want to holiday out there I cannot imagine. The smell alone!"

"It doesn't smell, Mum." It did smell, of course, of flowers and fruit and salt air, but that was not what she meant.

"Really," she went on, as if I hadn't said anything, "if you must live there, you should be pleased that there's some money coming in. Those developers will make things more civilized for all of you – people with money for resort condos aren't going to put up with not being able to make video calls, for one. This is a good thing, Sally. I don't know why you'd want to try and stop it, except that you always were contrary. If it's something that's making someone a living, it's got to be bad. You never did have your feet properly on the ground, no wonder you're living somewhere that's as flimsy as your ideas."

I could feel pinpricks of tears starting up behind my eyes and knew that if this kept on I was going to lose my temper. "Okay, well, I have to go now, Mum. Other people need the laptop. I'll call again soon, okay."

"Maybe you can get a job at the resort, be able to afford your own computer."

"Give my love to Dad," I said and hit the big red disconnect button.

I managed to get to the toilet without having to run, but wasted the nice piece of dorado I'd had for lunch. I'd managed to calm down before the library door banged open.

"Anything?" Joseph Seru asked.

I shook my head. "I should have known better than to ask my mother. She's half the reason I left."

"Thank you for trying," Joseph said and I felt terrible. "None of us have any connections to anyone over there; you did what you could with what you have." I could see that he wanted to put his hand on my shoulder, do something to show me that he truly was grateful, but he knew me well enough to know not to. "We will endure, as we always do. Who knows? Maybe it won't be so bad."

"Maybe," I said, but I knew we both were lying.

* * *

"You're a filmmaker, aren't you?" The woman standing in the doorway of the library looked the worse for wear – an unhealthy rosiness in her cheeks which foretold a nasty sunburn, expensively dyed hair exposing mousy brown roots and hanging limply in the humidity. Typical *palagi*. She probably looked a lot like me, and I can't imagine she liked that much more than I did.

"Yes," I said, suspicious. Since they'd arrived, I'd tried to stay away from the developers as much as possible. I preferred the mediation of a screen if I was going to be confrontational.

"That's great," she gushed in the phoney tones of an MBA holder. "We're making some promotional materials for the new community and would love to get locals involved, people like you. It's a terrific opportunity for all of us."

Her greasy smile was making my stomach turn and my heart pound. I didn't want to be there, but there was only one door to the library, which was itself only the one room. I couldn't escape her grinning face. "Have you talked to *te sina o fenua*? If you want local involvement they'd be the ones to work with."

She shook her head and looked at me like I was a naïve teenager. "The council members are old-fashioned, they just want everything the same as it's always been. They don't understand the importance of keeping current, of modernizing this community. That's why we're here, to make sure that New Tuvalu has all the advantages technology can bring." She looked around the library, her eyes resting on the bulky computers and the blinking satellite modem. "You must appreciate that."

"I'm not going to make an advert for you," I said, wishing I were anywhere but in this conversation.

"Don't think of it as an ad," she said, taking a step toward me. I felt myself push back into my chair, and I could see in her face that she noticed it, too.

"I'm not interested," I said. My mouth felt like it was full of sand.

"Fine," she said, stepping back, and the tightness in my chest loosened slightly. "But you have to realize that without people like us this place is never going to move beyond being an overgrown fishing raft. Is that really what you want, to live like someone in a National Geographic documentary?"

"Get out," I said, my voice barely above a whisper. Thankfully, she turned and walked back out into the heat of midday and I let my head drop into my hands. It was bad enough that they'd taken the beach, and were building a resort no one who lived here would enter from anything other than the staff door. But did they have to act as though just because I looked like them that I would think like them?

* * *

They ended up hiring some overseas firm to make their film. They earned their money – it was very well done. It made the developers look like a cross between Oxfam and Médecins Sans Frontières. I cried throughout the whole six minutes.

"It could be worse," Joseph Seru said. We watched it together in the library – the developers had provided an advance screening copy to the council.

"How?" I asked. "I can't see anyone wanting to help us now. How do you say you don't want better communications, more jobs, a thriving economy? How do you say you just want to be left alone?" I was trembling, and tried the old breathing exercises to calm down.

Joseph was quiet for a moment, and I couldn't read the look on his face. Finally he said, "We can't stop it, Sal. This is my home, but it isn't mine. I wish things were different but wishing doesn't make the fish bite or the rain fall. At least they are letting us stay."

"Damn it, Joseph," I said, my voice breaking. I didn't bother trying to fight the tears. "We are human beings. We're entitled to a place of our own. It's their fault that you had to leave Tuvalu in the first place, with their pollution and greed. And now … now they're taking this away, too?"

He looked at me and I thought I saw a trace of anger cross his face, then it was gone.

"I know you mean well, Sal," he said. "But there's nothing to be done. We have to make the best of what we've got. We've been doing that all along. New Tuvalu used to be rubbish. Now it's so beautiful that people want to come here from all over the world. Maybe we were too good at building something out of nothing, because, now, everyone wants what we've got."

He walked out of the library. The next day I learned that his daughter Mary had gone to work for the development as a sales manager. I tried not be angry, tried to remind myself that she had the right to her own decisions, that we all have the right to decide for ourselves how to live our lives. It was hard, though.

* * *

"Sally, it's rude and hurtful and you have no right to say those things." Mary Seru was a small woman, but she wasn't timid. She had planted her hands on my desk and her angry face was far too close to mine.

"I have a right to my opinion," I said, my voice about a third as loud as hers. If she hadn't been so horribly close to me, she probably would never have been able to hear me.

She shook her head. "Of course, but you don't have a right to plaster your opinion all over the blog like it's the gospel truth. Ugh." She let out a breath and stood up straight. I felt my chest expand a little as space opened up between us. "Some of us have to live here, you know."

I felt like she'd hit me. "I-I live here."

Her face softened slightly. "I know," she said. "But it's different for you. You can go home. The rest of us..." She looked out the window of the prefabricated building. It was another beautiful day in the South Pacific, the sky a clear blue, the warm breeze stirring the leaves of the potted trees. "The rest of us don't have a choice."

"This *is* my home," I said. "We all worked so hard to make this place livable. That's why I don't want to see it turned into just another generic resort. Your father understands. I don't see why it's so hard for you."

"My father feels sorry for you," she said, and I was fairly certain she didn't intend for it to be insulting. "Because you have no proper family connection, no people. But I can see that you're just like them." She jerked her head in the direction of the construction. "You don't even really like it here. All you can see is what this island came from. At least the developers see it for what it is now. At least they're honest enough to say out loud that they want a taste of a forbidden exotic life, to visit the world of us noble savages. And they're willing to trade those things we don't have in order to get what they want."

I guess she'd given up trying to be nice and I could see anger in her face. "You have no right to tell us what we should do with our lives and our island, Sally. You aren't the voice of this community. You never can be." She took a step towards me and I could see dark spots in my vision. I paid attention to my breathing and hoped I would be able to forestall a panic attack. "Just leave it alone."

* * *

Mary didn't come by to see me again. I didn't post anything on the *Spitball* again, either. I gave the login and password to Kevan Tulley and when Joseph asked me why I'd stopped running the blog I made up some excuse about it taking up too much of my time. He didn't press it.

The construction took eighteen months and for a little while I thought there might still be hope. But soon there were fewer boats going out to fish each day, fewer pickup games of soccer, fewer weaving circles. Then there were people wearing business suits and housekeeping uniforms. A fleet of rickshaw taxis sprung up. Two restaurants.

By the time the last condo was sold, I barely recognized the place. There was broadband all over the island now, so I borrowed the laptop and called my mother from my small hut. Her wide face filled the screen and she forced a smile with tight lips.

"Sally," she said, "I told you things would improve once that resort got going, didn't I? Aren't you glad your impotent little protest didn't accomplish anything, hmm?"

"I'm coming back," I said, unwilling to let this conversation go on any longer than absolutely necessary. "I've got a job lined up at the Film Archive in the capital; I won't have time to come down to Nelson before I have to start. Sorry."

I expected an "I told you so" or an "I knew you'd come crawling back," but Mum just frowned.

"What on earth for?" she asked eventually. "That island of yours is finally a decent place to be. Why would you want to leave now?"

I shrugged. I didn't know how to explain that everything that had once made living on the island appealing was gone. It was no longer unique, no longer special. Even its remoteness was now just an illusion, shattered by ubiquitous wifi and twice-weekly scheduled flights.

But that wasn't the real reason I couldn't stay. I'd thought that a people whose home sank into the sea was the perfect community for me. I shared a spiritual connection with them, we had a fundamental similarity. They were lost, I was lost – I'd thought we could be lost together. But Mary was right – I wasn't really like them at all. They had no choice, they could never be anything but a people displaced from their home by forces beyond their control.

I wasn't a tourist, but I wasn't a New Tuvaluan either. I had options they would never have, and I always would. Nothing I could do would change that, not for me and not for them. And now that I knew it, every time I looked at one of my neighbours, that gulf between us was all I could see. For the first time since I stepped on to the SPIT, I felt trapped.

"Well?" Mum said, impatience written all over her face. "Why come back now?"

I looked past the screen out the window, to the potted palm trees rustling in the warm breeze, and the core of pressed plastic peeking out through breaks in the grass and sand. Once it had been a symbol of how things that no one wanted could become central to an entire community. For the New Tuvaluans, it was a base on which to build a future. But to me it was now just another place I didn't belong.

I brought my focus back to the screen. "Homesick, I guess."

Alabanda

Kevin Martens Wong

IT WOULD ONLY BE MANY, MANY YEARS LATER when they would finally allow the people of the Lion City without Lions to ask just where in the world all the Eurasians had gone – and even then, between the people and them, neither would quite have a satisfactory answer, because in the end, no one, really, was quite sure. Yes, undoubtedly, the official story that would later emerge was true to a large degree. Better hopes and better prospects in Perth and London and New York and San Francisco; new worlds to explore in Tokyo and Shanghai and Christchurch and Delhi; a new, old home, even, to be found in the progenitor lands, in Lisbon, in Amsterdam, in Edinburgh, in Middleburg, where great journeys had begun some five, four, three hundred years prior. But ask any Eurasian, Upper Ten, Lower Six or any number in between, and they will tell you that for five, four, three hundred years, the best thing about us is just how good we are at keeping secrets.

Let the politicians have their promises, their sweeping newspaper headlines, their official, state-sponsored wikis with their clean, grand histories, battles for merger and separation, wars and wars and wars. Let the big men have their wars. Let God have their universe, and rightfully so, *Deus donu di seu kung tera*. But let the Eurasians live in peace. *Desah Jenti Kristang fikah seguru. Jenti di dos mundu.* They have always walked between two worlds, and because of that they know the true value of knowledge, the true ways of power. *Rikeza di mulera. Rikeza sigredu.* Even Kristang, the mother language, was rarely taught to the young, to the extent that in the theses and the journal articles, it was reported as nearly extinct, moribund, devastated by the meteoric rise of English. A secret language, the *bela-belu* would say, the old Eurasian men and women in the 2010s when people started to ask what had happened, when indigeneity returned to its rightful place in the world. We didn't teach it to our children, because it was our secret language, said the *bela-belu*, in the same way that they said that everyone had gone to Perth, everyone had left, there was nothing more, nothing left here to see. *Nus sa linggu mai, nus sa linggu sigredu.* Our mother language. Our secret language.

But he was young, and he did know the language, and he knew why. He knew where all the Eurasians, all the ones you don't read about in the censuses, all the ones protected by their families, their people, had gone. He knew where all of his people, the Last People, had gone, and he knew why.

Eli sabeh. Kauzu eli papiah Kristang, eli sabeh klai birah kaza. The greatest secret of them all. Those who speak the creole, the patois, the language they called broken, the language they called original Portuguese, the language that was hidden in plain sight, will know that the ways home are similarly broken, that the ways back to the origin are similarly beyond Portugal, beyond this space, beyond this time, yet so easy to find if you know what you are looking for.

What was he looking for? He was seventeen when he failed Chemistry and Math and Physics and was nearly held back a year in college. Sixteen when he kissed his first boy. Fifteen when he went missing for three days because a cashier at the supermarket had told him that foreigners from Europe like him were the cause of all the frustrations in the world after he tried to buy cigarettes from her with his elder brother's NRIC, which still also said *Eurasian*.

And he was eighteen when he learned the mother language, and learned where he should go, and why.

His *kanyong* and his *susi* of course, his elder brother and sister – they had succeeded at seventeen, soared at sixteen, flowered at fifteen. They had found their places in the Lion City without Lions, a doctor-to-be and, according to the *Straits Eurasian Advertiser*, Singapore's best cricketer since the golden age of Serani sporting giants in the 1970s. They would bring pride to the family; they would learn different secrets, different trades. Different ways to be the same as everyone else, so different and so much the same.

But he had a different place. A different path. A different *kaminyu*. A different thing to search for.

There was no National Service call-up for him, once he was eighteen, once the decision was made, once he had learned the mother language to a sufficient degree, and his *aboh femi* was satisfied that he would do her proud. *Koitadu*, you didn't know? Every *fila-filu* finds some way to make their family proud when you come from a Eurasian family, whether they are an atheist, a chain smoker, a homosexual or anything else under the sun and moon and five stars. And this was how he would make them proud. No NS call-up, no medical school, no gold medal at the SEA Games. No HDB flat. No CPF. None of that needed. This was different. He was looking for something different.

Bos buskah 404, said his *aboh femi*, when the day came, and he was ready to go, and they were all at the bus stop, his *kanyong* and his *susi* with her new *noibu muru*, his uncles and aunts, his three baby cousins, his parents, even the maid and the dog and the cat. *404*, said his *aboh femi*, pronouncing each syllable in the mother language as she kissed his forehead goodbye. *Kwa-tu-sen-tu kwa-tu*, as if he were still a child, reclined on her lap at Christmas in front of the tree, spreadeagled on the church pew because the Good Friday mass had entered its second hour and he was not allowed to kiss Jesus's feet because he had just recovered from Hand-Foot-Mouth for the second time. She still thought he was bad with numbers, although he was sure that he knew that she knew that he knew that it was better to be bad with numbers, better because this was what he had been really looking for his whole life.

They say their goodbyes to him, kiss his curls, pat his bag, slip him the buttons and pins that he has always festooned himself with, and cry with him for a while. And then, it is him, and his tears and fears, and his secret, growing pride – he is alone at the bus stop, him and his thoughts and his mother language and his dark-brown Lower Six skin. Not waiting for 404. Not just yet. *Nenang*. First the feeder, 633, which takes him right through Runway Boulevard, where he spent so many years with Argus, and Ethan, and Wira, and the old minority gang from Airbase Secondary that he will never see again, because this is not their journey. One last, rounding look at the Plab, at the neighborhood he has called home for all eighteen years of his life.

A second change, to 134, a long, winding journey through the dilapidated estates of Marine Parade to the flood barricades and the last functional entrance of Tanjong Katong MRT. The MRT itself, then, a third *kaminyu*: from brown line to the ancient green, and from the green line to the twists and turns of the H-shaped turquoise. The right platform at Bahar Junction is far harder to find than the number 404, but he finds it anyway. In a blink, he is at Tawas, and the 172 is trundling up. The fourth and last change, and the one, he has been told, is often the most difficult, not just because the 172 route is almost as ancient as the green line, but because it weaves through the only part of the city that still remains relatively wild, that has never been tamed into the straight, clean rows that have characterised the Lion City without Lions since the Collapses in the early 2020s. The wild must still scare some people, he muses, because he finds this fourth and final part of the journey easy, straightforward, untamed because there is nothing to tame inside of him to begin with.

The 172 deposits him at the edge of New Bidadari cemetery. Wide, windswept, whole, and absolutely and completely deserted; the cemetery area is clean, clear, unSingaporean, as far away as you can get from the city on an island that is literally a city surrounded by flood barriers and breakwaters. There is no one else in sight, though he knows, as his family does, that there are many out of it; this is their resting place, after all. And how fitting it should be, for those who believe in another world, like he does, because he knows it exists. Because it is here that he finally is ready to find what he is looking for, even though it is not marked on the bus-stop pole. 172 and 405, as it has been for decades; there is no service 404, and there has not been since the turn of the century.

And yet, there has been. There has been every second Friday of the month, rain or shine, since 1969. Not at all like your other Singaporean buses, your 134s, your 172s, your 633s; 404 arrives erratically, sometimes an hour early, sometimes four and a half hours late. Driven by Eurasians, says his *aboh femi*; he knows better than to think like that, although she is probably right. But he came prepared; its earliest reported arrival in the last five years was 08:56 in the morning, and so he ensures that the 172 has deposited him at New Bidadari at 08:38. Lucky as always, he has been, third child of five, and first in this generation in his family to make this great journey; it is 08:51 when it comes into view, a bus like any other in the Lion City without Lions, only conspicuous by a lack of service provider logo, or any kind of detail, really, to be found on its exterior. It pulls up in front of him; he is the only person at the bus stop.

"*Undi bos ta bai*?" says the driver, a young woman, and definitely (his *aboh femi* was right) definitely Eurasian, although her accent is from ... somewhere else. And that's the thing, isn't it? Everyone's from somewhere else, in the end. And he knows what to say. Because only Eurasians will know what to say.

"*Alabanda*."

It means many things in Kristang, depending on whom you ask, and nobody is quite sure which is correct. Some say it means *the other side*. His *aboh femi* always insisted that it meant *neighbour*. But he knows it means both these things, and something else to him as well.

There. Over there. The other world. The neighbouring world.

See the 404 shut its doors, him safely aboard. See it move off, slowly, picking up pace gradually as it ambles its way down the broad lanes of Lim Chu Kang Rd, now restored to its former glory after being used as an emergency runway during the flooding of Changi Airport in 2031. *Alabanda*, he thinks. *There. Over there.* The bus picks up speed. The grassy fields and flower farms stream past. *There. Over there.*

Desah nus bai alabanda. Let us go there, over there, somewhere. His *aboh machu*'s last words, as his life crumbled away in the hospital, seven years ago; his *aboh machu*'s face, now, flashing between orchids, and tombstones, and streetlights whizzing past. *Life here is over*, said Argus, one day, when they were in Secondary Three and the cats had all died again because the water supply was contaminated. *Have you ever seen anything like it*? He'd told his *aboh machu* about it, and his *aboh machu* told him about Lisbon, in the fourteenth century, and Middelburg, in the sixteenth, and Melaka, in the eighteenth.

Bida sempri ta brigah kung morti, his *aboh machu* said. Life is always fighting with death. Always wrestling with it. One must win, inevitably. One always wins.

Keng sempri ganyah? Bos lembrah keng? Who do you think always wins?

Orchids, and tombstones, and streetlights; and then, not suddenly, but still quite suddenly, stars, and other things, whirling and twisting in the space between dimensions, and starlight, the light of places he has never seen, the colour of time and the texture of probability. Things shift and change; the bus is in the Middle In-Between, the *Miu Intresmiu*, the place between universes, still travelling, and that's it, that's the last that he will ever see of his home for a long time, orchids and tombstones and streetlights. *Ja fikah strelaneru*, he says to himself in his mind, still seeing his grandfather's face in the paradoxes and the temporal eddies that bloom and implode around them. *You've become an astronaut.*

Do we have to become astronauts? *Mistih fikah strelaneru*? he remembers saying to his *aboh machu*, when he was in Secondary Three, after all the cats died and Braddell and Toa Payoh were poisoned.

For what reason? his grandfather said. *Pra ki kauzu*?

The ride is smooth, and easy, and his view of the multiverse is unobstructed. *Kauzu bida sempri ta brigah kung morti. Because life always fights with death.*

And right now, death is winning in our world. Agora morti ta ganyah na nus sa mundu.

"*Bos teng bong*? You alright back there?" says the driver. He starts a little; in Singapore, now and always, bus drivers rarely talk to their passengers. But he's not in Singapore anymore, and will not be for a very long time. He relaxes. "*Teng*," he says. "*Kantora chegah na Alabanda*?" He wants to arrive now. He wants to see the world, his world now.

"*Seti ke oitu minutu*," says the driver. Seven or eight minutes; he expected hours. "*Santah seguru*."

"*Sertu*," he says, smiling back tears, remembering in spite of himself his *aboh femi*'s favourite phrase. Not *santah seguru* – sit securely, sit safely – but *santah kaladu*. Sit quietly. Take the universe in. The driver is whistling something, a melody he doesn't know, but which he assumes is from Alabanda.

Santah kaladu. Alabanda. He does as he's told, even though he's sixteen and he can make decisions for himself. His mother is white-faced, *teng midu, teng tantu midu*. His father is frowning, making the decision for him. The school has said that there's nothing wrong, that a kiss is a kiss, that boys will be boys, that a little more sexuality education would help, but he knows his parents' fears, and their prejudices go much deeper than that. He knows that there is no place for him there, in their world anymore, later confirmed by the way his father howls after a good drink later at night, one good one, *tokah bebeh seng feng*. One good one. Perhaps he was the bad one; perhaps he was the one who had to go away. The nightmare, the nightmare about his mother waking up to find him dead, when he is the one dreaming; it makes no sense to him, for one whole year when he is seventeen, and yet it does. He understands, even though he doesn't. *Santah kaladu. Alabanda*. The way they didn't talk to him for three days and three nights. Three nights he was gone, when the lady thought he was European. *Santah kaladu. Santah seguru.*

Through it all, his *aboh machu*'s face swims into view, a cloud of green, growing thoughts, a brighter island amidst the gloom.

Jenti Kristang mudah tantu. He didn't believe it until years after his *aboh machu* was dead, but he did what he had to do, as his ancestors had done for generations, from Lisbon in the fourteenth century, to Middelburg in the sixteenth, to Melaka in the eighteenth. Everyone was fleeing; everyone was running from something. *Jenti Kristang bai prumiru*. We go first. We always go first. *Kontu olotu desah kung nus, nus desah kung olotu*. We go where they want us. Wherever that is. As long as we are wanted. As long as we are treasured. *Rikeza di mulera. Rikeza di korsang.*

Desah nus bai alabanda. His heart soars and flowers. The bus is accelerating. And then –

"*Ja chegah*," says the driver, in the voice of one who has said this hundreds of thousands of times, and never tired of it, because of who she gets to say it to, each and every time. *They have arrived.*

And why should she be tired of it, anyway? Because the first glimpse of a new entrant to the universe known as Alabanda is of the great purple structure rising straight up into the air to the left, arcing over their head, a craggy, racing outcrop of rock in the shape of a slithering, swirling train of smoke, culminating in a sharpened, pointed tip angled toward heaven over the glittering aquamarine waters to their right.

"*Kema draku*," he says, in wonder. Like a dragon.

And the driver smiles. "*Chadu mbes*." He is the smartest she's seen in a while, indeed. "*Porta Draku sa Rabu*." The Dragontail Gate. Around it are gliders, flyers, all sorts of small, dainty craft, as if constructed out of flame-of-the-forest leaves and paper; next to them, something skims across the water, delicate and spindly. He wants to call it a *barku labalaba*, a spider-boat; the flame-of-the-forest gliders are *Albi fogu abuah*; the Dragontail Gate is *Porta Draku sa Rabu*. There are names. Names for everything. *Nomi pra tudu*. And as he thinks them, he thinks freely, and clearly, and he is blinking back tears; for this is their world, the world of the Last People, a world where the names of things can be in any language, but can be in his language, his heart, his mind's eye. Those people in those gliders, those flyers, that *barku labalaba* – they are all his people.

We had to go somewhere, when no one wanted us, when things became bad, when the world was collapsing. And so we came here. Into this story. Into this world.

"*Bos teng bong*?" says the driver, repeating her earlier question with a smirk.

"*Teng* … *teng*…," he says, wonderingly, trying to find a word that describes exactly how he feels at this moment. For he has everything here. A home. A place to be free. A place for everyone who doesn't fit. A place beyond the places. A city, rising in the distance, a city alive and free, dressed in every colour probable and every texture known to humanity across the multiverse.

But he also doesn't have everything. He wants to turn back, but he cannot. He doesn't know how to remember where he came from. He doesn't want to remember. He doesn't know if he can ever forget. *Kontu eli bai alabanda*, he remembers his *aboh femi* saying, the night after the kiss, *eli impodih birah kaza*. If he goes there, he cannot come back. Why does the 404 pull up empty every second Friday? Because that's the unspoken rule. That's the deep secret, that Eurasians in every time and space know. People of two worlds, yes. *But once you go to the other world, to the other side, you cannot come home. Kontu bos bai alabanda, impodih birah kaza. Kauzu bos nadi kereh birah. Because you won't want to.* From Lisbon in the fourteenth century, to Middelburg in the sixteenth, to Melaka in the eighteenth – who actually went back? Who actually wanted to go back? And that is why, later, he will know, as you do now, that Eurasians are a small, small number in all the worlds, because in all the worlds, they end up asking the same question. *Where in the world did all the Eurasians go?*

And the answer is always the same. Here, there, everywhere and nowhere.

Alabanda.

One day, the legends say, the legends that nobody knows about, when the seas finally recede and the oceans became rivers once more, the Eurasians will return, back to where they came from. One day, they will come home to both worlds they were part of, after everyone else has gone, the Last People, because they never belonged, and they could never find their home.

But even the wisest and bravest of the Eurasians know that there is a secret within the secret.

That the secret is a lie. *Ja mintirah. Jenti Kristang mintirah tantu*.

Because the seas will never recede. The oceans will never become the rivers they once were. The world he was part of will never be the way it was. Neither will this world ever be home to him.

Instead, something new will always be there, waiting. Something new. Another bus. Another city. Another world. Another meeting, another mixing. Another people. Another thing broken, and another origin. Another story, and another thing made old. It never ends. And it always begins again. A *kaminyu* ends. A *kaminyu* begins.

But for someone to see that, for someone to want to leave that first world, and to take up their backpack, wait for that bus 404, out in the middle of nowhere; that's hard. That's really hard. You have to be out of here. You have to be nobody. You have to be another, an Other. You have to be over there, *santah seguru, santah kaladu*. Don't say a word, because there is no place for you and your noise, you and your dreams of being an astronaut, a Kristang astronaut (who ever heard of such a thing?) of being somebody to this place, someone that this place can love, because this place doesn't understand you. This place doesn't know you.

Santah kaladu, sayang. This place doesn't want you. At seventeen, it didn't want him because he couldn't pass Math, and Physics, and Chem; at sixteen, it didn't want him, because he kissed a boy, fully, lovingly, wholeheartedly; at fifteen, it didn't want him, because he didn't want to be who they wanted him to be.

And at eighteen, he doesn't care anymore. Because he will go where he wants to. And be who he wants to be. Hasn't that always been true of the Eurasians?

"*Aiyoh, sayang*," says the driver. "You ok? *Bos teng bong*?" *Are you okay*? But it also means, *what do you have?* The city is swimming clearly into view now, the city by the sea, that place here, there, everywhere and nowhere. He takes a deep breath. *Sertu*. There is only one thing that he is really certain of.

"*Teng bong*," he says, finally, his eyes looking back toward the Dragontail Gate, and now toward the city, looming before them. I'm good. And he's good because he knows. *Eli sabeh. Kauzu eli papiah Kristang, eli sabeh klai birah kaza*. He does know the way home after all. He knows the *kaminyu*, leading him far away from home, there, over there, far far away, and home to himself. The *kaminyu* leading him over there, into this story, into this world where he can really be who he has always been, and who he can grow into being.

Alabanda.

Here, there, everywhere and nowhere. Now you, too, know the secret of where the Eurasians have gone, and where in the world they can truly just be.

All That Water

Eris Young

IT TURNED WHITE, the interlocutor. Eyes wide, light-brown in its skin leaching away, allowing only a single meaning, stark.

Sanga tensed: violence was rare on first contact. But not unheard of. The woven surface of the platform creaked as Sanga, along with the rest of the interpreters, made ready to leap aside into water rutilated with protective reed and root.

But the interlocutor took a step back, and Sanga realised xyr mistake. The threat was not a threat, but adrenal vasoconstriction. An autonomic response. One that, by necessity, Sanga's people had long ago discarded. The yellowgreen beating in xyr chest receded.

And it was shocking, wasn't it? Since the very earliest of the histories, that bright road painting the night sky had brought them visitors of every stripe imaginable. These stranger-species came bearing information – news of policy changes, trade agreements, distant wars on the frontiers of Unified Space. News that the benefactors, confined as they were to their own vast domain, could not access without the likes of Sanga. In return these stranger-species, many and various as the stars in both physiology and language, asked for minerals, dyes, basketry, gene- and medtech, clean water.

So by what providence, what infinitesimal chance was it that these aliens, these stranger-species, should also be bipeds, and walk erect? Should also have hairless bodies, smooth skin in shades of umber and sienna? To Sanga, the interlocutor was like glimpsing xyr reflection off a still pool: a limpid green surprise, breathtaking.

The interlocutor glanced behind it – behind *her*, at a safe guess – towards the massive old ruin, twenty lengths away, already teeming with her people and their makeshift dwellings. No one had lived in that haunted, half-sunk place for a thousand years. But no reed platform was big enough to contain the multitudes streaming each day from the massive patchwork hull of the stranger-ship, faintly visible even now through the daytime atmosphere. They poured downwell like water from a burst levee. It seemed almost fitting, too: that these dwellers-in-metal should make that place their temporary home.

Metal-dwellers clumped, watchful, at the edges of the ruin, clinging to the vine-strewn curve of its side and shy of the dim tangled water all around. The interlocutor's hair swung in a sheet as she turned, draping her skull. It caught the sunlight like falling water, and made Sanga want to touch it.

<?????,> the interlocutor said, pale-voiced. A vocal communicator, then: Sanga's purview. Protocol dictated the stranger-species initiate, but Sanga took a breath and stepped forward from the gathered knot of xyr fellow interpreters. Xe heard someone suck their teeth in disapproval, but chose to ignore it.

Sanga knew the sense of trust xe felt was an artefact of evolution, nothing more. The impulse to relax xyr muscles, allow xyr heartrate to slow, dangerous temptation: a muddy, deceptive orange. The interlocutor was still an alien, stranger-species, however familiar her physiology.

But trade must begin, one way or another. And trade couldn't occur without communication.

Sanga tried customary greetings in four vocal linguae francae common to the system. Nothing.

The interlocutor pointed at her own chest. <?????.>

Xe mirrored her, saying, <Sanga.>

* * *

It took only seven rotations – and one neural-plasticity soak – for Sanga to learn <Pidin>, the language of the metal-dwellers. This was a mellow-gold, wise number of rotations, but it was small reassurance compared to the language itself, which was flat, greyish and sparse. Pidin was atonal, and utterly devoid of gesture, even nonmanual expression. It made Sanga wonder if the aliens even looked at each other while speaking.

<Rajih> called herself a <xenoanthropologist>. She was the only one on her entire vessel. Sanga wondered what it would mean to be alone in this way. Rajih was taller than Sanga and most reed-dwellers, and less melanated. Though Rajih's hair was black and shiny as the surface of a bog pool, some of her people apparently shared Sanga's hair texture. Sanga was startled to notice no webbing between Rajih's fingers and toes. She laughed when xe pointed this out, a greeny-brown sound like water splashing through the roots of a tree:

<I guess we don't need it…>

Then her eyes slid, again, to the water surrounding the platform, her face falling back into the greyish, tired expression it assumed at rest.

Again, again, Sanga felt it: the dense, yellowy jolt, like stepping through a hole in the mat at night, at the metal-dwellers' familiarity and strangeness. They had not come here under the auspices of a Union commission, and that alone was enough to mark them out. If their physiology was an indicator, then their mode of travel was a distant cousin to what the reed-dwellers' ancestors had used. But in the histories, the ancestors had settled here, in the land of reeds, at the end of a long, desperate flight from a dying planet. So how – and where – had the metal-dwellers survived for so long? Nevertheless, they had survived, and without guidance from any established species. This explained Rajih's ignorance of protocol, the ugliness of their vessel.

Rajih would stare at the water, mouth slightly open in a pinkish expression, like she didn't quite understand what she was seeing. She'd find an imperfection, a bump in the mat where one reed split into two, and rub a finger absently over it, while she and Sanga conversed in her grey, lifeless language.

Sanga was overcome with a sudden urge to teach her. Not the benefactors' rarefied, ephemeral speech, but the reed-dwellers' everyday tongue, which fit their shared physiology like a well-tied wrap-skirt. Xe wanted to see if Rajih could produce its eight tones, its facial gestures. To shake that grey stillness from her face.

But it would take Rajih far longer to learn Sanga's native tongue than it had taken xem to learn Pidin. And, Sanga thought with a purplegreen flush of guilt, that was not the work of an interpreter. Shared anatomy, that deceptive sense of kinship, had already eroded so much of the necessary distance. If Sanga spoke for xemself, negotiations could – would – be compromised: it had happened before, in living memory, once or twice. If Sanga spoke for xemself, xe could not speak for the benefactors.

So xe stilled xyr face, controlled xyr vocal cords, and did not ask to touch Rajih's shining hair.

* * *

Finally, Sanga was fluent enough in Pidin for communication to begin. Wearing xyr beautiful speaking garments, xe hefted the calling stone: a chunk of silver-flecked granite as big as xyr head, strung on a rope tied to the edge of the platform. A historian – Tilang, a third cousin of Sanga's – knelt on a neighbouring platform, with a clear view of both Sanga and the carefully-chosen stretch of water between them: clear of reeds, with clean sand on the bottom and no surface glare. With a nod from the historian, Sanga tossed the stone into the water.

Splash, splash, splash! Stones were thrown from neighbouring platforms, one after another, away into the distance. Rajih's face, a wavering question lost under the music of stone and water, was a tender yellowpink interrogative.

And then, too late, Sanga understood. In a yellowgreen flush, xe realised that Rajih did not know about the benefactors. She had lived, after all, with only her own species for company. Did she even suspect that anyone else might live in the land of reeds? But before Sanga could warn her or reassure her, the benefactor arrived, its dark soft bulk appearing silently beside the platform, just below the surface.

Once again, the colour drained from Rajih's face, her fists clenching in visible fight-or-flight. Sanga heard a snort of disdain from Tilang on the other platform, but if the benefactor itself noticed, it took no offence. Indeed, the first thing it expressed was surprise and delight: a warm rill of excited pulses directed at Sanga. In the flowing, golden-brown tones of an elder addressing a younger, the benefactor exclaimed at the luck that had brought the new bipeds. These metal-dwellers must at least be the same genus as the reed-dwellers: they might expand each other's gene pools nicely! Perhaps, it suggested – the gold in its tone shading into a canny orange, its patterns delicate and oblique like a matchmaking auntie – Sanga might like, with this shiny-haired emissary…?

Sanga's heart leapt even as xyr ears burned with unexpected, muddy-purple embarrassment. Xe was relieved Rajih couldn't understand the benefactors' language, and doubly relieved when the benefactor signalled its desire to begin speaking.

Xe shook out xyr arms and legs to make sure the speaking garments were draping right, and planted xyr feet, bending at the knees in a neutral position. One deep breath in, one out. In, out.

The benefactor started speaking, and Sanga began to move.

At once xe felt xyr sense of self start to slip away, edged out by the demands of xyr augmented working memory. It was always like this: plunging into an algal pool. Eyes, ears, whole body occupied entirely by a vivid, enveloping medium, and no thought to spare for what might be going on above the surface.

* * *

At the end of the exchange, Sanga emerged from xyr interpreter's trance, aching limbs and rasping throat, speaking garments heavy with sweat. Xe could just see a faint ripple to the southwest: the benefactor making its way back out to sea. Tilang had gone home.

Xyr brain contained only a pale, buzzing residue of the words that had passed through it: waste water, phytoplankton. Twelve months – two months – six months. Please.

Xe slumped onto the platform and chewed a cake of seaweed jelly, sighing as xe felt it replace protein, electrolytes, carbohydrates. Reed creaked behind xem, and Sanga jumped. Rajih still stood there. She stared overwater at the ruin where her people were living, teeth worrying her lower lip. Judging by her expression, the first round of negotiations had not gone especially well. A mauvish, sympathetic twinge: Sanga had grown up with the benefactors and xe still found them intimidating sometimes.

<Is something wrong with your raft?> Sanga croaked.

<No.>

Rajih drew a shaking breath. She spun to face Sanga, eyes suddenly alight. She said, all in a rush, <I want to go back your way.> You-plural-possessive: the way of the reed-dwellers. <Can you show me?>

Sanga blinked. Washed-out with fatigue, limbs weighted a dense redbrown, xe wanted to lie down and sleep right on the platform. But, with a little mossy trickle of surprise, Sanga found xe wanted *more* to swim with Rajih.

* * *

A tight-weave basket had to be found for Rajih's bracelet, which couldn't touch the water. On close inspection, what Sanga had taken for a knotted piece of fabric was actually a strip of material clasped by a thin, highly-polished stone, black and square. Rajih was anxious of this ornament, but struggled to explain why:

<It's very valuable – um, useful, to my people. Very … hard to make?>

Rajih shrieked – gasped, laughed – as she lowered herself into the water. The floating basket trailed behind them as they swam, tied on a cord to Rajih's wrist. She ducked and splashed, smoothed her hair back from her shining face, round and alive as a child's. As if they swam not in a brackish lagoon but in a telomere soak, the water rejuvenating her. At Rajih's smile, Sanga felt a mirroring tug on xyr own mouth – evolutionary programming or not, it was irresistible.

Rajih moved frog-style through the water, haltingly. Sanga had to take her shoulders to guide her around obstacles. Her smooth hair brushed xyr hand like fine seagrass.

She dawdled, gazing around at floating algae mats, raised grain paddies with their rich, dark loam. And down at their limbs, intertwined under the surface, dappled in shifting patterns of light and shade.

Sanga watched, too. Xe darted a glance up at Rajih's face, and startled yellowgreen: Rajih's eyes were closed, her smile clear-gold, beatific. Her face, upturned, had dried in the sun, save for two tracks of moisture, welling and falling from the corners of her eyes.

* * *

Rajih climbed, reluctantly, back up the side of the ruin, careful of the rusted skeleton under thick vegetation. Then she turned and held out a hand to Sanga.

Xe hesitated. Protocol – and practicality – demanded stranger-species and planet-dwellers keep apart during trade negotiations, which hinged on each side taking the other at face value, offering only what they were comfortable offering, regardless of what they had. But Rajih knew nothing of custom, or the practicalities of contact. It was easy – too easy – for Sanga to simply take her hand.

The noise, crowd, smell were unbelievable: a pulsing, frantic redyellow. The metal-dwellers must have been packed like salted shrimps into their patchwork vessel, creeping through that boundless void of sky, generation after generation.

People shouted to Rajih and gazed at Sanga, their curiosity a soft, naked russet, like the inside of an ear. There were nearly as many desalination-filtration setups as people: at least one for every dwelling – flimsy pale things that had popped up quick as mushrooms after a monsoon. Plant life, enclosed in tents made of fabric transparent as water, carpeted every surface, even atop some of the sturdier dwellings. The metal-dwellers had put up inscrutable grey spires, too, bristling metal, high enough to pierce the sky, and strung together with smooth, black ropes. No stranger-species had stayed here long enough to build before. Sanga's curiosity burned a hot and vivid magenta.

Every effort seemed to be in service of creating the most basic food and shelter. Every built thing was a threatening white or lifeless grey. Sanga wondered if Rajih's people weren't totally colourblind: had they given it up? Had they spent so long in their cramped metal vessel that they somehow no longer needed it? That thought was a muted-red wavelet of sadness.

The metal-dwellers were taller than the reed-dwellers. They appeared sexually dimorphic, though Sanga spotted one or two who might be like xemself. Their skintones and eye colours bespoke genetic diversity, yes, but they were skinny too, lacking muscle. And most had a pallid, uneven cast to their skin that hinted at multiple vitamin deficiencies.

A wash of yellow unease, brush of a sea-snake in the dark, raised the hairs on Sanga's neck.

Maybe Rajih didn't know that she was undermining her people's position, compromising negotiations, by bringing Sanga here. But it was obvious to Sanga, seeing this place and what they had made of it, that negotiations had been unequal from the start.

Rajih's people may be interstellar travellers, but this was no diplomatic or trade delegation: there were too many children and elders, too many unhealthy. They'd brought no news or knowledge to trade. The metal-dwellers were not explorers or merchants. They were refugees.

* * *

Sanga didn't see Rajih for four rotations. Negotiations, if they could still be called that, ground to a halt: Rajih simply stopped coming, or her people had stopped sending her. The benefactors, for their part, kept to their great cities in the deeper water. Sanga imagined them conferencing silently together in their kaleidoscope language.

A net-filter perimeter was set up. The metal-dwellers were allowed to fish, and to occupy three nearby reed-platforms. The magnitude of these accommodations seemed lost on the metal-dwellers. Only three percent of the planet's surface was above water: an archipelago of marshy islands used for growing rice, lotus, malanga, water-spinach. Platforms, such as the reed-dwellers lived and worked on, needed a natural bed to anchor them, and most were occupied already.

To house the metal-dwellers for any length of time, to convert their waste, feed or teach them to feed themselves, to say nothing of the nutritional soaks so many of them clearly needed? Well.

A handful might indeed strengthen the reed-dwellers' gene pool, yes. But just those settlers occupying the ruin would soon outnumber the reed-dwellers entirely.

The truth, brittle and pale as bleached bone, was that these people had nothing to trade in return for their lives.

* * *

It was raining when Rajih finally reappeared. A thatched awning had to be erected over the platform. Through the dim, wavering air, Sanga could see the metal-dwellers raising great grey cones of tarp between the tall metal spires, like dying flowers, to catch the water as it fell.

Rajih carried smudges under her eyes the colour of grief: the sight started a pale tightness in Sanga's chest. Rajih clutched a rigid translucent box, something dark clattering inside. She gazed at the platform surface, avoiding Sanga's eyes. Xe hesitated, then bent to pick up the calling stone.

<Wait— > The words were tired, heavy as stiff orange clay.

They sat, side-by-side, their feet in the water. Sanga's brown, webbed ones beside Rajih's, pale and small.

<It took me a while to figure it out.> She nodded at Sanga's speaking garments, each panel richly dyed with snail, weed, root, and beetle. <How you talk to them. It's like a dance.>

Water whispered down all around them.

<It's joyful. Until I came here, I never knew what joy was. I knew relief, when we found this place, after so long. Satisfaction, I'd be able to do the job I'd trained my whole life for, that my mentor, and her mentor before her, never lived to do.>

Rajih was paddling in circles, working her way towards something. Sanga let her.

<We could tell this place was habitable, beforehand. But we thought we'd have to fight for it. And then we came down, and your lives here were so beautiful. You just shared everything with us.>

Sanga waited.

<I know my history. My ancient history. That first day, when I saw you standing on the platform, your people all around watching us come, I think I knew it would come to something like this.> Her words were thin, squeezed out through a tightened larynx.

<Rajih— >

<They're making me do it.> She choked out, with a hollow, grey laugh., <That's the worst thing. I'm the anthropologist, I have a rapport with the – with you all. So it has to be me.>

She looked at the box in her arms like she wanted to fling it into the water. Sanga held out a hand, xyr heart tapping out a running, pinkgreen beat.

<Show me.>

<I told them, Sanga. What it would mean for us to interfere like this – to offer you this as a trade. Your whole way of life is going to change.> You-singular-possessive: Sanga's life.

Xe thought, *It already has.*

<But I couldn't make them see. Because this is all we have. What does it matter, they said, if it means we survive? If it means this doesn't have to be the end for us?>

Rajih's face was wet, her hair plastered down with rain, like dark seaweed.

Inside the box: a wide, flat piece of stone, the size of Sanga's hand with the fingers spread. Polished and thin, like Rajih's bracelet. She pressed something on the side. The thing made a chirp, like stone striking stone.

But even before Rajih began to work it, Sanga knew what the object meant. Because it was a deep, fertile black. The colour of rich soil, of the sky. The colour of potential.

Biographies & Text Sources

Ali Abbas
An Absolute Amount of Sadness
(Originally Published in *Fitting In*, Mad Scientist Journal, 2016)
Ali Abbas is the author of *Like Clockwork*, a steampunk mystery published by Transmundane Press. His shorter fiction has been published by Mad Scientist Journal, Transmundane Press, Death's Head Press and Darkhouse Books, and has featured on Every Day Fiction, Scarlet Leaf Review and Crimson Streets. Ali maintains a blog at aliabbasali.com and a full list of published works and free-to-read stories can be found on his author page.

Celu Amberstone
Refugees
(Copyright © Celu Amberstone, reprinted by permission of the author. Originally Published in *So Long Been Dreaming: Postcolonial Science Fiction and Fantasy*, 2004)
Celu Amberstone (born in 1947) is a Canadian author of fantasy and science fiction, and she is of Cherokee and Scots-Irish descent. She earned a bachelor's degree in cultural anthropology and a master's degree in health education. Her books include *Blessings of the Blood: A Book of Menstrual Lore and Rituals for Women* (1991) and *Deepening the Power: Community Ritual and Sacred Theatre* (1995).

Mary Antin
From Plotzk to Boston
(Originally Published in 1899)
Mary Antin (1881–1949) was an author and immigration rights activist. Born in Polotsk, in what is today Belarus, Antin immigrated to the United States when she was 13. Living in Boston and then New York City, she wrote of her assimilation into American culture in her 1912 autobiography *The Promised Land*. The book reflects her experiences of American life and of Jews living in the Russian Empire. The book's success launched her lecture career, in which she focused on immigrant issues.

Bebe Bayliss
Point of Entry
(First Publication)
Bebe Bayliss is an American-born Canadian author who writes in all lengths and genres. She also writes as Rowan Avery Holt, and co-writes with Gini Koch. Bebe has stories featured in excellent anthologies including *Dragonesque* from Zombies Need Brains and *Immigrant Sci-Fi* from Flame Tree Publishing. She lives in British Columbia with a very tall husband and a very small dog. Find her at bebebayliss.com

Christine Bennett
A Foot in Two Worlds
(First Publication)
Christine Bennett is a Jill-of-all-trades – photographer, former web developer, library technician, records manager, author, artist and whatever else she decides to learn, do and become. She recently

completed her BFA at the Alberta University of the Arts, majoring in fibre and textiles. An award-winning visual artist, Christine enjoys supporting others in artist alley and craft selling communities. During the day she administers a corporate photo library. Christine, her husband and budgie live in Calgary, Alberta, Canada on traditional Treaty 7 lands.

Otto (Eando) Binder
The Teacher from Mars
(Copyright © 1941, 1969 by Eando Binder; first appeared in *Thrilling Wonder Stories*; reprinted by permission of Wildside Press and the Virginia Kidd Agency, Inc.)
Otto Binder (1911–1974) was an American author, born in Michigan to Austrian parents. He wrote in the genres of science fiction and nonfiction, producing books, short stories and comics. He is known best for being the co-creator of Supergirl and the writer of scripts for numerous Marvel and other comic books. Overall he wrote more than 4,400 stories under his own name, and more than 160 others under his pen-name Eando Binder – a name he used originally for stories co-written with his brother Earl Andrew Binder (1904–1965), derived from their initials: 'E and O'.

Ben Blattberg
How Rigel Gained a Rabbi (Briefly)
(Originally Published in *Diabolical Plots*, February 2019)
Ben Blattberg is a software developer, improviser and writer currently living in Texas, as long as there are no followup questions on any of those indisputable facts. This story was inspired partly by William Tenn's 1974 novelette *On Venus, Have We Got a Rabbi* – or at least by the title, since he hadn't read Tenn's story before writing this one. His other stories have sporadically appeared in *Podcastle*, *Pseudopod*, *Diabolical Plots*, *Apex Magazine* and other venues.

Hjalmar Hjorth Boyesen
The Man Who Lost His Name
(Originally Published in *Tales from Two Hemispheres*, 1877)
Hjalmar Hjorth Boyesen (1848–1895) was born in Fredriksvern, Norway. Boyesen studied German and Scandinavian literature at the Universities of Leipzig and Oslo before moving to the United States in 1869. There he became a professor of languages at several prestigious universities. He was a prolific writer of both academic and fictional works, his most popular of which were based on Norwegian culture. His best-known work is his 1874 novel *Gunnar: A Tale of Norse Life*, which is considered the first novel by a Norwegian immigrant in the United States.

Fredric Brown
Keep Out
(Copyright © 1954, by Fredric Brown, copyright renewed 1982, by the Estate. Appeared originally in *Nightmares and Geezenstacks* and reprinted by permission of the Estate and its agent, Barry N. Malzberg.)
Fredric Brown (1906–1972) was born in Cincinnati, Ohio. An author of science fiction, fantasy and mystery, Brown is known for being a master of the 'short short' story form, and for incorporating humour and surprise endings into his works. His stories appeared in numerous science fiction and speculative magazines. His story 'The Arena' is considered one of the best science fiction stories of the early twentieth century, and it was later adapted into a 1967 episode of *Star Trek*. Brown also published numerous novels, including *What Mad Universe* (1949) and *Martians, Go Home* (1955).

Abraham Cahan
Yekl, A Tale of the New York Ghetto (Chapter II)
(Originally Published in *Yekl, A Tale of the New York Ghetto*, 1896)
Abraham Cahan (1860–1951) was a Jewish American author, socialist newspaper editor and politician. Born in Paberžė, in the Russian Empire (now Lithuania), Cahan became associated with the revolutionary movement that was emerging in Russia in the late nineteenth century. After his residence was searched by police for radical publications, Cahan emigrated to the United States. Cahan helped found the American Yiddish publication *The Forward,* which became a powerful voice of the Jewish community and the Socialist Party. His writing and public speaking on immigration issues and socialism positioned him as a leading figure of the radical Jewish left.

Judi Calhoun
Fallon Storm
(First Publication)
Judi Calhoun is an Artist, College Adjunct Professor, Elementary School Art Teacher and Author of Urban Fantasy, Horror, Murder Thrillers and Literary Essays with nearly 100 short stories published and included in numerous fiction and nonfiction national magazines and anthologies such as *Metastellar, Kaleidoscope, Appalachian Journal, Blue Moon Literary & Art Review, Crimson Street, Murder Ink*, newsroom crime series by the N H Pulp Fiction, Great Jones Street's collection of award-winning fiction and several anthologies sponsored by the John Greenleaf Whittier museum. Judi is also a cover artist for several major publishers. Follow her artistic adventures at judiartist2.wixsite.com/judisartwork.

V. Castro
RingWorm
(First Publication)
V. Castro is a two-time Bram Stoker Award-nominated Mexican American writer from San Antonio, Texas, now residing in the UK. As a full-time mother, she dedicates her time to her family and writing Latinx narratives in horror, erotic horror and science fiction. Her most recent releases include *Mestiza Blood* and *The Queen of the Cicadas* from Flame Tree Press and *Goddess of Filth* from Creature Publishing. Her forthcoming novels are *Aliens: Vasquez* from Titan Books and *The Haunting of Alejandra* from Del Rey. Connect with Violet via Instagram and Twitter (@vlatinalondon), TikTok (@vcastrobooks) or www.vcastrostories.com. She can also be found on Goodreads and Amazon.

P.A. Cornell
El Bordado
(First Publication)
P.A. Cornell is a Chilean-Canadian writer who penned her first sci-fi story as a third-grade assignment (for those curious, it was about shape-shifting aliens). While her early publications were in nonfiction, she has been steadily selling short fiction since 2016. A member of SFWA and 2002 graduate of the Odyssey Writing Workshop, her stories have appeared in several professional anthologies and genre magazines, including *Galaxy's Edge, Cossmass Infinities* and *ZNB Presents. Immigrant Sci-Fi Short Stories* is her second appearance in a Flame Tree anthology, the previous one being *Compelling Science Fiction Short Stories*. For a bibliography and social media links visit pacornell.com.

Yelena Crane
A World Away and Buried Deep
(First Publication)
Yelena Crane is a Ukrainian/Soviet-born and USA-based writer. She incorporates influences from both her motherland and adopted home soil into her work. With an advanced degree in the sciences, she has followed her passions from mad scientist to science fiction writer. Her stories appear in *Nature Futures*, *DSF*, *Third Flatiron*, *Dark Matter Ink* and elsewhere. Follow her on Twitter @ Aelintari and yelenacrane.com.

Indrapramit Das
The Moon is Not a Battlefield
(Copyright © 2017 by Indrapramit Das. Originally published in *Infinity Wars*, edited by Jonathan Strahan. Reprinted by permission of the author.)
Indrapramit Das (aka Indra Das) is a writer and editor from Kolkata, India. He is a Lambda Literary Award-winner for his debut novel *The Devourers* (Penguin India / Del Rey), and a Shirley Jackson Award-winner for his short fiction, which has appeared in a variety of anthologies and publications including Tor.com, *Slate Magazine, Clarkesworld* and *Asimov's Science Fiction*. He is an Octavia E. Butler Scholar, and a grateful member of the Clarion West class of 2012. He has lived in India, the United States, and Canada, where he received his MFA from the University of British Columbia.

Deborah L. Davitt
We Are All of Us
(Originally Published in *NewMyths #51*, 2020)
Deborah L. Davitt, daughter of a German immigrant and a US serviceman, was raised in Nevada, but currently lives in Houston, Texas with her husband and son. Her prize-winning poetry has appeared in over fifty journals, including *F&SF* and *Asimov's*. Her prize-winning prose has appeared in venues such as *Analog* and *Galaxy's Edge*. For more about her work, including her poetry collections, *The Gates of Never* and *Bounded by Eternity*, and her forthcoming chapbook, *From Voyages Unending*, please see edda-earth.com.

James Frances Dwyer
The Citizen
(Originally Published in *Americans All*, 1920)
James Frances Dwyer (1874–1952) was an Australian author. Working as a postal assistant, Dwyer became involved in a scheme to make fraudulent postal orders and was sentenced to seven years in prison from 1899. There he began writing, and after his release he moved to London, then New York. His writing career flourished in the United States with publications of numerous short stories and novels primarily within the genres of mystery and adventure. He is considered one of the most successful authors of his time who immigrated from an English-speaking country to the United States.

Greg van Eekhout
Native Aliens
(Copyright © Greg van Eekhout, reprinted by permission of the author. Originally Published in *So Long Been Dreaming: Postcolonial Science Fiction and Fantasy*, 2004)
Greg van Eekhout is an American author of science fiction and fantasy for adult and middle-grade readers. Born in Los Angeles, he is of Indo (Dutch-Indonesian) descent. One of his best-known

works is his short story 'In the Late December' (2003), which was nominated for a Nebula Award for Best Short Story. His stories have appeared in numerous speculative publications including *Asimov's Science Fiction* and *Magazine of Science Fiction & Fantasy*. His debut novel, *Norse Code*, was published in 2009. His middle-grade science fiction novels *The Boy at the End of the World* (2012) and *COG* (2019) were nominated for the Andre Norton Award for Young Adult Science Fiction and Fantasy. *COG* was listed as one of the 100 Best Books for Kids by the New York Public Library. His most recent work is the mythological fantasy novel, *Fenris & Mott*. For more information about Greg van Eekhout, visit his website: www.writingandsnacks.com.

Louis Evans

Babies Come from Earth

(Originally Published in *The London Reader*'s Motherhood issue, December 2019)

Louis Evans comes from Earth. It's crowded, but comfortable. His work has also appeared in *The Magazine of Fantasy and Science Fiction*, *Nature: Futures*, *Analog SF&F* and many more. He lives in New York City with two cats and his spouse, who is fond of reminding him: "We made a decision. We knew what it meant." Louis' story in this anthology was also notably reprinted in *Fusion Fragment* in 2021, and has been published in three other languages. Find out more about his work at evanslouis.com.

Sui Sin Far

The Wisdom of the New

(Originally Published in *Mrs. Spring Fragrance*, 1912)

Sui Sin Far (born Edith Maude Eaton, 1865–1914) was a British American author of Chinese descent, whose work focused mainly on the Chinese American experience. Moving several times as a child between England, the United States and Canada, Sui Sin Far witnessed severe xenophobia and prejudice. She began reflecting her immigrant experiences in her writing from a young age. Living in the United States as an adult, her stories described everyday life for Chinese Americans and pushed for their acceptance in society, during a time when the US government banned immigration from China through the Chinese Exclusion Act.

Illimani Ferreira

Warhorse

(First Publication)

Illimani Ferreira is one of those Latinx immigrants living in the United States they yell about on Fox News. He is based in Coastal Oregon where, having grown up in Brazil's central savannas, he is trying to figure out whether or not he is a beach person. His short prose can be found in different speculative publications. He also published a humorous science fiction novel titled *Terminal 3*.

Beáta Fülöp

Of Aspic and Other Things

(First Publication)

Beáta Fülöp is a Hungarian-Luxembourgish aspiring filmmaker and writer. She has been living abroad since she was six and speaks seven languages, but prefers to write in English. After dropping out of school, she spent years reading up on storytelling, with a special interest in representation of minorities. She is looking forward to using this knowledge by telling stories that will make people happy, ideally starring queer and disabled protagonists. Beáta has won a place in Queer Sci Fi's flash-fiction collections *Innovation* and *Clarity*. 'Of Aspic and Other Things' is Beáta's first published short story.

Sarah Rafael García

Associate Editor

Sarah Rafael García is an author, community educator and performance ethnographer. As a child of immigrants and first-generation graduate, she has over 15 years of experience as an Arts Leader in Orange County, California. She is the author of *Las Niñas* and *SanTana's Fairy Tales*, which is now a required Ethnic Studies text in the Santa Ana Unified School District in Southern California. She is also co-editor of *Pariahs: Writing from Outside the Margins* and *Speculative Fiction for Dreamers*. Her poetry, essays and fiction have been published in various publications. García is the founder of Barrio Writers, LibroMobile and Crear Studio – all art programmes initiated as a response to build cultural relevance and equity for BIPOC folks in her community. As of 2020, her community projects collectively established the LibroMobile Arts Cooperative (LMAC). Currently, she splits her time between writing, stacking books and curating digital archives and BIPOC art exhibitions – she gives credit to her parents' GED education and the migrant labour that brought her grandparents to the US as the source of her perseverance and foundation to her accomplishments.

Elana Gomel

Danae

(Originally Published in *Shoreline of Infinity*, Issue 25, August 2021)

Born in Ukraine and currently residing in California, Elana Gomel is an academic with a long list of books and articles, specializing in science fiction, Victorian literature and serial killers. She is also an award-winning fiction writer and the author of more than a hundred short stories, several novellas and five novels. Her latest fiction publications are *Little Sister*, a historical horror novella, and *Black House*, a dark fantasy novel. Her forthcoming novel is *Nightwood*, based on Ukrainian folklore. She is a member of HWA and can be found at citiesoflightanddarkness.com and social media.

Eileen Gonzalez

The Remaking of Gloria

(First Publication)

Eileen Gonzalez is a Connecticut-based freelance writer and the daughter and granddaughter of immigrants. Among other things, she is a contributing editor at Book Riot, and she is constantly fiddling with her own fictional universe, of which this story is a part. Her favourite things to write about, in both fiction and nonfiction, are issues pertaining to identity, belonging, and advocating against injustice. When not writing, Eileen collects comic books, watches entirely too many cartoons, and plays with her dog, Poppy.

Roy Gray

Rumblings

(Originally Published in *Asteroids! Stories of Space Adventure*, 2020)

Roy Gray's parents fled Nazi persecution in 1939. Roy's writings and 'poetry' have appeared in magazines such as *Interzone* (~2000), *Shooter* (#4, 2016), *Pulp Literature* (2018) and *The Antihumanist*, 2021; anthologies such as *Queer Weird West Tales* (2022, ed. Julie Bozza); journals, trade press and online. This Roy Gray didn't write any erotic poems you'll see on googling him. Roy's chapbook *The Joy of Technology* (Pendragon Press, 2011 – now a self-published ebook) could persuade you otherwise but there are many Roy Grays and this Roy's poetic efforts remain decidedly chaste.

Alex Gurevich
Eater and A
(First Publication)
Alex Gurevich grew up in the former Soviet Union with family roots in Russia and Ukraine. In 1989, he immigrated to the United States, where he earned a Ph.D. in Mathematics from the University of Chicago. He went on to become a Wall Street trader. Alex is the founder of HonTe Investments and the author of two investment books: *The Next Perfect Trade* and The Wall Street Journal bestseller, *The Trades of March 2020.*

Zenna Henderson
Deluge
(Copyright © 1963, 1991 by the Literary Estate of Zenna Henderson; first appeared in *The Magazine of Fantasy and Science Fiction*; reprinted by permission of the Estate and the Virginia Kidd Agency, Inc.)
Zenna Henderson (1917–1983) was an American author of science fiction and fantasy, as well as an elementary school teacher. She was born in Arizona and began reading science fiction from the age of 12. She published her first story in 1951 in *The Magazine of Fantasy and Science Fiction* and her novelette *Captivity* earned her a nomination for the Hugo Award in 1959. Often featuring middle-aged women as main characters, her work is considered pre-feminist, and she became a significant figure as a female author in the science fiction realm. Most of her stories concerned the fate of 'The People', a humanoid race of aliens forced to emigrate to Earth. These stories may well have been influenced by her experiences teaching in a camp where Japanese Americans were interned in Sacaton, Arizona, during the Second World War.

Betsy Huang
Introduction
Betsy Huang is Associate Provost and Dean of the College, the Andrea B. and Peter D. Klein '64 Distinguished Professor and Associate Professor of English at Clark University. Her work spans the overlapping spheres of US Multi-ethnic and Asian American Literature, Speculative Fiction, Genre Theory and Critical Ethnic Studies. She served as Director of the Center for Gender, Race, and Area Studies at Clark and was Clark's inaugural Chief Officer of Diversity and Inclusion from 2013 to 2016. She has published three books: a monograph, *Contesting Genres in Contemporary Asian American Fiction* (Palgrave, 2010), and three co-edited essay collections: *Techno-Orientalism: Imagining Asia in Speculative Fiction, History, and Media* (Rutgers, 2015); *Diversity and Inclusion in Higher Education and Societal Contexts* (Palgrave, 2018); and *Asian American Literature in Transition, 1996–2020* (Cambridge, 2021). Her work has appeared in *The Cambridge Companion to Asian American Literature, Journal of Asian American Studies* and *MELUS*, among others.

Jennifer Hudak
The Taste of Centuries, the Taste of Home
(Originally Published in *khōréō*, 2021)
Jennifer Hudak is a speculative fiction writer fuelled mostly by tea. Her short fiction can be found in publications such as *The Magazine of Fantasy & Science Fiction*, *Fantasy Magazine* and *khōréō*. Her work has appeared on both the *Locus Magazine* and the SFWA recommended reading lists, and

has been twice nominated for a Pushcart Prize. Originally from Boston, she now lives with her family in Upstate New York where she teaches yoga, knits pocket-sized animals and misses the ocean.

Jordan Ifueko
Oshun, Inc.
(Originally Published in *Strange Horizons*, 2017. The right of the Author to be identified as the Author of the Work has been asserted by them in accordance with the Copyright, Designs and Patents Act 1988.)
Jordan Ifueko (born in 1993) is a Nigerian American author of fantasy and young adult fiction. The daughter of Nigerian immigrants, Ifueko was born in California. She grew up listening to West African folktales from her mother, which have influenced her writing. Her best-known work is *Raybearer,* a young-adult fantasy novel that was inspired by her heritage and was published in 2020. It has received numerous accolades including a nomination for the Andre Norton Award. Her short stories have appeared in *Strange Horizons.*

Frances Lu-Pai Ippolito
A Satchel of Seeds
(First Publication)
Frances Lu-Pai Ippolito (she/her) is a Chinese American writer in Portland, Oregon. Her writing has appeared or is forthcoming in *Nailed Magazine*, *Buckman Journal*, Flame Tree's *Asian Ghost Short Stories*, Strangehouse's *Chromophobia*, *Startling Stories*, Not a Pipe's *Stories Within*, *Mother: Tales of Love and Terror*, *Death's Garden Revisited* and *Unquiet Spirits: Essays by Asian Women in Horror.* Frances also co-chairs the Young Willamette Writers program that provides free writing classes for high school and middle school students.

Jas Kainth
Voices from Another World
(First Publication)
Jas Kainth currently lives and works in the West Midlands as the Head of English in a secondary school. Her short stories 'A Taste of Home' and 'The Writer' are available on Amazon published under the name of Jas K. Her poems are available via her Instagram: jas.k.writes. She is particularly interested in writing about human experiences and relationships. Her most recent works have delved into the challenges experienced by immigrants who try to create a new life in an alien country.

Lee Yan Phou
When I Was a Boy in China (Chapters XI and XII)
(Originally Published in *When I Was a Boy in China*, 1887)
Lee Yan Phou (born in 1861) was born in China and later immigrated to the United States. He attended Yale University and graduated in 1887. His best-known work is his 1935 autobiography *When I Was a Boy in China.* The book discusses Phou's experiences as a young Chinese boy studying in New England. Phou is known for being the first Asian author to publish a book in English in the United States.

Ken Liu
The Paper Menagerie
(Copyright © 2011 Ken Liu, first published in *The Magazine of Fantasy & Science Fiction*, Mar/Apr. 2011.)
Ken Liu (born in 1976) is a Chinese American science fiction and fantasy author. Born in China,

Liu immigrated to the United States when he was 11. One of his best-known works is his silkpunk fantasy series *The Dandelion Dynasty*. His short fiction has been published in speculative journals including *Lightspeed, Clarkesworld, Asimov's Science Fiction* and numerous others. He has also been awarded the Hugo, the Nebula, World Fantasy and other accolades for his writing.

Samara Lo
A Rosella's Home
(First Publication)
Samara Lo is an author from Sydney, Australia. She was the recipient of the Copyright Agency-WestWords fellowship 2022 and the WestWords Emerging Writer's Residency at Varuna House 2021. She was a judge for the 2022 Aurealis Awards and has appeared in panels and workshops for writers such as the Art Gallery of NSW's Emerging Voices program. Her short fiction appears in *Daily Science Fiction*, *BAD Crime Anthology* (2022) and *The Living Stories Anthology* (2021).

Kwame M.A. McPherson
I Need To Keep It Moving
(First Publication)
Kwame is a 2007 Poetic Soul winner and 2020 Flash Fiction Bursary Awardee for The Bridport Prize: International Creative Writing Competition. A qualified life-long learning trainer, he has conducted creative writing workshops internationally in Toronto, Canada; London, England; and Kingston, Jamaica; specifically at the Kingston Book Festival, as well as partnering with the National Library of Jamaica. His self-published books have been purchased by the University of West Indies Bookshop, and his stories have been collected and displayed in the university's Archives Department.

E.C. Osondu
Foreword; *Memory Store* and *Sacrifice*
(Stories Originally Published in *Alien Stories*. Copyright © 2021 by E. C. Osondu. Reprinted the permission of The Permissions Company, LLC on behalf of BOA Editions, Ltd., www.boaeditions.org. All rights reserved.)
E.C. Osondu is a Nigerian writer and Professor of English at Providence College, Rhode Island, USA. He is the author of two novels – *This House Is Not for Sale* and *When the Sky is Ready the Stars Will Appear;* and two short-story collections – *Voice of America* and *Alien Stories*. He is a winner of the Caine Prize, the Pushcart Prize, the Allen & Nirrelle Galson Prize and the BOA Short Fiction Prize. His work has been translated into many languages, including Japanese, Italian, Icelandic, Belarusian and French. George Saunders describes Osondu as 'A vital voice in the short story, telling us new truths with deep humanity.'

Simon Pan
Ysarin
(Originally Published in *Cast of Wonders*, 2022)
Simon Pan resides in Canada where he masquerades by day as an undergraduate student of microbiology and immunology and by night as a writer of speculative fiction. When not writing or studying, he is busy staying active or collecting overdue library fines. In 2021, he was a recipient of the Lions Mountain Literary Scholarship for Young Writers and his work has appeared in *Daily Science Fiction* and *Cast of Wonders*.

Constantine Panunzio
The Soul of an Immigrant (Chapter IV)
(Originally Published in *The Soul of an Immigrant*, 1921)
Constantine Panunzio (1884–1964) was born in Molfetta, Italy. Aged 14 he joined the crew of a merchant ship and worked at sea for four years, sailing throughout the Mediterranean. Panunzio later immigrated to the United States in 1902, where he became a Methodist minister, author, social worker and professor of sociology. In his writing, he reflected on his struggles as an immigrant and his experience of living in Boston's Italian neighbourhood, the North End. His work earned him recognition from the New York World's Fair Committee 1940 for being an immigrant who made outstanding contributions to American culture.

C.R. Serajeddini
I Will Be Mila Tomorrow
(First Publication)
C.R. Serajeddini is a British Kurdish author of fantasy and science fiction. Inspired by her background, her work borrows from Kurdish history, and Mesopotamian and Persian mythology, often interwoven with fantastical and extra-terrestrial elements. She's currently working on her first novel, a YA Space Fantasy featuring a kick-ass heroine. When she's not busy exploring imaginary worlds, she enjoys hiking the mountains and coast with her family and gazing up at the stars. Preferably with a steaming mug of tea in hand.

Bogi Takács
Four-Point Affective Calibration
(Originally Published in *Lightspeed*, February 2018 (Issue 93). Edited by John Joseph Adams.)
Bogi Takács (e/em/eir/emself or they pronouns) is a Hungarian Jewish author, critic and scholar who's an immigrant to the US. Bogi has won the Lambda and Hugo awards, and has been a finalist for other awards. Eir debut poetry collection *Algorithmic Shapeshifting* and eir debut short story collection *The Trans Space Octopus Congregation* were both released in 2019. You can find Bogi talking about books at bogireadstheworld.com, and on various social media like Twitter, Patreon and Instagram as bogiperson.

Kanishk Tantia
White Berry, Red Berry
(First Publication)
Kanishk Tantia is a BIPOC and neurodivergent immigrant from India who currently lives in San Diego, California. His work has been published by *Solarpunk Magazine*, Flame Tree and *Dark Matter Magazine*. He works closely with The Dread Machine's editing team and can often be found lurking in their discord. You can also find him on Twitter @t_kanishk, or on his personal website, kanishkt.com.

Tehnuka
Potential
(First Publication)
Tehnuka (she/they) is a Tamil writer and volcanologist from Aotearoa New Zealand. She uses words to make sense of the world and, when it doesn't make sense, to make up new worlds. Her published short stories and poetry often explore themes of immigration, identity and relationships with the environment. Tehnuka likes to find herself up volcanoes, down caves and in unexpected places;

everyone else, however, can find her online at tehnuka.dreamhosters.com or as @tehnuka on Twitter, and some of her speculative stories in *Reckoning*, *Worlds of Possibility* and the *Imagine 2200* climate fiction collection.

Demetra Vaka
A Child of the Orient (Chapter XX)
(Originally Published in *A Child of the Orient*, 1914)
Demetra Vaka (Demetra Kenneth Brown, 1877–1946) was a Greek American author. Born on the island of Büyükada in Turkey, Vaka felt a strong affinity for Turkish culture and reflected this in her writing. Vaka left home to escape an arranged marriage and immigrated to the United States. Living in New York City, she worked for a Greek newspaper called *Atlantis,* then later became a French teacher at the Comstock School. One of her best-known works is *Haremlik* (1909), comprising studies of ten Turkish women. Vaka reflected on experiences from her childhood in her 1914 novel *A Child of the Orient.*

Francesco Verso
The Green Ship, translated by Michael Colbert
(Originally Published in Italian as 'La nave verde' in the anthology *Figli del Futuro* (*Future Fiction*), 2018. Originally Published in English in *The Best of World SF #1*, edited by Lavie Tidhar, Head of Zeus, April 2021)
Francesco Verso (Bologna, 1973) is a multiple-award-winning science fiction writer and editor. He has published: *Antidoti umani*, *e-Doll*, *Nexhuman*, *Bloodbusters*, *Futurespotting* and *I camminatori* (made of *The Pulldogs* and *No/Mad/Land*). *Nexhuman* and *Bloodbusters* have been published in Italy, US, UK and China. *I camminatori* will be published by Flame Tree Press as *The Roamers* in Spring 2023. He works as editor of Future Fiction, scouting and translating the best SF from 12 languages and more than 30 countries. He's the Honorary Director of the Fishing Fortress SF Academy of Chongqing. He may be found online at futurefiction.org.

M. Darusha Wehm
Home Sick
(Originally Published in *Use Only As Directed*, Simon Petrie and Edwina Harvey eds. Peggy Bright Books, 2014)
M. Darusha Wehm is the Nebula Award-nominated and Sir Julius Vogel Award-winning author of the interactive fiction game *The Martian Job*, as well as over a dozen novels including the Andersson Dexter cyberpunk detective series and the humorous coming-of-age novel *The Home for Wayward Parrots*. They are a member of the Many Worlds writing collective and their short fiction and poetry have appeared in many venues, including *Strange Horizons*, *Fireside* and *Nature*. Originally from Canada, Darusha lives in Wellington, New Zealand after several years sailing the Pacific.

Kevin Martens Wong
Alabanda
(First Publication)
Kevin Martens Wong is a gay, non-binary Kristang Singaporean speculative fiction writer, teacher, linguist and archeoastronomer. His first novel, *Altered Straits*, was longlisted for the 2015 Epigram Books Fiction Prize, and his work has also appeared in *LONTAR*, *The Second Link*, *The Tiger Moth Review*, *Suspect*, *NonBinary Review*, *Transect*, *entitled* and the Light to Night Festival. He is the founder of *Unravel: The Accessible Linguistics Magazine* (unravellingmag.com) and *Kadamundu:*

The Spice Road Review (kadamundu.com), and composes and performs original music in Kristang under the name Kabesakevlar (soundcloud.com/kabesakevlar). He currently runs his own freelance coaching and consulting initiative, Merlionsman (merlionsman.com).

Anzia Yezierska
The Fat of the Land
(Origially Published in *The Century* magazine, 1919)
Anzia Yezierska (1880–1970) was a Jewish American author, born in Mały Płock, Poland (then part of the Russian Empire). She immigrated with her family to New York City in 1893. Drawing from her own life, Yezierska's writing dealt with the experiences and struggles of Jewish immigrants in Manhattan, and the costs of assimilation. Exploring the lives of Jewish women in particular, her work initially struggled to find a publisher, however she soon gained success when one story appeared in *Best Short Stories of 1919.* Yezierska also published several novels, her best-known being *Bread Givers* (1925).

Eris Young
All That Water
(Originally Published in *BFS Horizons* magazine, 2022)
Eris Young is a queer, transgender author of speculative fiction. Their work has appeared at *Pseudopod*, *Fusion Fragment*, *Escape Pod*, *Metastellar* and others. The story featured in this anthology, 'All That Water', came first in the 2021 British Fantasy Society short story competition. They edit fiction at *Shoreline of Infinity* magazine, were the writer-in-residence at Lighthouse Bookshop from 2019–22 and in 2020 received a Scottish Book Trust New Writer Award for fiction. They have degrees in linguistics from UCLA and Edinburgh University. They are currently working on their debut novel, a queer historical fantasy titled *Raised in the Shade*.